Georgia

LOVE IS JUST PEACHY IN
FOUR COMPLETE NOVELS

GINA FIELDS
BRENDA KNIGHT GRAHAM
SARA MITCHELL
KATHLEEN YAPP

BARBOUR
PUBLISHING

Heaven's Child © 1998 by Barbour Publishing, Inc.
On Wings of Song © 1995 by Brenda Knight Graham
Restore the Joy © 1992 by Sara Mitchell
A Match Made in Heaven © 1994 by Kathleen Yapp

ISBN 1-58660-969-6

Cover design by Robyn Martins.

All Scripture quotations, unless otherwise noted, are taken from the King James Version.

Scripture quotations marked NIV are taken from the HOLY BIBLE, NEW INTERNATIONAL VERSION®. NIV®. Copyright© 1973, 1978, 1984 by International Bible Society. Used by permission of Zondervan Publishing House. All rights reserved.

Scripture quotations marked NKJV are taken from the New King James Version. Copyright © 1979, 1980, 1982 by Thomas Nelson, Inc. Used by permission. All rights reserved.

Published by Barbour Books, an imprint of Barbour Publishing, Inc., P.O. Box 719, Uhrichsville, Ohio 44683, www.barbourbooks.com

Our mission is to publish and distribute inspirational products offering exceptional value and biblical encouragement to the masses.

ecpa Member of the
Evangelical Christian
Publishers Association

Printed in the United States of America.
5 4 3 2 1

Georgia

Georgia

Heaven's Child

Gina Fields

Chapter 1

guess you're wondering why I'm here."

Randi Thomas looked at her great-aunt, Molly O'Bryan, from across a small table in her favorite family restaurant in Columbus, Georgia. "You're ht. I am wondering."

Thirty minutes earlier, Molly had arrived unexpectedly at the pediatric prac- e where Randi worked as office manager and announced she was taking Randi lunch. Randi hadn't expected to see her aunt again until the family reunion next ne. The last one had been only three weeks ago.

Molly took a dainty sip of coffee, then set her cup back in its saucer. "I'm here, andi, to offer you a job managing Simple Treasures."

The older woman's announcement surprised Randi. "But I thought you en- oyed managing the shop yourself."

"I'm seventy-two years old and more than ready to relinquish some of my responsibilities to someone else. Namely, you. Oh, I'm not going to retire com- pletely." Molly's light blue eyes took on a dreamy look. "But I am going to spread my wings and fly a little, do a little traveling."

Randi felt a bit confused. Molly rarely left her beloved novelty shop, Simple Treasures, in anyone else's hands except her late husband's grandson. "It sounds interesting, Molly. But what about Paul? He's the only person you've ever allowed to look after the shop in your absence." Randi had never met Paul O'Bryan per- sonally, but she figured he must be a pretty decent guy since Molly thought so highly of him.

"Paul does help out occasionally on the weekend if I need to be away," Molly said. "But during the week, he's far too busy with his own work to manage a nov- elty shop."

Randi paused, taking in her aunt's hopeful expression. Finally, she said, "I don't know, Molly. My and Colby's lives would be so different."

"Oh, Randi," Molly immediately responded, "you would love living in Serenity. It's such an adorable little town, and the people there are all so nice and neighborly."

Randi listened while Molly continued singing praises of the small North Georgia mountain community she'd called home for the past seventeen years. As Molly explained the benefits of managing the shop, Randi had to admit to herself

they sounded pretty good. She wouldn't make quite as much money, but living w
her aunt in the rambling Victorian-style house where the shop was located and
having to pay rent would more than make up the difference. But that wasn't w
attracted her most about Molly's offer.

When Molly finished talking, Randi trapped the right side of her lower
between her teeth and glanced out the window to the crowded parking lot, c
sidering all the older woman had said.

This could be just what Colby needed. As a widowed single parent, Ra
sometimes put in fifty-plus hours a week at work in order to make ends m
Managing the shop would mean shorter hours, which would allow her to spe
more quality time with her six-year-old son.

But what about Colby's problems? Randi knew his learning disabiliti
wouldn't bother Molly. But how would she feel about having a very hyperactiv
very unpredictable little boy in her unique shop filled with irreplaceable, painstak
ingly handmade crafts and pottery?

After a long, thoughtful moment, Randi turned back to Molly. "Before I con
sider your offer, there's something I need to tell you about Colby."

Molly propped her elbow on the table and rested her chin between her thumb
and forefinger, giving Randi her full attention.

Tucking her shoulder-length, dark brown hair behind her ear, Randi dropped
her gaze to her tea glass. As always whenever she was forced to talk about Colby's
handicap, her chest tightened.

"Molly, Colby is mentally challenged. According to a psychological evaluation he had about a year ago, he has some pretty significant learning disabilities."

"Colby? I can't believe it."

Randi met her aunt's surprised expression.

"I would have never guessed it," Molly added.

"Trust me, I was shocked, too. And I'm his mother." Sometimes, Randi still
wondered if the doctors hadn't missed the mark when they'd diagnosed Colby, and
a small part of her refused to believe he wouldn't one day overcome his learning
disabilities.

A brief silence passed, then Randi explained, "You see, Colby is an articulate
and outgoing child. The doctors explained that when a mentally challenged child
has high vocabulary and socialization skills, learning disabilities can sometimes
be hard to detect before they reach school age and are forced to apply themselves
academically."

Molly's eyes filled with compassion. "Randi, you know that will make no difference to me."

"I know. But there's something else. He also has attention deficit hyperactivity disorder, which means he's extremely hyperactive. He takes medication

r it, which helps. But he's still a pretty busy little boy. So I'll understand if you
want to think about your offer some more or withdraw it completely."

Molly reached across the table, placed her hand over Randi's, and with a
warm, understanding smile said, "My offer still stands."

Smiling, Randi squeezed her aunt's hand. "Give me a week to think about it."

❀

Eight weeks later, Randi cruised through Serenity's light midafternoon traffic,
observing a few of the charming mountain community's features: a small hardware
store on the right, a one-story brick bank building on the left, a quaint roadside café.

The right corner of her mouth tilted up in a half-grin when she spied two of
Serenity's 942 residents sitting in folding metal chairs outside the local farmer's
market. Both male, both in overalls. One of them leaned over and spit in the
plastic cup he was holding.

A little piece of heaven on earth. Randi recalled the words Molly had used to
describe Serenity, a lush little valley nestled in the Blue Ridge Mountains just a
stone's throw from the North Carolina line. The mountains rose like a fortress
wall on all four sides of the small town, seemingly shielding it from the harshness
of the modern-day world. It was a far cry from Columbus, and a thrill skipped up
Randi's spine as she envisioned her and Colby's new life here.

Rousing from his nap in the passenger seat, Colby raised his head and blinked
his sleepy eyes. "Are we there yet?"

Randi ruffled his light brown hair. "We're there."

This brought Colby up completely from his drowsy state. "Where's the big
house?"

Randi smiled. He was so excited about coming to live with Aunt Molly in
"the big house."

"I mean we're in Serenity," she explained. "Before we go to the big house,
we're going to get something to drink and use the bathroom." *And get something
for this headache,* she added to herself. The nerve-wracking drive over the winding
mountain roads had brought a persistent throb to her temples.

Randi turned into the parking lot of a convenience store and stopped next to
a blue pickup with ladder racks attached to its bed.

Colby frowned. "Don't the big house have a bathroom?"

"*Doesn't* the big house have a bathroom."

"That's what I said," Colby defended himself.

Randi decided to just let it go. She got out and met her son in front of the
car. "The big house has several bathrooms," she explained. "But I'd hate for our
first words to Aunt Molly to be, 'Hi. Where's the bathroom?' "

Randi was still looking down at Colby when the door of the store flew open.
All she saw was a flash of red and green before she was knocked backward. She

9

expected to feel the impact of the rough, hard cement, but she suddenly foun herself cradled in the arms of a giant instead.

"Hey! You guys watch where you're going!" called the man's deep voice.

Randi turned her head toward the objects of the man's command to see two adolescent boys, one in a red shirt and one in a green, jumping on bicycles. "Sorry Paul!" one of the boys yelled back. "We're running late. Gotta get home or Mama gonna kill us."

"If you don't kill somebody else first," he mumbled as he set her back on her feet.

Randi quickly searched for Colby and released a silent sigh of relief when she found him standing beside her. She then turned to her rescuer and found herself eye level with the pocket of a man's blue T-shirt. Tilting her head back, she scanned broad shoulders, a thick neck, a short beard and mustache, a straight, Roman-shaped nose, and locked onto mossy green eyes. A faint outdoor woodsy smell tickled her senses.

"Are you okay?" the stranger asked.

Randi opened her mouth, but it took two full seconds to find her voice. When she did, it was shaky. "Yes. Thanks for breaking my fall."

He narrowed his eyes and studied her, his brows dipping in a disconcerting frown. His gaze made Randi uncomfortable—and warm. She looked down and grasped Colby's hand. "Come on, Son. You can pick out a soda."

As Randi led her son into the store, the strangest feeling stole over her.

Déjà vu?

A light tingling sensation, like the flutter of tiny angel wings, traveled up her spine.

Weird, she thought, shaking her head.

Randi glanced down and noticed Colby still looking back. She tugged on his hand. "It isn't polite to stare."

When they walked out of the store, the blue truck and the giant were gone. Randi washed two white tablets down with a grape soda and was pulling out of the parking lot when she remembered the intended bathroom trip.

"Mom, who was that man back there?"

Oh, no. Here we go again. Randi groaned inwardly. Sometimes Colby was a bottomless pit of inquisition. Aloud she said, "I don't know, Honey."

"But you said 'don't talk to strangers.' "

"I know, but that rule doesn't always apply to grown-ups."

Colby held on to his confused expression. "But he picked you up."

"Those boys who ran out of the store weren't watching where they were going and ran into me. The man just kept me from falling. That's all."

Colby hesitated, his young voice thoughtful. "I seed him before."

"I've seen him before."

"You did?"

"That's not what I meant." Randi sighed, her shoulders slumping. "I've never seen him before, and neither have you."

"Uh-huh." Colby's eyebrows disappeared beneath his bangs as he bobbed his head up and down.

Randi really didn't want to continue the argument, so she took a detour round it. "I know where you think you saw him. Do you remember the book we read last week about the lumberjack, Paul Bunyan?"

"Yeah."

"That's who he looked like to me."

"Sorta," Colby reluctantly conceded, but he didn't look too convinced.

Aunt Molly's house and shop were two miles east of Serenity and, from the road, barely visible through a shield of tall hardwoods. Randi made the trip up the long blacktop driveway slowly. Red roses climbed the white picket fence leading up each side of the gently curving drive. She rolled her window down, inhaling the sweet scent mingled with that of the freshly mowed lawn, and watched with delight as Colby bounced up and down on the seat, clapping his hands.

"Mom, it's soooo pretty."

"I know," she agreed. This was the closest she ever expected to come to her second dream of owning her own country home. Her first dream of being a full-time mom had ceased to exist when Eddie died.

Randi had been to Molly's home in Serenity only once before, thirteen years ago. Then a fifteen year old devastated by her father's sudden death, Randi had been invited to spend a couple of weeks with her great-aunt that summer. A special bond had formed between Randi and Molly during that time, and it had grown stronger over the years despite distance and separation.

The massive two-story house had the same effect on her as it had then. It took her breath away.

The outside had recently been redone in pristine white vinyl siding with hunter green shutters and a matching green tin roof. The front porch, sitting beneath three dormer windows, spanned the width of the house. Azaleas and miniature hollies stood guard in front of the green latticework around the bottom of the porch, and two large rocking chairs were evenly positioned on each side of the bevel-paned door.

Colby was out of his seat belt and out of the car almost before Randi came to a complete stop. "Colby, wait!" She jumped out and ran after him.

As Colby bounced up onto the porch, the front door opened and Molly stepped out. Her eyes twinkled with delight as she bent down to greet him. He didn't stop until he had his arms wrapped around her neck. Their laughter was music to Randi's ears as she climbed the five steps leading to the porch.

"Aunt Molly, we comed to live with you!" Colby declared.

"I know, and I've been so excited I could hardly wait." Molly played "Buggy Buggy" up Colby's stomach with her fingers, bringing on another round of laughter.

When Molly stood, she embraced Randi, then held her at arm's length. "How are you, Randi?"

"I'm fine. Glad we finally made it here."

"That makes two of us." Molly smiled down at Colby. "Well, maybe three."

Molly held open the door, then followed Randi and Colby into the shop portion of the house. Lining the wall to Randi's left were several shelves of clay pottery. Shelves in the middle of the shop held a variety of handcrafted items including two dulcimers, a fiddle, and a banjo. Along the back wall behind the checkout counter, a stairway with a polished oak handrail led to the second floor. A door at the bottom of the stairs led to the shop's office, and to the right were two large racks of handmade quilts.

As Randi strolled around the shop looking over the fine-honed crafts of the "mountain folk," as Molly would say, a deep sense of nostalgia fell over her like a soft, warm blanket. She picked up a clay pitcher and, with her thumb, opened the folded tag tied to the handle.

"You'll find tags like that on each item in the shop," Molly explained. "They tell the story behind the product and its maker. As I told you when I came to Columbus, every item in here is crafted by northern Georgia and southwestern North Carolina mountain folk."

Randi set the pitcher back in its place and smiled at her aunt. "How long do you think it'll take before I graduate from being a 'flatlander' to one of the 'mountain folk?' "

Molly laughed. "Knowing you, a day. Two at the most."

Molly led the way through a door on the right to a small family room and on through swinging doors into a light, airy kitchen with a small claw-foot table in the center. The scent of freshly brewed coffee and something sweet and spicy greeted Randi. She took a deep breath, inhaling the pleasant aromas, then felt Colby tugging on the leg of her modest shorts. Looking down, she found him squirming from one foot to the other, rubbing his knees together.

"Mom," he whispered loudly, "I have to use the bathroom."

Suddenly, a vision of the reason she forgot the bathroom trip at the convenience store evolved before her—a handsome face and mossy green eyes.

"It's right through here." Molly led the way to a short hallway at the back of the kitchen.

When Colby returned skipping, Molly bent and straightened the elastic waist of his shorts. "Would you like some cookies? I just took them out of the oven."

"Yes!"

"Colby," Randi scolded gently. "I didn't hear a single magic word."

Colby stood up straight, folded his hands behind him, and rocked back and forth on his feet. "Yes, Ma'am, please, and thank you."

During the next thirty minutes, while Randi and Molly drank coffee and Colby inhaled cookies and milk, Molly filled Randi in on general information that was sure to be helpful to her as she and Colby established themselves as citizens of Serenity. Randi held her breath every time she had to stop and remind Colby not to interrupt. But Molly seemed to take it all in stride, stopping from time to time to answer his eager questions.

The grandfather clock in the family room chimed, announcing five o'clock. Molly rose and carried her cup to the sink. Randi followed suit and reminded Colby to do the same with his glass and plate.

Turning to Randi, Molly said, "On Thursday nights I usually go out to eat with a few of my friends; then we go to the senior center for a game of canasta. Will you be okay while I'm gone, or would you prefer I stay here tonight?"

Randi almost sighed with relief. "You go ahead. Colby and I will be fine. We need to get unpacked and settled anyway."

"I thought so. I think you will find everything in proper order. We can go over the schedule tomorrow after you get Colby registered for school. The refrigerator is full, so please feel free to help yourself." Molly patted Randi's shoulder and headed for the door, then paused. "I almost forgot. You remember me telling you I was having a portion of the second floor redone for expansion of the shop, don't you?"

Randi nodded.

"Well, someone will be here in a few minutes to go over the renovations with you. He'll probably come to the back door, so don't be alarmed."

Randi smiled at her aunt. "I'll try to remember I'm not in the city and let him in."

"Well," Molly said with a twinkle in her eyes, "I hope you have a good evening."

"Thanks. I hope you do, too."

After Molly left, Randi took a few minutes to reacquaint herself with the elegant country house. Three bedrooms and a bathroom, as well as a back door leading to a wide porch, were located down the short hallway at the back of the kitchen. She noticed Molly had prepared the two bedrooms facing each other at the end of the hallway for her and Colby. Another short hallway in the back left corner of the kitchen led to Molly's room, another bathroom, the laundry room, and a side entrance. On the right side of the kitchen were two doors: one that led to the family room, the other to the small office adjacent to the shop.

Tour finished, Randi unloaded the suitcases from the car and began unpacking. When Colby entered his bedroom, he jumped on the full-sized bed and started bouncing on his knees. "Look, Mom! A whole bed!" He had referred to his twin bed in the Columbus apartment as "half a bed."

"I see that. But you can't bounce on the bed. We have to treat things in this house just like we treated our things back in Columbus."

Colby looked a little disgruntled but complied with his mother's request just the same.

Once Randi had Colby's clothes unpacked, she picked up her suitcase and moved to the room across the hall. Colby followed on hands and knees, pushing a yellow toy dump truck.

When Randi opened her suitcase, her gaze fell on her wedding picture, laying faceup on top of her neatly folded clothes. Suddenly and unexpectedly, like hundreds of thousands of times before, a vast wave of loneliness swept over her. It had been almost seven years since the accident. Would she ever stop missing Eddie?

She sighed. Probably not. Because she had a small carbon copy of him playing on the floor at her feet.

Colby was so much like his father. Same light brown hair, same hazel eyes, same sparkling personality. Reaching for the photo, she eased down on the quilt-covered bed. As she stared at the smiling man looking back at her, she got lost in his memory. He had been her first date, her first kiss, her first love.

A smile touched her lips as she thought of the day she told him they were expecting a baby. She had been a little nervous at first because they hadn't planned to start a family so soon. They were both only twenty-one and had been married just a little over a year. But to her delight, Eddie had been just as thrilled as she, and the following week he had walked around like a proud peacock. His mother even commented that he acted like he was the only man in the world who had ever fathered a child.

One week, Randi thought. *Probably the happiest week of his life, then he died.*

Her smile faded and an old familiar ache rose in her throat as she recalled that horrible day. Eddie and her brother Mike had left that morning to go on an all-day deer hunting trip. That afternoon her brother had returned, not with her husband, but with a police officer to inform her that Eddie had accidentally fallen out of his tree stand and broken his neck. In an effort to comfort her, the officer said, "I know it's no consolation right now, Ma'am, but he died instantly. He didn't suffer."

But she had suffered. During the months that followed, all she could do was go through the motions of living. She ate properly for the baby's sake; she slept when she could. But without Eddie, she just felt dead inside. And her grief had kept her from feeling any real connection with the child growing inside her.

She had never felt so scared and alone as the day she went into labor. She had cried her heart out as her brother drove her to the hospital. While her mother held her hand in the delivery room, she had lashed out at Eddie in anger for dying and leaving her to face parenthood alone.

But when the doctor had laid that kicking, screaming little boy in her arms, something inside her came back to life. She wasn't sure if it was because she felt a part of Eddie had been given back to her, or knowing another flesh-and-blood human being depended on her for life and survival, or simply the mother's love she had always heard about but never experienced until that moment. All she knew was she had a reason to go on living.

She thumbed the simple gold wedding band she still wore on her left hand. On that day, she'd promised herself and her deceased husband that she would protect their son and meet his needs—whatever it took. And she had done her best to keep that promise, although sometimes it seemed no matter how hard she tried, her efforts as a parent fell short.

Her gaze drifted to Colby, still playing, making motor sounds with his mouth, totally oblivious to the pain piercing her soul at that moment.

Eddie never got the chance to know his son. And Colby would never know his father. Sometimes, life just wasn't fair.

Her vision blurred. *Oh, Eddie. Why did you have to go and forget to fasten the stupid strap on your tree stand?*

Chapter 2

A loud knock at the back door pulled Randi out of her reverie. She wiped away a stray tear and returned the photo to the suitcase. "Colby, you stay here while I go answer the door." Taking a deep breath to regain her self-composure, she left the room.

When Randi opened the door, her heart all but stopped. The man who had rescued her from falling at the store stood on the back porch. He now wore a royal blue cap with the words "O'Bryan Construction" stitched in white letters above the bill.

A hint of surprise skimmed across his face when he recognized her. "Hello, Ma'am." He grasped the bill of his cap and tipped his head forward. "I didn't think I'd be running into you again so soon."

Randi swallowed. "Nor I you."

"I'm looking for. . ." His eyes narrowed in much the same way as they had at the store earlier. Then suddenly his eyebrows shot up. "You! You're Randi!"

Randi's grip on the doorknob tightened. "Do I know you?"

"Not really. I'm Paul O—"

A sharp gasp cut off his words. Randi turned to find Colby standing in the hallway, his toy dump truck dangling from one hand. With his mouth the shape of an O, he looked beyond her to the man.

"Colby," Randi said, "I thought I told you to stay in your room."

Colby's wide-eyed gaze didn't waver as he said in a stunned voice, "Woooow. Mom, you was right. He really is Paul Bunyan."

Randi whipped back around, fixing her own wide-eyed gaze on the stranger. A hint of amusement danced in his eyes, and a smile toyed with the corner of his mouth. His left brow inched up his forehead.

Randi's tongue felt ten inches thick and dry as a desert. It tripped over obstacle after unseen obstacle as she tried to explain to the man her son's assessment of him. "When we saw you at the store today, ah, Colby thought you looked familiar. I mean, he insisted he had seen you before, and, ah, last week we read the story of Paul Bunyan, and I sort of suggested you. . .look. . .like. . .him."

The stranger's face broke into a wide grin.

He's laughing at me, Randi thought. And for some reason, that bothered her.

He tilted his head to the side and, looking beyond her, placed one booted foot inside the door and started toward Colby.

Randi stepped into his path. "I don't recall asking you in." Less than ten inches separated them, and she had to practically point her chin to the ceiling in order to meet his gaze. She estimated he towered over her own five feet three inches by a foot or more and outweighed her by at least ninety pounds. But she was determined to stand her ground. He wasn't getting near her son until she knew what his intentions were.

He pulled off his cap, his smile bringing laugh lines to the outside corners of his eyes. "Oh, excuse me. I was about to introduce myself when this young man here mistook me for someone else. I'm Paul O'Bryan, Ma'am, Molly's stepgrandson."

He slipped around her and walked right in, just like he owned the place, leaving her feeling a bit chilled as he took with him the heat emanating from his body.

She stared at the place he had just vacated while the name registered. Paul O'Bryan. Molly's grandson. *The one she adores. The one she thinks hung the moon!*

She pivoted just as he kneeled in front of Colby, leaving her with a view of his herculean back. His dark blond hair was neither too long nor too short, just brushing the collar of his T-shirt in back and touching the tops of his ears on the sides.

"Hey, Sport," he said, his voice just as rich and smooth as she remembered from the store. "I hate to disappoint you, but I'm not a lumberjack. I build houses."

Colby glanced at her, then looked back at Paul. "Mom says 'don't talk to strangers.' "

"Your mom's right. But since I've introduced myself to her, maybe she'll give you permission to introduce yourself to me."

They both looked at her, Paul having to twist his upper body around. Randi relaxed her death grip on the doorknob slightly. "It's okay, Colby. This is Aunt Molly's grandson."

Paul turned back to her son. "So, you're Colby." He tapped Colby's chest with his forefinger.

"Uh-huh." Colby bobbed his head up and down. "Colby Edward Thomas."

"Well, Colby Edward Thomas, I'm glad to meet you. My name is Paul." He placed his cap on Colby's head and pointed to the toy truck. "That's a fine-lookin' piece of equipment you've got there. Can I see it?"

Randi watched the exchange between the two as Colby handed the truck to Paul and went into a wordy explanation about how to operate it. *Can he tell Colby's handicapped?* she wondered.

"I see you two have met."

The voice behind Randi startled her. She turned as Molly stepped through the open door.

Paul rose, handing the truck back to Colby, and faced Molly. "I thought you had canasta at the senior center tonight."

Molly fanned the air once with her hand. "The building is flooded from last night's rain."

Paul hooked his thumbs in his back pockets. "I'm not surprised."

Molly's face lit up, as though she were suddenly struck by a bright idea. "I'll bet neither of you have eaten. Why don't you two go out and discuss the renovations over supper, and I'll fix Colby a hot dog here?"

"Oh, boy!" Colby skipped to Molly and grabbed her hand.

"That's not necessary," Randi injected.

Molly laid her hand on Randi's arm and said with a bemusing smile, "Yes, Dear, it is. Trust me."

Something in the way Molly said those last words set off a warning bell in the back of Randi's mind. She got the feeling there was something her aunt hadn't told her.

Paul released a long breath from puffed cheeks as he watched Molly and Colby retreat to the kitchen. "I think we've been had."

"I think you're right." Randi crossed her arms in an effort to put a barrier between her and this mountain of a man.

Turning back to her, he said, "Well, let's go grab a bite; then we can talk."

"Couldn't we talk here?"

"Yes. But I'm rather hungry right now, and this could turn out to be a lengthy discussion."

"Well, I'm not really hungry, so—" At that moment, her stomach chose to protest, and a loud rumbling sound came from beneath her folded arms.

His rakish left brow arched up once more. "Your stomach disagrees."

Randi sighed, reluctantly giving in. "Okay. Let me get my purse."

When she returned, Paul opened the door and stepped back to allow her to go out ahead of him. "We'll take Babe," he said with a grin.

As she walked past him, she shot him a quizzical glance at his reference to Paul Bunyan's blue ox. But when she stepped outside, her jaw dropped. "Babe" was the same blue pickup she had parked next to at the convenience store earlier, only at that time she failed to notice the words "O'Bryan Construction" printed on the doors.

❀

When Paul eased his truck to a stop in front of the small roadside café Randi had passed on her way through town earlier, she could hardly wait to get out of the truck. His size alone made the cab seem half its actual width. Being a single mother, she had made a rule long ago not to let anyone intimidate her, but she had a feeling that rule could be broken when it came to Paul O'Bryan. Something about him made her want to put her guard up.

As Paul led her through a maze of tables covered with red-checkered tablecloths, practically everyone greeted him by name, and Randi encountered more than a few questioning glances. The folks of Serenity, it seemed, were curious about his dinner companion.

He guided her to a corner booth near the back. After the waitress took their order, he leaned back, resting one arm along the back of the seat. "I take it Molly didn't tell you I was coming by the house tonight."

Randi, her hands in her lap beneath the table, unconsciously twisted her wedding band with the fingers of her right hand. "She told me someone was coming to talk about the upstairs redecorating. I didn't realize it was going to be her grandson."

"Don't feel bad. She didn't tell me you were the new manager of the shop either."

His comment confused her. What difference did it make to him who Molly hired to manage her shop? "What did she tell you?"

"That the new manager's name was Randy. Naturally, I assumed from the name you were a man, and Molly didn't bother to tell me otherwise." He chuckled. "She even let me work on the rental cottage in back of the house for two weeks, thinking I was getting it ready to be the new male manager's quarters."

"You mean she let you do all that work for nothing?"

He shrugged. "It was going to have to be done anyway."

Randi caught her right lower lip between her teeth for a few thoughtful seconds, then asked, "Do you think her deception was intentional?"

"With Molly, who knows?"

After the waitress delivered the food, Paul bowed his head and closed his eyes briefly. Randi respectfully ducked her head and tried to remember the last time she had asked God's blessing on her food. She couldn't.

When Paul raised his head, he seemed interested in only one thing—eating. Randi tried to remain patient while he finished man-sized servings of roast beef, mashed potatoes, black-eyed peas, and corn bread. Despite the rumbling in her stomach earlier, she moved her plate aside with only one-third of her chicken sandwich gone.

After what seemed like an eternity, he pushed away his plate and folded his arms on the table. He stared down at his half-empty tea glass a thoughtful moment, turning it with his left hand; then he raised a serious gaze to her. "Mrs. Thomas, why did you come to Serenity?"

His question caught her completely off guard. Bewildered, she frowned. "Excuse me?"

"We have very few of the conveniences you're used to. There are no theaters or malls at our back door. About the only pastime for kids is playing on the Park and Rec ball teams, and that can't come close to competing with what you're used to. I guess I'm wondering if you've thought about all you're giving up. I mean, coming here from Columbus is like coming to a foreign country with an entirely different culture. We don't even speak the same language as you."

Somehow, Randi stopped her chin before it dropped. Never in her life had she been given the third degree like this, especially from a practical stranger. Apparently, he wanted to send her back to where she came from. But why?

Stay calm, she warned herself. After all, this was Molly's beloved grandson. She couldn't afford to offend him.

Considering Molly's high opinion of Paul, Randi did something totally out of character. She bared her soul.

"Mr. O'Bryan, if you're wondering whether or not I'll make a good employee for Molly, let me assure you I'm well qualified. For the last three years I've been the office manager in a practice that consisted of eight pediatricians. And living in a city isn't as glamorous as you think. I left my home at seven each morning and usually didn't get home until six or seven each night, fighting traffic both ways. I was fortunate if I got to spend one hour with my son before tucking him into bed each night.

"When Molly offered me this job, I thought maybe a prayer had been answered. So I left my good-but-time-consuming job and probably the only apartment in Columbus I could afford to come here, because I think Serenity will be good for my son."

He seemed totally unaffected by her speech, so she continued. "Look, I have yet to figure out why I'm even sitting here having this conversation with you, but for some reason Molly thinks it's necessary. And I've got sense enough to know that, considering how she feels about you, you could probably convince her to send me packing. Or make it hard enough on me yourself to make me want to leave. I would like to think, however, that you're a fair man, and you won't do anything to keep me from doing the job I was hired to do before I even have a chance to prove myself. Anyone deserves that."

His expression changed then, his brows dipping in thought.

Randi felt defeated. She closed her eyes and massaged her temples.

"You're right, Mrs. Thomas. You do deserve a chance."

Surprised at his words, she opened her eyes and studied his expression. His features now appeared softer, his eyes kinder.

"So you won't fight my staying?" she asked.

He shook his head. "No."

She let go a sigh of relief. "Thank you."

He leaned back, crossing his thick arms and tilting his head to the side. "I think there's something else Molly's failed to tell you, though."

"What's that?"

"That I own the shop."

The shock was too much for her. Before she realized what she was doing, she flattened her palms on the table and leaned forward, rising halfway up out of her seat. "You what?"

Silence—except for the soft sizzle from the grill behind the counter.

Randi sensed she was being watched and glanced around to find approximately twenty-two sets of eyes aimed at her, forks, glasses, and tea pitchers held frozen in midair. She eased down in her seat and waited until everyone returned to their own affairs, then leaned forward and whispered, "What did you say?"

His eyes danced with amusement. "Judging by your reaction, I don't think I need to repeat myself."

Randi picked up her water and tried to wet her parched throat. It didn't help. When she set her glass down, she was still hoarse. "Let me see if I've got this straight. My aunt hired me to manage her shop, only the shop doesn't belong to her, but to her grandson, who isn't exactly thrilled by the idea of a woman from the city managing his shop." Then an even more unpleasant thought hit her. "Oh, no. If you own the shop, then you also own the house. That means I'm living in your house."

She waited for his confirmation.

He made her wait.

His cocky smile made it almost impossible to hold her simmering temperament in check. Leaning back, she crossed her arms. "I don't see what's so funny."

"Sorry." He took a sip of tea, obviously trying to camouflage his mirth. His gaze remained fixed on his glass as he set it down. "It's just that your reaction was so. . . ," he searched for the right word, then targeted her with his eyes, "electric."

She opened her mouth to respond, then snapped it shut. No one had ever told her she was electric before.

Something across the room caught Paul's attention. Randi turned to find two teenagers motioning for Paul. Sliding out of the booth, he said, "Excuse me just a minute."

Randi watched while he made his way to the youths' table; then she scooped up the ticket and headed toward the cash register. The least she could do was buy his supper since he was going to be looking for a new manager for his shop tomorrow.

Dusk had already arrived when she walked outside. A deep sense of melancholy stole over her as she opened the truck door and climbed inside. People here didn't even bother to lock their vehicles in the center of town. She'd be leaving this safe little haven before she even got a chance to fall in love with it.

"What am I going to do?" she whispered to herself. Her job and apartment were gone, and her savings could keep her and Colby going three months at the most. What if she couldn't find another job in that length of time?

She was still looking out her window contemplating her situation when the driver's door opened, flooding the cab with light as Paul climbed inside. "Sorry about that," he said. "As you get to know the people here, you'll find—"

"I'm afraid that won't happen, Mr. O'Bryan," she blurted out before she could stop herself.

Paul set the truck in motion. "What do you mean?"

"I mean I'm leaving first thing in the morning."

"Why?" Paul's voice remained calm and even.

Randi's didn't. She crossed her arms, putting up her barrier. "Because this whole thing is a farce. I didn't know you owned the shop, and you don't want me managing it."

"I didn't say that."

"You said you didn't think a woman from the city could adapt to Serenity."

"No, I didn't. I just asked a few questions."

"Well, your questions implied—"

"You misunderstood. Molly is really excited about having some free time on her hands. I just didn't want her having to go through the trouble of finding another manager if you had second thoughts a couple of months down the road."

"Well, she won't have to wait a couple of months. She can start looking bright and early tomorrow morning."

Paul eased the truck onto a wide place along the side of the road and killed the ignition.

"W—what are you doing?" she wanted to know.

He turned on the overhead light, laced his hands in his lap, and glared at her. "I'm going to let you have your say; then I'm going to explain a couple of things."

"I don't see the point, but go ahead. I'm listening."

He waited several more seconds, apparently making sure she was going to remain silent, then he stared straight ahead. "My ownership of the shop and house is in name only. As far as I'm concerned, it's still Molly's."

The tenderness in his voice as he spoke of Molly touched Randi, and she suddenly understood his motive behind his lecture earlier. In a more gentle voice she said, "You look out for her, don't you?"

He grinned, shaking his head. "I think Molly just humors me and lets me think I take care of her. I've never known a woman more capable of taking care of herself, or a better businesswoman."

"You may really be taking care of her when I get through with her tonight," Randi joked.

He gave her a sweeping smile, bringing laugh lines to the corners of his eyes.

Then his smile faded. "The other thing I wanted to explain is that I once lived in a large city for a short time. I felt like a caged wild animal."

"So you figured my coming here was like taking an animal that had been in captivity all its life and turning it loose in the wilderness."

"Something like that."

"I gave this move serious thought, Mr. O'Bryan. I feel you judged me prematurely."

"Maybe I did. Anyway, judging people isn't my job, is it?" Without waiting for an answer, he added, "I owe you an apology. I'm sorry."

Randi considered his earnest expression, then said, "Apology accepted. I'm sorry I exploded at the restaurant. I was just shocked to learn you own the shop."

"That's understandable." Their gazes met and held for the space of three heartbeats. "I hope you'll stay," he said softly.

Randi glanced out at the darkness beyond her window, escaping his intense gaze. "I don't think so."

"You said you quit your job and gave up your apartment. What have you got to lose?"

She caught her right lower lip between her teeth, thinking. What did she have to lose? What did she have to go back to? She could stay with her mother until she found another apartment, but she didn't want to do that. Her mother had already done more for her and Colby than Randi could ever repay. And what about her main reason for coming to Serenity?

She turned back to him. "Mr. O'Bryan—"

"Paul."

"Okay, Paul. If I had only myself to think about, I'd be gone in a heartbeat. But I have to think about my son. For that reason, I'll stay."

"Good. I'm glad." He wiped imaginary sweat from his brow. "I think you just saved my hide."

"Why's that?"

He grinned. "Because, considering the way Molly feels about you and Colby, she would skin me if she thought I had run you off." He switched off the overhead light and set the truck back in motion.

Randi couldn't keep the right corner of her mouth from easing upward. She didn't know exactly when her discomfort with Paul started slipping away, but she suddenly realized the truck cab no longer seemed too small.

As Paul eased to a stop behind the house, he turned to her. "Can I ask you a question?"

"I suppose so."

"Is Randi your real name, or is it short for something?"

"Why do you ask?"

He shrugged. "It's a little unusual for a woman, and a little confusing if that's all you know about a person."

"It's short for Miranda. When I was born, my brother was three. Randi was the best he could do. It just stuck."

"Miranda," he pondered with a reflective nod. "It's a pretty name."

For some reason, his words brought a strange little flutter to her stomach. She fumbled for the door handle. "Thank you." Then she remembered. "We never got around to talking about the upstairs redecorating."

"I'll come by tomorrow after work. I'm sure you and Colby need to get settled."

Relieved, she said, "Yes, we do. See you tomorrow, then."

Opening the door, she jumped out. As she started to close it, Paul said, "Hey, wait a minute."

She pulled the door back and stuck her head inside the cab.

He held out her purse. "You forgot something."

"Thanks."

❀

After putting Colby to bed and reading a short story to him, Randi walked into the kitchen to find Molly trying to escape to her room.

"Oh, no, you don't. You're not going anywhere until we talk."

Molly slipped on an innocent face. "Oh, is there something we didn't cover today?"

Randi planted her hands on her hips. "Yes, there is. Why didn't you tell me Paul owns the shop?"

"Did I not tell you?" Molly's hand went to the side of her face. "I guess memory starts failing at my age."

Randi tucked her hair behind her right ear and crossed her arms. "Molly, this is me you're talking to. Stop trying to tiptoe around the issue."

"Oh, all right." She took her hand from her face and fanned it once at Randi as she stalked to the table. Pulling out a chair, she ungracefully plopped down. "I can see you're not going to let me get a wink of sleep until we have this conversation." She put her forearms on the table, placing one hand on top of the other. Randi took the opposite chair.

"When Paul and I decided to hire a manager, you were the first person I thought of," Molly explained. "I didn't tell you because I was afraid you wouldn't accept the job knowing you'd be living in his house and working in his shop instead of mine."

"You're right, I probably wouldn't have. After all, I never knew the man before tonight."

Reaching across the table, Molly covered Randi's hand with her own. "Let me tell you about Paul and how and why his ownership of Simple Treasures came about." Molly's voice betrayed a deep affection for Paul. "When Clayton had his first stroke nine years ago, he made an almost complete recovery, but the insurance company canceled his health insurance. When he had his second stroke, and it was clear he wasn't going to get better, I was devastated. The shop started suffering because, at the time, I wasn't able to run it properly.

"Clayton was very sick the year before he died. He had to have round-the-clock medical attention, which meant putting him in a nursing home. The costs were outrageous, and our money soon ran out. Paul found out I was about to lose this place because I couldn't pay the property taxes, so he bought it, thus saving the shop and house and giving me the funds I needed for Clayton to get the care he needed."

"Was it necessary for you to sign your property over to him before he would help you?" Randi asked. "If he's the man you say he is, he would have helped without asking you to sign it over."

"He didn't ask; I insisted. Paul was fighting his own battle trying to keep his grandfather's construction company going, but he would have helped. As a matter of fact, he begged me to let him help without my putting the property in his name. But I absolutely refused."

Randi sighed, considering Molly's words. "Okay. So the guy has a big heart. And he does seem to have a soft spot where you're concerned; at least that's one thing we have in common."

Molly smiled. "Paul is very protective when it comes to people he cares about."

"I can understand where he's coming from." Randi paused, thinking of her son. "I want to know if there's anything else you haven't told me, Molly. I don't want any more little surprises."

"If I think of anything, I'll let you know. Now I'm going to turn in for the night." Molly rose and started to walk away, apparently finished with the conversation. She stopped at the hallway and looked back with an impish smile. "You know, this is going to be interesting."

The warning bell sounded in Randi's head again. She narrowed her eyes. "What's that supposed to mean?"

"Oh, you and Paul. You two are the most independent people I know." With a shake of her head, Molly continued down the hallway.

A little perplexed by Molly's comment, Randi wandered to her room and started getting ready to turn in. As she picked up her purse from where she had thrown it on the bed, she noticed several dollars sticking out of a small side pocket. She frowned. It wasn't like her to be so careless with money. Pulling out the bills, she counted. Twelve dollars. Exactly thirty-two cents more than the cost of her and Paul's supper.

Chapter 3

H ow did your first day go?" Molly asked as she entered the shop office the following afternoon.

Randi looked up from the ledger she was working on and smiled. "Wonderful. I can't remember ever enjoying a day at work this much."

Molly sat down in one of the two chairs in front of Randi's desk and crossed her legs. "As you know," she said, her voice taking on a businesslike tone, "we have a girl who comes in daily at two o'clock so you can do your office work. There are also two college students who help out on Saturdays, so you don't need to worry about staying around all the time on the weekends. Of course, we're closed on Sundays." Molly uncrossed her legs and leaned forward, pinning Randi with her gaze. "Randi, I hired you to manage Simple Treasures, and I have no doubt you'll do a great job. But I don't want you to do too good of a job."

Randi frowned. "I'm not sure I follow you."

"I don't want you in here working when you need to be spending time with Colby. How you manage the shop, I'll leave to your discretion. Just remember, you don't have to impress anyone, especially me."

When Molly and Randi finished discussing business, Molly insisted on taking Colby for ice cream, despite Randi's arguments that it was too close to supper.

After they left, Randi found four chicken breasts in the refrigerator next to a tossed green salad. She arranged the chicken in a baking dish, smothered it with barbecue sauce, then popped it in the oven alongside four baking potatoes.

Satisfied supper was under way, she stood in the middle of the kitchen and listened. Silence. She was alone and, for the first time in weeks, relaxed.

She wandered to the back porch. The small one-story rental cottage sat a couple hundred yards behind the house. To the right, adjacent to the cottage, was a covered well. A pebble walkway, lined on each side by a flower garden, led from the porch to a gazebo. And beyond that, the mammoth Blue Ridge Mountains started their journey upward until they seemed to touch the sky.

Slipping her hands into her jeans' back pockets, Randi leaned against the post at the top of the steps. She closed her eyes and took a deep breath. No heavy gas fumes, no fuel-laden smog. Just clean, fresh air laced with the light, sweet fragrance from the flower gardens. No blaring horns, no screaming sirens, no one yelling profanities from their car windows at whatever had traffic stopped a mile up the road. Instead, the wind whispered softly through the treetops.

She opened her eyes and spied a squirrel, its cheeks bulging, scampering up an oak tree near the gazebo. She watched the animal a few minutes, then gazed up at the mountains. Even with the late afternoon sun shining down on them, they were shrouded with a misty blue gray blanket.

"Beautiful," she mused aloud.

"I agree."

Randi gasped and whirled around at the sound of Paul's voice. He was leaning in the doorway, his arms crossed over his broad chest and one ankle crossed over the other, the toe of his work boot resting on the floor. The dusty knees and thighs of his jeans bore the signs of his day's labor.

She placed a hand over her chest, trying to catch her runaway heart. "You just cheated me out of ten years of my life."

He smiled. "I hope not."

Rugged, Randi thought. *No. Not just rugged. Ruggedly handsome.*

Surprised at her private observations, she turned back to the mountains. "I was just looking at the lovely view," she said, hoping her voice didn't betray her slight breathlessness. She could feel the porch give under the weight of his easy shuffle as he moved to join her at the top of the steps.

"Just wait until October," he said, hooking his thumbs in his back pockets. "When the sun hits the mountains like it's doing now, you'll almost think they're on fire."

"It sounds beautiful."

"It is." He glanced her way, then just as quickly looked away. "I didn't see Molly and Colby."

"They've gone for ice cream. I'm afraid she's going to spoil him."

"She probably will, but she knows where to draw the line. I don't think she'll let him get the upper hand on her."

Randi tucked her hair behind her right ear and looked up at him. "It's not Molly I'm worried about. I don't stand a chance when those two put their heads together and make plans."

Paul chuckled.

Randi pushed away from the post. "You ready to go over the renovations?"

"Yep."

"Where do you want to start?"

"How about upstairs in the room itself?"

After going over the redecorating project, Randi and Paul returned to the kitchen. Randi opened the oven door and checked the chicken, stabbing each piece with a fork. But when she closed the oven, she had no idea if the food was done or not. Paul's presence totally threw her off balance.

"I guess a few more minutes won't hurt," she said, placing the fork back on the spoon rest.

Just then the back door flew open and Colby came running into the kitchen, sliding to a stop when he saw Paul.

Paul kneeled with one knee on the floor in front of Colby. "Hey, Sport."

Colby didn't say a word but turned and ran to his room. Molly, who was just entering the kitchen, stepped to the side just in time to avoid a collision. Paul raised a questioning brow at Randi. She just shrugged.

When Colby reappeared, he had Paul's cap in his hand and moved at a much slower pace. He stopped in front of Paul with his head lowered and dejectedly held out the cap. "Mom said I forgot to give this back to you."

Paul ruffled Colby's hair. "You can't give it back."

Colby lifted his head and focused his wide eyes on Paul. "I can't?"

"Nope. I gave it to you. I have this rule, you see. Once I give something away, I never take it back. It's yours forever."

Does that include your heart? Randi had no idea why the question popped into her head. She wasn't prepared for the onslaught of perplexing emotions this man was arousing in her.

"Thanks!" Colby threw himself at Paul, wrapping his chubby arms around Paul's wide neck. Paul couldn't keep his balance and ended up sitting in the floor with Colby in his lap, his throaty laughter mingling with Colby's bubbly giggles.

When the laughter died, Paul and Colby picked themselves up from the floor.

"Paul, you don't have any plans tonight, do you?" Molly asked.

"Not really."

"Good. Then you can stay for supper." Molly started pulling plates out of the cabinet and setting the table, apparently considering the matter settled.

Randi checked the chicken once more and, satisfied it was done, took it out of the oven. After they all sat down, Molly asked the blessing.

"I'm not hungry," Colby announced a few minutes into the meal. "My belly's still got ice cream in it."

Randi shot Molly a quick glance before looking at Colby. "I'm not surprised. I'll cover your plate, and you can eat before you go to bed."

Molly turned to Paul. "Are you—?"

"Hey, Aunt Molly," Colby chimed.

Randi put her hand on Colby's arm. "Colby, Aunt Molly was talking."

"As I was about to say, Paul, are you going—?"

"Know what, Paul?" Colby cut in again.

"Colby," Randi said firmly, "you're going to your room if you interrupt again."

Colby propped his elbows on the table and plopped his cheeks in his hands.

Paul watched the pouting boy for a minute, then said, "Tell you what, Sport. If you can sit there and not interrupt while we grown-ups finish eating, you and I will go in the family room and watch the Braves while the womenfolk clean up the kitchen."

Colby's face lit up. "Can we play a game?"

"That depends on whether you can make it through the rest of the meal without interrupting."

"I will!"

Bristling, Randi glowered at Paul. Just who did he think he was, taking control of a situation between her and her son?

Paul, in turn, just sent her a wink and turned back to Molly, which irritated Randi even more.

"As I was saying," Molly started for the third time. "Paul, are you going to sit up with Reverend Phil and cook the pigs tonight?"

Paul took his second roll from the bread basket. "You know the reverend. He thinks the pigs can't cook without me."

"It's more like you think the pigs can't cook without you." Molly turned to Randi, who was totally confused, and explained. "Tomorrow the church is having an all-day fund-raiser barbecue. Several of the men from the church are going to sit up tonight and cook the pigs."

"Oh," was the only reply Randi could think of.

Colby opened his mouth to speak. Paul froze, fork in midair, and fixed his eyes on the boy's round face. It wasn't a mean or threatening look—just a steady gaze that said, "Don't forget our deal."

Colby closed his mouth and remained silent for the rest of the meal, swinging his short legs underneath the table.

Randi was amazed and, she had to admit, a little impressed. She and Colby usually engaged in a small tug-of-war game when he decided he wanted to be the center of attention, which was often. But Paul's tactic had worked, and she found her irritation at him slipping away.

Colby retrieved a few of his favorite toys and games from his room, then skipped to the family room in front of Paul while Randi and Molly started gathering plates from the table. After they put the last dish away, they made their way to the family room.

Paul's and Colby's attention shifted between the television and a board game that was on the floor between them. Colby's oversized cap dangled sideways on his head.

"Come on, Ump. It was outside by half a foot," Paul argued with the chubby man in blue on the tube.

"Yeah, by half a foot," Colby echoed, and Randi couldn't help but smile.

Paul noticed Randi and Molly standing at the door and checked his watch. "Sorry, Sport, but it's time for us to clean up our mess. I've got to go home and change before I go roast pigs tonight."

Molly bent to pick up a stray toy soldier at her feet. "Randi, you walk Paul out, and I'll help Colby put his things away."

Paul didn't argue as he brought his large frame up off the floor, his movements as graceful as a mountain lion.

Colby jumped up. "I want to walk out with Paul."

Paul straightened Colby's hat. "Maybe next time, Sport. Aunt Molly needs your help right now." With that, he followed Randi to the back porch, pulling the door closed behind them.

Randi turned to him. "Thanks for entertaining Colby."

"I think it was the other way around. I don't remember ever having that much energy."

"You probably didn't."

Paul's brows knitted. "I don't understand."

"Colby has ADHD, attention deficit hyperactivity disorder. He has to take medication for it."

"Oh." Paul gave a thoughtful nod.

"Molly knew about it before she hired me. I hope you don't have a problem with it."

"Of course not. He's a great kid."

She was relieved to see open honesty in his eyes. "Thank you," she said.

Paul dug keys out of his pocket. "I've got to run. They'll be looking for me at the church."

"Hold on," Randi said as he started down the steps. She dug several bills out of her pocket. "Here's the money for my supper last night."

Paul held up a palm. "No. My treat."

"No, really—"

"No argument." He cupped her hand with his and pushed it back toward her. Upon contact, their gazes locked—and Randi's world tilted.

She lowered her hand. "Well, if you're sure—"

"I'm sure."

Randi watched as he climbed into his truck and drove away with a wave of his hand. Since he owned the shop, it was only fair to at least tell him about Colby's ADHD. But that's where she drew the line. She didn't want to risk Colby being treated differently because of his learning disabilities. Besides, she wasn't about to give up hope that, with time, Colby would eventually overcome his handicap.

She stood there awhile longer, trying her best to get a handle on the conflicting emotions at war within her. Since Eddie's death, she had not even been remotely attracted to another man—until now. Being near Paul O'Bryan was like being caught up in a whirlwind. He evoked feelings in her that confused and scared her.

Realizing her thoughts were taking her to a place she didn't want to go, Randi shook herself mentally. *I don't need this. Not now. Not until Colby gets better.*

With that last thought, she turned and went back inside.

❁

Randi didn't see Paul again until she and Colby slipped into the pew next to Molly at eleven o'clock on Sunday morning. Colby insisted on sitting in the middle. Randi had begged off coming to Sunday school, giving the excuse that she didn't want to push Colby too much since tomorrow was the first day of school.

It didn't surprise her to see Paul singing in the bass section of the choir. She picked out his strong, mellow voice immediately. He wore a sport coat and an oxford shirt opened at the throat. No tie.

As Randi scanned the smiling faces of the singers lifting their voices in songs of praise, a longing started tugging at her heartstrings. She felt as though she were being drawn up in a glass bubble, like an outsider looking in. She was once part of a group like this. She once sang in a choir, even sang an occasional solo. She once prayed and studied her Bible daily. In fact, prayer and Colby had been the only things that got her through the year following Eddie's accident.

She had remained faithful in attending church on Sunday mornings. But as time passed and life went on, her sometimes fifty-hour-a-week job and single parenthood gradually edged out her daily visits with God and, eventually, her participation in the choir. Now, as she observed the apparent joy radiating from each face, she realized just how distant she had grown from God, and a chilling thought crossed her mind. *What if He hadn't had time for me when I needed Him most?*

When the choir finished their last song and started assembling themselves among the congregation, Paul sat down next to Randi. Before she knew what was happening, Colby jumped up and squeezed in between her and Paul. As Paul put his arm along the back of the pew behind Colby, his knuckles brushed her shoulder, leaving behind a warm spot where he had touched her.

Randi caught bits and pieces of the sermon, but more than once she found herself distracted by a pale blond who kept glancing back at her from two pews up across the aisle. A young boy who appeared to be a year or two older than Colby sat next to her. Randi quelled the urge to squirm under the woman's repeated scrutiny.

After church, Paul got caught up in the crowd, so Randi tried to make her escape. She had almost made it to her car when she heard him calling her name. She turned as he came trotting up.

Holding his hand out to Colby, Paul said, "Hey, Sport. Give me five." Colby slapped Paul's hand and giggled. Then Paul turned to Randi. "I wanted to invite you to bring Colby to Sunday school next Sunday. I teach his age group, and I'd love to have him in my class."

"We'll see," she answered a bit too quickly.

"Well, I'm still beat after sitting up all night before the barbecue. I'm going home and crash for a couple of hours before the service tonight. Are you coming?"

"I don't think so. I need to get Colby in bed early since school starts tomorrow."

"That's right. Who's his teacher?"

How could she get around telling him Colby was in special education? *Think, Randi, think.* "He's in Mrs. Green's homeroom."

"She's a nice lady."

"That's the impression I got when I met her during Colby's registration Friday."

Paul hesitated, trapping her gaze with his. "I'll see you tomorrow evening, Miranda."

Her name rolled off his tongue like a smooth melody. Usually she insisted on simply being called Randi. But this time, for some reason, she didn't.

"Okay," she said.

As Paul turned to go, Randi noticed the pale blond standing in the front of the church watching her again. Puzzled, Randi returned her gaze. There was something sad in the way the woman looked at her.

Intending to introduce herself, Randi took a step forward. But the woman turned away and walked in the opposite direction, leading the little boy who sat with her in church by the hand.

Chapter 4

On Monday morning, Colby bounced into Mrs. Green's room with his superhero backpack bobbing along behind him. Mrs. Green looked up from a cluster of six year olds and gave Randi the A-OK sign. With nothing else left to do, Randi made her way outside to her car.

She drove away cautiously, as parents and children were walking up the sidewalk. At the end of the school drive, an officer was directing traffic. Randi stopped and waited for the go-ahead sign.

As she accelerated to make a left-hand turn, a dog darted into the path of her car. Automatic reflexes caused her to jerk the steering wheel to the right. The next thing she knew, she was looking through the broken windshield at the front of her car, crinkled like an accordion against a power pole.

She grabbed her head. "What happened?" Then it came to her. Pushing the button on her seat belt, she tried to open the door but it wouldn't budge. She scrambled to the passenger side, ignoring the pain shooting through her left temple. As she reached for the door, it flew open and the traffic officer appeared in front of her.

"Are you all right, Ma'am?"

"I'm fine. Did I hit anyone?"

"No, Ma'am. Everyone out here's fine."

Relieved, Randi slumped in the seat.

"I'm going to call an ambulance to check you out," the officer said. "Is there anyone I need to call for you?"

"Please call my aunt, Molly O'Bryan, at Simple Treasures Novelty Shop," Randi said. "Be sure you tell her I'm fine, and ask her to call a wrecker service. I'm new in town and have no idea who to call."

Within minutes the ambulance arrived. An emergency medical technician urged Randi to lie down on a gurney. She closed her eyes and tried to convince her head to stop hurting.

"Are you sure you don't feel any pain?" the EMT asked as he put one hand under her knee and raised it while pushing on the bottom of her foot with his other hand.

"I'm fine." She didn't mention the bump she had taken on the left side of her head, fearing she would be hauled off to the hospital in the ambulance.

"Are you okay?"

Her heart skipped a beat at the sound of Paul's voice. Opening her eyes, she found him bending over her. "I will be when they get through poking around on me."

Paul turned to the EMT. "Is she going to be okay?"

The EMT shrugged. "Everything seems to be all right, which is amazing considering the shape her car is in."

Randi raised her head and glanced at her pitiful little automobile. A man from Mel's Wrecker Service stood shaking his head as he examined the front. Randi dropped her head back onto the cot and sighed. "Can I get up now?"

"Sure," the EMT told her as he filled out a paper on a clipboard. "We just need your name, address, and telephone number; then you can be on your way. But if anything comes up and you start experiencing any pain or discomfort, please check with your doctor."

"Thank you. I will." Randi sat up and filled in the required information. When she stood, she swayed slightly.

Paul quickly slipped his arm around her. "Are you sure you're okay?"

"Yes. I just got up too fast. Let's go see about my car." Paul kept his arm around her as they walked to her car.

The man from Mel's Wrecker Service had the bill of his cap trapped between his thumb and forefinger and was using the other three fingers to scratch the top of his balding head. "This your car, Ma'am?"

"I'm afraid so."

"Good thing you had your seat belt on."

"How did you know I had it on?"

" 'Cause if you hadn't, you would have gone right through the windshield."

Paul's fingers dug into Randi's side. Being ticklish, she jumped.

"Sorry," he mumbled, dropping his hold on her and hooking his thumbs in his back pockets.

Randi supplied the man from Mel's with her name and phone number, then turned to Paul. "How did you find out about the wreck so fast?"

"Molly called."

"Then she's not coming?"

"No. I'll take you back to the house."

"That's okay; I'll call a taxi."

Paul grinned. "We don't have a taxi in Serenity."

Realizing she had no other choice, Randi asked, "Are you sure it isn't too much trouble?"

"No trouble at all."

"Okay. Let me get my purse."

Paul held her upper arm while she retrieved her purse and walked to his truck. He didn't release her until she was in the passenger seat reaching for her seat belt.

"Do you feel like running by the job site?" Paul asked as he climbed in the truck. "It's just up the road, and I need to check in with my foreman."

Randi shrugged. "Sure."

"No belated aches or pains?"

"I'm fine. Thanks."

Five minutes later, Paul turned onto a dirt drive, his truck kicking up dust clouds when it left the pavement. He stopped near the skeleton of a long, two-story building where several men in hard hats were working. "You're looking at Serenity's first low-income apartment complex," he said, switching off the pickup. "This won't take long."

After they got out, Paul came around the back of the truck to meet her. As he stepped up to her, he reached into the truck bed and pulled out two hard hats. Before she could react, he plopped one of the oversized hats onto her sore head.

"Ouch!" Her hand flew to the side of her head.

Paul froze. "Wait a minute. You hit your head in the wreck, didn't you?"

"It's just a little bump. No big deal."

He tossed the hats back into the truck bed and reached for the sore spot with his right hand. She tried to back away, but he gently circled her upper arm with his left hand and pulled her toward him. "Did you tell the EMT about it?"

"Really, it's nothing."

He pulled her hand away and replaced it with his own, his touch feather light as he threaded his fingers through her hair. Suddenly, his eyebrows shot up. "Land sakes! You've got a knot as big as a goose egg!" He opened her door. "Get in."

"W—what are you going to do?"

"Take you to the doctor."

"Oh, no, you're not."

"Oh, yes, I am."

She crossed her arms and stood her ground.

And he stood his. "Look, you can get in, or I can put you in. Either way, you're going to the doctor."

His voice was low and calm, but the determination in his eyes told Randi he would do exactly what he said. In order not to make a scene, she climbed into the truck, pulling her arm away when he reached to help her. After he climbed in and closed his door, she turned on him. "I am not going to the doctor!"

"We'll see. Fasten your seat belt." With that, Paul set the truck in motion.

※

Randi stormed into the kitchen and started pacing. After spending most of the day in the clinic, the doctor had sent her home with a handful of sample pain tablets and advice that she have someone wake her several times during the night.

"I told him I was fine!" she mumbled. If her head did not hurt so badly, she would scream. She was without a car and in debt to the ambulance service. And now, thanks to Paul, she had a doctor bill she couldn't afford to pay.

She heard him try to open the door and waited for a knock so she could tell him to get lost. Instead, she heard a key turning the lock. Looking heavenward, she gave a palms-up gesture. *Of course, he's got a key. He owns the place.* She pushed her hair behind her right ear and crossed her arms. "Well, he doesn't own me."

The fact that Paul was smiling when he stepped into the kitchen just riled her that much more. "I hope you're happy. Molly's gone in her car, and I have to be at the school in fifteen minutes to pick up Colby."

Paul leaned back against the cabinet, crossing his arms and ankles. "Molly's going to pick up Colby."

Randi blinked. "She is?"

Paul nodded. "I called her from the clinic."

"Oh." A pause, then a meek, "Thanks."

His grin broadened, making his eyes crinkle.

Randi scowled. "What's so funny?"

He just chuckled.

"Let me guess. I look electric, right?"

"Sweetheart, right now you could light up the whole state of Georgia."

Chapter 5

I will not let Paul O'Bryan upset me again," Randi muttered to herself the next morning as she gingerly pulled a brush through her hair. She was going to have to remember who Paul was: the owner of the shop she now managed. Even if he didn't have a right to force her to go to the doctor, he did have the right to fire her if he found reason.

She fastened her hair at the nape of her neck with a gold clasp, then headed for the door in search of Colby. He should have been in for inspection by now.

A glance in his room told her he wasn't there. She started toward the kitchen but stopped short of entering when she heard his giggle, followed by Paul's low chuckle.

"Mom don't let me sit on top of the cabinets."

"Your mom's got a good point," came Paul's smooth voice, "because you could fall and get hurt if you tried to get up here by yourself."

"What if she catches me? She won't give me a ticket."

"Ticket?"

"I get tickets for being good. Then on Friday, I get to trade them in for something special."

"I'll tell you what, if you don't tell her, I won't tell her. It'll be our secret."

Randi peeked into the kitchen. Paul was standing with his shoulder and back pointed toward her at an angle, slipping a tennis shoe onto Colby's short foot. Paul wore casual khaki slacks and a green cotton shirt, not his usual work jeans and T-shirt.

"Can you tie your shoes?" Paul asked.

"No, but me and Mom's been workin' on it."

"Show me what you can do."

Colby lifted his foot to the countertop, tied the string once, then placed his hands in his lap and looked up at Paul.

"You've got the first step down pat. Let me show you how I learned to tie my shoe. You make two rabbit ears." Paul made a loop with each side of the string. "Then you do the first step all over again with the rabbit ears." He followed through.

"That's easy." Colby lifted his other foot to the countertop and, after three tries, tied a perfect rabbit-ears bow.

The scene moved Randi, and she tried to swallow the lump rising in her throat.

Paul lifted Colby to the floor. "How do you like Mrs. Green?"

"Mrs. Green's not my real teacher. I just go to her for—"

Randi popped into the kitchen. "Good morning!"

"Good morning," Paul and Colby chorused.

Colby looked up at Paul, put his hand over his mouth, and giggled. Paul winked at Colby. The pair looked as though they shared a well-guarded secret, and Randi struggled to keep from laughing.

Colby ran to her and stuck his foot out. "Look what I did, Mom. All by myself."

Randi kneeled. "I am very proud of you." She hugged him, then held him at arm's length. "I think that deserves an extra ticket."

"You have to give Paul one, too. He showed me how."

Randi glanced at Paul, noticing the merriment dancing in his eyes, then looked back at Colby. "I think you're right." She stood, opened a drawer, and tore two tickets from a fat roll.

Colby grabbed his ticket and headed to his room to add it to his ticket jar.

Taking the remaining ticket, Paul pulled his wallet from his back pocket and flipped it open. He stuck the ticket inside, then slipped the wallet back in his pocket, giving Randi a wink.

Molly joined them, and the women cooked breakfast while the men set the table. After they all sat down, Molly said, "Paul, would you bless the food?"

Paul nodded, and everyone bowed their heads.

"Dear Lord, thank You for the many blessings You have given us," he prayed earnestly. "We especially thank You for keeping Miranda safe when she had the accident yesterday. We ask for Your guidance and safekeeping throughout this day, and ask that You bless this food for the nourishment of our bodies. Amen."

"Amen," Molly repeated.

"Amen!" Colby added.

"Amen," Randi mumbled, feeling guilty. She hadn't even taken the time to utter a prayer of thanks to God for protecting her when she had wrecked.

Paul took a biscuit then held the bread basket out to Colby. "How's your head?" he asked Randi.

"Much better, thanks."

"Did you hear from Mel?"

"Yes, and it's not good. The frame of my car is warped beyond repair." Randi turned to Molly. "Do you mind if I borrow your car to take Colby to school today?"

"That won't be necessary," Paul answered. "You and I can drop Colby off. I need you to ride to Blairsville with me today."

Randi stopped spreading butter on her biscuit and trained a wide-eyed gaze on Paul. "I have to work today."

"You will be working. We need to pick out supplies for the shop renovations."

Both fear and excitement gripped her at the thought of spending the day with Paul. "Molly, why don't you ride to Blairsville with Paul and let me stay here and look after the shop?"

Molly gave her a smug smile. "Can't. I have a friend coming to have lunch with me today."

After the meal, Randi helped Molly set the dishes in the sink, then walked outside with Paul and Colby. A new white van with the words "Simple Treasures Novelty Shop" written on the door in silver script was sitting where she had expected Paul's truck to be.

"Catch." Paul tossed a set of keys to her when he had her attention.

She grabbed the keys out of the air. "What's this?"

"A van for you."

She froze. "Paul, I can get my own vehicle."

Paul took a deep breath and exhaled, turning to face her. "It's not for you personally. It's for the manager of the shop, which just happens to be you right now. When you leave—"

"What do you mean, when I leave?"

"Excuse me. If you leave, the van stays." He spun and continued toward the van. "If you don't believe me, I'll show you the invoice. I ordered it two weeks ago."

Warmth crept up her neck and over her face. What on earth made her think he would go out and buy something as costly as a van just because she wrecked her car anyway? Venting her frustration and embarrassment, she mocked him under her breath, bobbing her head from side to side like a disgruntled child. "If you leave, the van stays."

Suddenly Paul stopped, as though he had heard, and turned narrowed eyes on her.

She met him with a smile. "Coming, Master."

He grinned. "Good girl. If you behave, I might stop and get you a treat on the way home."

Randi rolled her eyes and caught up with him. "You drive." She pushed the keys toward him. "Colby, you can sit in the front."

"Oh, boy!" Colby took off running toward the van. Randi helped him fasten his seat belt, then climbed into the seat behind him.

Colby chattered nonstop to Paul during the ride to school while Randi silently renewed her vow to stay cool and calm. When they arrived, she got out and opened the door for Colby. To her surprise, he hopped up on his knees and wrapped his short, fleshy arms around Paul's neck.

"Bye, Paul."

Paul gave Colby a warm smile. "Bye, Sport. Have a good day."

Randi bent down for a hug and kiss, then gingerly climbed into the front seat as Colby took off skipping toward the school building.

"Thanks for straightening Colby's clothes this morning," she said once they were on their way. "How much damage did you have to repair?"

Paul smiled. "Well, let me see. We rebuttoned the shirt, straightened the waist of the pants, moved the heel of one sock from the top of the ankle to its proper place, and put the shoes on the right feet." He shook his head. "He's something else. We could learn a lot from kids like Colby."

"What do you mean, kids like Colby?" Randi's couldn't keep the note of defensiveness out of her voice, but Paul didn't seem to notice.

"He's so full of life and gets excited about the smallest things. It doesn't take much to make him happy." He hesitated, then added, "It says a lot about the way he's been raised."

"Thank you." Randi took a deep breath, deciding now would be a good time to call a truce. "I'm sorry I lost my temper yesterday. It's just that I'm not used to someone else. . ." She paused, realizing if she finished the sentence it would point out that she felt he had been overbearing.

"Butting in and making decisions for you," he finished for her.

She looked at him, considering the laugh lines crinkling the corners of his eyes, and said, "Well, that's not exactly what I was going to say." She couldn't help it—she smiled. "But you've got the idea."

Paul chuckled, but as his laughter died, his expression turned serious. "I understand. But not telling the EMT about your head wasn't a wise decision."

She quelled the urge to argue. "I guess you're right. Anyway, I'm sorry I got so worked up. Yesterday was just unusually eventful, to say the least."

His mouth tipped in amusement. "No problem. I kinda like your spirit."

Her heart fell. He was laughing at her again. Why did she care so much about what he thought?

"I understand your family still lives in Columbus," Paul continued.

"Yes. My mother is a substitute teacher, and my brother, Mike, is an attorney in a small law firm. My dad died when I was fifteen."

"Sorry."

"Thanks. What about you? Do you have any relatives in Serenity?"

"Nope. There's just me. My parents were hit and killed by a drunk driver when I was ten. I have a few relatives out West, but I don't see much of them."

"Molly told me about your parents. I'm sorry."

"Thanks. Grandma died two years later, and it was just Granddad and me until he married Molly." He grinned. "She took some getting used to, but now I consider her my closest family."

Randi's lips circled up. "I imagine Molly did take some getting used to." A small silence passed; then she decided to satisfy her curiosity about something. "Paul, when I first saw you at the store, then again at the house that same evening, I got the feeling you thought you knew me from somewhere. I visited Molly for a few days thirteen years ago after my father passed away, but I don't remember meeting you."

"I wasn't living in Serenity then." He hesitated, glancing her way, then back to the road. "The first time I saw you was at your husband's funeral."

Randi frowned, thinking back. "I'm sorry. I don't remember meeting you."

"Actually, we didn't meet. Molly was about to introduce us when—"

"I passed out," Randi interjected.

Paul nodded.

Randi looked down at her hands, drawing in a deep breath, then releasing it. "Well, believe it or not, life does goes on."

※

Just before noon, they walked out of the hardware store in Blairsville with everything Paul needed to refurbish the upstairs portion of the shop. "I'm ready for lunch," he said as he put the last gallon of paint into the back of the van. "How about you?"

"Sure," Randi agreed, hoping it was within her budget.

Paul drove to a street lined with small shops and parked in front of a store called the Pet House. Next to the door was a small fenced-in area with four puppies inside. A sign hanging on the fence said "Adopt-a-Pet."

Randi struggled to keep her voice calm as she asked, "Is this a joke?" recalling what he said about getting her a treat on the way home if she was good.

Paul's eyes followed the direction of her pointing finger. He looked at the window of the store, then back at her with a raised brow. His shoulders started shaking; then his deep, hearty laughter rumbled up from his chest. Before Randi realized it, she was laughing along with him. Then their gazes met and held as they both sobered.

"That's the first time I've heard you laugh," he told her. "It suits you."

Randi glanced down. She couldn't remember the last time she had felt so carefree and lighthearted.

Struggling with the reality of what was happening between her and Paul, she took a deep breath and raised her head, trying to keep her voice steady. "Well, when you said lunch, I had no idea this was what you had in mind."

Paul pulled the keys from the ignition and used them to point over his shoulder. "What I had in mind was lunch at the Trolley."

Randi looked across the street at a building painted to look like a black-and-red trolley. She met Paul at the back of the van, and his large callused hand swallowed hers as they crossed the street. But the second they stepped up to the door of the restaurant, he let go.

After sharing a companionable meal, Paul and Randi left the restaurant. Instead of stopping at the van, Randi headed straight for the fenced-in area outside the Pet House. She loved animals, but where she and Colby had lived in Columbus, the apartment manager allowed no pets.

She bent down and picked up one of the puppies. The dog had long ears, large white front paws, and was the scrawniest of the litter. Smiling, she held the pup up in front of her. "Hey there, little fella."

Suddenly, the puppy jutted his head forward. Randi turned her head, laughing and wrinkling her nose just in time to dodge the dog's tongue.

Then she noticed Paul. He stood leaning against the van door, arms and ankles crossed, staring at her with a strange, unreadable expression. Was he upset with her? Did he think she was wasting his time by taking a few minutes to play with a puppy? Maybe he didn't like animals. She returned the puppy to the fenced-in area.

Paul pushed away from the van and sauntered over to the fence. Kneeling, he took the time to scratch each pup behind the ear. He chuckled as they all fought for equal attention.

Randi watched the interaction. Maybe she was wrong. Maybe he did like animals. But why had he looked at her in such an odd way. *Who cares?* she asked herself.

A small voice in the back of her mind replied, *You do.*

As he stood, he asked, "Are you ready to go?"

"Yes. I need to get back in time to pick up Colby."

Paul held the keys up in front of her. "This time, you're going to drive."

The thought of driving the van for the first time with him in it didn't appeal to her. "I'll wait." She pushed his hand away and started toward the passenger door.

Paul stepped off the curb into her path, causing her to stumble into him. His free arm snaked around her as he continued dangling the keys in front of her. Even with her feet on the curb, she had to tilt her chin to look into his eyes. They danced with amusement.

"You seem to have a habit of falling into people's arms," he said.

His closeness set her heart to pounding. She was certain he could hear it. Pushing away, she said in a jesting tone, "Very funny." She grabbed the keys, marched to the driver's side, and opened her door. "Maybe I won't unlock your door," she teased. "Just let you find your own way home."

He narrowed his eyes, trying unsuccessfully to contain a grin. "You wouldn't dare."

She arched her brows. "Oh? Wouldn't I?"

He started around the front of the van.

"Okay, okay." She held her hands up in surrender. "I'll unlock the door."

Feeling giddy, she slid behind the steering wheel; then it hit her what she'd just done. She'd just flirted with him.

The reality was so startling, she dropped the keys twice before successfully getting them into the ignition.

❁

"Do you have time to drop me off at my office before you pick up Colby?" Paul asked as they approached town.

"Sure, I have a few minutes."

She followed his directions to a modest gray office building with several pieces of heavy equipment sitting behind it.

"Come in and meet Edith," he said. "If you ever need to find me during the week between eight and five, she'll know where I am."

Randi nodded and followed him into the office.

Edith was a friendly woman with short, prematurely gray hair and, if Randi didn't miss her guess, a very efficient secretary. She handed two phone messages to Paul, briefly explaining their contents.

"Excuse me while I return these calls," he told Randi, then disappeared through a door at the back of the small reception room.

When Paul returned, Edith picked up a paper she had turned facedown on her desk and held it out to him. "Sorry to be the bearer of bad news."

Paul took the paper and studied it a moment. Grimacing, he said, "The zoning board's at it again, huh?" Looking at his secretary, he added, "Call the commissioner and set up a meeting."

Randi had no idea what they were talking about, only that it sounded important. She hated to interrupt, but she had her own business to take care of. "Excuse me," she cut in. "I need to go pick up Colby."

"I'll walk you out." Paul gave the paper back to Edith and followed Randi outside.

Just before she reached the van, he wrapped his hand around her upper arm and turned her to face him, taking her by surprise. She released a soft gasp as she looked up at him.

"Miranda." His voice was low, hypnotizing.

She swallowed. "Yes?"

But he said nothing—just looked at her, holding her spellbound with his intense gaze.

Despite her efforts to resist, one foot inched toward him of its own volition. He reached up and tucked a stray strand of hair behind her ear, his knuckles lightly grazing the angle of her jaw as he withdrew his hand. Then he dropped his hold on her and stepped back, hooking his thumbs in his back pockets.

The spell was broken.

"I just wanted to tell you not to be in a hurry to replace your car. The van is entirely at your disposal."

"Paul, I can't—"

"Please." He stopped her. "That's what I bought it for."

The plea in his voice left her unable to argue. "Thanks," she whispered.

"I guess I'll postpone the work on the shop until next week since the Labor Day weekend's coming up. Maybe I'll see you at church Sunday?"

"Maybe." Randi looked away, hoping to hide her disappointment. "Thanks for the lunch." She turned and walked quickly to the van.

As she drove away, once-dormant feelings broke through the wall she had spent seven years building around her heart. A wall that had started to crumble when she fell into the arms of a green-eyed giant just five short days ago.

She fought back tears and spoke to Someone she had not spoken to in a very long time. "Dear God, please don't let me fall in love now. I have to think of Colby."

But she had a sinking feeling it was already too late.

Chapter 6

O ne week later, Molly left for a two-week trip to Alaska. Randi bid her aunt farewell that morning, feeling confident everything would run smoothly during her absence. By noon that day, Randi was afraid everything would run too smoothly. Only two customers came into the shop that morning, neither of which bought anything.

Restless from the stillness, Randi went into the kitchen to fix some lunch, leaving the door open in case the bell on the shop entrance signaled the arrival of a patron.

After searching the cabinets and refrigerator, she decided she wasn't all that hungry, after all, so she made her way to her bedroom. She retrieved her Bible and an ink pen from the nightstand and, taking them back to the shop, sat down on a stool behind the checkout counter.

She had been trying to read her Bible over the past few days, trying to reconnect with God. But her mind, it seemed, would always wander from the text she chose.

"Today, I'll let God do the choosing," she said, closing her eyes and sticking her thumb between two pages. She flipped open the book, then opened her eyes, and Psalm 51 lay before her.

She read the entire psalm, then went back and read verses 10, 11, and 12 again. She underlined the three verses, then read them a third time.

"Create in me a clean heart, O God; and renew a right spirit within me. Cast me not away from thy presence; and take not thy holy spirit from me. Restore unto me the joy of thy salvation; and uphold me with thy free spirit."

A tear fell as Randi whispered, "That is my desire, God."

Placing her head on her folded arms, Randi poured her heart out to God, wanting so much to feel His presence dwelling inside her. She had no idea how long she sat there with her head bowed when it finally happened. A tiny spark ignited in the center of her heart; then God fanned it into a flame, spreading joy and peace from her head to her toes.

When she rose, she looked up through tears and whispered, "Thank You, sweet Jesus."

She still had no crystal-clear, carved-in-stone answers concerning Colby's handicap or what the future would bring for Paul and her. What she did have, though, was the blessed assurance God would help her find her answers, even if the search was a long and painful one.

❀

Thirty minutes after Randi closed the shop that afternoon, the phone rang.

"Hello, Miranda."

Her pulse quickened. "Hi, Paul."

"I just thought I'd let you know something's come up and I'm not going to be able to come by tonight and finish painting the upstairs bathroom."

"Do you want me to finish it?"

"No," Paul quickly replied. "It's not that big a deal. I'll finish tomorrow evening."

"Okay."

He hesitated, as though thinking, then said, "Well, have a good evening."

"You, too."

Randi hung up the phone with a smile. "He thinks I can't paint." She shrugged and went in search of Colby.

Randi and Colby went through their regular routine of supper, homework, reading, bath, and a mild debate over Colby's bedtime coming too soon. Thirty minutes after she tucked him in, she peeked into his room and found him fast asleep. She locked the downstairs doors and made her way upstairs to the unfinished room. The only thing lacking was a coat of paint on two walls. What could be so hard about that?

Before starting the task, Randi opened the window for ventilation. She was about to put the roller to the wall for the third time when she froze. Something was wrong with her fresh coat of paint.

"What in the world?" She took a closer look. "Bugs!"

Tiny black insects were coming through the window screen and planting themselves in the wet paint. Randi closed the window and repaired the damage before resuming her task.

A few minutes later she closed the door in order to get to the area behind it. She was on the stepladder trimming the last few feet next to the ceiling with a paintbrush when she started feeling dizzy. Taking a deep breath, she tried to continue, but the room started to sway. She put the brush down and eased off the ladder.

"What's wrong with me?"

The room started spinning, and she reached for the doorknob. If she could just make it downstairs to the sofa.

She took one step; then everything stopped spinning and turned black.

❀

"Miranda, can you hear me? Miranda?"

46

Paul gently tapped Randi's cheek. "God, please let her wake up. Please." He sat next to her on the edge of the family room sofa where he had carried her after finding her lying on the bathroom floor upstairs.

Relief washed through him when her eyes fluttered open. "Paul?"

He stilled his hand on her face and stroked her cheek with his thumb. "Yes, Miranda, I'm here. Thank God, you're awake."

"What happened?"

"You passed out from paint fumes."

"Oh."

"How do you feel?"

She frowned. "Like I just woke up after passing out from paint fumes."

Paul shook his head. "What am I going to do with you?"

"For starters, you could help me up."

"You need to lie down a few more minutes."

Wide-eyed, she stared up at him, and he could almost see the wheels inside her head turning. Finally she said, "I'll meet you halfway. Help me sit up."

He studied her huge, dark eyes, considering her request. Reluctantly, he yielded. "Promise you won't try to stand for awhile?"

"Promise."

Paul slid off the sofa and bent over her, slipping his arm beneath her shoulders and supporting her head with the palm of his hand as he eased her up. He then sat down next to her and watched intently until he was sure she wasn't going to faint again. "Are you sure you feel okay?" he asked.

She nodded.

"Good!" He jumped up, slapping his palms against his jean-clad thighs in the process, and took three swift strides to the fireplace. He paused, hands on hips and back to her, then turned and took three quick steps back to the sofa, dropping to his knees in front of her. He grasped her upper arms firmly and shook her gently. "Are you crazy?!"

"No," she answered calmly.

"What were you thinking, painting in a sealed room?"

Randi blinked twice. "I guess I wasn't thinking."

"Obviously not!"

"Shhhh." She put her finger to her lips. "You'll wake Colby."

Paul noticed a twinkle in her eyes. The right corner of her mouth eased up, then the left. She was smiling at him! *Did the paint fumes get to her brain?* "What's so funny?"

"You are," she said, obviously trying to stifle laughter. "We're doing a role reversal here. You're acting like me." Her laughter started to fade. "At least, how I would have acted before this afternoon."

Paul sat back on his heels, placing his palms on his thighs. "What about this afternoon, Miranda?"

"Do you have a minute?"

He considered her serious expression. "Sure," he said. He rose from his knees and sat next to her, resting his arm along the back of the sofa behind her.

Randi's gaze drifted to her hands lying in her lap. "Do you remember that first Sunday Colby and I visited your church?"

"Yes."

"Well, while the choir was singing, it occurred to me that I had lost touch with God. 'Fell by the wayside,' as Molly would say. I didn't do anything bad or morally wrong," she wanted him to know. "But I did get my priorities mixed up and put a lot of things before God. I've been trying for some time now to find my way back."

"And?" He held his breath.

She looked up at him with a radiant smile. "And today, I made it back."

He pulled her into his arms and cradled her head against his chest with one hand, his heart swelling with emotion. "Welcome home." He kissed the top of her head and gently squeezed her, then replaced the spot his lips had touched with his bearded cheek.

His homecoming hug was too short-lived as Randi pushed away and cast her eyes shyly downward. "Thank you, Paul. I knew you would understand."

The fact that she could be so bashful touched him that much more. Reaching up, he cupped her jaw with his palm and urged her head up. Her warm breath caressed his face. He moved his thumb up and lightly caressed her temple, drinking in her smooth complexion, her dark round eyes, her small straight nose, her slightly parted lips. She was the closest thing to perfection he had ever seen, and at that moment he knew he had stepped through a door he would never walk out of. Sometime between that day at the convenience store and now, this fiery-eyed, pint-sized woman had slipped into his life and stolen his heart.

Just as he opened his mouth to express his feelings, her eyes widened and she pushed away. The words Paul wanted to say got caught up in his throat. "Don't move," he said instead. "I'm going to go straighten up upstairs."

Disheartened, Paul climbed the steps. Judging from her reaction, she didn't share his feelings.

❀

Paul did allow Randi to walk him outside after he put the finishing touch on the upstairs bathroom. She turned to him as they stepped out onto the porch. "I hope I didn't make a mess of things upstairs."

"The only thing you made a mess of tonight was yourself."

She ducked her head. "I'm sorry."

He tipped her chin and leveled his gaze at her. "You scared me, Miranda. Promise me you'll not do any more redecorating unless I'm here with you."

"Promise." Randi took a deep breath, glancing away and breaking contact. "I thought you were going to be tied up tonight. What happened?"

"I finished early and thought I'd stop by and check on you and Colby. I'm glad I did."

"Me, too."

"And by the way, the walls you painted look great."

She turned back to him and smiled, feeling a little lightheaded, but not from belated effects of the paint fumes. "Thanks."

After he climbed into the truck, she threw up her hand. He returned her wave and drove away.

Leaning against the top post, she closed her eyes and whispered, "Dear God, I'm not ready for this."

Chapter 7

The following afternoon, Randi breezed through the swinging doors into the kitchen to find Paul and Colby entering the room from the back hallway. She came to an abrupt halt.

"Hi, Miranda." Paul smiled.

"Hi. I was just coming outside to check on Colby."

"Mom, can Paul stay for supper?" Colby cut in. Both adults looked at Colby, hesitating. Colby turned to Paul. "Please stay, Paul. You can use your ticket. Mom'll let you."

Paul and Randi glanced at each other, unable to contain their smiles. Paul pulled his wallet from his back pocket, flipped it open, and pulled out the ticket. "Well, Mom, what do you say? Can I use my ticket?"

Randi shook her head. "I can't believe you kept that. Of course you can stay, if you don't mind waiting. I've been so busy I haven't had a chance to start cooking."

"What do you think, Sport?" Paul said, looking down at Colby. "Should we help Mom out and cook supper?"

"Yes!"

"Paul," Randi said. "I'm not sure that's a good idea."

Paul glanced up at her with a raised brow. "You don't think I can cook?"

"It's not that. I assume you've never tried cooking with a. . . ," she paused, guarding her words in Colby's presence, ". . .with a six year old as full of life as Colby."

Colby clasped his hands together beneath his chin. "Please, Mom. Please, please, please, please."

"I'll take full responsibility if the omelet burns," Paul added.

"It's not the omelet I'm worried about getting burned," Randi said.

"I understand, and I promise to be careful." Paul held out the ticket.

Randi hesitated, the right side of her lower lip caught between her teeth. "Okay," she finally agreed. She took the ticket from Paul and bent down, cupping Colby's chin in her hand. "Listen, Son, you have to be good and mind Paul."

"I'll be good, Mom; I promise." Colby stood innocently with his hands behind his back, tugging at her heartstrings.

Randi straightened and faced Paul. "He's not to get near the stove while it's hot, okay?"

"I'll be good, Mom; I promise." Laugh lines creased the outside corners of his eyes as he mimicked Colby, and Randi's heartstrings were pulled tighter.

"Well, I guess I'd better get back in there," she said. "It's almost time to close up."

Thirty minutes later she walked back into the kitchen to find the table set with ham-and-cheese omelets, toast, and applesauce. The smell of warm bread woke her taste buds.

"Who's gonna pray?" Colby asked as he climbed into his chair.

Paul leaned with his forearms on the table. "Who would you like to pray?"

"Mom."

Randi's eyes stretched wide with surprise. "I'm not very good at praying out loud."

Paul held his hand out to her. "We're behind you."

Colby sent Paul a confused frown. "We're not behind Mom."

"I meant we'll pray silently with her while she prays out loud," Paul took the time to explain.

Satisfied, Colby erased his frown and smiled. "Okay."

As they joined hands, Randi silently asked for God's help. He didn't let her down, and she was amazed at how easily the words came as she spoke, right up to the "Amen." When she raised her head, Paul squeezed her hand and smiled. Her pulse quickened in response.

Colby and Paul dominated the conversation during the meal; then they all three pitched in to clean the kitchen. Paul and Randi were putting the last dishes away when he looked down and asked, "What can I do for you, Sport?"

Randi glanced down to find the outer seam along the thigh of Paul's blue jeans bunched in Colby's fist.

"Will you stay a little while and play with me?" Colby asked.

Paul's gaze darted to Randi, then back to Colby. "I think you need to ask Mom how she feels about that."

Colby turned to her. "Can he, Mom?"

"Sure he can, if he wants to," Randi answered, looking down at her son.

"What does Mom want?" Paul wanted to know.

The question brought Randi's head up, more sharply than she wished. She wanted to kick herself when she opened her mouth and nothing came out. Clearing her throat, she finally managed, "I'd like for you to stay." Then, not wanting to give away the least of her feelings, she added, "Colby enjoys your company."

Paul glanced away. "I see."

She crossed the room and reached inside the cabinet, pulling out a canister. "Why don't you and Colby go on into the family room? I'll make some coffee."

"Come on, Paul," she heard Colby say.

She intentionally took her time digging in the drawer for a scoop, although she knew one was inside the coffee canister. When she turned back around, Paul and Colby were gone.

By the time the coffee started brewing, she had collected the senses Paul had scattered when he asked her if she wanted him to stay. She headed toward the family room, but Colby's voice stopped her short of entering.

"Do you like my mom?"

After a short silence Paul answered. "Sure I do, Sport."

"If you marry her, you can be my daddy."

Another brief pause, then, "Colby, Son, you had a daddy."

"I know, but he's in heaven. He can't ever come back and see me."

"It's not because he doesn't want to, Sport. It's because Jesus has some very important things for him to do in heaven."

"I guess so." Colby sighed.

"I'll tell you what. For now, why don't you and I be best friends?"

"For real?"

Paul chuckled. "For real."

Randi put one hand to the wall, bracing herself as a sinking realization settled deep in the pit of her stomach. There was a lot more at stake here than her feelings alone. Colby was beginning to think of Paul as a father figure. Why had she not seen it coming? He was her son, for crying out loud. Did her feelings for Paul run so deep that they clouded her judgment, not to mention her motherly instincts? What was she going to do now?

She closed her eyes and took a deep breath, trying to compose herself. When she walked through the door, a lump lodged in her throat. Paul sat on the sofa watching TV with his hands laced behind his head, his long legs stretched out in front of him and crossed at the ankles. Colby sat beside him in exactly the same position, only Colby's short legs barely reached to the edge of the sofa.

She sat down on Colby's vacant side. "Who's winning?"

Colby looked to Paul for assistance. Paul mouthed the word, "Braves."

Colby turned back to his mom. "Braves."

"That's good," she said, giving him an apologetic look in the process, "but I'm afraid it's your bedtime."

"Ah, Mom, let me stay up. Just five more minutes."

"Sorry. No can do. Run and get your pajamas on, and I'll be in to help you brush your teeth in a minute."

Colby started to leave, then stopped, his disheartened expression turning hopeful. "Paul, will you read me a story?"

"Colby," Randi said, "you've taken up enough of Paul's time tonight."

"I don't mind if you don't," Paul told her.

Colby clasped his hands beneath his chin. "Please, Mom. Please, please, please, please."

"Okay," she yielded. "Just for tonight."

"Oh, boy!" Colby shouted, skipping out of the room.

Randi picked up a throw pillow and hugged it to her stomach. "You don't know what you just let yourself get talked into."

"What can be so hard about reading a bedtime story?"

"You'll find out." She yawned and sent him a sleepy smile.

Paul stood. "I guess I will. Why don't you take advantage of the break and lie down for awhile?"

"I just might do that."

Colby returned and gave his mother a good night hug and kiss, then slipped his hand in Paul's.

"Don't forget to brush your teeth," Randi reminded him, and as soon as they disappeared through the door, she plumped up her pillow and lay down on the sofa.

For once, sleep came quickly. Because for this hour, for this minute, everything she dreamed of was close by, in a little room down the hall.

❀

An hour later, Paul carefully eased off the edge of Colby's bed and tucked the covers under his chin. As Paul reached to turn off the lamp, Colby halfway opened his sleepy eyes and said, "Please leave the light on. It keeps the monsters away."

Paul's brow dipped. "There's no such thing as monsters, Colby."

"Uh-huh." Colby bobbed his head. "They took my daddy away."

Colby's words bruised Paul's heart. What was Colby talking about? What monsters lived inside his head that he thought robbed him of his daddy?

"Good night, Best Friend Paul," Colby mumbled as he snuggled farther down in the covers. "I love you."

Paul tried to swallow the tightness in his throat. "I love you, too, Sport." He planted a kiss on the top of the boy's head, then stood a few minutes looking at the child who, like his mother, had staked a claim on his heart. Then he eased out of the room, silently vowing to find a way to help Colby chase his monsters away.

Paul found Randi fast asleep on the sofa. She was lying on her side with her hand wedged between her head and a throw pillow, her knees drawn up, and another pillow hugged to her middle. He turned off the overhead light and TV, leaving only the lamp on the end table shining above her head. Sitting down in a recliner, he rested his chin on top of the steeple he made with his fingers and watched her.

This is what I want, God. To see her face first thing every morning and last thing every night. I want to be the father her son longs for. I want to take care of them and protect them—for the rest of their lives.

The question was, what would it take to get her to return those feelings? Paul closed his eyes. *Help me, Father. I've never been down this road before. Please show me what to do.*

As Paul opened his eyes, an enlightening thought crossed his mind. This had all happened so fast. Maybe too fast for her. Perhaps if he gave her time, she'd eventually grow to love him as he loved her.

Deciding she'd be well worth the wait, he rose and ambled to the sofa, dropping to one knee. The apple-blossom scent of her hair invaded his senses as he pushed a stray strand away from her face. Giving into his desire, he risked lightly touching her soft, smooth cheek with his lips.

❀

Something warm and fuzzy tickled Randi's face, causing the corner of her mouth to twitch. She slowly opened her eyes and thought she must be dreaming, because Paul was there, smiling at her.

"Hey, Sleepyhead," he said.

His warm breath permeated the air between them, pulling her into pleasant reality. He was really there. "Did Colby finally go to sleep?"

"Yes."

"How many?"

"One."

Her eyebrows rose.

"I had to read it three times," he confessed.

"You did good. He talked Molly into five stories the first time."

Paul chuckled. "Don't think he didn't try. How about you? Did you have a good nap?"

"Mmm hmm."

"I hated to wake you, but I need to get going."

She sat up and rubbed her eyes. "Thanks for your help tonight, both with supper and Colby."

"I enjoyed it." He stood and held his hand out. She took it, but when she stood, he let go.

As they stepped outside, Paul said, "Don't cook supper tomorrow night. I'll bring pizza."

Randi opened her mouth to protest, but Paul cut her off. "Boss's orders. You've been working too hard."

She stood at the top of the steps and watched him drive away, thinking about the events of the evening. Was he attracted to her or not? She couldn't tell. He was sending mixed signals.

She turned off the light and went back inside, more confused than ever.

Chapter 8

Saturday evening after Molly returned from her Alaska trip, a fierce storm passed through Serenity. Paul phoned Randi the following morning and asked her to teach his Sunday school class, stating he needed to help a friend cut a tree off his house.

Reluctantly, Randi agreed. She had never taught Sunday school before, and thoughts of the task gave her butterflies.

Two hours later, she stood in Paul's classroom, smiling as she inspected the Noah's Ark visual on the wall. The first day she met Paul, she would never have guessed he taught a Sunday school class of six and seven year olds. But the more she learned about him, the more she admired his huge heart and gentle spirit.

"Ricky!"

Colby's excited voice interrupted her musings. She turned and found him running toward the door. She started after him but paused when she saw the pale blond standing in the doorway holding the hand of the little boy who always sat with her in church.

Randi approached the woman, whose light blue eyes were totally void of expression. Her delicate beauty made Randi feel like a piece of chipped stone on display next to a rare jewel. Her hair turned under at the shoulders, and her skin was fair and smooth as a porcelain doll's. But, as Randi noticed that first Sunday she saw the woman, there was a sadness about her.

Randi turned her attention to the little boy. It was the first time she had been close enough to see his facial features, and her breath faltered in her throat. If she didn't miss her guess, he had Down's syndrome. No wonder his mother looked so sad.

Leaning forward, Randi placed her hands on her knees. "You must be Ricky."

Ricky nodded and sent Randi a wide grin. "Where's Uncle Paul?"

Randi silently prayed the small shock waves the little boy's question sent through her didn't show on her face. "He's helping a friend get a tree off his house."

Her explanation seemed to satisfy Ricky.

Colby, who was standing beside Ricky, reached up and put his arm around the taller boy's shoulders. "We're friends at school."

"Well, I'm glad there is going to be someone Colby knows in the class today," Randi said.

"Come on, Ricky, you can sit with me," Colby told his friend as they made their way to the table in the center of the room.

Randi stood and extended her right hand to the woman. "I'm Randi Thomas."

The woman grasped Randi's hand with cool, impersonal fingers. "I'm Marcia Cooper, Ricky's mother. . .and Paul's friend," she said in a voice that was just as expressionless as her eyes.

Jealousy pierced Randi's soul. Just how deep did Paul and Marcia's "friendship" go? Forcing a smile, Randi said, "It's nice to meet you, Marcia."

Marcia didn't return Randi's greeting but glanced toward the table where Ricky and Colby sat chattering away. "I'll let Ricky sit in the adult class with me today. He doesn't work quite as fast as the other children."

She started for the table, but Randi stopped her by placing a hand on her arm. "I wish you would let him stay."

Marcia looked back at Randi and started to respond, but Randi spoke first. "I understand."

A frown creased Marcia's smooth forehead.

"How else do you think my son knows your son so well after only three weeks of school?" Randi added.

Marcia thought a moment. "Mrs. Rice's class?"

Randi nodded and let Marcia digest the information a few seconds before saying, "I've never been a Sunday school teacher before. I would appreciate it if you would stay and help."

Marcia gave Randi a sad smile and nodded.

By the time Randi finished with the lesson, the butterflies in her stomach had landed and she found herself enjoying the robust group of children. During the remainder of the class, she and Marcia moved around the table answering questions and helping the children with their take-home artwork.

Randi was putting the last of the Sunday school books on a shelf after the class had been dismissed when she sensed someone behind her. She turned to find Marcia and Ricky had returned to the room.

"Mrs. Thomas," Marcia said, glancing at Randi's left hand. "I assume it is Mrs."

"Yes, Ms. Cooper, it is. I'm a widow. And please call me Randi."

Marcia nodded. "I just wanted you to know I appreciate your welcoming Ricky so openly. I never know how people are going to react toward him. Sometimes I get the feeling parents don't want their children to be his friends."

"I know. I've been there myself. While Colby's handicap is one people don't initially see, there were a couple of his classmates in Columbus, where we're from, who figured out he was a slow learner and had no qualms about pointing it out to him, as well as to the rest of the class."

The corners of Marcia's mouth eased up, although the smile never quite made it to her eyes. "You can call me Marcia, and it was nice meeting you, Randi."

As Randi watched Marcia and Ricky go, she felt oddly that there was a possible friendship in the future between her and the seemingly sad woman. But that didn't make Randi less curious to learn what Marcia's definition of "friend" was when it came to Paul.

She looked at Colby, who was occupying himself at the table with a coloring book and crayons. "Are you ready to go to the auditorium, Sport?"

Great, she thought. *Now I'm beginning to sound like Paul.*

That afternoon, Randi was folding a basket of towels when her thoughts turned to the closeness that had developed between her and Paul over the past two weeks. He had fallen into the routine of sharing supper with her and Colby each evening before traipsing upstairs to work on the shop renovations. But on the weekends, he insisted they all go out and eat. And he never seemed to tire of her son's endless questions or incessant chatter.

Randi sighed. That she was in love with him, she had no doubt. And from his actions lately, she felt he at least had feelings for her. But she had a lot more to consider than her heart alone.

The sound of the doorbell made her jump. When she opened the door, her breath caught in her throat. Paul stood on the back porch wearing a navy blazer, khaki slacks, and a light pink shirt open at the collar. As he stepped through the door, he brought his clean, pine-forest scent with him.

Randi felt drab. She had on old jeans and a red button-up shirt, and her hair was in a ponytail that hung through the opening in the back of an Atlanta Braves cap.

Paul smiled, glancing at the cap. "Are you a fan?"

Confused by the remark, Randi frowned.

He pointed at the red A stitched above the bill.

"Oh," she said. "Eddie was, big time. I don't remember him ever missing a game." She touched the cap. "I should have changed. You look so. . .handsome."

"You're beautiful just the way you are."

Randi felt the warmth of a blush.

He glanced down the hallway. "Where are Colby and Molly?"

"They went to the park for the afternoon."

He reached for her hand, weaving his long fingers through hers. "Come on, let's take a walk."

Randi's pulse started racing. He had never held her hand in such an intimate way before.

They strolled along the edge of the backyard beneath tall hardwoods that were just beginning to put on their colorful fall wardrobe. They paused and watched a squirrel, its cheeks packed with nuts, scamper up a hickory tree, then bounce from limb to limb until it disappeared into the forest.

Paul leaned against the tree, drawing Randi around to face him. "Miranda, I need to talk to you."

She saw the intensity in his gaze, heard the hope in his voice, and knew what was coming. "Oh, Paul," she whispered.

Raising her hand to her mouth, she spun and put two steps between them. What should she do? She wanted a future with Paul, more than anything, but not if it meant taking time away from Colby. After an eternity of seconds, she turned back to him, her heart heavy.

His countenance fell. "Wait a minute. Don't tell me I was wrong." He pushed away from the tree. "I was beginning to think. . .hope you had feelings for me, too." This time it was he who turned away. "I'm sorry if I assumed—"

She put her hand on his shoulder, stopping him, and urged him to face her once again. Wetting her lips, she swallowed. "You assumed right, Paul."

"But?" He waited, obviously sensing her inner turmoil.

Reaching out, she encircled one of his hands with both of hers. She cast her eyes down and watched as she ran her thumbs back and forth across his knuckles, as though the task required every ounce of her concentration. "Paul, every decision I make, every single move I make, I have to stop and think of Colby first. You see, he's not. . .he's. . ." The words were there, right on the tip of her tongue, but she couldn't voice them.

Taking a deep breath to steady her voice, she decided to cast a shadow over the truth. "Last year in kindergarten he had trouble keeping up with his classmates academically. Trying to get him back on track is demanding a lot of my time and attention. I just don't know if I have time to nurture a relationship right now."

He placed his hand on the side of her face and urged her chin up with his thumb. "I'll do all the nurturing."

She took a step back. "Paul, a one-sided relationship wouldn't be fair to you. I'm afraid you'd eventually end up hating me and resenting Colby for coming between us."

He searched her face for the space of five heartbeats. "Miranda, I'll not ask you for a commitment right now."

"You won't?" For some reason, that disappointed her.

"Why don't we just take things slow? Take a little more time to get to know each other, and give me a chance to spend some more time with Colby?" He caressed her cheek with his thumb. "I know you've got a lot to consider, and I'm willing to wait until you're ready, no matter how long it takes."

"You'd do that for me?"

"Yes, I would. What I'm talking about is not temporary, Miranda." When she drew back, he quickly added, "Don't panic. I'm not proposing either. Not yet anyway."

She gazed up at him, considering what he was offering. He was telling her, without actually saying the words, that he loved her, wanted a life with her. Yet, he wouldn't pressure her or make demands she wasn't ready to meet. He simply loved her, without condition. She'd be a fool not to accept such a rare and beautiful gift.

In a breathless whisper she said, "Okay."

"Okay?"

She nodded. "Yes."

"Yes," he repeated as he pulled her into his arms, completely lifting her off the ground. She reached up and circled his neck with her arms, burying her face in his shoulder.

When he finally set her down, he pulled back just enough to look into her eyes. "I've never felt this way for anyone before, you know."

Randi opened her mouth to say, "Neither have I," but caught herself, shocked at the revelation. She had loved Eddie, with all her heart. But there was something different in the way she felt about Paul. Something deeper. Something more profound. But she wasn't ready to tell him that.

Fixing her eyes on her hands, now resting on his chest, she searched for just the right words. "Eddie has been the only man in my life, Paul." She unconsciously started twisting a button on his shirt. "Come to think of it, I've never even been kissed by another man, other than a peck on the cheek." She raised her eyes to his. "I just wanted you to know that."

He raised a hand and circled the back of her neck with his long fingers. "May I have the honor of breaking that record?"

The intensity of his gaze branded her with anticipation, making her heart beat erratically and her voice husky when she answered, "Yes."

As their lips touched, so did their hearts. Warmth traveled from the top of Randi's head to the bottom of her feet, like liquid sunshine. And she knew, in the very depths of her soul, she would love this man forever.

But there was another person in her life who occupied a place she wasn't quite ready to let Paul enter—her son. And for that reason, she was determined to take things slowly.

When they drew back from each other, Paul led Randi to the gazebo and pulled her down on the bench beside him, draping his arm around her shoulders. She laid her head on his shoulder, and they sat for a few minutes in blissful silence. Then Randi's curiosity got the best of her.

"Paul?"

"Mmm?"

"This morning, Marcia Cooper introduced herself to me as your friend in a very distinct way. What was she trying to tell me?"

"Oh, boy." Paul took his arm from around her and slid to the edge of the bench, leaning forward with his elbows on his knees.

Randi scooted forward, pushing her hair behind her ear and aiming questioning eyes at him.

Paul took a deep breath, then exhaled slowly. "Marcia and I were friends in high school."

"Friends?"

"Okay, we dated. But it was never serious. After graduation, I went away to college and she married my best friend, Jason Cooper. A few years ago, Jason left Marcia and Ricky. I felt sorry for Ricky because his father ran out on him, so I tried spending some time with him.

"Marcia mistook my affection for Ricky as affection for her. When I realized it a couple of months ago, I talked to her and told her the feelings she was looking for from me just weren't there. That they stopped at friendship. But she didn't take it very well." Paul met her gaze. "I really don't think her feelings for me run as deep as she thinks. She was very much in love with Jason, and I think she's just looking for someone to fill the void he left in her and Ricky's life."

"I see."

He quirked a brow. "Jealous?"

"Yes," Randi confessed.

He threw his head back and laughed, then pulled her close. "I love an honest woman."

Chapter 9

The following evening, Randi was helping Molly put the finishing touches on supper when Colby's squeal alerted her. Drying her hands on a towel, she quickly made her way to the backyard where she had left him playing a few minutes before. Molly followed.

With his O'Bryan Construction cap dangling sideways on his head, Colby sat in the yard with his chubby arms around a lively brown puppy. Paul stood close by, eyes full of laughter, watching the pair.

"What in the world is going on here?" Randi asked as she approached.

At the sound of her voice, the pup froze. He cocked his head to one side and perked his ears, wrinkling the white diamond on his forehead as he curiously looked up at her.

Randi kneeled, holding a hand out to the dog. "Hi there, little fella."

The pup took a quick leap into her arms, the tag on his new collar making a faint tinkling sound. She laughed, barely catching him before his tongue made it to her face. His shiny coat bore the feel and smell of a recent bath.

As she scratched the puppy behind his ear, it dawned on her she had seen him somewhere before. "Hold on." Her hand froze as she turned narrowed eyes on Paul. "This is the puppy from the pet shop in Blairsville, isn't it?"

Paul shrugged. "I plead guilty."

Randi urged the pup back to her son, who was shifting impatiently from one foot to the other. Standing, she smiled up at Paul. "I'm glad he found a good home."

"I am, too. Even if it did take him awhile to get here."

Randi's chin dropped. Paul reached out and pushed it up with his finger. "I wanted to get Bingo potty trained first."

Randi threw her arms around his neck and gave him a hearty kiss on his lips. "You're wonderful!"

Paul chuckled. "I think I'll go back and get the rest of the litter."

Molly cleared her throat. "I hate to interrupt you guys, but supper's ready."

Randi glanced at Molly, and Molly motioned with her head toward Colby. Looking down, Randi realized the motive behind her aunt's interruption.

Colby had stopped playing with Bingo and was looking up at her and Paul with a quizzical expression. She could almost see the list piling up inside her son's head. *Oh, boy*, she thought. *I can count on playing twenty questions tonight.* Aloud she said, "Let's go eat."

Hugging a stuffed polar bear Molly had brought him from Alaska to his chest, Colby scrambled onto his bed. As Randi pulled the blanket up to his chin, he trained his wide hazel eyes on her. "Mom, why did you kiss Paul?"

Randi was expecting the question, so she was prepared. She sat down on the edge of the bed. "Because Paul and I have become special friends."

"You mean like boyfriend and girlfriend?"

"I guess you could say that."

"Are you going to marry him?"

Well, I thought I was prepared. She took a deep breath, then exhaled. "That's something that can only be determined by how our friendship grows."

Colby's brow wrinkled. "Huh?"

"To make it simple, I don't know."

"He'd make a good daddy," Colby said with a hint of hopefulness.

"You know, you're probably right. But we'll still have to wait and see how things go. Now, good night, sleep tight, and don't let the bedbugs bite."

As Randi started to leave the room, Bingo raised his head and whined from the rug at the foot of Colby's bed.

"Good night, Bingo," Randi said.

Late the following afternoon, Randi dug through the clutter in Colby's backpack in search of homework. How one child could accumulate so much in only four short weeks of school, she did not know.

"Ah, there it is." Randi pulled the homework folder from the backpack, but when she flipped it open, her hands started trembling. She pulled a slip of paper from the inside folder pocket and read the words "Special Olympics Participation Form" in bold black letters across the top. The body of the letter explained when, where, and how the event would take place, and the bottom read, "Does your child have permission to participate? Check Yes or No."

She chewed on her right lower lip. If she agreed to let Colby compete in the games for mentally and physically challenged children, that would, in a sense, be the same as admitting he was permanently handicapped—like giving up hope. Was that fair to Colby? On the other hand, he had asked several times over the past week if he could participate. Was it fair not to let him?

Randi sighed, her thoughts muddled. She rarely had trouble making decisions, except when it came to Colby.

The back door opened, and she crammed the permission form into a nearby drawer. Colby ran into the kitchen weighted down with a new ball bat, glove, and ball. Paul and Molly, all smiles, followed.

Colby held up his prized possessions for Randi to see. "Look what Paul got me, Mom. He says I can play on his T-ball team!"

Colby's announcement left Randi a bit shocked, but she tried not to let it show in front of her son. "These things Paul gave you are very nice. I hope you told him 'thank you.' "

The equipment hit the floor with a clang as Colby turned and wrapped his short arms around Paul's legs. "Thank you, Paul! Thank you! Thank you! Thank you!"

Paul peeled Colby off his legs and stooped to the child's level. "A hug will do just fine, Sport." Colby clamped onto his neck.

When Colby turned to retrieve his equipment, Randi leaned forward and placed a hand on his shoulder. "Colby, I think you misunderstood about playing on Paul's team. Baseball season doesn't start until spring, which is still several months away. We'll talk about your playing then."

"We have a short fall league here," Paul told her. "It gives the kids something constructive to do before cold weather hits. I thought Colby would enjoy playing."

Randi looked at Paul, opened her mouth, then closed it, not trusting herself to reply in front of Colby. Instead, she said to her son, "Why don't you go wash up and get ready for supper?"

Molly helped Colby pick up his new equipment. "Come on, Sweetie. I'll go with you." She shot Randi a warning glance on the way out.

As Paul stood, Randi crossed her arms and turned on him. "Why did you do that?"

Paul looked taken aback. "Get him the T-ball equipment? Because I wanted to."

"That's not what I mean. Why did you tell him he could play T-ball?"

"You mean, you don't want him to?"

"You don't understand. He could get hurt."

"It's just T-ball, Miranda. We don't even use a regular baseball. The ball we use is soft and—"

"That's not what I mean," she said for the second time, her voice steadily climbing the scale.

Paul held his hands out, palms up, his voice pattern following hers. "What do you mean?"

"You shouldn't give him permission to do something like play on a T-ball team without checking with me first."

Paul stared at her for several long, silent seconds. Then his shoulders slumped and he hooked his thumbs in his back pockets. "Okay," he conceded. "I'll tell Colby. . .something. I'll find some way to tell him he can't play."

Randi turned her back to him and strode to the stove, lifting the lid from a pot of boiling potatoes and stirring. Steam rose, circled her head, then disappeared under the vented stove hood.

"Miranda?"

She looked back over her shoulder.

"I really don't know what to do here. Do you want me to leave?"

His questioning eyes filled her with guilt. How could he know about Colby when she hadn't told him? She immediately closed the distance between them and circled his waist with her arms. "I'm sorry, Paul. I shouldn't have lashed out at you. There's something you should know about Colby. Don't say anything to him until I've had the chance to tell you."

Relief washed over her as Paul wrapped his arms around her with his familiar squeeze. "Whatever you say," he said softly. But she feared she heard a trace of uncertainty in his voice.

❀

When Randi went to summon Colby and Molly for supper, Paul sat down at the table, crossed his arms, and contemplated what had just happened. This was a side of Randi he had not witnessed before. Sometimes he noticed her being a little overprotective of Colby. But weren't all caring mothers protective of their children to a certain extent?

Still, it bothered him that she would get so upset over him asking Colby to do something as simple as play T-ball. Wasn't one of the purposes of their slow courtship so he could spend some time with Colby?

Paul released a disgruntled sigh. It had been a long time since he had had to ask anyone's permission before he did anything. He wasn't sure he could get used to the idea of consulting Randi every time he wanted to do something for or with Colby. He wasn't sure he wanted to.

❀

Tension hovered over the table during supper like the clouds of a brewing storm. Randi was actually a little relieved when Paul retired to the family room while she helped Colby with his homework at the kitchen table. And even more relieved when Molly made the excuse she needed something from the market.

"Okay, Colby," Randi said as she placed the wide ruled notepad and large pencil on the table in front of him. "Same thing we did last night. ABC's twice." The nightly routine thrilled neither of them, but Randi knew it was necessary.

She pointed to each letter on the worksheet the teacher had sent home, said each letter slowly, then waited while he copied it.

Colby struggled, grasping the pencil so tightly his knuckles turned white. But no matter how hard he tried, he still couldn't make many of the letters legible. However, Randi always displayed patience—until tonight. Tonight, her anxiety over the earlier disagreement with Paul had left her in an unpleasant mood.

When Colby came to the dreaded *u*, he first wrote a distorted *y*.

"That's not right. Try again," Randi urged.

Colby grasped the pencil even tighter, struggling still; then he squeezed his eyes shut and hit his temple several times with the palm of his free hand. "I can't."

Randi stilled his hand with her own. "Yes, you can, Colby. Think."

"No! I can't remember *u!*"

"Yes, you can."

Colby threw the pencil across the room and turned tear-brimmed eyes on his mother. "No, I can't! I'm stupid! Toby said I was, and everybody believes Toby!" Colby jumped up and ran for his room, slamming the door behind him.

"Colby!" Randi ran after him, but a large hand captured her upper arm and stopped her just as she reached the hallway.

"Whoa." Paul's voice rose and fell. "Take it easy, Mom."

"I need to go to him, Paul. He's never done this before."

Paul moved his hands to her shoulders. "Let me go. I think you and he need to step back and count to ten before you face-off again."

Moisture clouded her vision. She raised a trembling hand to her mouth. "Oh, Paul, he can't even count to ten."

Paul gathered her in his arms. "Shhh, Honey. Don't cry. I'll go spend a few minutes with him and see if I can get him settled down."

Randi pushed away, knowing Colby needed comforting right now more than she did. Nodding, she wiped her wet face with the backs of her hands. Paul pulled his handkerchief from his pocket, closed her fingers over it, and kissed her forehead before heading to Colby's room.

A few minutes after Colby's door closed behind Paul, Randi slipped into her room and withdrew a large manila envelope from the bottom drawer of the nightstand. She took the envelope to the family room and set it on the end table as she sat down on the sofa. Then, propping her elbows on her knees and her chin on her fists, she waited. That's exactly how Paul found her when he walked into the room twenty minutes later.

"How is he?" she wanted to know as Paul sat down beside her.

"He's fine. Waiting for Mom to come and say good night."

Randi picked up the envelope and held it out to him. "This is a psychological evaluation on Colby that was done a little over a year ago. It will explain everything."

He took the envelope, and she got up and started for the door.

"Miranda?"

She stopped, looking back.

"I hope you don't mind. I told Colby he didn't have to finish his homework tonight. I'll go talk to the teacher in the morning if you want me to."

"I don't mind, Paul." Then she made her way to her son's room.

Colby was already in his pajamas. He sat in the middle of the bed cradling his polar bear in one arm and petting Bingo with his free hand. Randi joined Colby and Bingo on the bed, ruffling Colby's hair as she sat down. "How's it going?"

Colby's chin quivered. "I'm sorry I yelled at you, Mom." He jumped to his knees and clamped his arms around her neck.

Watery-eyed, Randi returned his hug. "I'm sorry I was so impatient."

Colby sat back down. "What's impa. . .im. . . ?"

"It means I got in too big of a hurry."

"Oh."

"Are you ready to say your prayers?"

"Paul said 'em with me."

"Okay. I still get to tuck you in, though. Bingo, you have to sleep on your own bed."

Colby helped Bingo off the bed while Randi turned down the covers. After a good night kiss, she eased out of his room and back into her own.

She pulled Paul's red-and-white high school letter jacket out of the back of her closet and slipped it on, pushing up the long sleeves to reveal her hands. She had found the jacket while she was unpacking the day after she arrived. Raising her arm, she inhaled the soft leather, then, smiling, thumbed the stripes on the top of the sleeve. He was a four-year letterman in baseball. She pulled the front together and made her way out the back door and into the brisk night air.

Stopping in the middle of the pebble walkway, she looked up at a sky so brilliantly clear she could see the Milky Way. She marveled at a God so big He could speak such an awe-inspiring galaxy into existence and still take the time out to listen to the prayers of someone as small and insignificant as she. But He did, and that was just one of the many beautiful things about Him.

"God, I am really confused about Colby," she said. "I'm afraid if I treat him like he's handicapped, then I'm giving up on him. But if I treat him like he's just as normal as the next child, then I'm afraid I'll push too hard, like I did tonight."

Closing her eyes, she waited. She smelled the mustiness of the damp earth and felt the caress of the cool night air on her face. She heard the katydids competing with two whippoorwills and a truck rumbling up the highway. But God was silent.

She opened her eyes and looked heavenward once again. "Okay, God. I know You have a reason in this, whether Colby's condition is permanent or temporary. But You're going to have to show me what to do. It's just more than I'm capable of figuring out on my own."

A gentle breeze stirred the night air. *"Trust in the Lord with all thine heart; and lean not unto thine own understanding. In all thy ways acknowledge him, and he shall direct thy paths.*" Randi remembered the verse as one she had read recently in her daily devotions, and with the remembrance came a blanket of calm that quieted her conflicting emotions.

"Lean not unto thine own understanding." She sighed, resigning to the revelation that God was going to make her wait for her answer. "I'll try to remember that, Lord."

She turned and started back toward the house just as Paul came through the door and started down the steps toward her. He circled her with his arms, lacing his fingers at her back.

"I hope you don't mind my borrowing your jacket," she said. "I found it stuck in the back of my closet."

He smiled. "It looks a lot better on you than it does on me."

"Oh, I think I would have to disagree. What position did you play?"

"First base, when I played."

"Which was probably always."

He shrugged modestly. "Come here." He pulled her closer, raising one hand to cradle her head against his chest. "I put the report back in your room."

She nodded.

"Thank you for sharing it with me. It helps me see things more clearly."

"Tell me what you think, Paul. Honestly." She closed her eyes and waited for his answer.

He shifted to kiss the top of her head. "I think you have the most special little boy in the world, and I couldn't love him more if he were my own flesh and blood."

She pulled back enough to see his face, relieved at the sincerity she found there. "Oh, Paul, now you know why I don't want him to play T-ball."

"Miranda, I know you want to protect Colby, but you can't shield him from the world. He needs to learn to cope with life—not hide from it. I think you should let him play."

"But what if he gets hurt, or one of the other children makes fun of him?"

"I can't promise you that won't happen. But I can promise you I'll do everything in my power to see that it doesn't." He tucked her hair behind her ear. "You believe me, don't you?"

"Yes." And she did. Suddenly, she was so full of love for him she couldn't contain the words any longer. "Paul, I—"

"Look!" He jerked his hand up and pointed to the sky over her shoulder.

She whipped her head around just in time to see the fading silver thread of a shooting star. "Wow! It's been a long time since I've seen one of those."

"Make a wish."

She met his gaze with a dreamy smile. "I wish you and I and Colby could find a mountaintop all our own and escape the rest of the world and all its troubles."

He cupped her jaw and caressed her cheek with his thumb. "Life's not about escaping, Honey. It's about accepting."

Randi's shoulders slumped. Did he always have to be so practical? "I know. But a girl can dream, can't she?"

"Of course. As long as you separate dreams from reality. And speaking of mountaintops, I want you, Colby, and Molly to come to my cabin tomorrow night for supper. It's not quite the mountaintop, but it is pretty peaceful up there."

"My, my. A mountain man who can cook. How fortunate can a girl be?"

"I can throw a steak on the grill and bake a potato. Anything more complicated you'll have to provide."

"A steak and potato will do just fine, Sir. But I suppose I could throw in a dessert."

"Good. It's time I show you and Colby where I live."

Chapter 10

Colby ran into the kitchen the next morning lugging a large, thick notebook containing Eddie's old baseball card collection. "I seed him, before, Mom! I knowed I did! I seed him before!"

Randi set a bowl of steaming oatmeal on the table, not even attempting to correct his jumble of grammatical errors. "What are you talking about, Colby?"

"This is where I seed Paul before!" He laboriously lifted the open notebook to the table and pointed to a card in the center pocket of the clear plastic page.

Randi took a spoon from a drawer and placed it in the bowl. "I think you're mistaken. It's probably just someone who looks like Paul."

Colby's eyebrows disappeared beneath his bangs. "No, Mom. It's Paul."

Randi looked at the card. Colby's short finger covered the face, but, to her surprise, the name on the bottom of the card was "Paul O'Bryan." She slid the card out of the pocket, and Paul, in an Atlanta Braves cap and uniform, stared back at her. He had a mustache but no beard. Even then, his smile brought laugh lines to the corners of his eyes. She turned the card over and read the stats, which were astounding. He spent two years at Middle Georgia College and two at Auburn University, batting over four hundred each year. It appeared he was drafted by the Braves just out of college, but there were no major-league stats.

Why did no one tell me about this? she wondered.

"Can I have my card back?" Colby interrupted her thoughts.

"Can I keep it for a few days, Colby? I promise I'll take good care of it."

Colby frowned and, although a bit reluctant, said, "Okay."

"Let's not say anything to Paul about this just yet. In a day or two you can ask him to autograph it."

This seemed to satisfy Colby, and he lugged his notebook back to his room. Randi slipped the card in the front pocket of her cotton shirt.

✿

After returning from taking Colby to school, Randi sat down at the kitchen table across from Molly. "Got a minute?"

Molly closed her newspaper and laid it next to her coffee cup. "Sure, Dear."

Randi slipped the card out of her shirt pocket and placed it in the center of the table. "I want you to tell me about this."

Molly's expression grew clouded. She picked up the card and slid her thumb

69

across Paul's name, then glanced back up at her niece. "Come with me; I want to show you something."

Randi followed Molly upstairs to a door located in the back corner of the large room that was under renovation for expansion of the shop. Reaching up, Molly withdrew a key from the top of the doorframe and slipped it into the door. After meeting with a little resistance, she turned the key and opened the way to the back portion of the second floor. She then led Randi through a maze of cardboard boxes and various memorabilia to the back right corner of the attic. Randi was shocked at what she found there.

Several dozen bats, each one looking like the Jolly Green Giant had used it for a toothpick, several worn baseball gloves, baseballs, and two large boxes full of trophies. In a daze, Randi picked up a trophy and read silently, "Paul O'Bryan, MVP, Serenity High, 1984." She set the trophy down and picked up one of the mutilated Louisville Sluggers, running her fingers over the splintered end. "What were these bats used on?"

"Gravel."

"Gravel?"

"Randi, baseball was how Paul dealt with his parents' death. Oh, he was good. He still holds several high school records here, and a couple of his college records have yet to be broken. But it was much more than just a game to him. He wrapped himself up in it in an effort to ease his pain." She touched Randi's shoulder, drawing her attention away from the bat. "Come here." She motioned with her head toward the back of the room.

Randi followed Molly to a window where dust particles danced lazily in the morning sun's rays.

Molly circled Randi's shoulders with her arm and pointed to the asphalt driveway behind the house. "That drive was gravel until a few years ago. Clayton told me Paul would come home from school, grab his bat, and head outside. He would pick up piece after piece of gravel and send it sailing off into the field with his wooden bat. Clayton said the only thing that ever broke the rhythm was when he would stop long enough to wipe tears away with his shirttail.

"As you saw, he went through quite a few bats. But as far as I know, Clayton never complained. He said when a bat started getting thin, he would go to the hardware store, buy a new one, and bring it home along with another bag of gravel."

Randi could see it in her mind's eye. A little towheaded boy, bending, picking up, hitting. Bending, picking up, hitting. Pausing to wipe tears from his dust-stained face. Then bending, picking up, hitting. Trying his best to dull his grief with each swing of the bat. Randi wiped a tear of her own.

"From the time his parents died," Molly continued, "Paul worked toward one goal only—to play professional baseball. The year he left here to go to college on a baseball scholarship, Clayton and I were sure he was destined to reach that goal. So when he called us and told us he had made it, we really weren't all that surprised.

"He played first base in high school and college, but for his first major-league game he was put in center field for a player on the disabled list. It had been raining that day, and he went back for a fly ball. He didn't realize how close he was to the warning track, and when his feet hit it, he slipped and fell, crushing his left shoulder. After his second surgery to repair the damage, he was told his professional career was over.

"He really had a rough time dealing with it. Baseball was the one thing Paul always had control over. When he lost that, he thought he lost everything. Then he became friends with a child named Ben, who died several years ago of leukemia. I think that little boy helped Paul see that we can't always choose the path we take. Sometimes God has a different plan."

Randi took a deep, shuddering breath, thinking about Paul's past. After losing his parents at a tender age, he spent his youth chasing a dream, only to have it snatched away the minute he caught it. Yet, at some point, he had accepted it and moved on.

Last night he had told her it was okay to dream, as long as you separate dreams from reality. Was she still chasing a dream, grasping at a false thread of hope that Colby would someday overcome his handicap?

She didn't know anymore. Didn't know what it would take for her to figure it out. She felt like she was standing at a fork in the middle of the road and didn't know whether to bear left or right.

"Trust in the Lord with all thine heart; and lean not unto thine own understanding. In all thy ways acknowledge him, and he shall direct thy paths."

The verse from the night before came back to her, and she silently prayed, *Dear God, I'm trying. But sometimes it's so hard.*

Randi had no idea how long she had stood there lost in her thoughts when Molly interrupted. "Are you ready to go back down? It's really hot up here, and I could use a little cold water."

Randi nodded and followed Molly back down.

Once back in the kitchen, Randi picked up the baseball card from the table, went into her room, and closed the door behind her. She slipped the picture between two pages of her Bible, then moved to what had become her special prayer place beside her bed, asking God to give her grace to accept His will for Colby.

❈

Paul tossed the last steak on the grill, then glanced down his driveway once more as the pleasant hickory smoke drifted up from the grill to float around his head. He was eager to know what Randi thought of his home.

A few minutes later Randi eased the van to a stop behind Paul's truck. Paul gave Colby their customary "Give me five" greeting, kissed the cheek Molly offered, then greeted Randi with a big hug and a light kiss on her lips.

"I'll watch the steaks, Paul," Molly offered. "Why don't you go show Randi and Colby your home?"

Colby raced for the door ahead of Paul and Randy. Just as the couple was about to step onto the carport, the boy released an ear-piercing scream. Paul and Randi ran to the door and into the kitchen, followed immediately by Molly.

Colby threw himself at his mother. She scooped him up as he wrapped his arms around her neck and his legs around her waist, burying his head in the crook of her neck. "There's a monster in here, Mommy! Don't let it get me! Please, don't let it get me!"

"Colby," Randi consoled, "there's no monster in here."

"Yes, there is!" Without raising his head, Colby pointed toward the wide entrance leading into a high-ceilinged den. "Please take me away! Don't let it get me!"

Randi glanced into the den, then spun and ran back outside with Colby.

Baffled, Paul looked into the room to see if he could figure out the source of Colby's fear. He found it above the mantel on his rock fireplace: the mounted head of his prize twelve-point buck that he had killed two years ago—Colby's monster.

Eddie had died in a deer hunting accident, so Colby must think the deer had taken away his daddy.

Paul took the mounted deer head down, placed it in an extra bedroom, and locked the door. He went back outside to find Randi at the edge of the yard still trying to calm a sobbing Colby while Molly looked on helplessly.

Paul made his way to Randi and Colby. He ran his hand over Colby's head. "Look at me, Colby."

Colby, face still buried against Randi's neck, tightened his grip.

"Colby," Paul continued, "I took the deer down. I'll not put it back up until you say it's okay."

"Did you hear that, Colby?" Randi urged Colby to raise his head by nudging him with her own. "Paul took the monster away. It can't hurt you now."

Colby raised his head enough to venture a peek at Paul and said between hiccups. "I–is it really g–gone?"

"It's really gone. Let's you and I go have a talk, man-to-man."

Colby reached for Paul, leaving his mother's arms.

Paul ruffled his hair. "Since you're such a big boy, I bet you would rather walk."

Colby, the end of his forefinger in his mouth and his lashes beaded with tears, bobbed his head up and down. Paul set him down and started leading him along the edge of the yard.

Randi started to follow, but Paul said, "Sorry, Mom. No girls allowed on this tour."

❀

Randi watched Paul go, leading her son by the hand. She wasn't sure if she liked Paul's tactic or not. He had a way of stepping into a situation and taking charge. But Colby was *her* son. What could Paul possibly say to him that he didn't want her to hear, or that she hadn't already said?

Randi helped Molly finish supper. They were setting the last of the food on the table on the screened-in back porch when Paul and Colby returned.

Although Colby had calmed down considerably, he ate very little and glanced at the door throughout the meal as though he feared the deer would reappear. After the meal was over, Paul found some paper and a drafting pencil for Colby to draw with while the adults cleaned the kitchen.

Once the dishes were put away, Randi turned to Molly. "Excuse us just a minute." She cupped Paul's arm with her hand and led him outside.

The second they were out of sight, Paul pulled her into his arms. "You read my mind."

Randi pushed against his chest, dodging his kiss. "Behave, Paul. We really do need to talk."

He pulled his head back in pretended exasperation. "Talking's no fun."

"I know. But it's necessary sometimes."

Paul sighed, releasing her and taking her hand as they started strolling toward the front yard.

"How did you know Colby was afraid of the deer?" Randi asked.

"Friday night when I put him to bed he told me to leave his light on to ward off the monsters that took his daddy away."

"A couple of years ago, Colby asked me how his father died," she explained. "I told him, and he's been afraid of deer ever since." They walked a few more steps in silence, then Randi asked, "What did you tell him while you were walking?"

"I told him deer weren't monsters. That they were very gentle creatures and wouldn't hurt him."

"Did you convince him?"

"Not quite. But it's a start. The rest of the time we watched a few birds and squirrels and talked about man stuff. You know, fishing, sports. . .T-ball." He glanced at her from the corner of his eye.

She couldn't help but smile. His conversation with her son sounded harmless enough. She even felt a little ridiculous now at being so concerned in the first place.

They ambled across the lawn without speaking for a short time, listening to a bobwhite call repeatedly to the wind whispering through the treetops.

"Miranda, have you ever explained to Colby that the deer didn't take his dad from him?" Paul asked.

Randi frowned. "I tried at first, but it didn't seem to do any good. Why?"

Paul hooked the thumb of his free hand in his back pocket. "It just seems to me it would be better to encourage him not to be afraid of something instead of going along with him when he's frightened."

"Paul, you can't explain away fear."

"I'm not talking about explaining it away. I'm talking about encouraging him not to be afraid. If you play along with him, like you did after my mounted deer scared him, then he gets the impression the monsters exist not only to him, but to you, too. It's sort of like validating his fears."

Randi had to admit Paul made sense. She sighed, "Boy, on a scale of one to ten, you must rate me about a three when it comes to motherhood."

Paul stopped and drew her around to face him, placing a large hand on each side of her head. "You listen to me, Miranda Thomas. I think you are the best mother in the world. And being a good mother, you follow your heart where Colby's concerned. No one can fault you for that. All I'm saying is it sometimes takes a different perspective to find the solution." He shrugged. "I could be wrong. But I'll always express my feelings to you, because I think that's the way it should be between two people who care for each other. I expect no less of you."

One corner of her mouth tipped up. "You know what I think? I think you're the most wonderful man in the world."

Paul grinned. "I like the way you think."

She slid her palms up his chest and laced her hands behind his neck. "Know what else?"

He narrowed his eyes. "Is this a trick question?"

"Nope."

"Then shoot."

"I love you."

Surprise fell over Paul's face like a boulder dropped from a housetop. "What did you say?"

Bashfully, she ducked her head. "You heard me."

"No, I don't think I did."

"Yes, you did."

He tipped her chin, forcing her to meet his gaze, an impish gleam sparkling in his green eyes. "I want to make sure I heard right."

Randi pushed against his chest and tried to step back. "Paul, you're impossible."

He slipped his arms around her waist, halting her retreat. "And?"

She continued struggling, even though her efforts proved futile. "And you're stubborn."

"That, my dear, we have in common. And?"

"And I can't think straight when you're this close to me."

A smile touched his lips. "And?"

Finally she gave up and relaxed. "And you're the most incredibly handsome man I know."

"Mmmm. Getting better all the time. And?"

She paused, her breath caught in her throat.

Paul lowered his head but stopped with two inches between them.

Randi's voice was no more than a husky whisper as she said, "And I'm hopelessly in love with you." She reached up and pulled his head down to close the small gap between them.

Just before their lips touched, she heard Paul whisper, "Thank You, God."

Yes, she silently agreed. *Thank You, God, for sending this incredible man to me.*

The kiss grew in intensity, igniting a spark inside Randi, threatening to fan it into a flame. Breathless, she pulled back. "I think we'd better get back to the cabin."

"I think you're right." He weaved his fingers through hers as they started for the door. "After you take Colby to school tomorrow, spend the day with me."

"Paul, I'm not so sure I should leave the shop."

"Let's ask Molly to cover for you for the day and the evening."

"The evening?"

"I've got to go to Blairsville and look at a job; then the rest of the day will be ours."

"What about Colby?"

"I'm not trying to get you away from him. I'm just asking for one day with no interruptions. It's important to me."

The right corner of her mouth eased up. "I'll have to ask the boss."

Paul drew her close under his arm as they stepped onto the carport. "You take care of Molly, and let me worry about the boss."

Randi tilted her head and grinned up at him. "No way. I'd rather take care of the boss."

Chapter 11

When Paul finished with his business in Blairsville the next morning, instead of heading back to Serenity, he took Randi to Dahlonega, a small town in the foothills of the Blue Ridge Mountains. The center of the town graced a Gold Museum that was once the county courthouse. Along the street circling the museum were a wide variety of craft and antique shops.

Paul and Randi took the liberty of window-shopping for awhile; then he led her down the corridor of a mini-mall and into a shop with a sign on the door that read "Sam's Gold Shop." The shop held several long glass cases of gold jewelry, and the walls were heavily decorated with a wide variety of Native American artifacts.

Randi picked up a red, blue, and yellow child's feather headdress. "Colby would like this."

Paul held up a child's tomahawk. "What about this?"

"I don't think so. I don't want to refurnish the house."

An elderly Native American with a braid hanging down his back left the trinket he was working on and approached Randi and Paul. His wrinkled skin looked rough and weatherworn. A baseball cap adorned with a conglomeration of fishing paraphernalia sat atop his gray head.

"Sam Barry," Paul said, "I'd like you to meet Miranda Thomas."

Reaching up a gnarled hand, Sam surprised Randi by grasping her chin between his thumb and forefinger and turning her head from side to side. When he finished inspecting her, he nodded once to Paul. "This one has spirit, huh?"

"She's got spirit, all right," Paul answered with one shake of his head.

Sam released her chin, and Randi gave Paul a "hmm, thanks" look.

"Come here. I want to show you something." Sam captured Randi's arm and led her to a glass case holding engagement rings and wedding bands. Paul followed.

The elder unlocked the glass case and placed a solitaire engagement ring and the matching man's and woman's wedding bands on top. The bands on all three were braided gold. Both wedding bands had three diamonds along the top, each diamond nestled inside a braid.

"There is a story here," Sam said.

Paul picked up the woman's band and examined it. "Tell us."

Not wanting to seem impolite, Randi laid the headdress on top of the case, picked up the engagement ring, and twisted the band between her thumb and forefinger. The diamond twinkled as it caught the overhead fluorescent lights.

Sam picked up the man's wedding band, presenting it to Paul and Randi. "The braids represent three lives joined together. So do the three diamonds. A man, a woman, and a child. As each new child is born into the family, a new diamond is added."

Randi's suspicious eyes targeted Sam's.

Sam apparently read her mind. "Pfssst." He waved a hand toward Paul as though dismissing him. "Paul didn't tell me you had a little one. You did."

"I did?"

Sam cackled, merriment dancing in his brown eyes as he held up the child's headdress.

Randi grinned. "You got me, Sam. That's a beautiful story. From where did it originate?"

"From Sam." He jabbed at his inflated chest with his thumb. "There's not another set like this in the world."

"They're lovely." Randi returned the ring to the countertop and started strolling around the shop. Even if she were hoping and wishing, she didn't want Paul to know it.

Before long, Paul stepped up behind her. "You ready to go?"

Randi nodded, and they left the store with the child's headdress—but no rings. She tried to convince herself she wasn't disappointed.

✼

Paul and Randi arrived back in Serenity as dusk was falling and stopped for a bucket of fried chicken before going to Paul's cabin. They picnicked on a quilt covered with multicolored hearts at the edge of Paul's front yard and now sat gazing at the star-spangled sky. Paul leaned back against a tree trunk with his legs stretched out and crossed at the ankles. Randi, wrapped in a leather coat belonging to him, sat nestled in his embrace with her head and back against his chest. He had put on a sweatshirt to ward off the night chill.

Randi knew Paul was wondering why she had been so quiet since leaving Dahlonega. Since they had looked at the engagement rings in Sam's shop, she had spent a lot of time thinking and a lot of time feeling guilty. As hard as she had tried not to, she couldn't help comparing the intensity of her feelings for Paul with the feelings she'd had for Eddie.

"Penny for your thoughts," Paul said softly, as though reading her mind. His warm breath against her ear sent a pleasant tingle up the back of her neck.

"Haven't you heard of inflation?" she teased.

"I'll pay the balance in kisses." He planted one on her temple.

She sat up and spun around to face him, curling her legs to one side. "As tempting as that offer is, I'm going to have to defer payment for a few minutes.

There's something I need to tell you." She paused, swallowing. "Paul, we've never talked about Eddie."

The toothpick in Paul's mouth stopped moving. He took it out and tossed it to the grass. "Miranda, I'm not going to try to take Eddie's place."

"I know." She placed her hand on his bearded cheek and studied his serious expression. "There's something I need to say to you, Paul. Something that goes deeper than a simple 'I love you.'"

Paul drew up his legs and wrapped his arms around his knees, leaning forward so that their faces were a mere three inches apart. Even in the moonlight she could read the intensity in his gaze.

"I loved Eddie—deeply," she continued. "When he died, something inside of me died right along with him, something that for the past seven years I thought was gone forever." She pressed her palm to her chest, desperately wanting him to understand the meaning in her next words. "But when I saw you, a giant of a man standing in front of that store the day I arrived in Serenity, I began to come back to life. And at this moment, I feel more alive than I've ever felt before."

His fingers grazed her jaw as he circled the back of her neck with his hand. He searched her face with eyes so full of emotion that Randi felt like the most loved and the most beautiful woman in the world.

"Oh, Miranda."

His husky whisper brushed her face and wrapped around her senses like a warm, protective cocoon. He said nothing else but pressed his lips to hers in a kiss that told her more than words could say. Randi circled his neck with her arms and answered his unspoken vow with fervor.

They pulled away, both breathless, and pressed their foreheads together. "Miranda, there's no words to describe my feelings for you. I love you so much."

"Oh, Paul, this has happened so fast, it's sometimes scary to think about."

"Then don't think about it, my love, just accept it."

She drew back, looking into his eyes. "I have to confess I sometimes feel guilty. It took a little longer than two days to figure out I was in love with Eddie."

Paul raised a brow. "You mean you knew this when you had been here only two days?"

Meekly, she nodded.

"Why am I just now finding out about it?"

"Because of Colby, and the attention he needs from me, I fought my feelings for you with every ounce of strength I possessed."

"Satisfy my curiosity. At exactly what point did you know?"

"The night you came to talk about the upstairs redecorating. When you sneaked up on me while I was admiring your beautiful mountains, I turned around and thought you had to be the most handsome man on the face of this earth. At that moment, I knew deep down I was falling in love with you."

Paul kissed her palm, then held it against his chest.

"What about you, Paul?" she asked. "When did you know?"

"It started the first time I saw you."

"Paul, the first time you saw me was at Eddie's funeral."

"I know. I remember standing there watching you at the grave. It was the most helpless feeling in the world. I don't suppose anyone told you who carried you to your brother's car after you passed out, did they?"

She thought a moment. "You?"

He nodded.

"Then that's why—"

"Why what?"

"The day you caught me at the store, I got this strange feeling like I'd been there before. You know, like—"

"Déjà vu?" He found the word she was looking for.

Smiling, she nodded.

"Then I guess your instincts were on target," he said.

"Getting back to the subject. Paul, you can't be saying you fell in love with me at Eddie's funeral."

"No. But I am saying a seed was planted in my heart that day. It lay dormant for the past seven years, until the Lord knew you were ready to love again. That day you fell into my arms at the store, that seed was touched by sunshine for the very first time. It was watered and nourished and started to grow. I started falling in love with you that day, Miranda. If that sounds corny, I'm sorry. It's the way I feel."

Randi had to remind herself to breathe. "It's the most beautiful thing I've ever heard in my life."

She figured the logical thing for him to do now would be to kiss her again. Instead, he rose in one fluid motion, pulling her up with him.

He stood facing her, taking both her hands in his. "I'm only planning to do this once in my life, so I want to be sure and do it right." Then he kneeled on one knee.

Randi's jaw dropped as he released her hands to fish something from his jeans pocket. He withdrew the braided engagement ring and held it up between his thumb and forefinger.

"Miranda, will you marry me? Give me the honor of being your partner for life and a father to your son."

Randi sank to her knees and sat back on her heels, her eyes fixed on the ring, her voice caught up in her throat.

Paul lifted her left hand and held the ring one inch from her third finger. "Miranda, Honey, if you don't hurry up and say 'yes,' you're going to give me a heart attack."

Randi raised her eyes to his as a happy tear escaped. "Yes."

He slipped the ring on next to her wedding band. "Yes," he repeated. "I love that word, and I love you."

"Oh, Paul, I love you, too."

They came together in an embrace as their lips met to seal their promise of love.

❄

The next two weeks were no less than pure ecstasy for Randi. She and Paul got their blood tests, their marriage license, and started making plans for a November wedding. Randi even felt confident she was finally coming to terms with Colby's handicap, and she agreed to let him play T-ball.

With each passing day, she felt her life was closer to perfect than it had ever been.

Chapter 12

Paul felt Randi's eyes on him and looked up. She sat across from him, elbow on top of the kitchen table, chin in hand, fingernail of her right pinkie caught between her teeth. He smiled and winked, and as he expected, she bashfully cast her eyes down. He returned to the last few morsels of his supper, resisting the urge to make his way around the room to kiss her since Molly and Colby sat around the table, also.

Colby, decked out in his Little Braves T-ball uniform, sat swinging his legs beneath the table with his cheeks propped on his fists, waiting impatiently to get to his first T-ball game.

After Paul drained the last of his tea, he asked Randi, "Did Colby get home with his Special Olympics permission slip?"

Molly stood and held out her hand to Colby. "Come on, Sport. Let's you and me go load your T-ball equipment in the van."

Colby jumped down and ran out of the room ahead of Molly.

Paul watched them leave, a little confused at the hasty exit. They still had plenty of time to get to the game.

"How did you know about the permission slip, Paul?" Randi asked.

"I'm on the Special Olympics Organizational Committee. I was going over the list of athletes the other day and noticed Colby's name was missing. I thought he may have lost his form between here and school."

Randi rose and withdrew a paper from a drawer and handed it to him, then started removing plates from the table.

Paul glanced at the permission slip. "You need to get this filled out and back to the school, or Colby won't be allowed to participate."

Randi, dishes in hand, stopped halfway to the sink. "Colby's not participating." She continued toward the sink.

The pain in her eyes sent an ache to the center of Paul's chest. He knew Colby's limitations were sometimes hard for her to deal with. But he wanted her to see she wasn't helping Colby by trying to shield him from everything. He stood and circled the table, waiting for her to set the plates in the sink; then he turned her to face him, resting his hands on her shoulders. "Miranda, why won't you let Colby participate?"

She glanced away. "I don't know. I just can't."

He placed his palm on the side of her face and forced her to look at him. "Miranda, Colby being in special education is nothing to be ashamed of."

She pushed away, a flash of indignation sparking in her eyes. "Ashamed? Paul, I'm not ashamed of Colby."

Paul sighed, hooking his thumbs in his back pockets. "Maybe that wasn't the right word. I just want Colby to grow up proud of who and what he is, regardless of his strengths and weaknesses." He could see she was fighting tears.

"I'm just not ready to put him in Special Olympics yet," she said. "I keep hoping. . ."

Paul wasn't sure how to respond. His instincts had told him more than once that if he pushed the wrong button, Randi's fierce overprotection of Colby could be a touchy subject between them.

Randi continued pleading her case. "Look, I'm trying. Okay? You can't expect me to change overnight."

He pulled her to him, hugging her. She circled his waist with her arms and buried her face against his chest.

"I know you are, Honey," he reassured. "We'll talk about it later." He kissed the top of her head and gave her his gentle squeeze as he closed his eyes. *Dear God, please show me what to do to help her.*

He held her another minute, rocking her from side to side before releasing her. "I guess we'd better go. The game can't start without the coach and the all-star player."

Randi looked up and smiled weakly, then withdrew her arms from around him and turned to go. When she rounded the hall corner, Paul folded the permission form and slipped it into his back pocket, just in case.

The Little Braves' dugout and bleachers were close to first base, the opposing Little Rockies' close to third. Ricky Cooper being on Paul's team didn't surprise Randi in the least. Marcia Cooper taking a seat next to her on the bleachers did. Molly sat on Randi's other side.

The beauty of T-ball was that outs and runs weren't recorded. Instead, an inning was over after each child on each team had batted once. It was nearing the end of the first inning when Colby came up to bat. Paul was coaching first base.

Randi's chest tightened and her teeth almost brought blood from her right lower lip as she watched. It took five swings of the bat before Colby finally knocked the ball off the tee; then it rolled straight to the pitcher, who then tagged Colby out right before he touched first base. But that was okay. The coaches and fans on both sides cheered for both players.

Paul held his hand out to Colby. "Way to go, Son. You really did a good job hitting the ball."

With a wide grin, Colby slapped Paul's hand and trotted back to the dugout. Randy sighed. Paul calling Colby "Son" sounded so wonderful.

When the Little Rockies came up to bat the second time, their coach appeared unhappy with two calls made by the umpire early in the inning. Near the end of the Little Rockies' batting order, the third-base player for the Little Braves and the runner for the Little Rockies tagged third base at practically the same time. It was so close, Randi didn't envy the umpire. She would have called it a tie. But the umpire called what he saw, and he saw the third-base player reach the base first. "He's out!"

Red-faced and angry, the opposing coach stalked onto the field and up to the umpire. "What da ya mean, he's out? He was safe by a mile!"

Randi couldn't hear the seemingly unperturbed umpire's reply.

"Don't tell me to sit down!" the coach screamed. "I'll sit down when I'm ready!"

The next words of the umpire could be heard by all. He went nose-to-nose with the coach. "Get in the dugout and sit down, Bill, or you're out of the game!"

A hush settled over the crowd. Observers, coaches, and players all grew so quiet Randi could hear herself breathe as Colby left his position in left field and walked up to the angry coach. She stood and was about to jump from the bleachers when Molly grabbed her wrist and urged her back down.

"Let the coach handle it, Mom," Molly said, then gave her a determined nod, daring her to argue.

Randi turned her attention back to the field as Colby stopped in front of the coach. Paul stood outside the dugout and watched.

"Why doesn't he do something?" Randi muttered under her breath.

Colby tilted his head to the side and peered up at the coach from under the bill of his cap. "You don't 'pose to act like that in front of us children, Mr. Coach. It makes Jesus very sad." Then he turned and walked back to the outfield.

The coach's chin fell to his chest as he watched Colby retreat. The umpire broke into a smile, and low chuckles rumbled through the crowd. A man stood up behind Randi and yelled, "Way to go, Kid! More of us parents should have your nerve!" The man started clapping, and within seconds every single person in the stands was on their feet clapping, cheering, and sending up shrill whistles. Randi stood and joined the crowd. She had never been so proud.

When the cheers settled, the coach, still standing in the center of the field, faced the crowd. "I'm sorry, folks. I'm going to ask my assistant to finish the game as I'm going to remove myself. I'll try my best not to act so inappropriately in the future." With that, the coach walked off the field and took a seat on a grassy hill away from the crowd, and the game resumed.

The next time Colby came up to bat, he made it to first but was tagged out at second.

As Colby stepped up to the plate during the third inning, Randi heard the little boy waiting next in line to bat yell, "Okay, Colby! See if you can make it past first this time!"

Paul aimed a stern frown at the child and said, "That's enough, Toby."

Randi wondered if the little boy was the same Toby who called Colby stupid at school, then reprimanded herself for immediately disliking the child.

Colby swung twice, missing both times. The third time his bat barely grazed the ball, and it dropped right in front of the tee.

"Foul ball!" the umpire called.

The fourth time Colby swung, he hit the ball dead center, causing it to shoot past the pitcher and second baseman into center field. Colby, with a million-dollar smile, took off for first base. Randi, Marcia, and Molly sprang to their feet clapping and cheering. Paul, jumping up and down, his big arm moving like the propeller of an airplane, was already motioning Colby to go to second base.

Colby rounded first base, but just a few feet short of second base he tripped and fell face forward, sending up billows of red dust all around him.

When the dirt settled, his tiny fingers were just inches from second base. The opposing team's assistant coach took advantage of the situation and instructed his center fielder to move forward and tag Colby out, which she did. Paul and his assistant ran to Colby's aid while Randi stood with her feet glued to the bleacher, unable to react immediately.

Then Randi's greatest fear became a reality.

Toby ran up to Colby where he lay with dusty tears running down his face and yelled, "Colby, you're stupid! You can't do nothin' right!"

Colby sprang to his knees, balling his short fingers into fists and screamed back, "I am not stupid, neither!"

"Yes, you are!" Toby chided. "You're in the dummy class at school, and that makes you a retard! I don't want you on my team no more!"

Once again the crowd grew deathly quiet. Paul, his face stoic, looked at Toby and said calmly, "You won't be playing on Colby's team anymore, Toby. You're out for the rest of this season."

Randi didn't know how many fingers and toes she stepped on as she scrambled down the bleachers. She saw and felt only one thing—Colby's pain. She rushed onto the field, slamming the gate back against the chain-link fence with a clang. She ran to Colby and jerked him up. Colby wrapped his arms and legs around her as she walked stiffly off the field.

Randi stopped in front of Molly, who had climbed down off the bleachers. "Could you please take us home?"

Molly directed her glance past Randi's shoulder.

Paul's hand circled Randi's arm and he turned her to face him. "Where are you going?" he asked.

"To take Colby home where he belongs."

"Miranda, let him finish the game."

"Mom, please let me stay," Colby begged.

Randi chose not to hear her son's plea. Through clenched teeth she said just above a whisper, "No, Paul. He has no business here. If you had listened to me to start with, this wouldn't have happened."

Paul sighed, dropping his hand. "Go ahead, Molly. I'll find a ride home."

Randi walked briskly to the van.

❁

Not at all pleased with his mother, Colby jumped out of the van and ran in the house ahead of Randi. Randi's shoulders slumped. "Thank you for bringing us home, Molly."

"Do you need me to stay a few minutes?"

"No. Go on back and pick up Paul. I'll see you later." Randi got out of the van and made her way to the house as Molly drove away.

Randi found Colby belly down on his bed with his chin propped on his stacked hands and his cap tilted sideways on his head. She sat down on the bed and started to rub his back, but he rolled out of her reach, resuming his same position with his face turned away from her.

"Colby," Randi started, choosing her words carefully, "I know what Toby said to you hurt your feelings, but—"

"I'm not mad at Toby no more! I'm mad at you!"

His words pierced her heart. "Me? Why?"

He rolled off the bed and faced her. " 'Cause you wouldn't let me finish the game."

"Colby, I was trying to protect you. I didn't like the things Toby said to you."

"What Toby said to me was just dumb ol' words! And Paul said dumb ol' words can't hurt nobody!" He swiped a tear from his dusty cheek with the back of his hand.

Randi didn't know what to say. Why was it Paul seemed to have all the right answers and she all the wrong? It hurt so much to think she could be the source of Colby's pain. She was only trying to protect him.

"Do you want me to fix you something to eat?" she asked, hoping to shift gears. "Molly made a batch of peanut butter cookies today."

"No. I want to be by myself 'til Paul gets here; then I want to see him."

Randi closed her eyes. She dreaded Paul coming. There would be words between them, she was sure. He was always trying to involve Colby in one thing or another, and when she resisted, his patient persistence usually won out in the end. But today proved her concerns justified. She had a feeling Paul wouldn't see it that way, though.

She opened her eyes. Her son now stood facing her with his arms crossed and lips pursed. "Okay, Colby," she said. "You can stay in here and chill out for now." With that she left the room, wishing she could jump right into tomorrow, skipping what was sure to come later today.

※

An hour later Randi heard the muffled sound of the van doors closing. Colby was out of his room, out the back door, and running toward Paul by the time he stepped away from the van. Randi approached at a much slower pace, putting off the inevitable every second she could.

"Did we win?" Colby asked.

Paul lifted Colby to his hip. "Both teams won." He tickled Colby's stomach, conjuring up a round of youthful giggles.

As the laughter died, Paul glanced at Randi, then back at Colby. "Why don't you go on inside with Aunt Molly? Your mom and I need to talk."

"But I want to stay with you, Paul."

He set Colby on his feet. "Not right now, Sport. I'll catch you a little later."

"Okay." Colby sighed, slipping his hand in Molly's. "Will you fix me some peanut butter cookies?" he asked, sending another pang of guilt through Randi's chest.

"Come on." Paul motioned with his head. "Let's go for a walk."

Randi crossed her arms and fell into step beside him. Neither spoke for several minutes. Finally, Randi decided to break the silence. "Paul, I don't think Colby should play T-ball anymore."

"And I think you're wrong."

Randi stopped. So did Paul. They faced each other. Paul's reply surprised her. He had never been so blunt with her. She took in his tensed jaw and knitted brow. He was upset with her.

"You saw what happened today," she argued. "How could you put him back out there, knowing it could happen again?"

"Miranda, can't you see what you're doing to him? Half the time you're pushing him to be something he's not, and the other half you're trying to shield him from what you're trying to push him into being."

Randi had to close her eyes and let Paul's words unscramble in her brain before she understood what he was saying. She tried to drown out the voice inside her head screaming, *You know Paul's right!* She was Colby's mother. She knew what was best for him.

Opening her eyes, she tucked her hair behind her right ear. "I'm trying to protect him, Paul. I'm his mother. That's my job."

"And I'm going to be his father."

"But you're not his father yet!"

Randi would never know why those cruel words slipped through her lips. One thing she did know, though. She would have given her life to be able to recall them and take the hurt from Paul's face. Her shaking hand rose to her mouth and tears sprang to her eyes. "Oh, Paul. I'm sorry. I don't know what made me say that."

She reached for him, but he backed away, holding his palms up; then he turned and marched toward his truck. Running after him, she grabbed his arm and forced him to look at her. "Paul, I didn't mean it."

He refused to look at her, and she felt as though an invisible hand reached inside her and started squeezing her lungs. She could hardly breathe. "I love you, Paul." She made each word deliberate.

Paul turned wounded eyes on her. "It was you who said a one-sided relationship does not a happy couple make. Do you remember that?"

"Yes," Randi whispered.

"I'm beginning to understand what you were trying to tell me. You've put a wall up around Colby, and you refuse to let me in. Well, I can't play daddy from the sidelines. In the long run it wouldn't be good for Colby—or us." Breaking eye contact, he looked straight ahead with a sigh. "If you need me for anything, you know where to find me." With that he started to walk away.

"Paul." Her voice was small and shaky. He paused, turning back. She slipped her engagement ring off and held it out to him in a trembling hand.

He stared at the ring for an eternity before lifting his gaze to hers. "I can't take it back, Miranda. It belongs to you." His shoulders sagged, as though his energy suddenly deserted him. He looked over her shoulder toward the mountains, and the wind lifted an unruly lock of hair from his forehead.

He could have been a thousand miles away when his gaze drifted back to her, and he said in not much more than a whisper, "When you're ready to share your whole world with me, Miranda, let me know. Maybe then we can start over."

Then he was gone.

She curled her fingers around the ring and brought her hand to her chest. Bowing her head, she squeezed her eyes shut. A tear found its way to her clenched fist.

Oh, dear God, what have I done?

Chapter 13

After bringing Colby home from school the following afternoon, Randi sat at the kitchen table nursing her twelfth cup of coffee for the day. The night before, she had gone through the motions of preparing Colby for bed, then retreated to the sanctuary of her room and cried into the early morning hours.

Chin in hand, eyes closed, she was trying to talk herself out of a headache when Colby came dragging his T-ball bat mercilessly across the wood floor with no regard whatsoever for his mother's throbbing temples.

"Can I have my card back, Mom?"

Randi opened one eye. "What card?"

He sighed, as though she should know exactly what he was talking about. "You know, the one with Paul on it."

"Oh." Randi nodded. "I'll go get it."

She forced one foot in front of the other until she made it to her nightstand. She had intended to mention the card to Paul, but timing hadn't been on her side, especially over the past few days. Picking up her Bible, she flipped it open and started to take the card out, but for some reason, her attention was drawn to the verse directly above Paul's pictured head—Ecclesiastes 3:11. She read the verse silently twice, then in a whisper.

" 'He hath made every thing beautiful in his time: also he hath set the world in their heart, so that no man can find out the work that God maketh from the beginning to the end.' "

She looked up as Colby dragged his bat into her bedroom. Bingo followed like a loyal trooper. Randi attempted a smile as she gave the card to her son. "You need to put this back in your notebook, Colby."

"But you said Paul would sign it."

"You can take it back out when you see him again." Silently she added, *Whenever that will be.*

"Okay."

The doorbell sounded as Colby skipped out of the room. Wearily, Randi traipsed to the door. When she opened it, her eyes widened in surprise. "Marcia. Ricky." She looked from mother to son and back again. Stepping back, she said, "Come in."

Ricky took off in search of Colby while Marcia stepped through the door, eyeing Randi. "You look as bad as Paul."

"You've seen Paul?" Randi asked anxiously.

"We had a Special Olympics meeting at school this afternoon. I have never in my life seen him so depressed—or grouchy. Now I know why. Trouble in paradise, huh?"

Randi's shoulders drooped. "You were at the ball game yesterday. You saw what happened."

Marcia nodded.

Randi led Marcia to the kitchen. "Well, after he got back to the house, everything just fell apart. We don't always see eye-to-eye when it comes to Colby."

Colby and Ricky skipped into the kitchen, Colby still dragging his bat, Ricky carrying Colby's T-ball glove, Bingo still following. "Mom, can we go outside and play?" Colby asked.

"Do you want to sit on the front porch and watch them play a little while?" Randi asked Marcia.

"Sure."

Randi and Marcia rocked in two rocking chairs and watched the boys take turns batting, then racing to try and get the ball before Bingo claimed it.

"You know, Randi," Marcia said, "when Jason left me, it wasn't because of another woman or because he fell out of love with me. It was because he couldn't accept Ricky having Down's syndrome. I don't think it would have hurt half as much if our son had not been his reason for leaving."

Randi didn't respond. The old familiar heaviness settled in her chest.

"Please don't think I'm trying to meddle in your and Paul's business," Marcia continued. "I just see two very dear people hurting. It's a hurt I've experienced, and I want your story to have a happier ending than mine."

Randi took a deep, quivering breath and released it. "Marcia, I'm so confused. My common sense tells me Paul's right most of the time. But when I see Colby hurt, it tears me apart inside. How do you cope?"

Marcia put her elbow on the chair arm, resting her chin between her thumb and forefinger. She hesitated, as though thinking. "When I have trouble dealing with it, I force myself to erase his handicap and look at what's inside."

Randi's brow wrinkled in befuddlement.

Marcia nodded toward Colby and Ricky. They were laughing as they tried to convince Bingo to relinquish the ball. "Look at them," Marcia said. "They're perfect."

Randi's frown deepened. How could this woman say they were perfect?

"A smile in their direction and they're your friends for life," Marcia said. "That's a pretty reasonable price to pay for loyalty. They love the way that God intended us to love—without condition, asking nothing in return. The mold they come from is unique. They're heaven's special children, and they are perfect because God made them. And God doesn't make mistakes." Marcia swallowed. "God doesn't look at them and say, 'You're different.' He looks at them and says 'You are My child; from you will spring forth many blessings.' That's the beauty in our boys, Randi. And I would hate to see something so beautiful come between you and Paul."

A tear escaped and slid down Randi's cheek, taking with it the confusion clouding her mind, driving the fog from the meaning of the message sent to her just a few short minutes ago. *"He hath made every thing beautiful in his time."* That's what Paul had been trying to tell her. Colby was beautiful, and it was a shame to hide such beauty behind the wall of her heart, never allowing it to touch the world. So many blessings would be missed.

She wiped her face with her hands, new hope springing up within her. "Marcia, I need to go find Paul. Do you mind—?"

"I'll be glad to watch the boys."

Randi stopped halfway to the door. "Marcia, Paul told me—"

"Water under the bridge," Marcia smiled. "Go get your man and be happy."

As Randi reached for the door, the phone rang. Randi could hear Karen, her afternoon clerk, on another line.

"I'll get it," Marcia offered.

"Thanks." With that, Randi retrieved her purse from her room and headed for the van.

She drove to Paul's office, knowing Edith could tell her which job site Paul was on. As she stepped through the office door, the phone rang. Edith smiled at Randi as she picked up the receiver. "O'Bryan Construction."

A brief pause, then, "Why, yes. She's right here." The secretary held the phone out to Randi. "It's for you."

"Randi," Marcia's voice came over the line in a rush. "Colby's missing."

"What?!"

"When I went back outside after answering the phone, he was gone. I tried to get Ricky to tell me what happened, but he was so upset he didn't make much sense."

Randi tried not to panic. "Did you check the house? He couldn't have gone far in such a short time."

"Yes. He's not in the house. I'm afraid he's wandered off into the forest."

"I'm on my way."

Randi slammed down the receiver. "Edith, Colby's missing. Call Paul and tell him to get to the house as fast as he can." As she ran for the door, she glanced back over her shoulder. "And tell him to bring every one of his men with him."

❀

"Ron, I've got to leave," Paul told his foreman one hour after returning to the job site from the Special Olympics meeting. "There's something I've got to take care of."

"Sure thing, Boss," Ron replied as he hefted a two-by-four to his shoulder. "See you in the morning."

Paul ambled to his truck a much humbler man than the day before. After a sleepless night and an entire day of silent prayer, he had to acknowledge the error of his ways. It had been nothing but wounded pride that made him leave angry at Randi last night. He now realized she was not only trying to come to terms with Colby's handicap, but she had made great progress in her attempts.

I expected too much too soon, Paul berated himself. He would give himself a firm kick in the seat of his pants, but God was doing a good job of that already.

Somehow he had to set things right with the woman he loved. And he was prepared to beg, grovel, do whatever it took to get that ring back on her finger and her back into his arms.

As he approached his pickup, he broke into a trot. His truck phone was ringing.

❦

When Randi got back to the house, she found Ricky sitting on the cottage steps holding Colby's ball glove to his chest, rocking back and forth and crying. "I–I sorry Colby g–got lost. I–I sorry."

Randi kneeled before the tortured child, laying a hand on the side of his tear-dampened face. "Ricky, Honey, no one's blaming you. We know it wasn't your fault."

Turning to Marcia, she said, "You stay with Ricky. I'll comb the edge of the woods."

Marcia looked torn, so Randi reassured her. "Your son needs you. Please try to convince Ricky no one blames him."

At that moment, Paul's truck came skidding to a stop behind the house, followed by two more trucks packed with men. Paul, his foreman, and two other men jumped out of Paul's vehicle, and a total of seven more men poured out of the other trucks.

Randi ran to Paul. They met each other halfway, wrapping their arms around each other.

"Miranda, what happened?" Paul wanted to know.

Randi pulled back. "We're not sure. We think Colby wandered into the woods. Ricky's so upset he can't tell us anything."

Paul looked toward the cottage steps where Marcia sat rocking Ricky in her arms. "Fire and Rescue is on the way," he said. "They'll organize a search party when they get here. I'll try to talk to Ricky."

Randi watched as Paul walked to the steps and crouched down in front of

91

Marcia and Ricky. Paul and Ricky talked back and forth several times; then Ricky bobbed his head up and down and pointed toward the woods where Ron and the rest of Paul's employees were searching. Paul smiled at Ricky, ruffled his hair, then made his way back to Randi.

"It appears when Marcia went inside to answer the phone, Colby went around the house looking for you. Ricky followed him as far as the backyard, but he's had so many warnings not to go into the woods alone he stopped and went back to the front to wait for his mother." He pulled Randi into his arms. "We'll find him, Honey. I promise."

Fire and Rescue arrived with lights flashing and sirens blaring. Within a matter of minutes, a plan was put in motion and search teams formed.

Molly arrived home from a shopping trip in the midst of the chaos and ran to the gazebo where Randi sat with Marcia and Ricky. Randi stopped wringing her hands and jumped up, throwing her arms around Molly.

"My dear, what on earth is going on?" Molly questioned.

"Colby's lost in the woods." Randi briefly told Molly what had transpired since Marcia arrived that afternoon.

Molly grasped Randi's shoulders. "You listen to me, Miranda Elaine Thomas. We will find Colby and he will be fine."

Paul, who had been directing the teams where to search since he knew the area so well, left his group and came to the gazebo. "I'm going into the woods with a team in a few minutes," he told Randi. "We need to cover as much ground as possible before nightfall."

Panic seized Randi. She gathered the front of Paul's shirt in her fists. "Paul, when it gets dark—"

He took her fists in his large hands and kissed them. "No, we won't stop. When it gets dark we'll do a shoulder-to-shoulder search."

"Can I go with you?"

"You need to stay here. Your face is the first one Colby needs to see when he's brought out."

Trying to draw strength from Paul's positive words, Randi conceded with a feeble nod.

"Miranda, was Colby wearing a coat, by chance?" Paul asked.

"No. He had on a sweatshirt, jeans, and tennis shoes. Why?"

Paul didn't answer.

Randi fought to keep her voice calm. "Paul, it's been reasonably warm today. He won't freeze, will he?"

Paul pulled her into his arms. "There's a cold front moving in tonight. We're supposed to get our first frost."

"Oh, no." She would have crumpled to the gazebo floor if Paul hadn't been holding her. But she soon collected herself and pushed away. "You'd better get going. Colby needs you out there. And so do I."

"Keep your chin up, Love. We'll find him." Paul hooked his hand around the back of her neck and kissed her soundly before joining his team.

As dusk started falling, the volunteers regrouped for the shoulder-to-shoulder search, where several searchers walked with all their shoulders touching through the darkness, aided by powerful flashlights. This method of search made it less likely to bypass a small body that might be lying on the dark forest floor.

Paul once again made his way to Randi before going back into the forest for the shoulder-to-shoulder search. She still sat in the gazebo with Molly. The two women had convinced Marcia to take Ricky home and away from the traumatizing excitement.

Paul flopped down next to Randi. "How are you holding up?"

Randi shrugged. "I'm trying."

Thunder rumbled from mounting clouds in the western sky as cold air collided with warm. Randi covered her face with her hands and leaned into Paul. He responded by embracing her. "Oh, Paul," she cried. "Colby's afraid of storms."

"Who called the television station?" Molly asked, springing to her feet.

Randi jerked her head up. "I don't want to talk to anyone."

Paul helped Randi to her feet. "Get Miranda inside, Molly. I'll deal with the media."

Once inside, Randi paced as she waited. Lightning pierced not only the dark sky but her heart as well. Each peal of thunder tore at her soul. She wanted to scream at the building storm. She wanted to run outside and shake her fist in the face of each dark cloud and dare it to cause her son any more discomfort than he already had to be feeling. Never had her world looked so dark. And although Molly sat at the kitchen table praying, Randi had never felt so alone.

As news of Colby's disappearance traveled throughout the small community, volunteers started trickling in. Within two hours, over two hundred people were buzzing between the house and woods in an effort to find Colby.

As though heeding her warning, the storm passed. Minutes turned into long, agonizing hours, and Molly finally convinced Randi to lie down when the grandfather clock in the family room announced the arrival of 2:00 A.M.

She went into Colby's room and lay on his bed. Pulling his stuffed polar bear to her face, she inhaled. She smelled superhero bubble bath and baby shampoo. Pancake syrup and chocolate milk. And. . .what else? She inhaled a second time. Yes, peanut butter cookies.

She hugged the bear to her breast. She was numb. Whether from fear, lack of sleep, or both, she didn't know, nor did she care. Because if she were not numb, the pain would be more than she could bear. Too spent to cry, she finally closed her eyes and prayed, "Dear God, please let Paul find Colby, and please keep Colby safe until he does."

"For he shall give his angels charge over thee, to keep thee in all thy ways."

Randi couldn't remember if she had read that verse recently or heard it in a sermon. She just knew it was there, and the Author had never broken a promise to her.

Her body finally gave way to fatigue, and in the hour just before dawn she drifted into a fitful slumber and dreamed of a woman in a soft white dress watching over her son.

Chapter 14

Paul, Ron, and two other men were still shining their lights on the forest floor just before dawn. Tired, wet, and cold, Paul no longer felt his hands or feet, and he knew Ron had to feel the same. They were the only two members of the rescue team that had not swapped out every two hours during the night.

As Paul started up a steep incline he wondered for the hundredth time how far one little guy could go. Statistics said no more than a two-mile radius. Statistics also said a child would seek shelter close to something like a boulder or log. But it seemed they had searched out every boulder and log on the mountain—twice. The mountains were full of sharp ledges and holes obscured by heavy foliage, but Paul refused to think in that direction. The sun would be up soon. They would find Colby then. They had to.

Ron tripped over a stump but quickly pulled himself up.

"Why don't you go out and rest for awhile?" Paul suggested.

Ron shook his head. "No. I'm fine. Let's keep moving."

Paul took two more steps on the damp leaf-covered ground, then stopped, holding up his hand. "Listen." The other three men froze, and Paul heard it again, a soft whining sound.

"Ron, did you notice a little brown dog at the house yesterday evening after Colby got lost?" Paul asked.

Ron thought for a second. "No, I didn't."

"Let's go." Paul tore through the woods in the direction of the whining, his flashlight throwing a haphazard beam over the forest floor. The others followed closely.

The whine became a bark as they approached the top of the hill, which led to a sharp descent. Paul stopped at the top of the ridge and directed his light downhill. There he found Bingo on the lower side of a huge uprooted tree, his large paws resting on the top side of the trunk. "Down here!" Paul yelled.

Paul made his way down the slope, half standing, half sliding. He leaned over the log, and there lay Colby, gray and motionless, his face, arms, and legs curled into the crevice of the tree trunk and the ground.

Paul jumped the log and put his fingertips to Colby's neck. "I'm getting a pulse, but it's weak." He put his ear to Colby's mouth. "He's breathing, but it's shallow. Ron, radio the guys at the house and tell them to let Miranda know we're coming out. Tell them to make sure the medics are ready to roll when we get there." He looked at the man on his left as he shucked his coat. "Help me get him out of those wet clothes. I know it's risky moving him, but I'm afraid if we wait for a stretcher, we'll lose him."

After they stripped Colby of his damp clothing, Paul placed his coat over him and gently picked him up.

Ron added his coat to Paul's precious bundle, then picked up Bingo and cradled him in one arm. "You did good, Boy."

"Okay," Paul said. "Let's go!"

❁

A jolt jerked Randi from her state of half-sleep. She opened her eyes to find Molly bending over her, shaking her.

"They're bringing Colby out," her aunt said. "Paul found him."

Randi was up and sprinting out the door in a flash, Colby's bear still held close.

It was several excruciating minutes before Paul appeared running from the woods, hugging a bundled-up Colby to his chest. Randi waited next to the open back door of the ambulance. Paul jumped in the vehicle in one graceful motion. Randi and two EMTs immediately followed. One EMT pulled the doors closed as the other slapped the window behind the driver. As the ambulance fled away, Paul tenderly eased Colby from his arms onto the gurney.

❁

"Colby has suffered severe hypothermia," the doctor explained. "His body temperature was eighty-six when he was brought in. We're giving him warm fluids intravenously and through a tube leading from his nose to his stomach. We've brought his temp up to ninety-two, but he's still unconscious."

"Is he going to be okay?" Randi asked.

The doctor pulled off his glasses and looked at her from beneath bushy, connecting eyebrows. "I can't make any promises, Mrs. Thomas. As low as his body temperature was, even if he does pull through, there is a possibility of brain damage. We're doing everything we can, but the rest is up to Colby." He pointed heavenward with his glasses. "And Him."

Randi reached for Paul's hand and found it. "Can I see him?"

"Sure. But only for a few minutes and only one visitor at a time."

Paul slipped his arm around Randi and kissed her temple. "We'll be praying."

She nodded and made her way down the hall, stuffed bear still in hand. When she entered the ICU room she clutched her stomach, unprepared for the sight of her lively, robust son, now lying motionless, pale, and gray, fighting for his life.

As the doctor had said, there was an IV in his hand and a tube in his nose. He also had something that looked like cellophane wrapped around his head covering his hair.

The nurse punched the buttons on the IV pump and smiled at Randi. "I'll leave you two alone for a few minutes. Just call if you need me. I'll be right outside."

Randi crept to Colby's side, easing down in a chair beside the bed. With a shaky hand, she placed the bear on the pillow next to his head. When she grazed his face with her fingertips, she cringed at how cool it felt.

She inhaled, trying to steady her voice. "It's Mom, Colby. Paul and Aunt Molly are in the waiting room. And Grandma Janet is on the way. I tried to get Aunt Molly to go home and get some rest, but she's as stubborn as always. She says she's right where she needs to be when you wake up."

Randi knew she was rambling, but she didn't know what else to do. "You know, Bingo stayed with you in the forest. He even showed Paul where you were. I don't think I'll ever complain about him getting on the bed again."

She sighed, unable to think of anything else to say. Moving her hand from his face to his clenched fist, she noticed he was grasping a stiff piece of paper. She pried his fingers open and straightened the paper. It was Paul's baseball card. Randi smiled sadly. "It looks like Bingo wasn't the only one with you."

The nurse returned, smiling compassionately. "Why don't you go lie down in the waiting room? We'll let you know if there's any change." The nurse apparently sensed Randi's reluctance to leave and added, "You have to go, Mrs. Thomas. We have to limit visits in the ICU to ten minutes an hour."

Before rising, Randi gave her son a lingering kiss on his cool, clammy cheek. "I leave him in Your hands, God," she whispered, caressing Colby's face. "Please take care of him."

She made her way to the pediatric ICU waiting room, where she found Paul and Molly. She sat down on the lumpy sofa next to Paul, and he put his arm around her, pulling her close.

Drawing her legs up, she curled into Paul's side and lay her head on his shoulder. She held out the crumpled card for him to see.

"Where did you get that?" Paul wanted to know.

"Eddie collected baseball cards. Colby found it."

Paul said nothing.

Randi let her arm rest across his stomach. "I'm sorry about what I said to you—when was it?" She frowned, thinking. "Night before last. I didn't mean it. I was just hurt for Colby. I promise it will never happen again. Can you ever forgive me?"

Paul laid his cheek against the top of her head. "Forgive you for what?"

Hearing that, Randi closed her eyes.

When Randi woke it was dark outside the waiting room window, and she and Paul were alone. She raised her head. "Where's Molly?"

"Gone to the cafeteria for supper."

She sat up, rubbing her eyes. "No word on Colby?"

Paul shook his head.

Ten minutes later, the doctor came in and Randi sprang to her feet. Paul rose and stood behind her.

The doctor pulled off his glasses and smiled. "There's one spirited young man down the hall demanding to see his mother."

Randi grasped the doctor's upper arms. "You mean—" She couldn't finish.

"He's fine. Not even a frostbitten toe. He'll probably be out of here by tomorrow evening."

Randi looked up. "Thank You, God." Then back at the doctor. "And thank you." She gave the doctor a bear hug, catching the stout man off guard.

"Small wonder her son's so spirited," she heard Paul say.

Randi released the doctor and headed for the door. She was two steps down the hall when she backed up and stuck her head in the waiting room, giving Paul an impatient look. "Well, what are you waiting for?"

Paul raised a questioning brow to the doctor, who nodded his consent. Paul reached for Randi's offered hand, and she practically pulled him down to hall to ICU.

Colby was sitting up in his bed and chattering nonstop to the two nurses preparing to move him to a regular room. The tube in his nose and the cellophane on his head were gone, but he still had the IV in his hand.

"My dog's name is Bingo, and my first best friend's name is Paul, but he's gonna be my daddy when he marries my mom; then Ricky will be my first best friend."

The nurses were trying to hold their laughter at bay so they could do their job. Randi and Paul looked at each other, shook their heads, and smiled as they moved to opposite sides of the bed.

Colby's face lit up when he saw them. "Hey, Mom! Paul! They're gonna drive me to my new room in this bed, just like a real go-cart."

"Sounds like fun." Randi leaned over and hugged him. Paul followed suit.

Randi sat on the edge of the bed, brushing Colby's bangs from his forehead. "Colby, I'm sorry you got lost. I know you were scared."

"I wasn't a-scared. A lady stayed with me."

"A lady?" Paul asked.

Colby bobbed his head. "Uh-huh. She had on a white dress that didn't even get wet in the rain. She told me a bunch of people were looking for me and that they would find me. Then she let me lay my head in her lap, and I went to sleep, and I just now waked up."

A thoughtful frown creased Paul's forehead. "Must have been your guardian angel." He ruffled Colby's hair, then glanced at Randi and shrugged.

A knowing smile touched her lips.

After the nurses left with Colby, Randi and Paul stepped out into the hall.

"Randi!" a female voice called.

"Mom!" Randi ran to meet her dark-haired, dark-eyed mother with an embrace. "He's going to be okay, Mom. I have never felt so blessed."

Janet held Randi at arm's length. "I had a feeling he would be. We prayed all the way up here."

"Then Mike came with you?" Randi asked about her brother.

"No. He's coming up in the morning."

Confused, Randi looked over her mother's shoulder to see who the other part of "we" was. She couldn't believe it when she saw Eddie's mother and father coming down the corridor toward her. After Colby's birth, they had gradually distanced themselves from her and her son. Although they never said why, Randi felt it was because they could see so much of their dead son in their only grandson.

"Mary. Sam." Randi greeted and hugged them. "Thank you for coming. Colby's going to be fine."

"Oh, thank God." Mary grasped Randi's hands. "I'm sorry we've not paid much attention to Colby in the past. I hope we don't make the same mistake in the future."

"That doesn't matter now. What matters is that you're here, and Colby's going to get better." Randi squeezed Mary's fingers. "There's someone I'd like you all to meet." She stepped back, and Paul stepped forward. "This is Paul O'Bryan; he's. . ." She stopped herself before introducing Paul as her future husband, remembering she and Paul hadn't had a chance to talk about their broken engagement. Realizing she had to say something suitable but unassuming, she finished with, "He's a very special friend of mine and Colby's."

❀

Three days later, Randi sat on the back steps of the house, her heart full of both joy and sorrow. God had spared Colby's life, and for that she would be forever thankful. But she and Paul still hadn't had a chance to talk about their engagement. And it seemed he didn't want to.

He had come to see Colby twice since he came home from the hospital two days ago, but he left after only a few minutes, stating there were things he needed to do.

Janet Harris came through the back door and joined her daughter on the steps. Randi took the glass of grape soda her mother offered but didn't drink it.

"Want to talk about it?" Janet asked.

"About what?"

"What's keeping you and Paul apart and miserable?"

Randi's nose and eyes started burning. "Oh, Mom, I said something terrible to Paul the night before Colby got lost. I thought when we were together at the hospital we could get past it. But it looks like he's not ready to do that yet. I'm beginning to wonder if he ever will be."

"Have you tried to talk to him?"

"I can't get him to hang around long enough. And even if he did, I'm afraid he wouldn't listen."

"Miranda, I've never known you to be afraid of anything in your life."

Randi's voice quivered. "I've never loved anyone the way I love Paul."

Janet slipped her arm around Randi, and Randi laid her head on her mother's shoulder. "Listen to me, baby girl," Janet said. "Do you remember when your daddy used to catch you and Mike doing something you weren't supposed to be doing, and you two would stand before him and vow never to do anything wrong again?"

Randi nodded.

"Do you remember what your daddy would tell you?"

Randi closed her eyes and thought back, then opened her eyes and raised her head as the words came back to her. The right corner of her mouth eased up. "Show me; don't tell me."

"Exactly."

A budding new hope flowed through Randi. "And I know exactly what to do to show Paul how much I love him. But there's something I have to take care of first."

❀

The following afternoon, Paul stepped up to the back door of the house and wiped his sweaty palms on the thighs of his jeans. Randi would probably tell him to get lost, but he was willing to risk it.

When she introduced him to her mother and Eddie's parents as a special friend, not as her fiancé and Colby's future father, he felt like she'd kicked him in the stomach. She couldn't have hurt him more if she'd called him their enemy. Apparently, she wasn't ready to unbreak their engagement.

And what had he done since then? Run, like a wounded animal dodging the hunter's bullet. He knew if she told him their relationship was over, it would take the life right out of him.

He took a deep bracing breath as he raised his hand to knock on the door. Love had completely knocked his simple, well-organized life off balance. A week ago, if anyone had told him he was a coward, he would have laughed in their face.

Well, he was still running; only now he was running in the right direction—to her. Somehow he had to convince her they were meant to be together. He loved her too much to let her get away.

He rapped on the door. A few seconds later the curtain moved and Molly peeked out.

Jerking the door open, his grandmother crossed her arms and leveled him with a look of indignation. "Paul O'Bryan, you're a big buffoon!"

"Save the lecture, Molly," Paul said with a touch of irritation.

"Don't you get smart with me, young man!"

Impatience caused his shoulders to slump. "I'm sorry," he said sincerely. "I need to see Miranda."

"Oh, you do, do you? Well, I'm afraid you're too late."

His chest contracted. "What do you mean, too late?"

"She and Colby have gone back to Columbus with her mother."

Molly's announcement deterred his anticipation but not his determination. "Give me her address. I'll leave right now and go get her."

"Did you forget you've got Special Olympics tomorrow morning?"

Placing his hands on his hips, Paul released a long breath from puffed cheeks. "Yes, actually, I did. I'll leave as soon as it's over."

Chapter 15

What happens when we die?"

Randi looked down at her son, silently rehearsing what she planned to say. This conversation was long overdue.

"Let's sit down, Colby." She dropped to the grass next to Eddie's grave and circled her drawn-up knees with her arms. Colby flopped down next to her and crisscrossed his legs.

"When we die, our bodies go in the grave," Randi explained. "But there's another part of us. The part that thinks, feels, and loves. That part of us is called our soul, and it's the part of us that goes to heaven to be with Jesus."

"Who takes our soul to heaven?"

"God sends one of his angels to get us."

Colby frowned, thinking, then said, "So the deers didn't take my daddy away?"

"No, Honey."

"Are angels good?"

"God's angels are."

A small silence passed, during which Randi raised her left hand and looked at her wedding band. She slipped it off and held it up for Colby to see. "Your daddy gave this to me when we married. Now I'm giving it to you. When we go home, we'll put it in a metal box in the bank where it will stay safe until you're grown."

Colby frowned, not too keen on the idea of getting something just to have it put away. "Can we take it out and look at it sometimes?"

Randi smiled. "Of course."

"Is Paul gonna be my daddy now?"

Randi chewed her right lower lip before answering, "I don't know, Colby. I said something to him that wasn't very nice, and he may have changed his mind about marrying me. But regardless of what happens between us, I'm sure he'll still be your best friend."

Colby's countenance fell. "I'd rather him be my daddy."

"So would I."

Randi reached out and, with her fingers, traced the engraved name on Eddie's headstone. As a tear slipped down her face, she made a confession that lifted a burden she had carried for seven long years.

"I was so angry with you for leaving me, Eddie, but not anymore. I forgive

102

you, as I know you've forgiven me. Thank you for sharing your life and your love with me." Taking a deep, shuddering breath, she lifted her eyes to the heavens. "And thank You, Father, for all the special blessings You've sent my way, especially for my son."

A deep-seated peace flowed through her like the current of a gentle mountain stream. She no longer stood at the fork in the road; she had stepped onto the path leading right. She had reached that point of acceptance. Acceptance of Eddie's untimely death, acceptance of Colby's handicap, and acceptance of Paul's place as Colby's new father—if he still wanted the position.

Closing her eyes, she relished the serenity of a quiet moment, then opened her eyes and looked back at the headstone. "Good-bye, Eddie. Rest in peace."

A little hand curled around her fingers. She looked down into bright hazel eyes shining beneath a crown of light brown hair and smiled. Rising, she pulled Colby up with her. "Come on, Son. It's time to go home."

❀

Randi peeked out from her hiding place behind the concession stand as Colby's class marched onto the football field. She saw Colby break away from his teacher and dart across the field, not stopping until he had his short arms wrapped around Paul's legs. The look of shock on Paul's face brought a smile to Randi's lips. Paul lifted Colby to his hip and glanced around the field and into the stands. He spotted Molly, Janet, and Mike and his wife Kathleen, and waved to them. He continued scanning the crowd until he had to lower Colby to the ground and turn his attention to the Special Education director, who was taking the microphone.

Randi drew her head back and took a deep breath as Marcia came running up. "You ready?" Marcia asked.

"No! I can't believe I let you talk me into this. When I called and said I wanted to volunteer, I had something like handing out ribbons in mind."

"You'll do great," Marcia responded with a lot more assurance than Randi felt. "Sounds like they're about ready for you." Marcia turned and walked toward the platform.

Randi raised her hand to watch the diamond of her braided ring sparkle in the sun. Glancing heavenward, she said, "Well, God, here goes." She gave Him a "thumbs-up" sign before stepping from behind the concession stand and climbing the steps of the platform. She knew exactly where Paul was, could feel him watching her, could sense his surprise. But she didn't dare look at him just yet for fear she'd lose her nerve.

The director announced into the microphone, "If everyone would please rise, we'll now have our Special Olympics oath."

Randi placed her hand over her heart and said the Olympic oath with the crowd.

"Let me win.
But if I cannot win,
Let me be brave in the attempt."

Everyone remained standing, right hands in place, while they pledged to the American flag. Marcia then took the microphone and announced, "Our national anthem will be performed today by Randi Thomas, the mother of Colby Thomas, one of our local athletes."

Randi accepted the microphone, opened her mouth to sing but had to stop. "Before I sing, there's something I have to say. When I first learned my son was handicapped, I was devastated. Like most parents I had dreams of him becoming a doctor, lawyer, or scientist. I denied the physician's findings and tried to make my son into what I wanted him to be. It took almost losing him to make me realize what a precious blessing God had given me.

"I know during my son's life he will experience discrimination and prejudice, and as he grows he will know there are limits to what he can do, as there are for any human being. But he will also know. . ." She paused, knowing what she was going to say was taking a chance, but it was a chance worth taking.

Her gaze settled on Paul, and for a moment in time, no one else existed. "He will know his parents love him and that they are proud of who and what he is."

She forced her attention back to the crowd. "Moms and dads, when you take your children home tonight, hug them and tell them you love them and that you're proud of them. Because, truly, each and every child on this earth is a special blessing from heaven."

She then sang, her mellow alto voice rendering every man, woman, and child motionless. When she finished, she searched the faces of the crowd and noticed several people wiping tears. ·

Paul met her as she stepped off the platform. "Miranda, we need to talk."

If what Paul had to say was bad, Randi didn't think she would have the courage to stay at the games. If what he had to say was good, she couldn't guarantee she wouldn't jump into his arms and smother him with kisses. She didn't want to risk either reaction in a crowd. "Not right now, Coach. We've got games to play."

Between Colby's turns in the events, Randi helped with the softball throw. By day's end, Colby wore a first-place ribbon for the soccer kick, a second-place ribbon for the softball throw, and fourth-place ribbons for the long jump and the fifty-yard dash. Randi's cup of joy overflowed as he walked proudly around the field displaying his ribbons.

The children were leaving the field and Randi was putting soccer balls in a bag when strong, muscular arms circled her waist and pulled her back against a hard chest wall. She turned with a smile and pushed Paul's hands down to his sides. "Paul O'Bryan, behave."

"My patience has run out. Let's go someplace where we can talk."

"We've got all this equipment to put away."

"We've got a group of high school students to do that. Now let's go."

"But it's almost time to pick up Colby."

Paul laced his fingers through hers and started pulling her off the field. "Molly and your mom are picking him up. Now don't argue with me, or I'm going to throw you over my shoulder and carry you to my truck."

Randi didn't argue.

❈

Paul drove Randi to his cabin. Before she could step out of the truck, he was at her door. He slipped one arm under her knees and one beneath her shoulders and picked her up, spinning her twice while their laughter rose to mingle above their heads. He carried her to the edge of his front yard before setting her on her feet. His hands rested on her waist, hers on his chest.

Then his smile faded. "Miranda, I was a fool to walk away from you that night after the T-ball game, and I was a coward to avoid you after you brought Colby home from at the hospital." He shrugged, hesitantly, then confessed, "I panicked. I love you so much; I couldn't bear to hear you tell me our relationship was over."

Wide-eyed, Randi gaped at him. "What on earth do you mean?"

"When you introduced me to Eddie's parents as your friend, I was afraid you didn't want to give our love another chance."

Randi dropped her forehead to his chest. "That's exactly what I thought about you when you didn't make an effort to discuss our engagement after Colby came home from the hospital."

Paul slipped his thumb beneath her chin and forced her to look at him. "You mean we wasted these last five days? Come here." He pulled her close. "I've got to make up for lost time."

He started to kiss her, but she resisted. "Listen to me, Paul. I need your level-headedness when the mother in me can't see what's best for Colby. I need your strength when I see someone mistreat him or take advantage of him. I can't promise you I'll always agree with you where he's concerned." She brought her left fingertips to her chest. "But I can promise you I will love you with all my heart forever. Knowing that, are you willing to start over?"

Paul lifted her left hand, turning it from side to side so the stone on her engagement ring caught the afternoon sun. Then his eyes locked onto hers. "Your wedding band?"

"It's in the safe deposit box, waiting for Colby to grow up and fall in love."

She didn't explain further; she didn't need to. His kiss, warm and tender, told her he understood.

When he drew back, his eyes looked misty. "Miranda," he said, "my love for you is like the band on this ring, never ending. I don't want to start over. I want to marry you just like we planned." His beautiful left brow eased up his forehead. "Unless I can talk you into marrying me as soon as we can find a preacher."

Randi's right hand found his cheek. She searched his face for a sign that he was teasing. She found none. "Are you serious?" she asked to make sure.

He kissed her palm. "Yes. We already have the license. Your family's here. I can call Reverend Phil. You can go to the house and put on a dress. What do you say?"

Her smile brightened and her eyes glistened with happy tears. "I say we need to go tell Colby he's going to get a new daddy tonight."

Two hours later, Randi stood before God and family and placed her entire world, son included, in the palm of Paul's hand. Paul wrapped fingers of love around that world and placed it in the center of his heart, with a vow to cherish and protect it for the rest of his life.

And two worlds became one.

Epilogue

Eight Months Later

Assembled around one of the tables at the Spring Sports Award Banquet were Randi, Colby, Molly, and Janet. Paul sat with the other coaches at the front tables next to the podium. He had coached a Little League team of eleven and twelve year olds during the spring Park and Rec season.

Randi still worked occasionally at Simple Treasures during busy times, but shortly after her and Paul's wedding, her mother moved to Serenity and now managed the shop. Of course, Randi was always on hand when Paul needed her to run an errand for his construction business. But for the most part, she simply enjoyed the role of wife and mom.

Paul stepped up to the podium and cleared his throat before speaking into the microphone. "The final award is the Sportsmanship Award voted on by all the coaches." He paused, glancing Randi's way with a brilliant smile and wink. "Now, I don't like to think of myself as someone who shows partiality. But tonight, I must confess, I am particularly proud to present the Sportsmanship Award to my batboy and my son, Colby Thomas O'Bryan."

Colby stopped fidgeting when he heard his name. His mouth formed an O, and his eyebrows disappeared beneath his bangs as he eyed the trophy Paul held in his hand.

Molly nudged Colby. "Go on and get your trophy, Sport."

Colby turned to his mother. "Come with me."

Randi shook her head. "No. You're a big boy. You go by yourself."

He grabbed her hand and tugged. "You have to, Mom, please."

"Come on, Mom," Paul said into the microphone.

Randi stood and allowed Colby to pull her to the podium. Colby, still in wide-eyed wonder, reached for the trophy as if it were a precious jewel. Paul lifted Colby to stand on the table, and the crowd applauded.

Randi captured her husband's hand and pulled him back two steps, out of range of the microphone. "Do you think you can bring this meeting to a close soon?" she asked from the side of her mouth while she gazed proudly at her son.

"What's the hurry, Mom?" Paul asked from the corner of his mouth.

"Colby's spending the night with Mom and Molly."

Out of the corner of her eye, Randi saw Paul's eyebrows jump up. "We're as good as outta here."

※

Paul was already pulling Randi into his arms before the cabin door closed behind them. It took some effort on her part, but she finally broke away from his first kiss. "Paul, behave."

"I don't wanna. I have you all to myself tonight, and I intend to take full advantage of it." He continued to pursue her, backing her into the den where his prize buck had been returned to its place above the mantel at Colby's insistence a week ago.

Randi knew he was headed for the sofa, and if he got her there, she would totally forget her surprise.

She pushed harder. "Wait a minute. I have something for you."

He pulled his head back. "For me? What is it?"

"Well, it's something to wear."

He rolled his eyes, his thumb and forefinger finding the zipper at the back of her dress. "Honestly, Miranda, I don't want to try on clothes tonight. I'd much rather—"

She pressed her fingers to his lips. "It's not for you to wear, Silly. It's for me to wear."

He forgot the zipper and pulled her hand away from his mouth. "Let me see if I've got this right. Colby's spending the night with Mom and Molly, and you bought something for you to wear—for me."

She nodded.

"Well, what are you waiting on? Go change." He turned her and gave her a playful slap on the backside.

When she walked back into the den, he was looking out the window with his back to her, bracing himself with one hand against the window frame. The sleeves of his white dress shirt were rolled up to his elbows, and the thumb of his free hand was hooked in his back pocket. The sight of him still caused a giddy flutter beneath her ribs. Would he ever cease to take her breath away? No, she decided, not ever, no matter how many years together God blessed them with.

She stopped in the center of the room. "Well, what do you think?"

When he turned, his smile immediately disappeared. He strolled over to her, circling her once while inspecting the green dress hanging in billows over her slim body.

Randi struggled not to laugh. One thing Paul couldn't hide was his feelings, and from the look on his face, right now he was feeling totally confused.

He cleared his throat and loosened his tie. "Ah, is that the latest style?"

"Well, it is for me. At least for the next seven months anyway."

His eyes traveled down the dress and back up; then his jaw dropped. "You mean. . .you're going to have, er, we're going to have. . . ?"

"Yes, we are." The left corner of her mouth joined the right corner in a sweeping smile.

Suddenly, and with a "Whoop!" Paul gathered her in his arms and twirled her around, but just as suddenly he returned her to her feet and stepped back. Placing his hand on her flat stomach, he said, "Oh, no. I didn't hurt you, did I?"

Randi grabbed his tie and pulled him to her, tilting her chin in order to look into his adorable, handsome face. "No, you didn't. As a matter of fact, the doctor said there's no reason I can't continue all normal activities, as long as I stay off skis and roller skates."

Paul grinned, slipping his arms around her and backing her down the hall. "He did?"

"He did."

Paul paused and looked heavenward. "Thank You, God, for all my blessings."

Randi laced her fingers behind her husband's neck. "Mine, too."

Paul kissed his wife until he had her backed into their room; then he closed the door.

GINA FIELDS

Gina is a lifelong native of northeast Georgia. She is married to Terry, and they have two very active sons. When Gina is not writing, singing, or playing piano, or doing a hundred homemaking activities, she enjoys volunteering for Special Olympics.

On Wings of Song

Brenda Knight Graham

Dedicated to Charles—
"More today than yesterday, less today than tomorrow."

I would like to thank the following who were
so helpful when I was writing this book:
Virginia Bonnette, Suzanne, Fairlight,
and Rebecca Dover, John Knight, and Eric Peck.
Thanks, Charles, for that hike into Tallulah Gorge!

Chapter 1

Connie Jensen looked up from writing in her bright new record book to scan the little faces of her eighteen students and try to connect names with them. She had given them each an art assignment. Some weren't paying it much attention while others puzzled over blank sheets and a few plied crayons or pencils with feverish zeal, shoulders hunched over their desks.

There was Marie, such a pretty little girl but with straggly, dirty hair; Sammy Craven, clean and shining with a mother's obvious care; Richard with his tongue at the side of his mouth as he toiled with his pencil. Connie had so looked forward to this very day, finally having her own class of children, though she hadn't really planned on first graders. She simply wouldn't let anything put a stopper on her joy, not Mr. Donovan with his strict ultimatums nor Zena Furr, fellow teacher, with her negative predictions.

She would teach these children to read! In a glow of romanticism she pictured herself surrounded by bright-eyed children, maybe sitting on a big rug with them all looking up to her, all excited as it came their turns to read from crisp new books.

It might be hard for a few weeks to prove to Mr. Maury Donovan, Pine Ridge Elementary's principal, that she could teach retained first graders and slow second graders as well or better than anybody. But he would see very soon that just because it was her first year teaching did not mean she was incompetent.

She couldn't help it that Mr. Donovan was out of his office the day she was hired, nor could she help it that the school board chose to hire her for this Georgia mountain school without his consultation. And she certainly couldn't help it that he seemed to resent her—as an impostor maybe? Her home in Augusta was only three hours away. He'd asked her why she hadn't stayed nearer home her first year teaching—as if she needed to hold her mother's hand or something.

But she wasn't going to hold her mother's hand, and she didn't intend to hold anyone's hand. Right now she didn't even want her fiancé, Henry Segars, always suggesting what she should do. In fact, the whole reason for her being here, she supposed, was to get away from Henry. She felt smothered by him somehow, and she had to get some perspective on things before they married. She had to know she really loved him.

A cracking snap interrupted the room's studious hum as a boy near the door broke his pencil. It wasn't just the lead that broke, but the whole pencil popped right in the middle. She wouldn't have believed it on little Marie's word alone, but she turned her head in time to see the boy laying the pieces down side by side with a look of near pride on his otherwise blank face. The kid certainly had strength in his hands. She ran her finger down her class roll. That was Rob Fenton, a retained first grader. Zena, teacher of the other first grade class, had already warned her he would never learn to read or write.

Before she could go see about Rob, two little girls stood at her desk, puzzled looks on their faces.

"Miss Jensen, what d'ya mean draw somethin' we like to do? I can't draw nothin'."

"Me neither," said the other.

"I just mean make a picture. Don't you like to make pictures?"

"No, Ma'am. Don't know how. You gon' show us?"

"Well. All right. Suppose I really, really like flying kites. Well, actually I do like flying kites, so it's not just supposing. I'll draw a girl out in a big, big wide pasture. Let's give her some long hair blowing in the wind. Like this. Now. She's holding a string, and at the end of that string a diamond-shaped kite's flying way up in the sky. You see? Now that wasn't hard. What do you like to do?"

"Mostly watch TV."

"And maybe have hamburgers," said the second little brown-eyed girl.

Groaning within, Connie flipped her long silky black hair out of her face, smiled at the little girls, and said, "There, you see? Make a picture of what you just told me. Watching TV and eating hamburgers. You can do that. And don't forget the ketchup."

Mr. Donovan had made it very clear he wanted a minimum of art and music presented to the first three grades at Pine Ridge Elementary School. That meant leaving art and music to the special teachers who came to Pine Ridge twice a week for forty minutes with each class. He didn't approve of classroom teachers using what he called frivolous activities to teach mathematical facts and reading skills. He said the activities themselves would get all the children's attention. She hoped he'd soon realize that children absorb through all senses—and the more senses the better.

She knew literacy was still a major problem in affluent America, even after computers and all kinds of modern methods had been tried. Now there was a big drive to go "back to the basics." But that didn't mean teachers should forget all that had been learned about child psychology, did it? Connie wondered just how much Mr. Donovan really knew about how to motivate children. As young as he was, he couldn't have been out of school more than ten years.

Yet there seemed a wider gap for some reason. Instead of his seeming too young to be a principal—which his looks would imply—he almost seemed too old! A principal was supposed to be a leader of teachers, wasn't he? Hadn't Mother always bragged about how her principal gave teachers a chance to suggest and object? Mr. Donovan was more of a narrow-minded squelcher!

"Our main aim is to teach these children how to read," Mr. Donovan had said at a teachers' meeting, pounding his fist for emphasis.

Even now Connie felt the sting of disapproval in his blue stare when she'd raised her hand and objected to his minimizing the use of music and art. He didn't stare long. He barked back at her that these children were going to learn to read, as if she'd intended anything different, and that leaving off extraneous subjects was the way he would make sure of it. She glanced at the other teachers. Could they really be as placid and agreeable as they all looked?

Mr. Donovan was a large man with a deep voice, and his eyes. . . Well, if he weren't so horrible, she'd have thought they were beautiful, such a deep blue in his tanned face. No one could deny he was a striking man as handsome went. But already he'd lived up to Mrs. Haburn's warnings to Connie. Connie's landlady had said for Connie to wear her armor at all times, because Mr. Donovan, a former air force pilot, was apt to run his school like a military camp.

Connie wondered if it wasn't a case of "bark worse than bite" and planned to go right ahead using music and art to teach reading. It would be fun and exciting for the children, and they would learn faster. She wasn't planning to make teachers such as Zena feel bad about having failed these same children last year. She only planned to motivate the boys and girls to the point that by Christmas everyone, especially the children themselves, would wonder if it could be the same class.

All her life Connie had known she would be a teacher. Even at the age of eight, she and some cousins had played school under her grandparents' house in Aiken, South Carolina. Remembering, she could smell the mossy dankness, feel the smart when she whacked her head against a floor sill, and the humiliation when Grandmother had shooed them out for pestering her favorite laying hen. Connie, always taller by inches than her peers, had been given much credit for being "responsible," which was often a burden since hers was the name shouted in exasperation when they got into mischief. But she, nearly always the teacher, had enjoyed quizzing her cousins in spelling and sums.

Now she knew there was so much more to teaching than quizzing. Like getting to know how her students thought—her motive behind this present assignment. Connie fluffed wrinkles out of her cotton skirt as she went around her desk and proceeded to peer over her students' shoulders, viewing their pictures. All in all, what she saw was amazing, though perhaps not helpful in character analysis— hamburgers, televisions, stick trees, and people with oversized feet and ears. But Marie had drawn herself swinging. Connie smiled at the great amount of hair the little girl had put on herself. She looked up at Connie and whispered, "I made my hair like yours." Connie promised herself as she moved on that soon she would wash Marie's hair.

Sammy Craven was only doodling on his paper and put his hands over it quickly as she approached. But Richard. . .why, Richard's picture had a house, a dog, and a truck with a child riding in the back. Really good images.

"You like to ride in your father's truck?" she asked and was rewarded only with a shy, lopsided grin that didn't tell her anything.

Connie checked her roll one more time before writing down her attendance count. One boy, Billy Ray Spence, was missing. Somebody at preplanning had said something about the Spences. Oh, yes, it was Mrs. Gurdy, the heavyset teacher who wore hats to school. She'd said to watch out for the Spences.

There were several Spence families represented at Pine Ridge, and the children were absent a lot, but when they were there they were troublemakers. If one was picked on by another student, and his brother, sister, or cousin found out about it, there usually were consequences. Nothing really terrible had happened, but several children had been bruised up by fighting Spences.

Connie stole a look at Richard, still bent over his picture. He was a Spence, too, but she couldn't imagine him in a fight.

"No, Rob!" she said, suddenly hurrying from behind her desk, but not in time to stop that child from deliberately breaking a little girl's pencil. She took him gently to a corner and explained time-out to him.

Rob followed her back to her desk. While she was in the midst of explaining to him again why he should stand in the corner, the door flew open and in walked Mr. Donovan, towering over a squirming boy he held by his collar, a scowling boy with his hair sticking out over the tops of his ears. Though blood was trickling down over the boy's lips, his expression defied any sympathy.

"Miss Jensen, this is Billy Ray Spence. He had a fight on the bus this morning and now, as you see, has a substantial nosebleed. Do you think you can handle this?"

She wasn't sure whether he was challenging her, almost with glee, or anxious that all go well. Either way, she bristled at the implication that she might not be able to handle it, even though her stomach was churning at the smell of sweat and blood. "Of course! Go to your desk, Billy Ray, and put your head back. I'll bring cool paper towels. Thank you, Mr. Donovan. I'll take it from here."

"Are you sure?"

"Yes, I'm sure."

She showed Billy Ray how to hold a wet paper towel with a firm pressure against his upper lip and went about trying to get Rob to stay in one place. It was apparent that a time-out corner wasn't going to mean anything to him, but she had to find some way of keeping him occupied. How could she teach anyone in the room with Rob wandering all about pulling hair and breaking pencils? A whimper of, "Teacher, teacher" followed him around the room.

She finally gave him a lump of modeling clay and told him he had to stay at his desk to play with it. Praying he would, she hurried back to Billy Ray. The bleeding was stopped. He'd wadded the bloody towels up and thrown them toward the trash, missing it by a mile. She looked at him, then the wadded towels, and decided not to discuss trash right now.

"Billy Ray, I've asked everyone to make a picture to start with this morning, a picture of something you like to do. I want you to draw it on this paper with your pencil. I'll give you a little more time while the rest of us get started on a reading lesson."

He tore the paper in two pieces, wadded each of them, and threw them toward the trash. "I don't make pictures," he said. "My cousin, Richard, makes pictures. I make bloody noses."

She wanted to laugh but managed not to. "Billy Ray!" she said in the most authoritative voice she could muster. "I do not allow behavior like that in my room."

"Good," said the boy, both fists balled tightly where they lay on his desk. "Then tell them 'at makes me come to leave me alone. I'll stay to home."

"I'll do no such thing, and you'll straighten that back of yours like a brave boy and show me you know how to learn. Now here's another paper. Please get started."

Her knees were quivering as she went back to her desk and began talking to the class about the letter *A*. But she thought she'd have no more trouble with Billy Ray. She was wrong. When she went to pick up his picture, she was horrified. No wonder he'd had to sharpen his pencil several times. He'd covered the whole sheet with a black screen punctuated by stabbed holes. "That's what I like to do," he said, shoving the paper at her. "I like to make things go black."

❀

Connie's head ached dully as she left the building that afternoon and crawled into her car. As she tooled around curves going north to Mrs. Haburn's, she began to feel a little better. The mountains were still there in spite of her hectic day; the blue mountains with the autumn reds beginning to stain saddlebacks and ridges. From one high curve she looked down on a little valley populated with a white house, a big brown barn, rows of apple trees, and a bright green pasture where black cows grazed, confined within a white fence. But even better than those story-book scenes were the wild ones like the old rusty gate twined by a brilliant red vine, or the small waterfall rushing from dark woods to catapult down a black rock face, roaring like a baby lion.

She felt much better by the time she turned off the Clayton Highway into Mrs. Haburn's driveway, which plunged steeply down to the pond, ran along beside it a moment, then rushed upward again to stop by her screened-in porch where an orange-and-white cat was giving himself a leisurely bath. As Connie tugged her books and supplies out of the seat, the screen door slammed and Mrs. Haburn herself, walking with her usual decided limp, bumped down the steps, lugging an armload of odd items.

"Go put your things up and get changed," she ordered with a smile almost as wide as her hat. "We're goin' fishin', an' I don't want no argument. I've even got us a snack here 'mongst all this stuff. Hurry and change. You look plumb tuckered out. Oh, and those telephone messages can wait. Henry said you could call him tonight, and Mr. Donovan can sure wait a little while."

"Mr. Donovan called?"

"Yeah, but don't you worry. You go put on them jeans an' come on down. I'm gonna teach you how to catch a fish."

Connie looked past Mrs. Haburn's squat waddling figure to the rippling pond that reflected clumps of bulrushes, a little rugged dock, and a cloud-flecked blue sky. Beyond the pond, blueberry bushes ambled in crooked rows, their zillions of tiny leaves a rich wine red. The hill that banked behind them was in shadow now, but dogwoods and maples flamed red amongst the pines.

Yes, she'd go fishing.

First, she tried to call Mr. Donovan, but his line was busy, and she dashed on out. The afternoon was too gorgeous to waste. As she ran down toward the pond with wind whipping hair away from her face, she tried to forget Mr. Donovan's stern look of disapproval and doubt when he'd brought Billy Ray to her classroom.

Chapter 2

Connie munched happily on a sweet little Yate apple while Mrs. Haburn baited and rebaited her hook, splashing more and more fish into her bucket. As long as she kept eating, Connie reasoned, Mrs. Haburn wouldn't bug her to try a hand at fishing. Connie looked down between her dangling feet to her reflection in the murky pond. A cloud of dark hair around a blob of white face was about all she could see.

"What were you telling me about this apple, Mrs. Haburn? You caught a fish about that time and forgot to finish your story."

"Oh. I'm bad about that. Not finishin' things I start. I was just sayin' my papa owned a great orchard an' he prided himself on growin' old-fashioned apples. Taste of a good tart or sweet apple brings back the good ole days like nothin' else. I like Jonathans and Yates the best. When the farm sold after he died, I dug up a few of his knee-high trees so's I could grow my own little orchard. Over yonder, back of the blueberries.

"The trees are good bearers. An' real popular. All I have to do is set up a table with small baskets of apples by the road and afore noon I'll have sold 'em, every one. That's a busy road there. My blueberry sign does the trick for me in July, too. Everybody around loves my blueberries. They're sweeter'n most, freeze good, too. 'Course in the fall o' the year, when color's at its peak, it's hard to get onto this road and that's pretty aggravatin', you know.

"I don't worry too much, since I don't drive anyway and don't have a car. But I have to worry for my drivers. The Lord sure were good to send you, Connie Jensen. When you said you'd pay part of your rent by runnin' me for groceries, to the doctor, and specially to church every Sunday, I could have stood on my head. There now, that's the kind of fish I were a-lookin' fer."

Mrs. Haburn flopped an eight-inch catfish within a foot of Connie. While Connie scrambled up, the older woman chuckled low in her throat. "You can throw that core you've done wore out into the water, hon. The fish'll eat it right up. Then you'll have a hand to get that fish off the hook for me."

There was a pause. Mrs. Haburn peered around at Connie's face and promptly began pulling the fish toward herself. "Or, then again, maybe I'll do it myself. Here, just let me get that other pole goin' fer you now. It's time you drowned a few worms. You gotta have somethin' pleasant to tell your Henry tonight, ain't ye?"

Connie giggled softly, knowing full well Mrs. Haburn was trying to get her to start talking about Henry. What would she tell Henry tonight? She could tell him about Richard's nice picture, about Marie's sweet nature, about Zena, her new teacher friend, and about that adorable, neat little girl named Joyce who wanted to mother everyone, even Billy Ray. Except she didn't want to talk to Henry about Billy Ray.

It was funny that she never wanted to talk to Henry about problems. She didn't know why. He wasn't an unkind person, certainly. He just never seemed quite able to understand. Probably because he didn't have problems himself.

"I were afraid you mightn't be a very good fisherman, being from the city," Mrs. Haburn commented as she threaded a worm onto a hook. She showed Connie how to toss it in and watch the cork set itself upright in the middle of multiplying ripple rings.

Connie jerked herself out of a daze just in time to clutch the pole as the cork began to swirl and dive. She wanted to dislodge Mrs. Haburn's preconceived ideas about her. But after losing her bait several times and, worse, catching a pearl gray fish and being totally unable to touch it, Connie was convinced Mrs. Haburn was right about her. She laid down her pole and watched her landlady, who sat flat on the dock with big boots stuck out before her, pulling in a hefty mess.

"Mrs. Haburn, what will you do with all these fish?"

"Oh, maybe have my whole church to supper one night. That Henry of yours might even be there. And you needn't be so shy. I do have eyes, you know, an' I've been watchin' that fine ring of yours turn sun rays into rainbows."

Connie's frown turned to laughter. "Mrs. Haburn, you should have had a dozen children for all your energy and mothering instinct."

"I'd a'sure taken a dozen if they'd a'come. But me an' my ole man only got two. I guess that's just all the Lord trusted us with."

"You really set a lot of store on what the Lord thinks about everything, don't you, Mrs. Haburn?"

"Of course. Don't you?"

"Well, not as much as you, I guess." Connie placed her hands, palms down, behind her and leaned back to look up at the sky fringed by hills on either side. Far overhead a tiny jet raced ahead of its stream of vapor, and a minute later its own sound droned along, trying to catch up.

"Sometimes I wish I were more dedicated," she continued. "More. . .more sure of what God's like and everything. I mean, I'm going to heaven. I know that. But people like you who are so happy right now make me wonder if I'm missing something."

Mrs. Haburn began winding in the fishing lines. "If you are missin' somethin'," she said, "you'll find it. If you search for it with all your heart, Lord always meets you halfway. Are you gonna come with me to church on Sundays?"

"I. . .sometimes maybe. But. . ." Connie didn't know exactly how to tell Mrs. Haburn she wanted to be left alone. She didn't mind taking Mrs. Haburn places. That was their deal. But she didn't intend to be involved in everything Mrs. Haburn did. She was only her chauffeur. Mrs. Haburn must have read her mind. The woman was uncanny!

"You have many other things to do, I know. I know, Hon. But it would please me very much. My own children are both way up there in Maine, you know. Why they both had to go so far is beyond me, but they're happy where they are. Anyway, give me a hand here. My, my, there's a chill in that air, don't you think? Let's get these things put up and set out some supper. I put a pot roast on, an' it should be just about gettin' tender."

❈

Later, Connie showered, wrapped her head in a towel, and, tucked warmly into a soft terry robe, stood as near her room door as the hallway phone would reach as she returned her calls. She hoped Mrs. Haburn would be so busy at her crocheting that she wouldn't listen to her.

First, Mr. Maury Donovan. Might as well get it over with. She tensed as she heard the ring at the other end of the line, relaxed as it rang over and over with no answer, and finally laughed softly to herself with relief. But of course, this was the school number and Mr. Donovan would have gone home long since. And he wouldn't have intended her to call him at home. It was probably nothing that couldn't wait 'til morning anyway.

She dialed Henry's number and instantly could see his dear solid self, dressed in a suit and tie and smelling of cologne. Well, no, he'd have changed by now into tee shirt and shorts. She glanced at her watch. Good. It was 7:30. His favorite newscast was over.

She tried to sound eager as she answered his questions about her first day at school. But the eagerness in her voice had only to do with her children, not with Henry. She stared down at her ring, beautiful even in this dark corner, as she listened to his soft voice begging her to break her contract and come on home. She was touched. It wasn't like Henry, who was always so organized and together, to be begging.

But she couldn't relent. She would not give up this chance to be herself. And so, again and again, she heard herself saying, "Henry, no. I can't, Henry. It's only for a year, you know. You're so busy with your job at the bank anyway, you'll hardly miss me once you get used to it. Just wait and see."

"Persistent, ain't he?" spoke Mrs. Haburn from her comfortable chair in the den when she heard the phone click into place.

"Mrs. Haburn! Please! Don't eavesdrop!" Connie tried to hold back some of her irritation, but it wasn't easy.

"Why, my dear, what can you expect with both of us livin' in this snug little house? You don't expect me not to care what happens to you, do you?"

"Care, yes. But meddle, no! I came here—"

"To get away from meddlin'? Well, I'll try to be good. But. . ." She adjusted the folds of the afghan she was creating and smiled up at Connie, who'd come to stand over her, hands on hips. "I'll try to be good," she finished lamely, seeing Connie was really not being funny at all.

🕸

There was a peremptory note on Connie's door when she got to school the next morning. Mr. Maury Donovan wanted to see her in his office. Well, she wanted to see him, too. She wanted to talk to him about Rob Fenton. Surely she hadn't been hired to be a baby-sitter!

Thinking of this helped her square her shoulders as she spoke to his secretary and entered the principal's office, only to find Mr. Donovan busy on the phone. He barely acknowledged her with an uplifted finger. She paced, irritated at having to wait when there was so much for her to do. There were those reading activity sheets to copy before school, and she wanted to rearrange the desks into a big circle instead of rows, and wet a big sponge for children to "plant" rye seeds on. She itched to get started!

Finally she sat down on a leather chair and took a minute to look at Mr. Donovan's diplomas and military awards. Somehow she was surprised to also see beautiful sky pictures—sunsets, a full moon with a pine bough brushing it, and one bright photo of sky divers coming down in formation. Maybe she'd misjudged the man. He couldn't be hard-hearted and like such beauty, could he? Then she noticed a small photo, a close-up of. . .could that be Mr. Donovan? She stood to inspect it more closely. It was Mr. Donovan! He was dressed in skydiving clothes, wearing the most radiant smile. Connie looked at it and then at the man now scowling into the telephone. They couldn't be the same person. But they were. She started visibly as his voice raked across her shoulder.

"Miss Jensen, I called you in because I felt we had a few points that might need clearing up. Sorry to keep you waiting. This won't take long."

She faced him, telling herself, *Stand straight now for the firing squad.*

Mr. Donovan looked at her hard, then shook his head as if to rid himself of a fly.

"For one thing," he continued, "the next time I leave word for you to call I would appreciate your responding promptly."

"Yes, Sir." She spoke automatically and then flushed in fury at being humiliated. This was to be nothing but an old-fashioned lecture.

"As to what I was calling about. . ." He had come around his desk to stand before her, and she had to will herself not to move back a step. She wouldn't let him know he intimidated her that way, that his very largeness fairly took her breath away. "I perceive you don't agree with my methods, Miss Jensen. In fact, I feel you were defying me by starting out your class with artwork, however simple, after I specifically demanded you leave art and music to the time slots allotted to them. I know you disagree, and you have a right to your own opinions. But only your opinions. I'm principal here. And I will not tolerate having my rules blatantly ignored. Life will be much more pleasant for both of us if you recognize that and simply follow my instructions."

She had tried to keep eye contact. She felt that was very important in being respectful to him as well as to herself. But somewhere along the way she began seeing his face as it was in that little picture, and something about the contrast was so comical that it was all she could do to keep from laughing. She had to drop her eyes, and when she did she saw his beat-up tennis shoes, wet with dew. The man was wearing nice slacks and a sport coat, but those shoes. . . She couldn't resist smiling.

"Miss Jensen, why do I get the feeling you're not listening to me?"

His eyes were stern and hard when she looked up. She flashed him a brilliant smile.

"Mr. Donovan, I've heard every word. I'll try my best to abide by. . .your rules. But I wish you'd reconsider. The children so need—"

He was opening the door. He was showing her out! Her cheeks stung with angry warmth as she struggled to be polite, wishing him a good day. Suddenly she remembered her own request and spun back around.

"What about Rob Fenton, Mr. Donovan? He's obviously mentally challenged and needs to be in a special class. Surely he's not going to be in my room all year!" That's not the way she'd meant to say it. But it was out now.

"No, Miss Jensen, he is not. Only for half of each day. He will be bused to another school where his special education teacher has a room. But the board hired her late, and we've been asked to give her a week's preparation time. Don't tell me one day has done you in, Miss Jensen?"

She caught her bottom lip between her teeth for a second. So, she really did have a lot to learn and he knew it.

"I. . .I'm sorry. Of course it's no problem. I was only concerned about the child. Mr. Donovan, if I could just use some art with Rob. . .and Billy Ray."

Mr. Donovan's jaw tensed. "No art, Miss Jensen. I don't expect a miracle with Rob Fenton. But I do expect the rest of your children to be reading by the first of the year." He was all but shaking a big finger in her face!

She willed her voice to stay steady, though her eyes glinted with dangerous lightning. "You mean you've given up on Rob Fenton? I think I could teach him some skills if I were allowed to use—"

"I don't give up on anyone!" he shouted, then turned and raked a hand through his hair as if he were remembering something. Heading for his desk, he said over his shoulder, "Miss Jensen, please let me know if there's anything within the parameters I've laid out that my office can do to help you. Now, if you will excuse me, my phone is ringing."

When the door closed on her, Connie wanted to beat on it, but instead she turned down the hallway toward her room, mimicking him as she mumbled, "The parameters I've laid out."

Zena appeared beside her, falling in with her fast stride. "Boss got to you this morning, huh?"

"He sure did."

"Well, don't let it eat on you. He's that way. Some days are worse than others. You'll learn how to get along without crossing him."

"I'm not sure I want to. He needs to be crossed. He's all wrong. Children need to *like* learning, Zena."

"Oh, Connie, that's just stuff they teach you in those education classes. It doesn't work in the real world. You have to do what the principal says, or after a year of misery, you'll be out!" Zena made a slash across her own throat with one finger to illustrate her point.

"And let me give you another bit of advice. Not that you look very interested right now. And I know you're wearing an engagement ring, too. But just in case, don't get any romantic ideas about Mr. Donovan because he's only interested in light relationships. I should know."

In total surprise, Connie turned toward the wispy little blond. "You?"

"Yes, I went out with him a few times last year. And he was a perfect gentleman. But, believe me, he doesn't intend for anyone to get near that heart of his. So save yourself some pain, okay?"

Connie unlocked her classroom door, shaking her head. So strange. She'd never dreamed of having any romantic ideas about that man. Heaven forbid! Right now she heartily wished she'd stayed in Augusta, Georgia.

Chapter 3

From her bed, Connie watched the very early Sunday morning light reveal the character of her corner room. She could hardly believe how right she felt about this room in only a few weeks. . .its scents, textures, bright pillows in a chair by the window—everything.

There was an abundance of space for books, even in her bedstead. The bed had belonged to one of Mrs. Haburn's children, and the headboard doubled as a bookcase. A desk of some dark wood topped with shelves nearly as high as the ceiling occupied one wall, while near the door a corner cabinet cozied into a space it didn't exactly fit. She eyed the cabinet and the corner and decided at least one of them was a bit crooked.

The room lightened some more, and Connie could study the new wallpaper job, which left a lot to be desired in the way of perfection since, as Mrs. Haburn had put it, her young friends from church had "thrown it up for me one weekend." Connie smiled at the video that played through her brain of many hands at work that had never before attempted the skill of papering around windows and light sockets.

Her attention turned to a favorite focus in the room, a picture of a couple praying in a field, a pitchfork stuck in the ground by the man who held his hat reverently in front of him. Behind the woman, who wore a long dress and apron, was a wooden wheelbarrow piled high with hay. She also was bowed in prayer. It was a familiar piece of art, but Connie couldn't remember the name of it. *"Evening Prayers?"* She'd have to ask Mrs. Haburn, who had offered to take it down so Connie could have the space for hanging her own choice of picture, but so far she hadn't wanted to replace it.

The picture was so peaceful, so inspiring, so like what Mrs. Haburn would choose to hang. She'd already invited Connie to pray with her each morning "to get her day off to a good start." At first Connie was hesitant, not wanting to be held to such a rigorous morning schedule. But Mrs. Haburn was so sweet and persuasive, Connie decided she could at least do it for awhile. The little woman was so energetic she put Connie to shame. She was up cooking breakfast no matter how early Connie got up, was constantly making applesauce and canning it or trundling a wheelbarrow of leaves to a mulch pile. And when Connie got home from school, often Mrs. Haburn was up by the road, vigorously selling apples, extolling their goodness as if they were made of pure gold.

Sunlight-patterned leaf shapes printed themselves against Connie's curtains, maple leaves that she knew were turning red, but seen through the curtains they were only shifting shadows on blue cotton. Suddenly she sat upright, then ran to her front window to pull back the curtain and peer through the maple tree to the steep hillside rising from the other side of the road. Gauzy vapor clung in low spots between house and road, and Connie caught her breath as she spied a rabbit sitting not twenty feet from her window, nibbling on some grass.

"I've got to get out of here and see everything," she breathed to herself. "I bet the pond is gorgeous about now."

As she slid into jeans and T-shirt, she could hear Mrs. Haburn talking. *Must be on the phone,* she thought. Maybe she could slip past her unnoticed.

But Mrs. Haburn wasn't on the phone. She was talking to a smoky little fire she'd started in her kitchen heater. Though she was bent over, prodding a weak flame as Connie crept by, she called out cheerily, "Have you some breakfast in no time, Dearie. This fire's for comfort, you know, not cookin'. You go on and have yourself a little walk, an' when you get back I'll have you some pancakes an' coffee. You like sorghum? Don't know? Well, you'll be for findin' out soon. Have a nice walk now, you hear?"

Connie made a wry face as she left the house, the cat trailing along behind her. Couldn't she move around here without being noticed? But Mrs. Haburn was so kind, too.

Shaking her head as if to clear her mind of such thoughts, Connie explored the hillside beyond the pond. She sat down on an old log, while the cat stalked little creatures and played in the noisy leaves.

She knew she'd done the right thing coming to this community, choosing this "jumping-off place," as Daddy called it, for a home. Yes, even taking the job at Pine Ridge seemed a good idea right now, in spite of Mr. Maury Donovan. But still she had such an unsettled feeling. If Henry wasn't the one for her, then who was? And, after all, could she be a good teacher?

As she idly pulled bits of bark off her sitting log and tossed them teasingly at the cat, she wondered what it would be like to be really at peace with her world like the couple in Mrs. Haburn's picture or like Mrs. Haburn herself.

Lord, I really want to be the person You planned me to be. I really do. Connie rubbed goose bumps on her arms and started back down to the pond.

Vapor hovered close over the water with a silvery, eerie appearance. Connie ambled along, enjoying the smells of bulrushes, dewy grass, and some unnameable spicy scent that seemed to come with autumn. The cat pounced on something that turned out to be a little frog. Connie knelt to inspect the victim. Pitying him, she threw him back into the pond, hoping he'd survive, though part of one leg was gone. Watching the perfectly symmetrical circles twinkle outward from where he'd splashed in, she suddenly wondered if he'd been a toad instead of a frog. *I may be more dangerous as an ecological sympathizer than to ignore it all and let it fix itself!*

When she got back, pancakes and coffee were ready. They had never tasted so good. Maybe it was the sorghum.

Mrs. Haburn rubbed her hands together in childish excitement and exclaimed, "I just know this is the day you're going to church with me. I just know it!"

"Well, actually. . ." Connie hadn't planned to go. She really wanted time alone. But her going seemed to mean so much to Mrs. Haburn. This little woman was so bright-eyed and so wistful and had already asked several times. The least Connie could do was go to church with her. And it couldn't help but be good for her. "Yes, I'll go with you this time," she answered cautiously.

Mrs. Haburn ignored the caution and began to vigorously clear the table. "I can't wait for you to hear Reverend Stone. I know you're gonna like him a lot. He an' Mrs. Stone aren't that much older than you, an' they're simply the dearest people. Don't know how to discipline their own children, but other than that they're really fine."

"Reverend Stone wants us all to call him Phil, but you know, I just can't do that. He's the age of my own boy, or younger, but I can't feel right calling my preacher Phil. That just ain't right. But all the young folks do, you know. Next thing, the way everyone's demanding this right an' that an' changin' old traditions, schoolteachers won't even be called Miss or Mrs. anymore."

Connie had to laugh at Mrs. Haburn's wonderful grumbling good cheer. "Oh, that'll be the day, Mrs. Haburn. With concerned citizens like you still around, I doubt that'll happen."

❦

The church was charming, a white frame building with a steeple pointing to a sky which, that day, was bluer than any Connie thought she'd ever seen. The church was only about three miles toward Clayton from Mrs. Haburn's house and was atop a small hill, like a beacon for all to see.

"I raised my children in this little church," rattled Mrs. Haburn, gathering her Bible and Sunday school book and hunting for the door handle as Connie turned off the ignition. "We got married here and here's where my husband's buried. It's a pretty important place in our lives. Well, I know the building itself ain't the church, but it is pretty special, you know. Well, anyways, here we are."

Connie persuaded Mrs. Haburn to let her sit in on her own Bible study class that first time. "I don't know a soul here but you, and I came to church to be with you," she insisted.

"You need to make acquaintance with other young folks," said Mrs. Haburn over and over, but finally she agreed.

Connie was almost overwhelmed with questions by Mrs. Haburn's friends. It wasn't just her life history they wanted. She grinned to herself when finally she and Mrs. Haburn were seated in church. They'd have wanted her great-grandfather's history if she'd known it. Mrs. Haburn was mild beside some of them.

She peered sideways at her landlady just in time to catch Mrs. Haburn winking, then flashing a beaming smile toward the pulpit. Expecting to see Mrs. Haburn's beloved Reverend Stone, Connie looked up, too, just in time to lock eyes with the distinctly startled, deep blue eyes of Maury Donovan, the minister of music, as he announced an opening hymn.

She looked swiftly at Mrs. Haburn, but she was innocently searching for the hymn number in her book, the little devious woman. She knew if she'd told Connie who was directing music she'd have never come!

Connie tried not to look at him. But how could she sing joyfully without looking up at the leader? Every time she did, there was Maury Donovan, an astonishing Maury Donovan. She could not believe what was happening. This Mr. Donovan was nothing like the man she met every morning at school, scowling his way along the corridors, shaking his big finger, and passing down rule after rule.

This Mr. Donovan was glowing, yes, positively glowing with happy energy as they sang "He Keeps Me Singing." He really and truly looked as if he believed totally what he was singing. But how could he possibly believe that "Jesus swept across the broken strings, Stirred the slumb'ring chords again" when he went about making everyone miserable all week?

She was relieved when the singing was over and the big disturbing figure of Maury Donovan, resplendent in suit and tie, settled himself on the front pew with a row of wiggling little boys. Now she could listen to the little preacher Mrs. Haburn had talked about so much.

Or could she? She had to keep pulling herself back from thinking about the strange double life of Maury Donovan as she tried to hear Reverend Stone's sermon, his first in a series on the Beatitudes. She could see why Mrs. Haburn liked the man. He was so warm, eloquent, and down-to-earth, so humble, and yet so confident.

She wished she were a better listener. And she would have been, she knew full well, if it hadn't been for that looming set of shoulders in a dark gray suit on the front row; the dark head often bent to whisper to a little boy beside him. It wasn't fair that he was in this part of her world, too.

But she didn't have to come to church with Mrs. Haburn. She'd just go elsewhere. But why should she? Why should it matter one way or the other? She looked down at her ring, twisted it to make rainbows gleam in a ray of sunshine coming through one of the many tall windows. Why wasn't she sitting securely in church with Henry right this minute?

Oh, Lord, please help me concentrate on worshiping You. And don't let me get addled over that aggravating man!

"So good to have you with us today, Connie," said Reverend Stone as Mrs. Haburn introduced them after the service. "Mrs. Haburn's like a mom to a bunch of us, and her friends are our friends. Sure hope you like us. Say, we're like a big family around here, and some of us nearly always go out to eat after church. How about you and Mrs. Haburn joining us, hmmm? We're going toward Toccoa today to a friendly barbecue place. We'd like it if you'd come."

"Well, really, that's very kind of you, but I thought—"

"You know, Connie, that's not a bad idea," piped up Mrs. Haburn at her elbow, "seein' as how I never got any dinner cooked before we left. We'd only have a sandwich if we went on home. That'd be too bad now, wouldn't it?"

The woman was insufferable! Connie's mouth dropped open and Mrs. Haburn nodded to Reverend Stone as if that was a sure assent. Before Connie knew what was happening, she and Mrs. Haburn were being ushered to the church van where, of all the downright impossible situations, Connie had no choice but to sit beside Maury Donovan. Since there were too many passengers in the van, the seating was very tight, and Connie squirmed against the unforgiving window, wondering why she'd allowed herself to be persuaded like soft butter, led away like a starving stray—or some such awful figure of speech. She vowed she'd never again let Mrs. Haburn talk her into anything.

Mr. Donovan put his arm loosely around her as he talked to a young woman on his other side. He was totally unconscious of her, yet she was so uncomfortable that her palms were sweating, and she decided she'd concentrate on Mrs. Haburn. She could see Mrs. Haburn's peppery hair bobbing just in front of her as she talked loudly with Reverend Stone. The preacher was driving, and one of his sons was talking to him at the same time, but he never missed a bit of what Mrs. Haburn was telling him about one time when she had chickens, and a fox got in her henhouse and couldn't get back out before the chickens pecked his eyes out.

"Some kind of justice there," laughed Phil Stone to his wife, Margie. There was a general babble as the van traveled to the other side of what Phil Stone said was Mile-Long Hill, a long, steep stretch down into a V and back up as high again. Ed's Barbecue was set among some pines, a simple structure with no great view or claim of atmosphere. "Just plain good food," said Dave Olds, a young man who gallantly offered to help Mrs. Haburn out of the van.

If Mr. Donovan had even looked at her the whole trip, Connie wasn't aware of it. But now, as they both waited to climb out of the van, he turned to her, his eyes demanding her full attention. Was there a hint of amusement twinkling in their blue depths and tickling at the corners of that wide mouth? She smiled uncertainly. For one moment she actually had the feeling she was going to reach up and brush strands of hair back from his forehead, but thankfully her arm was pinned so tightly she couldn't impulsively commit such an awful goof.

"Sorry about the tight quarters here, Miss, uhm, Miss Jensen, I believe it is? Good thing it's no farther or you might have disappeared into that crack. Mrs. Haburn, what are you feeding your boarder, ghost rations?"

Was he patronizing her or trying to be funny? Either way he'd failed. She couldn't think of anything to reply and was saved the trouble by the young Stones, demanding that Mr. Donovan please, please sit with them in the restaurant. Once in there, they appeared to have a hilarious time telling jokes and corny riddles.

From the table where Connie sat near a large buck stove, it seemed Maury Donovan was having the most fun of anyone. His spontaneous laughter escaped in sudden roars and drew everyone else to it as cats are attracted to heat. He couldn't help laughing, it seemed, and no one else could resist laughing with him. Except Connie, who resisted pretty well. If there was anything she hated worse than a cranky person, it was a hypocrite in any form, and that's evidently what this Maury Donovan was. If he had such a sanguine personality, why did he keep it hidden under a cloak of pessimism at Pine Ridge Elementary?

Phil Stone got up and walked among the tables, talking not only to members of their party but to other diners as well. Was there anyone the man didn't know? One might have mistaken him for a restaurant host instead of a guest, but the manager was obviously happy and unthreatened by this small man with a big smile and a hard, warm handshake.

As Connie observed him hunkering down beside a table full of young folks, she wondered how he and Maury Donovan had gotten teamed up. Was it a temporary situation? Had Phil not learned yet what an impossibly negative person Mr. Donovan was? Or was he trying to help Mr. Donovan? *That could be dangerous,* she thought. When he stopped at Maury Donovan's table, he began cleaning up the mess his own boys had made as he said, "You're a good man, Donovan, to let my sons worry you like this."

"Oh, never mind, Phil. I can take it for a few minutes. You have 'em all the time. No offense, guys," he finished, winking at his little friends.

"Tell him, Mr. Donovan. Tell Daddy about your jumping. And tell him what else you said."

"Uh-oh, I smell a big question coming," said Reverend Stone, leaning closer.

"It's just that next Saturday I'm going to be in a formation sky dive down in Gainesville, and I wondered if you and Margie and the boys would like to come watch."

"Now that's an interesting offer." Phil Stone carefully piled little butter wrappers in the middle of the table and wiped his hands on a napkin, rubbing them extra long.

"Can't we, Daddy? Please?"

"You haven't been jumping lately, have you, Maury?"

"No. Wind's not been favorable. Besides, it's very difficult to get a formation team all set up. Why? You afraid I've gotten rusty?"

"No. Not that. I just hadn't heard much about your sky diving lately. Wondered if you'd quit."

"You hoped I had?" Was there an edge of irritation in Maury Donovan's voice?

Connie looked at Mrs. Haburn, and they both spoke at once on separate subjects, then laughed at themselves, knowing they were trying not to listen to the preacher's conversation. Connie welcomed the interruption of a young woman named Jean who left her table with other young people to sit down and make friends with Connie. But she only half listened to Jean's comments on why she wanted to be a forest ranger.

Maury Donovan was a sky diver? What else? And why, if children loved him so much, couldn't he be a shade more lenient? She could hear his answer to that one. He wanted them to be good readers. Beginning, middle, end. And he believed he had all the answers for achieving that, the arrogant man!

Chapter 4

Connie managed to get the farthest backseat riding home and didn't know how the trip to Toccoa Falls was concocted, didn't even realize they were headed toward Toccoa instead of Hollywood until the van turned at the entrance to Toccoa Falls College. She'd been chatting merrily with Jean about their families and about Georgia's parks. Now they wound along quiet college streets, arriving finally at a beautiful stone structure beside the Falls Trail entrance.

"There's where we should have had dinner," said Dave Olds, "at the Gate Cottage Restaurant."

"We'll do that next time," responded Phil cheerily. "There's no end to the possibilities around here."

"This place looks too fancy," said Mrs. Haburn as Maury Donovan helped her alight. "I think that barbecue'd be hard to beat."

"Well, I guess we could be kidnapped real easy," said Jean as she and Connie finally crawled out of their backseat and looked around. "I had no idea we were coming here, but I'm glad we did. I love this place. Have you ever been here, Connie?"

"No. My family used to vacation up here a lot. In the Georgia mountains, I mean. But usually we went to Helen and up that direction more. I don't remember this. It is wonderful, all these tall, thick trees and the rocky stream. And we can't be far from town."

"And do you hear the waterfall? Do you see it? Look above the trees! This is the highest waterfall east of the Mississippi. Not the widest, or the one with the most water running over, but the highest. It is really something."

Connie caught her breath and clasped her hands tightly together as she approached the foot of the waterfall. She felt fine spray misting her face as she watched rainbows at the fall's base. Shielding her eyes, she looked far, far up where rushing liquid thunder spilled over a sheer precipice. It was almost as if it were gushing right from the sun-whitened sky.

Great rocks, like a giant's toys, lay tossed about in the foaming stream. One young couple had climbed atop a huge boulder, and Mr. Donovan was taking their picture with the waterfall in the background. Margie Stone pulled off her shoes and squealed at the shock of cold water as she waded in the edge of the stream.

Her boys, Sunday pants rolled to their knees, clambered over the giant's toy rocks all the way to the other side of what some would call a wide creek. Margie screamed for them to start back but couldn't make herself heard above the roar. They were climbing toward the top of the waterfall as their mother looked about for her husband. Phil Stone had walked with Mrs. Haburn, and the two of them were far back down the path, sitting on a bench.

Connie began to pull off her shoes to go after the boys when Mr. Donovan dashed past her, taking the stream in only three great leaps. Soon he returned with one squealing and kicking boy under each arm.

She could hear Mr. Donovan's voice above the roar, admonishing the boys as he pointed to the top of the waterfall. "That's 186 feet up, and when you fall from that high, there's nothing left but a broken body."

"Is that what happens if your parachute won't work, Mr. Maury?"

Maury Donovan playfully bumped the two boys' heads together and shrugged as he thrust them at their mother.

Connie turned her attention quickly to the waterfall so she wouldn't meet Maury Donovan's eyes as he turned away from the boys. The rushing water, playful in the sunshine, was flanked on each side by dark hemlocks and by hardwoods brightening with autumn color. Its beauty was shadowed by a fearsome dignity that filled her with a deep sense of awe. She would not admit to herself that she felt a considerable fascination for this big mountain of a man, too. No, she would not admit that even in her most private thoughts.

She didn't want to leave and was, in fact, one of the last to turn away from the waterfall and head back along the creek-side trail to the parking lot. She planned right then to come again with her camera, though she knew she'd be disappointed in her pictures. She would never be able to capture the majesty of the scene. Even after she followed the others, she kept turning back to look once more at the magnificent waterfall that seemed like a living thing to her.

She stopped to read a prominent historical plaque. In November 1977, thirty-nine people had been killed when the dam above the waterfall burst and dumped Kelly Barnes Lake on Toccoa Falls College, a four-year Christian college. Today the college was still there, stronger than ever, with many newly built dwellings and many stories of bravery and faith.

"It was one of the saddest, most freakish accidents that's ever happened around here," remarked a deep voice at her elbow.

She started visibly, totally unprepared for the height and breadth of Maury Donovan sidling up beside her with his hands in his pockets like a little boy.

"It was terrible," she agreed. "I can't help thinking how awful it must have been for the parents of those students, not knowing for perhaps hours whether their children and grandchildren were alive or not."

"I was young when it happened. My parents brought me with them to help clean up one day. It was truly, to use a trite expression, awesome. The house we worked on had been totally ruined. It was the home of the school's dean, I think."

"Was any of the family rescued?"

"Yes. Miraculously, all of them were. The parents and two children were separated when the bank of water hit. The father and his little daughter were slammed out of the house, into the rushing torrent. His wife and son were trapped inside where they scrambled up on top of some cabinets, with only their chins above water. They said it was an eternity during which each pair thought the others were in heaven. When they found each other, they were full of praise to God."

"But what about the thirty-nine who weren't rescued? They were Christians, too, weren't they?"

"Yes. That part's harder to explain. I guess we shouldn't even try. One of God's mysteries. Actually, you know, the families of those who had lost someone in the flood were praising God, too. I didn't really understand it, and later on I understood it even less."

Connie looked up at him, surprised at a note of bitterness that had crept into his voice.

They walked now along the Falls Trail, following the quietly chattering stream. It was such an innocent creek today. But behind them the roar of the waterfall was a reminder of how powerful water can become when gathered together.

"You mentioned your parents. Do they live near here?"

"My mother does."

"Your. . .father?"

"He's deceased."

The two little words fell like stones—no, like heavy rocks. She looked up at him, expecting an explanation. But he'd turned his head and was watching the flowing water.

She cleared her throat and wondered what to say. School, of course. Their only common ground. No, not school. Anything but that.

"What does it feel like to sky dive? I've never known a sky diver before."

Her question took a moment to drive from his face a look of rare vulnerability. But quickly the pain or fear vanished like a shadow, leaving the same self-assured blue gaze she was used to. "How does it feel just before, during, or afterward?"

"Any of the above. I don't know." She walked quickly to keep in step with his long strides.

"When I'm heading up into the sky, my equipment all ready, my heart starts thudding like the airplane's engine and I'm scared to death. When I stand in the lineup and know my turn is coming up, I have a bitter taste in my mouth and I wonder why I'm doing this one more time. Then as I float down under the parachute, I'm at total peace. Nothing matters at that moment. Not even the harsh mysteries.

It's like being a baby again with no cares at all, yet having adult sensitivity to beauty and exhilaration as the world comes up to meet me. Afterward? Well, I feel cleaned out for awhile, with an afterglow of freedom. Then the gnawing begins again. Wanting to do it all over."

"Wow! Sounds like a consuming hobby."

"It used to be my career, Miss Jensen. I'm sure you've heard I was a pilot in the air force. I was still in the reserves during Desert Storm. I guess I can't get it all out of my blood."

"But now you're a principal and a minister of music and I don't know what all else. I guess you can do most anything you want to."

"Do I hear a hint of disapproval? As if you think I'm only an actor or something?"

"We're all just actors, aren't we? Didn't Shakespeare say that? But I was only wishing—"

"Yes, Miss Jensen?" They were nearing the rest of the group, and Maury Donovan paused to look down at her. "What were you wishing?"

"That the Mr. Donovan I see right now would be in his office tomorrow when school opens."

One dark eyebrow lifted. His jaw firmed; his shoulders straightened. "And of course I will be. Or are you implying I'm not the same person on Sunday as on Monday?"

"I'm just thinking about little Billy Ray and how much he needs to do things that are fun to help him learn, things like beating rhythms on an old milk jug, drawing pictures no matter how black—whatever can help him get rid of some of his anger."

"Miss Jensen, don't you ever take a day off? As your principal, I definitely do recommend it." His tone was light but edged with seriousness. He was ignoring her off-the-cuff plea for Billy Ray.

She put her hands on her hips. She was about to be too bold and she knew it, but she couldn't stop herself.

"You know, Mr. Donovan? You'd do well to use your Sunday personality all week."

"You are saying I'm a hypocrite. Well, you're right. Sure. So is everyone else. But the Lord loves us, even so, I reckon."

She couldn't argue with that. But she longed to chip this big rock of a man somehow, to make the real man step out from behind all his masks. The true Maury Donovan, she had a feeling, would let her try many methods to reach Billy Ray.

"Come on, Mr. Donovan, I want to sit next to you. Come on!" yelled the littlest Stone, grabbing his big hand.

He looked back at her with an odd look of regret, it seemed. She took a deep breath and followed.

※

When the van deposited them at the church, Connie and Mrs. Haburn rode straight home, Mrs. Haburn talking nonstop about how she'd never told Connie a lie; she'd just never mentioned anything about who the minister of music was, and anyway he really wasn't all that bad. Look how the children loved him, and wasn't the waterfall wonderful, and didn't she just love the Stones? Connie nodded at the right places and laughed appropriately, but her mind was not focused on what Mrs. Haburn said.

After she phoned Henry, she picked up the yellow cat and ambled down to the dock where she watched their reflections, threw in bits of stick, and chewed on a green reed. Finally, she felt better. She couldn't say why because she didn't know what had bothered her in the first place. Was it Maury Donovan's bull-headedness? Or his fleeting look of wistfulness, or despair, when he'd spoken of his father? Or was the real disturbance that she'd spent even one minute worrying about Mr. Donovan, one way or the other?

"I can't see for the life of me how a person as utterly distasteful as that man could have such nice qualities," she said to the cat, smiling as the cat's ears flicked with the movement of her breath across them.

Chapter 5

In the following weeks, Connie avoided Mr. Donovan as much as possible, making sure she was never the first or last one at a teachers' meeting. She attended church with Mrs. Haburn but made sure they had their own lunch plans. Mrs. Haburn was so glad Connie would go to church with her that she didn't make much complaint, especially when Connie joined a Sunday school class and even helped Jean give a shower for a bride-to-be. Mrs. Haburn seemed content that her boarder had made friends with those "her own age," so all was well.

Connie had not given up on wanting to teach her own way. But she decided to go along with Zena and do everything possible to keep from causing unnecessary friction at school. It seemed sort of dishonest, but maybe the other teachers were right to agree with Mr. Donovan, then quietly do their own thing to a degree. *It's all for a good motive,* she reminded herself, *to teach these children to read, write, and do their arithmetic.* She thought the less she saw of Mr. Donovan, the better all the way around.

But she hadn't reckoned on Billy Ray.

She'd read with horror of the growing number of children across the country appearing at school with weapons. But that was in places like New York, New Orleans, and Los Angeles. Never would anything like that happen in a rural Georgia setting.

One gorgeous blue October day, she found Billy Ray wrapped in sullen anger, and she told him to draw a picture of what had upset him. She returned to her desk feeling very good. *Every teacher needs to practice psychiatry,* she thought as she prepared to work with a reading group.

Suddenly there was a slight movement at her elbow. She turned and gasped. "Billy Ray! Where did you get that knife?"

"It's mine. My pa gave it to me."

"Close it and hand it to me. Now." Her voice was steady. She was sure it was.

The young boy before her didn't move one of his blond hairs, and his blue eyes held hers without a blink. The pocket knife he grasped in his right hand at a menacing angle was no more than a foot away. Could she be fast enough to grab his wrists before he slashed her? If she failed, the knife could split her face or gouge her chest. Her brain went wooden; her hands felt like sawdust. She remembered the many times Billy Ray and other boys had been pulled apart on the playground when he'd attacked them for some slur on his family. He was fast, and he'd never shown any compassion.

"Billy Ray, what is the problem? Why are you doing this?"

"Because I want to. And you can't stop me. No one can touch me or they'll be in trouble, big trouble. You can't make me do nothin' I don't want to do." Connie had never seen so much hate in one place as she saw staring from this eight-year-old boy's eyes. A fleeting vision of those eyes gleaming through prison bars made her shiver.

"The trouble will be toward you, Billy Ray. You cannot get away with this. If you'll just lay the knife down this very minute, I'll talk to your parents and try to work something out so you don't have too bad a time. But if you don't, I can't promise—"

"Your promises ain't worth a thing. Ain't no one alive keeps a promise. Richard, tie her up. Here." Billy Ray reached with one hand to pull a rope from his pocket.

Connie grabbed for Billy Ray's wrist but missed. The knife came at her with terrifying force, but she lunged backward in her desk chair, slamming against the blackboard, her hands crossed over her face. She heard Marie scream, "Don't hurt her, Billy Ray!"

At that moment the door flew open and Zena stood there, one hand clapped to her mouth, the other one pointing to Billy Ray, who held the knife over Connie like an ice pick.

"Call for help," said Connie as calmly as she could. She realized all the other children had retreated to the back of the room near the playground exit and were huddled together, their little white faces splotched with dark eyes of fear. All were at the door except Rob, who stood in the middle of the room with both fists clenched and his eternal blank stare fixed on some high point on the blackboard.

"Call for help," Connie said again as Billy Ray nonchalantly began wiping his knife across his jeans and folding it together.

"Help!" said Zena in a whisper, her face as white as cottage cheese.

Connie, having secured the knife by now, as well as having gotten a grip on Billy Ray's shoulders, steered his body with amazing ease toward the door.

"Never mind, Zena. I'll go for help. Please stay with my children or get someone else to. I'll be back soon, class. Please, everyone, sit at your own desk. Rob. . . Joyce, see if you can help Rob, will you?"

She knew it was only because Billy Ray had recognized he was cornered that he was following her direction. Halfway down the hallway he might bolt away from her, but she really didn't know what else to do. He'd given his whole violent act up when Zena opened the door. How might it be another time?

Connie tried to ignore her own thundering heart. She had to be calm, she just had to be. No matter how bad this looked, how bad it really was, she was positive they must not send Billy Ray away. She knew she couldn't lie for the child, but could she convince Mr. Donovan to give the boy a second chance? She had to. She just couldn't give up on Billy Ray now. If they sent him away, it would be like agreeing with him that yes, Billy Ray, you really are a very bad boy. And that's all he would ever be.

Mr. Donovan, as usual, was on the telephone, but something in the faces of teacher and student arrested his attention, and he did not delay in getting off the phone.

"What's the problem?" he asked, looking at Connie, who continued to keep a hand on Billy Ray's shoulder and shook her head when a chair was offered her.

"Billy Ray needs to spend the rest of the day with you, I think, Mr. Donovan. Here's the knife with which he threatened me. I think he had no idea how serious it was." Connie imagined she must sound pretty shaky. Her tongue was so numb and her lips so dry that she was having a hard time speaking.

" 'Course I knowed. I ain't no dummy." Billy Ray's face was smudged with dirt, and it made his scowl even darker.

Mr. Donovan's voice was like a coarse rasp. "Am I to understand this child threatened you with an open knife, Miss Jensen?" Seeing her nod, he continued, "Was there a witness other than the children?"

"Well, Miss Zena Furr heard my children scream and came. When Billy Ray saw her, he started folding his knife up. He did not hurt me."

Mr. Donovan looked hard right into her eyes, then squeezed her arms, ending with a lame pat as his hands fell away. "I'm glad you aren't hurt," he said simply.

He dropped to one knee and placed big, firm hands on the boy's shoulders. "Billy Ray, you and I will have to talk. You stay with me now."

He looked up at Connie with a gray look around his mouth. "Go on back to your room and reassure your children. I'll take care of this. And I'll talk to you later."

"But I—"

"We don't need you anymore, Miss Jensen. You may go."

Just when she thought he was so human, so kind, he started yelling at her! She didn't know what she should have done for Billy Ray, but she knew she'd failed him somehow. As she walked back down the hallway, she wondered if it would have helped for her to have spent more time with the child, given him a stump to hammer nails into. That had helped some children. Would she ever have a chance to help Billy Ray now? Her throat ached with the need for tears. But she couldn't cry now. There were the other children.

"Oh, I'm glad to see you whole and unscratched. That child is a terror, isn't he?" Zena had stood up when Connie walked in. The children were as quiet as hunched-over statues. Even Rob was at his desk.

"Don't say that, Miss Furr! He's just—a disturbed little boy. We're all fine. Or we will be once we talk about this. Richard, are you okay?"

The rope was on her desk where Richard had dropped it when Zena had opened the door. Now Connie perched herself on a cleared spot next to it. "Come here, Richard. I need to see you're all right," she said. Was she wrong not to have told Mr. Donovan that Richard had been slightly involved also? The boy was so innocent and so sweet, she wanted to take him in her arms and cuddle him like a baby left too long crying. But of course she knew better than that.

The child didn't come at first. She didn't press him. Instead she talked in a normal voice to all of her students, allowing them to ask questions as they were ready. But she kept the dark-eyed little boy, his breathing quick and shallow, in her peripheral vision. Finally, when he thought she didn't notice, he slid from his seat and crept toward her. She wasn't sure what he would do until she felt his clammy hand pat her arm. She slid off the desk and enveloped him in her arms and heard the whole class shift in their seats. Soon they were all surrounding her, and tears crept down her cheeks. All this time Zena had stood near the door silently watching. Now she winked and quietly slipped out.

❀

The day lasted an eternity. When her class went to lunch, Connie saw Billy Ray sitting with Mr. Donovan in a corner of the cafeteria. Anyone might have thought they were just having a cozy chat. But she knew better. The sadness in her stomach took away her appetite completely, even though there were chicken nuggets, one of her favorite lunches.

Mrs. Gurdy had brought a container of some kind of cooked greens and a bottle of pepper sauce. In her wide hat, she went about giving some to each teacher. Connie was glad there wasn't much left when Mrs. Gurdy reached her. Mrs. Gurdy patted her shoulder as she started to leave.

"Miss Jensen, you needn't spend any precious time worryin' about that mean little Spence boy. Why, he'll be sent off to Alpine Unit in Demorest so quick you won't even know it. I'm surprised he hadn't already been taken after he stole my billfold last year." The last sentence she whispered loudly into Connie's ear, then looked apprehensively at Richard eating at the other end of the table.

"Thanks, Mrs. Gurdy," mumbled Connie. Anything to get the woman to leave. Connie looked around at her children, some of whom had heard every word Mrs. Gurdy said, though Richard seemed totally occupied with crumbling bread into his dessert. How could she save these children from insecurity and fear?

As soon as school was out, Connie rushed straight to Mr. Donovan's office to see what he'd decided to do about Billy Ray. She was surprised to learn he had let Billy Ray go home on the bus.

He raked a hand through his thick hair and sheepishly cast his gaze toward the toes of his tennis shoes. "Against my better judgment. But I'm going up there in a few minutes. I told him I'd be there before or soon after his bus arrives. You know, he's more excited about my coming to see him than he is afraid of what I may say. Kind of humbling, isn't it?"

"He's. . .he's starved for love, I think."

"Funny you can say that after what you've been through. Are you really all right?"

"Oh, yes, I'm fine." He peered down at her with such a look of concern that she felt her cheeks go warm. "I'm fine," she repeated as he scowled and took a few paces back and forth.

"What about Richard Spence? These children stick together."

She'd been afraid he'd ask. She'd decided she was right not to bring the subject up, but now. . . Richard couldn't help what had happened.

"Miss Jensen! Don't try hiding anything from me. I have to know everything."

"Yes. I know. Richard didn't do anything at all. . .until Billy Ray called out to him. And then he came very slowly and. . .took the rope Billy Ray told him to tie me up with. But just then is when Zena popped in. Richard is scared out of his wits. Mr. Donovan, he let me hug him after I talked to him awhile.

"Oh, don't scowl. I know hugging is against the rules. But I had to! This was severe circumstances. Anyway, when I hugged him, it was as if I could feel every nerve in his little body quivering." Even now, talking about it, her eyes moistened. "You. . .we won't have to do anything to him, will we? He only did what Billy Ray said to do. He had to."

"Yes. But what might Billy Ray tell him next time? But. . .no, I hope we won't have to do anything, but you know it isn't entirely up to us. I've talked to Mr. Miles, county superintendent, and I'm to get back in touch with him after my visit to Billy Ray's this afternoon. A lot depends on the attitude of the parents, you know. Billy Ray's and Richard's."

"Have you ever talked to them before?"

"Yes. And only about trouble. With Billy Ray's brother, Lavon, and with Billy. You see, Miss Jensen—"

"You can't send Billy Ray away, Mr. Donovan. I can manage him; I know I can."

"Miss Jensen, again, it isn't our place to decide. That should be a comfort to you, that you're not sending him away. He got into some trouble last year and would have been placed in a special class in Demorest this fall, but there wasn't room. He's on a waiting list. But this episode will change things, I'm sure. They'll make room somehow."

"Please, Mr. Donovan, can't you do something to keep him here?"

"Well, I'm going to talk to the parents. If they could really convince us they'll make a difference in their care and control of Billy Ray, then. . . . I hate looking like trouble. That's how it will be when they see me coming. These parents, and many more, too, don't come to PTA meetings, so I never see them until there's something wrong. I really do wish we could make home visits when things are okay. Then these times wouldn't be quite so bad. But there's no way we could. There's no time for the personal touches. Yes, they'll know there's trouble when they see me coming."

Connie watched her principal's face sadden as he talked, and a seed of admiration took root. "I would really like to go with you to see the children."

"I don't think that's wise, Miss Jensen."

"I don't care whether it's wise! It's the personal touch you're talking about. I need to go. I need to go for myself if not for Billy Ray. I feel like. . .I know I've let him down."

"No! Not you. Of all people, you have not let him down."

Connie was astonished at the certainty in his voice after all his belligerence and criticism.

"You have not let the boy down, Miss Jensen. And you really don't need to be exposed to any more trauma today. Look, if you need a ride home, I'll get someone to take you or at least ride along with you. I know you must be shaken up."

"Yes, I'm shaken up. But the only thing that's going to make me feel better is to let Billy Ray know that what he did has not made me hate him. Please, Mr. Donovan. Let me go with you."

He turned and walked around his desk to stare out the window, his hands in his pockets. She thought of him as he was that Sunday at Toccoa Falls with his hands in his pockets, only then he'd been so much more relaxed. He'd reminded her that day of a little boy. Now he was a man full of tension. Irrelevantly, she noticed he hadn't had his hair cut lately and it was curling above his wilted collar.

As he whirled toward his desk, snatching up the phone, his mouth set in a hard line. "I'll call the sheriff and have a car accompany us, just to be on the safe side. I'll be a few minutes making arrangements if you want to finish up in your room."

She smiled brightly as she left his office, her steps suddenly much lighter.

Chapter 6

Connie squirmed in the passenger seat of Mr. Donovan's blue pickup. If only the man would chitchat, maybe they could both relax a little, but she'd run down a lengthy list of starters, getting nowhere, and now hasty glances showed that her principal's jaw had hardened. Staring straight ahead, he whipped around mountain curves. How much farther could it possibly be and still be in their school district?

They arrived at Richard's house, a small building bulging with children, and talked to his mother, who stood, arms akimbo, in the doorway and never invited them in. The pudgy woman vacillated between fear and defiance, but she did give them reasonable assurance that Richard would not be playing or associating with Billy Ray and that she'd watch him closely.

Turning away from Richard's home, Mr. Donovan skillfully steered the car over winding gravel roads until they finally turned onto a steep, red clay driveway that was little better than a gully. On top of a sharp knoll was a dilapidated, single-wide trailer surrounded by a collection of vehicles in various stages of deterioration. A curtain moved at one splattered window as they parked under a vast oak tree, the place's only redeeming feature.

"They're here," Connie reported.

Mr. Donovan only grunted as he slid from under the wheel. But as they approached the door, which appeared to have been bashed in several times, he put a supportive hand under her left elbow and whispered, "Let me do the talking." For once, she didn't want to argue.

Trisha Spence had squinty eyes set in a splotched face ruled by a long irregular nose. Her hair was dark, but it was hard to tell whether it was black or brown, it was so laden with grease. The lighting in her cramped living room was extremely poor, but Connie couldn't help observing a plate with a half-eaten, moldy hot dog atop a TV, dirty clothes strewn on the floor, and a roach boldly crawling over food debris on the kitchen counter. Her stomach lurched.

There was no place to sit even if Trisha Spence had invited them to—and she most decidedly had not. Clad in a faded, oversized shirt and tight pants, she folded her arms across her chest and stared deadpan while Mr. Donovan explained their reason for being there.

"I don't know nothin' 'bout that," replied Trisha concerning Billy Ray's use of a pocket knife.

"Is Billy Ray here yet?"

"Naw. Bus ain't come yet."

"Mrs. Spence, I can't say too much about how serious this is. We can't jeopardize our teachers and children by allowing someone like Billy Ray to carry dangerous weapons."

"It were only a knife. Just a knife. Every kid has to have a knife."

"Not if he threatens his teacher with it. Are you listening to me? We could be in the hospital right now with Connie Jensen bleeding from lacerations to her face and arms, and you stand there staring somewhere behind me at nothing. Where is your husband?"

Caught off guard by the question, Trisha Spence let her eyes cut ever so slightly to her right, though her head never moved. Swallowing, she repeated as if she were a robot, "Mr. Spence is delivering wood today, other side of Clayton and won't be back until late. I'll tell him all about it."

"That's not good enough."

"What do you want me to do, then? Billy Ray will get his whippin' if that's what you want!" For the first time, a splash of pinkness spread across her face, and she bit a swollen lip as if dealing with some remorse.

Connie stepped to her side. "That's not necessarily going to do any good with Billy Ray, Mrs. Spence. He doesn't mind pain in the least, I think. Not physical pain. I brought some of Billy Ray's pictures. I think I know a little of what's bothering him if you'd let me show you."

"I ain't got no time for such as that. We work hard to send our young 'uns to school, and from there they got to make it on their own. There, he be comin' now. Don't look like nothin's botherin' him."

Connie was close enough to hear Trisha's sigh of relief.

Billy Ray came bouncing in, red cheeked, eyes sparkling. "Hi, Mr. Donovan! Hi, Miss Jensen! You came. You really came! Want to see my chicken? I got me a chicken cooped up. He's real smart. I'm teachin' him how to count to four by peckin'." Could this merry child possibly be the same one who'd threatened Connie that very morning?

Trisha Spence grabbed the boy by both arms and shook him violently. "Hush that foolishness now an' pay attention like you've been taught. When your pa gets holt to ye, I reckon you'll listen up then. What d'ya mean, showin' that knife to yer teacher like you thought o' hurtin' her? Ain't you got no sense? But o' course not. You're sorry like yer brothers, not a sound, thoughty one among you. Might as well to be saddled with a pack o' wolf pups. Now you turn aroun' an' 'pologize to this pretty lady. Right now."

Having delivered this lengthy speech, the woman stepped back, replaced her arms across her chest, sealed her lips, and stared at the three awkward people before her.

Connie's arms hung limply, Billy Ray stared up at her in a mixture of defiance and ignorance, and Mr. Donovan towered over them all, his dark brows meeting.

"Sorry to scare you, Miss Jensen. It were only a joke," said Billy Ray, donning an angelic smile.

"Thank you, Billy Ray, but—"

"Son, this is not a little matter like passing a note or running in the hall. This involves safety to other people as well as yourself." Mr. Donovan had knelt as he talked so he'd be at eye level with the boy.

"Don't call him son. You ain't our father," said the older boy, Lavon, who had slid in behind them. Connie felt something against her and, looking down, stared right into the grimy, pixie face of the boys' kindergarten-age sister. The little girl smiled and took her hand. Connie wasn't sure if the child was trying to protect this strange woman who'd come to her house or if maybe she was seeking protection herself.

"You folks could be in a great deal of trouble here, and it would be smart of you not to be picky about little phrases you don't like."

Mr. Donovan was losing his patience. He stood up and stared down at Billy Ray, whose blue eyes were unblinking. How did he do that, stare so hard without blinking?

"Mrs. Spence, I'll be in touch. You can send Billy Ray to school tomorrow, but someone will search him, and there'd better not be anything harmful on him. He's under review for a school change already, and any more signs of rebellion can only make matters worse."

"He won't do nothin' like that again. His pa'll probably half kill him tonight."

"But, Mrs. Spence, you don't understand—" Connie began, but Mr. Donovan placed a very firm hand on her arm and shook his head.

"We'll be going now," said Mr. Donovan.

"You know there's a sheriff's car down by our road?" asked Billy Ray chattily, following them away from the door. "T'll probably be a deputy sometime. Reckon I could get a ride in that car?"

"I wouldn't try it right now, Billy Ray," said Mr. Donovan. "I had that car sent in case there was any trouble here we couldn't handle. Make sure we don't need to call them again, understand?"

"Yes, Sir. But wow! Right here by my road. Pretty car. Say, you were gonna look at my chicken, weren't ya?"

It was while Connie and Mr. Donovan were walking back around the trailer after peering in at Billy Ray's white chicken that they saw the face of Mr. Spence at a back window. Mr. Donovan did not break his stride in the least, and Connie didn't know until they were in the truck whether he'd even noticed.

"Yes, I saw him. I knew already he was there, but I'd decided not to push it today. I have a tendency to tackle a week's work in one day, but I thought better of it this time."

"So Mr. Spence is a week's work?"

"He sure is. Say, I'm starved all the way to my backbone. We're not far from Lakeside Restaurant on Tallulah Lake, and I think they'd be serving dinner by now. Go with me?"

"Well. . .sure. Not dinner, thank you. Mrs. Haburn always cooks. But I could handle a cup of coffee about now."

"I thought so. You look a little like death on a cracker, you know."

"Thanks very much."

"No offense. Anyone would after seeing all that horror. Makes me want to choke someone when I see children having to cope with such filth and disrespect, probably downright abuse. It keeps going on, too. They'll grow up and have children who will live the same way. Unless you and I break the pattern."

Connie looked at him quickly, then broke into a genuine friendly smile. "You think there's hope for Billy Ray, don't you?"

"I'm going to do my best."

❀

Mr. Donovan took the scenic gorge loop and stopped at the old overlook building on their way to the restaurant. Since the new road had bypassed this overlook, businesses had shriveled, and the long, cliffside building was ghostly with shrill gusts of wind rattling its boarded windows. Connie stood with Mr. Donovan at the vine-grown guardrail, awed by the depth and character of the gorge as they talked about rock strata, the hardy little trees growing up the sheer gorge wall, and the distance from one craggy cliff to the other.

"It never looked any farther to anyone, I guess, than it did the day Karl Wallenda, the Italian tightrope walker, crossed it."

"You saw him do that?"

"Well, not exactly. My parents were here and my mother was pregnant with me at the time. It was 1970. Everybody was here, they said. His cable was 1,100 feet long and the rock-studded river flowed 2,000 feet below, as it does today. That is, what's left of the river after being dammed into lakes Tallulah, Rabun, Burton, and Seed."

"I can't believe they actually saw him. I don't think I could look even if I were present for something like that." She laughed self-consciously. "Even circus tightrope walkers scare me."

He turned toward her, the wind whipping his black hair about his eyes, his collar askew. "You would have looked if you'd been here," he said. "Mother said the man was like a magnet, drawing everyone's absolute attention. It was as if they might make him fall by not looking hard enough. Spectators tried to hold their breath as if that would help him, but of course they couldn't. It took a very long, tedious time. But he made it all the way and came back. Then fell to his death someplace else, Italy, was it?"

"Where did he walk across the gorge?" asked Connie.

"Down river a ways. Between here and the power plant. You can still see where the cable was attached. Maybe I can show you sometime. Right now I need that food."

As Mr. Donovan ate a heaping platter of fried catfish, French fries, salad, and hush puppies, Connie sipped coffee, enjoying the view. Afternoon sun danced on Tallulah Lake and twinkled off windshields as dozens of cars traveled the new four-lane bridge. The two talked very little, but somehow Connie didn't feel threatened or uncomfortable. She was convinced Mr. Donovan really wanted the best for Billy Ray, and it changed her attitude toward the man.

When they left the restaurant, Mr. Donovan turned south, but he'd barely gotten straight in the road before he turned left into a gift shop parking lot.

"Something wrong?" Connie asked.

"No. There's something I want to show you."

Before she knew it, Mr. Donovan had given her a gentle push, and they were on their way along a winding nature path out to an open promontory. The gorge yawned before them, compelling their respect and admiration. Hemlock and pine mixed with autumn reds grew up the canyon walls. Down in the blue gray distance, a thin splash of water drew itself down the rocky riverbed like the silver path of a paintbrush held in the unsteady hand of a small child. There were blobs of pools and squiggles of rapids and violent turns, but it was all so far away Connie had to wonder if it was really water when she couldn't hear it. Mr. Donovan said there were several falls down there, yet she wasn't ever positive that the roar she heard was water and not the wind.

"It's like seeing a different side of someone's face," he said to explain their need to see this view also.

But her thoughts had reverted to Billy Ray.

"I know what I could do!" she exclaimed, turning toward him, her brown eyes sparkling. "I could teach Billy Ray separately for awhile. In-house suspension, you know? Maybe the review committee would let us continue if it worked out. Please, would you let me try?"

Connie was encouraged that he didn't immediately pick her up and throw her over the cliff. But she saw storm clouds gathering on his rugged face. "Where would you do this?"

"Why. . .I guess in your office. Wouldn't that be the best place?"

He grinned. "Not if you want to use your haphazard approach to teaching, Miss Jensen."

She blushed. Haphazard! So that's what he thought! It seemed a good thing just then to sit down on a convenient bench and become very occupied with studying the other side of the gorge. Was that hemlock growing right out of a rock? It certainly looked like it.

He sat down beside her. "So what kind of methods would you use? To teach Billy Ray, I mean? After all, you'd still have your whole classroom, and you can't be two places at once."

Thankful he was at least talking about it, she plunged into sharing some of her ideas. With Billy Ray, maybe she could experiment, try some of her art and music ideas, and prove to Mr. Donovan how helpful they could be.

"I just can't believe that you are so against things like measuring salt to learn math or dressing up as characters and acting out a story in reading. This is the beginning of the twenty-first century, and these methods have been taught in education classes since back in the Dark Ages, all the way back to the 1960s anyway. You've told us to hold science, health, and home ec for upper grades, but don't you know the children need stepping-stones to prepare for later learning? And we can use those subjects to teach reading and arithmetic."

When she dragged her eyes away from the gorge and looked at Mr. Donovan, she was startled at the naked pain in his face. Or was it sorrow or defeat? Something was vastly wrong for him, she knew that. She hugged herself against a chilling breeze and half whispered, "I'm sorry. I was way out of line. Should we be going now?"

"No. No, you weren't really out of line. I asked for it. And no, we can't go yet. I. . .I need to tell you something."

He was quiet so long she thought he'd forgotten what he was going to say. He dropped his head into his hands at one point as if he had a headache.

"It's all right, you know," she said, not knowing what to say but sure she must do something. "Whatever it is, you don't have to tell me, really."

That made him smile. "You're not the world's greatest psychiatrist, that's for sure."

"I think I'm pretty good," she returned, squaring her shoulders.

"Extremely modest, too," he added. His smile faded. He seemed to gather himself together for a great undertaking. "I don't know why I'm telling you this," he said finally, watching a bird circle far below as he leaned forward, elbows on knees.

"Well, if you must tell me, then get on with it," she said, laughing nervously.

He smiled at her as if she were a naughty child who had just done something nice. "Thank you. I will, then."

She waited, pulled her sweater closer around her, picked up a pinecone to examine it, and waited again. When he cleared his throat and began talking, she squeezed the pinecone so hard it left marks in her hand.

"I know I'm unreasonable in allowing so little extracurricular activity around the school. Sometimes I wonder why I still have a job, and I know I wouldn't if it weren't for my mother and her politics. She watched this job like a hawk and made sure I had it as soon as I'd taught a couple of years. She knew I wanted more than anything to make sure every child in my care learns to read. And she knew what started that desire in my life.

"You see, my father couldn't read. Oh, he was the smartest man I've ever known. And no one but the two of us and my mom knew he couldn't read. Why, he even memorized a Sunday school lesson every week and taught a class! But if someone ever asked him to read anything, of course he'd always forgotten his glasses or had a piece of dust in his eye or had a sudden coughing spell. I got very angry at him once because he couldn't read, and I yelled at him that I would teach him myself.

"He did let me try. But nothing I did ever worked. He simply could not distinguish phonetic sounds. I used flash cards and tried to drill letters and words into him. Many an evening I began my own homework at eleven because of working with Dad all evening. And he hated it. Sometimes it seemed as if. . .he hated me, too. We got so frustrated with each other, my mother finally stopped it all."

Connie tried, like the Wallenda spectators, to hold her breath as Mr. Donovan crossed his own gorge full of rocky feelings. She was afraid he would turn back into his old raspy self before he told her everything. But in a low rumbling voice he continued.

"I was away at college when it happened. Dad developed pretty bad angina. He kept nitroglycerine pills ready all the time and was, as always, the life of any gathering, the muscle of any work job, and the epitome of happiness. He loved his garden better than almost anything except Mother and spent nearly all his waking hours preparing soil, planting, or harvesting.

"That's where Mother found him one day when she got home from the grocery store. He was facedown in the dirt, one hand gripping his nitroglycerine bottle tightly. He was too far gone for CPR to revive him, and he died on the way to the hospital. When I got there, Mother was hysterical and all she could say was 'He had his medicine. Why didn't he take it?' I looked at the bottle, which she said he'd just gotten the day before. It was a new bottle with a childproof cap and. . . well, you see, he couldn't read the directions for opening, and apparently, in his pain, just could not figure it out."

Connie ached for the man beside her who was so obviously still grieving for a father dead now ten years. She couldn't say anything. To speak seemed as out of place as getting up to make an announcement in the middle of a preacher's sermon. After what seemed several minutes, she laid one slim hand on the seat beside him, and, without a word, he laid one of his big ones over it. For long minutes they sat that way. Connie didn't consider that it was anything unusual until they stood to leave. Then she realized she missed his big, warm hand.

❀

Neither of them spoke on the return trip to Pine Ridge. Once there, she expected him to say, "See you tomorrow" or some such trite farewell and leave her to start her car alone. But he jumped out and met her at her door. Before she could fish her keys out of her bag he placed hands on her shoulders as he had done earlier that day. Then, it had been to be sure she was all right after Billy Ray's threat. Now, he held her shoulders firmly as he said, "Thank you, Connie."

Then with no warning he leaned over and kissed her. She tasted the tracks of salty tears on his lips, yet his lips were so strong and so good. With a whirlwind of new feelings chasing each other through her head and her heart, she watched him walk away.

As she drove home, she touched two fingers to her lips and laid the hand he'd touched against her cheek. He was such an odd man, and there was so much more to him than she'd realized. *I've seen his face from a different angle,* she thought, remembering his comment about the gorge. But no matter what, she wouldn't even hint to Mrs. Haburn that she'd changed her mind one little bit concerning Maury Donovan.

When she turned her car in at Mrs. Haburn's and plunged down the little steep road, she had the feeling something more was going to happen before the day was over—that as full as it had been, there was still more. Mrs. Haburn was in the kitchen and announced cheerfully they'd have to go to the grocery store if company was coming for the weekend.

"But are we expecting company, Mrs. Haburn?"

"I forgot I hadn't even told you. You're so late or I would have told you long ago. Anyway, Henry called. Said he'd be here Friday evenin'. Now you don't worry about a thing, Child. I'll take care of things around here, and you can just relax and enjoy your friend. I've already figured out we can have chicken pie Friday night. No man alive has ever not liked my chicken pie. And Saturday lunch we can have fried chicken if you don't think that's too much chicken. An' I guess you two would be goin' out Saturday night, but if you want to eat before you go we could have country-fried steak and mashed potatoes, one of my favorites. And of course roast beef on Sunday. . ."

Connie closed her bedroom door behind her and pressed fingers against her eyes. Taking a deep shuddery breath, she walked over to her maple tree window and stood for awhile staring out before opening her attache case of papers.

Later, as she went to bed, she prayed for Billy Ray and for wisdom concerning Henry. Even with her room darkened, she could still imagine the picture of the praying couple in their field and wished that she could be as confident when she prayed as they seemed to be.

She was almost asleep when she realized Mr. Donovan had called her Connie.

Chapter 7

Henry arrived right on schedule at six o'clock Friday evening, smelling of his usual cologne and full of quiet cheer. He was genuinely happy to see Connie. She tried hard to appear glad to see him, too, though there was something very wrong about the whole thing, and she knew it. They went to a movie in Toccoa after eating Mrs. Haburn's wonderful chicken pie. Henry did most of the talking going and coming and seemed satisfied with Connie's very lame comments.

Saturday morning they strolled down to the dock, and she tried to explain Billy Ray to him without actually telling him about the knife. She just said Billy Ray had gotten into too many fights and was to be in some form of suspension for several weeks, and the principal was going to teach him himself from lesson plans she prepared for him. Which was all true. Mr. Donovan had made up his mind he was going to teach Billy Ray himself, and for three days now that had worked out fine. But Henry didn't really hear much of what she said. He did hear her story about washing Marie's hair and how very happy the little girl was, flipping her beautiful brown hair about and feeling of it as she did her work.

"Connie, you're not supposed to be washing hair. You're not a beautician; you're a teacher! What next?"

If he only knew!

After lunch they went to Clayton and rode out Warwoman Road, enjoying the autumn color splashed up the slopes of Screamer Mountain, exploring a portion of old railroad bed dating back to the Civil War, and eating chocolate bars while passing between sweeping skirts of thick, dark hemlock in a little park. As long as there was plenty to talk about other than personal feelings, Connie could have a reasonably good time. But deep inside she felt guilty, as if she were cheating Henry.

Referring to a delightful North Georgia guidebook she'd picked up, Connie asked Henry if he'd rather go to Mark of the Potter on the Soque or go all the way to Helen, Georgia's alpine village, maybe even up the scenic Russell Highway.

"Hmmm. Doesn't really matter," said Henry. "Only let's don't go as far as Helen. I came to see you, Connie, not to sightsee. Let's find a nice place to sit and talk."

Even after that comment, Connie, who was driving, put off serious talk by jabbering about landmarks they passed, filling Henry's ears with mountain trivia in which he had no interest. They drove all the way back to Clarkesville, turned up the Lake Burton Road, had cinnamon rolls and coffee at Batesville General Store, then backtracked to the Mark of the Potter. By the time they arrived at the old gristmill made into a gift shop, the afternoon was old for Connie in more ways than one.

Connie usually liked to browse around and see all the beautiful crafts. She particularly enjoyed watching pottery being formed by skilled craftsmen. But she quickly realized Henry was miserable. Pottery was far from his cup of tea. That's when she suggested they go out on the deck and throw some of the provided feed in the river for the fish. Wonderful, long sleek trout frisked or hovered in the stream, and Connie giggled at the sport they made of a handful of feed.

"It's good to hear you laugh, Connie," said Henry, laying an arm across her shoulders. "I've missed your laughter, you know. I. . .I'll be so glad when you come back. Things aren't right when you're not around."

Connie tossed in the last little pellets of feed, then turned her back to the railing, lightly shedding Henry's arm. Taking a deep breath, she plunged into truthfulness.

"Henry, things are never going to be the same again. If I could make this easier I would. I've tried to think of a good way to do it. But all I know is to tell you straight out. I. . .I just can't. . .marry you, Henry."

He seemed so intent on watching the fish she thought for a minute he hadn't heard her above the roar of the water and his own concentration. But finally he turned toward her, and she was startled at the white pain in his face. "You've found someone else, I suppose."

"No. But, Henry, I don't believe I love you. Not the way I should. I care for you a whole lot. But. . .that's not good enough."

"When did you realize?"

She wouldn't have known before he asked, but now she said, "When you chided me for washing Marie's hair."

"But, Connie, I'm sorry about that. I just—"

"No, Henry, it's all right. Only. . .you see, we're so very different, and I don't think we'd be happy. I was proud of washing Marie's hair, and it thrilled me to see her feeling pretty. It was important to me. I'm sorry, Henry; but here, I'd better give you your ring back."

"Not here, Connie. Wait until we get to the car. You might drop it in the river. Come on. Let's go."

❦

Connie could not understand why Henry couldn't have humored poor Mrs. Haburn a bit and stayed long enough to eat her beautiful dinner. But Henry grabbed his things up from Mrs. Haburn's sewing room where he'd slept and was gone in minutes.

"Something wrong with my nose?" asked Mrs. Haburn, staring at the firmly closed door. "I didn't smell nothin' wrong with that steak."

Connie laughed halfheartedly. "No, no, it wasn't the steak, Mrs. Haburn. It's I who doesn't smell so good."

Mrs. Haburn whirled so quickly she immediately began massaging her arthritic neck, but at the same time she eyed her young boarder with open curiosity. Breaking into a contagious cackle, she declared, "Well, you smell like a rose to me. And. . .is Henry gonna be callin', d'ya think?"

"No, I don't think so." Connie's eyes brimmed with sudden tears, and Mrs. Haburn hugged her very tightly. She had the good sense, for once, to say nothing at all.

🌸

Connie was amazed at Mr. Donovan's determination, his persistence in teaching Billy Ray, as days and weeks went by with so little progress. For whatever reason, the review board had not yet transferred Billy Ray, and Connie felt that Mr. Donovan had a lot to do with it. But if he didn't make some progress soon, teaching Billy Ray addition facts, spelling, and how to write. . .

Mr. Donovan's secretary was out for the day so Connie left her class under the care of the school's roving aide for a few minutes and went to see if she could help Billy Ray. She didn't mean to eavesdrop but paused indecisively at the door.

"Billy Ray, there are some things you just have to learn," said Mr. Donovan in a tone that sounded as if he'd said it already at least a hundred times. "Don't give me that deadpan stare either. I know and you know that you can do this. Come. C-O-M-E. Come. As I've told you, letters make up our code, and you have to break it to communicate. I'm letting you in on the secret. Go, G-O. Come, C-O-M-E. Now you have to learn the difference, or when your girlfriend writes 'Come,' you'll go instead."

"Don't never plan to have a girlfriend," grunted Billy Ray. "My pa said I don't need none of this stuff to get along. Weren't for my mama, I'd be workin' with him."

A tense silence followed. Connie gripped her hands together, wondering if she should go in or turn very quietly and leave. She jumped as something heavy crashed. Flinging the door open, she saw Mr. Donovan's face ablaze with anger and Billy Ray crouching defensively. Mr. Donovan had knocked his own chair over and now proceeded to set it back up, a sheepish look overcoming his anger.

"I ain't done nothin'," blurted Billy Ray. "You gonna put me in jail for not learnin' C-O-M-E, come?"

Connie stared at the little boy, then at Mr. Donovan's astonished face. The two adults burst out laughing and Billy Ray's ears turned very pink.

After that, Connie was much more respectful of Mr. Donovan and his rote method. On the other hand, Mr. Donovan broke down and asked her advice quite a number of times, though she couldn't tell that he ever used it. She could see that he seemed less like a charging bull these days, and that helped the school's general atmosphere.

Other teachers noticed a change in Mr. Donovan, too, and marveled to Connie how he must have a soft spot for tough little boys. Zena Furr even went so far as to say she thought he had a soft spot for Connie because he let her get away with some things he'd never allowed them to do, like planning a musical Thanksgiving play that required an hour of practice each day for two weeks. Or allowing her to teach Billy Ray how to play a harmonica, which was a huge thrill to both Connie and her pupil. Billy Ray was seldom seen after that without the mysteriously donated harmonica at his lips. Mr. Donovan said Miss Jensen should have been in Singapore instead of teaching him to play, but there was a small twinkle in his eyes when he said it.

But whatever Zena said, Connie couldn't feel Mr. Donovan had a soft spot for her. Not when week after week he spoke to her only professionally and never seemed to recall their conversation at the gorge. In church group meetings, his laughter seemed to quiet when she entered the room. All she could think was he'd been awfully sorry he kissed her and he hoped she'd forget all about it. After all, it was only a momentary departure from reality in the heat of overwrought nerves.

But she couldn't forget—not his firm, vibrant kiss nor the warmth of his big hand protecting hers, accepting her sympathy, as they had sat by Tallulah Gorge.

One day while standing in front of his desk waiting for him to get off the phone so she could explain Billy Ray's lesson plan, she idly scanned his big planning calendar flopped open right before her eyes. She didn't mean to be snooping; she just happened to see that the following Saturday was a flying day. Sky divers were scheduled to land at 2:30 P.M. at Gainesville's small airport. She didn't know exactly when she decided for sure she was going, but when she woke up that Saturday morning, there was no doubt in her mind, and she dressed with as much excitement as if it were Christmas morning.

Connie was glad she'd added an extra layer of sweatshirt under her jacket when she saw ice on the pond. Driving to Gainesville on such a clear bright morning was a pleasure even with the sound of Mrs. Haburn's cautions ringing in her ears: "Wherever you're going, drive carefully, watch for ice patches, and be very careful on bridges." Of course she didn't know where Connie was going or she would really have been full of cautions.

That morning Connie had prayed with Mrs. Haburn as usual, and it was pretty hard not to tell her landlady about her exciting adventure, but she didn't dare. Besides, there was hardly time after she related all the cases at school for which she wanted Mrs. Haburn to pray. Rob was there only half days, yet he vandalized the other children's pencils and work when he was there. Sammy Craven was doing very well as long as she worked closely with him. He was pretty lazy, she'd decided. There was Joyce, so much brighter than most, who could read and write now, but needed strong motivation.

And then there was Richard, who had become sullen since Billy Ray's absence from the classroom. Richard no longer made happy detailed pictures; whatever his assignment, his paper was covered with ugly monsters. And, of course, she wanted Mrs. Haburn to pray for little Marie, who'd learned to read and wanted a new book every day.

As Connie drove, thinking of all her prayer requests and how Mrs. Haburn took each one like a precious responsibility, she smiled to herself. To begin with, Connie had prayed with Mrs. Haburn to make her landlady happy. Now, Connie realized, she herself wanted prayer time. *Maybe this is what growing as a Christian means,* she thought. She'd always wondered about that lofty phrase, "growing as a Christian."

She shopped a little in Gainesville, had lunch, and soon afterward headed for the airport. She wasn't sure where at the airport she should go but soon spotted a small knot of people over to one side staring at the sky. That must be the place. She shyly stationed herself a short distance away, close enough to hear some of the others' comments but far enough away so they didn't have to feel they must talk to her.

It was so, so bright, even with sunglasses. Connie stared up into the sky, seeing nothing but clear, unclouded space entered occasionally by small planes approaching or departing. *That group of spectators has to be awfully dedicated to stick to this activity for very long,* she thought, rubbing her neck.

"Roger was wishing they could have done formations today," said one vigorous young woman with her sleeves pushed up as if it were late spring instead of early December.

"I know. Jock, too. Of course it's not the same for him since he never jumps anymore, but he loves to fly the plane. Makes him feel he's still part of the group. And he gets so excited when they do the formations. He's always so keyed up nights before that he can't sleep a wink."

Connie thought the second speaker was probably about forty, an attractive woman wearing a hand-knit beret of bright red with matching mittens, which she was constantly removing and replacing. When she wasn't taking her mittens on or off, she was lacing her fingers or putting her hands together as if in prayer.

Suddenly Connie realized the woman in the red beret was speaking to her. "Do you have someone in the sky, Honey?" she asked.

"Oh, no. I mean, well, yes, I am watching someone, but he doesn't even know

I'm here. It's just my school principal. I'm a teacher and I thought—"

"Of course, of course. You must work for Maury Donovan, then."

"Well, yes, how did you know?"

"He's the only principal in the group, that's all," said the woman, walking over to introduce herself. "I'm Jock's wife, Betty Friedman. We all like Maury Donovan. But he and my husband are especially close. They were in the service together, even though Maury's a lot younger than we are."

"I'm Connie Jensen. It's very nice to meet you. Isn't it about time they were coming down?"

"Oh, it varies, you know. They may have run into some air pockets or something and decided to fly up over the lakes before they jump. When those four get together, you can never tell what they're going to do." Betty laughed with her head thrown back, her eyes constantly scanning the skies.

Connie relieved the crick in her neck by looking around at the rest of the spectators. One man was a chain-smoker. Another one cracked crude jokes, one right after another. Connie noticed Betty, though she didn't voice any complaints, simply did not even smile at the man's jokes. One very pretty woman looked old enough to be a mother to some of the jumpers. Could that be Maury's mother? She tried to see some resemblance but couldn't, for the woman was small and blond.

"Are you ever worried, I mean really worried, about your husband when he's up there?" asked Connie of Betty Friedman.

Betty looked into her eyes briefly before turning her face back up. "Yes. I worry. It's impossible not to sometimes. But he dearly loves to do this. More than anything. And I just decided a long time ago I'd rather come and watch than sit home and worry. Everyone has to make their own adjustments to things like this. But I believe we're happier than folks who only stay home and watch all their sports on television. Oh. . .I see the plane now. That's our plane." She showed Connie, pointing a red hand, her voice shaking with excitement.

Connie had trouble seeing the plane very well, the glare was so bad, but she could hear it. "Sounds as if it's stopping," she said uneasily.

Betty laughed. "Jock's letting the jumpers out. There's one. . .two. . .three. He doesn't really stop, but it does sound like it. Now, there he goes to circle and come back down."

"But. . .where are the jumpers?"

"Can't you see them? They're only specks yet. But it won't be long before you'll hear Maury Donovan singing. He always sings when he comes down. Reminds me of that beautiful piece of music called 'On Wings of Song.'" She cut loose right that minute, humming strains of music Connie had never heard before.

"Not that Maury sings that song. I've never even heard words for it. But the way he sings so happy and free makes me think of 'On Wings of Song.' I'm not really crazy, Connie, just wacky," she said, one red-mittened hand shading her eyes from the sunshine.

Connie glanced at the woman beside her, drawn by her enthusiasm; then she studied the skies again. Now she could see them! Even as she watched, funny blobs or dark specks developed into colorful umbrellas as one by one the parachutes opened. There was a cheer from the whole little earthbound audience. Then almost a reverent silence settled on them so that, sure enough, as Betty had said, they could hear Maury Donovan's rich bass belting out " 'There's a land that is fairer than day, and by faith I can see it afar. . . .' "

Connie shivered and pulled her jacket closer as she stared steadily at the descending parachutes. It was amazing how slowly they came down. She was wishing Maury Donovan would sing again so she could try to tell which one he was when Betty pulled at her arm and pointed him out.

"That one," she said urgently, "the one with the red-and-white canopy."

First of all, Connie was astonished when the jumpers landed so neatly on their feet amid billows of colorful silk. Then she was suddenly envious as several of the women ran to embrace their men at various landing places around the airport. She noticed the little blond woman, though excited for them, did not budge from beside the chain-smoker. They were just friends of the jumpers, she supposed. She watched the jumper with the red-and-white canopy and saw only Betty Friedman in her red beret running over to him to hug his neck.

Having decided to disappear quietly, Connie couldn't wait to get her car cranked and be away from there. She wouldn't stop long enough to tell Betty good-bye or hear all the glowing reports and, mainly, she wouldn't talk to Maury Donovan, and he could think whatever he wanted to when he found out she'd been there. It had simply been a matter of good healthy curiosity, that's all. She couldn't have lived with Mrs. Haburn for three months without acquiring a huge case of inquisitiveness.

She fumbled with her keys, her fingers cold in her gloves. At the moment she finally slid the key into the ignition, a shadow seemed to pounce on her car and she gasped out loud. The shadow turned out to be a fully suited Maury Donovan minus his parachute, his face glowing like sunrise on Easter morning.

Having done a spread eagle across her side of the windshield, he jerked her door open and pulled her out. Very deliberately, he slid her sunglasses from her face and tossed them into her car, then enveloped her in the biggest, warmest hug she'd ever known, nestling his face in her hair and gently rocking with her for long minutes. Airport sounds—droning of a plane overhead, shouts of other happy sky divers, and flapping of a wind sock—drifted about them as they clung to each other.

When Maury Donovan whispered, "Will you go with me to get a bite to eat?" Connie nodded her dark head against his cheek.

In a friendly sandwich shop they huddled over a booth table talking about the jump. Maury's face was still glowing, and his descriptions of the total peacefulness and exuberance in the ten-thousand-foot descent lit sparkles in Connie's eyes as well.

"People think our biggest thrill is in watching the earth from the air and, of course, that is a lot of fun. It's so beautiful from up there. You don't see the trash anymore, or wrecked cars, or abandoned buildings. Everything is green or brown, spiky or soft looking in fascinating squares and rectangles as pasture, fields, or forests rise to meet you. But better than what I can see is what I feel up there. I feel stripped of all encumbrances, Connie, so I can really praise the Lord. It is just incredible!"

The waitress brought his sandwich and fries and he ate ravenously, explaining between bites that he never ate anything before a jump. "Far too excited to eat. Haven't had a bite since last night. Just some orange juice this morning."

"Mr. Donovan, you're going to need more than one sandwich, I think," said Connie softly.

He wagged a finger at her and tried to speak, but his mouth was too full. Finally what came out was, "You've got to call me Maury when we're away from school. Can't you do that?"

"Yes, of course I can. . .Maury."

"Now that's better. And, yes, I think I will have another sandwich, maybe two more. Don't you want anything?"

"No, thank you. I'm only an earthling, you know, and can't be expected to have your heavenly appetite."

He laughed with her, but in the middle of the laugh his eyes dropped suddenly to her left hand and impulsively he reached for her ring finger, rubbing the empty finger with his thumb. "I've been wanting to ask. . .what happened?" he asked.

"We. . .just. . .aren't suited for each other. I gave him his ring back long ago. In October."

"I knew it was missing but didn't know why. Guess I was kind of bashful about finding out."

"You, Maury? Bashful?" She laughed and shook her head.

"Under every tough skin there is a boy, Connie," he said, chewing more thoughtfully now.

"Speaking of boys, you've sure made a difference for Billy Ray. Isn't he doing pretty well now?"

A cloud crossed his face. "Let's don't talk about school, Connie, please. But, since you asked, yes, the boy's doing fine. Just needs lots of attention. More than he'll ever dream of getting in that cesspool where he lives."

"Maury!"

"Well, it is. And you're the one who brought up this subject."

"Well, I'm sorry; I'll change it. Does your mother ever come to watch you jump?"

He was in the middle of a big bite, but Connie thought he took an extra long time finishing the bite before he answered. Then it was a curt, "No." Nothing more, just no.

She was baffled and would not let it drop. "Why not?"

"Because she chooses not to. That's all."

She didn't know how to respond and simply folded and refolded her napkin until he mentioned something about the wind, and soon they were talking about flying again.

When they went back to the airport to get her car, the place was quiet as a school in July. The wind sock wasn't even flapping, and planes tied in their places didn't look as if they'd ever be airborne again.

"Far from the circus atmosphere of a couple hours ago," commented Maury, unfolding himself from under the wheel to see her into her own car. "But then we can't stay on mountaintops or at a circus. The Lord made us to have highs and lows and lots in between. I think what I need now is about seventy-two hours of sleep. But I'll see you in church tomorrow."

"With your eyes open?"

"Maybe I can prop them open with sixteenth notes," he answered, playfully pulling one eyelid up. He leaned elbows on her open window and she thought he might kiss her, but he only squeezed her shoulder with a big hand, then stood back and waved her off.

Why didn't he want to talk about his mother? she wondered as she started home. The more she thought about it, the more indignant she became. The man had drawn too many lines. Don't talk about school; don't talk about my mother; just talk about flying, mainly just flying. Well, Zena Furr was right, Connie decided. She did need to leave Mr. Maury Donovan well alone.

Chapter 8

In spite of all her wise cautions to herself, Connie did hope very much to see Maury at church, but she didn't see him for more than a minute privately. He directed the choir in a wonderful rendition of "When I Survey the Wondrous Cross," which brought tears to her eyes. And his face was far from sleepy as he led congregational singing. She imagined he beamed right at her several times, and she knew her smile gave away the fact that she liked his glances very much.

When church was out, she walked slowly beside Mrs. Haburn, who not only was hobbling worse that day, but was compelled to have a long chat with everyone she met. Suddenly Maury was beside them, explaining quickly that the preacher needed him to take a carload of youth to a Bible drill meet that afternoon. "I'll see you soon," he said over his shoulder as he hurried away.

Mrs. Haburn had a bad bout with arthritis in her neck and left knee that afternoon, and they decided not to get out in the evening air to go to church, though Mrs. Haburn worried that dear Reverend Stone would think she didn't want to hear his promised message on angels.

Connie didn't see Maury until Monday morning and then only to give him Billy Ray's lesson plan very hurriedly since he had put a caller on hold and her own class was waiting. She didn't think too much about it that day. It was really what she'd expected, knowing the routines of school days. But by the end of the week when he hadn't called or spoken privately to her, she began to have forebodings. She had no right to expect anything more than a friendly nod from him, yet her disappointment deepened every day. How could she have totally misread his feelings expressed in a kiss, a touch of the hand, and a hug?

❀

Mrs. Haburn had baked her fruitcakes right after Thanksgiving so they'd have time to season really well before Christmas. Now, on December 13, she was ready to make fudge if, as she said, the weather would cooperate with her. And if Connie could help get her ingredients together. She needed some walnuts and she was out of vanilla. Would Connie pick those up after school?

"I'll not only pick them up for you; I'll help you crack the nuts," said Connie cheerfully as she left for school in predawn darkness. It was her week to be on bus duty.

The first sign that day that everything was going wrong was when Richard wet his pants. She was trying so very hard to teach him how to read. Why, if he could make pictures of anything he wanted to, couldn't he learn simple words like *run?* In chin-hard determination, she refused to let him leave her desk until he completed one whole page of reading, which was actually only six lines. When he said he needed to go to the rest room, she simply restated that he must stay there until he finished. Then he wet his pants, and she had to go to the school's front office to find dry clothes.

While she was in the office, Connie saw the sheriff enter Mr. Donovan's office, a hard-looking deputy with him. She didn't understand what they were there for since she was in such a hurry to see about clothes for Richard, but the news spread rapidly. Seems they'd arrested Billy Ray Saturday outside a grocery store where they found candy bars and crackers, goods for which he hadn't paid, stowed in the pockets and lining of his jacket. They'd let him go with a severe reprimand and return of the goods, but this morning he'd done the same thing at another store.

"I think he's going to have to go to reform school, if they take them that young," said Zena while their children played at recess. "You know he's not safe to have around, Connie!" she remonstrated, seeing the defeated look on her friend's face.

Connie looked at little Richard, Billy Ray's cousin, sitting alone against the playground fence, and for the first time wondered if there really was any hope for either of them. Richard's parents had never offered any more support since they'd been questioned concerning Richard's part in the knife threat, and Billy Ray's parents were totally uncooperative. If it hadn't been for Mr. Donovan, Billy Ray would have already gone to the disciplinary class in Demorest. Maybe, just maybe, he could stall the review board one more time.

But this was one time too many, the sheriff said.

Connie tried to be truthful but gentle in explaining to her children what had happened for, of course, they found out and were full of questions. Marie was the one most upset. She cried for an hour, her head down on her desk, sobbing over and over, "They'll make the dogs chase Billy Ray."

Marie wasn't consoled by anything Connie could say whether she explained that Billy Ray wouldn't be chased, wouldn't be in jail in the first place, or that he would be back in just a few weeks for good behavior. But finally little mothering Joyce hit on a comforting thought when she said, "Marie, Billy Ray can run faster than a deer, and if those dogs do get after him, he'll leap high over a fence and be long gone."

Connie shuddered at the influence of television on her children. Most of all, she mourned losing Billy Ray. She wanted to lay her head down like little Marie and just cry, but of course she didn't have that privilege.

Mr. Donovan came to her room to report what had happened, almost as if they'd had no other communication about Billy Ray, as if he were simply the principal reporting to the teacher of a delinquent student, nothing more.

She almost forgot about walnuts and vanilla, and she didn't remember until she'd slowed as usual to turn in by Mrs. Haburn's apple sign. In the nick of time, she accelerated and drove on toward Clarkesville.

She was so tired that she didn't feel like hurrying. The store was merry with Christmas supplies, and she took her time looking at all the nuts, choosing walnuts from a loosely filled barrel, collecting some navel oranges, and admiring miniature Norfolk pine, ready-dressed as Christmas trees. She and Mrs. Haburn had bought a Christmas tree the weekend before, but she wondered if Mrs. Haburn would like one of these tiny trees to put on the dining table. About then she heard someone say the name Maury and she glanced around.

Two women were standing in front of the cabbages, catching up on the news. One was a tall spare woman with a loose-fitting coat, short iron gray hair, and bright blue eyes.

"Maury's doing fine, thank you. He's still principal at Pine Ridge."

"Any young lady friend I haven't heard about?"

"No. Maury dates but never settles down to liking only one. I'll probably be a grandmother when I'm too old to spoil the grandchildren!"

So this spare-framed lady with iron gray hair was Maury's mother! Connie studied the Christmas trees even harder, hoping it would appear she was trying to choose the healthiest one.

"Well, have a merry Christmas now. Tell that handsome hunk of a son hello for me. Maury's always been one of my favorites."

"Merry Christmas to you, too, Susan," said Mrs. Donovan.

Connie had found Maury's mother! Driven by either an insatiable curiosity or something even stronger, she followed the woman all through the store, up and down the aisles. She collected a half buggy full of groceries Mrs. Haburn hadn't requested, including the Norfolk pine and, in the meantime, observed subtly how Mrs. Donovan seemed sad and lonely, though some people did speak to her. She put very little in her cart, things easily prepared for only one person.

Connie longed for some chance to introduce herself to the woman but could not think of any courteous way of bringing it about. Even if she could, what good would it do? They couldn't discuss the thing that haunted Maury so, the death of his father caused by his illiteracy.

When Connie arrived home, Mrs. Haburn was fit to be tied because Connie was so late. The bustling little woman rattled all through supper about that and other things. "We didn't need all that stuff. I just asked for walnuts and vanilla, and I don't know why you got all them things. Not that we can't use 'em, mind you. You'd be surprised how quick I can run out of things. Like flour, for instance. Since you went hog-wild, it's a good thing you thought to get flour because I might have been sendin' for some in a couple o' days. All the Christmas bakin', you know. I need to make cookies for your class, Connie, maybe gingerbread boys and girls. You need to tell me exactly how many of each."

And, of course, Mrs. Haburn couldn't be huffy long while that merry little Norfolk pine was smiling at her from the center of the table. Connie was glad one good thing had come out of this dreary day. If it was dreary to her, how much drearier was it to Billy Ray, placed in a strange foster home? She wondered what he might be doing about now, probably sulking and making his foster parents miserable. Whoever they were, they needed a lot of prayer! She wished she could take Billy Ray his own box of gingerbread boys. Would she be allowed to do that?

The next afternoon when she dragged her bone-weary self into her room to clean up after finishing her bus duty responsibilities, Maury Donovan followed her. Without a word, he picked up a broom and went to work. She straightened up the desks, rehung a fallen poster, cleaned the blackboard, and snapped all the smudgy work sheets into her attaché case to take home and grade. The principal had sat down on a corner of her desk by then and was watching her.

"I think Billy Ray is vastly better off where he is," he said. "He's with a good family. We've had children they kept before, and I've always been impressed with their care. He goes to the Alpine Unit in Demorest where they're trained to care for disturbed children. It's pretty much as usual for him except. . .well, I know his teacher's not nearly as pretty nor as talented as the one he left behind."

She was so astonished at his compliment she couldn't think of what to say. Clearing her throat, she asked, "Would it be all right if I take him some of Mrs. Haburn's cookies?"

"I think so. I'll give you the directions. The family's in Clarkesville, not hard to find."

"You've been to see him?"

"Of course. Had to get him settled in, you know. Connie—"

"Yes, Sir?"

"Please don't 'Yes, Sir' me right now."

"We're still at school, Sir."

"Well, then, let's go somewhere."

"I don't think so. I. . .I'm very busy with all these papers to grade."

"I see. Connie, look, I know I've been unkind lately. I just want a chance to explain."

"You don't need to do that. It's totally unnecessary. Would you lock the door for me? My hands are full. Papers to grade and forms to fill out. Papers, papers,

papers. If they think of even one more thing teachers are supposed to do, I'm sure we'll all just combust and go up in smoke."

He smiled at her grumbling humor and took it as encouragement, striding down the hall beside her.

"I have a few more things I have to see to here. Then I could come to your place. Or, if you'd rather, I could come later and take you to Toccoa or Clarkesville for dinner, maybe try Taylor's Trolley in Clarkesville. I bet you haven't eaten there."

"No. But I don't plan to go out tonight, Mr. Donovan. I'm going straight home and climb into my ugliest clothes, and I don't intend to see anyone." She was shocked at how good it felt to be rude to him. Smiling her frostiest, she walked out, leaving him with a very surprised look on his face. If he thought he could treat her like a friend one day and last year's Easter egg the next, he'd better think again.

When Connie got home she really did climb into her ugliest clothes. Mrs. Haburn was busy making delightful gingerbread boys, but she didn't seem to need any help, so Connie gratefully went to the pond alone, that is, with only the cat.

She sat down in Mrs. Haburn's rusty old chair out on the dock and watched the water for thirty minutes until its peaceful influence began to invade her being. Looking at trees rippled upside down, tiny waves from a winter wind or from stray leaves skidding onto the pond's surface, and the trace of a bubble path where a turtle swam helped her get things back into proper perspective. Whatever proper perspective was. She only knew that Maury Donovan was not a man she should lose her heart to, and she hoped she hadn't already done it.

The sun was going down. Long, dark shadows enveloped the little valley. She was thinking how everything turned purple as night was coming on when a flash of light arrested her attention. Light shot into rainbow colors for a second off a windshield as a vehicle turned in at Mrs. Haburn's driveway. She thought someone was using the road to turn around, then realized it was Maury's blue pickup. Her heart thudded with instant hope before she scolded herself. Well, if he really wanted to see her, he could come all the way to the pond. She wasn't budging.

However, as he approached, she did get up and met him onshore. She felt too vulnerable sitting alone in that chair on the dock.

He held a hand up as if to defend himself. "I know you said not to come. But I had to."

"Well, I was just getting ready to walk. Come on. We'll circle the pond five times."

"That's my limit?"

"It'll be dark by then."

"I don't mind darkness. Stars will be out tonight." By now they'd made half the first round, and he was actually having to speed up to keep in step with her.

"I met your mother yesterday," she said, taking control of the conversation.

He exhaled noisily. "You talked to her?"

"No. But she was talking about you. A very nice-looking woman with short grayish hair. She looked a little like you, I think. She's proud of you, Maury."

"For no reason. And she's definitely not always proud. There's one whole part of me she wants nothing to do with."

"What's that?" She looked at him for the first time as they approached the dock and kept going around.

"My eternal desire to jump out of planes."

"Oh."

"She wants me to be stable, staid, and responsible. She wants me to be respected in the community. She wants me to be all that my father wasn't and much, much more. And she's afraid. Mainly she's afraid."

"Afraid?"

"Yes. She loved my father so very much and she lost him. She doesn't want to lose me, too."

"Did you tell her about Billy Ray? Do you talk to her about things that happen at school?"

"No. I do not!" His voice went harsh. They walked on in silence, and the cat fell in behind them on their third round. By and by he said more softly, "I don't ever talk to my mother unless it's necessary, Connie. She and I just don't get along. She despises my flying and I must fly. That's why. . .that's why I'm afraid of you."

"Afraid of me?" She stopped. Blueberry bushes hunched down in purple rows behind him, and in the distance, the dark hill cut a stark shape out of a crimson sky. She couldn't see Maury's face very well, but she knew he was quite serious.

"I'm afraid because I can't give up flying, Connie. And any commitment I could make would require that. I don't think I can live without being able to fly and jump. It's my freedom, my joy."

"Who said you had to give it up to make a commitment? And who asked you to make any commitment?"

"Connie, you can tell how things are going. I. . .can't help myself when I'm around you. And the last thing in the world I want to do is hurt you."

"I see. Well, just walk on off then, Maury Donovan. Now. I don't understand why we're having this conversation. In case you think for some bizarre reason that I have some sort of feeling for you and you were about to hurt me, you can think again. I can take care of myself. And if you don't mind, Sir, I'd like to finish this walk by myself. This warm, dear cat is all I need." She scooped up the cat and marched on around the pond.

"Connie!" He grabbed her arm; she jerked it away. "Connie, I'm sorry if I said that all wrong. Look, I'm a big dunce."

"Yes, you are! For once you're absolutely right. You're a dunce because you think you can get away from commitments by hanging between earth and sky. Well, you can't!"

"Now wait a minute. I do make commitments. How do you think I keep a school running?"

"Not very well. That's how. You hate being a principal more than anything."

It was nearly dark now, and in her fury she didn't notice the uneven spot along the bank. She tripped and would have probably tumbled down into the pond if Maury's strong arms hadn't caught her in an iron grip. She thought she heard bones cracking, he squeezed her so hard. When he set her on a level surface and let her go, he stood still over her a minute, a towering dark figure, his face shadowed, his breathing uneven. Her last angry whiplash had taken the last spark out of her, and now she wished she could take it all back. But it was too late. Maury Donovan grunted something that she didn't understand and walked briskly up the hill to his car, where gravel spun under his tires as he left.

That know-it-all man! That infuriating, egotistical man! Why did I have the rotten luck to fall in love with someone I don't even like? She borrowed a hand from cuddling the cat to swipe at hot tears.

Chapter 9

The Christmas holidays were terribly long. Connie thought it would be so wonderful to be home learning about her sister's college experiences and sharing with Mother some of her problems with the children. And, of course, visiting the neighbors, going to her own church, carrying fruit baskets to the shut-ins, and caroling on Christmas Eve. But this year nothing was the same. Her sister was furious with her for "doing Henry" so badly. Her parents didn't understand either, though her father did remind her, "To thine own self be true," implying that, understood or not, she had to stick to her own resolves.

And everywhere she went, whatever she was doing, Maury Donovan was never far from her thoughts, though she knew miserably that he wasn't thinking of her. If he had been, he would have done something about it by now, whether he was afraid of losing his freedom or not. After all those things she had said to him, he'd probably never give her one of those wonderful smiles again. She'd considered apologizing, but too much of what she'd said was true. She was only sorry she'd said it all, but she couldn't take it back. She'd have to do as he did and cover her feelings with activity.

Mother helped her create a touching bag, filled with cardboard letters and numbers and household objects to use in games with her slower children. She read thirstily from her new book by Gilbert Morris and from a volume of Robert Frost poetry, and she even helped give a birthday party for her eighty-year-old grandmother.

But still the days were far too long. She wondered what Mrs. Haburn was doing, and if her children from icy Maine had arrived home in time for Christmas. She was glad she'd finally confided in Mrs. Haburn her feelings for Maury Donovan. At least now someone knew, someone who would pray for her every day. She realized more than ever how important it was to have someone praying for her. Of course Mother would have prayed if she'd known. She was tempted to tell her, too, but it seemed as if one person knowing was all she could stand. How could she explain to Mother that she had fallen in love with the man about whom she'd written such irate letters?

She persuaded her parents she should go back to Mrs. Haburn's the Friday before school started. Her mother was really upset about it, but Connie's dad defended her, saying it would be a lot safer not to be traveling on Sunday at the end of a big holiday and, anyway, she needed time to get settled in before starting back to work.

Connie's reason for going back, if she were honest with herself, was a slight hope that she might catch a glimpse of Maury Donovan.

But the minute she turned into Mrs. Haburn's driveway, she knew she wasn't going to place herself anywhere that Maury Donovan might be until Sunday morning.

It started snowing after church Sunday. On the way home, flakes kissed the windshield, then whirled at them in fuzzy fury. Connie was thrilled, never having lived where it snowed much before now. She was also glowing inside from the warmth of the big smile Maury had shot at her as he began the song service that morning. Maybe he would come over and walk in the snow with her.

Of course she knew he wouldn't. And he didn't. Not that day nor the next three days when the snow was so thick on the ground there was no getting up Mrs. Haburn's steep driveway. Good thing Mrs. Haburn had a healthy stack of wood on the porch for her kitchen heater. Even in that protected place, the women had to knock snow off the logs before bringing them in. The logs hissed with dampness when they were first added to the fire.

The kitchen table was a cozy spot for playing Scrabble, eating popcorn, and just talking over mugs of cocoa. Outside, Connie formed a snowman, complete with carrot nose and top hat. Mrs. Haburn, who wouldn't step past the porch, told all sorts of stories about the good old days when it was safe to eat snow cream and when the pond froze so thick a cow could cross it. All in all, it was a really wonderful time. But Connie was ecstatic when the sun came out.

The first few days back in school tried Connie's endurance considerably. All the children were like tightly wound tops, and by the end of the second week Connie was beginning to wonder if the rest of the year was going to be like that. All the excuses of too much candy, too much confinement, and too much spoiling had been worn out. When she woke in predawn darkness on Friday morning hearing rain on the roof, Connie groaned, buried her head deep in her pillow, then saw a vision of bright-cheeked children playing various homemade band instruments. She sat up in bed excited at the challenge. Yes! Today they would have a band. She'd been saving materials for just such an occasion.

Connie thought Maury Donovan would be tied up in a board meeting nearly all day, and besides, he hadn't stuck his head in her room once all week, so why should he today? Anyway, the children needed a healthy outlet for their pent-up feelings, and she intended to make it available.

There were five drummers that day; they made their drums from oatmeal boxes. Rob even held the drum she made for him and awkwardly beat on it. His ear-to-ear grin at hearing his own noise made Connie want to hug him. There was a little boy behind those blank eyes!

Marie was leader of the comb section because she could carry a tune so well. Combs encased in plastic wrap tickled children's lips as they hummed into them, making a sound not too dissimilar from the droning of bees.

Only five children made shakers with juice cans and dried pinto beans. But it sounded as if their whole wing of the building might just fall in. And all to the shuffle of six or seven sand-block creators.

The project was quite a success, even if Richard could never be persuaded to play a drum, shuffle sand blocks, or anything, and simply sat at his desk drawing spiders. Spiders were his thing to draw that day.

But success or not, an entire morning devoted to making and playing band instruments was not recognized as good teacher planning. When Mr. Donovan heard the ruckus coming from Miss Jensen's room, he steered his visiting board member toward the other end of the building. However, the noise was so obvious that the member, an elegant silver-haired woman, insisted they check in on it.

Connie would never forget the look on Maury Donovan's face when he opened her door that day. She saw his total surprise, followed by delight, quickly curtained by dismay and horror.

The children hadn't been happier all week. At that particular moment they were in excellent form, Connie thought, for they were marching in step to a lively recording of "The Grand Old Flag," with one little boy carrying the stars and stripes and everyone but Richard and Rob playing their new instruments. Desks were arranged so the band could wind among them, making a longer parade route, and Connie herself had gotten carried away at the moment and was standing up on one desk, directing. She used a fly swatter for a baton, that being the best she could lay her hands on quickly.

Connie left her directing to meet her guests, but she didn't stop the band from playing until Mr. Donovan yelled at her with the voice of an enraged bull. His thunder scared their visitor almost as much as it did Connie, but the children kept on marching. However, Connie was able to have them in their seats and quiet in less than sixty seconds and that so impressed the silver-haired woman she forgave her for her light approach to teaching. Of course Connie didn't hear the woman tell Mr. Donovan that he was to be commended for allowing teachers of various personalities some freedom. If she had, she would have understood even less why he was such a bear about the whole thing.

When Connie responded to Mr. Donovan's summons and sat before his desk, she saw no humor around his mouth nor in his sky blue eyes.

"I thought we understood each other about teaching methods, Miss Jensen."

"Yes, Sir. But the children have been extremely restless all week, and sometimes you just have to let them relax."

"They can relax when they get home to their cartoons," he said in a blistering voice. "Relaxing them is not our job. Our job is to be sure every one of them knows how to read!"

"Oh, but they do. All of them are doing pretty well now except Richard and, of course, Rob. Speaking of Richard reminds me. . . What's this about Billy Ray being moved to another foster home? Are his parents making inquiries? When can he come back here?"

"Miss Jensen, do not try to swerve from the subject! Oh dear, what was I talking about?" He wearily drew a hand across his forehead.

She smiled benignly and slid to the front of her seat. "I was asking about Billy Ray, Mr. Donovan. When do you think he could come back?"

Mr. Donovan swiveled his chair toward a window behind him and dropped his dark head into his hands. His shoulders vibrated like a pecan tree having its nuts shaken down. He was laughing at her! Well, that was better by far than anger. When he finally turned, he'd mustered some semblance of solemnity, but his eyes were moist.

"Billy Ray is better off where he is. His teacher is an acquaintance of mine, a really good man. And, no, I don't know when Billy Ray will get out. The disciplinary committee wouldn't allow me to negotiate with them at all. Lots of times children are in Alpine for a whole year, but it's usually at least half a year. Anyway, as I said, he's actually better off where he is."

"You don't really believe that. You don't believe Billy Ray is better off where he is. You've seen my children's scores and you know very well they're improving remarkably. Oh, sure, I make mistakes. That parade was out of line—actually, they were in step very well, if I do say so—and I won't digress like that again. But you can't believe Billy Ray is better off in a school where he's bound to be hearing curse words from other ill-reared children, where he must arrive every morning convinced he's a doomed and terrible child."

"Miss Jensen! Hey, that's not the way it is at Alpine. If you will just listen a minute. Calm down, will you?" He had come around the desk and propped on the edge of it, looking down at her with a worried frown. "Hey, don't go to pieces on me. I'm counting on you. Listen now. You want to visit Billy Ray? I'll give you the new directions, okay?"

When she left there several minutes later with directions in her hand, she felt giddy with relief. Not that she'd escaped Maury Donovan's lecture on impromptu bands, but because she was going again to see the little boy who'd so oddly won her affection. And because Maury cared enough to help her, even if it were only professional caring.

❀

She began visiting Billy Ray regularly every Wednesday afternoon. He'd never trusted her, but she hoped that would change. At least he devoured Mrs. Haburn's huge tea cakes she took him. That first visit, Connie took a dozen cookies, thinking he could save some for his foster brothers and sisters. He ate all twelve in her presence. After he'd eaten six she began pleading with him to share, but he grunted that they were his and he wanted to eat them himself. She worried all the way home that he might have gotten sick. Next time she took only six. He looked very disappointed when he opened the box and ate the six as quickly as Connie might eat one. It was on the third visit he began to talk a little.

"I don't like this place."

"I know. I don't either."

"But you should like it," he said, looking up at her with those wide blue eyes.

"Why should I like it?"

"Because you're a grown-up. Grown-ups like all bad and awful stuff."

She smiled. "Sorry, Billy Ray. I guess I'm odd. I don't like this place because you're not happy here. Can you tell me why you're not happy here?"

He considered a minute as he played with a napkin his foster mother had laid by his frosted juice before she'd gone out with the other children. "Well. It's a nice place. No one whips me. Nothin' like that. Just that. . .I do miss my fam'ly. An' I don't like bein' so clean. We have to take a bath every night!"

Connie choked back a giggle. "I'll do my best to get you back to Pine Ridge. No promises about the baths, though. Are you being very exceptionally, unbelievably good?"

He was scornful. "You know I'm not."

"Well, I want you to be. That's how you'll get to go home, see? And I want you back in my classroom. I miss you, Billy Ray. I need you to help me with Richard. He's been so—"

"Don't you say a bad word about my cousin!" The calm blue eyes blazed.

"Okay, okay. But I'm worried about Richard. I want to help him. And I know you could make the difference."

"How's. . .Mr. Donovan? I thought he'd come to see me. Last foster home they put me in, he came."

Something stirred in Connie's brain.

"Oh, you know principals," she said. "They have so much to worry about. But he remembers you. He made arrangements for me to come."

"I'd rather he'd come himself. Is he gone flying instead?"

"Flying! How do you know about that?" Connie closed the magazine she'd been flipping through.

"He has pictures on his walls. He flies and he jumps with parachutes. He's a really brave man."

❀

In bed that night, Connie thought about what Billy Ray had said, that Mr. Donovan was a "really brave man." Maybe he was brave, but bravery in the skies wasn't doing Billy Ray any good while he stayed cooped up in that little house and cramped yard so far from his family and from his pet chicken. She must persuade Maury Donovan that he needed to visit the little boy again. It would do Billy Ray so much good to see his hero, to know he cared that much.

But apparently Mr. Donovan didn't care that much. Connie couldn't get any commitment out of him for a one-hour visit. She used the guilt complex angle, the pleading pose, the all-American-duty argument, but all to no avail.

But Billy Ray would still see his hero. She'd cooked up a scheme that would help her feelings as well as Billy Ray's, she hoped.

It had stung her over and over, thinking of Maury Donovan assuming that she might be falling for him. On top of that was the implication that of course she would "make him" stop skydiving if they were engaged. Such a male chauvinist, right here in the twenty-first century! He should have lived in the nineteenth century instead, except then his skydiving thrills might have been a bit tamer.

Would she be afraid for Maury to sky dive if she were engaged to him? Probably so. But she hoped she might be like Betty Friedman and have faith when the time came. Not that she thought that time was coming. Somehow, though, it was important to prove to Maury Donovan that flying was not such an all-powerful big deal to her. The only way to prove how she might react would be to place herself once again in the middle of the action. Only this time, she'd get closer to the action. She'd fly with the pilot and take pictures of the jumpers as they left the plane. And she'd have lots of colorful pictures to give Billy Ray to have for his very own.

She was so pleased with her plan that she could hardly contain her excitement as she purchased fast film and a new zoom lens. For practice, she took a zillion pictures of the children swinging, running, and climbing on the playground. She visited photo shops, bugging owners with her questions, and even audited a class at North Georgia Tech in Clarkesville for several weeks. In the meantime, she tracked down Betty and Jock Friedman and talked them into letting her try her scheme. Of course she only told them she wanted pictures for Billy Ray. They could think whatever else they wanted to, but she did ask them not to tell anyone her plan, not even Maury Donovan. They were really nice folks, and she believed they'd keep her secret.

❀

When the appointed Saturday in early March finally arrived, Connie's eyes only blinked once at dawning light before she bounced out of bed and ran to her front window to see if there was fog on her mountain. All she saw were baby clouds that would soon burn off. She dressed in a hurry, explained to Mrs. Haburn she had a busy day in Toccoa, and moved on without even any breakfast. She thought that not eating would be prudent.

❀

Mrs. Haburn watched half-hidden behind a curtain as Connie left. What could she be up to? If Connie weren't such a sweet Christian, Mrs. Haburn would almost think she were a criminal the way she'd been sneaking around. Connie had made sure Mrs. Haburn had her grocery list ready on Friday this week, and they'd already been to town. So she couldn't complain. But no one could stop her from wondering and worrying. This sudden trip had to have something to do with that unpredictable Maury Donovan.

She'd warned Connie from the very start about Maury Donovan, but only as a principal, not dreaming she'd develop any deeper relationship. Granted, he was really quite appealing in a rough kind of way. There was something about him she just couldn't help liking herself. But he was mixed up. Didn't seem to have his life in focus.

"Guess I'm awful picky, Lord," Mrs. Haburn whispered. "Henry is stable and focused, even if on himself. And we didn't want him. But this man. He's gonna break Connie's heart. I feel it. But, dear Lord, as old as I am, You'd think I'd remember to ask for help and quit worryin'. I guess I'll never learn, hmmm?" She eased her aching knees to a rag rug before a well-worn old stuffed chair and continued talking out loud, the cat coming to purr ecstatically, curling around one sweatered elbow.

❀

Connie turned on her radio to hear the weather news as she headed toward Gainesville. Seemed silly going so far to get on the plane. Since Maury and his friends would jump over Toccoa's airport this time, why didn't they get on the plane there? But Jock's plane was in Gainesville. He said they would all start together there.

"Clear, beautiful skies," chatted the weatherman. "Perfect day for doing whatever makes you happy. Plant those bulbs. Cut your firewood. Enjoy the sunshine while you can." She smiled. Planting bulbs was what she should be doing. But instead, she was going flying!

She was scared and excited. Was this a tiny bit of how Maury might feel about now? Almost unconsciously she began to sing the old hymn Maury seemed to like so much: "There's a land that is fairer than day, and by faith I can see it afar, for the Father waits over the way, to prepare us a dwelling place there. In the sweet by and by. . ."

Chapter 10

Jock Friedman hadn't been happy about Connie's flying with him that day. But letting her go had seemed the human thing to do. And Jock was a warm-hearted individual who didn't say no unless he absolutely had to. He should have told Maury about it, though. That was the least he could have done for his friend to save him from the jolt as they were all boarding. Maury either hated her dreadfully or loved her, Jock was sure, for his tan turned to chalk, and he almost jerked the woman's arm off trying to get her out of the plane.

This was the teacher Maury had told him about, the one he'd groaned over as he told his friend, "What if this is the one? But I can't give everything up just now. I'm not ready." Jock grinned, remembering. Could be his friend, Maury, had finally been stung enough he'd realize some things are worth making arrangements for. Of course Jock couldn't say very much about that because his Betty had made all the adaptations in their life. But right now he'd leave the sky and never sweep it again if that's what it took to keep Betty.

As he looked down on apple orchards, pastures, and sprawling developments, he wondered why all the jumpers were so quiet. They couldn't communicate without shouting because of the wind noise caused by the large opening ready for them to exit. But they usually tried, or some did. He'd never flown such a quiet group as this. He glanced around and saw only stony faces. All of them were angry. Oh, boy. And the woman his wife had talked him into flying, Connie Jensen, was white as bleached sheets.

❀

"Get her a baggy, will you, Maury?" he barked. It was the most humiliating moment in Connie's life. And there was more to come.

She blamed her sickness, not only on the throbbing motion but also on the heat. It was so nauseatingly hot in that plane. She managed to get her jacket off, but the nausea clung to her until she felt weak as melted butter. Or maybe it was the noise. It was such a pounding, shuddering noise made by wind beating around the large door opening. Or was the bright light making her sick? The searing intensity of it invaded her completely. She couldn't wear dark glasses and take pictures, and so the light pinned her in place like a speared butterfly. Grabbing the baggy again, she lost the breakfast she hadn't eaten and thought limply that this was far worse than being seasick.

She heard Jock's shouts pointing out landmarks as they approached Toccoa—Lake Louise, Hartwell Lake Road, Tugalo Reservoir, Currahee Mountain—and she tried with rubbery fingers to get her camera ready. Sick or not, she'd get these pictures. She wouldn't let a little nausea stop her. She snapped a few pictures of the jumpers lining up. It was an awesome thing, sixteen men lining up in the seatless DC-3. Of course there wasn't room for one straight line so they wove their line, or lines. Every man knew exactly where he belonged.

One jumper knelt on the floor of the plane by the door on the left side of the fuselage near the tail. Periodically, he stuck his head out the opening into the wind stream and looked down at the ground. Jock had just told them they were flying at 10,500 feet. When this jumper kept sticking his head out, Connie was forced to use her baggy again. Seeing his face out in the wind stream was worse than a ghost movie; his skin actually blew so his cheeks looked hollow and folds appeared near his eyes and sideburns. Twice he signaled Jock to turn the plane slightly, then finally yelled, "Cut!"

As Jock pulled back the throttle on the engine, the spotter, as they called him, grasped the front inner edge of the doorframe and swung his body outside the plane. Connie clung to her camera as if it could save her and tried closing her eyes tightly but opened them again in spite of herself. What next?

In seconds there were three men outside the plane, clinging to edges of the opening with bare hands. This was worse than any nightmare Connie had ever had. She tried to remember why she'd had this harebrained idea and couldn't. But she took pictures. It was the only way to keep from fainting.

Teeth chattering from nervousness, Connie cautiously took a look at the faces of the men lined up inside the plane. They were all perfectly quiet, each one staring straight ahead, each suited in bold-colored nylon, some with a tight fitting sort of headgear with goggles, others bareheaded. Each jumper pressed his chest and arms tightly against the beach pack or parachute of the one in front of him and stood with his left foot forward and right foot behind. All this was as Jock had explained it to her with diagrams many hours ago on safe earth. She wanted Maury to look at her. Just once. But he was like a person in a trance, his eyes trained on the man ahead of him.

The very last jumper in line, a short, small man with a crew cut, suddenly snapped, "Hot!" Connie couldn't agree more but realized immediately that was a code word. Now the jumpers were rocking and yelling, "Ready! Set! Go!" As they rocked, the middle floater, one of the three men outside the plane, pushed his hips farther out into the airstream, then rocked back toward the inside, pulling himself by the doorframe, then out again. All the jumpers rocked simultaneously toward the door, then back.

Connie clenched her bottom lip in terror. She was too scared now to be sick.

The whole plane was rocking horribly, and she herself was only a couple feet from the door. As everyone shouted, "Go!" she put her camera to her face and began clicking. In seconds, when all sixteen men were gone, she sagged forward in exhaustion.

"You all right, Connie?"

"Sure, Jock. Fine."

"I'll try to get you in position for some shots of their formations if I can. Hold tight."

"Don't worry," Connie breathed.

"You know, to them these seconds are a long time. You have a feeling of eternity when you're out there free-falling. Sometimes you're flying horizontally with the earth, and time stands still, though you're still going a good 110 miles an hour."

Connie sucked in air. "They're going. . .that fast?"

"Oh, sometimes 200 when flying vertically. But they'll slow to a mere 10 or 15 miles an hour when their canopies are up. But there now, Connie, if you'll lean near the opening, you can get some shots of their sixteen-man diamond. She's a beaut! Oh, wow!"

Connie was glad Jock was so enthusiastic that he didn't notice how timid she was about getting near the door. She did see the diamond made up of men in bright suits holding to each other a little like children making angels in the snow. It was spellbinding, as were the subsequent four-man diamonds that formed out of that one. It was perfect timing and maneuvering.

"Amazing, isn't it?" shouted Jock, letting out an involuntary yodel. "Only God could make creatures that coordinated!"

"Yes. Only God," said Connie. She guessed that about now Maury Donovan had that look of pure joy on his windblown face.

As Jock landed the plane, Connie wished that she'd stayed on the ground and watched the formations from below. It would have been much prettier and a lot less harrowing. Her bravery had turned out to be purely wimpy, and she shuddered at what Maury must think of her now. Well, she'd tried. At least she'd have some pictures for Billy Ray, albeit wobbly and blurred.

Connie knew she must still look shaken when Betty Friedman, who had driven up to be part of the ground excitement, offered her a ride back to Gainesville to get her car. "But first we'll all have lunch together here in Toccoa," said Betty. "The celebration after the jump is my favorite part." Her brown eyes shone with inner light.

While the men got out of their suits, Connie and the Friedmans watched airport activities. Still feeling a bit queasy, Connie headed for the rest room and literally ran into the tall, spare lady she'd identified months earlier as Maury's mother. Stepping aside in confusion, mumbling apologies, Connie then moved toward the door, but the woman touched her arm.

"Wait," she said. "Didn't you fly today with my son? I thought I saw you getting on Maury Donovan's plane."

"Yes. Yes, I. . .I took pictures," answered Connie, glad her camera was still around her neck.

"Oh. I see. I don't suppose you'd be able to give him a message for me? I'm Mrs. Donovan, Maury's mother."

"How do you do? I'm Connie Jensen, a teacher at Pine Ridge."

"Yes, of course, I should have known," said Mrs. Donovan, seeming to make a quick assessment of Connie's appearance. "Will you give my son a message, please?"

"Why. . .yes. But he'll be back soon, I think. He's just changing."

Mrs. Donovan nodded impatiently. "Tell him I'll expect him for supper tonight. About seven. I must run now."

"Sure. I'll tell him," said Connie, feeling stupid since by then Mrs. Donovan was several fast paces toward the outer door.

Inside the rest room, Connie stared at her pale, tousled look. No wonder Mrs. Donovan had eyed her so strangely. She pulled a brush from her bag and began to work at smoothing a million tangles out of her hair.

At Bell's Restaurant, Betty insisted on Connie's sitting at a table with her and Jock. They'd been seated only a moment when Maury slid into the fourth seat. His face was glowing with excitement as he turned to Connie exactly as if he'd never been grumpy or tried to throw her off the plane.

"How did you like it?" he asked.

"After I got through the ground attack it was really fine," said Connie, lifting her chin stubbornly.

"A bit airsick, weren't you?" Maury's mouth wasn't smiling, but his eyes were.

"Oh, she was quite plucky, that one," said Jock, setting his menu down. "I think she's already got her color back, don't you, Maury?"

"Don't tease the poor woman, you guys. She did do it, after all. That's more than can be said about me," said Betty wistfully, her full lips slightly pouting.

The next hour was so pleasant with Maury close by, exclaiming over the joys of free falling and successful formations, Connie almost forgot the message she was to deliver. When it came to her, she impulsively laid a hand on Maury's and leaned toward him.

"Did you know your mother was at the airport, Maury?"

"No. She couldn't have been. She doesn't ever come. It makes her very sick."

"But she was there. I met her."

His eyebrows went up. "You did?"

"Well. It was an accident. I ran into her." In spite of herself, Connie couldn't keep from giggling as she replayed the scene in her mind. "But anyway, she remembered seeing me get on your plane, and she asked me to tell you to please come to supper about seven."

"You're sure she didn't say she'd expect me to come to supper?"

"Something like that," she agreed, folding her napkin.

Betty Friedman broke the silence that had fallen on them. "One of you guys get the waitress's attention. I want a big fattening dessert and some coffee. Connie, what would you like? Peach cobbler and ice cream? Or a hot fudge brownie?"

Connie groaned, then laughed. "Just coffee, I think."

Much later, as Connie confessed the day's adventure to Mrs. Haburn, it occurred to her again how Mrs. Donovan's message had been like a splash of cold springwater on their party. Had she intended it that way? Or did she really want to rejoice with her son and just didn't know how? If she was afraid of flying, well, Connie could understand that part! But refusing to accept something as important as this was to Maury, that was another matter.

❦

Soon after Connie retrieved her photos from the drugstore, she took them to Maury's office to show him. Though he'd teased her good-naturedly at the after-jump lunch, she didn't know for sure how her flight test had turned out until he looked at those pictures.

"I can't believe you really did that," he said, flipping through the stack of photos.

"Did what? Took such terrible pictures?"

"No. Went up with us that day. I. . .never realized it would mean so much. Even if you did so generously feed the bag," he remembered with a chuckle.

She flushed self-consciously. "I was pretty disgusted with myself that day. For being such a wimp, you know."

"Connie you're so far from being a wimp, you wouldn't even know one if you saw one." He looked up from the pictures as he spoke, and Connie saw admiration in his eyes. The horrors of the flight were well worth that look!

He glanced at a wall clock then and said, "Here, you better take these—quick. I've got work to do here. Mrs. Gurdy is coming in a minute. But. . .oh, yes, by the way, when you deliver those to Billy Ray, you'll need new directions." He put his hands behind his head and leaned back in his squeaky desk chair, looking smug.

"Why? Why new directions? Another foster home?"

"Yes. One near here. He's been so good, they're transferring him back."

She squealed in excitement and clasped her hands together. "Oh, thank you, thank you!" she exclaimed. "Tell me. Tell me right now where he is."

"You realize how much more work it will be for you having him here? And he's not the most grateful little guy I've seen!"

"Oh, but, Maury. . .Mr. Donovan. . .he wants to come back. He's going

179

to be good because he wants to stay here. I really believe that boy's going to do something great someday."

"Well, I hope it's a good great. Hope he doesn't end up in the state pen. Anyway, I'll have to do as before and incorporate his studying into my office routine. Just prepare individual lesson plans for me to use, please, along the lines you're using with your other children right now, until we see how far he's progressed while he was gone."

"May I go see him today? It might help the transition."

"No. Because the fact remains Billy Ray did pull a knife on you. There's no kind of security at this foster home, and it's in a pretty remote area. I can't let you go, not yet."

She was going to ask him about the home, but Mrs. Gurdy came bustling in, her usual hat pushed back a little farther than usual. "Well, I guess you know your troublemaker's coming back," she announced, looking at Connie as she plopped into a winged chair.

"No. Just Billy Ray," murmured Connie and, with a parting look at Maury, she left.

As she hurried down the hall, questions zinged around in her head: *What about Billy Ray's parents and the other children? Who had gotten Billy Ray freed from Alpine? Maury?* What other secrets was he saving under that thick hair of his?

❀

That week at church, several young adults were trying to organize a hike down into Tallulah Gorge before the weather got warm. They wanted Maury to be their guide. He'd done it before, they said, and knew the best way to go. Besides, according to several, Maury was the guy you'd want around if anything went wrong.

"And he's really a lot of fun, too," one young woman added, sounding a little defensive. Connie couldn't help smiling, thinking of Maury's moods of grim concentration that shadowed the moments when love of life itself shone from his face.

Maury agreed, with reservations. It meant pinning down a Saturday three weeks away, which might turn out to be a jewel of a flying Saturday, Connie knew. If a choice had to be made, she knew which way he'd go, and it wouldn't be hiking.

With growing excitement, Connie looked forward to the hike. Maury had told her that afternoon months ago when they looked into the gorge that he'd show her the way down sometime. She'd like to have had him alone, but this was far better than nothing. After all, they'd both shied away from private meetings since his brutal pronouncement by the pond, thwarting something before it could begin. Connie still felt a strong pull between them, and she prayed every day that if Maury Donovan were the man for her, God would unkink the ropes that kept them knotted away from each other.

Billy Ray had turned into a model student. His foster mother sent him to school every day with his hair clean and combed and, after a few bouts with old classmates who'd forgotten how strong Billy Ray was, he began arriving with an unbloodied nose, too.

It was obvious to Connie that he nearly worshiped Maury Donovan. Billy Ray was even making progress in learning his addition facts with Mr. Donovan's strict rote teaching. He'd set Billy Ray to work, then be on the phone, working on his reams of paperwork, or even stepping down the hall to visit a classroom. Billy Ray would have the work done on time and brightly ask for more.

Sometimes Connie managed to leave her children with an aide long enough to play a game with Billy Ray using her touching bag of letters and numbers. But soon that was totally unnecessary. Billy Ray had broken the code.

Connie and Mrs. Haburn began picking Billy Ray up for Sunday school each week. Maury cautioned Connie not to get so involved with a pupil; then he himself began interesting Billy Ray in his boys' mission group. Billy Ray made quite an impression on teachers and children at church. For awhile it looked as if they might have to leave him at home for the sake of other children who'd never heard such language at church. But he began improving, and Phil Stone insisted they give him more time.

"If the church can't minister to little guys like this, it's not much good, is it?" he asked.

❀

"I guess I'll renew my contract," said Zena in the teachers' lounge one day. "At least I know sort of what's expected here."

"If we have the same principal next year," said Mrs. Gurdy.

Connie almost spilled her coffee. "What do you mean?" she blurted out.

"Why, I'm surprised you don't realize, as much as you've been in and out of Mr. Donovan's office. It's obvious a change is brewing. For one thing, his mother is on the board of education, and if she got him this job, then I reckon she can move him to another as well. I know she's called him three times lately about something, and she's not one of your chatty kind of people."

"I don't think that indicates he'd be making a change, Lora," put in one of the other teachers.

"No. But a visit from the superintendent with a prospective principal in tow might be."

"How could you know a man was a prospective principal?"

"I know one when I see one," said Mrs. Gurdy smugly. "And it wasn't a man either."

Connie couldn't forget this conversation, though she'd never set great store on what Mrs. Gurdy said. Still, the woman did have an uncanny art for knowing things no one else had heard or seen. She'd probably have been a good police detective. Now Connie couldn't decide whether to sign her contract for another year. She'd never intended to stay more than one year, but where would Maury be, and was there any hope he'd ever love her the way she loved him? If she left, there wouldn't be a chance. Yet if she stayed, she might just be asking for another year of misery.

She was thinking about this as she walked down the hall one afternoon, responding to a call from the principal to come to his office. He hadn't raked her over the coals lately, and it was about time, she guessed. She'd taught Marie how to sew on buttons last week and he'd probably found out about that. Or he was upset because Richard, as bright as he seemed to be, still could not read other than the words *it*, and, *see*, and *I, me, you*.

When she walked into the office, she knew something was terribly wrong. And it wasn't just because Maury Donovan was standing at his window, staring out at the mountains. There was a heavy feeling in the air. She sat down quietly and waited a few minutes, then cleared her throat. He spun as if he'd been shot. His face had lines as deep as the gorge, lines that had not been there the day before, and his hair seemed extra black against his pale face. He touched the corner of his desk as he moved toward her, never releasing her from his gaze.

Pulling her to her feet, he held her against him, and she felt him shaking. "It's Jock," he whispered hoarsely. "He crashed. In the mountains."

"Jock? But that can't be! He is so careful!"

"Careful isn't enough. Here, you'd better sit down."

"How? How did it happen?" Connie asked, dreading the details.

"I don't know except that he crashed in the mountains, and he was dead when rescuers reached him. They called me because I was his best friend. They want me to. . ."

"You have to tell Betty?"

He nodded, and her own eyes stung with tears for both of them, for all of them. Dear Jock! So compassionate, funny, and bright! Gone—just like that!

"Connie. . .please. . .go with me."

"Yes. Of course I will."

It was the hardest thing she'd ever done in her life. But Betty made it easier for both of them. It was as if she'd always known it would happen sometime. She cried. But she didn't go into hysterics. In the end, she was down on her knees in front of Maury, comforting him, or trying to.

Maury couldn't be comforted. Betty wanted him to sing at the funeral, but he refused. Connie understood. It would have been entirely too hard. But she didn't understand the way Maury shut others out and withdrew into himself. He was a

Christian, and Jock had been a Christian. Jock had died doing what he wanted to do. So what was there to be bitter about? And who was he bitter toward?

It sounded as if he thought God should have reached down and become pilot of the plane when Jock had his heart attack. Instead He had smiled from the sky and watched him fall. Maybe Maury felt that way about his father's death, too, as if God should have opened that bottle of medicine for him.

More and more distance formed between Maury Donovan and those around him. He was like a bear routed early out of hibernation or a cornered rattlesnake. The sunshine had left his eyes.

Chapter 11

When Billy Ray was placed again in Connie's room, she was nervous. It wasn't that she was afraid of Billy Ray. She'd never believed Billy Ray felt personally malicious toward her anyway. She was nervous because she didn't want him to lose all the emotional ground he'd gained, and she wasn't sure how she should deal with him.

As far as that went, who did she know how to deal with? Quiet, bright Richard, who could make a beautiful picture of a kite but couldn't spell it? Or Rob, who could only write his name on good days? Or Marie, who could read circles around everyone now and needed so much more challenge than time seemed to allow? Just as her mother had predicted, Connie felt that after a year's teaching she knew less than she had when she'd started.

Connie had been shocked to learn from Maury that Billy Ray's whole family had moved and left no forwarding address. They hadn't taken his pet chicken. Worse than that. They'd left it to starve, and Maury had found it in the corner of its pen, a rotten mass of feathers. He'd had to report this to Billy Ray since he asked continually about his chicken. But the boy so adored Mr. Donovan that he had appeared to work through all this trauma and be happier than he'd ever been before.

Now, for whatever reason, Mr. Donovan canceled his sessions with Billy Ray. Mrs. Gurdy said she'd known all along he wouldn't stick to such a routine. What principal would, or should, as a matter of fact? A principal should do his job, teachers theirs. Connie personally was convinced it was because of Jock's death. He needed more time, she supposed. She wasn't Billy Ray's choice, but she'd have to do her best, that was all, whether Billy Ray liked it or not.

Most teachers had trouble with their pupils talking too much. That hadn't been Connie's trouble with Billy Ray before his suspension. It was when he hadn't talked he'd become frightening. Now, though, he seemed actually pretty glad to be back in his own desk at last. And he talked a lot.

He found he could get the attention of the whole class by telling stories he made up. Everyone's favorite was the tale about Billy Ray and his pa, killing a wildcat with their bare hands. Connie saw this storytelling as a building time and let him have a good bit of freedom. But she began to notice that more and more of his fantastic tales were centered around sky divers in some way or another.

"I know a sky diver myself," he concluded a story one day. "I'm not telling who it is, but I can tell you this. He's gonna let me go with him one of these days. Sometime I'll see him come whizzing down like Superman. Whoosh!" Billy Ray stood on his desk and demonstrated a quick descent to the delight of the other children.

"Okay, okay, Billy Ray," said Connie. "Enough of that now. Let's get back to when we use capital or uppercase letters. If Billy Ray had been writing his story..."

Another time Billy Ray confided in Connie as he stood at her desk while she checked his workbook. "Mr. Donovan's gonna take me skydiving. He promised. You'll see, Miss Jensen."

"Sure, Billy Ray," she countered, trying to make light of it.

Had Maury really promised to take Billy Ray to watch the skydiving? She was sure he hadn't. Or hadn't meant to anyway. She needed to ask him, but nowadays there never seemed the right moment to ask him anything.

When she learned from Jean that Phil Stone had persuaded Maury to keep his promise to guide their young adult church group on a hike down into Tallulah Gorge, Connie was surprised and excited. He hadn't given up everything, after all. And surely that day she'd have a chance to ask him just what he'd promised Billy Ray.

❀

The day they'd chosen dawned chilly but clear and ice free. Mrs. Haburn grumbled good-naturedly as she prepared oatmeal and cheese toast. "Foolhardiest thing you've done yet, outside of flying in a plane with the door off. What will it be next? Planning any underwater adventures? Just don't tell me about 'em. You know, you're likely gonna break a leg and have to hobble around like me. Or break your head on a rock an' have to be spoon-fed the rest o' yer life. Do you really want that?"

"No, Ma'am." Connie laughed. She was in bubbling good spirits. "I'll be totally and absolutely careful. I promise."

❀

As a person looking down from above becomes familiar with Tallulah Gorge's facial features, its rugged lines, idiosyncratic curves, its quirky smiles and frowns caused by differing light effects, the gorge becomes a very good acquaintance, a memorable character. But if a brave soul descends into the gorge, its very heart is exposed. This person learns not just what the gorge is like, but what it's made of, what makes it endure. And the acquaintance of surface comments becomes the friend of shared hopes.

This was the philosophy with which Maury entertained his group as he approached the gorge. Parking on a lonely promontory, he said jovially, "Here we are." He seemed more himself than he had in weeks.

The group looked around dubiously. The road by which they'd neared the edge wasn't highly traveled. On this chilly morning no one else was around, only a lone hawk, circling against a blue sky. Before them a sign warned that those who descended the gorge did so at their own risk. "Maybe this isn't such a good idea," said one or two, peering over the precipice.

"Oh, come on, folks, you knew when we started out this wasn't the thing the general public does. We've got on the right shoes; Maury knows the way. Let's go." Jean wasn't about to be stopped from this adventure.

The path Maury chose for them, the one most frequently used, he said, zigzagged down approximately 2,000 feet to a rock-lined riverbed. Connie wasn't at all sure it could be called a path in the usual sense. It certainly wasn't a walking path, only a sliding one for stretching, sideways steps only! Bushes and wind-toughened trees, slickened by hundreds of hand grips, grew between scarred ancient rocks. A foothold here, a handhold there, were sometimes plain to see, sometimes hard to be imagined.

Connie was glad she'd chosen jeans rather than corduroy shorts. Her knees would have been raw by the time she got down if she hadn't. She paused and propped against a jutting rock to swipe her sweatshirt off, exposing her bright blue T-shirt. Tying sweatshirt sleeves around her waist, she inched down to the next foothold.

"It's about as rugged a path as we can manage without needing special climbing equipment," Dave Olds remarked as he accidentally knocked dry leaves onto Connie's head.

"And I dread to think of pulling myself back up," said Connie, shaking trash out of her hair. "I'll be wishing I weighed about fifty pounds less. Is there any other way back up?"

"Don't think so," laughed Dave.

"Down by the power plant there's a rusty cable car," called Maury from below. "But we're coming back out on our own speed."

"Did you hear that, Dave?" Connie passed the message up.

"Tell him to speak for himself," said Dave.

Winded, hot, bruised, and scraped, the ten adults scrambled down over the last laurel-caressed black boulder and onto the canyon floor. Several sat down as soon as they could. Connie's knees were quivery, but she wobbled over to the water's edge to peer into a frothy pool fed by one of many small cascades. Staring at angry water made her dizzy, and she turned away only to find herself staring up at Maury's dark face. He smiled and put an arm around her to steady her.

"May not be that much water compared to what there was before 1910 or whenever they dammed the river, but it's more than you'd want to get trapped in." Maury glanced around at others who had ambled over, including them in his remarks.

"Trapped in?" asked Connie, glancing behind her.

"Yes. You get in one of these big holes and you can't get out; the sides are so steep and slick."

"Has that ever happened to anyone?" asked Jean, a touch of challenge in her voice.

"Yes, afraid so. A honeymoon couple a few years ago got in a pool. . .I suppose they thought it would be a nice whirlpool. Anyway, they never got out. They were found dead from exposure."

"Maury! You're making that up. No one found them for that long?" Dave wanted to know.

"There aren't that many people coming here all the time, so they had it to themselves for far too long. And you'd be surprised how quickly total exposure to harsh elements can deteriorate a person. All right, Dave, maybe I've got my story wrong a bit. Maybe there was a storm that made it worse. Anybody else remember?"

"Not exactly. But I remember it happening," spoke up one of the others. "Seems things like that are always happening to honeymooners, doesn't it? Love is dangerous."

"Can be," said Jean, cutting her eyes toward Connie and Maury.

"On the other hand, love can rescue the perishing," quipped Dave with a grin at his own wit.

"And the main thing is, the gorge awaits us," said Maury, waving a go-ahead signal as he strode off.

Maury's being abrupt was nothing new. Still, Connie wondered if the teasing had goaded him into rushing on. She wanted to hide her own pink blush and only hoped that anyone who might have noticed would blame it on exertion.

While the trail into the gorge hadn't been a walking trail, the one downstream was nonexistent. Since there was nothing but rocks and water, there was little to call a path. Maury's long legs stretched easily from one rock to another over rushing water, and the rest followed, not daring to lag behind for fear they'd get stranded. It reminded Connie of following a maze. Some ways seemed as good as others, but the wrong choice could lead you to a dead end. She had to do some fast thinking, as well as use fast footwork, to keep up.

She kept wishing there was time to stop and feel the unbelievable, perfectly round, smooth craters in some of the rocks that had been shaped, Maury told them, by pebbles and water beating rhythms on them for hundreds of years. But there was no time to pause until they finally came to a wide, solid rock beach that slanted toward the base of the cliff.

"There's the old lookout building, way up above us," said Jean, head tilted back. "I remember coming there when I was little. That was the main road then. Mama used to give my brother and me each a dime to look through the telescope."

"Yeah. Me, too," said one of the other women. "I can't believe I'm looking up at it from so far below. My mother wouldn't have dared let me do this. Still wouldn't if she knew." She giggled. "Oh, look, is that a weasel, Maury? I know that's a weasel!"

Maury and others watched with bated breath as the long furry creature slid out from a stunted laurel on the other side of the water, looked around, then slunk back into hiding.

"That's a weasel, all right," pronounced Maury, and Connie wondered to herself if there was anything he didn't know.

Connie found another perfect rock hole the size of a basketball and sat down beside it to run her hand around in its smoothness. Funny how the mere feel of something could be soothing, calming. Wouldn't she love it if her schoolchildren could have in their playground just one enormous wonderful rock like this with mysterious craters! But even if such a rock were available, there'd be some safety regulation against it.

"I've always wanted to come down here," said Jean, sitting down beside Connie. "Maury's right. There have been some pretty grim stories of awful things happening to people who didn't use good judgment. But isn't it beautiful down here?" She lay back on the hard floor, the better to enjoy watching the sky framed by pine-trimmed edges of canyon far above.

"It is beautiful. It's wonderful!" agreed Connie.

"Connie! Jean! Come on, let's go on down farther. Maury says watch out for ghosts. Aren't you coming?"

The women looked at each other and laughed. "We're afraid of ghosts!" Jean answered. "Besides," she added to Connie, "I'd just like to slow down and absorb some of this."

"I know." Connie lay back beside her friend, shielding her eyes with one arm, idly watching birds circling halfway up the depth of the gorge. To which world did those birds belong? Were they below their world or above it? Probably they could live in either or both. Did Maury know some of their freedom when he floated earthward at a dreamy ten miles per hour?

When another member of the group pulled Jean to her feet, insisting she go with them, Connie stayed where she was. Adventure was exciting, but she could do with some absorbing, as Jean called it. A gust of wind blew down the canyon, and Connie shivered as she pulled her sweatshirt back on. It didn't take long when she stopped moving to realize the air wasn't so warm, after all. Stretching out on the natural pavement, she drew a sigh of contentment.

"Can you imagine it in a month or two with all those laurels and rhododendrons blooming?" asked Maury, startling her so much that she almost jerked a knot in her neck.

"It must be glorious," she said, recovering her composure, at least outwardly. "More than glorious, because it already is that. Didn't the others need you to guide them down the gorge? What was that about ghosts?"

"Oh, Dave has my instructions. They don't need me. As to the ghosts. . .you may never know." His grin was full of mischief.

"And I suppose you think you've raised my curiosity now and I'm going to go leaping down the canyon."

"I hope not," he said. "Sitting here on the beach beside you is vastly more appealing than running after you right now."

She covered her crimson face with both hands, then peered between her fingers at the bulk of him sitting so very near, apparently engrossed in studying the sky.

"Since you're our guide, tell me what it was like here back at the turn of the century."

"Well, terribly busy. Hotels, several of them, full in season. A train affectionately called the TF made a run every day. Big spenders came from all over the world. It was the place to be. And Wallenda in the '70s wasn't the first to walk across it on tightrope, you know. There was a tightrope walker back in 1915 or something who was paid by a big hotel to come walk across. My grandmother remembered that."

"Your grandmother?"

"Yes. She died five years ago. And, speaking of bustling, I can remember myself, as Jean does, when that lookout building up there was as busy as a shopping center."

"Wow! And you look so young," she teased him as she sat up. She pushed her hair behind her ears, then flipped the glistening length of it over her shoulders, all the time watching his smile involve every groove and plane on his face.

"You idiot," he said, a warm light in his eyes.

Neither of them spoke for a few minutes, just enjoying sounds of rushing water, a leaf sliding across rock, the faraway drone of a plane. And each other. Then perhaps the plane reminded Maury of Jock. A shadow fell across his face.

"This place always makes me think of the song 'Rock of Ages.' I need to be able to hide myself in that Rock about now."

"Can't you?"

He ignored her question. "You know, it could be my time to go next."

The air was charged with question marks. What did he expect her to say?

She took a deep breath. "Sure. It might be me, too. Knifed by one of my students."

"But you'd be doing your job."

"Yes. I'd be doing my job."

"I'd be out having fun if I died skydiving. My mother says it's an unreasonable risk."

"Well. I guess she's kind of right, isn't she? Depends on what angle you look at it from. Your mother's called you, then?"

"Oh, yes. Several times lately."

"Do you think you should stop skydiving, Maury?"

"No! I'm not stopping!"

She was shaken by the harshness in his voice.

"I'd be only a shadow of myself without skydiving. That's where I get my inspiration. That's where I'm really me."

"Maybe you're looking at the wrong place for your inspiration," said Connie, leaning over her knees so her hair fell around her like a curtain.

"Maybe. I've been thinking the same thing. Maybe I've been worshiping creation instead of the Creator. But, Connie, I'm so confused right now, I can't sort it all out."

"You will. I know you will."

"I'm glad you know it." He stood and shoved his hands deeply into his pockets.

"Remember, God gives songs even in the night, Maury. I read that in Psalms not long ago. This is a night for you, but maybe you'll find a beautiful song in it."

"You should be a poet, the way you think," he said, turning gentle again as he knelt and reached for her hand. "Connie, I have to make a change. I can't go on fighting within myself all the time, feeling like a hypocrite half the time, a misfit the rest of the time. I know you're not going to understand this."

Her mind raced ahead of him. So he *was* giving up the principal's job. Mrs. Gurdy was right. Well, wasn't this what she'd prayed for? That he'd be put in the right spot? But now she didn't want him to leave.

"Connie, did you hear me?"

"I'm sorry, Maury, what?"

"I said I'm giving up my church job."

"Your church job? The one you love most?"

"Who said I loved it most?"

"I did." She stood up. "Maury, you can't!"

"I can. I already talked to Phil Stone."

"Maury, why?" The intensity of her question was written all over her face. To her it seemed as if her question echoed back and forth, clanging against walls of the canyon.

"I've got to become focused," answered Maury. "I've done a terrible job this year, as you well know. There are children in every grade who can hardly read road signs, much less anything else. I've got to do better."

"Quitting your music job is going to make that right?"

"I need more time to take special courses, make more resources available to teachers. You know what a rat race it is, Connie. Besides, you know I couldn't make it on my part-time musician's salary. I can't give up my school job."

"This isn't about money, and you know it."

"What, then?" His eyebrows shot up.

"It's about a debt, but not a monetary one."

His jaw was firm, his arms across his chest. "I suppose you're beginning to use your psychology on me now. Well, would you explain what you're talking about?"

She took a deep breath. "Maury Donovan, if you could teach every child in Georgia how to read, it wouldn't bring your father back. Don't you know that?"

His eyes widened as if she'd struck him. "That's not what I'm doing. That's got nothing to do with it."

"Yes, it does, it most certainly does. And maybe teaching every child to read is a worthy goal, but your motive is not. Your heart isn't in teaching or administering, certainly not administering. And I don't think God asked you to do something you don't have a heart for."

"Oh, you don't, do you?" He gripped both her arms and stared deep into her eyes. "Just what business did you have coming along, confusing me so, anyway? I knew where I was going and everything until you walked into my office."

"Well," she held his gaze steadfastly, then whispered, "maybe I'll be gone soon."

He sighed. "I knew you wouldn't like my decision. I don't like all of it myself, mainly because. . . I know you've realized how I feel about you. You'd have to. And I wish more than anything—"

"What, Maury? What do you wish more than anything?" Her face had gone from a flushed pink to white.

"That I could answer that question," he answered. "If only I knew the one thing I wanted more than anything."

She looked down at the toes of her hiking shoes and dabbed at a tear behind the drift of her hair. "You will someday," she said firmly. "I think I should be honored you cared enough to tell me a second time that you don't want to care. Somehow, right now it doesn't feel particularly good."

"Connie." His hands were warm on her shoulders, and she looked up because she couldn't help herself. She'd never before realized his eyes held varying shades of bluish lakes, each with many depths. "Whatever you think about me, know this. I want the very best for you. Contrary to the way I came across in September, I think you're a jam-up person—yes, a jam-up teacher—and I'd recommend you to anyone."

"Of course you'd send along a bottle of aspirin for my next boss, too, I suppose," she said with a grin as she heard their noisy friends returning up the canyon.

"The biggest bottle I could find," he said, letting his hands slide down her arms before he turned away.

"Maury, you clown, nary a ghost lured us into that rusty cable car!" Dave yelled before they could even see him.

"Yeah, Maury, you promised us ghosts!" cried Jean.

"Didn't you see the wreck hanging from a tree above you? Now wouldn't you think there'd be a ghost floating around somewhere? Tell me how anybody got out of that car alive or dead? And I see you found yourself a sign."

" 'Men At Work.' Don't you just love it?" yodeled Dave, lugging an orange caution sign rusted by years and weather. "I'm going to put this up outside my garage."

"Oh, boy, what a lie that will be," muttered Jean, and everyone laughed.

Maury pointed out to them the exact spots where Wallenda's cable had been attached, while they munched on candy bars he magically pulled out of a small pack. For Connie, the sweet candy might just as well have been bitter medicine. She was glad when they began the strenuous climb out.

As she stretched herself beyond what she thought she could and dragged herself up over impossible spots, her mind kept returning to things Maury had said, such as "I knew you wouldn't approve of this," meaning his giving up the church job. How had he known that about her? But it was so true. "Oh, Maury, no, please, you're dropping the wrong job!" she wanted to plead. But her main plea was, "Maury, don't shut me out!"

Back home, sitting on her log in the woods above the pond, she realized soberly what she'd learned about herself. She wanted to marry a man who put God first. Henry didn't put God first. Neither did Maury.

"But I love Maury," she whispered in the shadows.

It was Monday morning before it dawned on her she'd never asked Maury if he'd promised to take Billy Ray to watch skydiving.

Chapter 12

The month of May progressed rapidly. Connie felt like a piece of birch bark in a river of time approaching a mighty waterfall, with nothing to stop her from plunging over in the powerful rush of water. On the other hand, time froze in cameo segments. She would always be grading papers at her book-crammed desk at Mrs. Haburn's, looking up now and again to see the picture of prayers in a field. Or she would always be listening to Joyce and Marie, Sammy, and others, reading their very first "chapter" books. She would always, all her life, be settling Rob in his chair one more time.

Blueberry bushes bloomed. Connie hadn't ever considered how blueberry flowers might look. They were tiny, pinkish bells, very dainty, but the most amazing thing was their profusion. If all those flowers developed into berries. . . Well, it was no wonder Mrs. Haburn could sell so many, make pies, and still can, jam, and freeze quarts and quarts of berries.

Outside Connie's bedroom window, "her" maple tree threw leaf shadows again like delicate hands against her curtain. On the hillside beyond the road, glossy laurel bushes were decorated with puffy clusters of faint pink umbels, and rhododendrons bloomed. Wild azalea, or honeysuckle, as Mrs. Haburn called it, flamed orange and lemon in the woods.

Connie hadn't signed her contract for the next year. She knew she couldn't teach under Maury Donovan another year. Instead, she accepted a position in Augusta and was back and forth several weekends, making arrangements. It was going to be nice to be near home again, she told herself. One weekend when she and her mother were talking, she spilled out her feelings about Maury Donovan.

"I was wrong to try to persuade you to marry Henry when you didn't love him," said Mrs. Jensen. "And now you've learned what the other side of un-returned love is like. I'm truly sorry."

"It isn't even that simple," said Connie. "If it were unreturned love, I could accept it more easily, I think. But he loves me, Mother, he does love me! Yet he will not commit himself because. . ."

"Because?"

"Because he thinks he'd have to give up his dangerous adventuring if he married. And I think, more than that, maybe—I don't know—that he's decided on a course of life, and he doesn't want me or the Lord changing it for him."

"I wish we could have met him. I'm sure he's a really good man. You said he has this thing, this mighty cause, to be sure the children learn to read. And that is a wonderful cause, Connie!"

"Sure. But he's let the cause become more important than the children. And he works so hard with so little joy. It just doesn't seem as if he were meant for that job."

"But he has to decide that."

"And he has. He's decided about the job and about me."

"Oh dear! I am sorry. But I'm glad you're coming back here."

"Me, too. But I'll miss Mrs. Haburn so much."

Mrs. Jensen's eyes darkened. "She's been a better mother than I have been."

"No, Mother, don't say that! She was simply herself, a really wonderful woman, always there when I needed her. And I don't know why I'm talking in the past tense. I have two more weeks of school."

Two more weeks! Only two more weeks to teach "her" children. It would be a relief in some ways. But. . .

"I wish I knew what to do for Billy Ray, Mom. He was a different child for awhile when I was taking him to church and Maury was working with him. At first when I took him to Sunday morning church, I had to keep close watch to keep him from making spitballs out of my bulletin. Then, later on, he really began to listen, I thought. But now since Maury resigned all his jobs at church and doesn't even go anymore, Billy Ray doesn't want to go either. Worse than that, he's up to his old tricks at school. Friday he stole Marie's homework and tore it to shreds right in front of us all—just pure meanness."

"From all you've told me, you're doing everything there is to do, Connie. You have helped him an awful lot. Remember that."

"Yes. But it's not good enough. I don't want to leave him unhappy. I tried to get him to play his harmonica the other day and, after several refusals, he finally said he'd buried it."

"Buried it?"

"Yes. Said he would never play it again and when I said he just had to, he said Mr. Donovan doesn't sing anymore so he doesn't play harmonica anymore. What could I say?"

"Honey, be careful. I'm really not sure that boy should still be free after his attack on you."

"Oh, Mother, I'm not afraid *of* him! I'm just afraid *for* him."

❦

It was the last week of school, and the children were incredibly loud and unmanageable. One day in the midst of reading exercises that weren't exciting even the brighter students, Connie suddenly clapped her hands for attention and announced they should put their books and papers all away. Startled little faces stared back at her.

"I mean it. Put them away," she said. "We're going to make something instead. Puppets." She went to the storage room and came back with a stack of paper plates and a package of tongue depressors. "I want you each to make a puppet of who you'd like to be. Think real hard first of who you'd really, really like to be. You can make a puppet of a famous person you admire, or you can make one of, let me see, a fireman, a policeman, the president, a secretary—"

"A teacher?" asked Marie.

"Sure."

"A car thief?" asked Billy Ray without a smile.

She gave him an evil look and ignored his question. "When you've finished your puppets, class, I want you to be ready to put it up in front of your face and tell us about yourself, the puppet self, the one you would like most to be. Okay? Now get your crayons out and do your very best job."

The children were as noisy as ever, but now they were at least accomplishing something. Connie sat down at her desk to work in her grade book, pleased that even Rob was occupied for the moment as he held a purple crayon awkwardly like an ice pick and slashed at the plate.

Feeling herself being closely watched, she raised her eyes to look into the solemn face of Billy Ray. After all these months, he could still slip up on her like a scout in moccasins. She narrowed her eyes. "What is it, Billy Ray? Why aren't you working on your puppet?"

"Don't need a stupid puppet. You know what I want to be."

He was holding his hand behind him. Now he was pulling it out. For one frozen second she pictured herself again with that knife coming at her. Then she realized what he held was a tightly folded piece of paper.

"What is that?" she asked, moistening her lips.

"It's a copy of Mr. Donovan's letter about the skydiving Saturday. I want you to take me. Please?"

"Where did you get that?"

"From Mr. Donovan's office. While he was gone I just made a copy, that's all. Please, Miss Jensen?"

"Billy Ray, you should never take things like that. It's stealing as sure as. . . stealing a car. And you've already asked me about going to see the skydiving." How many times had Billy Ray asked already? If only he knew how much she wished she could take him, but it was impossible. She wanted to get through this job and leave with as little contact with Mr. Donovan as possible.

"Why can't you?"

"Because. It's in Gainesville, a long ways. And I have so much to do, getting ready to move soon. Come on now. Why don't you make a puppet of a sky diver, Billy Ray? Maybe someday you can be one. You could join the air force like Mr. Donovan and. . ."

Connie told Zena about the episode later on as they watched their children at play.

"If Billy Ray wants to see Mr. Donovan jump so badly, why don't you take him? You've done everything else for the boy. Or is it that you like Mr. Donovan too much to be in his vicinity?"

"Oh, Zena, I wish I could have taken your advice and never thought two things about that man!"

"Well," said Zena, rolling a candy wrapper into a tighter and tighter ball, "sometimes advice, particularly mine, is just totally lost on people. Anyway, this is a case of filling the big desire of one very underprivileged boy. If he'd asked me, he could just forget it because I don't do stuff like that. . .help people out, I mean. But you. . .you will be really sorry you didn't."

"Maybe so. I'll think about it. And, Zena. . .that's not true about you. You have helped me all year. I couldn't have made it without you."

Zena smiled brightly and began to call her children in. "Good luck!" she said over her shoulder.

Connie slept fitfully that night and woke early the next morning. She sat by her window, looking up through maple leaves to the dark tree line beyond the highway and the gray sky brightening the hillside's rim. A whippoorwill was singing down beyond the pond somewhere.

"Should I take him?" she whispered against the grayness at her window. "Maury would never believe I was just bringing Billy Ray. He'd think. . . But what does it matter what he thinks? After next week I'll never see him again anyway. So I can have puppet shows and I can take Billy Ray to see the skydiving."

When Connie finally realized about nine o'clock that Billy Ray wasn't coming to school that day, she was relieved. Perhaps he had conveniently gotten sick for these last few days and she would be safe from his brooding, belligerent hurting and from taking him to Gainesville.

Maury Donovan came in while the children were waxing dramatic with their puppets. He stood rigidly near the door, a dark expression on his face. Connie moved toward him but paused to reseat Rob. When she stood again, Maury was gone. Her own disappointment rattled her. *Even his lectures are better than nothing at all,* she thought.

That afternoon Connie sat on the dock swinging her legs above slightly murky water while Mrs. Haburn fished. Occasionally Connie threw out crumbs for the ducks, who swam majestically about, their dark green and black feathers glistening in the sun.

"Had a letter from my daughter today. She's found another job."

"Oh. That's nice. I guess."

"Means she won't be coming here for the summer."

"And you'll have an empty house. Mrs. Haburn, I'm sorry—"

"Now, now, don't go being sorry for me. Lord's taken care of me every turn in my life. And He will this time, too. Still wish you could be here for blueberry season, though. You've never seen any prettier blueberries than mine. You can see the trees are plumb loaded down."

"Yes, and they'll be ripe before too long, won't they? Maybe—"

She didn't finish her sentence, for at that moment Maury Donovan's blue pickup flashed down the hill.

"Hmmm, wonder what he wants?" murmured Mrs. Haburn.

Connie jumped up and ran toward him, knowing instinctively that something must be badly wrong.

"You don't know anything about Billy Ray?" asked Maury.

"Billy Ray? No! I supposed he was sick. Why?"

"His foster mother says she sent him to school. He hasn't been home all day."

"Maybe he's gone hunting for his family."

"Maybe. Just wondered if you had any other clues. It's too early for the police to be very involved, you know, but I'm worried."

Connie wondered silently why he was worried now when he'd ignored Billy Ray for the last few weeks.

"Can you think of anything he's said that might help me find him?" urged Maury.

"Well, I know what he wanted to do more than anything. He's been asking me to take him and I kept telling him I couldn't. He wanted to see you sky dive Saturday. It's all he thought about."

"Oh. Do you think he might hitchhike? Would he know where to go?"

"He's awfully smart. Yes, I think he'd figure that out. He wouldn't realize how hard it would be to get thirty or forty miles. But he wanted to go so much, I don't think much of anything would stop him if he got started. I. . .had decided to take him, but he wasn't there today for me to tell him. I thought he must be sick."

"You know Billy Ray never gets sick," said Maury with no sympathy as he ran back to his truck.

"Maury, wait!" cried Connie. "I'll come with you."

He turned back for half a second, then strode on up the hill. "Suit yourself," he growled.

Connie returned from making a very brief explanation to Mrs. Haburn to find Maury so impatient she barely had the door closed before they were away like a streak of blue up the driveway.

After conferring with Billy Ray's foster family and with representatives from family and children services and the sheriff's office, Maury and Connie began their own search along the hilly Gainesville Road. They asked frequently at houses and businesses but found no trace of a boy tall for his age, towheaded with, according to his foster mother, a five-dollar bill in his pocket. "I know he took it. It was change from when I bought gas," the woman said. "I put it on the refrigerator and now it's gone."

Gradually Maury's brittle edges began to smooth off a bit. "Sorry I was so raspy," he said to Connie as they drove along, scanning both sides of the highway. "It's not your fault he's missing. It's mine."

"Not just yours. It's circumstances. Billy Ray knew his parents had left. What a horrible rejection that was! Even if they were terrible, they were his parents, you know. His foster parents are good people, but they have five other children already. He'd been placed there in an emergency, and he knew he could be moved again anytime. Maybe he'd begun to find some stability at school, but now it's ending and the summer stretches ahead."

"You do have a way with words, Connie Jensen."

"And you are the one who matters most to Billy Ray, Maury."

"And I let him down, quit the church, and turned into a bear. Didn't I?"

Connie didn't answer. She searched the roadsides for any possible clues. Would someone be so irresponsible as to give a young boy a ride and not try to take him back where he belonged? The thought of the kinds of people who might pick him up for their own pleasures or gains made her shudder.

Billy Ray walked all day Thursday and nearly all day Friday, but it was slow going since he had to stay out of sight all the time. A couple of times Friday he did get short rides. He wasn't afraid of much and certainly not of strangers. His own father would have scared him but not strangers.

One of the strangers who gave him a lift was an elderly man on his way to the supermarket. Billy Ray told him he'd stayed home from school to take care of his mother and she needed some ginger ale and some antacid real, real bad. That ride saved him five miles of trudging. The next one earned him a few more. Again, he didn't ask for much. He didn't want this man smoking a cigarette and looking sort of zonked to suspect his story wasn't true. What he liked about that ride was the dog in the backseat, a big, mean-looking German shepherd. He never growled at Billy Ray a single time and the little boy took that as a good sign.

By nightfall Friday, he'd passed Alto and was very glad. He didn't like being anywhere near that place where big boys went to correctional school. They were the same as in jail at that place. Pa had always yelled at him and Lavon that they'd go there someday. Twenty more miles to Gainesville, and his legs were so tired they could hardly move anymore, and blisters burned on both heels. But he had to keep going, had to. He couldn't expect any rides on this big road, especially at night.

He walked, scrambled, and slunk along the edges of woods, high banks, and deep ditches. By now, he knew that his foster mother would have reported to the school that he wasn't sick at home. He'd bribed his foster brothers and sister not to tell anything until they were asked. He'd given one some cough drops, one a pair of pliers he'd found by the road, one his only good shirt, but hardest of all, he'd given away his sleek, silver harmonica. He'd told Miss Jensen he wouldn't play anymore, that he'd even buried it. But that wasn't true. He'd played every private moment he'd had.

He wished he had his harmonica right now. He'd play it to the stars and the moon. He put his hand in his jacket pocket where his harmonica would have been and felt instead the five-dollar bill.

Smiling in the darkness, he thought of breakfast. He would have breakfast in the morning. He finally got so tired he couldn't walk straight so he crawled into a culvert, curled an arm under his head, and, in a fetal position, went sound asleep.

❁

Connie knew Maury was searching Friday every chance he could but, even after school, he didn't ask her to help him, so she went on her own hunches. She didn't have any better success than she had on Thursday. Finally she went home and slept very poorly, rising before dawn to start toward Gainesville. If Billy Ray had made up his mind to go to the Gainesville airport in time for the eleven o'clock sky show, then somehow he would be there. And she would be, too.

When a semi full of empty chicken crates roared past her down below Alto, she had no idea that inside the cab a lonesome driver was listening with the greatest concern to a small boy's tale of his traumatic experience.

"Do you think my father's alive, Mr.? Can he still be alive?"

"Yes, yes. The fall out of the house didn't kill him instantly so he's probably going to be fine. Why was he working on his new house so early on Saturday morning?"

"Well, because something had to pass inspection or. . .I'm not sure. Mama didn't want him to. She cried and screamed at him, but he went anyway."

"And your mama followed?"

"Yes, Sir. She put me and my baby sister in the car and lit out after him. Only by the time we got there, Daddy was lying—oh, it was awful! So she sent me to call an ambulance. Only a neighbor must have already called. When I got back they were leaving. In the ambulance. I yelled and waved my arms and ran after them, but it kept going and going."

"But you're sure it turned toward Gainesville? There's a good hospital in Habersham County, too."

"It went this way. I'm sure. Oh–h–h–h. I hope my daddy's all right." Real tears called on more tears, and soon Billy Ray was shaking with sobs.

"Say, you know, you never told me your name," said the burly driver after a time.

"William Spencer," answered Billy Ray promptly, wiping his nose on a sleeve.

"Good name. Mine's Cliff Wheeler. Well, now, William Spencer, we're gonna be at that hospital in no time an' I'll go with you to the desk an' make sure they let you right in where your family is. Bet your mom's about frantic now worryin' about you. Good thing I'm ridin' empty so we can whiz up these hills."

"What do you carry in this thing?" asked Billy Ray, twisting in his seat belt.

"Chickens. Baby chicks to fill the chicken houses, broilers when they're ready for processing. Going to market, you know, so you can have that good ole fried chicken."

"I had a pet chicken once," said Billy Ray wistfully. His mind was working overtime. How would he shake this driver once they arrived at the hospital? He'd have to be fast, that was for sure. The blisters would just have to hurt. He couldn't believe how lucky he was to get a ride all the way to Gainesville. Now all he had to do, after getting away from this nice driver, was find the airport.

Chapter 13

A s Connie parked at the airport early that Saturday morning, she remembered the first time she'd come here and how exciting it had been to see the parachutes coming down, especially that one with the red-and-white canopy. How happy Maury had been that day!

Pulling herself back to the present, she had to wonder if Billy Ray was anywhere in the vicinity. Maybe he had gone searching for his family. No one knew yet. But she had a feeling, a strong feeling, that Billy Ray would be at the airport soon.

She spied a telephone booth and hurried toward it. Just maybe Maury might know something by now. Of course he probably was anywhere but at home. He'd either be searching for Billy Ray or getting ready to fly.

As she waited for an answer, she scanned the skies from the phone booth. Clear and gorgeous. The sun's rays brushed pink on the horizon. It would be a wonderful day for Maury to parachute. But if they couldn't find Billy Ray, he wouldn't enjoy it at all.

A female voice answered huskily. Connie was confused. Had she dialed the wrong number? Was Maury's mother with him? Not on a flying day! She hung up and left the phone booth as if a bee had bitten her.

She sat in her car, oblivious now to the sunrise, the drift of a wind sock, or to early morning walkers using a runway for their track. She hugged herself against a chill and realized her teeth were chattering. It was the end of May, not that cold.

Now she understood clearly why Maury hadn't asked her to help him hunt for Billy Ray yesterday. He'd already had plans before Billy Ray complicated things. No wonder he'd been so indifferent whenever she mentioned his doing something with Billy Ray the last few weeks. All this time she'd thought he was still mourning his friend and trying to make sense out of his life. And of course he didn't want to get serious about her. Oh, no! Because he had someone else all along. How could she have been so. . .naive?

And what should she do now? To leave was most appealing. But there was still Billy Ray. Maury wasn't hunting for him, so she had to. She must stick to her post. That's all she had to worry about right now. Stick to the airport like a veritable private eye until she saw that little blond-headed boy.

Nine and nine-thirty came and went. People were beginning to arrive for the show. Connie recognized a few faces and felt a pang of her own grief for Jock and

Betty, who should have been there. Seconds ticked away. Where was Maury? Aside from everything else, Maury was a faithful person. He wouldn't willfully let his team or anyone down once he'd made a promise. He just didn't make promises very readily. And where, oh, where was Billy Ray?

Raising Jean's binoculars one more time, Connie scanned the whole airport and was about to lay them down with a sigh when a gasp escaped her instead. There he was! Billy Ray. Getting out of a blue pickup truck. Maury's! Maury ran inside the building, leaving Billy Ray behind but not alone. Who was that with Billy Ray? It wasn't his foster mother, certainly not his mother. Short curly blond hair, bright pink cheeks, arm across Billy Ray's shoulders. They disappeared inside the building. The voice she'd heard on the phone, she was sure, went with that curly blond hair. Connie fought nausea.

❦

"You should have stayed to see what all happened, Dearie," soothed Mrs. Haburn later that day as she poured Connie a bracing cup of tea. "You know, you owe that much to Maury Donovan. You shoulda let him explain."

"I don't guess I owe him very much. He cut the strings, if there were any, pretty thoroughly. Only I just wouldn't let go. In my mind I was still hoping. I know that now. I couldn't confront them down there, Mrs. Haburn. As long as Billy Ray was okay, I thought I should leave. Anyway, to tell the truth, I didn't really think much. I was so stunned, so. . .overwhelmed. . .I couldn't."

"Tell me again what she looked like."

"Oh, Mrs. Haburn, she was beautiful! Curly blond hair, a gorgeous figure."

"Could be a lot of folks, includin' Dolly Parton and Barbara Mandrell," said Mrs. Haburn, setting some cream down for the cat.

"Oh, don't try to make me laugh. This isn't funny!"

"Sorry, Honey, I know it ain't. Just hate to see you so sad."

The phone rang and both women looked at it hanging there on the wall like a living, breathing intruder. At the third ring Mrs. Haburn answered it. Her face lit up.

"Oh, hi, Billy Ray. I've heard a lot about you. Yes, sure you can speak to Miss Jensen. Right here she is."

When Connie hung up, her eyes were dull. "He's okay, so I should be glad. It was time for Maury's plane to go up so he told Billy Ray to call me. Maury had called earlier and I wasn't here yet. You must have been outside."

Mrs. Haburn nodded. "Went down to check on the blueberries."

Connie sat back down. "He said Miss Tatum was real nice and would let him stay at her place tonight because his foster mother already said she doesn't want him back. I'm not sure how he knew that, but I don't guess it matters. Anyway, he wasn't worried at all, just kind of breathless with excitement, getting ready to go watch the sky show. At least his dream is coming true."

"Oh dear, I think this calls for another cup of tea," said Mrs. Haburn, gathering Connie's cup.

"No. No, thanks, Mrs. Haburn. I've had enough tea. I need something else. I'm going for a walk."

"You should have learned how to fish. That's the best unkinking thing to do," said Mrs. Haburn, who was rewarded by Connie's watery smile.

Connie watched the ducks for a few minutes, but they were becoming very snobbish and discourteous since she hadn't brought them any crumbs. She walked between rows of blueberry bushes and paused to lift one branch, heavy with green berries. Something soft pushed gently against her leg, and she bent to scoop up the yellow cat. "Left your cream to come comfort me, did you?" she asked, laying her cheek against the silken fur.

High up on the hill, she looked back east across the pond to where slopes of forest beyond the road basked in afternoon sun like green furry monsters cuddled up to sleep. Shadows darkened the dips and crevices of shoulders, haunches, and paws. Nearby, the pond lay motionless, mirroring a scene so much bigger than itself. A thrush sang somewhere behind her. The song that usually made her so happy now brought tears to her eyes.

"I've really been pretty useless lately, Lord, what with worrying about my own situation so much. But I know You're not through with me yet, and I'm depending on You to make something out of this mess. I don't even know what to pray for except. . .please be with me."

Shadows lengthened. A stiff breeze rippled the pond, zigzagging its reflections of trees and sky. More birds, inspired by the thrush, began to sing. Connie became aware of a spicy sweet scent carried lightly on the wind.

She would not think about Maury's exuberance after his jump and of someone else being there to catch the light of his joy. She would not think about Billy Ray happily skipping between the two of them. She would not think.

"Thanks, Lord, for bringing Billy Ray back and for taking care of him. Help him day by day to replace his hate with love. He's such a sweet little fellow underneath his cover. I hope. . . Send him a good teacher next year, please, someone who will believe in him. And give him a permanent home with security. I don't ask much, do I?"

She picked up a stick and tossed it where the cat was stalking, so startling the poor creature that he forgot his real prey and pounced on the stick instead, rolling over with it in his briery grasp.

"And, Lord, please take care of Maury Donovan," said Connie as she rose to follow her well-worn trail back down the hill.

Chapter 14

Connie had been back home in Augusta for two weeks. Those last few days at Pine Ridge after the children were out seemed nothing but an unhappy blur. Maury had been courteous, even kind when she had to talk to him professionally, but that was all. What little she learned about Billy Ray's being found was from Zena, who said the child was now staying temporarily with his caseworker.

When she got her first letter from Mrs. Haburn, she scanned it quickly for any mention of Maury Donovan. Even the smallest bit of news would be wonderful. But she didn't see his name anywhere. Billy Ray's name filled up the whole letter. What did Mrs. Haburn have to say about Billy Ray? But wait—what was this clipping? The announcement of a Miss Candace Tatum's upcoming marriage? Miss Tatum? She looked at the smiling picture and wanted to tear it to shreds then and there. Though she'd only seen the woman through binoculars that day, she was sure this was the same person. And Maury was marrying her? How could he after telling her. . .what had he told her? Was this the same man who couldn't get serious?

With a mixture of reluctance and insatiable curiosity, Connie began to read the wedding announcement and cried out in amazement. The groom's name was Edward Clark. A man's name had never looked so wonderful! She kissed the piece of paper that moments earlier she'd wanted to shred.

But back to the letter. What was this about Billy Ray?

"After you left," wrote Mrs. Haburn in a jerky kind of handwriting that sort of wandered downhill, "I was too lonesome. Not enough to do. I knew that little boy needed a place. And lots of love. I've got both. So I called that family services place. That Miss Tatum is the one I got. You'll remember her when you see her picture. She's Billy Ray's caseworker. A real nice person.

"Anyways, Billy Ray's living with me now, staying in your room. He's not near quiet like you, but he can sure catch a fish! He's almost as picky as you about anybody prying into his affairs, but I keep prying anyways. I'm not afraid of him at all, 'cause I just don't live that way. I may be a mite foolish, maybe a whole lot foolish, but I do want to do this."

Connie bit her lip. Miss Tatum was Billy Ray's caseworker. That explained some things. Her cheeks warmed at the very thought of how easily she'd jumped to conclusions. On the other hand, she still didn't quite see why the woman was at Maury's house answering his phone at six thirty in the morning. She read the letter over, amazed again at Mrs. Haburn's generosity and energy. What a wonderful place for Billy Ray if Mrs. Haburn could manage it. Billy Ray could outrun her coming and going, but if anyone could outwit him, it was Mrs. Haburn.

The next time she heard from Mrs. Haburn, her letter went on and on about how many blueberries she and Billy Ray had picked, how many picking customers they'd had, how fast a picker Billy Ray was, how many pints she'd frozen, how many canned, and how much jam she'd made. Connie was surprised there weren't blueberry stains all over the paper since she could easily picture Mrs. Haburn hunched over her letter, writing at the same table with buckets of blueberries.

But Mrs. Haburn had poured out her very best news at the bottom of the last page. In a different color of ink, words scrambled to the bottom of the page and climbed back up the sides. The handwriting was more atrocious than ever, written in such excitement.

"Glad I didn't mail this yesterday. Would have to start up a whole new letter if I had. Your prayers and mine are done answered, Connie! We knowed that fine Maury Donovan weren't happy being a principal. Well, listen to this. Reverend Stone preached a sermon today that made everyone want to give whatever they had to the Lord, even if they went to the poorhouse. And what some has to give is more than money.

"Mr. Maury Donovan was there. He's been coming to pick me and Billy Ray up for church ever since you left. Well, I could tell Maury was awful fidgety. I thought maybe he was in a hurry or had a stomachache or at least a bad case of chiggers. But when Phil gave the invitation, guess who was the first one down that aisle? Maury Donovan! He talked to the church, told us he was sorry he'd been so wishy-washy, and that he knew now that God wanted him to be a minister of music, that he'd tried to get out of it long enough. Get this. He's going to seminary in September!"

Connie burst out into excited screams. It was unbelievable! Yet it was true. She grabbed her sunglasses from the hall table and went jogging. She simply could not stay in the house knowing such big news; she had to get outside and be doing something. If only her mother were home, someone to rejoice with her.

When Connie got back from running two miles, she read the letter again and again, smiling at Mrs. Haburn's closing that was scrawled along the side of the page: "Now I've run clean out of paper. You take care, Honey. Love and prayers, Hilda Haburn."

She'd write Mrs. Haburn back right now; that's what she'd do. Or should she call? She'd do both!

❁

She wondered if maybe Maury would call her, now that so much had changed.

But weeks went by and the only news she received was from Mrs. Haburn and Jean. Maury would be moving to Louisville, Kentucky. He was working with their church until he left sometime in August. Also he was working at the school, getting it in tip-top shape for the new principal who, at last report, hadn't been found.

Could she call him? Not when he'd made it so abundantly clear he didn't want to get involved with her. Yet some of his reasons had been removed, hadn't they? Maybe not all of his reasons. No, she couldn't call, no matter how much she wanted to.

It was a hot, sizzling day late in July when Mrs. Jensen called Connie to the phone. A familiar deep voice said, "Hi! Connie? Maury here. I need to see you." Just like him not to beat around the bush.

She took a deep breath. "When?"

"Ten minutes? I'm at the airport. Flew down with one of the guys. We're jumping this afternoon."

"Give me thirty minutes. I'll meet you at the airport."

Ten minutes indeed! The crazy man! No word in all this time, then suddenly, "Meet me in ten minutes!" She smiled to herself. She was going, wasn't she? But not before she changed from shorts to an ankle-length gauzy blue skirt and white T-shirt. After fastening her favorite gold earrings in place and giving her dark hair a brisk brushing, she dashed out the door.

He was bigger than ever and his eyes bluer. He'd even grown a beard, a neatly trimmed one. He was gorgeous. She smiled uncertainly as she started toward him, but his face lit up when he saw her and he leaped to his feet, covering the distance between them in three big strides.

"Connie! Oh, you look so. . .very wonderful!"

"Thanks very much," she said stiffly, putting out a hand.

His smile faded and dark brows knit together. "We need to talk, and this place is too noisy."

"Come on," said Connie. "I'll take you for a ride."

"No. Let's just walk outside. Our jump is in another hour or so. I need to stay close. Anyway, I want you to listen to me, not drive."

"You're still jumping, then?"

"Yes. This will be the last one for a long time. I'm going to be a student again—"

"Mrs. Haburn told me the wonderful news. Maury, I'm so glad! I can tell you're happy. Your face is so much more relaxed, at peace. What I can see of it," she ended on a tease.

He rubbed a hand across his bristly jaw and grinned.

They walked around the end of the building where they could see several small planes tied down. The sky above was clear blue, and the wind sock was barely moving.

"Augusta is always like this in July," Connie said. "Humidity and mosquitoes thick enough to butcher for supper, my daddy always says. You can see why in the old days everyone who could hopped on a train and went to the north Georgia mountains."

"Augusta has its calling cards, too," said Maury, grinning down at her.

"Tell me what happened, Maury."

He drew a deep breath, then slowly exhaled, hands deep in the pockets of his light khakis. "It still seems too big to confine to mere words," he said. "When I finally let go and told God He could have all of me—school, flying, you, everything—He put the pieces in place for me. I'm on His timetable now. It's like I've been released from a ten-year confinement. I've lost a lot of time worrying about what couldn't be helped. . .like my father's death. But God's taking it from here."

"Your mother?" asked Connie.

He sighed. "She doesn't like my going into the music ministry and was bitterly opposed to my giving up the principal's job. Maybe someday she'll accept it all. I hope so."

They'd gone around the building now. Maury stopped at a corner and leaned against the wall. "Connie, I don't think I've a right to say anything to you, but I. . . well, I know you misunderstood some things."

"Such as?" The pain had returned, and it made her harden her chin and straighten her back.

"Well, Mrs. Haburn says you called my house early in the morning that day—"

"Yes, and a young woman answered the phone. I remember the sun was just coming up."

"Miss Tatum. She's Billy Ray's caseworker. She was hunting for Billy Ray the day before, and I knew it, though we hadn't been together." He saw her disbelief but shoved on. "She'd given me her number in case I heard anything. We did not spend the night together, Connie!"

"So what happened?" she asked.

"I'd called all the area hospitals and told them to report to me anything to do with an eight-year-old blond boy's injury. Well, they called that morning from Gainesville's hospital and told me this weird story about a chicken truck driver who'd brought a boy in to see his parents; only the parents weren't there, and the boy had disappeared while the truck driver was inquiring. I knew it had to be Billy Ray. Doesn't it sound just like him?"

For the first time they smiled together, mutually enjoying the scene they could both so easily picture.

"Well, I called Miss Tatum right quick as I'd promised to do, and she said she'd be right there. She must have been up and dressed already. She came so quickly I was still pulling my socks on. Right after she got there, the phone rang. I nodded for her to please answer it because she was nearer, and I assumed the call would be about Billy Ray anyway. I guess that was you."

"It was."

"Connie, I'm sorry. I didn't even know for a long time that that was you or think of how it seemed to you."

"You didn't know I went to the airport, too?"

"Not 'til recently."

"How did you find Billy Ray?"

"Looked everywhere between that hospital and the airport and finally spied him sitting on a curb looking totally tuckered out. You should have seen him when I pulled up beside him!"

"I would have liked that."

"Connie, there was never anything between me and Miss Tatum—never. It was so far from my mind, I was staggered when Mrs. Haburn showed me how it seemed to you."

"Does it really make any difference now?" she asked.

"I hope so," he said, putting a finger under her chin to make her look at him. "I hope you can forgive me for all the times I've hurt you. I want your forgiveness, Connie."

"You have it, Maury. Really."

"But that's not all I want." He hadn't moved his hand.

"What else?"

Heat waves shimmered a foot above the asphalt. A light plane touched down and coasted to a halt. But for Connie the world had stopped. She wanted to believe what she saw in Maury's eyes, that hungry, wistful look. That look that made her feel like the most desirable woman in the world. But was all this real or was she dreaming?

Slowly Maury placed his hands on her shoulders, then framed her face with them.

"I'm so completely in love with you; I've been missing you every minute you've been gone and kicking myself for making such stupid mistakes. My only defense is, God hadn't knocked sense into me yet."

His face was only inches away now. His eyes were filled with warm light that made the blue sparkle like sunny lakes. His lips touched hers very, very gently, like a plea. Then, finding her submissive, he kissed her again, and she nestled against him with a sigh that was almost a sob.

"This is what I came for," he said.

"Silly. You came to jump, remember?"

"No. That was just my excuse. You know what this means?" he asked against her hair.

"No. What does it mean?"

"It means I'm very, very serious about you. And I hope you can be serious about me."

She laughed softly. "Serious?"

"Serious. As in, will you marry me?"

She pulled away from him, the better to study his face. "Maury? Are you sure you want such a burden?"

He laughed. "I not only want you; I need you, burdens and all. I love you, Connie."

"I love you, too, with all my heart. Yes. Yes! I'll marry you." Impulsively, she stood on tiptoes and kissed him.

Behind them someone noisily cleared his throat. "Maury! Time to suit up!"

Maury cupped Connie's chin in one hand. Her eyes now were alive with dancing lights. "I won't go if you really don't want me to. I'm willing to stop jumping right now if that's what it takes to win you."

"It was never my idea for you to stop skydiving, remember? I'll be waiting when you come down. Now, you'd better run!"

There were several jumpers, but they weren't prepared to make formations, only to come down singly. Connie wished she had Jean's binoculars and vowed she'd get some of her own. It was quite awhile after the jumpers were out before Connie could be sure which one was Maury, but as soon as she spotted him, she began trying to figure out just where he'd stand down so she could be nearby.

He was almost down when she heard his big voice singing in the sky, belting out an ecstatic melody for all to hear: "Then sings my soul, my Saviour God to thee, how great Thou art, how great Thou art!"

"He's coming down 'On Wings of Song,' " she whispered, knowing without a doubt she'd follow him wherever the Lord sent him.

BRENDA KNIGHT GRAHAM

Brenda grew up near Clarkesville in Northeast Georgia, but has lived for the last thirty-five years in Southwest Georgia's Cairo where her husband Charles is a veterinarian. Mother of two and grandmother of two, she is active in her church and community. One of her passions is literacy missions and she is thrilled to see God at work in students of English as a second language as well as adults learning to read. Brenda has written several books for adults and children. She enjoys playing with her grandchildren, traveling with her husband, and creating crossword puzzles.

Restore the Joy

Sara Mitchell

Prologue

Death lurked in the room where a man lay in a huge tester bed, breathing in labored gasps. His complexion beneath the full black beard and mustache was waxen, the flesh clammy. His eyes opened and fixed upon a weeping woman sitting beside him.

"Do you understand?" he repeated hoarsely with great effort. "Do you understand why I had to do it this way?"

The woman fingered the lace of her cashmere breakfast jacket, then reached and laid her trembling hand over his where it lay clutching the bedclothes. "I understand, Everett," she murmured in a tearful voice. "Please try not to tire yourself now." Her voice caught, and she turned her head aside so the man would be spared the sight of her stricken face.

She was a lovely woman, with rich black hair gathered in a bun on top of her head and fashionably fuzzy ringlets framing her face. But deep unhappiness and shame had left their marks. She had had to pay a heavy price to be with this man, and she knew that, as he prepared himself to meet his Maker, he was trying to atone for both their sins.

"You. . .and Harold. . .will be. . .comfortable," he was gasping out now, his breathing even more labored. "Won't have to worry about yourself. . .or our son."

"Thank you," the woman whispered humbly. He might have built her this mansion and showered her with material possessions, but she had always known about his feelings of guilt.

"Must do what's fair, what's right." For a minute he rested, gathering the strength to finish. "I can't rest in peace. . .through eternity. . .with the VanCleef name tarnished. This—this will help restore honor. . .to rightful. . .heirs."

His chest rose heavily and fell, and his eyes closed so he did not see the fresh pain washing into the woman's face. Suddenly he roused and with surprising strength gripped her hand. "But I did love you, Gwinette. . . ." His parched lips parted in a smile and the unfocused eyes assumed a satisfied, faraway cast. "Got you the window like I promised, didn't I?"

"Yes, Everett, you got me my beautiful Tiffany window. And I love you for it." Tears crowded her throat and she stopped, her heart breaking.

"Only one other window like that. . ." His eyes dimmed now, and the strength went out of his grip. "It's still there, I imagine. . . . I wonder. . .if she ever forgave

213

me. . . ." The words died away, and his hand slipped from her fingers to the heavy silk counterpane.

He died an hour later, and the sober attending physician laid the covers over his head and put a comforting hand on the woman's shoulder. She waited until the doctor left the room, then walked slowly around the bed to pick up a document lying on a table. Carefully and quietly, she found the safety deposit box Everett had kept hidden in the secret place at the back of the closet.

It would be so easy to destroy the document, to tell the lawyer Everett had changed his mind and dictated a new one to her. But she couldn't. She had given herself to Everett, thereby blighting her reputation and his, so she could not destroy his feeble effort to redeem himself.

She had this house—with the window she had coveted from the moment she saw its twin at his home in New York—and she had their son. Everett had been as faithful to her as he knew how to be. In the end, though, it hadn't been enough. Man's faithfulness alone never is.

Chapter 1

Dear Emily,

Just thought we'd drop a line and let you know we've made it as far as Virginia. Beautiful scenery—it's great having all this freedom to go and come as we please. Keep the home fires burning.

Love,
Mom and Dad

What home fires? Emily Carson thought with resigned humor as she read the postcard from her parents. The little square frame house she had lived in all her life had been sold three months before. In its place, Dad had purchased a monolith motor home, complete with every luxurious appointment known to man. He and Mom had kissed Emily good-bye, asked her to maintain contact with her younger brother Jimmy-Joe, and taken off for parts unknown.

Emily dropped the postcard in the round straw basket she had purchased to hold the sporadic remembrances from her mother. *Let's see—today's note makes three, so that's about one a month.* She sighed.

It was a hot, lazy day in early June. School had just been released, with shouts of freedom from the students and gasps of relief from the teachers. Emily Carson was a teacher, only she had not gasped in relief. She missed her kids already because for the past five years it was from them—and them alone—that she drew meaning and purpose for her life.

A plain, quiet girl with straight, nut brown hair and solemn brown eyes, Emily had learned early in life to combat her poor self-image and lack of popularity by working as hard and as long as she could. Gainfully employed since the age of fifteen, she had opened her own bank account when she started college. Now at twenty-six, she had—thanks to her parents' radical lifestyle transformation—her own apartment, a compact car, and an overwhelming sense of loneliness.

The loneliness was harder to ward off in the summer months, and since school let out the previous week Emily had taken to driving around the south Georgia countryside. She never drove with a destination in mind; if a road looked inviting, she simply turned and followed it. Narrow country lanes of packed clay or sand crisscrossed paved county roads, which intersected the larger state highways she invariably left to follow those other winding, bumpy lanes and roads. Eventually she would happen onto a signpost, and when she was ready, she'd wander back toward Sylvan, the sleepy, slow-moving town where she had lived all her life.

Today her beat-up Toyota headed east, where forests of pine, fields of corn, soybeans, and tobacco, tumbledown shacks, and one-corner communities all blurred together as the miles ticked away on the odometer of the car. She would have missed the house outside Timmons altogether if it hadn't been for rays of sunlight striking off one of its windows directly onto Emily's windshield. Wincing, Emily glanced over to the right to see what had caused the sudden glare and caught her breath. The car swerved as she jammed the brakes, then backed up with careless haste and stopped dead in the middle of the ancient dirt road upon which she had been traveling.

Half hidden by towering oaks and elms, almost strangled by overgrown azaleas, rhododendrons, and a healthy crop of weeds, a house straight out of nineteenth-century Victorian America resided in faded splendor right there before Emily's incredulous eyes. In that first astonishing moment of discovery, all she saw was that the two-story structure was constructed—incredibly for south Georgia—entirely of brick. Then, as her delighted eyes moved over the gables and steeply pitched slate roof and the wooden gingerbread porches, her gaze fell at last on the huge bay window. In spite of the accumulation of dust and dirt and years of neglect, the sunbeams had found this diamond in the rough and offered it to her—plain old Emily Carson.

She had never seen a window quite like this one. She had never seen a *house* quite like this one. With careful but eager movements, she stepped across a ditch and picked her way through beggar's-lice and tall scratchy grasses and a multitude of other undesirable weeds to stand in front of the bay window.

The side panels were of clear beveled glass panes. Matching smaller panes created a frame for the center panel, which was of leaded glass. Emily reached trembling fingers and gently smoothed away some of the layers of grime. A shimmering, soft shade of luminous lemon gold appeared.

Clumsy with excitement, she used the hem of her shirt to clean a larger space, and a moment later her eyes confirmed what her brain refused to believe: The front panel of leaded glass depicted an intricate floral pattern, complete with leaves and branches intertwined in glorious, richly hued colors. Lips parted, breathing suspended, Emily stared at this vision of delight with the growing seed of an idea clamoring to take root.

She wanted this house. More than anything else on this earth, she wanted this house. She wanted to restore it, uncover all its dignity and charm and elegance, resurrect this huge, decaying ghost from out of the past and give meaning and purpose to her own life as well. She would live here and become something beyond plain old Emily Carson, abandoned and rootless. She needed this house.

This house needed her.

An unfamiliar, tantalizing emotion bubbled up and through her. She stood a moment longer, staring at the house, hands clasped to her chest as if to keep her heart from bursting through. Then she whirled, scrambled into her car, and tore off down the dirt lane with unladylike haste.

※

Over the next weeks Emily Carson acquired three things. The first was an alarmingly large dog whom she dubbed Ivan the Terrible. Ivan had just passed his first birthday and was housebroken. The second was a scruffy, flea-ridden kitten. Two former students begged Emily to save the animal from its dismal, but certain, fate.

Her third acquisition was the house.

Upon closer inspection of the latter, Emily learned that the room with the beautiful bay window must have been a library. Floor-to-ceiling shelves on two walls, empty now of books and coated with dust and dead insects, clued her to this snippet of information.

Upstairs, she also discovered traces of former residents—someone who must have camped out in a couple of the rooms for awhile. Emily stuffed empty beer cans and filthy litter into a sack and stomped angrily downstairs. If any wandering hoboes made a return visit, she'd toss them out on their ears. This was her house now.

She planned to restore it one room at a time as finances permitted. The library would be first—except for her hidden treasure of a window. That jewel she would save for last.

Where had it come from? She had seen stained-glass windows before, but only in churches, and even those did not resemble the one here. And it was hers now. Hers to savor, hers to dream over and wonder about its past.

By the middle of July, Emily was sanding down the mantel over the fireplace with the belt sander a man at the Timmons hardware store had recommended. The wood, she was told, was mahogany, although the bookshelves and molding were oak. Fingers now as red and rough as the sandpaper on the tool she was using, Emily nonetheless delighted in each new discovery she made about her new home. Solid oak floors, five fireplaces including one in the kitchen, large airy rooms fringed with intricate crown molding and filled with sunlight—every day she stumbled onto a bonus she was sure had to be the last.

Buying the house may have taken almost every penny in her savings account, but it was worth it. It was doubly worth it considering the weeks of trouble and uncertainty and tedious searching and waiting before this glorious palace was hers. . .all hers.

Emily rubbed her hands hard against the small of her back, sitting on her heels to rest a minute as her mind idly mulled over the past hectic month. If it hadn't been for a nice but nosy old man shamelessly eavesdropping in the county courthouse that day—

From outside came the sound of a car door slamming, and Emily twisted her head. What on earth? She wasn't expecting the electrician until tomorrow. He had checked and repaired the existing wiring already, but Emily wanted some new outlets, and he had promised to drop by in the morning.

"Anybody home?" a man's voice called out a moment later, and Emily stood up with a sigh. She might have known it! This was probably one of those disgusting vagrants who made free with other people's property. Well, he had a surprise in store.

"In here," she answered grimly, rising to her full five feet six inches and preparing to intimidate with her best stern schoolteacher's demeanor. She shoved a few straggling locks of hair out of her face, then froze.

Like Emily, the man was wearing jeans, but his weren't covered with sawdust. A shaft of sunlight glinted off sandy brown hair, revealing deep chestnut highlights among the rebellious waves spilling haphazardly about his face. Although he obviously tried to control his hair by keeping it cropped about the ears and neck, the first impression was quite dramatic. To Emily, he resembled the statue of an ancient Greek warrior.

His eyes, warm and a startling shade of green, were amused. Emily realized with a start that she was staring. "I'm sorry," she apologized, and grinned sheepishly. "I wasn't expecting anyone—especially someone who looks like you."

"Someone who looks like me?" the stranger repeated with a charming, white-toothed grin. "What does that mean, or should I ask?"

Emily laughed. "Oh, nothing special, I assure you. My first thought was that you were one of the bums who had used my home for a pit stop sometime in the past." She tilted her head to one side and studied him. "But somehow I don't think you're a bum. . .and you're definitely an improvement over the plumber. He was about fifty years old and that many pounds overweight. The termite man was just the opposite—in his twenties and skinny as a maple sapling. He also chewed tobacco."

As she talked, she ticked the numbers off on her fingers, enjoying the frank appreciation of the man's response without analyzing why she felt so free to tease. "The roofing man wasn't too bad, but he had a wife and four kids. He showed me their pictures."

"Well, I'm not married, I'm thirty-three, and I don't chew tobacco. And I'm definitely not a homeless vagrant."

"You're not overweight either," Emily couldn't help adding, and they both laughed.

The stranger began prowling slowly about the room, eyeing it with entirely too much interest to suit Emily. Stroking the mantel with a proprietary hand, she watched him with the wariness of a mother dog defending her pups. He ran a finger along a section of the molding she had sanded down, then knelt suddenly to examine the tongue-and-groove hardwood floors.

"What did you want?" Emily prodded, his easy silence making her somehow nervous.

The man dusted his hands and turned back to her. For a minute he studied her in silence, then remarked casually, "I understand you've bought this old place. Is that correct?"

"Yes." Emily stared back, her own gaze speculative. "How did you find out—and why do you want to know?"

"I asked in Timmons. Apparently you've generated more business—and gossip—than they've enjoyed in a decade or more."

He sounded half-amused, half-bemused, and in some confusion Emily turned and picked up the belt sander from the mantelpiece. "Everyone has been. . .mostly helpful. Look, I don't want to be rude, but I am busy, as you can see. If you're trying to sell insurance or something, you're wasting your time. I've spent every dime I have in the world on this place, and every dime I hope to make in the future as well."

"I'm not an insurance salesman." He paused, then added, "But you do need adequate, specialized insurance on a place like this. It's financial suicide not to."

"I'm not stupid," Emily replied stiffly. "It's insured. Now if you don't mind. . . who are you and would you please hurry up and go?"

One thick sable eyebrow shot up, and a chuckle echoed deep in his throat. "Yes, Ma'am!" His gaze wandered over the room again, ending with another examination of Emily. A strange expression flitted through his eyes, but his voice remained pleasantly bland. "The Realtor—a Mrs. Davis, I believe—told me you were doing most of the work yourself."

Emily's chin lifted. "Yes, I am."

"You've taken on an overwhelming project, you know. Do you have any idea what you're demanding of yourself to try and do it alone?" He hesitated, then spoke as if choosing his words with more than usual care. "There are businesses devoted to this kind of work, and it seems like it would be prudent to take advantage of their expertise. As a matter of fact—"

"All they would do is take advantage of my pocketbook," Emily retorted. "Besides, I want to do it myself." She waved her hand with the sander in it. "I don't think I've done too badly for a rank beginner in home restoration." She flashed him a determined grin. "I realize I jumped in the deep end before I learned more than a dog paddle, but I'm not a klutz. Besides, I couldn't afford to hire someone who had to be paid to do what I'm doing for free. I told you it took every penny

I had to buy the place."

Her own gaze roved fondly about the room, ending on the window—her pot of gold, the reward for the hours and days and weeks of labor. She was saving the window to do last because the anticipation of what it would look like kept her going long after her body begged for rest. "But it's worth it," she whispered almost to herself. "Oh, it's worth it."

She abruptly became aware that the stranger was watching her with a peculiar expression, his body posed in an attitude of unnatural stillness. Coloring a little, she started to change the subject, but even as she opened her mouth, he moved, walking in swift, sure strides across to her window.

"What's this?"

There was sufficient excitement in his voice for Emily to become alarmed. She didn't want to share her window with anybody. It was her secret, and no one else—especially some nosy stranger—was going to poke around and discover what lay beneath the concealing layers of grime.

"It's a window," she understated.

The man tossed an impatient glance over his shoulder. "It's more than just a window, and I think you know it."

He reached into his hip pocket and withdrew a neatly folded white handkerchief. Before Emily could reach him, he had carefully cleaned off a six-inch square, revealing a deep-wine-colored rosebud. Inhaling sharply, he muttered something Emily didn't catch because she was too busy scurrying over and grabbing his arm.

"Leave it alone!" she snapped, too desperate to be polite. Her fingers dug into a forearm covered with soft, curling brown hair, but the muscles beneath were as hard and unyielding as the oak banister out in the hall.

His hand came up to cover hers. "I'm not going to hurt your window." He withdrew his hand and moved away. "It is yours, I take it? According to the Realtor, you paid cash and closed the deal as fast as the reports came in attesting to the basic soundness of the place."

"Yes. It's mine," Emily stated flatly. "I found it and spent a week unearthing as much as I could of its history at the county courthouse. I found the real estate company who handled it, and they sold it to me. I'm going to restore it and turn it back into the thing of beauty it used to be, and no one is going to stop me."

Her impassioned speech rang into the hot stillness of the day.

"You feel pretty strongly about it, don't you?" the stranger commented after a moment, his voice and green eyes suddenly softening.

"Yes," said Emily. "I do." She was amazed at how much she was letting a perfect stranger see, but she sensed on a subconscious level that he posed a threat of some kind. Perhaps if he were convinced of her dedication and determination, he would go away and leave her alone.

"About five months ago my parents up and sold the only home I've ever known," she elaborated. "They bought themselves one of those mile-long motor homes and took off for the wild blue yonder. My brother joined the Air Force. He just shipped out to Germany, and I probably won't see him for three years."

Hands planted on her hips, head held high, she stared the man straight in the eye. "This house is all I have in this world that means something to me besides the dog and cat that got dumped on me a month ago. I need it—and it needs me. So, I don't know who you are or what you want, but if it has to do with this house, forget it. I'm not interested."

"My name is Simon Balfour, and I'm afraid I am here about the house, and I'll have to have your interest whether desired or not." His disconcerting green eyes probed hers briefly, but then, to Emily's amazement, Simon bowed his head and closed his eyes as if he were about to offer up a prayer.

For the first time Emily knew fear, and she found herself wanting to pray, too. Although she had come to an awareness of her need for God while in college, she had never felt a compulsion to bother Him overmuch with petty day-to-day details of her life. She had always felt the Lord had more important things on His mind than the niggling problems of Emily Carson. Right now, however, her problems loomed with the significance of the last trumpet call, and she found herself sending up a desperate plea for divine intervention in her behalf.

Simon Balfour opened his eyes and looked at her again, this time with pain—and pity. He turned abruptly away. "There's a title dispute," he declared without looking at Emily.

"Title dispute?" she echoed stupidly.

Simon turned back, his face a mask of frustration. "Yes. I'm sorry. If it's any consolation, I feel like I've just booted a baby bird out of its nest, from what you tell me of your parents."

"There can't be a dispute. It's legal. Mildred didn't say anything." She stared at him, so stunned she couldn't even take offense at what he had called her.

"Why don't we go sit outside on the steps, and I'll explain?" Simon suggested.

As they walked across the creaking, slightly sagging porch, Emily's shell-shocked gaze wandered over the wild beauty of the front yard. "Prove it," she demanded suddenly. "Give me some proof of your allegation or I'll throw you off this property. *My* property, I might remind you."

"I don't have any proof with me right now," Simon admitted slowly, a spark of reluctant amusement lighting his face at her outrageous threat. "I came out here to meet you, introduce myself." Amusement spread as he surveyed Emily from the dust-streaked, frazzled braid unraveling down her back to the equally dust-streaked, frazzled sneakers on her feet. "Just to satisfy my curiosity, how would you go about throwing me off your property?"

Emily put two fingers to her lips and whistled with the easy expertise of a ten-year-old boy. In a minute, Ivan came bounding across the yard through the three-foot-high weeds. One Sunday afternoon, Emily and her friend Barb had passed the time speculating on Ivan's ancestry. They stopped after Great Dane, German shepherd, collie, and Doberman pinscher, deciding the effort was fruitless and it was easier just to call the animal a gigantic mutt. His back came almost to Emily's waist; his face, almost shaped like that of a Great Dane, had the longer hair of a shepherd. He looked horribly ferocious and had a bark to send shivers down the spine of a sumo wrestler, but it was all show. He retained the gregarious personality of a puppy. Of course Simon Balfour didn't know that.

The man's eyes opened wide at the sight of the dog, who leaped up the steps and stopped short when he saw Simon. Ivan growled, then barked twice—his invitation to play. Emily stood with arms crossed and a smug expression on her face. She gave Simon Balfour credit, however, for although he looked uneasy, he didn't bolt.

"Nice dog," he intoned dryly, holding out his palm for Ivan to sniff.

"Sometimes," Emily murmured back provocatively. Ivan turned from licking Simon's hand to whining playfully around Emily's feet, acting about as threatening now as he actually was. When Emily's eyes met Simon's again, she smiled reluctantly. "Okay. So I couldn't throw you off the place, and my watchdog would welcome Genghis Khan if he offered to play catch first." She sat down abruptly, humor wilting as she shooed her pet away after failing to dodge his wet tongue. "Please. Don't lie to me. Tell me why you're here."

Ivan padded off with an injured air and collapsed with a loud sigh in the corner of the long porch.

"I wouldn't lie to you, Emily Carson," Simon promised with quiet sincerity. "Or to anyone else, for that matter."

"How noble," Emily retorted with a touch of acerbity. "Everyone lies if it suits his purpose to do so."

"You don't have much faith in people, do you?"

Emily shrugged. "I suppose not. No one has ever given me much reason why I should."

"What about God? Can even He earn your trust?"

Emily jerked her head around, wondering if she had heard right. Was he joking, being sarcastic? He met her astonishment and wariness with a clear-eyed serenity that was either completely guileless or the product of years of polished acting. "I don't see where my views on God have anything to do with the situation here," she finally hedged. "Are you stalling or something?"

Simon gave a rueful laugh and sat up. "I was perfectly serious in my question, but yeah—I was stalling." He paused. "I've discovered I have this tremendous aversion to hurting you. And I'm afraid, after talking with you these few minutes, that what I have to tell you is going to hurt you pretty badly."

"The title dispute. . ." She spoke the words as if referring to a repugnant, noxious weed. "Are you trying to tell me you're claiming this as your house?"

"Not exactly." He stirred restlessly. Emily sat unmoving, her very stillness betraying a fear she didn't want to admit. "It's my great-aunt, actually. She claims the house belongs to her by virtue of a will that—unfortunately—hasn't been found yet. The property was supposed to have been left in trust with the Realtors you dealt with."

Emily shook her head, trying to understand. "My real estate agent never said a word. Mildred didn't know anything about the place other than referring to it as the old deCourier place like everyone else in Timmons. We searched for the deed together. She was just as excited as I was. . . ." Emily's voice faltered. "It doesn't make any sense. In fact, I don't believe you." Bewilderment hardened to accusation. "You're just trying to take my house away from me so you can tear it down and build condominiums or something."

"No, I'm not." Simon's voice and face oozed compassion and regret, and Emily's suspicion faltered. "I don't understand about your Realtor, although she did mention something about her mother being her partner, but she's away for a three-month Mediterranean cruise. Maybe she would have known."

He fingered the wilting blossoms of a huge, lavender hydrangea planted by the front porch steps decades before. "All I know is what I learned from Aunt Iris, who might be seventy-six years old but has the finesse of a Sherman tank. She called my mother about a month ago ranting and raving about someone snatching her inheritance out from under her."

His gaze wandered over the yard as if he were imagining what it would look like all cleaned up. "Apparently some old codger who lives around here mentioned the sale to his sister, who is a longtime acquaintance of Aunt Iris. The woman commented on the sale in a letter to my great-aunt, who promptly declared war over it. Included in her campaign was a rather heated call to my mother—Iris's niece. Mother got hold of me and persuaded me to see if I could find out what was going on."

He sighed and muttered in an undertone, "I don't know why she didn't call my brother Geoff, but I suppose due to the circumstances. . ." He raised his voice and smiled at Emily, who did not return the gesture.

"Aunt Iris is a little less than five feet high and weighs maybe ninety-five pounds. But she's Attila the Hun and Queen Victoria all wrapped up in one package, and it's sort of hard to refuse when she gets a bee in her bonnet." In spite of herself, a smile tugged at Emily's lips. He sounded like a little boy and resembled one at the moment, the way he was toying with the flowers and avoiding her eyes, talking about this great-aunt as if she were some monstrous dictator holding a gun to his head.

"Anyway," Simon continued, "Aunt Iris swears there is a will somewhere in this house that stipulates the place has to remain in our family for a hundred years from the date of the will."

"Is that legal?"

"I've talked to my brother, who is a lawyer. If the will is found and is a proper will, then yes, it's legal."

"Why didn't your brother take care of all this, then? Why did your great-aunt want you to get involved?"

Simon heaved a bone-deep sigh, contemplated his jogging shoes, then faced Emily squarely. "She wanted me to find out the details so I could get rid of you before you did too much damage to the house. Aunt Iris wants it renovated as well, but she wants me to do it." He paused, then finished almost roughly, "You see, I'm a professional contractor, Emily, and head a company specializing in period home restoration."

Chapter 2

Emily jumped to her feet. "You won't touch my house! No so much as pound a nail or paint a single board! Get out."

"Miss Carson—Emily—"

Panicked now, Emily ignored him. "There's no aunt, no will—you just heard about my house and want it for yourself!" Her voice rose. Ivan, hearing the unusual sound of his mistress yelling, trotted over and nudged her with a damp inquisitive nose. Simon rose, too, and put his hand on Emily's arm. She knocked it away with a force that surprised both of them.

"Get him, Ivan!" she commanded the dog, her voice almost breaking now. "Attack, you stupid animal. He's trying to take away my house." Her gaze ricocheted around wildly, ending with Simon, who stood a little ways from her now, his eyes very green. The outburst died as abruptly as it had erupted, and Emily plopped back down on the top step, shoulders slumped in exhaustion and mortification. Ordinarily, she was not a passionate woman, not one who wore her feelings on her sleeve. She had a reputation as an easygoing, absentminded, tolerant creature with a heart like warm oatmeal. She never got angry, never lost her temper, and was frankly appalled to discover she had a temper.

But she had also never been as unnerved as she was at this moment.

Simon came down the steps and hunkered down in front of her, balancing on the second step from the bottom with the ease of a gymnast. "I am truly sorry," he repeated quietly. "It's a mess, and we're just going to have to work together to find a way out of it."

"You and your family can work any way you please," Emily responded in a tight, cold voice. "Until you present me with an affidavit proving otherwise, this is my property, my house. And I plan to keep on restoring it the way I please." She glared at Simon. "And you can tell your Attila the Hun of an aunt that just because it's your job and I haven't done it before, doesn't mean I can't restore my home just as well as you can."

Incredibly, Simon grinned. "So there," he finished for her and stood up. "Well. . .I think I'll take myself off now, since you're obviously not interested in negotiation at the moment. Not," he added with a rueful sigh, "that I blame you." He started down the steps, then stopped, turning back. "There's an old hymn I love. . .it reminds me that God's eye watches over us all the time—'His Eye Is

On the Sparrow.' I've been thinking about it the last few minutes, when I had to warn a sparrow that she might be kicked out of her nest."

He stared down at her for a moment longer, then loped off toward his car. Ivan bounded after him, leaping and running in circles and barking happily. Simon ignored the dog, but just before he climbed back inside his snappy little sports convertible, he looked across the yard at Emily one last time. She returned the look, refusing to move until he ducked into the car, started the engine, and drove away.

Emily had been working in the daytime at the house, then driving the thirty miles or so back to her apartment at night. After the confrontation with Simon Balfour, however, she determined to move in lock, stock, and barrel as fast as she could. Possession, after all, was nine-tenths of the law.

It took almost a week to transfer her belongings, during which time Emily also resigned her teaching position in Sylvan. She crammed most of her things into the dining room since she had no plans for entertaining until she finished restoring her new home. Her parents had told her she was welcome to the contents of the house they'd lived in for over thirty years. Emily never let them know how much their attitude hurt. They discarded it all—as if everything had the sentimental value of a worn-out shoe.

About like they discarded J.J. and me, Emily found herself thinking late one night. She kicked the crumpled sheet, rolled on one side and then the other, and finally fluffed her pillow so she could sit up and be miserable. And alone. Thanks to her best friend, she was acutely aware that she was a single woman, living alone.

Barb and Taylor Chakensis and their two children had helped her move, and Barb—a perpetual worrier—fretted over Emily. She made such a fuss over Emily's job situation, her isolation, and the possible reappearance of Simon Balfour that Emily herself was becoming paranoid.

"Look," Emily had finally said, "I've applied in Timmons for a teaching position, and I should have the phone in a few more weeks. Until then, if a motorcycle gang from L.A. decides to camp out here, I'll feed 'em lunch." She ignored Barb's rolling eyes. "At least I have Ivan."

Ivan. . . Emily sat up a little straighter in the bed, listening. He was barking again. Emily started to yell at him when her ear caught the faint sound of an idling car engine. Suddenly it revved up and gunned down the dirt road. Ivan barked three more times, and Emily finally yelled at him to hush. Honestly, did he have to bark at every car that passed?

"Give me a break, Dog," Emily groaned, plumping her pillow and flopping back. "I'm finally in a position where I don't have to listen to Mom and Dad fighting about what to do with J.J. I don't have to listen to creaking floorboards when people walk across the floor in the apartment above mine, or hear the water running down the pipes every time they turn on a faucet. I have a home of my own now."

But for how long? The uncertainty lingered even though she hadn't heard from Simon Balfour again. Emily tried to convince herself he had been a slick con artist who had discovered she couldn't be conned, so he had given up. And yet what kind of con artist talked about old hymns and. . .and called her a sparrow?

The metaphor hurt because sparrows were nondescript, pesky birds everyone ignored.

And yet. . .Emily had taken time to run by her church, where she rifled through the pages of an old hymnbook Mrs. Jenkins, the church pianist, unearthed for her. Why would a slick con artist talk about God as Simon Balfour had and refer to a song about how God watches over individuals as He does an insignificant bird? It had been a rather comforting song, actually, and when Mrs. Jenkins told her she was welcome to the hymnbook since the church used newer ones now, Emily had accepted the offer with thanks.

Ivan didn't bark again, and eventually Emily slid back into sleep.

The next morning was gray and sullen. Emily donned her jeans and an old, oversized T-shirt with an arrow on the front pointing down to her stomach and the word *Baby* printed above it. Another arrow beside it pointed upward with the word *Mother* printed at its point. Barb had donated the garment after declaring she would never need it again, teasing Emily about what would happen if Emily wore it in public. Emily had laughed and said it was going to be a work shirt, and if Ivan and Samson took offense, she could shove them both outside.

She had finished stripping and sanding all the wood in the library and was going to start painting it a lovely creamy gold color. It would be nice to wallpaper, of course, but that would have to wait. One day. . .

A light rain started when she had been painting an hour, and with a sigh Emily put the brush down to close all the windows but the two opening to the side veranda. Even if the shower turned into a downpour, the overhanging porch would keep the water from splashing inside and ruining all her work.

Sure enough, within the next hour the sky darkened and rumbles of thunder heralded a good old-fashioned summer storm. Emily ignored the sound and fury and continued to paint in long, even strokes just like the instructions recommended. It was actually sort of soothing, and she began humming a tuneless song to the rhythm of the strokes, oblivious to the rest of the world. She was so oblivious that she didn't hear Ivan's welcoming barks over the steady beating of the rain on the roof, nor the sound of the buzzer-style doorbell that didn't work half the time anyway.

Balanced on the top step of her new ladder, reaching to paint over the crown molding that framed the walls next to the ceiling, Emily didn't hear the footsteps scraping across the floor and pausing momentarily at the entrance of the library. When Simon Balfour's voice offered in approving tones, "This is looking good,"

Emily was so startled she let out a small yelp, jerked around, and promptly lost her balance.

She didn't know how he managed to move so quickly, but Simon caught her as she toppled, the wildly waving paintbrush missing his head by inches. His arms folded around her in a hard, bruising grip, and for just a moment he held her tightly against his chest before setting her gently on her feet.

"I'm sorry. I suppose I should have kept ringing the bell, but I was getting soaked out there and, besides, I was concerned about you." He stopped, his gaze dropping to the paint-spattered T-shirt, then lifting to search her face.

Emily was still too busy recovering her breath as well as her balance. She lifted her hand to swipe at her hair, saw that she was still clutching the brush, and laid it carefully down across the top of the can of paint. What on earth was he doing here? She straightened slowly, using the brief seconds to marshall her scattered senses. Her eyes lifted to meet Simon's, where the blankness of a stone wall had replaced the engaging air of apology and concern and interest.

That threw her all over again, and instead of demanding to know what he was doing she gaped at him, not understanding the aura of disapproval, almost censure, that hovered behind the carefully expressionless face.

"I wasn't aware of your condition," Simon said finally after a moment of uneasy silence. "It's none of my business, but I don't think it's such a good idea to be perched up on ladders, much less inhaling all these fumes without adequate ventilation."

"Just what," Emily demanded incredulously, "are you talking about? I'm as healthy as a Berkshire hog at the county fair, and you're right; it is none of your business. Speaking of that, what are you doing here anyway?"

He was staring at her front again, so fixedly that Emily finally followed suit to see what was causing him to be so abominably rude. Color climbed hectically all over her cheeks; she groaned and covered her face with her hands.

"I will never tell my best friend Barb about this," she mumbled from behind her splayed fingers. "This is one of her old maternity tops she gave me to work in. I'm not pregnant. In fact, I've never—" She stopped, so embarassed she wanted to leap through the open window and see if the rain would melt her. . .or maybe lightning would strike her dead. . . .

Simon was laughing. "I'm relieved you're not pregnant," he finally managed to say between chuckles. "I'm also just as pleased to hear about the other, even if that's none of my business either. Young women like you are a rare and wonderful species nowadays, and speaking as a Christian and a man, I'd like to ask you to marry me."

Emily jerked back, then realized he was teasing her. It was a kind thing for him to do, and it worked. She found herself laughing, the awkwardness and

228

humiliation of the moment dissolving. "If I wasn't so sure you were asking mainly in order to get your hands on my house, I just might consider accepting and teaching you a lesson," she tossed back.

Simon shook his head and proceeded to wander around the library examining her work. Emily found herself feeling like one of her eighth graders taking midterms. Would he truly approve of what she had done? More to the point—why did she care what Simon Balfour thought? Because she was so uncomfortable with the direction of her thoughts, she sidelined the whole issue. "I need to go check on my cat," she blurted. "He's not too wild about thunderstorms."

With cool dignity she marched from the room as if her hair were bound in a strikingly elegant coronet and she were dressed in a suit, silk stockings, and three-inch heels.

When she hadn't reappeared in ten minutes, Simon went searching, taking note of the fact that she had moved all her furniture in. The bulk of it was crammed in haphazard fashion in a room down the front hall: boxes stacked on top of each other and tables on top of tables, chairs with their legs stuck up in the air mingling with lamps and knickknacks and other odds and ends. Simon shook his head again, smiling a little at this evidence of Emily Carson's determination to stake her claim. *Hey, Lord, this is a lot harder than I thought it would be.* Why couldn't she be some hard-nosed female who could just be bought off with appropriate monetary compensation? Why a vulnerable, appealing young woman with gumption and grit and the most expressive pair of brown eyes he'd ever encountered?

"I'm storing it in here," Emily informed him from over his right shoulder.

He turned, taking note of the cat purring contentedly in her cradled arms. Not another furry animal to contend with. How many did she have anyway? She had mentioned the two last week, but Simon was rapidly coming to realize that Emily Carson was an unpredictable creature at best. She just might produce a rabbit or two from under the staircase if he wasn't careful.

"I can see that. What are your plans—a room at a time?"

Emily transferred the cat to her shoulder, where he draped about her neck as contented and limp as only felines can be. "Yes," Emily agreed almost defiantly. "One room at a time, and you saw for yourself how capable I am."

"How would you like a job working for me, then? I could always use capable, dedicated help." He watched her, wondering how someone with so expressive a face could be so wary and cynical about people.

"If that's a subtle way of reintroducing our previous discussion on a supposed title discrepancy, it worked." She gently dumped the cat on top of what was presumably a cushioned kitchen chair, residing at the moment on top of a coffee table. "Would you like a Coke or something to drink? And come find a chair somewhere. If we're going to fight, we might as well be comfortable."

"A Coke would be nice, and I didn't come wanting to fight you." He followed her into a small galley kitchen with ancient, grease-filmed gas appliances. A small dinette table with metal legs had been positioned under a window, with one of the mates to the chair Emily had put the cat on next to it. Simon backtracked the few steps to the dining room and helped himself to the chair next to the cat, who stared at him with unblinking disdain.

When he returned, Emily handed him a paper cup filled with ice cubes and cola. "I haven't unpacked dishes yet," she said, sounding defensive.

Simon shrugged amiably. "This is fine." He took a long swallow, put the cup down, and leaned forward on his elbows. "Emily, I flew up to Connecticut to try and persuade Aunt Iris to drop the whole thing. She's never even seen this place and has apparently looked on it as sort of a nest egg security for her old age all these years."

"Connecticut?" Emily spluttered. "Why on earth should someone from Connecticut be interested in a house in the backwoods of south Georgia?" She searched his face. "Can you prove any of this today?"

"Yes. I brought papers and letters and identification—I left them in the car, though." He stood, glancing out the window at the pouring rain. "Do I have to go get them right now?"

"No." She sighed. "You can wait until it lets up some. But I do want to see some proof of all this."

"I understand. In the meantime, can I explain the situation and try to convince you that I'm as frustrated by it all as you are?"

"I can imagine your level of frustration," Emily responded dryly. "How much profit would you realize restoring a place like this?"

"That," stated Simon a little too evenly, "was uncalled for." Emily ducked her head, but Simon knew she sensed the temper flickering beneath the words.

"I'm sorry." She traced the faint brown stain made from a too-hot pan, her gaze wandering around the room and settling on the stain again. "This was my fault," she murmured absently, as if Simon had asked. "I was twelve. Mom yelled at me about how clumsy and stupid I was. Then—like she always did—she turned around five minutes later and apologized. Another five minutes later she breezed out the door to go—I've forgotten where she went. . . ."

Her voice remained offhand, neutral, but Simon suddenly had the uncomfortable urge to wrap her in a tender embrace. He also had a feeling the scar on Emily's soul was as permanent as the scar on the table.

"Hey."

She lifted her eyes.

"We'll work it out, okay?" He lightly brushed the back of her hand. "I understand the sense of panic and desperation you must be feeling, and I really would like to avoid your losing your home. But unfortunately for us both, there's still Aunt Iris."

"Blood is thicker than water," Emily murmured, but there was no sarcasm in the observation, and she managed to give Simon enough of a smile to convince him she was merely trying to inject a lighter note.

"I don't think Aunt Iris has blood—not her own anyway," Simon returned. The ensuing laughter was strained, but somehow after that the atmosphere lightened, and when Emily offered to make sandwiches to go with the drinks, Simon agreed easily.

"From what I can gather, my grandmother couldn't have cared less about this property—but then she married my grandfather pretty young and had no need of it anyway." He took another huge bite of his ham-and-cheese sandwich. "Iris never married, though, and from what Mother tells me she's always had a 'thing' about the 'family estate.' I suppose, when you grow up in the Depression years, land is about as valuable as money in your pocket. Aunt Iris felt that as long as she had property down in Georgia, she would never have to be beholden to anyone or be totally destitute."

"Where did this"—Emily waved her sandwich—"family estate come from? Who built it? And why here in Georgia instead of Connecticut?"

Simon smiled across at her. The bruised look was fading from her eyes now, and she was almost as relaxed as her cat, who at the moment was sitting at his feet with a hopeful, expectant look on his face.

"I'm still working on that one. All my great-aunt can remember is her mother talking about a family scandal and amazement that she would even consider having anything to do with this property. I gather it was more or less a taboo subject for my grandmother and Aunt Iris, so little was said until their mother—my great-great-grandmother—had died. Some mention of the will and the property were made in her will, and Aunt Iris must have jumped on it like a spinster would an eligible male."

"Watch it, Fella. I'm a spinster schoolteacher and take exception to such remarks. Who needs men?"

"Such belligerence." Simon lifted his hands in mock surrender, relieved that she had recovered enough to tease like she had when they first met. "Does this mean I can't make you swoon with a display of all my muscles or my just-as-healthy bank account?"

Emily wrinkled her nose. "Yucch. You would doubtless impress the girls in my science classes, but it doesn't do much for me."

Simon gave in and dropped the last bite of his sandwich to the floor. It disappeared immediately. "I take it you disagree with the biblical observation that it is not good for man to be alone."

His gaze wandered over her smooth, high forehead, the huge brown eyes framed with dark lashes and several spatters of cream-colored paint, traced the line of her cheek and jaw back to her mouth, which at the moment was pressed in a tight line.

She was not used to such a frank, masculine survey. Simon found himself wondering why. She was not particularly beautiful, but there was nonetheless something incredibly appealing about her. "What put you off the male of the species?" he asked.

Emily pondered his question a moment, brow wrinkled in thought. "I never really thought about it like that," she confessed at last. "And it's not that I don't like men—I suppose I've just been occupied with other things."

She contemplated her fingers. "I've had a job of some kind ever since I was fifteen. There was never any time to date much or do all the other things the kids were doing." She began twirling the end of her braid round and round her fingers. "Besides, I have a younger brother who was pretty wild. I spent a lot of time trying to keep him—and his friends—out of trouble."

Emily flung the braid over her shoulder and stood up, dumping the trash in a paper grocery sack on the floor. "My parents had no idea what to do about J.J., and they quit trying. I finally persuaded him to join the Air Force, and he's in Germany now."

She turned back to Simon. "That's enough biography. What about the title dispute? What are you going to do now that your great-aunt refuses to give up her notion of a lost will?"

Simon stood up, too, dumped his trash in the bag, and came to stand in front of Emily. "I'm going to have to try and find the will," he admitted, inwardly wincing at Emily's expression. "She claims it's hidden somewhere in this house. I'd like your permission to search for it."

Chapter 3

Emily closed her eyes. She should have known what he was going to say, but she was so thrown by the whole situation her brain wasn't functioning. "I don't want you nosing around," she whispered, opening her eyes but avoiding looking at Simon. "And if I let you, and you find the will, it's like I'm signing my own death warrant."

"I know."

She hated it when he spoke like that. Why couldn't he be mean and obnoxious, a bully and a crass gold digger she could fight, someone whom it was easy to harden her heart against?

"But I also know I have to make the effort," Simon continued, his voice flat, expressionless. "And if I can't do it with your cooperation, I'll have to do my job without it."

Emily changed her mind. It was very easy to harden her heart against him. "Go ahead, then. But don't expect any help from me." She scooped Samson off the floor and stalked out the door down the long, narrow hall.

Moments later, Emily heard Simon come into the library. "Go away," she said without pausing in her strokes, her voice husky. "Go look for your stupid will."

"Can I help paint awhile instead? The way you're going about it, you're going to smack the brush through the wall any minute." Emily paused in midstroke, stared at the section of wall she had been painting, and winced. The strokes of her brush were short and abrupt, almost vicious, and as a consequence the wall was a mess. She laid the brush down, wiped her hands on a rag, and rubbed them over her eyes and face.

"I don't want your help," she muttered tiredly. "Could you please either look for the will or leave? I don't mean to be rude, but I'm not very good company right now." Her gaze bounced off his, then returned to a dejected contemplation of the floor. "I don't know why I'm apologizing. It's your fault I'm in this predicament."

Simon studied her with assessing eyes Emily was afraid saw a lot more than she was comfortable with. His next words confirmed it. "Someday I'd like to find out why you have so little faith in yourself and in other people. I'd like to change that, starting with teaching you to have faith in me and my intentions."

He leaned and picked up the paintbrush and placed it in Emily's hand, closing her limp fingers around the handle. "So I'm leaving you right now, giving you some space. I'll come back to start hunting for the will after you've had a little time to adjust. Try not to let your burdens get you down too much, little sparrow."

He left, but it was a long time before Emily could concentrate on painting the library wall. She tried to undo the damage she'd inflicted, but her heart wasn't in it. Grumbling vague threats, she ended up rummaging around upstairs, looking for Simon Balfour's stupid will.

How, she asked herself furiously as she sneezed and coughed through the dust and dim corners of the upstairs rooms, *am I supposed to concentrate on restoring my house when I can't even be sure it is my house?* If she found the stupid document before Simon did, she would burn it.

No. . . She wouldn't, couldn't do that, even if she could get away with it. She might not be the best Christian on the face of this earth, but she did know right from wrong. Even back in high school, before she committed her life to Christ, she had been unable to cheat on tests, or lie about her whereabouts, or experiment with drugs and sex. It had been such a relief to find out the reason why, thanks to a compassionate, caring college roommate. Her body was the temple of God, and He had laid out specific rules as to its care.

Somehow, though, in the last couple of years, the Lord hadn't seemed to figure as prominently in her life. She had been so busy working, so worried trying to keep J.J. out of trouble, and the last couple of months so. . .disillusioned with life and people that her faith had more or less taken a backseat.

Wiping her hands on her paint-splattered jeans, Emily trudged down the narrow hall into her bedroom. Over in the corner was the box holding all her important documents and papers. Emily rummaged until she came up with the folder holding all the papers on the house, tugged it out, and began reading.

For almost thirty minutes she sifted through legal jargon and page after page of photostated documents and certifications and contracts. Everything looked straightforward, as it should be: On July 10, she and Mildred Davis, Realtor, with a lawyer and secretary as witnesses, had signed all the papers for the property known as the deCourier estate over to Emily Elizabeth Carson.

Mildred's mother had handled the property for the past twenty years or so, but since she had been out of the country, the lawyer hadn't seen any problem with Mildred handling things. No one stepped forward protesting the change in ownership—and as Simon pointed out, virtually the whole town knew what was happening in the office of Shady Tree Realtors.

The only other names Mildred and Emily had been able to unearth in the dusty tomb of the records office at the county courthouse had been someone named VanCleef and some man whose first name was Harold (the last name had smeared to an indecipherable blot). The only other owner had been a woman name Gwinette deCourier.

Emily squinted at all the faded type. Where on earth did Simon's great-aunt Iris come into all this? What would happen when all the citizens of Timmons heard? And they would, Emily knew. Human emotions were fickle at best. Emily mentally vowed to gird her armor more tightly against whatever weapons Simon Balfour chose to fire at her.

A week passed. Emily worked with single-minded desperation, falling exhausted into bed at night. Her sleep remained restless, uneasy; and twice more Ivan woke her barking at passing cars. A random thought flitted through her mind that there was a lot more traffic out here in the country than she would have anticipated.

Simon returned late one afternoon, just after the whippoorwills began their haunting calls to each other from the woods surrounding the house. Ivan barked and galloped across the yard to meet him. Simon irritably ordered him to get down and go away, wondering again why anyone would want a dog the size and disposition of a bouncing kangaroo.

Emily met him at the door, looking even more like a ragpicker's child. "I wondered when you'd come back," she said, chin up and bristling with defiance.

Simon looked closer, noting the signs of exhaustion and apprehension her tired defiance couldn't hide. "I was going to give you a few more days," he replied, following her inside and into the front hall, "but every night my great-aunt calls both my parents in Florida and me at Timmon's one and only motel to see if I've found anything. And. . .since you're more or less being dangled on a fraying rope over a precipice, I decided the sooner we resolve things, the better for everyone."

"That was a lovely line," Emily murmured, looking both stunned—and close to tears. "You really sounded as if you meant it." She lifted a hand to mop at the perspiration trickling down her temple, and Simon noticed her trembling fingers. He frowned down at her, then peered over her shoulder into the library. "How long have you been working without a break?" he asked quietly.

Emily shrugged. "Since Barb left this afternoon. She and her two kids brought cookies and lemonade. I don't know. What time is it anyway?"

"It's going on eight o'clock. Have you eaten anything?"

"Lemonade and cookies."

His frown deepened to a scowl. "You're going to kill yourself over this place if you don't take better care." If he had an ounce of sense, he'd hunt out the wretched will and get it over with. . . . "Go clean up and put on some decent clothes. I'll take you into Timmons for a meal and come back in the morning to search for the will."

She stared at him as if he'd lost his mind, and Simon didn't blame her. He couldn't believe himself either.

"Do I have any say-so in the matter?"

Suddenly they grinned at each other, and the aura of tension evaporated.

"No," Simon promised. "If you don't do as I ask, I'll take you as you are. We might be refused service in the first couple of places, but I daresay someone will eventually overlook your extreme grubbiness."

"Thanks a lot. I'll go clean up—it will probably only take fifteen minutes or so. Do you want to wait in the kitchen? I don't have chairs set up anywhere else."

"I'll wait on the front porch. Take your time but hurry."

Simon sat on the porch steps, elbows on his knees, feeling buffeted by conflicting feelings of depression and guilt, excitement and determination. Never in his life had he found himself in such an untenable situation, and he didn't know what to do.

Bowing his head in prayer, he sent up a heartfelt petition for guidance and direction. Solomon had been granted the wisdom to handle two women who claimed the same child; surely he could come up with an approach to offer Aunt Iris and Emily Carson that would achieve a similar resolution. Unfortunately, with Emily he seemed to be losing his ability to remain neutral. He stood when he heard her footsteps crossing the porch, something very unnerving stirring deep inside as she came to stand quietly in front of him.

"I don't have any dresses unpacked," Emily gestured apologetically to her plain khaki slacks and the oversized turquoise sleeveless knit sweater. "Will this do?"

Simon studied her face, bare of any makeup, the vulnerability and openness of her nature shining out at him like a beacon. She had washed her hair and coiled it in a wet bun on top of her head. Drying wisps were already slipping out and feathering her slender neck and forehead, and they seemed to accent the slenderness of her form.

She was not beautiful—she was not really even pretty—but Simon felt a giant hand squeezing his heart. She was somehow beyond either of those trite descriptions, and all he could think of was that she was the most gallant person he had ever known. Her dark brown eyes were filled with worry and fatigue, but she had lifted her chin and was gazing at him with that tiny spark of defiance flickering away, distinguishable even in the purple shadows of early evening.

She had a rare beauty of spirit, yet such a thick veneer of disillusionment, the spirit was only allowed to shine at brief unguarded moments he was beginning to cherish. What had made her the way she was? And what was he going to do if and when he found the will?

Chapter 4

They ate at a steakhouse in Timmons, and Emily—with a challenging gleam in her eye—ordered the most expensive steak on the menu. She had just laughingly promised Simon she would too eat every bite when a medium-sized man with carefully combed hair and an intimidating scowl stopped by their table.

"Excuse me, but you're Emily Carson, aren't you?"

Emily looked up, smiling in surprise and anticipation. "Mr. Radford! How are you?" He was the principal of the junior high school in Timmons, and Emily hoped he was going to tell her about the position she had applied for. It had worried her to be without a job more than she had allowed Barb to know.

Mr. Radford ignored her question. "Miss Carson, I've been trying to get in touch with you for a week. You apparently had your phone disconnected in Sylvan and have yet to have one installed in your new place of residence." He paused and added bitingly, "It's very annoying, as I'm sure you agree."

Emily colored. "I finally had my secretary send you a letter Friday, but since I saw you here I thought I'd go on and let you know." Mr. Radford glanced at Simon, who was sitting without moving, watching Emily. "The teacher who was considering retiring changed her mind. There are thus no available openings at this time. Since you do have excellent references, we're keeping your name on file for midseason replacements. We'd also be happy to use you as a sub."

He glanced at his watch, then over toward the entrance. "It's a shame you don't have any training in foreign languages. The high school is looking for a Spanish teacher."

"I see," Emily said very faintly. "Thank you for telling me, Mr. Radford."

"I'm sorry, Emily," Simon offered after Mr. Radford left. "That's a tough break."

"Yes. First you and your will. Now this. God must not want me around here." Her chin lifted. "But I'm staying. I'll handle it—I'll find another job." She picked up her water glass and took a swallow, put it down and toyed with the silverware until the prickling tears receded and the hot poker in her chest cooled a little.

"Emily—look at me." Emily lifted dull brown eyes. "Don't shut God out, or convince yourself He's trying to crush you in defeat. It's not true—He cares very much what happens to you."

"His eye is on the sparrow, right? I found a copy of the song—it's a nice song." She stared down at her steak. "Maybe God does watch out for sparrows—I don't know. I do know He obviously has more important things on His mind than watching out for me." She lifted her gaze back to Simon. "So please don't try to convince me otherwise."

"No."

He said the word softly but with unyielding emphasis, and Emily felt a shaft of something hot and alien stirring to life deep inside her. "Exactly what do you mean by that?" she asked carefully.

"I mean you're wrong, dead wrong, and I'm going to convince you of it if it takes the rest of the summer. Or longer. I have a crew of well-trained men and women who can function on their own awhile."

He placed his palms flat on the table and leaned across, trapping Emily with his determined gaze. "You, on the other hand, have no job, a house that might not be yours, and the insane notion that God has turned His back on you. If anyone ever needed to be convinced that God has His loving eye on you at all times, you do. And since I feel responsible for at least half your problems, I plan to be responsible for the solutions as well."

"I want to go home, please." If he thought for one minute she was naive enough to fall for that approach. . . Abruptly, she shoved her chair back and stood. "Thanks for the meal, but I'm not hungry after all. Please enjoy yours—I'll get a taxi. See you in court, Mr. Balfour."

Shamefully glad to see signs of temper flickering across his face, Emily swiveled and marched out of the dining room. Her behavior was irrational, rude—totally out of character—and her parting shot childish. But right now she just didn't care.

Simon caught up with her outside.

"Come on," he said, his voice short, clipped. Cupping her elbow, he added, "I'll take you home."

Emily jerked free. "I'm not a helpless old woman yet! You can take me home only because it'll be hours before I could rouse a taxi." Stalking across to his car, she reached for the handle, then rounded on the man hovering at her heels.

All the suppressed rage and denied fear welled up and burst free. She glared up into his shadowed face, almost shaking with emotion. "I don't need you or your—your pity! And if you ever compare me to a sparrow again, I'll wallop you. They're disgusting little creatures nobody cares two straws about—and that song is wrong!"

His figure loomed above her, radiating temper and something even more ominous. "Maybe," he growled, "just maybe now's the time to do what I've wanted to do since the second time we met."

Suddenly his arms wrapped around Emily and she was held immobilized against a damp chest that smelled equal parts of aftershave, sweat, and rib-eye steak. Without warning his mouth covered hers, and Emily Carson, placid, easy-going schoolteacher, was kissed more thoroughly, more expertly, than she had been in her entire twenty-six years.

When Simon lifted his head at last, Emily gawked up at him, mouth tingling, ears ringing, and all around them moths and gnats fluttered in the wavering streams of yellow light from the restaurant parking lot.

"Oh," she stammered out at last, "I thought you were a. . .a gentleman. . .a Christian gentleman."

Simon stared at her as if he couldn't quite believe what he had heard. His gaze moved from her eyes to her mouth, and a muscle twitched in his jaw.

"Being a Christian doesn't mean I'm a eunuch, Woman!" He turned away with an infuriated jerk and braced his palms flat on the hood of his little green Jensen-Healy. Head bowed, breathing heavy, he stayed thus for several moments without speaking.

Emily considered and cast aside a baker's dozen comebacks, but she was bitterly aware that nothing could erase the unbelievable naiveté of her comment. Nor could she deny the fact that the kiss had somehow transformed all her anger to a far more frightening emotion.

What had possessed her to behave so? She had been kissed before, had even successfully repulsed the heated advances of one of J.J.'s drunken companions. What bewildering alchemy had Simon performed to metamorphose the plain, unexciting woman of humdrum lifestyle into a starry-eyed, pliable creature fairly throbbing with—with passion?

She didn't like Simon, she didn't trust Simon, and he was making her feel all sorts of violent emotions she never would have associated with passion and desire: anger, frustration, helplessness, fear. Yet when his mouth had covered hers, all those seething emotions had swirled into something so mindlessly bone dissolving that all she could do was gape at him like a bug-eyed frog and utter foolish banalities.

"What are you standing there for? Waiting for an apology—or seconds?" Simon snapped with unforgivable irritation. She had no idea what he must have read on her face, but after pinching the bridge of his nose between thumb and forefinger, he dropped his hand and said, quite gently, "Get in the car, Emily, and I'll take you home."

Emily obeyed without another word, and they spent the next moments in thick silence, the only noise coming from the muted roar of the Healy's engine.

Eventually Simon heaved a sigh. "Did I frighten you?" he asked, the words vibrating with an uncomfortable edge, even though he again spoke quietly. Emily wet her lips. "A little," she admitted just as quietly. "But I frightened myself more. I've never behaved that way in my life—I've never felt like that in my life." She almost smiled. "I've got a reputation of sorts as being disorganized but level-headed. Haphazard perhaps—but sane, calm, and dependable."

Simon snorted.

"Well, I have. . .I am," Emily retorted. She turned her head away and gazed sightlessly out at the dark, deserted countryside. "Ever since you came into my life, nothing has been the same, including me. I wish you'd disappear back into the wilds of Connecticut or wherever you came from and leave me alone."

"I've been on a location in Tennessee, and I'd like nothing better than to get back to the order and sanity of my own life. You've messed my life up as well, Emily Carson," he admitted. Then, after another uncomfortable pause, he added, "I haven't treated a woman like that since I was in my unregenerate teens. If my father were here, he'd likely be tempted to try and mete out the same discipline he did then." He gave a mirthless chuckle. "Especially now that I'm definitely old enough to know better."

Emily's curiosity overcame the sinkhole of apathy and depression into which she was sliding. "What on earth did you do—and how did your dad find out?" she couldn't help asking.

"I was seventeen, thought I was God's gift to the female sex, and came on a little too strong for Janie Beth. She told her folks; her dad called mine. . .and I was grounded for two weeks as well as being sole man on the cleanup crew for my dad's contracting business."

He smiled ruefully. "And in the evenings I had to paint the fence that surrounded Janie Beth's house. She wouldn't speak to me, but her parents let me hear an earful, as did her twitty thirteen-year-old sister. I remember begging Dad to let me out of at least that part of my punishment, but he just smiled, and I painted."

"What a monster of a father you must have."

She could just make out the swift turn of his head toward her before he returned his eyes to the road.

"Not at all," he refuted evenly. "I wouldn't have respected him like I do if he hadn't come down on me that hard. I deserved it." There was a fractional pause, then he added, "He disciplined me in love as a father should, Emily; he didn't punish me to vent his own frustration. Didn't your father do likewise for you?"

"I never needed much disciplining, and he quit trying with Jimmy-Joe after he ran away when Daddy whipped him the last time. He was only ten, but he was gone for two days. After that, I think Daddy and Mom both decided to pretty much consign him to whatever retribution he might reap if he was caught." She twisted her purse strap round and round in her hands. "But I know he and Mom cared for us as much as they could, in their own way, so don't go feeling sorry for me."

"It would be easier to feel sorry for a Venus's-flytrap," Simon grumbled beneath his breath.

The next instant they were both blinded by a car with its headlights on the bright setting, hurtling around a curve and approaching them fast—on their side of the road. Simon flattened his hand on the horn and wrenched the wheel hard to the right.

The other car swerved at the last moment and careened by them with inches to spare. It had not slackened speed at all, and they heard the tires squealing in the distance as it tore around another bend.

"Are you all right?"

Emily released her death grip on her purse and wriggled her fingers to restore the circulation. "I think so," she said shakily. "He must have been drunk."

"Or high as a kite on drugs. I was talking the other day to the proprietor at the motel where I've been staying. Apparently the police think there might be a gang operating somewhere in this county. Whatever happened to plain old moonshine?"

"There's a problem everywhere. Two of my boys were caught behind the bleachers last spring. It makes me furious and sad all at the same time to see lives wasted like that."

"I'm sorry about your job. I have a feeling that's probably what sent you off the deep end back at the restaurant, wasn't it?"

"It didn't help," Emily muttered.

A short while later they turned onto the dirt lane that led to her house.

"Is that another car coming?" she asked, squinting to catch what she thought had been the flash of headlights down the road and through the barrier of the trees.

"I don't see any lights." Simon pulled into the front yard and switched off the motor. In the sudden silence the quiet ticking of the cooling engine sounded inordinately loud. There weren't even any cicadas buzzing or crickets chirping.

And Ivan wasn't barking a welcome.

"I wonder where Ivan is?" Emily opened the door and got out without waiting for Simon. She put her fingers to her lips and whistled. The shrill sound rent the night, and after a moment she heard the faint barking of her dog. He was across the field, somewhere in the woods the two of them had explored, and Emily pressed her lips together. Some watchdog, but at least he was okay.

"Will you forget that dog for two seconds and listen to me?" Simon had come up beside her, but Emily hadn't noticed because, in spite of the moon, the darkness out here was as total as the blackest hole in the universe.

She wished she had remembered to leave on her porch light, especially when Simon commented on it. Emily ignored him and began making her way to the front porch, barely discernible in the faint light of a grudging quarter moon.

"Emily. . .I want to apologize."

The words floated across the yard and wrapped themselves around her feet, halting her indignant retreat. For the first time since Emily had walked out on him at the restaurant, Simon sounded like—Simon.

She waited, confused and tentative, listening to his steps swishing through the tall grass and weeds. When he was so close she could feel the warmth of his body, he stopped. Every nerve in Emily's body seemed to tingle with the awareness of his presence.

"Emily—" She heard a thread of laughter in the word. "I still disagree with your description of sparrows, but will you at least forgive me for everything else?"

The last of her indignation softened to a bewildering compliance, and Emily heard herself murmur back in just as whispery a tone, "I guess so." Then, her resolve stiffening slightly, she stepped back away from him and added with a hint of vinegar, "Maybe I'd better find out what you're asking forgiveness for. Your arrogance, your bad temper, or your—your—"

"My what, Emily?"

Oh, no, there it was again. That wretched note of laughter dancing through otherwise ordinary words, playing a pied piper tune on her heartstrings. Confound the man anyway. What had he done to her? "Your kiss!" she flung out recklessly as she braced herself for his laughter.

It never came. What did come was a very wet, very dirty Ivan leaping out of the night and practically knocking Emily down. He yapped and whined and panted, his forepaws leaving muddy trails all over her clothes, arms, and legs. His bullwhip tail snapped happily against Simon, who kept dodging about trying to avoid the affectionate welcome.

"Oh, Ivan, bad doggie! Where were you? Stop that—why weren't you guarding the house?" She laughed harder when Ivan turned to Simon, who snarled at the dog to leave him alone. Emily ordered Ivan to the porch. "What's the matter?" she intoned innocently. "Don't you like my dog?"

"Not particularly. He's about as lovable as a dead elephant, and he smells like a sewer."

"He smells like a dog," Emily retorted, stung by the acerbic answer. "He can't help that any more than you can help smelling like a man!" After one horrible second with those last words ringing in her ears, she added in a much smaller voice, "I didn't mean that the way it sounded."

Simon didn't answer. He had turned away, and he was laughing so hard the sound echoed back from the woods and fields. Emily decided his laughter was one part humor and three parts hysteria, with a dollop of resignation and frustration tossed in for effect. She walked slowly over to the porch steps and sat down on the bottom one. Ivan whined, but she told him to stay. Simon was at least partly right:

At the moment Ivan did smell a lot like a sewer.

"I give up," she heard Simon eventually gasp out between chuckles. "I think it's a waste of time trying to accomplish anything with you tonight. We can talk in the morning when I come back to start looking for the will."

The will. In the emotional turmoil of the past hour Emily had virtually forgotten the reason for Simon's presence in the first place.

He must have heard her involuntary gasp. "Try not to worry," he promised in a voice as dark and calm as the night. "And try to find it in your heart to forgive me—for everything—Emily Carson."

"Simon. . ." It was difficult to squeeze his name past the constricted muscles of her throat.

"Will you go inside before I leave and at least turn on the porch light?" His voice floated back across the yard. "With the dog I feel a little better about leaving you, but I'd still like to know you're safe inside."

How could someone who had made her angrier than she had ever been in her life turn around and make her feel more protected and, well, cared for than she had ever been in her life? "All right."

She stood listening until the sound of his car faded away. When Ivan poked his nose in her hand and pressed his wet body against her, she cupped his head and held him close. At this moment his presence, smell and all, was all that stood between her and a vast chasm of loneliness.

Chapter 5

Two days later Simon returned, driving—to Emily's outraged disbelief—a pickup truck that was towing a pop-up-style camper.

A wry smile lifted the corners of his mouth. "If your phone were installed, I would have called to let you know," he said, correctly reading Emily's indignation. Stepping past her, he looked around the empty foyer, into the freshly painted but still bare library, and finally back to Emily.

"It really bothers me, you know, you being out here by yourself with no way to call for help. Which is why, of course—" He gestured toward the camper. "This is my 'portable office' that I had one of my guys bring down from Tennessee. I borrowed the truck from the gas station to bring it here so Charlie could take my truck on back to Tennessee."

"You're as bad as my best friend Barb," Emily groused, at the same time feeling a shameful twitch of relief. "Look, the phone man will be here as soon as he can. Until then, you will all just have to add a few gray hairs to your heads. I've got a few myself after the other night."

"What happened the other night?" The small smile hovering on his lips suddenly widened. "Or are you referring to our cat-and-dog fight?"

Her cheeks warmed. "I'm referring to the fact that it took me almost forty-five minutes to find Samson, and when I did, he was as strung out as if he'd been tossed between two pit bulls, and then I heard—" Her voice skidded to an abrupt halt, not feeling up to facing any more of Simon's bullying concern.

"What did you hear, Emily?" He was looking really concerned now, and Emily grimaced.

"Oh, nothing that out of the ordinary," she tossed out. "Just a car that sounded like it was going to stop but changed its mind when Ivan barked."

Simon looked like a lovely white, puffy cloud suddenly burgeoning into a towering thunderhead, and Emily hastened to add, in an attempt to downplay the incident, "I'm sure they were lost and probably needed directions. If they had known Ivan was more of a puppy dog than a watchdog, I'm sure they would have come in and asked for coffee as well as directions."

"It's a good thing I decided to camp out here until I find the will."

Instantly her defenses sprang up. "I haven't granted you permission to move in." She wanted to kick his shins. "Just because I'm a woman doesn't mean I don't know how to take care of myself. Why do men always have to think like that?"

Good grief! What's the matter with me? Slapping her palms over her flushed cheeks, Emily averted her head. "Look what you do to me! Simon, I can't do this. I'm not constitutionally set up for these kinds of games."

"Neither am I," Simon drawled, looking faintly dangerous. "Let's kiss and make up and start all over." He reached out a lazy arm and folded her into his embrace. "I need to amend your way of thinking about men. Christian men anyway."

"There's nothing wrong with the way I think about men, Christian or otherwise." Emily shoved his chest. He was wearing a creamy yellow button-down chambray shirt and shorts instead of jeans. He smelled of soap and something minty, and with his green eyes boring into hers from close range, she realized a few other things about men she hadn't known before. She hadn't realized she could feel this way about one. "Simon, why are you behaving like this?"

His eyes softened, and he dropped a quick, undemanding kiss on her wrinkled forehead and released her. "I don't know," he answered with disarming honesty. "I find you very attractive, but you also frustrate and infuriate me more than any woman I've ever known. And with the situation over the house and Aunt Iris swinging back and forth between us like Edgar Allan Poe's pendulum, my behavior comes across accordingly."

Emily pondered him, nose wrinkled along with her brow as she mulled over the implications behind his words. Men had dated her infrequently over the past years, but usually it was because Emily needed an escort and asked for the date herself. No one had ever mentioned the fact that she was attractive.

She shook her head, and the freshly wound braid swung back and forth along her slumping shoulders. "Let's go find the will," she stated tiredly. "That's about all I can think of right now."

She started up the stairs without a backward glance, but when she reached the top she paused, turning back to Simon. "The next time you grab me and kiss me, you'd better be prepared to nurse a sore jaw."

A dangerous spark glinted in the enigmatic green eyes. "We'll see," he murmured, and they proceeded in silence to the room at the head of the stairs.

Three hours and three inches of dust and grime later, Emily called a halt. "We've searched every inch and it's not up here. It probably doesn't exist anyway. Why can't your aunt accept that?"

"You haven't met my aunt."

Tracings of dust and perspiration trickled down his face, emphasizing the lines of weariness. "Would you give up this house without a fight?"

Emily sighed and admitted painfully, "No. What are we going to do?"

Simon sank down onto the floorboards and leaned back against a wall. His grimy hands worried his damp hair, causing the waves to curl even more wildly about his face and ears. "I'm afraid," he finally said, the words dragging, "that you're going to have to talk to a lawyer."

❦

Bradley Lauderman's office consisted of two rooms over what used to be Sylvan's only theater. Emily had chosen to go to a lawyer in her hometown because she needed the emotional support of familiar surroundings. Barb's husband, Taylor, had recommended Bradley Louderman, as had her old principal Joe Southers, so Emily was hopeful of sound advice for what she also hoped would be a reasonable price. After her appointment, she planned to run over to the school and throw herself at Joe's mercy and beg him to rehire her, even as a janitor.

Simon had wanted to accompany her to this appointment. In the last several days, along with searching for the will, he had offered advice on everything from the security of her home to the refinishing of her home to refinishing herself. "Emily, you can't exist on a diet of cheese crackers and soup—you already bear an uncomfortable resemblance to a starving rock star, especially when your hair looks like that," he'd said. Emily had thrown the sticky paint rag at him and told him if he was going to criticize the least he could do was shave his head to control his own untidy hair.

In contrast to his earlier behavior, Simon was now scrupulously treating her like his kid sister. Emily knew he worried about her—and not just concerning her eating habits and casual appearance. The night before her appointment with Bradley Lauderman, Simon had also heard a car idling outside and told her about it. Peering through the window of his camper, he'd watched a car door open. When Ivan barked inside the house, it had immediately slammed shut and the car left.

Simon was subdued, even surly, all morning. He and Emily finally had it out over the matter, with Emily ending the discussion abruptly by bursting into tears. Even now, she squirmed when she remembered her behavior. Or at least that's what she kept telling herself. But she had a nagging suspicion that her real discomfort was with Simon's response.

Following her out onto the back porch, trapping her against the railing, he had taken her chin in his hand and just stared at her in silence for a long uncomfortable moment. "You're the most stubborn woman I've ever known," he repeated, only this time his voice crooned the words instead of shouting. "But you're also a rare and precious jewel, Emily Carson, even though you can't see it."

His thumbs brushed away her angry tears, and then she was free. "God help me," he muttered, "because I can see it, and that's why you scare me into losing my temper with you." Emily could only stare dumbly.

Simon turned away, so she was not totally certain of his last sentence. "And if someone tries to harm you in any way, God help me for what I would do to him," was what she thought he had said.

That sounded much too romantic and dramatic a statement for a man to make about a woman like her, so Emily tried to shrug the whole incident aside and focus her distracted senses on the encounter with Bradley Lauderman.

Shrugging Simon aside, however, was somewhat like trying to shrug off the Rock of Gibraltar.

Climbing the narrow steps to Bradley Lauderman's office, Emily found that her stomach muscles were clenching and her hands were damp. She opened the dusty, glass-topped door reluctantly, and from the other side of a cluttered desk, a young, smiling woman with dark curly hair greeted her.

"Hi. Emily Carson?"

Emily nodded, absorbing the sight of old, sagging chairs, the framed prints of different species of ducks hanging crookedly on the walls. Old magazines were scattered on the low table in front of the chairs. Her gaze swung back to the secretary, who had risen from behind the desk. She smiled into Emily's widening eyes.

"I'm due any day and look like a watermelon, I know. But Brad desperately needs the help so I'm hanging in there."

From behind a closed door a man's voice called, "Is that Ms. Carson, Gloria?" The door opened and a tall, slender man stepped through. He had a glorious thatch of straw-colored hair and blue eyes that crinkled at the corners. In spite of the fact that it was late summer, his skin was untanned, but he radiated energy and vitality. He held out his arm and shook hands with Emily. "Come on in. We don't stand on ceremony around here. Gloria, can you waddle across the hall and wheedle some coffee from Dave?"

"For you, anything."

As the secretary disappeared, Brad grinned down at Emily. "Dave's a CPA—has an office across the hall. He's so agreeable about sharing his coffeepot, we never got around to installing one of our own." As he ushered Emily into his private sanctum, he winked. "It also cuts down on the exorbitant rates I have to charge my clients."

Emily was charmed by his easy wit and manners. Some of her anxiety began to dissipate, and as she relaxed back into an old but comfortable leather wing chair she looked around. Brad Lauderman's office was a mess. All four walls were covered floor to ceiling with legal books, documents, and papers. They even surrounded the three metal filing cabinets, one of which had a drawer left open, a file tilted upward at an angle. Emily felt uncomfortably at home.

"Don't look so worried. All lawyers' offices look like this."

She met his teasing eyes with a grin. "Actually, it reminds me of my own place. Organized chaos."

"Exactly." He reached across his desk to a glass jar filled with all shapes and sizes of gum, from sticks to colored balls to Bazooka bubblegum and huge grape spheres. He caught Emily's rapt interest. "I gave up smoking and got hooked even worse on this." He gestured to the jar and popped one of the smaller balls into his mouth. Then he leaned back in his desk chair, clasping his hands behind his head and keeping his intent gaze upon Emily. "Now, what's the problem? I've been over all the stuff you had Roger Bates send me. Tell me everything. I don't have to be at court until noon."

Emily took a deep breath. "I'd better start off by method of payment. If I can't have my old teaching position back, I'll be an unemployed schoolteacher, with the reason I'm here a heavy albatross about my neck."

"That could be a problem, I agree." He leaned forward, glancing down at some papers on his desk before looking at Emily again. "Can you type?"

"Yes," Emily answered, though her voice was bewildered.

"Great!" Brad rubbed his palms together, a wide grin splitting his face. "Then I think we might have a solution to both our problems."

An hour later Emily was still protesting but much less vigorously. Bradley Lauderman wanted her to replace Gloria as his secretary for a couple of months.

". . .By which time you might have found another teaching position, and hopefully the situation with your house will be resolved." He blew a huge bubble, caught sight of Emily's poorly hidden amusement, and sheepishly grinned. "Sorry. I forget sometimes how unprofessional that must look." He swallowed the bubble. "I have warned you, though, that this could drag on for up to six months, depending on a number of factors."

"I know." Emily contemplated her neat but worn taupe pumps a minute, then looked back across the desk. "I still feel uncomfortable with the whole idea of a lawsuit, not to mention working for you while you're more or less working for me."

Brad smiled back in sympathy. "It might raise a few brows about conflict of interest, but we're in Sylvan, not Chicago, and the whole town has known both of us since we were in diapers." He swept a nonprofessional, frankly masculine survey over her person. "How is it that you and I have missed each other all these years?"

"I was probably still in pigtails chasing after my brother and his friends, making a pest of myself, and you were probably chasing after all the girls in high school making a pest of yourself."

"Hey—I'm not that many years your senior!" He picked up the notes he had taken in the past hour and studied them a few minutes. "If you've given me all the facts, there's a mere six years separating us. Want to complicate our relationship even further by having dinner with me tonight?"

"No." Emily shook her head in mock dismay. "I'm confused enough by this whole mess as it is and, besides, I just wouldn't feel. . .comfortable. Mr. Lauderman. . .Brad. . .do you really have to file a lawsuit?"

He instantly reverted to the seasoned professional lawyer. "Yes, Emily, that is the correct legal procedure. As far as I'm concerned, you aren't violating any biblical tenets about suing your brother, or whatever the phrasing is. You are merely following legal precedent for the express purpose of determining who has superior title to the property." He stood up, stretching his tall, lanky frame. "Trust me as your lawyer, all right? If you have any more questions about the religious end of it, why don't you talk to Sam Noland? Isn't he the minister of the church you attend?"

Emily nodded and stood up as well. "I don't feel comfortable about working for you either, even if you are deducting your fee out of my paycheck." She paused, then leveled a straight look at him. "You still won't be charging me what you normally would, will you?"

"Nope, but at least I'll have a secretary, and that matters a whole lot more to me than losing a few bucks." He came around the desk and held out his hand. "Let's shake on it, Ms. Emily Carson."

"But I haven't typed in years, and although I was a secretary for Mr. Evans when he was mayor, I was all of seventeen years old. I've probably forgotten—"

A stick of peppermint gum was thrust into Emily's mouth, and her hand was grasped in a warm, firm handshake. "Chew on that instead of problems that don't exist," Brad admonished her easily. He held her hand a little longer than was strictly necessary but immediately let go when she tugged. "Set up a time to get together with Gloria, and she can show you the ropes. Don't wait too long, though, or you might be winging it as you go."

His intercom buzzed, and he stretched a long arm to take the call. He held his hand over the mouthpiece and finished by saying, "Gloria will set up our next 'business' appointment—or you can do it yourself if she's gone into labor or something."

Emily left the office shaking her head in bemusement, and another hour later she left the building still shaking her head. Gloria had been so relieved she had thrown her arms about Emily and hugged her, then laughed at the awkwardness of her gigantic stomach. She had also asked if Emily had time to learn the ropes now, since she might not, as Brad pointed out, have another opportunity.

The job seemed simple enough. She would basically be fielding phone calls, typing up wills, filing, and a couple of times a week walking the two blocks to the courthouse to file a client's papers with the clerk of the court when Brad was unable to do it. Because she was still trying to restore the house herself, and because he wasn't that overloaded with cases, she would only be working three days a week, leaving her plenty of time to work on her home.

"Since the paperwork from the lawyer who handled the closing on your property indicates that you have good title to the property, keep on with the sanding and painting if that's what cranks your engine," Brad had reassured her.

Chapter 6

Emily decided to detour by Barb's house instead of going straight home. She hadn't seen her friend or been able to talk to her in a week, and although she might fuss and worry, Barb was a marvelous sounding board. She also had down-to-earth common sense, easing Emily's mind over Simon's ubiquitous presence in her life. Taylor, in fact, verbalized their relief that Emily wouldn't be isolated anymore.

Today, however, when Barb opened the door she gave a relieved shriek, grabbed Emily's arm, and hauled her into the house. "Mark, turn down the stereo!" she yelled, and as they passed the table in the entrance hall, she swiped up a newspaper. "Look at this." She thrust the paper under Emily's nose. "Look at it! I've been out of my mind worrying."

Emily read the headlines, mouth dry. "Car Overturns on County Road—Kills Two Passengers." The subtitle noted that a second wrecked car had been found abandoned near the site of the accident, with several pounds of cocaine and two boxes full of pornography found in the trunk. Identities were being withheld on the dead passengers until more details were known.

The wreck had happened on the road that led to Emily's house. The time of the accident had been on the night she and Simon had almost been run off the road.

"That doesn't mean it was right outside my front door, Barb," she began somewhat weakly.

Barb, who had poured herself a glass of iced tea and grabbed a couple of doughnuts while Emily was reading, promptly slammed down the glass. "Front door, my great-gramma's nightshirt! When are you going to come to your senses, Em? The world is not a safe place anymore, especially for someone like you."

"I can take care of myself."

"That's just the problem," Barb argued. She sighed and gulped the tea and doughnuts; then she tried to make her point. "You've always had to take care of yourself, and you have no idea how really vulnerable you are. Simon won't be around forever, you know. Someday, something is going to happen, and you're going to realize you need other people, and they won't be there—especially when you've isolated yourself out in the boonies."

Emily drove home through a late-afternoon thundershower, moody and depressed. Not only was she unnerved by the newspaper article and Barb's consequent flapping, but she was even more upset by her friend's observation on her own self-reliance.

Emily had always prided herself on her independence, her ability and determination to do anything she set her mind to, even if she had the knack for biting off more than she could chew. She hadn't really had much choice. It didn't do to try and depend on other people—they only let you down eventually, as she had learned throughout her lonely life. It was simply shortsighted to depend too heavily on other people when the only person she could really count on was herself.

Sure, God figured in it all somehow, Emily supposed. And maybe in some remote sense He cared about her. But she couldn't worry Him with all her problems when the world had so many worse ones, could she? Wars, famines, diseases—the Lord depended on her to keep the oils of her own unremarkable life running smoothly, freeing Him for all the big-time stuff.

It was far better to be kind and friendly to everyone, live by the Golden Rule, but never expect or hope for anything in return. That way, she would not be disappointed and let down when something happened like Simon Balfour appearing out of the blue and threatening to take her house away from her.

A long rumble of thunder pealed across the rain-soaked countryside, and a thin streak of lightning zigzagged across the sky. *Simon makes me feel about like this storm,* Emily reflected as she slowed down to allow for the torrential onslaught. Telling her God had His loving eye on her all the time, promising he would help find solutions to her problems. Ha! Simon *was* the problem, with his grass green eyes and his silver tongue. . .calling her a sparrow and. . .and kissing her like. . .like he couldn't help himself any more than Emily could control her own response.

I won't be an easy mark. I may be easygoing—but I'm not an easy mark. She turned onto the dirt lane that, because of the rain, was a sea of mud, and wriggled her tense shoulders. She wouldn't be an easy mark as long as Simon kept his hands to himself.

It was an infuriating admission, but she might as well be honest with herself. She was attracted to the man, regardless of all the circumstances muddying her life as the rain muddied the road. She was almost glad he hadn't found the will yet, not because it meant she would keep her house, but because it kept him near.

Okay. . .she was a borderline easy mark and would just have to try harder.

Pulling into the yard, Emily sternly ordered her heart to be relieved instead of depressed that Simon's car was gone. Ignoring the lack of an umbrella, she slogged up the porch steps, drenched and dreary—and gasped in alarm. Ivan sprawled limply in the corner, not even a flicker of movement from his tail greeting her. He had been sick, and specks of foam lined the corners of his mouth. She rushed to his side, heart hammering. "Ivan, what happened? What's wrong?"

A vet. She needed to call a vet. She was scrabbling frantically in her purse for the key when the brutal fact hit home: She had no phone.

"Ivan," she sobbed beneath her breath. "Lord, please don't let anything happen to Ivan."

Another crack of thunder and a simultaneous lightning flash heralded a fresh downpour. Paying no attention to a note taped to the door, Emily unlocked the house, ran to her bedroom, and yanked off the spread. Halfway down the hall she stopped, remembering how Samson hated storms.

She dropped the spread, ran back into the dining room, and found the cat in his hiding place behind the boxes. Scooping him out, she took him to the kitchen and poured him some milk, spilling half of it all over the counter in her haste. After reassuring him that the storm would pass and begging him to forgive her for leaving him, she dashed back down the hall, grabbing the spread as she ran.

❀

Two hours later Emily drove home alone, having left Ivan overnight at the vet's for observation. Her hands shook when she at last unlocked the door and untaped Simon's note. He'd had to run off to Tennessee and would be back the next afternoon. He was sorry to leave her alone again.

Alone. Emily wadded the paper into a ball and called for Samson in a voice that did not sound at all like her own. When the cat wandered out to the hall and stroked himself against her legs as if he hadn't a care in the world, Emily finally broke down.

It did not occur to her that she might be in danger.

❀

The next afternoon she was getting ready to retrieve Ivan when Simon drove up.

"What's wrong?" he asked immediately, looking solid and secure and scruffy in faded cutoffs and a paint-stained T-shirt from Alaska advising, "Go kiss a moose."

Under any other circumstances she would have teased him about trying to emulate her own dress style. Unfortunately, not even her pain about Ivan dimmed the intensity of his discerning gaze or the attractiveness of his smile, which was fading fast in light of her awkward silence. "I have to go to town," she answered, nose buried in her purse. "You can come on in and start searching if you want to. I. . .I'll be back in awhile."

Firm fingers lifted her chin. "I asked what's wrong," Simon repeated gently. "You've been crying."

Startled, Emily pulled free, her hands clutching confusedly at her shoulder bag. "How can you tell?" she asked.

Simon stuffed his thumbs in the waistband of his shorts and contemplated her a moment. "Your eyes are slightly puffy and your nose is still red." His voice suddenly changed and became abrupt, almost cold. "Are you going back to the lawyer? Is what he told you yesterday so upsetting it made you cry?"

"No. . .Brad was very nice. In fact, I'm going to be his—" She stopped, unwilling to go into the details when all she could think about right now was Ivan. She started to brush past Simon. "I'll tell you about it later. I really need to go right now."

"You're going to be his what?"

Hard hands with a grip that was not gentle at all latched onto her shoulders and jerked her around. He held her at arms' length, and the look on his face was indescribable. "Emily, what have you done?" When she looked up at him un-comprehendingly, he shook her. "What have you done to keep this house, you idiot?" he repeated, his voice so full of fury and panic Emily's shaky composure erupted as well.

"Let go! What's the matter with you? Brad said it would be all right since it was Sylvan and not Chicago. I'm sorry if you don't like it, but it's really none of your business what I do." She squirmed uncomfortably, then gasped as he thrust her from him, whirled away, and banged his fists on the wall.

Indignation fizzling, Emily took one hesitant step and touched his shoulder. It was like touching one of the sun-warmed boulders by a river where she used to vacation as a child. "Simon?" she offered tentatively, wondering at the violent emotion she seemed to generate in him. "There was nothing you could do. It's a job anyway and will at least pay the bills. I told Brad I hadn't been a secretary since I was seventeen, but he was desperate because Gloria is due to have her baby any day. I'll be—"

Simon turned back around abruptly, and his arm shot out to steady her with an almost convulsive grip. "Did you say 'secretary'?" he demanded, a beseeching note beneath the question.

Emily tugged ineffectively at his hand. "Yes." Her own voice reflected her growing bewilderment. "Didn't I tell you?"

Simon released her, lifted a hand to his brow, and closed his eyes. "No," he murmured very quietly. "You forgot to mention that little fact."

"I'm sorry." Emily sighed distractedly. "It's just that I'm so upset about Ivan I don't really know whether I'm coming or going." She paused, gulped, and added, "Speaking of which, I do have to go. Dr. Moffat promised Ivan would be all right, but I won't believe it until he's back here. . . ."

Her voice started to crack and she bit her lip hard. Oh, no. She couldn't break down in front of Simon again. Besides, he didn't like Ivan. He wouldn't understand.

"Ivan? Your dog?" He stepped closer, and Emily tried to smile.

"Someone tried to poison him last night. I got him to the vet in time, but apparently it was touch and go for awhile." She swallowed hard. "I'm going to go get him now. Dr. Moffat kept him overnight for observation."

"Ahh. . ." With heart-stopping tenderness, he folded her into an embrace so radically different from his earlier behavior that Emily's defenses collapsed like the walls of Jericho. She clung to him, savoring the heady sensation of leaning on someone else's arms. It wouldn't last but a moment, she knew, but it felt so good. It felt so. . .nurturing. And she needed it so desperately.

"I'm sorry," Simon was whispering into her hair. "I know how much your dog means to you. What a rotten thing to happen on top of everything else." One hand stroked the long braid, her back, and shoulders, while the other held her close. "That's why you've been crying, isn't it?"

Head buried in the soft T-shirt, Emily could only nod.

✻

Simon continued to hold her, his own thoughts whirling and gradually steadying as he was able to accept that Emily was here, in his arms, and unchanged. There were still a lot of unanswered questions, however, and a lengthy examination of his own feelings would have to have top priority over the next few days.

Emily amazingly enough had not picked up on his initial train of thought concerning her relationship with the lawyer. *Thank heaven for that,* Simon told himself with grim amusement. What a fool he would have looked! He had lost control with her at least twice now, and although she was obviously still totally unaware of the effect she had on him, she was not a stupid woman. She was only confused, worried, and staggering beneath problems that would have defeated most other people.

Simon tried to serve his Lord in the best way he could, but it did not always come easy. He had accepted Christ as his Savior when he was fourteen and been a model student through high school and college. Then, after his father retired and Simon took over, channeling the business into one specializing in restoration, he somehow sidetracked onto the road of hard work and "loose women," as his mother had put it.

One day she had cornered him, sat him down, and looked him straight in the eye. "Son, do you eventually plan to marry and raise a family like your brother and sister have?" she had asked, casually enough so he hadn't immediately bolted.

"Yeah, one day, Mom. I'm too busy right now, you know. Twenty-seven's not exactly over the hill, and I'd like to have a good time for awhile yet, I suppose. . . ."

"Hmmmm. Well, when you do settle down, do you think it would be with a woman like the ones you've been—seeing—over the last few years?"

Not too much seemed to escape his mother, even if he hadn't lived at home since college. "Good grief, no!" Simon had exclaimed. "Not those women. . ."

She had leaned forward then, planting strong, work-roughened hands on her knees and fixing upon him her most serene, impossible-to-argue-with stare. "So what makes you think a pure Christian woman whom I presume is your idea of a suitable mate would have anything to do with a man who dates the type of women you do?"

He had never forgotten the lightning bolt of conviction that had electrified his senses. It had killed his former lifestyle as dead as the bolt that had struck a white pine in their backyard the previous year. Simon had never viewed women in the same manner since, nor treated them as if they were merely there for his personal gratification.

Over Emily's head he smiled. Emily would doubtless disagree. In the weeks they had come to know each other, he had wrecked her carefully constructed little world, bullied her, lost his temper, kissed her with a ruthless passion she had obviously never experienced, and just now had leaped to a regrettable conclusion for which Emily could justifiably take offense. What a mess!

And now that ugly leviathan of a dog had gotten himself poisoned. Who on earth would do such a thing, when Emily lived in such isolated splendor? And why? Some very unpleasant possibilities were nudging his brain, clamoring for attention and causing the muscles of his jaw to clench. Emily had not exactly made a secret of the fact that she lived out here all alone. And those cars—not to mention his talk with the county sheriff about a crash along Emily's road a few weeks back. He wondered if Emily knew about that.

Unfortunately, poisoning the dog might have been more than an arbitrary, haphazard piece of cruelty. Somewhere out there, somebody just might be planning for one Emily Carson to be his next victim.

Chapter 7

Surprisingly, Simon went with Emily to pick up Ivan, who was fine but subdued. Simon spent several minutes talking to Dr. Moffat while Emily paid the bill, made arrangements to bring Samson in to be neutered within the next month, and got Ivan into the car. She couldn't help but wonder why a man who was by and large disinterested in animals would want to talk to a vet. Even after Simon's reply to her query had been an evasive, "Just talking," she was so relieved to have Ivan back, she shrugged the matter aside.

Once they were back at the house and Ivan was ensconced safely in his favorite spot on the front porch, Emily announced that she was going to start painting the kitchen. As far as she was concerned, Simon was welcome to wear himself out looking for the will wherever he pleased.

"Brad said since the title at present establishes my clear ownership, I can work on the house if I want to," she announced defiantly, expecting a fight.

To her utter astonishment Simon agreed it was probably better that way anyway, but would she promise to break for lunch? He touched the back of his hand to her cheek in a gesture somehow more intimate than a kiss and disappeared upstairs.

❀

For the next two weeks they worked in relative harmony, pursuing their chosen tasks. Their work was interrupted only twice: once by a brief visit from Barb and then by the long-awaited installation of the phone line.

Emily decided Simon must be going over the entire house board by board, and at odd moments when she was particularly tired, she came to the conclusion he was dragging it out for the sole purpose of annoying her. Several days he prowled outside somewhere, and at other times he worked at a drafting table he'd set up in the library. A couple of times a week he worked outside in the camper in his on-site office, complete with impressive computer, modem, and printer.

Emily had a sneaking suspicion he was also secretly daydreaming about how he would restore her house. Her suspicions were confirmed late one Monday afternoon in early September, her third week as Brad's secretary.

It had been a long day, because she was accustomed to standing in front of a blackboard or painting walls, not sitting behind a desk answering the phone, typing, and—when she was bored because the phone hadn't rung—updating and reorganizing Brad's files. That day he'd warned her they could expect to hear from Iris Bancroft's lawyer soon, and then the judge could determine the date for their hearing.

As she drove home from work, Emily thought about how she hated the whole process. She felt dreadful knowing she was having to destroy an old woman's dreams, even though Iris was responsible for initiating the whole affair. Of course, from what Simon shared with her, his great-aunt was about as helpless an old woman as Emily was a candidate for Miss America.

Emily hoped the hearing would be soon. Brad was confident of a verdict in her favor, but that was only because as yet, Simon had not unearthed the will. As the weeks passed, Emily had grown more convinced the document didn't even exist, and she suspected Simon agreed, though he wouldn't say so.

She came to know whenever Simon's parents had heard from Iris. He never complained, but there would be a certain tension in the grim line of his mouth, and he would work with fanatical single-mindedness until lunch, when he was finally able to shrug aside whatever wounds the woman inflicted with her incessant goading. Privately Emily was grateful Simon had adamantly forbidden his parents from revealing Emily's new phone number under any circumstances.

He had reverted to the calm, courteous stranger she had first met, neither shouting at her and trying to tell her what to do, nor attempting to approach her romantically. When Emily realized she felt slighted by this decorous behavior, she was so angry with her unruly emotions she erected her own formidable barriers, mostly consisting of a combination of aloofness and determined cheerfulness.

Emily's musings were interrupted as she turned into her driveway. Climbing wearily out of the car, she saw Simon sitting on the front porch steps, incredibly enough tossing a stick for Ivan to fetch. While he had never made overt gestures of friendship to the dog, ever since the poisoning episode he had at least been civil, both to Ivan and Samson. Emily smiled as she walked across the yard.

Ivan loped across to her side, barking and posturing, as healthy as if he hadn't been inches from death less than a month ago. Emily hugged him and talked doggie drivel all the way to the porch, where Simon had risen to meet her.

"Hi." She always felt awkward and shy around him now, never knowing what to say. "Thank you for playing with Ivan. He gets sort of lonely now that I have to be gone three days a week."

"I know," was the dry retort. "He brought the stick over and whined for ten minutes until I finally gave in."

Emily smiled, hating herself for the warm flush she felt rising in her cheeks. "I'm sorry you think he's a nuisance."

"I'm getting used to both of them," Simon promised, stuffing his hands into the hip pockets of a pair of worn-out cords.

He followed Emily into the house and down to the kitchen. Gesturing her to a chair, he fixed her a glass of iced tea, then sat down across from her and propped his elbows on the table. "The question is, are you getting used to me, Emily?"

The question was soft but provocative. Emily searched his face, really looking at him for the first time since the day Ivan was poisoned. The green eyes were narrowed, full of light, but they revealed nothing. His hair was unruly, just brushing his ears and neck. Right now it looked as if he had just washed it, and the late afternoon sunlight highlighted the gold and chestnut tones Emily so envied. His tan had faded somewhat, and there were lines scoring his cheeks and forehead she hadn't noticed before. "I suppose so," she finally told him slowly. "Why do you ask?" Simon dropped his gaze a moment, contemplating the table as if it contained some secret message. Then the heavy, straight lashes lifted, and Emily found herself unable to avoid the piercing intentness of those eyes. "I want to help you restore the house," he told her, the words deliberate so she could not possibly misunderstand. "Not as the professional, not by bringing in my crew and taking over. Just me, helping you, because I've come to. . ." He hesitated, as if he were still picking his words carefully. "To care about this place almost as much as you have."

Emily, of course, was not surprised. She was, however, staggered by the tidal wave of relief surging over her. Had she somehow let slip these past weeks how uncertain she was of her ability to complete the project alone, how tired she was of juggling a job along with the restoration? Had the fact that she was still uneasy since the poisoning and thus was not sleeping well become that noticeable?

"Emily?" Simon prodded, reaching across the table and placing his hand over hers. "Please don't fly off the handle or start feeling threatened. You can use the help—you need the help. There's so much I know, so many ways I could help you, show you how to make the work go faster, look more professional." He smiled a little when she bristled. "You've done an outstanding job, Honey, but admit it. You are an amateur."

"I was going to give in gracefully," Emily grumbled, "but if you're going to adopt that kind of superior stance you can take your help and stuff it in one of the corners you keep poking in for the dumb will." They stared at each other for a moment; then both broke into relieved laughter.

"I was afraid you'd go for my shinbone," Simon confessed between chuckles.

"Well, I'm still afraid you're going to bulldoze over my feeble efforts, and then I *will* go for your shins."

Simon had no difficulty reading between the lines. "Emily," he promised softly, all laughter fading away, "until I find the will, and until the court says so, this house is yours, and Aunt Iris can foam at the mouth all she wants. I only want to help you and enjoy practicing my vocation for the sheer pleasure of doing so. Will you believe me?"

"I'd like to. But, Simon, what if you never find the will? You've been looking for a month now, and I know conducting business long distance isn't healthy even with all your fancy equipment. How much longer can your great-aunt force you to keep looking?"

Simon stood up, moved around Emily, and drew her to her feet. "I don't care if it takes the rest of the year." His hands moved warmly from her wrists up to her shoulders. "When are you going to realize that's only an excuse to be near you?"

"What do you mean?" Emily whispered, the question ending in a breathless squeak as he held her close and trailed soft kisses from her temple to her cheek.

"I mean," he murmured, "that I'm tired of pretending that I don't have any feelings. You've flitted around and struggled to feather your nest and chirped on about that lawyer you work for—and not once have you picked up on the fact that I happen to be very attracted to you. You, Emily Carson—not the house." He lifted his head, holding his mouth poised just over Emily's. "So. . .what do you have to say about that?"

Just before her eyes closed, Emily watched the teasing green glitter in Simon's eyes flare into something altogether different. Then he was kissing her, not with the almost angry passion of the first time, but with an exquisite blend of tenderness and restrained desire.

They broke apart abruptly when Samson jumped up onto the chair and meowed, causing Simon to start and pull away from Emily. She sank bonelessly into the chair, automatically picking Samson up as she did so.

Simon laughed shortly, his mouth quirked in wry acknowledgment. "Yeah, you striped and whiskered fleabag, you do have some competition for the lady's affections."

"He doesn't have fleas. He's wearing a flea collar," Emily responded with splendid irrelevance. It was as if she were spinning, feeling like a playful fall breeze suddenly swirled into a full-blown hurricane. She gazed up at Simon, struggling to comprehend what had happened.

Simon flexed his shoulders, sighed, and touched her cheek with the tips of his fingers. "Don't look so confused. This has been coming on since the first time I kissed you." He scrutinized her dazed features in something close to exasperation. "Don't tell me you haven't felt the tension between us, Emily, even if I have tried to keep mine under control."

"I felt it," Emily replied very low. "I just had no idea *you* would feel so. . .so strongly. . . ."

"You really have no awareness of yourself as an attractive woman, do you?" He raked his fingers through the thick waves of his hair in consternation. "You've mentioned as much before, but I suppose I didn't really believe it. I thought the reason you look the way you do was circumstances more than anything else."

Some of the dazed look sparked into resentment. "And what is that supposed to mean? I can't help it if I'm not a nubile teenager with the seductive charms of Aphrodite."

Simon threw back his head and laughed, a deep laugh designed to capture and hopelessly tangle heartstrings. "Ah, Emily, what am I going to do with you?" He pondered her now with the old teasing affection, and Emily felt fingers of red creeping up into her cheeks. "Put Samson down."

"What?"

Looking as if he were lifting a smelly bag of garbage, Simon reached for the cat and deposited him on the floor. Then he once again drew Emily to her feet. "You have something far more beautiful than a seductive figure and alluring manner, Emily Carson," he crooned in soft rhythmic syllables, his hands cupping her face, the thumbs gently stroking her cheekbones. "You have character. And purity. And an inner beauty that shines out to any man who is astute enough to see beneath the camouflage." Emily's hands had risen to tug at Simon's, but they fell helpless at her sides as he released her, then gently touched her braid. "This lovely hair you keep bound. . .the styleless clothes that reflect your poor self-image. . . your makeup-free face that gazes fearlessly out at the world and never reveals how lonely or unhappy you are. . . ."

His fingers shushed her as she tried to protest. "You might have convinced yourself and everyone else that you're a contented, quiet lady who could never stir even a ripple of passion in a man, but you're wrong." He smiled into her eyes. "And you know it now, don't you?"

Emily was saved by the bell, literally. The phone rang, and she flung herself away from Simon and scampered down the hall to her bedroom.

"Em? Brad here. Sorry I didn't make it back to the office before you left. I've got the date for your hearing and thought you'd like to know."

The blood pumping furiously through Emily's overheated veins chilled to an abrupt standstill. "When?" she managed to ask, then had to reassure Brad that she was all right, just tired, and no, nothing was wrong, before he would answer her question.

Simon was waiting at the entrance to her bedroom, leaning against the doorjamb with arms folded across his chest. He was scowling; all teasing and tenderness wiped away. "The lawyer, I presume?" he guessed after she hung up, his voice almost, but not quite, hostile.

Emily nodded. "The hearing is set for this Thursday," she recited, and she looked down at her hands, marveling that they were not quite steady. "Ten o'clock. Your great-aunt's lawyer will have notified her, so I guess I'll see both of you in court, as the saying goes."

Simon stared at her across the room, and it was as if a giant chasm had opened between them. "I guess you will," he agreed evenly.

Emily's chin lifted. "And you'll be flying to Connecticut as soon as possible?"

He sighed deeply. "Yeah. Emily." He stopped, a muscle twitching in his jaw. "I'll call you."

"There's no need—"

"There's every need!" He bit out the words, then looked as if he wanted to swallow them back. Turning on his heel, he stalked off down the hall, and a second later she heard the door slam.

Emily sank down onto her bed and buried her head in her hands.

❁

That night she jerked awake to the sounds of footsteps prowling around outside the house, then up on the porch. This time, except for Ivan and Samson, she was alone.

At first Emily was so frightened she clung to Ivan, holding the struggling, whining dog to her with her hand clamped over his muzzle so he wouldn't bark. It took several terror-filled moments for her to comprehend that insanity, and with a sharp little sob, she let Ivan go.

The dog tore off with a series of roaring barks that would have scared the stripes off a tiger. Emily would not let him outside for fear of what might happen, but at least there were no more footsteps, and after thirty minutes of growling and prowling, Ivan finally settled back down. Emily patted his head and told him he was a good dog, but she didn't sleep at all that night, falling only into a light doze around dawn when the only sound she had heard for hours was Ivan's quiet breathing.

First thing in the morning, she called the county sheriff and explained what had happened. The sheriff dispatched a deputy who tramped around the yard and poked about the porches searching for clues or signs of forced entry. He found nothing. After patting Emily on the shoulder and remarking kindly about women and their generally excitable constitutions, the slightly paunchy, slightly pompous patrolman left. So that day, instead of working on the house, Emily attached a leash to Ivan and embarked on a hike around the parameters of her property. Someone might be using her land for nefarious purposes, and as usual it was up to Emily to take care of the matter.

Gray skies hung like a damp, dirty sheet low and heavy in the sky. September usually wasn't as hot as August, but the humidity was still high enough to be cloying. The air was ripe with the pungent odor of vegetation and wet earth, but at least the wind was in the right direction to keep the paper mill fumes at bay.

Emily marched across the weed-infested field, intent on starting her investigation at a camping site she and Ivan had happened on one day. She kept Ivan leashed because she could not depend on him to stay close enough for her to protect. A

262

detached part of herself laughed at the irony. Ivan was supposed to be protecting her, not the other way around! Simon would definitely not understand.

She would not think about Simon right now. She would not. She would concentrate on searching for signs in her woods that should not be there—beer cans, a campfire—Emily didn't know what she was looking for, but she also knew if she stayed holed up in her house like a sniveling coward afraid of her own shadow, she would never forgive herself.

She tramped for hours through underbrush dripping with dew and the rain from two days ago, beneath silent, slender pine trees whose needles carpeted the forest floor. For awhile she followed the firebreak, but after sidetracking into the woods to search over the abandoned campsite she and Ivan had discovered in July, Emily struck off into the woods on the other side of the little clearing. Stumbling onto an old logging road made walking easier, but Emily had no idea where it would lead. She checked her watch and decided to follow it no more than thirty minutes, since by then she would doubtless have reached the limits of her property anyway. Someday, God willing, she would have to scratch up the funds to have the boundaries surveyed and updated.

The rutted, overgrown road wound through another quiet glade of pines, then meandered about the edge of a huge cleared meadow. Emily decided it was time to start back just as Ivan growled deep in his throat, then emitted a soft warning woof.

Startled, Emily turned, her eyes scanning the field and widening in astonished disbelief. Ivan barked again, louder this time, and with panicked swiftness Emily clamped her hand around his muzzle.

Unbelievably, parked at the far end of the field was a plane. It was small, without the bright colors tipping the tail or wings or body. There was a van beside it, and several men were taking boxes out of the plane and loading them into the van. For a frozen second Emily couldn't move, couldn't think, couldn't breathe. Drugs. It had to be drugs. It seemed beyond comprehension that she had stumbled onto such a scene, but she had, and all the seeming isolated incidents of the last months blended together to paint a deadly scenario.

Cars slowing and idling outside her house in the dead of night. A crashed and abandoned car full of cocaine and pornographic materials. The footsteps last night. Had her house—abandoned for years—been used as a drop-off point? Storage for their filthy cargo?

Emily had attributed the mess she had cleaned up when she moved in to relatively harmless hoboes. Now she wasn't so sure.

Ivan struggled, whining, and Emily felt the hair rise on the back of her neck. She had spotted the plane—but that meant they could also see her.

Emily grabbed Ivan's collar while her other hand stayed clamped about his mouth; then she turned and, as quietly as she could, crept back into the covering of trees. When the shadows of the pines and a curve in the road provided a modicum of safety, she ran, clenching Ivan's leash in a death grip.

She ran until her lungs ached and a stitch in her side doubled her over so that she had to stop and rest. Ivan whined and licked her face. He wasn't even breathing hard but sat by her panting easily, tongue dripping, waiting for his mistress to tell him what to do next. For one whirling moment Emily thought she was hopelessly lost, but as her labored breathing slowed, she caught the faint sound of the creek. Still breathing in hard stabbing gasps, she stumbled through the woods until they reached familiar territory.

Her immediate instinct was to grab the phone and call the police. Even in the process of dialing she hesitated, then slowly replaced the phone in the cradle. Was there any chance they'd believe her after the attitude displayed toward her this very morning by that deputy? Even if they did, Emily doubted she could retrace her path to the field. The plane would have left hours ago, and the van with its deadly load would be on its way to ruin more lives.

Emily pummeled her fists on the wall in frustration and despair. What could she do? She had had firsthand experience of what happened when a person got messed up in drugs, for she and a fellow teacher had caught two ninth graders smoking pot under the bleachers the previous spring, and when their lockers were searched, crack was discovered. One of those boys had been an honor student, with his whole life ahead of him. Now—

Emily picked up the phone again, willing to make a fool of herself for the sake of all the other schoolkids. Then another, even more unpleasant, thought struck: If the police went nosing around the area and found nothing, the jerks who were involved with the trafficking would probably know who had set the authorities on their trail.

She spent the rest of the afternoon and evening sanding kitchen cabinets, but the sweaty, backbreaking labor could not drown out the clamoring voices in her head, all telling her to do something different. So she ended up doing nothing at all. She spent another sleepless night—this time with the hammer by her bed as well as Ivan.

At least she had Ivan. When Simon returned, he and his aunt would be guests of Lamar Hansell, Iris's lawyer, so Emily could not depend on Simon's help anymore. That was okay by her. She wasn't stupid—and she had Ivan.

Tomorrow at work, maybe, just maybe, she could talk to Brad and ask him for advice.

Unfortunately, no matter what she decided, she still might end up in a burlap sack at the bottom of the creek, and Iris Bancroft could have the property free and clear, will or no will.

Chapter 8

Wednesday morning, Emily dragged herself to work. Brad, chewing on a couple of sticks of spearmint, barely spared her a second glance.

"Hi, Em. Glad you made it. You need to cancel all my morning appointments. Sorry about this. Rearrange them for. . ." He chewed even more furiously as he flipped through several pages of notes, his normally pleasant features distorted in a harried scowl. "For Friday, if you can. If they're going to be dead before then, have them come in as late this afternoon as you can—not before four."

He slapped the papers down and muttered something mildly profane, then apologized to Emily. "I have to go to Albany. Gloria left the reminder on my calendar, but she forgot to tell you so you could remind me of the note she left to remind me."

They grinned at each other. Emily was genuinely fond of Brad, for he was an easy person to like. He had been patient with her rusty secretarial skills, had praised her reorganization of his jumbled files, and never failed to remind her that her own case would turn out all right. Emily waved him out the door.

A little while later the secretary for Lamar Hansell called, and nebulous thoughts of drug dealers and death threats vanished from Emily's mind. Tomorrow. This time tomorrow the waiting and wondering would all be over.

What would the judge decide? Were Iris and her lawyer as confident as Brad that they would be the "winners"? How could anybody really win when either Iris or Emily would be devastated, whatever the outcome?

Over the past weeks at odd moments, Emily actually found herself praying for God's help. She even talked to her minister, Sam Noland, as Brad had suggested, marginally relieved when he provided her with some scriptural comfort. According to Pastor Sam, the apostle Paul flat out told the Romans they must submit themselves to the governing authorities—which was what Emily was trying to do now. A lawsuit offered the only alternative to determine legal ownership of the property. Emily's true trial, and manifestation of her Christian faith, would be accepting the outcome graciously.

Brad called at a quarter to five to apologize for not returning in time to go over the procedure for the next day with her. Emily tried to sound offhand, but Brad was too good a lawyer to be misled by her manufactured cheerfulness.

"Don't sound so worried," he counseled her kindly. "It's a fairly straightforward case without the will, Emily. By noon you can go celebrate." There was a pause; then he added hopefully, "Maybe I'll take off a couple of hours and celebrate with you."

Emily found herself wondering what Simon would think about that, so she told Brad with deliberate sweetness that she would love to celebrate with her favorite lawyer. Simon would have his hands full comforting his battle-ax of a great-aunt anyway.

❀

Thursday morning dawned a hot, cloudless day with a brassy sky promising rain by nightfall. Emily dressed carefully, remembering Simon's words concerning her appearance.

Her best, most sophisticated outfit was a suit, bought two years ago for the end-of-the-year PTA banquet. It was a lovely shade of cinnamon, and Emily bought it because it fit okay and had been on sale. She never considered the fact that it turned her into a monochromatic symphony, serving to reflect the truth of Simon's favorite nickname for her.

Her suit teamed with a jewel-neck ivory blouse; her hair carefully brushed, braided, and bound on top of her head, Emily dismally surveyed herself in the mirror. She'd wanted to look brisk and businesslike. But her mirror said she resembled a plain brown sparrow.

Would Simon be there? She had been astonished to find a postcard from him waiting in her mailbox yesterday afternoon, since he'd only been gone two days.

"See you Thursday," Simon had penned in a loose but neat script. "Don't worry about Iris. I'll take care of you, too. So will the Lord—go read Psalm 84:3–4. See you soon, little sparrow."

Emily tossed the card in the basket with the ones from her mother and forgot about it.

❀

Brad met her on the courthouse steps, told her she looked fine, then spent the next fifteen minutes alternately explaining the procedure and reassuring his apprehensive client.

"You act like you've been indicted for violating the Controlled Substances Act or something," he teased, attributing Emily's sudden jerk of dismay to more nerves. He wrapped a comforting arm around her shoulders, fished in his pants pockets, and pulled out a stick of wintergreen gum. "Here. That ought to help soothe the savage beast within."

The awful moment passed, and Emily managed not to blurt out her onerous knowledge of a plane loaded with some of those controlled substances. Then the door to the waiting room opened, and Mr. Hansell, Simon, and the smallest woman Emily had ever seen walked through.

At first glance, Iris Bancroft did not look as if she could possibly be Attila the

Hun in a ninety-five-pound package, as Simon had suggested. Silver hair styled in tight curls framed a lined, mahogany-tanned face devoid of makeup save two bright splotches of rouge on each parchment cheek. One gnarled, bony hand supported her slight weight on a cane while the other rested on Simon's bent arm. She was wearing a severely tailored street dress of a soft mauve color that, Emily admitted, was infinitely more becoming on Iris than Emily's own brown suit was on her. The hand-crocheted collar seemed to emphasize her age and fragility until she opened her mouth.

"So you're the unprincipled, land-grabbing opportunist trying to steal my property."

Simon groaned and the lawyer, who had shut the door behind them, smiled in weary resignation.

"Aunt Iris," Simon reminded the woman quietly but firmly, "the matter is going to be decided legally, and name-calling merely detracts from your own credibility."

Iris bridled at the reproof. She removed her hand from his arm and stumped over to where Emily and Brad were standing, flinty gray eyes fastened on Emily.

"I don't care if you're Cinderella," she snapped, her voice raspy but clear and strong. "That house is mine." She turned and shook the cane at Simon. "You promised you'd find the will and kick the upstart baggage out, and all you've done is let her make mush of your brains." She expelled a forceful sigh, then concluded, "I always told your mother you were a stubborn, willful brat. Seems to me you haven't changed much."

"Maybe we should wait in the hall," Lamar Hansell suggested.

Simon came up beside his great-aunt and laid an arm about her narrow, bony shoulders. "That won't be necessary," he promised, green eyes measuring Brad's close proximity to Emily. His mouth thinned, something primitive and raw flashing through his eyes. "Now that my aunt has vented her spleen, she'll behave with the utmost propriety."

Iris snorted, then swatted Simon's arm. "Don't try to put me in my place, Nephew. There's not a man alive capable of doing that!"

The two lawyers suppressed smiles, and everyone moved to sit down in some of the uncomfortable wooden chairs scattered about the room. Brad had not missed the look in Simon's eyes, and he discreetly chose a chair two seats away from Emily. She wanted to swat Simon like Iris had.

They spent a few minutes chatting in restrained, civil fashion, while Iris sat in queenly disdain and ignored them all. But Emily had seen a frightened glitter in her eyes, and when she took a dainty handkerchief from her purse, her hands were trembling. Emily was wretched.

Just before their case was called, Marylou Thomlinson, Mildred Davis's mother and partner, strode into the room, looking like an older copy of Mildred. She had the same brisk energy, the same tall, well-toned body and air of assurance.

"Sorry I'm late," she apologized with a smile encompassing everyone. "Will this take long, Lamar? I need to show a house at noon."

High noon, Emily found herself thinking with crazy humor. All they needed was the music and Gary Cooper. It would all be over by noon.

Emily only looked at Simon once, as they were all entering the courtroom. He was holding the door for everyone, and as Emily passed through with Brad at her elbow, Simon sliced her a look that would have frozen a welder's blowtorch. Emily couldn't conceal her pained confusion, and his mouth briefly softened. He and Brad exchanged glances; then Brad ushered her to her seat.

What had happened to the Simon who had promised to take care of her?

The procedure lasted only forty-five minutes. The lawyers presented their respective cases, and then the judge retired to his chambers to evaluate the claims before he made his decision. Emily knew he had already studied the case. She just hoped he would make his decision instead of delaying, which Brad had told her was a possibility for which she should prepare herself.

She had not been prepared for Marylou Thomlinson's revelations.

According to Mildred's mother, some twenty-six years ago—the very first year she received her broker's license—a man named Harold deCourier had come to see her. He was old and ill, with a very unusual request: He wanted Marylou to handle his father's property—the VanCleef estate—but according to the terms of his father's will, the property could not be sold out of the family for one hundred years from the date of that will.

Harold was, he informed Marylou with touching shame, VanCleef's illegitimate son, which was why his last name was the same as his mother's. The time limit would now be up in one more year. Twenty-six years ago Marylou had simply signed an agreement, then filed the whole thing in the back of a drawer, figuring she would probably never sell the property, so why worry about it?

She had truly forgotten the whole affair. Over the years, the old deCourier place just sat and rotted out in the country. Harold had died years ago. He had never married and left no will that anyone could find, so there the house sat.

Marylou never told Mildred. Why should she, since she never thought about it? Thus, Brad meticulously proved, Mildred sold Emily the property in good faith.

Emily listened in growing horror and consternation, especially since Iris Bancroft turned out to be the granddaughter of Everett VanCleef, and therefore the legitimate heir. At one point Emily glanced toward the older woman, sitting straight and dignified across the room. No emotion showed on the aging, aristocratic face, but Emily still felt like an unprincipled carpetbagger. She couldn't help it. Once Simon had asked if she would give up the house without a fight. She understood now why Iris was just as determined, and the knowledge was suffocating.

The judge returned, everyone rose, and Emily found that she couldn't take a deep breath. Ten minutes later it was over—and Emily had won. Because the will had not been found and because Harold had died without issue, the judge declared Emily's ownership more legally binding than the terms of the agreement between Harold deCourier and Marylou Thomlinson. Lamar Hansell and Brad shook hands, and Lamar went over to console Iris, who was sitting as if turned to a pillar of salt.

Simon bent over his aunt, whispering, but as Emily and Brad started to leave the room, he straightened and met them at the door. "I'd like to speak to you, Emily."

Brad lifted a tawny brow. When Emily nodded and managed to reassure him with a facsimile of a smile, he murmured that he would wait for her in the hall and left.

"I'm truly sorry for your aunt," Emily told Simon. "Seeing her in action, I can understand why you've had such a time of it." She paused, then added painfully, "Why didn't you explain to me?"

"I only found out Marylou's story two days ago. She was in the Mediterranean all summer, remember? Then, too, Aunt Iris believes in playing her cards close to her chest." He regarded her unsmilingly. "Especially now that she knows how I feel about you."

Emily digested those words in stony silence. "And how would that be?" she finally ventured. "From the looks you've thrown my way ever since you walked into the waiting room, I'd about decided I must have turned into the wicked stepmother instead of Cinderella."

A wicked glint appeared briefly. "I did warn you about her tongue, didn't I? At least you haven't had to listen to it for almost three months." The glint disappeared. "What's Lauderman to you anyway, Emily? Besides your lawyer and employer, that is."

Emily stiffened. "You have no right to ask me such a question. And now that the house is mine. . ."—she faltered, her gaze going in spite of itself to Iris—"twice over, I imagine you'll be going back to your own life."

"And prove I'm as undependable, as faithless, as everyone else in your life?" Simon asked very softly. When Emily's eyes jerked back to his—startled, dark, and vulnerable—he lifted his hand and touched her cheek. "You might have your property, but there's still some goings-on to be cleared up, aren't there? Besides—you haven't learned about God's faithfulness yet. I've decided He's appointed me as His representative on your behalf, so get used to the fact that you'll be seeing a lot of me in the future." He opened the door and held it for her. "See you soon."

Emily ate lunch with Brad but only because he insisted. Before they parted, Brad grasped her arm and waited until he had her full attention. "Emily, I wouldn't be worth the paper my degree was printed on if I didn't warn you about a couple of things."

Alarm filled Emily's face, but she relaxed a little when Brad gave her a wide, sheepish smile.

"Sorry. Maybe I should have phrased it in legal jargon. What I mean is that there is every possibility Iris is going to pursue the will. If it's found, you'll find yourself being served with your own lawsuit."

"Oh."

"And that brings me to my other warning." He loosened his tie, then crammed his hands in his pants pockets. "Be careful with Balfour. The man has his eye on you, Emily, and it isn't just because of your property."

Emily colored. "It's nothing serious, Brad. I'm not the sort of woman to inspire a man to launch a thousand ships for me. And regardless of what you may think, it is the house he's interested in." She smiled a little. "He just has a bee in his bonnet about teaching me a lesson about God."

"What?" Brad laughed suddenly and shook his head. "I've heard a lot of lines, but that one takes the cake. He might talk as pretty as a preacher, Honey, but that's not what he's got on his mind. I'm a man, and I know." He eyed her thoughtfully a moment and shrugged. "I entertained a few thoughts myself until I saw which way the wind blew. Go on home, Emily, but keep what I said in mind."

Men, Emily decided as she drove the twelve miles home, were as undecipherable as they claimed women were. As she turned onto the dirt lane, her spirits perked up a little. She was sorry for Iris, bemused and irritated by Brad and Simon, but she finally had a home. A home of her own. And now she could relax and get on with the rest of her life.

She had taken Samson in to Dr. Moffat the evening before for his neutering operation. Now the first order of the day was to call and make sure her cat was okay. Shaking her head and chiding herself for forgetting to go by the vet's after she left Brad, she also decided to take Ivan for a walk since she had left him inside this morning.

"Hope he didn't chew up anything else," she spoke aloud, feeling the accumulated hours of worry and tension sloughing off her back as if she were shedding a burdensome extra skin. "Poor baby. Maybe I'd better let him stay outside again. If he's learned—" The words died in her throat.

Jerking to a halt and flinging herself from the car, she ran to the edge of her yard and stared across the field, horror turning to desperation and spiraling fear. The flames were small as yet—but deadly, creeping with scorching fingers in a steady line across the field toward her house. Smoke curled and billowed in gray swirls, and the air had borne it aloft so that it filled her nostrils with the sharp, acrid scent.

Without wasting another second, Emily whirled and raced for the house. Her fingers shook so badly it took three tries to dial the emergency number. Thank God she had a phone now; Ivan was here in the house, and Samson safe at the vet's! She tried to calm the whining, worried dog as she explained the situation in a trembling voice to the calm man at the other end of the line. She managed to give directions, then hung up and began tearing her suit off in a panicked frenzy. The fireman had told her to evacuate and move herself and her car to the main highway, but Emily had no intention of sitting by and watching her property go up in smoke.

Yanking on jeans and a dressy, long-sleeved blouse she normally wore to church, ripping a nail as she struggled into socks and tennis shoes, Emily's mind raced as she tried to figure out ways to cap and destroy the flames. Carrying a bucket would be useless—like spitting in the wind. Should she try digging a firebreak? Starting backfires as firefighters did to combat forest fires? Hose down her yard to dampen everything?

She snatched one of J.J.'s old baseball caps she had saved and stuffed it over her hair to keep the braid up out of the way. Grabbing Ivan, she leashed him and then dumped him in her car in case the worst happened. "You'll be safe here." She patted his head and ran her hand briefly but soothingly over his quivering flanks. "I'll be back as soon as I can."

Stumbling and tripping, she ran across the field with a shovel in one hand and a wet rag to tie across her face in the other, sending up incoherent pleas to God, the firemen, Simon, and anyone else she could think of who might help. There was no way she could put out a fire alone, even though she was determined to try.

Sometime later she heard the keening of the fire engines, but she was too busy to be relieved. Smoke stung her eyes and burned her nose; heat scorched and blistered her face and hands as she dug into the earth and flung heavy shovelfuls over the flames; dug and flung until her back was on fire like the field and her hands were raw with sweat and blisters. She was much too preoccupied to notice a sinister figure creeping steadily out from the woods behind her.

The blow caught her at the back of her neck. She went down like a pine sapling felled by a single swipe of the ax. When the fire engines pulled up five minutes later, there was no sign of Emily.

❀

Consciousness returned by degrees, each more uncomfortable than the last. Her first sensation was the awful, searing pain in her head and neck. On the heels of the revelation came the awareness that she was being carried, flung over someone's shoulder like a bag of fertilizer. She tried to move, to scream; then the third realization that she was bound up inside some sort of sack hit her. She was as helpless as a chicken tossed into the gunnysack of a chicken thief.

After awhile, the labored breathing of whoever was carrying her altered to grunts of exertion, and she decided somewhat fuzzily that he must have been carrying her a long time because she wasn't that heavy. She was on the edge of passing out again when she was unceremoniously dumped onto the ground.

"It's about time," a muffled voice complained testily.

"Put a lid on it," was the sharp reply. "She might look like a skinny school brat, but you try carrying her on your back for forty minutes."

"Don't see why we couldn't just leave her in the field."

"Because that's a murder rap, you dumb scum! Orca made his feeling plain—or are your eyeballs so fried you didn't catch his reaction after that ball up with Frank and Pete?"

"Back off, Gumshoe." The voice came closer, and Emily's heart rose in her throat and tried to suffocate her. "Can we at least have a little fun with the dame? She's not much of a looker, but—"

Emily tried to close her ears to the spate of foul language that followed between the two. She tried to lick her lips, but she was dry-mouthed, parched with fear and thirst and the exertion of fighting the fire. *The fire! Oh, please, God, let the firemen get there on time.*

She wanted to struggle, to free herself from the blinding, scratchy burlap sack that kept her trussed-up and helpless. Some deep-seated instinct of survival kept her still; the subconscious voice warning her that movement of any kind would only draw unwelcome attention to her.

But she had to do something. She couldn't just tamely submit to her fate. It wasn't right. It wasn't fair. Never had she felt so helpless, so out of control. Even when J.J. had been at his most rebellious, she at least had been able to talk him into listening to her point of view. And when Mom and Daddy left, she had had the freedom to make a new home. When Simon came and tried to take it away from her, she had been able to fight back.

Now she was utterly and completely at the mercy of these thugs, and with that realization she fell into the darkest, blackest pit of despair in the universe. This must have been what Jonah felt like when he had been swallowed by the big fish. What had Jonah done to get out? Emily's conscious mind was coming and going now, flickering in and out like a bad camera reel of a 1930s film. Jonah and the whale. . .sparrows. . . Simon called her little sparrow because of that song. . .a song about a whale? No, it had something to do with God. . . . His eye is on the sparrow. That was it. . . . Jonah had prayed, and up out of the fish he came. But he was a man and she was just a little sparrow. . . . God wouldn't listen to her prayers. . .
"His eye is on the sparrow, and I know He watches me. . . ."
Help me, Lord. Send Simon before it's too late. . . .

Chapter 9

Emily was picked up again, roughly, and dumped with scant ceremony into the seat of some kind of vehicle. Through a semiconscious daze, she heard a new voice speaking in a high-pitched whisper.

"Hurry! They got the fire out and now they're looking for the girl!"

"Did you take care of that mutt?"

After a horrible pause the third voice replied in a grudging tone, "Yeah. I . . . took care of him."

Emily didn't notice the bouncing ride or the pounding pain in her head. Tears dripped down her cheeks, soaking her face as, heartsick, she grieved for her innocent pet. He had been slaughtered because she hadn't gone for help when she had the chance.

Ivan was dead, and she was probably next on the list, no matter what that other man said.

After awhile, they pulled onto a smoother road, and the bouncing and bumping ceased. The car picked up speed, but Emily had no sense of where they were or which way they were going.

Fortunately, the drive didn't take long. With a squealing of tires and a jolting turn that threw Emily against the door, the car jerked to a halt. Gravel voice—had he been called Gumshoe?—cursed the driver roundly; then Emily heard doors wrenched open, and she was hauled out feetfirst and once again slung over a shoulder.

She sensed the presence of the other two men walking on either side. She could hear multiple footsteps, smell the malodorous combination of sweat, cigarettes, and unwashed bodies.

"This is far enough," one of them finally whined. "It'll take her until tomorrow to find her way back as it is. Let's split, Man. I don't like this."

Suddenly Emily was yanked off the shoulder and then held suspended by two hands grinding into her arms like giant metal braces.

"I hope this little scare will teach you to keep your nose out of business that don't concern you. Next time we won't be so gentle." There was a harsh bark of laughter. "You might end up in the same shape as your dog." The clamps suddenly released her and she collapsed onto the ground. "Nice meeting you, Ms. Carson. If you value your hide and that pile of bricks, you better not venture too far out of it into the woods anymore."

The sound of footsteps retreated. A short while later the car engine roared to life and gunned off down the road. Emily was alone.

Silence lapped over and around her, gently lifting her up out of the dark hole and tugging at her dazed senses. Eventually she moved her hands and fumbled weakly with the corner of the sack, managing after several abortive attempts to tug it over her head. She winced as the late afternoon sun struck her eyes. How could this possibly still be the same day? Had it only been this morning that she'd learned she was the bona fide, one and only legal owner of that. . .pile of bricks? Shock and grief and a residue of terror stiffened her spine, and she forced herself to stand. It took a couple of tries.

"What a mess. . . ," Emily mumbled, her voice a quavering husky croak.

In the distance, she heard the faint drone of a plane, the plaintive call of a bird, a car. A car? Feeling like the scarecrow from Wizard of Oz, whose stuffing was scattered all over the field, Emily dragged herself a few steps, swaying and dizzy and trembling. They hadn't carried her very far that last time. Hopefully the road was close by.

She fought a stumbling, wavering path through waist-high goldenrod and milkweed, and prayed. Even though she was neither starving, nor a prisoner of war, nor dying of cancer, she hoped under these particular circumstances the Lord might incline His ear for a few minutes, if only until she was safely home.

The road proved to be an ancient county road, paved in the distant past with asphalt that was now cracked and crumbling, with weeds encroaching on the edges. If she were lucky, another car might pass by before next week. For the first time since she had been released, Emily's chin trembled. It was one thing to keep her sense of proportion when her life was on the line—it was another thing entirely when she was spared, but then was solely responsible for her continued well-being.

Simon. If only he were here. He would know what to do. He would take care of her. What was she thinking? She could take care of herself, as she had always done. She couldn't depend on anyone, including Simon Balfour. This was the man whose great-aunt wanted her home, who would doubtless be after Simon to keep on looking for the will regardless of this morning's outcome.

Iris Bancroft reminded Emily of the story in the Bible about the widow who kept nagging the judge until he gave her what she wanted, just to be rid of her. From what she had seen and heard of the elderly woman, the judge who this morning had ruled in Emily's favor might eventually reverse his decision just to get rid of Iris.

Simon would have his hands full with his great-aunt. He also had his own life to consider. Surely his team of specialists couldn't do all the restoration work in his absence; if they could, they'd go into business for themselves.

Besides, she had made it plain she wasn't interested. All that talk about being God's emissary was nothing but talk, just like Brad had tried to warn her. Men were a strange lot, but it was not in Emily to figure them out right now. She had all she could do to put one foot in front of the other and find out if there was a phone or a house at the end of the winding little road.

❀

A sunburned, dust-covered farmer driving a tractor pulling a flatbed of hay came upon Emily a half hour later. He helped her up, and she lay in the warm, sweet-smelling hay as the farmer urged the ancient chugging tractor to its limit.

The farmer's wife exclaimed over her, put her on a couch, and nursed her with hot tea. Then Emily was driven to the county hospital, where an extremely large, comfortable-looking nurse clucked over her smoke- and dirt-laden state. A doctor examined her and "harrumphed" a lot, but he refused to tell her anything. Emily was wearily trying to remember the name of her insurance agent in Sylvan to tell the nurse when the curtain shielding her from the other cubicles in the small emergency room was flung wide open.

Simon erupted into view, his body a coiled spring of tension and his eyes wild. "Emily, are you all right? Emily!"

"Sir," the nurse tried to protest in her best matronly tone, "you can't come in here right now—"

Simon did not budge. "I can and I have." He was at Emily's side immediately, his hand reaching out with trembling fingers to touch her cheek, still red from fighting the fire. "Emily." He couldn't seem to say anything else and stood gazing down at her with red-rimmed eyes. Emily stared back. "Simon. . ." She passed her tongue over her cracked lips. "How did you find me?"

For a minute his eyes closed as if in agony, and his hands clenched the side of the table with such force the knuckles gleamed white. "I drove out to see you—the firemen were just putting out the last of the flames. Your car was there, but no one had seen you."

He picked up her hand and held it, caressing her fingers, then lifted it to his lips. "We searched everywhere. Someone found an old baseball cap with some of your hairs attached, and your shovel, but that was it." He looked down at her with such naked pain that Emily was shocked out of her own pain and exhaustion. "I never want to go through those feelings again. I called the police, Barb and Taylor, Lauderman. . . ."

For the first time, the glimmer of a smile lightened his face. "Do you realize there are probably fifty or so people and officials in two counties combing the woods around your property for you? When the hospital notified the sheriff that a young woman fitting your description had been brought in, I burned up the road getting here."

Emily licked her dry, cracked lips. "I had no idea anyone would go to so much trouble," she whispered.

"How badly are you hurt?" he asked abruptly. "Can I take you home? Are you going to be up to answering some questions from the police—and me?"

"I'm all right. Mostly shaken. . .and a headache. The doctor hasn't really filled me in. . . ." Her voice faded and she bit her lip, her gaze dropping to watch her hands fidgeting with her blouse. "Simon. . .I think I've gotten in over my head this time. . . ."

His hands covered both of hers and stilled the agitated movements. "Whatever happened is not as important as the fact that I've got you here, now, and you're safe." He drew in a deep breath and his hand tightened reassuringly. "Were you assaulted, Emily?"

The question was voiced softly, almost offhandedly, but Emily was not too battered to miss the undercurrents, and suddenly she was as much afraid of what Simon might do as she was of the three thugs who had manhandled her and—and killed Ivan.

"Not exactly," she dragged out unsteadily. "They—I—was being taught a lesson." She tried to take a breath. "Ivan. They. . .they. . ." She couldn't go on, but Simon didn't need the words spelled out.

"I'm sorry, Emily." Leaning forward, he brushed his lips comfortingly over her forehead. "I wondered when we couldn't find him and hoped he might be with you." He waited a minute, then prodded in a gentle, coaxing tone, "Who is 'they,' Honey?"

"It would have been nice if you'd waited for us, Balfour."

A short stocky man in a khaki sheriff's uniform strolled over to stand at the foot of the gurney. "Miss Emily Carson? I'm Sheriff Travis Jessup. Mighty glad you're okay, Ma'am. Some of my men were getting ready to pen this fella here up in a cage—he was about as uptight as a renegade cougar." He hooked his thumbs in his gun belt and surveyed Simon and Emily. "Care to tell us about it, Ma'am? Doc Wilburn ways you're a mite battered about, but nothing near bad enough to stay unless you really want to."

"No." Emily allowed Simon to help her sit up, dangling her legs on the side of the gurney. "No, I don't want to stay here."

Both men waited in taciturn silence while Emily haltingly related her tale of terror. A time or two, Sheriff Jessup inserted a question, but Simon kept silent. His gaze never left Emily, and the hand holding hers refused to let go.

"And then they left and I made my way to the road, and the farmer—I don't remember his name—found me and brought me here."

"The only names you remember hearing are Frank and Gumshoe and another funny-sounding name you can't remember?" the sheriff quoted from his notes, watching Emily intently.

Emily nodded wearily, her head throbbing—her whole body was throbbing. Simon's hand held hers in a warm comforting clasp, however, which tightened when the doctor returned.

"She can go," he repeated, albeit reluctantly. "For the first twenty-four hours she probably ought to be monitored, maybe wake her every couple of hours through tonight—just as a precaution." He glanced from Simon to Emily and back again. "I take it this gentleman will see to those conditions?"

"You take it right."

The doctor winked down at Emily, patted her shoulder, and left. Simon held out his hand to the sheriff. "Thanks for everything. I'll get her settled first and then square things away as to addresses and procedures."

"Sure thing, Mr. Balfour. Miss Carson—I'll be in touch." He scratched his chin, looking uncomfortable. "I'm sorry 'bout all this, Ma'am. . . ." He touched his hat, gestured to Simon, and walked out.

Simon smiled down at Emily. "I'll be right back. Don't move."

When he came back a few minutes later, he looked grim, but the hands helping her to her feet handled her with exquisite gentleness. "I'm taking you to Barb and Taylor," he said. "They'll put us up until I can call my folks. By the way, we're going down there as soon as you're up to it."

He helped her walk toward the exit, keeping an arm about her shoulders and matching his stride to hers, talking in a soft, steady patter of words. "The sheriff and I decided whisking you off to Florida until this mess is cleared up a little would be our best option. No—don't shake your head at me. It's all been taken care of.

"Barb is something else, isn't she? When I got in touch with her, I thought she was going to come after me with her food processor—then I thought she was going to collar the FBI director himself if she had to hire a private jet to get there to do it."

Emily tried to laugh. That sounded like Barb.

Simon looked pleased. "She got on the phone and inside of thirty minutes had your entire hometown on its way over to start a search." He eased her into the seat of his Jensen-Healy, and they backed out of a parking spot marked "Ambulances Only," then drove slowly off down the street.

Emily leaned back in the seat, her eyes closing against the steady beat of pain, against the rapid tide sweeping her willy-nilly down a stream she was helpless to paddle against. "I can't go to your parents, Simon."

"Just rest, little sparrow. Just rest. I've got you now, and everything's going to be okay."

She rolled her head sideways, being careful not to jar the swollen lump. "Do you really think God has His eyes on sparrows?" she mused in a faraway, fading voice.

"I know He does." His hands clenched suddenly on the wheel, and his voice went rough and raw. "I couldn't have stood it otherwise." And on that note silence reigned.

�֍

They spent two nights with the Chakensis family. Barb and Taylor wanted Emily to move in with them, but Simon remained obdurate—the next day he was taking her to his parents' home in Florida. Friends dropped in to ask after her and offer aid and comfort, but the bulk of their advice centered around a central theme: Under no circumstances should Emily return to her house.

The police had been unable to find any sign of her abductors, although after hearing Emily's story about the plane, they combed the woods, looking for the open pasture. Emily had not talked to Sheriff Jessup since the day after the fire, so she had no idea if they had found any clues or not.

"I suppose there's at least a smidgen of good in being knocked out and hauled around like a sack of dirty laundry," she commented over supper that evening. "At least my story is taken a little more seriously. Now I'm not just a neurotic woman living alone and scaring myself to death with my imagination."

Simon paused in the act of taking a bite of his mashed potatoes. "Has someone been giving you that impression?"

"Not since I was bashed over the head," Emily provided hastily. Simon was becoming more and more possessive, and it was downright uncomfortable, if not awkward. She had never had anyone fuss over her before, treating her as if she were fragile and needed protecting. Part of her responded as a desert flower responds to spring rains, but the rest of her remained a wary, prickling cactus.

"The policeman who came out after I heard someone walking around outside the house one night treated me more or less like a feebleminded ninny." She abruptly became aware of three sets of eyes boring holes of recrimination into her and ducked her head guiltily. She had forgotten that they hadn't known about that incident.

"You heard someone walking around outside and didn't say anything?" Barb's voice ended in a shriek, and Mark and Lara put their hands over their mouths and giggled.

"Calm down, Honey," Taylor remonstrated his wife before turning to his children and adding sternly, "You two go take your baths and get ready for bed. You've got school in the morning."

"Em, why couldn't you be back teaching? Dump that house and come back here where you belong, where you'll be safe."

Emily very carefully laid her crumpled paper napkin by her plate and rose. "I have a very good job as Brad's secretary," she responded in a colorless monotone, "and as for belonging—I feel more at home in that house with Ivan and—" She

278

stopped as a rush of emotion threatened to engulf her. "Excuse me," she muttered and fled out into the backyard.

Simon followed her a little while later. She was sitting in a rope swing with a board seat Taylor had rigged for the children, her feet idly scuffing the dirt patch beneath it where all the grass had been worn away. She was staring fixedly into space with a closed, blank expression, but the hands clasping the rough hemp rope as if she were clutching a lifeline betrayed her inner turmoil. Without a word, Simon gave her back a gentle push and began swinging her, his hands warm and firm.

"I could accept it better if they had at least left his body," Emily offered almost inaudibly. "At least I could have buried him and grieved and gotten it over with."

"I know." His hands kept up the gentle pushing, but each time they pressed into her back for that brief instant of contact, they somehow conveyed a message of caring sympathy.

Emily closed her eyes a few minutes to try and savor the early evening and relax. Last night the wind had changed, bringing in a cool front and the deep blue skies of approaching fall. The breeze riffling through her hair with the motion of the swing smelled of dry leaves and smoke and mid-September. In front of her, the sun had just slipped over the horizon, leaving behind a pastel watercolor sky of pale orange and pink and blue.

Life should have been serene, like a happy child tossing tiny pebbles into a placid pool. But it took everything Emily had to keep from bursting into tears.

"Sunset's beautiful, isn't it?" Simon observed as if he knew Emily needed to changed the subject. "I think sometimes that God reveals Himself the most dramatically in sunsets and sunrises."

"I suppose."

"But I've also found He can reveal Himself just as dramatically in other ways—sometimes to my cost."

Emily swung up and back, up and back, and then gave in. "What do you mean?" she asked.

She heard Simon chuckle softly. "Sometimes that still small voice we Christians are supposed to cultivate is more of a first sergeant's shout when I'm not listening like I should." He gave her braid a gentle tug as he pushed her away. "Like when I lose my regrettable temper, or when I'm so blind with worry I forget."

"Forget what?" Emily found herself persisting.

Simon stopped the swing, and his hands closed over hers. He turned her, swing and all, to face him, holding her not only with his hands but with the compelling message in his eyes. "When I forget the faithfulness of God," he declared with the strength and depth of a mountain stream. "When I try to control all the circumstances, forgetting that He's promised to stay with us at all times—good and bad—so all I really need to do is trust Him to deliver me."

Chapter 10

Sheriff Jessup met them at Emily's house early the next morning before they took off on the short drive to Florida.

"Got a few leads," he informed them after inquiring after Emily's health and shaking Simon's hand. "We found the field they were using as an airstrip, but needless to say we found nothing else useful. We'll stake it out awhile just in case, though." He glanced around the library. "You did a nice job on this room, but why don't you clean up that window?"

"I'm saving it for last." Emily shrugged self-consciously. "It was sunbeams hitting that window and reflecting on my windshield that brought the house to my attention, and when I discovered the window, I knew I had to have this place."

She sighed. "But it's been a lot harder and more tedious then I dreamed it would be." She slanted a quelling look at Simon. "Imagining how beautiful my window will look when it's cleaned up is all that keeps me going sometimes."

"You've done a first-class job," Simon assured her. He nodded toward the window. "I've been itching to get my hands on it myself. I've restored period homes all over the South and have never come across a lead glass window of this caliber in a private residence. I'm pretty sure it's a Tiffany or LaFarge, but since Emily hasn't given me permission to check more closely, I have to suffer in silence." He smiled at Emily's look of astonishment, but now was not the time to pursue the matter.

"Have you found out any more about the low-life creeps who assaulted Emily?"

The sheriff nodded in satisfaction. "Her hearing the name 'Gumshoe' was a piece of luck for us. We've been in touch with the DEA and the FBI, and they both had this character on file." He contemplated his scuffed-up shoes a minute, hand stroking his chin.

"I wasn't too wild hearing that—means this is more than a bunch of locals out to make a few fast bucks. Gumshoe is a former private investigator, hence the nickname. His real name is Henry Parskoni. He apparently lost his license because of his cocaine habit—he's street smart and a real cynical son of a gun. He's also careful. I'm surprised he let the mention of his name slip by."

"What about the other guy Emily mentioned?" Simon asked.

"Nothing yet. But we do think we've tied this incident to the wreck that resulted in two casualties back in July."

"My mailman said there was a second car involved, and you had found some drugs inside it."

"Yes'm." He hesitated, then added, "High-grade stuff—and two boxes of the most disgustin' porno books and magazines I ever had the misfortune to see." He shook his head slowly, looking every inch the world-weary, battle-worn officer of the law fighting a war he couldn't win. "Whole country's straight on a road to the pit. It's the tip of the iceberg down here, since we suspect this area might be one of the drop-off points of a pipeline from South America. We figure on average, we only manage to seize about 15 percent of this garbage before it hits the streets." For a minute the three of them struggled with the weight of their helplessness; then Sheriff Jessup put his hat back on and moved briskly toward the front hall. "Well, I'll be going now that I've apprised you of the situation. Let me know twenty-four hours before you bring her back, and I'll assign some men to her."

"Thanks," Simon said. He looked as grim as the sheriff.

※

Emily hastily tossed some clothes in the suitcase Simon had brought in from his car. Barb had packed her some things the other day, but Emily, who had never given much thought to dressing herself up as long as she was fairly neat and clean, found herself wondering what Simon's parents would think of her. They'd probably think she was a mousy, colorless woman Simon had taken under his wing for incomprehensible reasons of his own.

As she knelt on the floor of her closet, she tried to bolster her drooping spirits. Why not just look at the experience as an all-expense-paid vacation to Florida with a very attractive man? It was too bad she didn't have an address for Mom and Daddy—she could have sent them a postcard.

She pushed her clothes aside and tugged at a box of summer clothes and other stuff she had never unpacked. A corner of the box seemed to be stuck on something, and she pulled harder, wanting to finish and be on her way so she wouldn't have to think any more about her motivation for giving in to Simon so easily.

There was an ominous sound of ripping wood, and with a muttered exclamation, Emily peered behind the tangle of clothes into the dark interior of the closet. Wonderful. One of the cardboard flaps on the box had caught on a loose panel or something in the wood. She carefully edged her fingers behind the flap and in between the splintering panel to try and disconnect them.

"Just what I need. Something else to repair!" Emily grumped aloud, stifling a sigh of frustration as she tried to feel what was going on. The closet didn't have a light in it, and she didn't feel like searching for a flashlight. With a sudden spurt of impatience, she tugged at the wood and the cardboard flap, scraping her knuckles as she did so.

A tearing, rending sound announced that the wood, as well as the flap, had pulled free of the wall. Emily yanked the box of clothes out of the closet and shoved the clothes on hangers out of the way. She was planning to stuff the displaced panel back, when her fingers encountered something cold and metallic in the space behind it.

The realization of what she had uncovered struck her a stunning blow, and with shaking hands she withdrew what turned out to be a metal strongbox. She backed unsteadily out of the closet and stood, black spots dancing before her eyes.

With a feeling of sick foreboding, she laid the dusty coffer on the floor. Incredibly, it wasn't locked, and after only a slight hesitation, it opened quite easily. Inside was a faded manila envelope, so old it was closed by old-fashioned strings tied around a button. Inside the envelope was a folded sheet of paper, with the heading "Last Will and Testament of Everett VanCleef" written in an elaborate, bold script across the top.

"What's taking so long?" Simon appeared in the doorway. "Emily? What's the matter? What's that?"

He crossed to her side, studying her face, but his gaze dropped to her hands when she mutely help up the will. "Oh, no," Simon breathed, a stillness coming over his body. "Why now?"

With careful fingers, he lifted the will from Emily's trembling hands and began reading aloud, his voice a somber, expressionless baritone. " 'I, Everett Peter VanCleef, being of sound mind and declaring this instrument to be my last will and testament, dispose of my properties as follows. . .' "

"Simon," Emily sighed in a wisp of an undertone, "I feel sort of funny. I think I'd better sit—"

She swayed; then Simon's arm was around her, and he was guiding her over to the bed. They sat down together, and his hand moved to the back of her neck. Pressing with gentle insistence, he made her lower her head almost to her knees.

He kept her there a few minutes while he massaged her neck, being careful with the still-tender bruise where she had been hit. "Easy, easy, Love," he quieted her with his voice and hand. "I'm sorry. . .so sorry. . . ."

There was the sound of rustling paper and then his other hand slid beneath her chin and lifted her back up. Emily was incapable of hiding the shock, the inertia of shattering defeat that revealed itself in her stricken eyes.

"I can't bear it," she choked out, her voice still nothing but a thready wisp. "I've lost everything. Everything. I can't bear it anymore."

"Shh. . .shh. You haven't lost everything, I promise."

Emily very carefully removed herself from his hold and stood up. "Brad warned me if the will were found Miss Bancroft would have a good chance of winning a second lawsuit." Her unseeing eyes fastened on her shoulder bag lying in a jumbled heap on the bed beside the half-filled suitcase. She picked it up, rummaging inside until she found the huge old brass key.

"Here." She held it out to Simon. "Take it. I quit. I can't handle anymore. I hope you enjoy restoring it." Her voice drifted off, then resumed in a vague, dreamy tone. "I wonder if Brad could use a full-time secretary. . . ." She looked around. "I'll try and move my stuff out as soon as I can."

Simon stood up, and with utmost gentleness took Emily by the shoulders and walked her down the hall into the kitchen. *She looks,* Simon found himself thinking in agony, *even worse than when she told me about Ivan. Lord, what can I do? She needs You now more than ever—because I don't know if she'll ever trust me again.*

Sitting Emily down in the kitchen chair, Simon fixed her a glass of water and told her to drink it. After pawing through the largely empty cupboards, he finally unearthed a half-empty box of animal crackers. "I want you to eat these while I finish packing your suitcase," he instructed Emily as he would a child.

Emily looked at the cookies and water. "All right, Simon," she said apathetically, her entire posture speaking so wrenchingly of defeat that it was all he could do to keep himself from grabbing her and wrapping her in a fierce embrace.

He strode back to her bedroom, shoved in the suitcase what few clothes remained to be packed, and slammed the lid shut. If she needed something else, he could buy it for her later, but right now he was determined to clear out and get Emily on the road to Florida.

He glanced around the bathroom, then prowled the downstairs to make sure everything was secure. Jessup had promised to keep an eye on the premises while they were gone, the vet was caring for the cat, and the post office was holding her mail. All Simon had to do was keep Emily from giving up completely.

He laughed a bitter, mirthless laugh. *Might be too late for that,* he thought, and he couldn't blame her. Why had she had to find that wretched will? For two cents he'd burn the thing and be done with it, but he knew that evasion and lies and pretense were never the answer.

Jaw firming in renewed determination, he returned to the kitchen. "Come on, Honey." He glanced at the barely touched water, the box of crackers still in the exact position he had left them. "We'll eat on the way." He put his hand beneath her elbow and tugged her up.

Looking neither at him nor around the house, Emily followed blindly. She was a lifeless, broken doll, and her once-vibrant, spunky personality lay in a crumpled heap somewhere deep inside her. She allowed Simon to lead her outside and down the steps, then over to the midsized sedan he had rented to make the trip more comfortable.

Emily slept most of the trip.

Nathaniel and Katherine Balfour had built a beachfront home years before on a tiny strip of a peninsula at the bottom of Florida's panhandle. Simon spent the bulk of the six-and-a-half-hour drive praying while he drove, watching Emily as much as he did the road.

She still looked poleaxed, like a zombie. Simon would have preferred tears, or even her unpredictable, almost humorous display of temper rather than this present lifeless state. Right now she reminded him of a snuffed-out candle.

Barb and Taylor had shed a goodly amount of insight into Emily's complex personality, her paradoxical blend of reckless confidence and the easygoing, phlegmatic woman so astonished by her own capacity for passion. As far back as they could remember, Emily had had to pretty much play a lone hand. Her parents should never have had children, Barb had contended forcefully, because they were both basically selfish people.

"They never neglected their kids or abused them exactly," she'd admitted. "It was more like they were just going through the motions of being parents, just waiting 'til Emily and J.J. were old enough to take care of themselves." She smacked her lips fondly at Taylor, who shook his head at her and returned the blown kiss. "I mean, they dropped her and J.J. off at church but never went themselves. And if Emily was receiving an award at school or something, her mom would slip in long enough to see Emily, then disappear before it ended so she wouldn't have to go backstage and be around all the other kids. Emily said once that kids make her mother nervous."

"You're making her sound like a coldhearted monster," Taylor remonstrated mildly.

Barb shrugged her plump shoulders. "You weren't as close to Emily as I was. She used to come over to our house after we became best friends in high school and just sit in the kitchen listening to Mama and me yak. She'd get the most wistful look on her face. Mama used to cry after she went home because she felt so sorry for her."

"I suppose work was sort of a substitute for her," Simon finished, his own heart wrenching as he thought of what Emily had become, and what she could have been had anyone taken the time and care to let her know she was special and loved.

"In a way," Taylor put in, his expression thoughtful. "I also think it was just as much an escape. At home she had indifferent parents and a wild, rebellious younger brother she spent most of her youth keeping out of trouble. At least at work she could be validated somewhat."

Breaking away from his silent reverie, Simon woke Emily as he turned onto the narrow road that ended at the gate of a state park encompassing the northern half of the peninsula. His parents lived a few miles south, and since he and Emily would be arriving in less than fifteen minutes, he knew Emily would need some time to compose herself. He also needed a few quiet moments to determine how best to proceed with their relationship.

He pulled the car to the sandy shoulder of the road and shut off the engine. He had known since the day she was abducted that he was more involved emotionally with Emily Carson than he had ever been with another woman—but he was uncertain about the future.

Was he ready to make the kind of commitment required to keep from destroying her? He knew things had reached a point where he would either have to back out of her life completely and take that risk—or be prepared to be bound to her the rest of his life. Did he love her? As if with a mind of its own, his hand slid across the back of the seat to trace a feather-light path across the crown of her head.

This morning at Barb and Taylor's house—another age ago—Emily had meticulously woven her hair into a neat French braid, and Simon had overheard her anxiously asking Barb if she looked respectable enough to meet his parents. His finger smoothed the silky soft layers, and he had to fight to keep from awakening her with a kiss.

Respectable! *God, I really need your guidance now. If this woman is the one You have chosen to be my mate, I need to know—I need a little more confidence not only with my own feelings, but hers.* He knew Emily still didn't place much trust either in the Lord or him. Actually, she didn't trust anyone. And yet he knew that at one time she had accepted Christ for her eternal salvation.

She stirred, head rolling toward him slightly so that the still-neat braid slid over his hand and spilled down the seat. Simon fingered the plait, wanting to bury his face in the softness with so urgent a need he had to force himself to move away from Emily completely. He had felt desire before and knew how powerful the sexual drive could be. But never had he felt the tremendous pull when tenderness was coupled with that desire. He wanted Emily with every drop of warm red blood in his body, but he also wanted to protect her, to shield her, to convince her that his feelings for her were more than raw passion.

He flexed his tense shoulders and drew a deep breath. He would definitely have to talk things over with his own parents, who thankfully were the loving, supportive parents God intended a mother and father to be. He bowed his head a minute and sent up his fervent petition, then slid back across the seat.

"Emily." He gave her shoulder a gentle squeeze. "Wake up, Love. We're almost there."

Emily lifted heavy-lidded eyes and blinked slowly, dazedly. Lifting her hands, she rubbed her eyes with her knuckles like a sleepy little girl, stretched, and winced at the stiffness of her muscles.

"Here," Simon offered, turning her with careful hands. "I'll massage some of the kinks out for you."

"Where are we?" Emily croaked, her voice still blurred with sleep.

"We're about five miles from my folks' home. You've been asleep over four hours."

"Oh." She sat up straight and twisted back around to face him. Her eyes were wide, very dark. "I wish I could just sleep forever."

Simon scowled. "I made a promise to myself that I wouldn't lose my temper with you anymore, Emily. But if you make any more statements like that, I'll be tempted to change my mind."

"I wasn't talking about suicide," she refuted with indifferent flatness. "I just don't have the energy to face anything or anyone right now."

Simon relaxed, and he gave her braid a tug. "My folks aren't 'anyone,' so you won't be having to face anything except a quiet, deserted beach and the tide tickling your toes. And some good Southern cooking to put meat back on your scrawny bones." He restarted the car and drove slowly along the winding asphalt, rolling the window down so they could smell the sea breezes.

"Simon?" Emily ventured in a small voice a few minutes later when he turned onto a bumpy lane of shifting white sand and gravel.

He turned his head, his ear caught by the soft uncertainty of her tone. "What, Honey?"

"Do you think they'll be angry with me for buying your great-aunt's house and causing so much trouble?"

He winced. "Emily," he ground out with commendable restraint, "you are not causing the trouble. You're an innocent victim, on all levels, and nobody blames you for anything. And my parents will love you—exactly as you are."

She turned her head aside, gazing out at the gnarled scrub oaks and pine scrubs and the dunes. It was a surprisingly wild and desolate stretch of land for Florida, but Simon had a feeling right now it matched Emily's mood exactly.

Moments later, his mother threw her arms around him and covered him in flour and laughter and kisses. A spare woman with gray brown hair and Simon's green eyes, she apologized unrepentantly as Simon tried to fend her off. "I'm making biscuits, but I guess I forgot in the emotion of the moment."

His father hugged him as well, then clasped his hand in a firm handshake. "You're looking good, Son." He looked Simon up and down; then his shrewd hazel eyes moved to Emily.

Although not a large man, Nathaniel Balfour had the wiry toughness honed by a life spent outdoors working at physical labor. He was almost bald, and wrinkles crisscrossed his tanned face, giving him more of the weathered look of a farmer instead of the carpenter he had been.

Emily stood quietly off to the side, watching with reserved solemnity while the wandering son was welcomed home. When Simon finally reached to tug her over, he could feel her stiffness and sense the awkwardness as if he were inside her skin.

"You would be Emily." Nathaniel Balfour stepped over to her and held out his hand. His wife elbowed in between and gave another floury hug to Emily.

"Don't be so formal, Hon," she admonished her husband with a wink to Emily. "Emily will get the wrong impression." She lifted the hem of the faded apron she wore and wiped some flour off Emily's arm. "Emily, welcome to our home. We want you to make it yours for as long as you like." She beamed at Simon with maternal indulgence. "Simon has kept us informed of your miserable state of affairs, and Nat and I feel what you need is a nest right now where you can feel safe and spoiled."

"You can also see if you can put a pound or two on her," Simon chimed in, reaching out a long arm and catching a stiff Emily next to him. "That way when I hold her I know it will be a woman instead of a baby bird."

Emily blushed, and Katherine Balfour gave a delighted peal of laughter. "What a silver-tongued wretch you are," she chided him. "Come on, Emily. I'll show you to your room before I get back to my biscuits. Simon, you and your father can bring in your cases. Supper's at seven, so you should have time to take her for a short walk down the beach."

Chapter 11

Emily followed Mrs. Balfour down a long cool hall, feeling off balance and strangely shy. This was not the kind of greeting she had steeled herself for, and Simon's parents were. . .were as nice as Simon himself could be when he chose.

"I hope this will be all right." Mrs. Balfour gestured to the small but light and airy room.

Emily nodded and smiled but couldn't think of a thing to say. The Balfour home was beautiful but not as elaborate as Emily would have expected. Built on stilts, with a rustic cedar exterior, wraparound porches, and a gable roof with one side extending over the back porches, it was a house to be lived in rather than show-cased. Simon had mentioned that his father had built it all himself, disdaining his eldest son's offers of help.

Though not a luxury resort, the house exuded a quiet charm, a welcoming comfort that seemed to reach out gentle hands and tug at Emily's bruised and battered heart. She turned to Simon's mother, struggling to find the words, and found the older woman studying her with such a wealth of compassion that Emily's eyes misted.

Horrified, she walked over to the window and looked out, saying the first thing that occurred to her. "What a wonderful view."

Katherine joined her and laid a work-roughened hand on her shoulder. "Emily, I have three children, and I love them all dearly. They live separate lives with their own families now, but whenever they have a problem, or just need to get away from things, they come here." She patted Emily's shoulder once more and then moved away.

"There's a phrase in the Bible I've always loved—the one hanging on the wall over there." She waited until Emily turned and found the small framed verse on the wall behind the rocker. " 'He reached down from on high and took hold of me; he drew me out of deep waters,' " she quoted with lilting softness [NIV]. "Simon has shared with us some of what you've been going through—I hope you won't mind. Nat and I both pray your being here will help you to feel the Lord drawing you out of those deep waters."

She walked out then, quietly shutting the door behind her, leaving Emily alone. For a long time Emily stood at the window and watched the waves lifting in white foamy crescents, then ebbing away from the clean sandy shore. If there were any peace this side of heaven, surely one could find it here.

If God were truly in His heaven and all was right with the world everywhere else, would it be asking too much for Him to make things all right in her own little corner of the world? A tear slipped out and dribbled forlornly down her cheek. Simon's parents seemed so nice. . .so much like—well, like a mother and a father ought to be. No wonder Simon was so confident, so sure that God was taking care of things. He had grown up with a family who seemed to demonstrate that kind of love every day.

From down the hall, Emily could hear the sound of their voices, the deeper bass of Simon's father's softening the lilting mezzo-soprano of his mother's voice. And Simon's voice, a mixture of rich black coffee and golden honey and Samson's soft fur. The Balfours were a unit, complete within themselves and safe from the isolation of not belonging.

Emily turned away from the window and sat down in the rocking chair, listening to the soothing rise and fall of their voices and the murmur of the sea. *I want to belong, too,* she finally admitted to herself. *God, I want to have a home and family, too.*

A soft but peremptory knock on the door interrupted her solitary reverie.

"Emily?" Simon's voice sounded from the other side. "Let's go for that walk on the beach. There's time before supper."

They strolled around the porch and down a boardwalk that ended at some dunes covered in grass and sea oats. The sand was cool and soft, sifting between Emily's toes and over her ankles as they wandered barefoot down to the deserted beach.

Waves lapped lazily, lifting in slight swells and then sliding onto the smooth shore like a wet, glistening sheet. The setting sun cast a silver sheen over the rippling surface of the waters, and the rest of the world was bathed in the opalescent flow of a September twilight.

"I love to come here," Simon admitted reflectively. "It doesn't seem to matter how majestic the mountains or how serene the woods—there's just something about the rhythm of the sea and the canopy of the sky that draws me closer to God."

He drew Emily's hand through his arm and hugged it to his side. "There's a verse—I think in Psalms—that talks about God wrapping Himself in light. That's what this scene reminds me of."

"It is peaceful." She closed her eyes, swallowing against the hard lump rising in her throat.

Simon paused, lifting his hands to cup her face and study it, patterns of green light shifting through his eyes like the waters of the sea. "Emily, share your pain with me. I want to help—please don't shut me out."

Emily tried to back away but was helpless against the strength of those gentle hands, the power of those eyes. Her feet sank into the damp sand as her heart sank into the shifting sands of Simon's moods. He was in turn tender and sensitive, tough and obdurate, wildly passionate. And running through it all, like the sunlight invading the surface of the water, was his abiding faith in God.

How could she fight against something her soul yearned for so deeply, something she found as impossible to believe in as the pot of gold at the end of the rainbow?

"Why do you have so much faith in God?" she blurted out, searching his face with haunted eyes.

Simon's fingers began caressing the shadowed hollows and soft curves of her face. "Because He loves me," he replied simply. "Loved me so much He was willing to sacrifice His only Son. He loves you just as much, Emily. Believe that."

"I know." She swallowed, trying to ignore the absent stroking of his fingers. "But it's hard to understand how someone like. . .well, like me rates anything beyond salvation. I'm not important. The world wouldn't come to an end if I did—and God has so many more important things to take care of than to be bothered with my small problems." She put her hands up and pried his away, moving back a few steps. "Besides, if He really cared about me," she said in a moment of honest revelation, "I wouldn't be having all the problems I am."

"Is that how you see God?" Simon questioned casually, without any hint of censure. "As the benign big genie in the sky doling out favors to His children to prove He loves them?"

"Of course not!" Emily flung back, stung in spite of his nonthreatening tone.

"Is that what your parents did for you?" he continued, still in the same gentle cadence that nonetheless trampled her abraded feelings like the hooves of a galloping horse. "Gave you all the things you needed—but never gave themselves?"

He saw too much. Somehow he knew too much. Maybe he'd picked Barb's and Taylor's brains. Emily turned on her heel and fled, walking down the beach and leaving a trail of damp footprints behind. How dare he pick and probe her psyche! With each word, he undermined the girders she had so painfully dragged into place over the years to protect herself. And in another moment, he'd have her bawling all over him like a baby.

She stepped on a broken shell and staggered, almost falling from the sudden pain. Glancing back, she saw Simon following her but without any pretense of haste or pursuit. It was as if he knew she had no place to go.

Stunned by the raw finality of that thought, Emily sank down in the sand, heedless of the grittiness and dampness. She couldn't escape him. She couldn't escape the person she became when she was around him. She ceased to be the detached, easygoing creature whose feelings were buried so deeply no one ever guessed at the depths or intensity. Instead she became hypersensitive, vulnerable—and ridiculously easy to provoke.

Simon sat down beside her. She could feel his eyes moving over her, but she kept looking out at the water, struggling to withdraw into herself and become as insignificant and unnoticeable as a shell fragment.

"Remember the other night when I was pushing you in the swing?" he asked, the question so unexpected that Emily's head swiveled toward him, her braid swishing across her back and flipping over her shoulder.

"Yes. Why?"

"We were talking about the sunsets then, too." He smiled, a slow smile with the warmth of a golden sunset reflected in it. "Like I said, there's something about being out here that brings me closer to God, and I want you to feel it, too." He relaxed back on his elbows, lifting sand and letting it drift through his fingers. "I believe I mentioned something about how the beauty and inevitability of sunrises and sunsets reminded me of the faithfulness of God."

Emily watched her toes, caked with sand, digging into its coolness as if to hide. "So?" she muttered.

"You never read the verse I asked you to read, did you?" Simon countered without heat. "If you had, you'd understand the point I'm trying to make."

"And what point is that?" Her determined show of indifference was a mistake. With a fluid swiftness so abrupt she didn't have time to react, Simon reared up and grabbed her shoulders, pinning her with his eyes. "No more," he blazed. "I won't let you withdraw anymore, Emily." He leaned forward, his breath fanning her cheek, and the words had no place to go but straight to her heart.

"You've been keeping God at a distance because you're so afraid. You're afraid He doesn't care enough about you to risk trusting Him, just the way you're afraid of me. You bottle up your emotions and give the world the tame, placid version of Emily Carson, and I won't let you get away with it anymore."

"Simon—"

"Well, I'm only a man, and someday I will let you down, or unintentionally hurt you, or fail you because I'm a fallible human being. But God won't ever do that—He can't. It's not possible. Your problem is that you just won't accept God's love for you—personally. And it's robbed you of all the confidence and peace to which you're entitled. It's robbed you of joy."

"I don't—"

"You might restore that house and think you're happy, satisfied, and secure, but it's a lie. Until you let God restore the joy of your salvation, you'll stay as empty and feel as abandoned as that old place was for fifty years." He leaned closer, and in the rapidly approaching night, his eyes seemed to burn with a fire so bright the sea and sky and sand receded into a single swirl of darkening shadows.

"You've got to open up and allow yourself to believe in that faithfulness, because it's as real, as inevitable, as wondrous as the sunset. He's not the One trying to take your house away, or burn it down, or destroy innocent animals, Honey. That's all man's doing. God is there, hand stretched out, just waiting for you to take it so He can carry you through."

He released her abruptly and sat back. Then, with a significance that took Emily a moment to grasp, he slowly held out his hand.

Emily sat in the sand, motionless, though her insides were as unstable as a vial of nitroglycerin. Simon was telling her something so significant, so life-changing, that she simply couldn't grasp it. And with his own outstretched hand, he was creating a vivid picture to illustrate the words he had just spoken. What would happen if she put her hand in his? Beyond that, if she symbolically put her hand in the Lord's as Simon wanted her to do?

And what would she do when Simon inevitably let her down, as he had warned her he would?

The silence between them stretched taut, shimmering like a hovering knife blade between Simon's hand and Emily.

She knew that if she refused this outstretched hand, her relationship with Simon—however uncertain it was right now—would be irrevocably altered. Like footprints washed away by a relentless tide, so their relationship would be washed away, the only thing left an impersonal, smooth expanse of beach as untouched, unmarked as before.

Emily had tried to convince herself that she was satisfied with being alone. She had created her world and populated it with people and activities to keep her busy. She had been a comfortable Christian, content to sing in the choir on Sunday mornings and praise the Lord for His goodness. At Easter she had even sung a duet from Handel's "Messiah" proclaiming that He would feed His flock like a shepherd. She had thought she believed it.

She realized now that her faith wasn't the size of a mustard seed. It wasn't even as large as one of these minuscule grains of sand. She also realized that the world she had created for herself would never satisfy her again.

Slowly, heart pounding, Emily lifted her arm and held out her hand. Her fingers trembled.

Hard, warm fingers closed around hers and drew her to her feet. Unnoticed, the last glimmer of sunlight slid into the ocean, and the deep blue sky darkened to the dusky purple a shade away from black. "For a moment," Simon breathed as he drew her into his arms, "I was really afraid." His head descended and his lips brushed the delicate lobe of her ear. "Ah. . .Emily. Shy and wary—my stubborn sparrow struggling so hard to build her nest. . .what am I going to do about you?"

"Halloo down there, you two!" Nat's voice caught on a sudden breeze and swirled down to them, breaking the mood instantly. "Dinner's on! Come and get it!"

Simon's arms tightened around Emily momentarily; then she was free. "It's just as well," he murmured as they brushed sand off their clothes and then picked their way across the drifting sand to the boardwalk. "Much more time out here with you and I might have gotten carried away. And if my dad found out about that, this time I might have to paint all your porches and be grounded forever."

A smile tugged reluctantly at Emily's lips, then withered. "You'll probably be painting them anyway," she reminded him, dullness coating the words.

He took her arm firmly as they began walking back down the boardwalk and up the stairs to the house. "We'll talk about it tomorrow."

※

Two days rolled by along with the undulating tides. Emily was stuffed morning, noon, and night with every kind of delectable meal Katherine Balfour could devise. In between she lolled about on the beach or in a huge old rocker on the porch. Nathaniel taught her the rudiments of chess and took her on long walks along the largely deserted beach.

To Emily's consternation and utter bewilderment, Simon left the house the first morning after they arrived. Katherine explained kindly that there had been some sort of emergency at one of his jobs—they had called after Emily had gone to bed, and Simon hadn't wanted to disturb her. She was to sleep in, rest, and be as lazy as an old hound dog napping in the sunshine. He hoped to be back within three days.

Emily accepted this development with equanimity. It was awkward, though, feeling as if she had been beached with Simon's parents like a piece of driftwood, but by lunch of the first day their natural warmth and genuine interest in her helped soften the awkwardness. She still couldn't talk too much about herself, or about the house and her abduction, but she did relax enough to fall back into a facsimile of her former serene, mild-tempered persona.

By suppertime the second night, she was calling the Balfours by their first names without any self-consciousness. She was even sharing in their evening devotionals, luxuriating in their naturalness, their faith that was as much a part of their lives as breathing.

And they included her as if she belonged.

Emily woke on the third morning with a smile on her face for the first time in six months. That morning Nat was going to take her surf fishing, and then Katherine was going to show her how to make the famous biscuits all the men in the family raved about. The first evening Simon had scarfed down four and would have buttered up and downed a fifth, but Nat swiped it right as Simon was reaching for it and ate it himself, his eyes twinkling at Simon like a cat lapping a saucer full of spilled cream.

With a single-mindedness developed from childhood, Emily managed to lay aside all the worries waiting for her in Georgia. She coveted the time spent with these two people who had welcomed her as if she were their own, coveted it with the greedy desperation of a pearl merchant whose oyster bed was going dry. Because, for all she knew, this would be the only time in her life when she would ever truly feel like a member of a family.

At odd moments, thoughts of her own family intruded, marring the brightness of the day as tarnish on fine old pieces of silver. Emily quickly banished them. She had long ago accepted things the way they were and saw no need to dwell on what hadn't been and could never be. But that was no reason to look this particular gift horse in the mouth.

She stretched beneath the covers, then kicked back the sheet in a sudden burst of energy. Nat had told her the earlier they got down there, the better the fishing would be, and Emily didn't want to keep him waiting. She opened the room-darkening shades covering the windows and gasped in dismay.

It was a little past seven, but there was no sun today. A glowering, slate-colored sky brooded over choppy, restless waters. The sea oats on the tops of the dunes waved wildly in response to a whipping wind, and Emily dropped into the rocking chair and plunked her head on the heels of her hands in dejection. So much for a lovely, relaxing day.

"Doesn't look good," Nat confirmed when Emily dragged out a little while later.

Katherine's normally pleasant face wore a concerned look today as she poured her husband a second cup of coffee. "What's the weather report now?" she asked, since he had just come back from the den where the television was.

"They're still calling it a tropical storm, since it hasn't turned into hurricane force yet, but if and when it does, we'd better get the boards up. It's stalled off the Keys, and there's no telling which way it will come."

Emily sat down and thanked Katherine for her cup of coffee. "Have you had many bad hurricanes here?" she asked.

"We've been luckier than a lot of folks," Nat answered and smiled comfortingly as he glanced up and caught the worry in Emily's face. "The last really bad one was a couple years ago. We lost a window and the boardwalk, but the house stood."

"Thanks to you." Katherine laid her hands on her husband's shoulders and kissed his cheek. "Over the years some of the other homes have crumbled like matchsticks from the worst hurricanes. But when Nat builds a house, it's for keeps."

Emily watched the love flow between them and felt a strange wrenching in her heart, a plaintive cry echoing in the barren wasteland of her soul. Nobody had ever looked at her like that or offered the almost worshipful support Katherine and Nat gave to each other. Unwillingly her thoughts strayed to Simon, but there was about as much future in daydreaming over him as there was daydreaming about her house. Both of them were slipping out of her grasp, and years ago Emily had given up trying to hold on to will-o-the-wisps.

After breakfast, Nat and Katherine moved to the den to monitor the weather reports. Emily decided to walk down to the beach since it wasn't raining yet. Somehow the bleak uncertainty of the day matched her mood.

Katherine gave her a windbreaker to wear because the temperature hovered in the sixties and, with the wind swooping about in erratic gusts, Emily would appreciate something to cover her arms. Katherine gave the younger woman a hug as she held the screen door for her.

"Don't wander too far. Things can deteriorate pretty fast in conditions like this." She smiled into Emily's downcast face. "Of course, thanks to the capriciousness of nature, things could also clear up, and this could turn into a mild breezy day. You just have to take each moment as it comes and trust in the Lord to see you through, regardless."

Emily knew she wasn't just talking about the weather. "I'm trying to believe that," she confessed sadly. "But it's awfully hard right now."

"I know." Her lined face bathed in concern, Katherine leaned suddenly and pressed a kiss to Emily's cheek. "And we do care, Emily. Not just because my son is fond of you, but because you're you."

A lump formed in Emily's throat and stuck. "Thank you," she whispered then fled.

Chapter 12

Emily walked over an hour, head down against the wind, hair hopelessly tangled as it was whipped and tugged about her back and in her face. She didn't care.

Hands stuffed in the pockets of her jeans, she watched her feet scuffing in the sand. There was no one out this morning, not even the elderly couple she and Nat had met and chatted with on previous mornings.

Beside her, the Gulf of Mexico churned, and on the horizon a lumbering trawler plowed through the heaving water like a dinosaur in a pond shrugging aside a spring zephyr. Emily paid neither the Gulf nor the ship the slightest attention.

The storm in her soul already blew at hurricane force, and she was so caught up in its fury, she was unaware that she was no longer alone on the beach. Only when her downcast eyes fell upon an extra pair of sneakers did she lift her startled gaze as she bumped into Simon's solid chest.

His hands fastened loosely on her forearms to steady her. "Hello, Emily," he greeted her, his face solemn. The wind was having a heyday with his hair, too, whipping it wildly about so the waves tumbled all over his ears, neck, and forehead. In contrast, his mouth remained a straight, unsmiling line.

Emily couldn't help it. She stared up at him, revealing all the confusion and wariness and hopeless longing. Simon groaned deep in his chest, jerked her against him, and kissed her.

"Why did you do that?" Emily gasped out when at last he lifted his mouth and set her a little ways from him.

"Because I wanted to. And don't ask me why, or I'll do it again just to shut you up." He snuggled the two unzipped panels of her windbreaker beneath her chin, the knuckles of his hands brushing the soft underside of her throat.

"What gives you the right—?" Emily sputtered, indignation and alarm kicking through her, but her protest was abruptly silenced as Simon carried out his threat. When he lifted his head this time, Emily was clinging to his neck and shoulders, legs weak as water.

"You are the most baffling, frustrating woman I've ever known." His fingers danced across the surface of her skin, skimming an electrifying message over her wind-stung face and the little pulse hammering in her throat. "And for some reason I'm attracted to you more strongly than I've ever been to another woman.

You, on the other hand, seem to think you're about as desirable as lukewarm cream of wheat."

"It's the truth." She slurred the words.

Simon administered a brief but firm shake. "Stop it!" he demanded, temper whipping through the words like the wind was their hair. "Look at me, Emily!"

She opened her eyes, hands moving to push against his chest in an effort to be free. "What are you trying to do to me?" she wailed, struggling to cope with the extreme shifts of his moods. "You cuddle me up, then tear me down. You kiss me, and then you yell at me. You tell me you find me attractive, and then you treat me like a scummy rag!"

❀

Simon was not fooled by Emily's display of temper. He might have succeeded in riling her enough to momentarily break her out of her misery and depression, but he had also confused and frightened her. That, of course, made him a stupid, insensitive jerk. *Help me, Lord.* If he weren't careful, he could lose the battle altogether, and hence the war.

There was something else he had to tell her, and because he'd been stalling, he had ended up muddying the issue by dragging feelings into it. But when he'd seen her walking out here looking so lost and alone, he couldn't stand it, especially when she looked at him with those huge dark eyes. God knew how desperately he was trying to control his feelings, but it was getting harder. When she found out his news, she probably wouldn't let him any closer than a mile.

"Emily," he allowed with a sigh, "I know I'm a first-class heel, even though all I wanted was to jar you out of your depression. I can't apologize for kissing you, but I will admit to lousy timing." He waited, but when Emily refused to respond, he took a deep breath and took the plunge. "There's something I need to explain, and after you hear what it is, maybe you'll understand why I'm behaving the way I am."

"That's a first-class excuse," Emily finally retorted, the words muffled because she had her hands over her face now.

Simon groaned. "Emily, are you crying on me?"

"No! Yes. What if I am? I feel like a yo-yo the way you're acting. It's. . . humiliating." She faltered, caught her breath on a sob, and tried once more to move around him.

"Emily. . .please. I'm sorry. Don't go in yet." He waited in agony, his eyes on her bent head and the rigid line of her back. After a long, painful moment, she slowly turned around, but she still wouldn't look at him. Simon allowed his pent-up breath to escape in a long sigh, and with a hesitant gesture of repentance, he reached and brushed his fingers across her cheekbone.

"I'm not providing you with a very loving example of God's faithfulness, am

I?" he observed, chagrin coating the words. "Unless you keep in mind that at least I do keep coming back, even if it's only to confuse you more."

She almost smiled. She lifted her head and faced him with an expression as blank as a sheet of fresh typing paper. "What else did you want to tell me?"

His eyes flickered briefly, but he didn't sidetrack this time. "I have something to tell you about Aunt Iris, and it isn't very pleasant, though I doubt it will come as a surprise."

"She's suing me." She made the statement matter-of-factly, but Simon knew her better. He opened his mouth, but Emily interrupted. "Why didn't you just tell me, instead of. . .initiating that. . .display a few minutes ago?"

Simon buried his hands deep in the hip pockets of the chinos he was wearing and gave her a candid answer. "I couldn't help it. You looked so lost and alone, and I was about to make it worse. I wanted to wipe away that lost look and wake you up to how I really felt. I know I'm coming across irrationally, and I do apologize for it." He dropped his gaze to his feet, then lifted it back to Emily's coffee-dark eyes. "But with God as my witness, I'll never deliberately hurt you. Never. Can you try to believe that at least?"

❀

After lunch Simon announced their decision to return to Georgia.

"Emily is going to need to talk with her lawyer, and I'm going to see what's happening with the sleazeballs trespassing on her land." He watched Emily grimly, hating the whole mess with a vehemence bordering on homicidal.

"Wouldn't it be better if she stayed with her friends?" his father commented.

Simon nodded his head at Emily, his expression remote. "You try to convince her. I gave up an hour ago." A muscle in his jaw quivered as he battled his frustration. "For two cents I'd leave her here, but knowing her, she'd simply hike down to the main road and hitch a ride."

Emily smiled across the room at him. "You're just a poor loser," she stated with false sweetness. "It may not be my home much longer, but while it is I plan to live in it. No slimy lowlifes are going to frighten me away, and—"

"The next time they might do more than frighten you," Simon interrupted harshly. "Why do you insist on being so pigheaded, Woman?"

"Simon," his mother interjected, doubt and dismay so blatant Emily turned her head away. "How about our tagging along with you? We could stay at Emily's—"

"No!" both Simon and Emily chorused in emphatic agreement.

"We don't need to go providing them with any more ammunition," Simon stated flatly. "I've talked to the sheriff. He promises around-the-clock protection, for awhile anyway—as long as he can. But I don't want you two involved. It's bad enough having Emily in the thick of it."

"I can take care of myself."

Simon sliced her an impatient look. "Like you did the day you landed in the hospital?"

Emily slumped in defeat. "I'll go make sure my bag is packed," she mumbled, walking past Simon with downcast head.

His father waited until Emily shut her door, then motioned for Simon to follow him into the kitchen while Katherine followed Emily. "Don't you think you're being a mite bossy?" he observed mildly, and Simon flushed.

"I can't seem to help it. She won't listen to reason. I know she's hurting, not only over the drug issue, but now this confounded lawsuit." He slammed his hands down on the counter, rattling the dishes drying in the drainer next to him.

"Why did she have to find the will? It's almost impossible to get through to her now. She's clammed up inside herself so tightly and so blindly that she has no idea of what could happen to her all alone in that big old mausoleum." He whirled and faced his father. "I'm beginning to hate the place, you know. Hate it because it's going to cost me the woman I—"

He stopped, stunned, and then groaned aloud, covering his eyes with the back of his hand. "I'm in love with her," he confessed and dropped his hand to stare across at his father. "If something happens to her—if Aunt Iris takes the place away from her—I don't know if I'll be able to stand it."

Nathaniel laid his arm around his son's shoulders. "I know. . .I know. You're just going to have to do a lot of praying—and as much protecting as she'll allow." He grinned a little bit. "But if you'll take the suggestion of the old man who reared you and suffered through your wild youth, try honey instead of vinegar. Emily might not be a militant feminist, but she's been on her own too long to fall tamely in line with your commands."

"If I try that approach I doubt I could maintain my Christian code of ethics, Dad," Simon responded dryly. "And Emily's . . .untouched."

Nathaniel lifted an eyebrow. "That's refreshing—and a relief from a parental point of view. I thought she looked—I guess 'unawakened' would be the word."

"And you don't know how badly I'd like to awaken her." Simon examined his fingernails, then met his father's smug expression. "That's right—gloat. You and Mom have been trying to marry me off for ten years now."

He contemplated his hands as if wondering whether he'd like to wrap them around Emily to caress her—or throttle her. "I suppose you realize that persuading her to marry me will be about as easy as the Arabs and Jews negotiating a truce in Jerusalem."

"I trust you'll control yourself, Son, and remember your Christian convictions, regardless of your feelings."

"I'm not going to seduce her, Dad, if that's what you're getting at." Simon straightened, giving his father the sort of stark honesty he had given him all his life. "I do want to make love to her, because I love her—even if I only acknowledged it this moment. But it's because I do love and desire her so much that I can wait. Do you have any idea what it means to me to know that if she'll marry me, I'll be the first—and only?"

"I know. I pray God will grant you that chance, if Emily is truly the woman He has picked out to be your mate." He cleared his throat, and his eyes were damp. "She's a pretty special lady. Your mother and I would love to have her as a daughter."

"Thanks, Dad." Simon squared his shoulders and moved toward the hall. "I'd better see what's keeping her and Mom. There's no telling what Emily may try. Being around her is like trying to catch hold of fog."

"Knowing your mother, she just might succeed. And then present your elusive lady to you for Christmas."

Chapter 13

The nearer they came to the Georgia border, the more nervous Emily felt. Simon was strangely pensive and even more strangely nonaggressive. He hadn't tried to talk her out of going to the house anymore, and he hadn't badgered her about how to handle the lawsuit and what she ought to say to Brad. If she hadn't been so worried about the future, Emily would have been hurt.

As it was, she found herself wishing Simon would at least talk to her, even if it was only about the weather, which was gray and drizzling and miserable. When she was looking out the window, all her mind did was scrabble frantically around the problems she faced, without offering any solutions. "Simon?" she finally asked, almost whispering.

"Hmm?"

"If I admit I'm a little bit scared, will you jump down my throat and say 'I told you so'?"

His hands tightened on the steering wheel, and he shot her a brief look that encompassed a galaxy of emotions. "Have I been that terrible, Emily?"

She puzzled at the hint of hurt, the nuance of despair. "You haven't always been sweet and understanding."

He scowled at that. "What do you expect when you insist on modeling yourself after a sitting duck?"

"Nothing, I suppose." She choked down the hurt and resumed contemplating the countryside.

A few minutes later Simon pulled off into a deserted roadside picnic area. A misting rain slid down the windshield, blurring the surroundings now that the wipers were no longer swishing back and forth. The atmosphere inside the car thickened until Simon commanded very quietly, "Come here, Emily." He pointed to the space beside him.

"Why?" Emily responded warily, her body stiffening with suspicion and a strange sort of excitement.

"Because I've decided to try my hand at being sweet and understanding for a change. Now come here."

"I didn't mean to hurt your feelings," Emily grumbled, but she undid her seat belt and slid over.

"That's better," he murmured huskily. "Now. . .put your arms around me and kiss me."

"What? What's that supposed to prove?" She floundered about, looking everywhere but at Simon.

He uttered a low laugh, picked up the end of her braid, and began winding it around his fist until she was forced to move right against him, their faces inches apart. "No problem," he breathed. "I don't mind kissing you. . . ."

His mouth closed over hers, and he kissed her with tender thoroughness and consummate skill. Emily's arms crept up over his shoulders and clung to him as she gave herself up to the incandescent cloud of feelings. She could feel Simon's heartbeat thundering, its wild cadence matching hers, and she marveled that she really did seem to affect him so strongly.

After awhile his hands released her, and he gently removed her arms from around his neck. "Now, relax and let me give you the reassurance you're so desperate for."

He held her head against his chest and stroked her hair, all the passion wiped away as if it had never been. "I'm trying, you see," he murmured above her head, "to teach you that you can trust me, at least physically."

Emily gradually relaxed, and at last closed her eyes with a low murmur of contentment. If only he would be like this all the time. If only she could trust him. She stirred restlessly, and his arms tightened.

"Be still," he coaxed. "Be still and rest, little sparrow. It's going to be all right. Everything is going to be all right. Because regardless of how things turn out, regardless of how you feel about me—God will be there, taking care of you." He paused, then added in such low tones that Emily wasn't sure she heard, "And so will I."

The next morning when Emily called Brad to tell him she'd be in to resume her secretarial duties, he did not try to hide his relief. He did tell her that they would also take the time to have a lawyer-to-client chat, but she was not to worry about a thing.

Emily wondered if Simon would fuss about her going back to work so soon, but he smoothly agreed with her decision, pointing out that she would be a lot safer thirty miles away in Sylvan anyway. Emily sourly reminded him that she was not a two year old who needed coddling and then clamped her mouth shut. She was feeling raw after a crying jag the night before. Somewhere inside her lived a two year old whose feelings were bruised because Simon had made no effort to console or coddle her.

She drove the miles to Sylvan in uneasy silence. It was really no wonder Simon acted so unpredictably around her. She pushed him away with one arm and clung with the other. Heat stole into her cheeks as she relived her unbridled response in the car coming back from Florida. Simon must think her a totally desperate woman willing to take any crumbs he cared to toss her way—and if the price was patting her shoulder and telling her things would be all right. . .well, he had come through with his end of the bargain.

It was no use. She was pining over him like the girls in her eighth grade classes pined over a high school junior. The only difference was that the girls had a better chance of landing a date with the junior than Emily did landing Simon Balfour. In spite of everything he kept telling her, he was still out of her league. Way out.

"Things are never that bad." Brad greeted her glum countenance with a cheery welcome smile that didn't try to hide his open relief. "Here. Have a stick of strawberry gum—a gal I met in Albany gave me a couple of packs."

"No, thanks." She tried to produce an answering smile as she put her purse under the desk, but it wavered. "Brad, I'm scared."

Brad's cheerfulness disappeared behind his bland lawyer's mask. "Let's just take things one at a time, all right? You worry about secretarying and let me worry about the legal matters."

That, unfortunately, was easier said than done, as Emily found out when she was sitting across from him later that afternoon. Brad did not try to confuse her by spouting off legal terminology, but he did not mince words either.

"As I warned you, Ms. Bancroft has filed in probate court to prove the validity of the will that I gather it was your dubious honor to find." He chewed a few minutes on his third stick of strawberry gum, drumming his fingers on his desk. "It was in a safety deposit box hidden behind the closet wall in your bedroom, Lamar told me."

Emily nodded. Her own hands were clenched tightly between her knees, and despite the pleasant coolness of the day, she could feel perspiration dotting her brow and dampening her palms. "Simon dropped it off at Mr. Hansell's office on our way to Florida. He figured the sooner we got it over with, the better."

"Hmmm," Brad replied unhelpfully. "Well, they certainly didn't let any grass grow under their feet, which I suppose isn't surprising after meeting Ms. Bancroft." He gave a reluctant grin. "Formidable woman, isn't she?"

"I don't stand a chance," Emily declared miserably.

"Now, now, don't insult your lawyer," Brad chided, but he didn't disagree with her. "I've got about three weeks to dig up some other court decisions that will support our position. You concentrate on being my secretary and keeping yourself safe." He looked across at her. "Are you staying with Barb and Taylor?"

"N—no." She couldn't face the alert look of suspicion that entered his face, and she dropped her gaze. "I'm staying at the house. Sheriff Jessup has assigned two men to guard the place, and I know the DEA is also—"

"Emily, that's insane!" Brad jackknifed up out of his chair, raking his fingers through the thick thatch of blond hair. "Where is your Sir Galahad, anyway? Or has he kissed you off now that the will has been found?"

Emily found herself unaccountably angry at the disparaging reference to Simon, and caution was thrown to the winds. "He most certainly has not 'kissed me off'! In fact, he's promised that as long as I live in the house, he won't leave until the men who abducted me are behind bars." The words resounded off the filing cabinets and hovered in the air like a burst of fireworks on the Fourth of July. Emily watched with dismay the incredulity and disillusionment wash over Brad's lean, attractive face.

"Not only does that make you a sitting duck for another abduction, or worse, but under the present circumstances, Balfour's presence could be construed as even more of a conflict of interest than your working for me."

"I don't know why the two of you insist on behaving like snapping turtles," Emily muttered, exasperated. "The main reason he's staying is because he's doing most of the restoration work now—and yes, it's because I gave him permission."

Brad sat back down and casually propped his feet on the desk, crumpling several papers in the process. "Snapping turtles, huh?" He contemplated the ceiling with a bland expression Emily hated. "Are you telling me Balfour has been suggesting libelous interpretations of my actions toward you—with no evidence to substantiate his claims, I might add?"

"Quit talking like a lawyer!" Emily retorted.

Brad burst into laughter. "Boy, have you got it bad! Do you leap as hotly to my defense with Balfour?"

Emily gave a disdainful sniff. "I have better things to do than sit around while you mock me. If our—consultation—is finished, I'm leaving. I need to go by the grocery store."

For a laid-back lawyer, Brad could move with startling speed, blocking the door before Emily had taken more than two steps. "Come down off your high horse, Emily. I was only teasing you, and you know it."

"Sounded more like harassment to me."

Brad folded his arms across his chest. "Stop talking like a lawyer," he mimicked.

Giving up, Emily finally laughed. She returned to retrieve her purse, aware that Brad was still watching her even as he stepped aside. Emily did not trust the look on his face at all—it reminded her of Simon. "See you day after tomorrow," she tossed out lightly.

"Okeydokey." Just before she reached the bottom stair he called to her. "Emily?"

She twisted her head around. "What?"

"Be careful with Balfour, will you? I don't trust him."

Emily's face closed up like elevator doors. "Neither," she enunciated carefully, "do I."

Chapter 14

The court date was set for the first week in November. Emily told Simon, and he watched her carefully circle the date on her wall calendar hanging in the kitchen.

Autumn arrived and the last of summer withered with the last of the honeysuckle and wisterias. Some of the bronze mums Emily had planted back in July bloomed, and Simon helped arrange them in a jar on the kitchen table. The monthly missive from Emily's parents showed a dramatic New England fall, and Emily taped it on the wall above the mums. Simon tactfully made no comment.

He spent most days working on a different area of the house from where Emily was, though anytime she asked for help, he willingly obliged. Most of his evenings were spent in his portable office.

One week he'd had to spend in Tennessee, tying up work on the eighty-year-old stone cottage. The two deputies had been reassigned due to lack of funds and staff, but Sheriff Jessup arranged their return while Simon was gone. Emily, quieter with each passing week, barely protested. Without telling her, after returning from Tennessee, Simon renegotiated the dates for his next job, postponing work until after Christmas.

Two days before the hearing, he was on the side veranda, applying a wood preservative to the yellow pine floorboards he had replaced. He was enjoying himself so much that it was almost easy to forget the reason he was able to do the work in the first place. Everett VanCleef certainly had built this place to last, for there was surprisingly little deterioration, even though the house had been unattended for almost fifty years.

Simon had repaired mortar joints in the bricks and, with Emily's permission, had hired a local carpenter to help replace a sill and several of the joists under the porches which had succumbed to rot. But other than three windowsills on the north and east side of the house that had also needed replacing, the exterior wood structures were fairly sound. Yep, Everett sure had wanted this house to last, and considering the terms of his feudal will, it shouldn't have been too surprising.

The will.

The hearing, now only two days away.

Simon plopped the brush down and sat back on his heels a minute, tension curling his spine. That wretched will!

Every time Simon caught Emily gazing at the leaded glass window in the library with agony in her eyes, it took every ounce of self-control to keep from cleaning the window himself, then falling at Emily's feet and confessing his love. More than anything on this earth, Simon wished for providential blessing to restore both woman and window to their light and beauty.

If I keep a lid on my temper and try extra hard to wait on You, Lord, is there a chance? And no, I'm not trying to bargain. I just can't help wanting to know, wanting—

"Simon. . ."

He jerked out of his prayerful reverie with a start, lifting his head to where Emily was standing just outside the French doors leading onto the veranda. In one swift, encompassing glance, he marked the colorless complexion and the way she was clutching the front of her sweatshirt with her hand. His eyes zeroed in on the hand, which was covered in blood.

He was by her side in two swift strides. "What happened?"

"I was trying to replace that broken pane—the one you picked up at the store yesterday for me. . . ." She gasped a little as Simon gently pried loose her hand and exposed the wound.

"Easy, Love." It was a nasty cut, a diagonal slash across the back of her wrist, and it was bleeding heavily. "Here—hold it up—that's it. . . ." He whipped his handkerchief out and placed it directly on the cut, applying a firm, steady pressure and talking to her in a low, soothing voice. "It's okay, Emily. It's okay. Come on, now, and let's get you to the bathroom and clean you up. At least it's the back of your wrist instead of the front." He gave her what he hoped was an encouraging smile. "You could have been a first-class klutz and gone for the artery."

"You're so reassuring," Emily muttered faintly. "I'm bleeding to death and all you do is make disparaging remarks about my abilities." For some reason—probably because she was tired and worried and still insecure, Simon realized—she took offense at his teasing remark instead of responding to him in kind.

After sitting her down, Simon lifted her chin with his free hand. "I wasn't denigrating your work," he promised softly. "You've done a great job, and I'm proud of you."

Her head lifted. "You are?"

Simon gazed down into her incredulous, suddenly smiling eyes. *Lord, I love this woman.* His fingers stroked a tender path across her soft lips. "Yes," he affirmed deeply, "I am. Now take a deep breath and lean on me. This is going to hurt."

He wouldn't allow her to work any more that day, bullying her into sitting on the veranda in a deck chair Barb had donated so Emily could watch him work. She submitted both to his doctoring and gentle dictatoring with such a hazy, dreamy acquiescence Simon wanted to shout aloud his feelings. She was softening, responding to him now. Soon, very soon, he would confess his love, and he prayed she would reciprocate. *I can't wait much longer, Lord.* He refused to speculate about the aftermath of the hearing.

They whiled away the afternoon in rich harmony, with Simon savoring every moment. As he worked, he shared stories of various homes he had restored and the sometimes hair-raising tales of the owners he'd had to contend with. Emily countered with similar hair-raising stories of her life as a junior high teacher, relaxing into the serene, warm, and compassionate woman she was when she wasn't feeling threatened.

❧

Early Wednesday morning, Simon drove Emily to Sylvan to spend the day and night with Barb and Taylor while he flew to pick up Iris. Emily had withdrawn again, treating him to the remote, polite facade she'd perfected since the trip to Florida. Simon hung onto his temper, but it was an effort. The thirty-mile trip seemed twice that long because of the grim silence that hung between them. Finally they reached Barb and Taylor's home.

"Heard any developments on the drug ring?" Taylor asked in a low voice while Barb dithered over Emily's bandaged wrist.

Simon shook his head. "Last week a plane was sighted taking off from a field two counties west of here, and a Customs agent managed to track it until bad weather closed in and they lost it. Nothing else has turned up so far, and we don't know if it's the same people or not."

He didn't tell Taylor—who would tell Barb—that a weekly check by Sheriff Jessup of the woods surrounding Emily's property had turned up evidence of a recently used campsite. That in itself was ominous but inconclusive, so Simon had chosen not to burden Emily or her friends with the information.

She wouldn't appreciate his decision, he knew. Abruptly, Simon wanted to pound his fist through a wall. He interrupted Barb by stepping in front of her and turning to Emily. "Walk me back to the car?" He cupped her elbow and smiled at Barb.

"Trying to flaunt your power?" Emily observed snidely once they were outside, and Simon counted to twenty.

"I know you're feeling pretty defensive and vulnerable right now," he returned very quietly, "but I wish you'd try trusting me for a change instead of automatically assuming the worst."

Emily flicked him one look of shattering pain. "I can't trust you. I won't." Her chin jutted. "And if your great-aunt wins tomorrow I'll pack my bags, and you won't see me for the dust."

The chill of her pronouncement rang in Simon's ears long after he drove off, and he knew the look on her face would haunt him the rest of his life.

307

❀

Taylor took the day off so he could drive with Emily and Barb to Timmons. It was a muggy day, so hot and close the crispness of autumn might have been a dream. In the Deep South, summer and fall often waged a contest throughout November, with the dreary dripping rains of winter finally ending the battle.

Barb had taken Emily in hand, forcing her to choke down half a grapefruit and a slice of cheese toast for breakfast and then picking out what she should wear to the hearing. Emily had brought along the brown suit and cream blouse she'd worn the first time, but Barb regarded the outfit with disdain.

"You don't need to look like you're going to prison, and that's about what all those neutral shades do for you." She began plundering her closet, muttering imprecations since her dress size was at least two sizes larger than Emily's. "Haven't you listened to anything I've tried to tell you over the last couple of years about your needing to wear brighter colors?"

"I'm not auditioning for a beauty contest, Barb." Emily sat listlessly on the edge of the bed, brushing out her hair with halfhearted strokes. Her bandaged wrist made this awkward, and the cut throbbed a little. "I frankly don't care how I look."

Barb ignored her. "Here—try this blouse. You'll have to wear the suit, but we can at least liven it up a little. With the jacket on and the way this blouse is supposed to drape in folds, no one will notice that it's a little big."

Emily eyed the brightly patterned blouse swirling in vivid shades of burnt orange, red, and sienna. When she put it on with her brown suit, the difference was startling. Emily glanced in the mirror and shrugged. "It's okay, I suppose. Thanks, Barb."

She sat in the backseat as they drove to Timmons, ignoring the glances Barb kept casting over the seat and the looks Taylor sneaked in the rearview mirror. She was clammy and cold in spite of the sultry day and wondered if she would ever be warm again. Brad had tried to reassure her yesterday before she left the office, but he was not hopeful and was too good a lawyer to lie. Emily could feel the shroud of hopelessness bearing her down, down into a cold pit of nothingness.

All her life she had wondered why she wasn't loved, what lack in her existed that kept her parents from loving her enough to provide her with the love and security her soul needed and craved. J.J. had fought his way to recognition, but all it had earned him in the end was trouble until he grasped the life ring of the Air Force Emily had tossed to him so desperately. He had never bothered to toss her anything in return, and Emily had learned to go her own way because no one would ever care enough to help her out.

And now, just when she had finally found something to call her own, something that needed to be needed—just like herself—it was going to be yanked away from her. *God,* she found herself praying, *God, what am I going to do? What's the matter with me? This is even worse than being held upside down in a bag, not knowing if I was going to live or die. I don't have a choice now—I have to keep on living, but Lord, I feel dead inside.*

When hope within me dies. . .I draw ever closer to Him. . . . The single line of melody whispered across her heartstrings, so faint and haunting that for a moment she actually caught her breath, straining to hear. *From care He sets me free. . . .* The music was stronger now, and the words plucked a little louder, sounding in her head like chimes. *His eye is on the sparrow. . .and I know He watches me—His eye is on the sparrow, and I know He watches me.*

The song. Simon had told her she reminded him of that song—that's why to this day he sometimes called her "little sparrow." It aggravated her, infuriated her, irritated her—but not until this moment did she feel the comfort and reassurance the nickname also offered. Emily had only been concentrating on the unflattering ramifications of being a sparrow—plain, brown, and not worth looking at twice.

Simon had tried to tell her differently, but she hadn't listened. She closed her eyes, bowing her head to force out all the other intrusive sounds. She wanted to listen now. She pictured the battered hymnbook Mrs. Jenkins had given her and tried to focus on the page on which the song was printed. There was something about being afraid, about clouds. Why had she just stuffed the book in a box of other forgotten paraphernalia when she moved out of the apartment? The words were hovering on the tip of her tongue, so close she could—

That was it! *. . .draw over closer to Him. . . From care He sets me free. . . . Lord, I would give anything—including that house, if I could draw closer to You and know You cared about me. Simon claims You do, and he certainly acts like he's got an inside track to Your ear, but then he's been a lot more faithful to You over the years than I have.*

The haunting melody deepened into the baritone chords of Simon's voice reciting another Bible verse. What was it? Something about salvation restoring the joy. . .

"Emily? You okay? We're almost there." Barb's voice intruded suddenly, shattering the melody Emily was straining to hear.

Emily lifted her head and forced a smile. "I'm okay, Barb. Believe it or not, I was actually praying."

Barb looked abashed. "I'm sorry, Emily." She reached a hand over the seat to Emily, and after a brief hesitation Emily's lifted in response. "Everyone has been praying for you, even the kids." She squeezed Emily's hand, then let it go as Taylor slowed to pull into the diagonal parking space in front of the stately, columned courthouse.

They were a little late, and when the three of them walked inside the same drab waiting room as before, it was already crowded with people. Their case was not the first one on the docket this morning, and there were a half dozen or so other equally nervous individuals all waiting their turn.

Everyone else blurred in Emily's eyes when she caught sight of Simon. For the past three months, they had lived like friendly next-door neighbors who worked together, and for most of that time Emily succeeded in regarding Simon in that light.

Now—with a single glance—everything had changed. He was sitting beside Iris, looking so solid and capable and masculine next to Iris's petite fragility that Emily's mouth went powder dry. He was wearing a charcoal-pinstriped suit with a mint green silk shirt and coordinating tie, the effect lending him an aura of leashed power and raw elegance Emily had never really noticed. The thick waves of his rich, nutmeg brown hair radiated health and vitality, and the same sizzling life leaped out of his eyes when he saw Emily.

Something sizzled in Iris Bancroft's gray eyes as well, but it was the cold sizzling of steam rising off frozen steel, and it was also frankly triumphant. Her snappy cardinal red suit, tailored gray blouse, and matching gloves made Emily feel like a frumpy dowager instead of the other way around.

Simon started across to meet her immediately. Brad, talking in the corner with Lamar Hansell, also caught sight of her. He excused himself, a grim, determined look behind his deceptively lazy, charming demeanor.

"How are you doing? Did you sleep at all?" Simon was asking her in a husky undertone, his gaze moving over her face, her hair, dropping to the suit and Barb's blouse. "That's a pretty blouse—lots better than the one you wore the last time."

Emily bit her lip to keep from smiling. He was trying so hard. "It's Barb's. You'll have to tell her you approve of her taste better than mine."

"Emily." Brad was at her elbow. "We need to discuss a few things."

For a spine-tingling moment the air froze into an aura rife with unspoken threats. Emily glanced from Brad to Simon, trying to comprehend why the hairs on the back of her neck were tingling, and why Simon looked—well, almost primitive, as if he were about to rip Brad apart like a ravaging wolf devouring a piece of raw meat.

Feeling uneasy and uncertain, she shifted her gaze over Simon's shoulder and met the frozen glare of Iris Bancroft head-on. But there was an arrested gleam there as well, an almost reluctant dawning of awareness Emily didn't understand any more than she did Simon's behavior.

Then the moment passed as Brad tugged her away and Taylor moved up beside Simon, asking him a question and forcing the younger man's attention.

"Brr." Brad shivered as he led Emily over to the only two vacant chairs left in the room. "Your watchdog is growling awfully noisily for someone who only wants to restore your house, Ms. Carson. He almost acts jealous, if you ask me."

"I thought you had something you needed to talk to me about," Emily reminded him, feeling the faint color staining her bleached-out cheeks.

Brad smiled a little but took the hint. He dropped down in the chair beside her, glanced off to the left, then deliberately lifted Emily's hand and held it comfortingly between his own. "Emily, you know this doesn't look good, but I wanted to remind you that we still have the option of filing a countersuit ourselves if the judge decides in the plaintiff's favor this time."

Emily shook her head. "I can't take anymore, Brad." She looked up at him hopelessly. "I know you've done the best you could—probably better than any other lawyer could have done—but if this goes the way I think it will, I'm throwing in the towel." She swallowed, then finished in a tone so low Brad barely heard. "Simon will do a better job on the house with me gone anyway."

Brad cursed softly but succinctly, then issued a gruff apology when Emily winced. She found herself noting with stunning irrelevance that Simon had never once used foul language or curse words in her presence. He liked ordering her about, lost his temper with her—even yelled at her, but never had he blasphemed or employed gutter language to vent his anger and frustration. He wasn't perfect and was honest enough to admit it, but Simon Balfour was a committed Christian to the core. She might not ever be able to trust him—but she did trust his faith.

"Emily!" Brad was jiggling her hand, and she looked at him, eyes wide and startled. "It's time to go. They're calling our case."

He kept her hand tucked in his elbow as they all moved toward the door. Simon shot Brad a murderous glare, and Brad merely deflected it with a provocative grin; but dread had reared up and grabbed Emily's throat, and she didn't notice anything.

She remained a motionless statue as the court was brought to order and the case presented. The judge retired once again to his chambers. No emotion ruffled the barren desert of her countenance when, as predicted, the judge returned to set aside his prior decision, determining that the validity of the will should prevail over Emily's later title.

Voices gusted around her like breezes, but she sat unmoving, feeling as if layers of clear polyurethane were being applied around and around her. She was present but unreachable. Barb's arm was around her, and Taylor was patting her shoulder. Brad said something, but he was talking to Mr. Hansell now and whatever he told her slid right off.

He came back a minute later and took her hand. "Listen, Em, I know what a blow this is. Why don't you hang up secretarying for me awhile and try to just rest—get your perspective back? Gloria will be able to come back in a week anyway, and I can manage until then." The voices around Emily rose suddenly, as if people were arguing, and a warm, strong hand on her arm was urging her to rise.

"Just leave her alone!" Barb was snarling. "Go gloat with your old biddy of a great-aunt!"

"I don't think you understand." The hand tightened, and Emily found herself standing. "I'm not asking your permission."

She was being led down the short aisle and out of the courtroom, and because it was Simon, her senses swam into a sharp, stabbing moment of focus. "Please leave me alone," she stated clearly.

"Not on your life."

"Wait a minute, Balfour!" That was Brad's voice coming closer again. "I need to—"

Simon halted, jerking around with Emily following like a boneless rag doll. "You don't need to do anything but back off," Simon suggested so quietly, so deliberately, that Brad did just that. "Whatever formalities need to be handled, you can either handle yourself or wait. I'm taking Emily someplace private, and I'm taking her now."

Emily wanted to summon up the energy to fling aside his hand and unleash the temper she had discovered she had after she met Simon. It stayed locked up somewhere in the frozen storage area of her heart, though, and she ended up allowing herself to be hustled out of the courthouse, down the steps, and into Simon's Jensen-Healy without even lifting her little pinkie.

"What about your great-aunt?" she inquired with polite detachment.

"Lamar is taking her to his home. We'll pick her up later." He drove several blocks to a small park and playground, parked, got out, and came around and helped Emily out. Keeping her hand firmly in his, he walked her over to a wooden park bench placed between two towering pines.

He sat down, then joined her, turning so he could watch her, his hands reaching out to grip her shoulders. "Emily." He sighed her name almost as if in prayer. "Emily, you don't have to lose the house. You don't even have to leave it." He shook her gently, forcing her eyes to focus on him so he knew she was taking in his words. "Emily, I want you to marry me."

Chapter 15

Emily was staring at him blankly. "You want me to marry you?" she parroted in a dull monotone. "Why? The house belongs to your great-aunt now. You can restore it however you like. Why marry me?"

"Because I'm in love with you!" he all but snapped. "Why else would I ask you to marry me?" His hands slid down her arms, then back up to cup her face. "Did you hear me? I love you."

For a brief instant something stirred inside her, as if a flickering spark buried so deep under the ashes was struggling to reignite. Then she shook her head, lifting her own hands to gently but firmly remove his. "You don't love me—you just feel sorry for me." She forced a painful smile. "It's okay, Simon. I'll be okay after awhile, but I appreciate the gesture."

She made as if to rise; then a startled gasp escaped her restricted throat when Simon jerked her completely off her feet and into his lap. He wrapped her in a firm embrace, his face thrust inches away from hers.

"I do not feel sorry for you, Woman!" he growled. "I said I love you, and that is exactly what I meant. I've never told a woman that before, and I hadn't planned on telling you yet. But now that I have, you'd better believe it, or we'll have the first shotgun wedding in America where the bridegroom's father is holding the shotgun instead of the bride's!"

"Nobody loves me like that," Emily whispered. "They never have—why should you?"

He groaned and began covering her face with kisses. "You are loved, Emily Carson," he promised fervently, feverishly. "You are lovable, and you are loved. By me, by all your friends—by your heavenly Father." His mouth found hers, and he kissed her long and deeply. "Marry me, Emily. Marry me, and we'll restore the house and our lives together."

"No." She began shaking her head and couldn't seem to stop. "No. You don't really love me, and I won't trap us both. Leave me alone, Simon, please. Take me back and leave me alone." When his arms merely tightened, she began to struggle, but the efforts were weak, sluggish, as if all her batteries had run completely down. "Let me go," she whimpered, perilously close to breaking.

Simon released her, watching with tortured gaze as she scrambled up and backed away, hands shaking as she straightened her rumpled suit and hair. His hand lifted, reaching out, pleading. "Emily—please try to believe me. I love you. As God is my witness, I love you as much as a man can love a woman. Love, Emily. Not pity."

The tears began then, a slow, hot trickle that slipped over the pooling rims and slid down her ashen cheeks. "I wish I could believe you," she sighed in a choked undertone. "I've always wished I could believe you." Lifeless, defeated, she stood in front of him, inches away, the tears falling unheeded. She might as well have been on another planet.

"We'll discuss it later." He took out a handkerchief and wiped his face, looking exhausted—but determined. "Let's go fetch Aunt Iris."

"I'd rather not. She won't want to be anywhere near me."

"You leave Aunt Iris to me."

❀

"I suppose you expect to be tossed out on your ear," Iris Bancroft announced in a reedy patrician voice, setting down her glass of iced tea and fixing Emily with a penetrating gaze. "You look like you're facing a firing squad."

"Aunt Iris—"

"Stay out of this, Boy. You've caused me enough trouble in the last months to put me on digitalis." Her ivory-handled cane thumped on the Oriental rug of Lamar Hansell's study. "I heartily disapprove of your actions, but of course you're aware of that, I daresay."

"You've made it pretty clear," Simon returned calmly. "But what you don't seem to understand is that I love Emily, and I'm going to marry her."

Iris surveyed him archly, the merest suggestion of a smile softening the severity of her lined, narrow face. "I understand quite well," she refuted and emitted a disdainful sniff. "Just because I never married myself doesn't make me blind, deaf, and dumb. You've been pie-eyed over this girl for months, and after seeing her at court today, it's plain as springwater she's just as pie-eyed over you."

Emily flushed, wondering if it were possible to feel worse. "Miss Bancroft—"

The older woman shushed her. "I've come up with the perfect solution," she announced, bracing her gnarled hands on the arms of the chair and leaning forward. "I've gotten too old for Connecticut winters, and although I can't say I'm overly fond of the South—such dreadful humidity!—I must confess it's likely to be easier on these arthritic old bones. I plan to move into," she paused, shooting Emily a shrewd, calculating glance, "into my house, and it will become my winter residence. Emily will continue living there until the two of you marry—I'm getting too old to live alone anyway. After the wedding Simon can either find me an acceptable cottage nearby or have one built."

She lifted her chin to an imperious angle and regarded the two stunned individuals before her. "The house will be my wedding present to you both.

314

Well? Are you both agreeable to that?" She examined Emily closely a minute. "I admit to being somewhat set in my ways, and I can't abide laziness and stupidity. But I daresay we'll get along fairly well—you're a teacher by profession, I understand."

"Yes, Ma'am." Emily found her way to a worn wingback sofa and sat down. "But you hate me. . . ." She shook her head in bewilderment. "I took your house away. . . ."

Iris hooted in derision. "Balderdash! I was mad, Girl, but I'd never met you. How could I hate you? The past few weeks, if you must know, I've reluctantly had to accept the fact that I maintain a grudging respect for you."

She marked Simon with an old-fashioned look. "Anyone who can catch and keep this footloose young devil has to have something besides a pretty face." She lifted her cane and pointed it at Emily. "You hide the looks you have, but it didn't fool me. And it obviously hasn't fooled my grandnephew. Well, Emily Carson? Is it a deal?"

Emily looked at Simon, who had started grinning, a wide grin that spread from ear to ear. She looked at Iris, whose stern, glacial demeanor was dissolving into wrinkles and twinkles right before Emily's disbelieving eyes. She looked down at her lap, trying to comprehend what was happening. *Dear God,* she found herself pleading silently, *what do I do now?* The cold, choking panic spread, freezing her veins—her heart.

She couldn't trust these people. She couldn't. One day they would decide she wasn't worth their while and would leave her stranded and alone again. "It won't work," she said, her voice small but set. "I can't do it."

Simon's grin faded and his green eyes narrowed to slits. "What do you mean by that?" he questioned very softly. Iris's back stiffened, but she held her tongue.

Emily made a short, jerking gesture with her arm. "I can't marry you."

"You love me, Emily. You can deny it until the cows come home, but you love me as much as I love you. If you'd stop being so all-fired defensive and prickly, you'd admit I feel about as much pity for you as I do the characters who hauled you off in a gunnysack." His nostrils flared when Emily shook her head. "I'm not above trying a little kidnapping of my own."

"Leave the girl alone," interrupted Iris sharply, surprisingly. "She's been through enough and doesn't need you browbeating her."

❀

A long, painfully tense moment followed. Simon measured both the truth of his great-aunt's words and Emily's infuriating mind-set. Throat tight, a muscle twitching in his cheek, he faced Emily down until she turned her head away.

A childhood memory came to Simon suddenly, wrenchingly: He'd caught a fledgling blue jay and wanted to keep it for a pet in the new birdhouse he'd just built. To make sure the bird didn't escape, he'd held it tightly in both hands and ran all the way home.

Excited, breathless, he'd called for his brother and sister, but when he carefully opened his hands to show them the bird, it was dead.

"I only wanted to keep it safe and give it a home," he'd sobbed to his father.

Dad had laid a comforting hand on his shoulder. "Son, sometimes the best way to help a fledgling bird is to just let it go, so it can learn to fly on its own."

"All right," Simon said now, his voice raw because he couldn't hide his pain. "All right, Emily. I'll leave you alone, give you some time." He reached out and brushed a tear from her cheek with trembling fingers. "But try not to take too long, little sparrow. I'm not as strong as you think."

They arrived back at the house a little before five o'clock. Simon muttered something about working in his portable office a little while. He shot Emily a brief glance and disappeared inside the camper.

The sultry day was finally cooling from a tentative afternoon breeze. Emily changed into some light cotton slacks and a three-quarter raglan sleeve pullover, then wandered around the house like a displaced ghost. Pausing in front of the stained-glass window in the library, her fingers gently traced along a dust-covered fragment molded into the likeness of a flower. Someday it would be a rich sunset hue. . .but she wouldn't be here to see it.

She meandered out onto the front porch, moodily scanning the burned field behind the house. Though still charred and blackened, nature was already healing the wound, covering the area with weeds and autumn wildflowers. Somewhere in the woods came the faint, far-off sound of a dog barking.

A dog? When this house was the only property for two miles in every direction? The faint sound echoed again. Emily froze, not moving, not breathing, her entire body straining to hear.

There! Over in the direction of the old campsite she and Ivan had discovered. Was it possible that they hadn't killed him? Could it be? If they hadn't really killed Ivan—

Even as her brain formulated the thought, her feet were in motion, flying down the steps and across the yard. "Ivan!" she screamed with every ounce of breath in her body. "Ivan! Where are you?"

From behind she vaguely registered Simon's voice shouting her name, telling her to wait, to stay away from the woods. She ignored him. Didn't he understand? She had to find out—had to see if she had heard a dog and if it had been Ivan.

She no more thought about drug rings or nefarious criminals or what had happened the last time she strayed into these woods than she heeded Simon's frantic yells for her to come back. Heart in her throat, she ran all the way across the field and plunged into the woods, calling Ivan's name as she fought her way through the underbrush.

She was halfway down the old logging road before Simon caught up with her. He snagged her shoulder, jerked her around, and held on grimly as she fought to free herself. Sobbing, pummeling, kicking, she finally managed to wrench loose. "I have to see!" she cried frantically. "Simon, I heard a dog bark—it might be Ivan. I have to see!"

"Emily—Honey, it's too dangerous. It's almost dark, and the woods are probably full of stray dogs." He advanced upon her cautiously, keeping his voice low and reasonable. "Come on, now. Let's go back to the house. You know you don't need to be out in these woods until the police—"

"I don't care!" she flung back. Her hair had tumbled out of its neat bun and spilled about her face and neck and down her back. Emily swiped at it, then turned away. "I have to find out!" she repeated, her voice breaking. She ran off, down the trail, with Simon at her heels.

Moments later she burst into a clearing, lungs on fire, eyes blurred with tears so that for a moment she had no awareness beyond her furiously pounding heart. Then Simon was there, his arm going about her shoulders and holding her to him in a bone-crunching hug.

"You don't listen too good, Ms. Carson," a gravelly voice chided from just behind her. "And now we got ourselves a problem."

Chapter 16

I t was two hours later, more or less. Though Emily knew it must be dark outside, with a blindfold covering her eyes, her mouth gagged, and her hands tied behind her back, her only certainty was the knowledge that she and Simon were still alive.

The van in which they'd been traveling had stopped. With cautious, surreptitious movements she wriggled her body, trying to loosen stiff, numbed muscles. Trying, less successfully, not to worry about Simon.

She couldn't hear anything but the sound of her own harsh, raspy breathing. Was he conscious yet? She remembered seeing two men coming toward them, remembered Simon trying to thrust her out of the way. Her frightened gaze had caught a blur of movement, and she had tried to call out to Simon.

She was too slow, too late. Something hard struck the back of his head, and the arm holding her had dropped away.

Emily had gone a little crazy then, but she recalled little except Gumshoe yelling hoarsely for them to either tie her up and gag her, or he'd take care of her the same way. Before the pimply-faced young man and swarthy-looking Latin-type had succeeded, Emily managed to scratch deep furrows across the young man's cheek, and the other guy would wear bruises on his shins for days.

Suffocating terror roared back through her. Emily choked back a sob, repeating in her mind like a litany: *We aren't dead yet.* The probability nonetheless loomed before her like a mushroom cloud, and so, ever since they had been tossed into the back of what felt like a stripped-to-the-bones van, Emily had been praying.

She prayed because she had no other hope, because Simon was unable to do so, and until he had groaned and moved awhile ago, she hadn't even been certain he was alive. She must not think about the feelings she had endured then.

In her head, she sang all the songs she had learned in choir over the years, and whenever the fear threatened to choke her and send her back into a nether world of screaming phantoms and leering demons, she thought of sparrows and all the verses Simon had quoted with such deep faith over the past months.

Simon. . .Simon, please be all right. Lord, please let Simon be all right. Help us, please. Give me the strength to endure. . . . God, please let me know You are there.

No legions of angels descended to set them free, and no fiery chariots swept

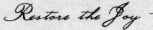

down to burn their unsavory abductors to a crisp. But a small, steady voice had surfaced from the deepest part of her being. *"I'll never change. You'll always have Me, and I will always be with you, My child. Just like salvation—My love is forever."*

Emily hung on to the Voice—and waited.

The van doors opened with a screeching jerk. Ungentle hands hauled them out, and a minute later she was unceremoniously dumped onto some sort of hard floor.

"Tie 'em both good," a voice grunted nearby. "And make sure this shack burns long enough to destroy any evidence."

"Alright, alright. . .whadya think I am—a dummy? And I know it has to look like an accident, right?" That was the young, pimply-faced man, the one who promised Ivan had been taken care of.

Heart racing, Emily struggled impotently against the bonds. This couldn't be happening; it wasn't real—

"Hurry it up, you two! I want to get outta here." Emily felt a rough rope passed around her middle, then her back was against Simon's and she realized they were being tied together. Bile rose in her throat, and in spite of the last hours of steadfast prayer, a strangled sob escaped.

Incredibly, she felt the muscles in Simon's back constrict, press harder against her, and his elbows, locked with the rope to hers, moved with the slightest of gestures. He was conscious! He was even aware of what was going on and was trying to reassure her.

Confidence and renewed determination flooded through Emily, spilling new life into her numb limbs and floundering heart. She couldn't see; she was afraid to try and speak; she could barely move—but now she could hope. *Thank You, Lord! Oh, thank You! Now please get us out of here.*

The smell of burning wood and sound of crackling flames jarred Emily momentarily out of her euphoria. She began to struggle convulsively until the urgent pressure of Simon's back and arms once again calmed her.

"That'll do it. Now let's split." A harsh guttural laugh grated their ears. "So long, lovebirds. You won't be gettin' in the way anymore, will you?"

A door slammed, and they were alone with the gathering strength of the fire radiating heat and terror.

The minute the door shut, Simon began speaking. His words were barely legible, hard to hear over the fire, and Emily realized he'd been gagged as well. But she responded to his voice like a morning glory to the sun.

"Prss magain' muh back," he ordered, and she understood immediately what he was trying to do. It had been a game growing up—kids sitting back-to-back and seeing if they could stand up without using their arms. Little did she suspect then how useful such a game could be. Without hesitation she matched the pressure against her back, bent her knees, and as she felt Simon rising, tried to counter with a similar move.

"Muh ft. . . ," she croaked, tumbling sideways because her ankles were bound. After a heart-stopping moment, she managed to regain her balance, and they stayed upright.

For another moment they stood motionless, recovering breath and gathering wits. "Jus' relak. Truh to jus' come wif me," Simon managed, the crackling flames and growing smoke fumes rendering comprehension almost impossible.

He seemed to be trying to edge in the direction of where they had heard the door slam, and it took only one step for Emily to realize they hadn't bound his feet like they had hers, probably because he had been unconscious at the time.

Simon seemed to realize about the same time that hers were bound, since she had had to hop instead of step. He moderated his step so she could hop without falling. Sweat poured down her body, soaking into her clothes, and she couldn't seem to stop the tremors in her arms and legs. But she stayed upright, close to Simon, and hopped.

Behind them the fire roared as it engulfed something even more flammable. Suddenly Simon ran into the wall, and she heard his muffled groan. Tears sprang to Emily's eyes. This was her fault. Simon was hurt and might die—and it was her fault, just like Ivan's death had been her fault.

Simon turned so that their hands could just touch the coarse, unfinished boards that made up the walls of the shack, already hot to the touch. Choking, gagging, Emily prayed.

Then she heard the doorknob rattle, and her bound wrists twisted along with Simon's as he struggled to turn the knob and open the door. When she felt it opening and pushing her almost off balance again, she sobbed against the restraining gag, feeling the inrush of cool air against her face, in her hair.

Simon did not waste time trying to talk anymore. Instead, he encouraged her through a series of firm but urgent tugs to follow him. As they jerked and hopped out the mercifully unlocked door, the sound of crashing wood exploded behind them, and part of the ceiling collapsed.

With a sucking roar of redoubled intensity, the triumphant fire devoured the interior of the shack. Emily felt the heat of it blasting her, searing her as Simon all but dragged her on his back the last few feet.

They were still too close to the burning structure when she lost her balance again and tumbled sideways, throwing Simon off balance, too, so that they both fell to the ground. She heard him grunt in pain, and she frantically struggled to get back up with him before he passed out. Too close—they were too close to the shack, and the flames and heat could still accomplish their deadly mission. And it was her fault.

Once again the firm, steady pressure of Simon's back quieted her, guided her. "Easy, Love," she thought he said, and in mere seconds they managed to regain their feet. With Herculean effort, Emily managed to keep from panicking again, blindly obeying the largely unspoken communication of the man to whom she was literally bound.

The analogy burst into her soul like the consuming brightness of flame. She was trusting this man with her life, not knowing where he was going, and she was unable to either see him or give him much aid on her own. He wasn't leaving her behind because it was her fault, or trying to make her feel guilty. He was only working to save her life.

And that was the way she should trust God, whom she could neither see nor hear. Nor did she know exactly where He was leading her. She certainly couldn't offer Him much aid on her own. All she could do was surrender, no longer resisting.

Just as she knew Simon would give his life to keep her from all harm—was struggling to do that right now—so she realized and truly understood for the first time in her life how much God cared for her. Cared for her so much that He sent His beloved Son to die for her, even though the fault was hers—not His.

She, Emily Carson, did matter after all. And there was Someone who loved her. . .who had always loved her. Loved her as she yearned to be loved. *Oh, Lord,* she prayed in everlasting gratitude, *thank You. Thank You for restoring the joy of my salvation—thanks for Your faithfulness in spite of me!*

After awhile she came to the more fundamental awareness that Simon was fumbling with the cords that bound their wrists. For several frustrating minutes he worked in silence, but it was no use. He muttered something unintelligible. "Muh fingehs. . .too big. . ."

Emily moved her raw, throbbing wrists back together and found his fingers with her own. She pressed, trying to tell him to let her try. His fingers brushed against her wrists and jerked, and Emily knew he was probably feeling the rawness and seeping blood.

"Ahm okay." She gagged again, so she quit trying to talk, focusing every atom of her concentration on working the knots in the slender cords free. Her back and shoulders burned, and behind them she could hear the snapping, crackling flames, smell the charred wood and choking smoke.

"Oo can do it. Take ur time. At's it." Simon coached her, soothed her, encouraged her as if they had all the time in the world.

I can do it, Emily ground out to herself. *I've done it before.* This was no different than the time J.J. and his stupid little friends tied her up when she was eleven and left her in the woods. She escaped then, and she could do it again.

This was no different, yet it was. Then, she'd been alone. Now Simon was with her. *And not only Simon,* she thought with growing excitement. *I can do it, because You're with me,* she prayed. *With Christ I can do all things.*

A moment later she succeeded in loosening the knot, and with a violent tug, Simon came free of the bonds. He worked with savage speed to untie the rope that bound him and Emily together.

"Almost home free, Love," he enunciated clearly, directly in her ear, and Emily knew then they would be. He twisted and dropped a kiss on the top of her head as he swiftly untied the gag and tugged off her blindfold.

Two minutes later they were both free and fell into each other's arms.

❋

They were sitting beneath a pine tree because Emily's leg had given out, and Simon was running his hands over her the same way she was doing him. "It takes more than a knock to keep me down," he consoled her with a white-toothed grin, barely visible in the flickering light of the fire. "I'm okay, Honey. Stop shaking now—I'm okay." He laughed a little. "I'm more worried about you than you are me, so how about if you reassure me for a minute?"

"I'm fine—just sore, mostly on my wrist where it was cut. And my jaw and shoulders hurt."

He lifted her wrists and rubbed his thumbs gently over the raw, blistered skin, then tilted the bandaged one up toward the fire to try and examine it better. The thick gauze bandage she had taped there that morning was crumpled, but at least it had been thick enough to protect the wound.

"What about the fire?" Emily asked, and they both turned to gaze at the remainder of the shack.

"It looks like it's just going to burn itself out, fortunately."

Even as he spoke, the two remaining walls toppled into the center of the fire, sending an explosion of sparks and flames shooting into the night. The building had been placed in a clearing, so there were no trees or even protruding branches close enough for the fire to refuel itself with a roar into new life.

Simon put his arm around Emily, and she dropped her head onto his shoulder. They sat beneath the pine and watched until the flames died, first to flickering tongues, then to a glowing pile of embers and a wavering column of smoke.

"We were supposed to be in there," Emily spoke at last into the night, and a spasm shuddered through her weary frame.

Simon hugged her harder. "I know," he agreed quietly. "But we weren't." He cupped her face and kissed her very tenderly. "Let's thank God for our lives, then see about finding shelter for the night."

They bowed their heads, and Simon offered an eloquent prayer of thankfulness that melted Emily's heart completely. How could she have been so blind not to know she was head over heels in love with this man?

She rubbed her damp cheek against his shirt, basking in the steady beating of his heart. Her fingers crept up to softly touch his beard-roughened cheek. "Simon? I've been praying—a lot—these past hours and you know what? Never has God been so real to me. I felt—really felt—His power and presence surrounding me, sustaining me. . .us. And everything you've been saying all these months suddenly made perfect sense."

Incredibly, his chest heaved, and a sob of utter relief seared her ears. Then his arms hauled her up and he kissed her, words and tears all mixing up together. Emily eventually managed to wriggle a hand between to cover his mouth.

"You haven't let me tell you something else." She laughed, breathless, her own eyes aching with tears of joy.

"What's that?"

"I love you with all my heart, Simon Balfour. . .and if you still want to marry a plain brown sparrow who doesn't feel insignificant anymore. . .she's yours."

"Oh, God, thank You!" Simon vowed, passion and relief making his voice shake. "Yes, yes, yes, you impossible woman—of course I still want to marry you."

"Even though I almost killed us both?"

He kissed her. "Hush. I love all of you, Emily Carson—including the impulsive, unthinking woman who has a thing for ugly animals."

Emily dug an elbow into his ribs. "Just for that—I'm only marrying you to stay in the house."

Simon grabbed a fistful of her hair and wrapped it around her throat. "That was my line, remember?"

Emily pulled his head down, and for the next few moments neither of them said anything. Eventually Simon lifted his head, his fingers smoothing her face. Cradled in his arms, surrounded by enveloping darkness, Emily knew she had found a home at last.

"Simon?"

"Hmm?"

"Let's make sure we clean the window before the wedding, okay?"

"No–o problem."

Epilogue

The day after Thanksgiving, Emily, Simon, and Aunt Iris were sitting on the front porch, rocking in three of the huge wicker rockers Simon had bought from the couple in South Carolina whose old country inn he would be restoring after Christmas. The sun had finally broken through the storm clouds, which had dumped an inch of rain Thanksgiving Day.

Emily rocked in blissful contentment, holding her husband's hand and watching the sunbeams streaming down into the dripping yard. "It was nice of Sheriff Jessup to phone the good news yesterday, even though it was Thanksgiving," she mused dreamily. Simon squeezed her hand.

"Without bail," Simon added. "All of them, including Gumshoe." His gaze moved lovingly over Emily, causing her to blush. "God sure moves in mysterious ways—using a murdering drug dealer to finally convince my wife," he leaned over and kissed Emily, "that she couldn't live without me—or the Lord."

Iris snorted. "If you two are going to start acting like a pair of billing and cooing doves again, I'm going back inside."

Simon chuckled and stood. "Don't move. Emily and I will go for a walk."

"Simon—it's too wet."

He ignored her laughing protests and hauled her into his arms, carrying her. "There. Quit complaining, Love. I want to watch the sun shining on our window."

"Oh." Emily relaxed, hugging him. "In that case. . ."

He carried her out into the yard, finding just the right spot to best savor their pride and joy.

"I like the purple iris best," Emily announced after a few minutes of rapt contemplation. "It's incredible the way the sun makes all the colors so rich and alive—Simon? What is it?"

He had cocked his head in a listening stance, turning his face to the field behind the house. He wasn't even looking at the window. In exasperation Emily twisted her head. "What are you doing?"

"I thought I saw—" He stopped, then gently set Emily down. "Yes. There, near the edge of the field. Something moved."

"Probably a rabbit."

"Nope, too big. Didn't you say you'd seen some deer—?" His voice died, the hand loosely clasping Emily's waist suddenly jerking her hard against him.

Emily peered across the field, and then she heard it: a weak but very definite "woof." And saw, very briefly, a large bony head. "Ivan. . ."

They tore off across the field, oblivious to the wet scratchy weeds and soggy earth, coming to a breathless halt to stare in disbelief at the animal whining weakly at their feet. Dropping to her knees, Emily gathered the gaunt, filthy dog into her arms, sobbing. "Ivan, Ivan. . . You're alive!" Ivan's bullwhip tail thumped weakly.

Simon was shaking his head. "I don't suppose we'll ever know what the old boy endured—or why they didn't kill him instead of dumping him somewhere. It's probably taken him all this time to find his way home."

Emily looked across at him, eyes swimming in tears. "He came home," she repeated, so choked with happiness and tears she could barely speak.

Simon grinned. "Well, I guess I'll have to change my way of thinking about ugly, smelly dogs, now, won't I?"

He knelt, his hand coming down to join Emily's, stroking Ivan's floppy ears and filthy head. Then he gently elbowed Emily aside and lifted the dog into his arms. Ivan licked his face feebly—and Simon didn't even grimace. "Come on, you ugly, overgrown moose," he said. "Let's go home."

And they made their way back across the field, to the welcoming, beckoning house.

SARA MITCHELL

Sara Mitchell, a best-selling fiction writer in the Christian publishing market, over the years has established a devoted following among her readers. The author of thirteen novels, she offers a consistently high quality of writing in her stories, whether genre inspirational romance, historical fiction, or complex historical suspense. Her novel *Virginia Autumn* was a 2003 Christy finalist in the North American Historical category. In addition to her fiction, Sara, a life-long music lover, has also written drama, musical drama, and skits. One of the earliest authors in the inspirational fiction market, her publishing credits are extensive, and her works have touched the lives of readers all over the world.

Two Sara Mitchell hallmark traits are her command of language and exhaustive research. Many of the story settings are drawn from her own travel experiences as the wife of a former career Air Force officer: She has lived in diverse locations from Georgia to Colorado to Great Britain, which allow for a high degree of authenticity in her books.

Sara and her husband now live in Virginia, within commuting distance of Washington, D.C., wher her husband works as a consultant. They are the parents of two adult daughters.

A Match
Made in Heaven

Kathleen Yapp

With love and smiles to David and Tamara.
You know why.

To Tamara McCumber,
for her patient explanation of the technical aspects
of the data communications industry.

Prologue

Your son would be a perfect husband for my daughter," Jane Grady announced to Katherine Forrest as they ate lunch together in a small, elegant restaurant in northeast Georgia.

"And your daughter would be a perfect wife for my son," Katherine agreed, looking at a picture of a stunning, red-haired young woman whose eyes sparkled with life. "What are we going to do about it?"

"Get them together, of course."

"How?"

"First, we'll pique their curiosity." Jane Grady smiled and sipped her sweetened iced tea.

"Every few days we'll tell them something intriguing about each other." Katherine Forrest smiled and sipped her lemon-flavored water.

"Exactly."

"What fun!"

"It will be a match made in heaven," the two matrons agreed as they bowed their heads, closed their eyes, and asked the Lord's guidance in their meddling.

Chapter 1

C.G. Grady had been told that she had one of those infectious smiles that made folks want to smile back. It started in her magnanimous heart, beamed through alert, Wedgwood blue eyes, and came out on soft, full lips over pearly white teeth that were near perfect, except for one incisor on the right, which barely overlapped its neighbor.

Women wanted to be her friends; men did, too. It was a rare day when C.G. Grady was not smiling about something.

Today was a rare day. . .she was not smiling; she was frowning, because she had just been told that Ashford Bank and Trust, for which she worked as manager of the Information Systems Division, was being acquired by a major bank in Atlanta.

"All twelve of our branches here in northeast Georgia will become part of Georgia National Bank in the middle of December," one of the vice presidents told her. "We are assured that most of our people will retain their present positions." He cleared his throat. "Most, but not all. Your performance during this acquisition could be a contributing factor in whether you stay or go."

The fifty-three-year-old vice president leaned forward over his uncluttered mahogany desk. "I certainly hope you will be one of those who will stay, C.G. How could we get along without your *joie de vivre?*"

C.G. was more concerned about how she would get along without a paycheck and wished she had more money in her savings account. She'd paid too much for the used car she'd just bought, and maybe she should cancel that New Year's cruise to the Bahamas she'd bought as a surprise for her parents.

"Do you know with whom I'll be working on merging the data information of the two banks?" she asked the vice president.

"Yes, his name is Drake Forrest. I just got a memo on him this morning. He's an independent communications consultant with an outstanding reputation."

Drake Forrest? She'd read about him not more than a month ago, in *Fortune* magazine. The article had said he was one of the best consultants in the country, constantly in demand by Fortune 500 service companies.

"I wonder what he's like to work with?" she thought out loud.

"Tough, I hear through the grapevine. Thorough, cost-conscious. Nothing stands in the way of his completing a job on schedule."

"Nothing? What about tornadoes, civil war, the discovery of gold in the parking lot?"

"Nothing," the vice president affirmed, and C.G. groaned while he smiled at her sense of humor.

She didn't mind hard work and long hours, but Drake Forrest sounded like a tyrant, albeit an exciting tyrant of such knowledge and reputation from whom she could learn a lot, if all went well.

Of course, if all did not go well, she could lose her job.

Returning to her own office, a carpeted, nice-sized room behind glass windows on the left side of the bank's luxurious lobby, she thought of the seven years she'd worked there. They'd been good years, and she'd learned and been promoted, until now her department—comprised of herself and two assistants—had responsibility for all data regarding account records, credit histories, and loan information for twelve separate Ashford Bank and Trust facilities.

She was good at her job and had been told so by her superiors many more times than once. But would the executives of Georgia National think so, too? Would Drake Forrest think so?

C.G. sat down in her chair behind her desk and reached for the blue leather New King James Bible on its right corner. Her fingers easily flew to Isaiah 26:3, the verse she'd read that very morning as part of her devotions: "You will keep him in perfect peace, whose mind is stayed on You, because he trusts in You."

I do trust You, Lord, she prayed silently, her eyes open and staring ahead at nothing in particular. *I trust You with all my heart and soul and mind. Help me in these trying days ahead. Don't let me goof up. I'm not a rich girl, and I need this job. I pray in Jesus' name.*

Knowing she'd better be prepared for the inevitable first contact, C.G. called her assistants, James Wyatt, who handled data operations, and Dottie Westfall, whose responsibilities were voice communications, into her office to tell them about the acquisition.

They were stunned.

"Are we going to be fired?" James asked. He was a short, wiry young man of thirty-one, two years older than C.G., and though hardworking and intelligent, he was not innovative or easy to get to know. C.G. expected he would never rise far in the corporate world.

"I certainly hope not," she answered his anxious question.

"New companies like to bring in their own people, C.G., or tighten up and let employees go."

"That's true."

"Don't worry about it, James," C.G.'s other assistant, Dottie Westfall, told him with a wave of the hand. She was a hefty woman with orangish blond hair, ten years older than C.G., and married to a career policeman with whom she had four children.

Dottie was brutally honest all the time, and she was perfectly content to be an assistant and nothing more. "I have enough responsibility at home," she had said to C.G. more than once, "taking care of four kids because Hank always seems to be on duty. If he put in as much time with his family as he does at the station, we'd have a good life."

"Just like you-know-who," C.G. had quipped, thinking of the breakup of her engagement three years before to an attorney who was also a workaholic. Randolph was forever striving to impress the senior partners at his prestigious law firm with how many hours he billed clients. The only time he had lavished attention on C.G. had been when he was trying to win her affections. Once the conquest was complete, and an impressive diamond shone on the third finger of her left hand, he had gone back to his real love: practicing law.

The engagement had lasted five months before C.G. had broken it off. By that time there had been no tears to shed, but she had learned an indelible lesson: Beware of men married to their careers; they can only handle one wife at a time. This thought brought her back to the present.

"We'll be working with a hotshot, independent consultant, a Drake Forrest," C.G. told her assistants, "who gets the job done regardless of how many bodies get strewed along the way."

James groaned, but Dottie laughed. "I can hardly wait to meet him," she said. She grabbed James by the shoulders and pushed him toward the door of C.G.'s office. "Come on, Partner, we'd better sharpen our pencils and straighten up our desks before Hotshot gets here."

"My desk is always neat," James protested as Dottie propelled him out the door.

C.G. smiled. They were good people, James and Dottie. *I hope their jobs won't be in jeopardy,* she thought, knowing it was her responsibility not only to make a good impression of herself but of her coworkers as well.

For the next two hours, she closed the door to her office, kicked off her shoes under her desk, and went over the information she was sure Drake Forrest would need. There was a lot. It would not be a quick and easy task to merge the information systems of the two banks. It was now the first week in August. To complete everything by mid-December was going to take some doing, but she would be ready.

She wondered when he would contact her.

❊

It was a nagging pain in her shoulders and neck that reminded C.G. she'd been sitting in one position for too long.

Standing and stretching, which felt deliciously good, she looked to the left, through the glass wall into the expansive lobby of the bank, and her eyes collided with those of a tall, strikingly handsome blond-haired man standing in the center of the room, who was staring in her direction.

She stared back, for though he wore a finely tailored business suit and carried an expensive-looking briefcase, he seemed—as he stood there, square on both legs, his expression fiercely serious—more like a conquering Viking warrior, transported out of history to capture this very room. And her.

Her gaze left his full head of windblown, sandy-colored hair and traveled over well-developed shoulders and chest, past slim hips, long legs, down to his wing-tipped shoes, then back up to his rugged face marked by large eyes and a prominent, slightly off-center, nose. His fierce look had been replaced by a rakish grin, and C.G. was humiliated that he'd caught her ogling.

Since no one else was paying him any attention, she quickly left her office and hurried toward him, knowing without a doubt that he was Drake Forrest, already here and ready to put her on a work treadmill she wouldn't get off for months.

A phone call of warning would have been nice, she thought as she stopped in front of him, a tiny bit breathless, and looked up, and up, into the most compelling blue eyes she had ever seen. Her heart stopped.

❀

Drake Forrest watched the woman walk toward him with a self-assured gait, and he liked what he saw. She was stunning and not too tall, with smooth, red hair swirled casually about her chin, pale, luminescent skin, and huge, vibrant eyes that held his attention.

Her stylish cream-colored suit, hemmed just at the knee and fastened at the waist with one large cloth-covered button, covered a slender body and identified the wearer as a woman of taste.

She belongs here in this sophisticated room, he thought, *surrounded by refinement and important business.*

The impressive mahogany desks, gold-framed nature pictures on the walls, healthy green floor plants, thick, sound-absorbing slate blue carpeting, tellers speaking in subdued voices, and even the seven-foot grandfather clock standing imperiously in one corner—all gave the impression that Ashford Bank and Trust was a proper place, a bank to be trusted to handle one's money wisely.

She was in front of him now, and Drake saw that her eyes were blue, her mouth small, and that her head came just about to his shoulders.

She smelled of Chanel No. 5, and the first crazy thought that entered his mind was that his mother would approve of her.

He also knew she would have a serious, romantic name like Elizabeth or Catherine. Not C.G. What kind of a name was that?

When he'd first been given the name of the person he'd be working with at Ashford Bank and Trust, he'd conjured up an image of a woman in combat boots, no makeup, and a mannish haircut. Not at all someone like the princess who stood before him now, all radiant and sweet-smelling.

"Mr. Forrest?" she asked in a voice that was pure velvet, as he had known it would be. She smiled, and her teeth, surrounded by well-shaped lips the color of Georgia Belle peaches (he loved Georgia Belle peaches), were white and straight, except for one, and it wasn't a detraction.

"Yes, I'm Drake Forrest, here to see C.G. Grady," he said, wishing he could delay his meeting with "that woman" and spend time instead with this exquisite beauty.

"I'm C.G. Grady," she said, giving him a smile that could stop a train on its tracks.

Shocked, and without taking his eyes from her heart-shaped face—because he never wanted to—Drake extended his hand to her, which she accepted and shook with delicate firmness. Only the strongest self-control kept him from raising her fingers to his lips.

"I look forward to working with you, Mr. Forrest," she said, her intelligent eyes assuring him she was capable of doing that well. "My assistants and I will do all that we can to help you."

"Good."

"If you'll follow me to my office, then," she said, gesturing toward it, "we'll get started."

Drake silently obeyed. Never a follower, always a leader—at the moment he was quite content to do as he was bidden.

In her office, he sat down in the low-backed chair in front of her desk and watched her settle herself, smoothing her skirt beneath her in the age-old tradition of women who cared about the appearance of their clothes.

He thought of what he'd been told about her at GNB: "C.G. Grady is smart as a whip and dependable. That's all we know. It'll be your decision whether we keep her or bring in someone else."

He couldn't tell yet whether she could keep up with his demands, but he would cut her no slack. Gorgeous and sweet-smelling though she was, either she did the job or she was out the door.

Chapter 2

M r. Forrest, what do you need from my division?" C.G. asked, noticing the strong set of his jaw, the straight, well-shaped nose, the way his eyes focused on her.

"The specifications for your computer system and its software, and a month's billing for voice and data communications."

"Of course. Shall I bring the information to you at GNB's headquarters in Atlanta?"

"No, just send it by overnight mail to my company." He handed her a business card, which she accepted, noting he worked in a prestigious area of north Atlanta. "If everything goes smoothly, Miss Grady, you'll find I'm an easy man to work with."

His strong, straight mouth edged up at the corners, but C.G. wasn't fooled. She knew there was more to that sentence, and she finished it silently: *And if it doesn't go smoothly, you're out of a job.*

"Georgia National wants this acquisition completed by December 15," he told her in a rich, deep voice that would do justice to Shakespeare. "And I don't want our part in it to cause any holdups."

"Nor do I, Mr. Forrest."

"Then I can expect the information I need tomorrow?"

"Yes, you may."

C.G. liked Drake Forrest's professionalism. He was direct and didn't waste time. There'd be no idle chitchat from him asking about her weekend or how her rose garden was doing. His no-nonsense approach was, "Here's the schedule; stick to it. And survive."

His presence filled her office with a potent masculinity, fostered by his self-confidence and strong, decisive body language—the way he moved, and stood, and took possession of the space in which he found himself.

Probably a little older than she, his rugged good looks and mesmerizing eyes started her nerves tingling whenever he spoke to her, and C.G. knew it would take some doing to concentrate on their work and not on him.

"I'm having an office prepared for you now," she said, wondering if he ever relaxed, cracked a joke, or was late in the morning. "Is there anything in particular you need in it?"

"Just desk space enough for my laptop computer, a phone, fax, printer, yellow tablets for my scribbling, number two pencils, felt-tipped pens in an assortment of colors, and any other general office supplies you can think of."

"No coffee?"

"Yes, definitely coffee. Thanks. I drink it black."

"Lunch menus from nearby restaurants? Pizza coupons?"

The corners of his mouth twitched, and he gave her a questioning gaze. "Whatever you think I'll need, Miss Grady."

"Please call me C.G."

"Which stands for?"

"C.G."

"Ah," he said, his eyes dancing with a mischief she was surprised to see. "A secret name?"

"Known only to my parents, minister, and doctor."

"Not to a husband?"

"No."

"Boyfriend?"

C.G. stood up without answering the question. "Drake—I assume I may call you that—name, rank, and serial number is all I can give you today." The rebuke was a gentle one, and she waited for his reaction. Her personal life was private and none of his business.

When his handsome, chiseled face relaxed in what could almost be called a smile—almost—she added, "I think we'll work well together."

Then the smile became thoughtful, almost enigmatic, and oozed over C.G. with all the devastation of hot fudge melting over ice cream. "I hope you'll say that four months from now, C.G. I have been known to eat alive those who don't live up to what's expected."

She laughed. "Then you won't find a meal here."

"Good."

Were his eyes twinkling? Under that stern personality, did there lurk a sense of humor? C.G. determined to find out, not entirely frightened by his gruff manner, but wisely respectful of him, as one would respect the territory of a predatory animal.

Her main goal was to hold her own against him and help James and Dottie to do the same.

Another goal, which might prove harder to realize, if he were not married, and if he kept looking at her the way he had been so far, would be to keep herself from being drawn into a personal relationship with him, because she had a hard-and-fast rule *never* to mix her business and personal life. *Never.*

"I'll start using that office next week," Drake told her, standing up.

"It will be ready."

He picked up his briefcase, laid it on her desk, opened it up, and handed her two sheets of paper neatly typed.

"I've made some notes about the areas we should cover first."

C.G. scanned them and saw nothing that would present a problem. She told him so.

"In that case, it's been a pleasure, C.G., to meet you." He gave her a broad smile that weakened her knees.

"Thank you, Drake."

After he left, her office felt unbelievably empty, and C.G. placed her hands on her cheeks, knowing they were warm, as a quick glance in the decorative, beveled glass mirror above her credenza verified.

Taking a moment to calm her accelerated pulse, she finally buzzed both her assistants and asked them to come to her office.

"I have a major assignment that needs to be completed yesterday," she told them.

Like it or not, they were up and running with Drake Forrest, and if they wanted to keep their jobs, they dared not miss a step.

❀

Drake left C.G. Grady's office and took the first ordinary breath he'd had in ten minutes. That's all it had taken for the woman to impress the life out of him and speed up his heart rate. He knew it was not going to be easy working closely with her without getting personally involved, which was not a good idea in a work situation, usually.

With C.G. Grady, he was sure it was going to be downright impossible, for she was intelligent as well as beautiful, organized as well as intriguing, businesslike as well as womanlike. And she wasn't afraid of him, which would make their getting to know each other a whole lot easier.

He laughed at himself for thinking, with a name of C.G., that she would be mannish and wear combat boots. *What could those initials stand for?* he wondered. Right now, to him, they stood for confident and gorgeous.

❀

The rest of Drake's day was filled with finishing up work for other companies so he could devote full attention to the GNB acquisition. The rest of his day was also filled with thoughts of C.G. Grady.

At his apartment that night, he was still thinking about her as he paced back and forth in his kitchen, restlessly watching a thick steak grilling on the Jenn-Air cooktop. He remembered the sheen of her hair and the charming, musical lilt of her voice that had made him want to hang on every word.

The juices from the T-bone sizzled on the stovetop and made him think she was feisty under her office decorum, and as he flipped the steak over with long-handled tongs, he wondered why there was not a man in her life. That had been the first thing he had looked for when he'd entered her office and she'd turned around to face him: a ring. There hadn't been one.

The beeper on the microwave signaled his baked potato was done, so Drake whipped it out, slit open the top with a Ginsu knife, and dropped in a hunk of butter the size of a golf ball.

When the steak was cooked, he added it to the plate with the potato, generously sprinkled them both with salt, and took from the freezer an icy glass mug in which he poured cold, whole milk. Taking a long, slow drink, he sank into a chair at his white oak kitchen table and began his meal.

Drake was a good cook, although his menus were few and basic. He was not into salads or quiche or casseroles. Meat and potatoes were his staple, along with fresh vegetables, an apple a day, and pecans. He loved Georgia pecans.

Savoring the odor of the medium-rare steak, he cut off one piece and plunged it into his mouth. "Mmmm," he groaned in satisfaction, then worked the melted butter through the baked potato before stabbing a forkful of that into his mouth.

Relaxing for the first time since he'd hit the front door of his large apartment in trendy, uptown Buckhead in north Atlanta, he looked contentedly around the cheerful breakfast nook with its white chair molding and white and burgundy wallpaper boldy striped. Through wide windows, their white shutters open, early evening light streamed.

Drake liked light and space, each room in the apartment having only minimal furnishings that were, however, big, comfortable, and always expensive.

He was outrageously successful at what he did, with the bank account and men's toys to prove it, but he worked hard and expected others around him to do the same. That would include C.G. Grady.

The classic beauty of her face surged back into his memory, and Drake knew he was in trouble. He couldn't stop thinking about her.

He rarely was without a date on the weekend. His little black book was filled with names and addresses of the women he'd taken out. Some had stayed in his life for a month or two; most lasted only a few weeks.

Their common appeal was good looks and intelligence. They were all career women who knew how to dress and speak and present themselves well. They had captured his interest quickly and just as quickly had lost it. They were nice but not impossible to live without.

Would C.G. Grady be different?

Time will tell, he decided, slicing more of his steak into bite-sized pieces, *that is, if she ever lets me get close to her.* And he knew, even in this short time of acquaintance, that he definitely wanted to get close to her.

Chapter 3

To stop thinking of C.G., Drake concentrated on devouring his meal, quicker than he'd been taught to as a boy, and as he did, he remembered a letter he'd received from his mother that day.

She and his father only lived fifty miles away, in a small town of twenty-one thousand in north Georgia, but she loved to write letters and send him tidbits of information she'd gleaned from newspapers and magazines that she thought would interest him. It was like having his own private clipping service, for his mother was an intelligent woman who understood pretty well the complicated world of communications through which he moved.

He respected his parents, and they got along well even though his mother did remind him now and then that he worked too hard (in her opinion but not his), and he should be getting married and having children.

At thirty-five, he guessed she was right, at least about the marriage and family, but he'd never met the woman who could make him forget his passion—business—for more than a few hours.

Picking up his mother's letter, he pulled from the white parchment envelope a single sheet of paper that had words carefully printed on it, and not a single comment from his mother, Katherine Forrest:

luscious hair
peaches-and-cream complexion
late twenties
smart and beautiful

Curious and puzzled, Drake turned the paper over. There was nothing written on the back to tell him who this intriguing female was. His natural inclination was to scrunch the paper into a ball and toss it in the trash as meaningless, except that his mother never sent him something meaningless.

He read the description again, then growled deep in his throat as awareness dawned on him. Snaring the phone from the hutch behind him, he called her.

"I know what you're doing," he said when a lyrical soprano voice answered.

"And what is that, Dear?" his mom responded.

"You're matchmaking."

"You're absolutely right."

"You admit it, without shame?"

"Freely. I have found the perfect wife for you."

Drake chuckled. "Mother, I'm a big boy. I hang up my clothes, pick out my own socks, and even know how to open a can of spaghetti. And, someday, I'll find my own wife."

"A good wife."

"Sure."

"A Christian wife."

He paused. "I suppose so."

He knew his mother was not at all sure he would find a Christian wife, and to be honest, it wasn't the first requirement to being attracted to a woman, though he certainly wasn't opposed to the idea.

An uncomfortable silence reminded Drake that his parents were concerned that over the years he had slipped away from the close relationship he had once had with God when he'd been a teenager.

It wasn't that he disbelieved—far from it. His priorities had just changed as he'd matured. He knew this attitude hurt his folks, and for that he was sorry, but a man had to live his own life. He still considered himself a Christian, albeit an inactive one.

"You haven't set up a time for me to meet this incomparable person, have you?" Drake asked, dreading the answer if it were yes.

"No, Son, not yet, but I'm working on it." The lilt was there in her voice. She had forced herself past the awkward moment.

"Please don't."

"You'll like her, I know. You have so much in common."

Drake was not going to fall into the trap of asking what they had in common. He wasn't going to cooperate at all.

"Mother, give it up."

"I can't. She's right for you. I know it. Her mother knows it."

"Her mother?"

"Yes, we go to different churches but attend a community Bible study and have become friends."

Drake groaned and stared up at the ceiling. The only thing worse for a man than having a matchmaking mother was having two mothers trying to manipulate him into matrimony.

"I love you, Mother, you know that, but please do not set me up with this stranger. Does she know what you and her mother are doing?"

"No, she doesn't. But she will."

"Mother—"

341

"Good-bye, Dear."

The line went dead and Drake's jaw turned to steel.

❀

C.G. Grady kicked off her leather low heels and collapsed onto the blueberry camelback sofa in her living room in which the ambience was defined by comfortable furniture, well-cared-for plants, stained-glass suncatchers hanging in the front windows, and brass-framed pictures of family and friends.

Hers was a country house, and she'd purposely decorated it to have a close, cozy atmosphere.

It had been a disturbing day at the bank, and never had she been more thankful for the quiet and solitude of her charming, eight-year-old house.

Propping her feet up on the heavy oak coffee table in front of her, she closed her eyes, loving to be here, where the antique clock ticked comfortingly on the mantel over the gas log fireplace, the air-conditioning hummed, keeping the temperature in the one-story, seven-room home a steady seventy-eight degrees, and the Crock-Pot on the kitchen counter gave out the tantalizing odor of a tuna-noodle casserole, her favorite. She loved casseroles.

C.G. breathed deeply and slowly, deciding that after a few more minutes of immobility, she would take a leisurely, warm bath with plenty of scented bubbles to soak away the day's stresses. Maybe then, she would stop thinking of Drake Forrest and how he'd looked in the lobby of the bank when he'd burst into her life at 3:45 that afternoon.

He was an interesting man and typical of the breed who put work above all else. Of course, she didn't know that about him for sure, but she'd be surprised if she were wrong. It was all there: the decisiveness, the single-mindedness, the fire in the eyes when discussing an important project.

Oh, yes, she'd seen it all before. In her uncle, in Dottie's husband, and in the man she'd been going to marry but discovered, before it was too late, that he would always put work before her.

And now here was another one, a driven-to-succeed man who would be her superior for months to come, a man who would hold the fate of her employment in his hand and would not understand if she wanted a life outside the bank.

Picking up the mail she'd dumped on the cushion beside her when she'd first come in, she found three bills and an elegant, ivory envelope with her name and address handprinted in her mom's lovely, distinguishable style.

C.G. opened the envelope, anticipating some tidbit of information gleaned from a newspaper or magazine and sent on for her perusal. Jane Grady, C.G.'s mom, often did this even though she and C.G.'s father lived less than a mile away. C.G. smiled as she pulled out a single slip of paper.

"What is it this time, Mom?" she said out loud. "A recipe? The dates of a play you want us to see? A new fact from history you know I'll question and. . ."

Her voice dropped off as she read the few words carefully printed on the page:

wavy, blond hair
mischievous eyes
strong
dependable

Curious and puzzled, C.G. frowned and turned the paper over. There was nothing on the back. She reread the few statistics. "*Who* has wavy, blond hair and mischievous eyes?" she asked the empty room.

Sighing, and not at all in the mood for a game, she decided to take her bath and then call her mom and find out what she was up to.

An hour later, refreshed and ravenous for dinner, she forgot to do so.

❧

The phone call came in at 11:58 A.M. the next day at the bank, just as C.G. was starting to think about lunch. She recognized the deep, resonant voice.

"Drake, good morning. How are you today?"

"Twiddling my thumbs, Miss Grady."

"I beg your pardon?"

"I didn't receive the information you promised me."

C.G.'s mouth dropped open. "It went out yesterday. Overnight, express mail."

"Yes, I received a packet from your office, but it wasn't what I wanted."

"What's missing?"

"Figures from all twelve of your branches. All I got were the ones for the main office where you work."

C.G. groaned. She had specifically told James and Dottie to include every branch of Ashford Bank and Trust. Why hadn't they?

"I'm sorry for the mistake, Drake."

"Did you personally handle this, C.G.?"

"No, I didn't."

"Why?"

The question was curt, and C.G. wanted to snap back that she did have other work to do, but she held her tongue, not about to shift the blame from herself to her assistants. She was in charge. The responsibility was hers.

"Let me look into the matter and call you back," she offered.

"Forget the call. I'll be there in an hour to pick it up."

"But, Drake—"

A rude click told C.G. the conversation was ended, and she decided right then and there not to serve him tea and crumpets when he appeared.

Chapter 4

C.G. called James and Dottie to her office. "We have a problem," she announced.

James's shoulders drooped. "What is it?"

"We were supposed to send figures from all twelve of our branches to Drake Forrest. Instead, he only received ones from our main office here."

Dottie grunted and poked James's arm. "I told you that's what he wanted."

"I'm sorry, C.G. We goofed. I goofed," James apologized, his gaze falling to the floor.

C.G. felt sorry for him, knowing he was a real team player, always willing to do whatever needed doing, whatever would please her.

When he'd first come to the bank three years before, he had asked to date her socially, but she'd let him know she never mixed her business and personal life. Besides, she was not at all attracted to him.

She came to learn that even though James treated women with great courtesy, he was not a lady's man, and was sensitive about his slight build and five-foot eight-inch height, as though that were why women didn't like him. Actually, she thought him nice-looking, with straight, brown hair and pale, sensitive eyes, and hoped he would find someone to love.

Dottie was a contrast to him, twenty pounds overweight, with short, kinky hair, fat cheeks, and a cheerful, never-get-discouraged disposition that sometimes drove James crazy. C.G. had always been able to count on Dottie. Until now.

"I'm sorry, too," Dottie added her apology to James's. "We'll gather the rest of the information and get it out stat."

C.G. forced a smile. "Yes, on getting the material together. No, on sending it out. As we speak, a disgruntled Drake Forrest is on his way here to pick it up."

James turned and ran out of the office.

❈

Thirty minutes later Dottie hurried into C.G.'s office and leaned over, palms down, on C.G.'s mahogany desk. Her cheeks were flushed. "I have the scoop on Drake Forrest," she said excitedly.

C.G. looked up from a file she'd been rifling through. "I don't need 'the scoop,' Dottie; I need the information he wants."

"James is finishing up. This is better. My cousin, Mattie, works for Georgia

344

National in Atlanta, and is dating a man who's worked with Drake Forrest on another project, and she says that he says—"

"Hold it, Dottie." C.G. put up both hands. "Is this gossip?"

Twinkly eyes accompanied a twinkly grin. "Of course not. It's ammunition, for you, as well as us. We're all fighting for our jobs here, C.G."

"I agree. Go ahead."

Dottie spoke softly and quickly.

"Drake Forrest. Thirty-five. Unmarried. No children. Born in Chicago. Grew up in Southern California. Graduated from Cal State Fullerton. Seven years with Citibank, at the end of which—get this: He was in charge of communications for the entire nation. Then he quit, went on his own, and in only five years has built a solid reputation as the best in his field."

"That's impressive."

"You said it. He's successful, rich, good-looking, and dates a different woman every month."

C.G. stood up. "We don't need to know about his women."

"Forewarned is forearmed."

"He's not pursuing us, Dottie."

Dottie shrugged. "Us? No. You? Time will tell."

❀

Exactly fifty-two minutes later, Drake Forrest strode into C.G.'s office and plunked his Italian leather briefcase down on her desk.

Startled, and surprised that he'd made it there so fast, C.G. looked up past a custom-tailored charcoal suit, gray shirt, silver tie bar, and a silver, burgundy, and black silk tie, her eyes finally colliding with his stormy blue ones. "You broke the speed limit, Mr. Forrest," she said sweetly.

"Did I?" His jaw flexed. "Don't you ever drive faster than you should, C.G.?"

"Never."

"Never?"

"Well, hardly ever."

He gave her a superior look, then asked, "Do you have the information I need?"

"That, and more I know you'll be wanting." From the way his eyes never left hers, C.G. felt a strange heat playing at the back of her neck as she handed him a heavy folder.

❀

C.G.'s smile softened Drake's heart as he took the folder from her. He liked the fact that she was mentally quick, could spar with words, and wasn't going to let him intimidate her, not that he'd planned to. It was just his nature to take charge of every situation.

His eyes skimmed over the data. It was exactly what he'd come for, and he was impressed that C.G. had gathered additional information for him before he'd asked for it. Now he could get back to his office and bury himself in it all, but he hesitated, not wanting to leave, and knowing why: He wanted to be with her.

"I think I'd better look these over now," he said, "to be sure everything's here."

"Of course," C.G. agreed. "Let me show you the office I've arranged for you to use while you're here and introduce you to Greta, my secretary, who will help whenever you need her."

"Fine."

She stood, and the rustle of her sage green silk dress pleased his ears as did the scent of her perfume when she passed him. Again, she was wearing Chanel. Again, his nostrils deeply breathed it in and evoked an image of warm, humid nights in the arms of a beautiful woman. C.G. Grady.

He followed her through the lobby and down a short corridor to a small office, furnished stylishly, but with no windows. Reading his mind she said, "I'm sorry we don't have a room with a view."

"No problem," he assured her. And it wasn't. "When I'm working, I'm not gazing out a window to look at daisies."

"Then the room is adequate?"

"Let's see."

He moved to the desk, opened its drawers, saw the well-stocked supplies he had requested, sat down in the high-backed executive chair, played with the computer, asked C.G. a few questions about the phone system, examined the printer and fax machine, then thudded the palms of both hands down on the desk as he stood up.

"It'll do fine." He was rewarded by a luscious smile that made him aware of how soft and inviting her lips were.

"I'll leave you to your work, then," she said and was almost out the door before Drake called after her, "You will be in your office, won't you, in case I have any questions?"

She looked down at a slim, gold watch at her wrist. "I was about to go to lunch. . . ."

Drake glanced at his Rolex. "It is that time, isn't it? Why don't we go together?"

"I. . .uh. . . ," C.G. stammered, and Drake almost galloped across the room to get to her.

"Are you going with someone else?"

"Well. . .no."

"Have errands to run?"

"No."

"Good." He took her elbow and escorted her back toward the lobby, their footsteps muffled by the thick, durable carpet. "Just guide me to a good restaurant. I'll drive." He grinned down at her. "Slowly."

After she'd picked up her purse in her office, Drake escorted C.G. to his black Corvette convertible, top up since rain was expected. He opened the passenger door for her and watched her get in, hoping he could keep his head when she was sitting close to him, her perfume filling his car, her dress shimmering in the sunlight streaming through the window, catching its hues.

Following the directions C.G. gave him and driving slowly (something he rarely did) through the downtown streets of Cheston, Drake saw that it was an ordinary, small town. There was nothing spectacular or memorable about it, except for the abundant pines, Bradford pear trees, crepe myrtles, and beds of saucy petunias, marigolds, and impatiens which brightened the landscape at practically every building.

"We're here," C.G. announced. "Turn right and park."

Drake did and found himself in the parking lot of a four-story hospital. Gazing up at the neat brick building, he said, "We're eating lunch at the hospital?"

"Yes. They have great food."

"You're kidding me."

"Would I do that?"

Drake got out of the car and was halfway around when C.G. opened her door.

"Stay where you are," he shouted, hurrying to help her out. "No woman riding in my car ever opens her own door."

C.G. gave him an appreciative gaze that warmed his skin clear to his shoes. "I'm not used to such gentlemanly care, Mr. Forrest. Please forgive me."

Drake stared into her vivid, blue eyes and wondered what was wrong with the men of Cheston that they would not give C.G. Grady the care she deserved.

"The food really is wonderful here," she said as they walked up the stairs to the hospital entrance, "and we can eat fast." They waited for the elevator to take them to the lower floor where the cafeteria was located.

"I thought you didn't like fast."

"Not in cars, but in food it's good, especially when one has something to do after lunch."

"Does one have something to do after lunch?"

"Yes, there's someone I must visit, but it will only take a few minutes. We won't be late back to the office."

"I certainly hope not."

They laughed then, and Drake knew that working with C.G. was going to be nothing but pure pleasure.

Chapter 5

D rake wouldn't have believed it, but he actually enjoyed his lunch. The beef pot roast was full of tender potatoes and carrots in a thick, brown gravy, the blueberry muffins were soft and warm, and the strawberry shortcake was as good as his mother made. It was hard not to go back for seconds of everything, but he settled for one more muffin. A particularly large one.

"Do you eat here often?" he asked C.G.

"Yes, because I'm here a lot, visiting members of my church who are sick."

"I see." *So,* he thought, *C.G. Grady is not only intelligent and capable, she's caring and religious, too.* Now he knew his mother would like her.

"The lady I'm going to see today had a mild heart attack four days ago, but she's recuperating nicely. She doesn't have much family living in the area, so a visit means a lot to her."

"And you don't mind coming to a hospital?"

She smiled. "Not at all. In fact, I get excited whenever I'm here. I think I should have been a doctor or a nurse."

Drake found himself curious to know what else she did with her free time, and he asked her.

"I love to read."

Her quick answer indicated a passion, and he liked that, always drawn to people who felt strongly about things.

"What kinds of books?"

"Almost anything: fiction, nonfiction, historical, contemporary, biographies. I really enjoy biographies. And Christian books."

Drake thought of his library and knew he had everything she liked on his shelves, except for the Christian books. He'd given them all away before he'd moved to this apartment—not enough room for everything, he'd told himself.

"What else?" he asked.

C.G. took a bite of lemon meringue pie and gazed thoughtfully out the window at the pretty garden area awash with scarlet red begonias around a gurgling fountain, then said enthusiastically, "I'm a big sports fan—baseball and basketball in particular."

"Really?" He was an avid Braves fan and had season tickets for the Atlanta Hawks. Maybe she'd go to a game with him if he asked.

He buttered his muffin, and C.G. watched his hands. They were strong hands, with long, solid fingers and well-manicured nails. The hands of a businessman. Yet, they looked like they could build things, hammer nails, lift furniture. Was he a man of brawn as well as brain? If so, her dad would like him; he was a physical kind of guy. Always building, tinkering around the house and yard.

Drake looked up and caught her staring at him. "Am I growing tentacles?" he asked with a grin.

"Actually, I was admiring your hands."

Drake choked on the last morsel of muffin while C.G.'s cheeks flamed. "My mother says I'm too honest sometimes."

He shook his head. "I wouldn't call that a fault."

"It gets me into trouble."

"Which I'm sure you get out of with grace."

C.G. grinned. "Not always."

"I'd like to hear of a few examples."

"I'll write you a memo—someday."

Drake cleared his throat. "So, you like my hands."

C.G. looked at her watch. "Time to go if I'm to visit Mrs. Weathers and still get us back to the bank by one."

"Are you always this conscientious of company time," Drake asked, "or just trying to make an impression on me?"

C.G. gave him a serious look. "I don't play games, Drake, not with the company or in my personal life." She stood up and took her tray to a moving conveyor belt, which returned it to the kitchen. Drake did the same, insisting on paying the bill, though C.G. vigorously protested.

"A quirk of mine, C.G., is always to pay when I take a lady to lunch—"

"You weren't taking me," C.G. argued. "This was a business lunch."

Drake's mouth turned up in a grin. "All right. You may pay the next time."

"Fine," C.G. declared, glad she had won that battle.

It was not until she had visited her church friend and was back in Drake's car that she realized there would have to be another meal shared with him in order for her to pay. She wasn't sure that would be a good idea since she was beginning to like more about Drake Forrest than just his hands.

The afternoon dragged by for C.G. She was acutely aware that Drake was just down the hall, going over her bank's records. She knew they were in order, that he wouldn't find anything amiss. Still, there was that nagging concern that a problem would arise.

It did.

Drake came into her office at three-thirty. He had discarded his suit jacket, but his tie was still straight and the sleeves of his shirt were still buttoned at the wrist.

"I need something right away."

C.G. was sure she was going to hear that phrase a lot in the coming days: right away.

"What is it you need?"

"The total number of analog data lines for all the Ashford Bank and Trust branches, including this one. We're going to change to digital lines, which means faster transmission and fewer errors."

"I had expected that. I think there are fourteen lines altogether, but let me make sure. I'll check the phone bills for the past month and get back to you."

"Today?"

"If I can, but it could take some time to find them buried in all those numbers."

He frowned and C.G. mentally recorded two of Drake's business priorities that she'd figured out: 1) Do it right the first time. 2) Do it as soon as you can. Simple. Like throwing the right meat to a hungry tiger. If she could manage to keep doing that with him, she just might keep her job.

"I'll wait here for you to get the figures," he said.

"Here?"

"Is there a problem with that?"

"No, except that it might take some time—"

"And you don't want me snooping around your office."

"Are you a snooper?"

Drake chuckled, despite trying not to. "Probably. A person's office tells a lot about him—or her."

C.G. gave him a saucy grin. "You could always just ask whatever it is you want to know."

"Yes, I could, but would you answer?"

"My life is an open book."

"And I enjoy reading as much as you do, C.G."

She walked hesitantly past him, not comfortable with leaving him there, in her space, though she wasn't sure why. The only personal things she had out were a photo of her and her parents on a sailboat, a small pewter Mickey Mouse from a favorite vacation to Disney World, and her Bible. What would he conclude from seeing those?

"C.G., are you all right?" Dottie stood up behind her small, square desk that looked as though a bomb had exploded on it. How she ever kept anything straight was beyond C.G.'s understanding. Still, her work was trustworthy.

"Yes, I'm fine," C.G. assured her with a halfhearted smile, trying to shake from her mind a picture of Drake meandering through her office. She went over to a beige metal cabinet. "I need the phone bills file to get the exact number of analog data lines for all our branches."

"Sure, it's in there."

It was not.

Dottie looked puzzled and C.G. stared at the ceiling in frustration.

"Where is it, Dottie? Drake Forrest is waiting for those figures."

"I have no idea, C.G." Dottie rifled through the drawer herself. "Believe it or not, my files are well-organized, but that file is not where it should be."

C.G. let out an exasperated sigh. "Could James have it?"

"I don't know why. If he took it, he didn't ask me first."

They both went to his office. He wasn't there. The file C.G. needed was not on his desk and she didn't want to go rifling through his desk drawers.

Fighting a rise in temper, C.G. said, "Let's see if Greta knows anything about it."

She and Dottie went out into the lobby to their secretary's immaculate desk at one end of the room.

"Greta," C.G. addressed the thirty-one-year-old woman, who stopped writing on a legal pad and looked up, her huge brown eyes giving them instant attention. "We're looking for the phone bills file. Have you seen it?"

Greta pursed her lips, thinking, then absently scratched shiny brown hair that hung straight down her back and was cut in wispy bangs in the front. She shook her head no. "Not since I put last month's bill in it."

C.G. groaned and glanced back to her office, just knowing Drake Forrest was pacing a hole in the carpet and had smoke coming out of his nostrils.

Sure enough, he was not sitting patiently in the chair waiting for her return. Nor was he pacing the floor. In fact, he was not even in her office, but was, as C.G. finally located him with her eyes, in the lobby, sipping coffee and talking with one of the tellers, Susie Black, a young, tall blond with an hourglass figure and a predatory reputation where good-looking men were concerned.

Chapter 6

Telling herself she didn't care how many gorgeous females Drake Forrest spoke to in the course of a day, C.G. turned back to Greta and asked, "Could James have the file we need?"

The secretary shrugged. "If he does, he got it himself. He didn't ask me to do it for him."

C.G. and Dottie exchanged worried looks. "Thanks, Greta," C.G. said as an uncomfortable churning began roiling up in her stomach.

She tugged on Dottie's arm, and they stepped away from Greta's desk. Through clenched teeth and low voice she said, "Dottie, I have to find that file. I don't think I'm being melodramatic here when I say our jobs are on the line. We've already goofed once. Now we can't even find a simple file. Where is James anyway?"

"Beats me. You placate our hotshot expert, and I'll beat the bushes for James."

C.G. exhaled in frustration. "This is only the second day of the acquisition procedure. We have months of this merry-go-round ahead of us. What's next, I wonder?"

"I don't envy you, having to work with Drake Forrest. He's intense, to say the least." Then her eyes lit up. "On the other hand, he's also one gorgeous male. That physique. That thick head of hair."

"Dottie, stop drooling. You're married."

"Yes, but you're not. Maybe in a few months you'll be. . .friends with Drake Forrest."

C.G. glowered. "No, Dottie, we will not be. . .friends. You know my rule about never dating anyone from work."

"Turning down a date with James was not difficult," Dottie muttered. "Saying no to a Hungarian vegetarian dinner with two-hundred-fifty-pound Walter from Accounting was also not difficult. But since there isn't another eligible man in this bank, in all of Cheston, and maybe even in the entire state of Georgia on a par with Drake Forrest, you may want to reconsider that ridiculous rule."

"It is not ridiculous."

"If it makes you pass up you-know-who, it is."

"You're an impossible romantic, Dottie," C.G. insisted and spun around to return to her office when she ran smack into the man of their conversation. Drake.

352

It was like hitting the Rock of Gibraltar at a full run.

C.G. collapsed, off balance, but was kept from falling to the floor by Drake's powerful arms that captured her against his chest, one arm around her waist, the other over her shoulder. As he saved her, he also stepped on her right foot. Hard.

"Ow!" she howled.

"C.G., I'm sorry." His expression was stricken as he leaned back and gaped down at the foot she was holding gingerly off the floor. "Are you okay?"

C.G. put her weight on the throbbing foot, but it gave way, leading her to clutch Drake's arms for support.

Then she was up in his arms, and he was carrying her toward her office.

Shocked, her breath taken away, she saw the smirk of delight on Dottie's face as well as the amazed expressions on the faces of every teller on duty.

"Put me down," she ordered Drake. "You're making a spectacle of us both."

"Who cares? I'm getting you to a chair."

"There are chairs in the lobby."

"Too public. I need privacy to assess the damage."

"Are you a doctor?"

"EMT. I've had training."

That shut her up and she relaxed in his arms, a little, but not too much. She didn't want to enjoy the ride, after all.

When they arrived in her office, Drake eased her effortlessly down on the chair behind her desk, and C.G. couldn't help admiring his strength that had gotten her this distance without his even being out of breath. Obviously his physical activities involved more than plunging papers in and out of a briefcase.

Once she was settled, he sank to one knee and gently removed her low-heeled shoe. His hands on her foot, and the sensation they created, almost took C.G.'s mind away from the very real pain she still felt.

"I don't think it's broken," Drake said, his fingers light in their examination. He gave her a reassuring gaze. "Wiggle your toes."

She did.

"Good." His eyes found hers. "Pretty toes."

C.G. tried to pull away from him, but he wouldn't let her go.

"Can you move your ankle? Rotate your foot in a circle?"

C.G. moved it slowly, but she winced as she did.

"Good girl. You're probably all right, but you could have a hairline fracture. Watch it the next few days for swelling or turning black and blue. For now, let's get it elevated, and we need some ice—"

"I'll get it." It was Susie Black, wide-eyed and beautiful, with an adoring smile on her bright red lips. "We have some in the freezer in the kitchen." Her long false eyelashes floated down to her cheeks, but Drake didn't seem to notice the seductive gesture.

"Thanks, Susie," he said, barely looking at her, even when she sashayed out the door with considerable movement in her lower region.

"Is all this really necessary?" C.G. questioned when Drake moved another chair in front of her and carefully placed her foot on it, which did make it feel better, she had to admit.

"Absolutely. I want you to rest it for at least a half hour."

"A half hour? Drake, I have work to do."

"Which can wait."

C.G. threw him an incredulous look. "Did I hear that out of your own mouth—saying work can wait?"

"You may never hear it again."

"That's what I thought."

"Special people demand special consideration." His eyes were almost smoky when he gazed at her, and C.G. blinked under their scrutiny, then looked at the wall. She was having little control over the effect he had on her.

Susie returned with a plastic bag of ice cubes and a towel, which Drake took from her, wrapped together, and delicately placed on top of C.G.'s foot, kneeling down beside her again.

"There, how does that feel?" He looked at her with such caring and concern, C.G. almost forgot to answer, and when she did, her voice was breathless. "Fine, thanks."

"Good. You just rest."

"Is there anything else I can do?" Susie asked, leaning over to peer at C.G.'s foot, her long silky hair brushing Drake's shoulder.

"Not for now, thanks," he answered her.

"You just come get me if there is."

"I will."

C.G. felt like throwing up.

After Susie left, Drake said, "I'm sorry I was in the wrong place at the wrong time."

She gave him a tiny scowl. "You were supposed to wait in my office."

"I got bored when you were gone long enough to handwrite those phone bills for the last two years."

"So you went for coffee."

"Yep."

"Was it good, or was it the company you craved?"

His surprised look almost made C.G. grab her letter opener and cut her tongue out. Her question had had just enough edge to it to make her sound jealous of Susie Black, and the look of amusement that danced in Drake's eyes made her want to evaporate on the spot.

"The coffee was too weak, actually. I prefer it stronger." His mouth twisted upward in an infuriating grin.

Is he only talking about coffee, or is this his assessment of Susie Black as well? C.G. wondered. Not many men could ignore Susie's considerable physical charms. Would that be enough to satisfy a man like Drake Forrest? She didn't know him well enough to know that—yet.

He stood up and loosened his tie. "I'm going to get you some aspirin," he said and was out of the office before C.G. could tell him she had some in her desk. She watched him go straight to Susie who gave him a magnificent smile, two aspirins, and a cup of cold water, in that order.

Drake brought the aspirin back to C.G., concerned that she was more injured than she was letting on, and he berated himself for his clumsiness in causing the accident.

"I really am sorry about hurting you," he said, standing beside her desk, watching her, noting the gentle flush on her cheeks and that her hands shook when she put the cup of water down. It would take a few minutes for the aspirin to work.

"Please don't worry about it. I should have looked where I was going." Her smile was generous and sincere, and Drake found himself more and more drawn to her.

There were two sides to C.G. Grady—the professional businesswoman who was sophisticated, capable, and conscientious; and the devout Christian, willing to give up her lunchtime to bring comfort to someone else and brave enough to have a Bible on her desk.

He'd spotted the Bible the first time he'd walked into her office and he had wondered if she were one of those Christians who witnessed easily of her faith. He admired that, because it had never been easy for him to do.

If she asks about my own beliefs, what will I tell her? he pondered, knowing his spiritual life was far from active at the moment.

"Oh, Mr. Forrest?" He heard the sound of Susie's tight, short skirt swishing over bare legs before he saw her, returning with a gigantic ceramic cup with a football logo on it.

"I made some more coffee," she said in her little girl's voice. "This is stronger. I hope you'll like it."

With eyebrows raised in surprise, Drake took the mug from her long slender fingers tipped with scarlet polish, then tasted the liquid.

"It's just right." He sighed after a long drink and was given a woman's smile far different than the one he'd just received from C.G. "Did you bring some for Miss Grady?"

The come-hither smile on Susie's lips died, and she didn't even look at C.G. when she said, "No, I didn't." She made no move to correct her oversight.

"I'd appreciate it if you would."

"Well, okay."

She oozed out of the office, and Drake turned to C.G. and shrugged his shoulders. He wanted to tell her that Susie Black meant nothing to him. How could she? She wasn't real.

Instead, he sat down, loosened his tie, and said, "Thoughtful girl." It was all he could think of to say.

"Isn't she?" C.G. agreed, thinking how much more human Drake Forrest looked with a cup of coffee in his hand and his tie loosened. Either the caffeine or the effect of Susie had taken the edge off his voice, and C.G. felt his male charisma even from the distance he was sitting from her and wished she didn't find him so appealing.

Chapter 7

Drake looked at his watch. "Only another few minutes, and then we'll see how your foot is doing."

"I'm sure it will be fine," C.G. insisted.

"Let's hope. In the meantime, tell me, did you find the information we need?"

C.G. took a long sip of the lukewarm coffee Susie had reluctantly brought her and wondered where in heaven's name Dottie was. Had she found James?

"The file will be here in a minute," she told him.

"A minute?"

"Yes. Dottie's taking care of it."

Drake gave her a long, silent assessment that made her nervous, as though he were reading her mind and knew she hadn't the foggiest notion where that important file was.

Needing to do something to break the spell of his gaze, she called James Wyatt's number and left a message on his voice mail to come to her office as soon as he got back to his desk. Where was that man anyway?

Turning her attention back to Drake, she said, "Since you must have other things to do, why don't I call you as soon as I have what you want."

She thought he'd agree and leave, but he didn't. Instead, he leaned forward on the chair, resting his elbows on his knees, his hands clasped loosely in front of him—those powerful hands with a sprinkling of blond hairs on their backs—and, after looking at her long enough to give her a thorough case of nerves, said gently, "Where's the file, C.G.?"

She gulped, looked around the office, out in the lobby, up at the ceiling, anywhere but at Drake Forrest. She had just discovered another of his attributes: dogged determination, an admirable trait, to be sure—but not when she was the one being dogged.

His silence demanded she finally bring her attention back to him, and she looked up, to his eyes, which forcefully held her gaze so she could look nowhere else. "The file. . .is. . ."

"Not here," another voice, breathless from rushing, finished her desperate sentence, and C.G. looked up to see James Wyatt stumbling into the office.

"James, just the man I need," she cried, leaping to her feet before she remembered her injured foot, which reacted to being bounced upon by shooting

357

pain clear to her kneecap.

"Ow," she groaned, falling back into the chair.

In a second Drake was kneeling before her, concern contorting his face while his hands protectively enfolded her injured foot. "Are you all right?" he asked anxiously, to which question C.G. closed her eyes to will away the pain before she opened them again and said, "Dandy."

She also managed to see that James's hands were empty, and her heart sank. Either he didn't have the file, or Dottie hadn't gotten hold of him yet to tell him about it.

James's eyes bulged. "What happened, C.G.?" He leaned forward to watch this stranger's hands on the foot of the woman he had at one time adored.

"I had an accident," C.G. explained simply.

"The accident was me." Drake explained further, standing after getting a reassuring nod from C.G. that she was all right.

"I ran into him," C.G. went on. "Didn't see him there."

"Didn't see him?" James questioned, looking up at the tall hunk of a man, the breadth of whose shoulders equaled twice that of his own. "Sorry I was out of the office when you needed me, C.G. Dottie told me you want the phone bills file."

"Yes, we thought you might have it." C.G. wished Drake Forrest had gone away, so he wouldn't know now that her department could not keep track of a simple file.

"I don't."

"Oh. Well, in that case. . ."

"But I know where it is."

"Fine." Her spirits soared. "Would you please bring it to me right away?" She looked straight at Drake, her "problem" solved.

"I don't have it."

C.G.'s eyes traveled slowly to James. "Where is it then?"

Her assistant began nervously swaying from one side to the other, like a teenager about to make a dreaded speech. "In Blue Ridge."

"Blue Ridge?" Her voice was half an octave higher than usual. "How did the file get there?"

"I gave it to Gwen Johnson yesterday. She was here."

"Who's Gwen Johnson?" Drake interrupted.

"Our branch manager in Blue Ridge," C.G. answered him, then asked James, "Why did you give it to her?" She hoped her tone did not give away the fact that the file should never have left the office.

"Gwen is setting up next year's budget and wanted to figure her communications costs—how much her branch's phone lines will run. Since the information for all the branches is kept here—"

"Yes, but, James, you could have made copies for her of what she needed instead of giving her the entire file." C.G. was trying to keep her patience. It was not like James to be casual with bank records.

James began to fidget. "Ordinarily I would have, C.G., but I was totally swamped getting that information out for Drake Forrest, fancy consultant, that he demanded immediately—out of all reason, I might add—as though we have nothing else to do around here but cater to him—"

With a perfectly straight face, Drake took a step forward and thrust out his hand. "By the way, I'm Drake Forrest."

James's face turned crimson.

"Go on, James," C.G. urged him, feeling guilty that she hadn't introduced the men earlier and saved James the humiliation he was now feeling.

"W—well," he stammered, his voice barely audible, his eyes downcast, "since there's a meeting of all the branch managers here on Monday, and Gwen said she'd bring the file back then, I thought I'd save myself some time and just give her the whole thing—"

"Couldn't she have made the copies herself and left the file here?"

James looked at C.G. as though she were a firing squad of one and he the victim.

"She could have," he answered stiffly, "but I made a quick decision and just gave it to her. How was I supposed to know that file was going to become so all-fired important overnight?"

"All right, James." C.G. was surprised at his show of temper. Usually he was utterly emotionless. Of course, having Drake present added to his embarrassment, and she didn't want to hurt his feelings any more. "As long as we have the file back on Monday that will be fine." She gave him a supportive smile, which he did not return.

Drake cleared his throat. "I'm afraid it won't be fine," he said.

C.G.'s body jerked and she turned to gape at him. Then, knowing that she and he were about to lock heads, she suggested to James, whose shoulders were drooping despondently, that he go back to work.

"What about the file?" James asked.

"I'll take care of it," C.G. promised, and James left without looking at Drake again.

But C.G. looked at him. In fact, her eyes were sparking and Drake knew they were going to tangle.

"That branch meeting is scheduled for ten Monday morning, Drake," C.G. began, her voice firm, "and I'll have the information for you then."

"That's too late."

"Why?"

She wasn't backing down, and he liked that, liked the fact that she wanted answers, sensible answers. She was not a "yes" person. She had spunk.

"I need to do a lot of work on this acquisition over the weekend," he explained, "and this information is crucial—now." He paused, then added, "So you'll have to go after that file tomorrow morning first thing."

"I'm sorry, but I can't. I have plans."

"Cancel them."

C.G. took in a breath of surprise. "What difference will another two days make?" she challenged him. "We'll have the file here, in this office, Monday morning—"

"And I will have lost two days' work."

"Two days? Surely you aren't going to give Sunday to this, too?"

"Sunday's the same as any other day to me," Drake informed her. He expected more fireworks but was surprised when C.G.'s expression softened.

"I'm sorry that's so for you. For me, Sunday is the most important day of the week."

Drake glanced over at C.G.'s Bible on her desk. "Do you spend your entire Sunday in church?" he asked, remembering how he had gone both morning and evening to services years ago.

"All but about a half hour when they unlock the doors and let us go for lunch," she replied innocently, and Drake knew he was being teased.

"All right, all right, I deserved that."

"Yes, you did, because whether I go once, twice, or all day, it's because I want to. It's exhilarating to be in God's house worshiping."

"Why?"

"It's where the power is. The Source I need to keep me energized. It's where the knowledge is to help me live my life day after day. And the people are wonderful. As close as any family. We care about each other. Take care of each other."

"But can't a person still be a good Christian and not go to church?"

"I suppose, but why would one not want to go? It's only for a few hours a week compared with all the other hours we give to ourselves."

"The Bible says we are the temple of God and His Spirit dwells in us."

It pleased him to see the surprise register on her face. Somehow it was important that she know he was not a total heathen.

"You know the Scripture," she stated.

"Sure. I grew up with it, read it, and studied it. I've even taught Sunday school."

"Do you still do those things?"

"I read the Bible every once in awhile, but I don't have time for church."

"Don't take time, you mean."

Her statement was not one of condemnation but of fact.

"That's right. But I'm definitely a believer. I still pray."

"When you can."

"Yes."

"You must be starving then," she said, her eyes dancing with life.

"Starving?"

"A big man like you has to eat food to stay alive, right? Well, a Christian has to have sustenance to stay spiritually alive." Her expression was kind. "I'm glad we're both Christians, Drake. That will make our working together even nicer."

Drake's sensitivity deflated when she didn't preach at him about what he "should" be doing, and he felt a stab of authentic guilt, knowing they were miles apart on the importance they placed on living the daily life of a Christian. While it obviously meant a lot to C.G., it hadn't been a meaningful part of his life for years, and no one was to blame for that but himself and his ambitions.

"I think you'd better call Gwen Johnson about that file," he said, wanting to change the subject. He was uncomfortable with the searching way she was looking at him. "Tell her we'll pick it up tomorrow."

"We?"

"Yes. I'm going with you."

Chapter 8

C.G. gasped. "It really isn't necessary for you to go with me to Blue Ridge. It won't take long to find the information I need."

"I'm going, too." The words were gentle but had the finality of an iron door clanking shut.

"To hold my hand?"

He gave her a long, steady look. "Does it need holding?"

C.G.'s cheeks flamed, first at the thought of holding hands with Drake Forrest, then with the realization that that's not what he meant at all. He was just letting her know he thought her incapable of accomplishing the simplest of tasks.

"It's a long ride there and up into the mountains," she told him stiffly. "Over two hours."

"No problem. While I'm there I can check out that branch's network interface and get their circuit identification numbers. I'll have to do that with every branch."

"So you'll know which one to disconnect?"

"Yes."

"Can't the branch manager tell you?" She wasn't at all thrilled with the idea that he wanted to go with her.

"There are usually so many circuits—one for data, another for business lines, burglar alarm, automatic teller machines, and a half-dozen other things—most managers haven't a clue which is which."

"I see." C.G. took up the phone and started to dial a number, then stopped. "Do you always work seven days a week?"

"If there's a job that needs to be done, yes. And to answer your next question, no, I am not a workaholic."

"Working seven days a week is giving a good imitation of one."

"I work hard, but I'm not obsessed with work. It's the thrill of meeting a challenge head-on and conquering it that gives me energy, that drives me—relentlessly is a good word—to complete whatever project I'm on."

"So the struggle means more than the accomplishment?"

"Exactly. Haven't you ever felt that way? Been particularly proud when something you've worked on, grappled with, turns out well?"

C.G. put the phone down and looked at Drake with new understanding.

"Yes, I have felt that way a few times," she admitted, "and I admire your dedication to excellence, Drake. But a man needs more in his life than work."

He leaned back in his chair. "I have more of just about anything I want because of the success I've garnered."

"Fine. When was the last time you took a vacation with good friends or family?"

A deep frown furrowed his brow, and C.G. picked up the phone, dialed the number of the Blue Ridge branch, and waited for the connection to be made. "Gwen Johnson, please."

From the corner of her eye she saw Drake stand up and begin a thorough examination of her office.

His eyebrows raised when he saw two bronze plaques commending her on career accomplishments.

He leaned closer to peer at a watercolor of a seashore she had painted herself four years before while on vacation at St. Simons Island.

Then he picked up from her credenza the only personal picture in the room, one of her and her parents on a sailboat, the wind whipping her hair back, all three of them laughing into the wind. The frown, which he'd had all this time, deepened, and when he set the picture down with a thud, she guessed it had been a long time since he'd had a vacation with someone he loved.

Gwen's secretary came on the line and told C.G. that Gwen was on a long-distance call but knew she was waiting and would be with her as soon as she could.

"Thank you," C.G. said and passed the information on to Drake, who came over to her desk and sat down on one corner of it, one foot firmly on the ground, the other hanging.

"I promised Georgia National I'd have this project completed in time for the acquisition to take place by December 15. That's only four months, C.G."

"Perhaps that was an unrealistic promise."

"Not at all. I can do it."

"Why the rush?" she asked, piqued.

"GNB needs a tax write-off this year."

Their gazes locked and held, and all sound in the bank disappeared.

❈

"So, where are the pictures of your children?" Drake broke the tension between them. Even though she'd told him she wasn't married, a woman her age sometimes had several children.

"I have none," C.G. answered.

"Boyfriend?" Drake remembered asking this question before and receiving no answer. He wanted to know more about her private life. The vacation picture of her and her parents bothered him—first, because he couldn't remember the last time he'd had a fun day of sailing, which he enjoyed, and second, he couldn't remember the last time he had been with his parents when the three of them had been laughing.

A sudden envy of C.G. and her family made his throat go dry. His folks were terrific people, yet he spent very little time with them.

Before C.G. could answer his question about her having a boyfriend, Gwen came on the line and they spoke a few minutes.

C.G. put her on hold and told Drake, "The file's at her home, but she's not finished with it. She wants to keep it 'til Monday."

"What's the earliest we can use it at her house tomorrow?"

"Do you mean before or after the sun rises?" C.G. quipped, and Drake worked hard not to laugh.

"See if nine o'clock is okay," he suggested, and C.G.'s look was not endearing as she nodded slightly and asked Gwen the question.

A moment later she put down the phone and said, "Nine o'clock will be fine. She offered us breakfast, but I assured her we would eat before we got there."

"We will?"

"Yes, you at your house; I at mine."

"Oh." She was letting him know she didn't intend to spend one minute longer than necessary in his company.

"I'll pick you up at your house tomorrow at seven," Drake said. "Then you can tell me about your boyfriend."

"Why don't I meet you here at the bank instead, and not tell you anything about the men in my life?"

"Men?"

"Figure of speech."

"Is your house on the way to Blue Ridge?" he asked.

"Well, yes."

"Then it's better I pick you up there." He smiled. "You'll have more time for breakfast that way."

❀

C.G. knew he was right, but she also knew she wasn't sure she should let him know where she lived. He'd probably come banging on her door at four in the morning, forcing her to get up to accomplish something for The Acquisition.

"I really think meeting here would—"

"Waste time, C.G., and we don't have an unlimited supply of that with this project. Don't worry that I'll come banging on your door at four in the morning to force you to do something for this acquisition."

C.G. gaped at him.

"What's the matter?" he asked.

She was not about to tell him he had just read her mind, but all her senses were heightened, as though she were preparing for mortal combat.

This man was like no other she had ever met: determined, single-minded, brilliant, and so downright attractive she was afraid to spend too much time with him, but she could hardly humiliate herself by letting him know that. Driving to Blue Ridge and back was not going to be easy.

"You'd better pick me up at quarter to seven," she said. "If we take Highway 60 to Blue Ridge, you won't go much over thirty-five or forty."

"I drive fast, remember?"

"Not on this road, you won't."

❧

She wrote out directions to her house and handed it to him, almost reluctantly, and Drake wondered why. Then a thought came to him. "Did you have plans for tomorrow?" He should have asked her before. Even for him, his attitude had been heavy-handed, and he wouldn't blame her for being miffed.

"As a matter of fact, yes, I did have plans."

"Hopefully you'll be back in time." He wanted to see a smile on her face.

"Afraid not. The singles' group from our church is going to Barnsley Gardens. It's an all-day trip."

"With lots of walking?"

"Yes."

"Then it's a good thing you're not going."

"What?"

"Your foot." He pointed to it. "You don't want to overdo so soon after an accident. Being with me will help your foot to heal."

"That's only fair, I suppose, since you're the one who crushed my foot to begin with."

Drake didn't need a billboard to tell him C.G. was not thrilled to be working on Saturday, and that disappointed him about her. He'd given more weekends to his career than he'd stayed home or vacationed. If a job needed doing, then he did it. No complaining. No pouting. That was why more people weren't successful at their occupation—because they wouldn't make the total commitment needed to be the best at what they did. And being the best was right at the top of Drake's intentions.

Maybe he was being a jerk to make C.G. work on Saturday and give up some activity at her church, but nothing was more important than this acquisition, not even C.G. Grady's social life.

Besides, he wanted to be with her.

Chapter 9

C.G. did not want to go to Blue Ridge with Drake, and the reason was simple: It was the weekend, and she had other plans.

When a little voice inside her head suggested she was attracted to the man, made weak by his very glance, and wasn't sure how well she would handle being with him in the close confines of his sports car for several hours, she tried to deny it. "I admire his intelligence," she argued out loud with the voice while standing at the closet, contemplating what outfit to wear the next day. "And I respect his success. That's it."

Her hand reached for an avocado cotton jumpsuit, and she held the gauzy thing in front of her to see if it would do for a special occasion.

Special occasion? Being forced to drive over two hours to do work on Saturday that could be done just as well the following Monday, with a man who was a tyrant, a slave driver, a man too dedicated to his work, a man who had little sympathy for mistakes made? Special occasion?

She slammed the jumpsuit back among the other clothes, and her lower lip jutted out. She was not at all happy she'd had to cancel going with the singles from church to Barnsley Gardens, just to work.

Her eyes flitted over her considerable wardrobe, stopping at a conservative brown skirt, then examining a practical white linen dress. Wrong, both of them.

She reached again for the jumpsuit, which was made of material that was soft, supple, and feminine. The color was perfect for her red hair; and for the long day ahead it would be comfortable and sophisticated after a fine gold necklace and earrings completed the ensemble.

Will he like it, though? she wondered, then groaned and glared at the person glaring back at her from the full-length mirror she stood in front of.

The phone rang, and C.G. was surprised that it was Jeffrey Brandon, a youth minister she had met at a retreat three months before in St. Augustine, Florida, where he lived and served with a large, affluent church. They'd spent some time together those few days, discovering mutual interests—the most important one being their shared faith.

Since then, he'd called her several times and they'd had nice conversations. He'd sent her a birthday card.

"C.G., I'm on my way to a week-long conference in Gatlinburg, Tennessee and will be going through Cheston Saturday afternoon. I'd like to see you. Maybe for dinner?"

C.G. didn't hesitate. "Sounds wonderful, Jeffrey."

"Good. What time should I pick you up?"

C.G. thought about her trip with Drake to Blue Ridge. She would surely be back no later than three o'clock, which would give her plenty of time to shower and change for dinner with Jeffrey.

"How about six o'clock?"

"Great. I'll see you then. You pick a place you'd like to go."

"Do you like barbecued ribs?"

"Sure."

"All right; then dress casual. I'll look forward to seeing you again, Jeffrey." And she would.

While she had dated a number of men both before and after her engagement to Randolph, there had not been any, other than her ex-fiancé, with whom she would have wanted to spend the rest of her life.

Not that she was all that interested in getting married anymore. It seemed every way she turned, she saw men who put career above all else, including family and God. Better to be single, she'd just about decided, than have a husband in name only.

She gave Jeffrey directions to the house, doing so easily since she'd just done the same for Drake, who was coming from the same direction.

How different the two men were: Jeffrey was dark-haired, thirty-two, five foot nine, stocky of build, and a man of considerable intellect who thought deeply and spoke slowly. Moved slowly, too, to the point of being indecisive.

Drake, on the other hand, was tall, blond, and definitely decisive. Though he drove fast and acted quickly, there was nothing about his personality that hinted at rashness or recklessness.

He was a man determined to be in control of every situation, who knew exactly what he wanted to do and when. Slow was not in his vocabulary, she was sure.

C.G. stopped the comparison there, choosing not to think how Drake speeded up her pulse while Jeffrey only made her comfortable.

❀

In the great room of his apartment that night, Drake took from his briefcase some papers that C.G. had given him at the bank. It was only eight o'clock, so he figured he could spend a couple of hours going over them, then hit the shower and go to bed. He wanted to be wide awake tomorrow for the work that was to be done—and for C.G. Grady.

He was uncommonly looking forward to going into the mountains to Blue Ridge. Since moving from California to Georgia three years before, he had been

367

single-minded in pursuing his career and had learned little about the uniqueness of his newly adopted state. Tomorrow would be an education in the north Georgia mountains as well as a chance to accomplish some business.

Throwing himself down on the wide, leather sofa, he stretched long, muscular legs over its seven-foot length. Wearing khaki shorts and a matching tank top, he had freedom of movement, which he enjoyed after the confines of a business suit, shirt, and tie.

For the briefest of moments he thought about wearing something similar for the trip the next day, but then thought, *No, I'll be on business, not a date.*

A date? With C.G. Grady? Now there was a thought to wake up a man.

He reached for a cold glass of iced tea from the coffee table beside him and held it firmly in both hands as an image of C.G. came to mind, not that she was ever far from his thoughts since the first moment he'd seen her walking toward him across the lobby of the bank.

There was something about her that captured his attention and wouldn't let it go. She was no more beautiful than a half-dozen other women he knew, nor more intelligent than they. Witty? Yes, with a saucy sense of humor and an intriguing sparkle in her eyes.

What was it that she had that the other women in his life had not, that made him determined to get to know her better?

He was honest enough with himself to know that the main reason he wanted to go with C.G. to Blue Ridge was to be with her. She could have gotten the file herself; he could have done his work alone at another time. But he wanted to spend time with her, see what she was like outside the office.

He knew it wasn't always wise to have a relationship with someone he worked with, but he'd never met anyone quite like C.G. Grady. He was drawn to her in a way that was disquieting as well as exciting.

With renewed energy, he began shuffling through the papers he'd spread out on the coffee table.

Finding that one was missing, he got up and went to his briefcase, rummaged through files, and that's when he found the letter he'd received that morning from his mother. He'd tossed it into his briefcase, thinking he'd find a minute or two to read it during the day, maybe at lunch. Only he'd taken C.G. to lunch, and after that his mind had been on her and not on his mother's letter.

He slit open the envelope; it was the same stationery she'd used for the last letter—white parchment. Again, there was a single sheet of paper. What was written on it this time was different, though, from the other:

sophisticated
college graduate with degree in marketing/management

comes from an old, respectable Georgia family
sings solos in church

Now he laughed out loud, read the qualifications again, and called his mother, the matchmaker.

"You might as well give up, Mother, because I'm not interested in meeting this 'perfect' woman, whoever she is."

"Drake, won't you even give her a chance?"

"No."

"No?"

"Pretty lady, I appreciate what you're trying to do for me, and I'm sure this woman is terrific, but I want to find my own wife."

"I've already found her."

"Mother. . ."

"She's perfect for you."

"No one's perfect."

"She is."

"Mother. . .'

"All right."

"All right, what? You'll stop your campaign?"

"For the moment."

Drake growled deep in his throat, recognizing that stubborn, determined streak in his mother, from which he got his own. He couldn't be angry with her, for he knew she only wanted what was best for him.

What frustrated him, though, was that she just didn't realize that mothers and sons look at women with entirely different eyes. He wondered if ever, in the history of the world, there had been a successful love match arranged by a mother for her son. He doubted it.

He adored his mother and would do anything in the world for her—but not this. A man had to choose his own woman.

"Let's change the subject," she suggested cheerfully, and he knew the furrows on her brow had relaxed. "Can you come for dinner tomorrow night? Your father isn't feeling well, and a visit with you would cheer him up."

"What's the matter with Dad?" His father had always enjoyed robust health.

"General malaise. I don't think it's anything serious, Dear. He just works too hard in the garden. Thinks he should have the strength and vigor of a twenty year old."

Drake chuckled. "As far as I'm concerned, he does. I've worked with him. His energy is phenomenal."

"I agree. Anyway, I'm going to fix his very favorite meal, beef stew, and if you come, I'll bake you a pumpkin pie."

"Mom, after all these years being married to Dad, you still want to make him happy. You baby him. And me."

"You're both worth it," his mother insisted, and Drake felt the love in her voice.

"I'll be there, Mom, tomorrow night."

"Good."

"What time?"

"Six?"

"See you then."

He hung up reluctantly, not wanting to sever connections with this woman who cared so deeply about him and his father, and others as well.

From the time he'd been a small boy, he had seen her compassion for anyone who needed her, whether the person was a neighbor, a relative, someone from church, or a stranger who had no one else to turn to.

He couldn't help comparing her with the women he'd been dating lately.

Claudia was a successful attorney who was a killer in court. She was smart and clever, but when she spoke of her clients, they were just cases, not real feeling, breathing people. He'd dated her only six weeks before tiring of her icicle personality.

Genevieve owned her own accounting firm, but while she was remarkably beautiful, that was her best asset. She was as humorless as the numbers she dealt with day after day. Their relationship had lasted four weeks.

Was it a generational thing? Were women his age too intent on building their careers to respond to the needs of others? Neither Claudia nor Genevieve had ever baked him a pumpkin pie, even though they had learned it was his favorite, and he had taken them to many restaurants and even cooked for them in his apartment. They hadn't cared that he loved pumpkin pie, especially homemade.

He picked up the sheet of paper his mother had sent him and stared at it. She liked this woman. Should he give her a chance?

No. He tossed it into his briefcase, intending to take it to the office and put it with the other one. There was no way he was going to give in to his mother's matchmaking. It wouldn't work. He knew it wouldn't work. But he couldn't throw away her loving attempt either.

Chapter 10

C.G. was disgusted with herself for forgetting to pick up her mail at the post office, and though it was after nine o'clock, she put on a pair of jeans and a short-sleeved blue blouse and drove the five minutes, unlocked her post office box, and reached inside.

There was only one envelope, from her mom. She smiled but did not open it until she got outside and into her car where she started the engine and felt the relief of the air-conditioning. August in the South was a constant battle against heat and humidity, and she let the motor idle as she read.

great personality
highly intelligent
a little rough around the edges
adorable
protective

C.G. felt guilty that she'd forgotten to call her mom when she'd gotten the first teaser. She really did appreciate all her mom's efforts to make her life more interesting.

She studied the words again, then suddenly laughed out loud as she figured out what was going on. Two minutes after going through the front door of her house, she called her mom, who answered on the third ring.

"I know who 'he' is, Mom," C.G. enthused.

"How could you, Chryssie?" her mom responded. "I haven't given you his name."

C.G. chuckled softly, first of all because her mom refused to call her C.G., her initials which she used in business because they sounded far more sophisticated than Chrysanthemum Geraldine, and secondly because she was pleased with herself for having figured out the mystery before having to ask her mom to explain it to her.

"Names don't matter," she said. "It's what he is that's important, right?"

This strong, dependable, adorable, mischievous, rough-around-the-edges, protective, wavy blond-haired creature with a great personality had to be—*a dog*— a cocker spaniel, no doubt.

About a month ago, her mom had expressed concern that she must be lonely, living by herself in a house out in the country without anyone to share it with. "You need a dog. For protection and companionship."

"I don't need a dog, Mom," C.G. had tried to assure her. "I'm fine by myself."

"Your father is concerned about you."

"I appreciate that—"

"And so am I, so we have an idea how to fill the emptiness in your life."

"There isn't an emptiness, Mom."

Her argument had not changed her mother's mind, obviously, since now she'd received two notes describing just the animal her parents thought she needed.

Well, maybe it won't be so bad to have a pooch to come home to, a loving, warm body to snuggle up to and tell my problems to after a hard day at the bank.

"I hope you'll like him, Chryssie," her mother went on.

"It may not be a case of whether or not I like him, Mom, but whether or not I'll have time for him. I'm not home very much."

"He'll understand."

"But I don't want him to be lonely when I'm gone."

"He's used to being alone, Dear."

"I'm just not sure I'm ready for that kind of commitment."

"I wouldn't worry about that until you've been around him awhile."

"But that's just the trouble, Mom. If he's as adorable and protective as you say, I'll fall in love with him for sure."

"That's the whole idea, Chryssie."

"Mom, I want to meet him before I make any promises to love him for the rest of his life."

"Of course, Dear. That goes without saying."

"Is he at your house now?" C.G.'s curiosity was growing.

There was a pause before her mom responded. "No, he's not, but I'll call you as soon as I can arrange for him to be."

"Tell me one thing more, Mom. Is he big or small?" C.G. was sure they were talking about a cocker spaniel.

"Oh, he's big, Dear. Very big."

C.G. frowned. She'd have to get out her dog encyclopedia and see what other blond, wavy-haired breed there was. An Airedale, perhaps? "Is he too big for my house?" she asked, not wanting the animal to feel confined.

"Time will tell," came the ambiguous reply.

"I have to go, Mom, but thanks for caring. I'm glad we're talking about a dog here, and not a man; because if you were trying to set me up with a man, my answer would be *no!* You know how I feel about matchmaking."

"Yes, I do."

"Remember Sandra Bishop? Her parents found her the perfect husband, and they got married and then divorced within six months."

"I remember, Chryssie, and that was sad. Well, I'll talk to you soon, Dear." Her mother hung up, almost too quickly, C.G. thought.

She felt lighthearted all of a sudden. The idea of getting a dog had taken her mind off Drake Forrest, the threat he posed to her career, and the even more immediate threat he posed to her sensibilities. Tomorrow wasn't far off.

❀

The day didn't start out to be a disaster; it just ended that way.

At quarter to seven in the morning, when Drake knocked on C.G.'s door, the sun was bright, the clouds were clear, and C.G. climbed into his black Corvette with a sense of optimism that nothing would go wrong today that would tarnish her business reputation in his eyes.

"I'd never been in a Corvette before until you drove me to lunch," she told Drake as she settled into the contoured seat and put her purse on the floor by her feet. "It's fabulous." And intimate, she could have added—just two seats and a small cargo space behind them.

The high-backed bucket seat enfolded her in a private world that included only one other: the driver, whom she could touch without even stretching out her arm.

Her eyes traveled over the luxurious red interior; her fingers touched the deeply grained leather upholstery.

She'd often heard that a car mirrored the owner, and in this case, it was certainly true: This magnificent machine of power and class *was* Drake Forrest.

Drake turned the key in the ignition and brought the mighty engine to life.

"I'll bet this car is fast," C.G. said.

"Sure is. Zero to sixty in—"

"Don't tell me," C.G. interrupted, her eyes noting the words *air bag* on the dash in front of her. That should have helped her breathe easier, but for some reason it didn't.

When Drake stepped on the accelerator, they zoomed down the narrow, tree-lined country road, and C.G. swallowed hard. She was not a speed freak.

"Do you know exactly how to get to Gwen's?" he asked. "We don't want to get lost."

"And lose valuable time."

"Time is money."

"Yes, but there are more important things."

He threw her a serious look. "Name one. Without money the world does not move. Deny that."

"I can't. Of course money is necessary, but there's the inner man to consider, too."

"Which sounds like too serious a conversation for this ride."

C.G. accepted Drake's closing of that topic, but she hoped that in the months they'd be working together he'd share something of his spiritual life with her.

Why people did or did not follow the Lord was fascinating to her. She loved to talk about it with anyone she met, and she prayed every day that she'd be an effective witness. Some wonderful experiences had come her way.

"I like your outfit," he said five minutes later.

"I like your shirt."

The truth was, she liked him *in* his shirt, which was exactly the same color green as her jumpsuit and fit snugly across his considerable chest. Like her dress, it was also short-sleeved, exposing his long, muscular arms—

"I hope we don't look like those old married couples who purposely dress alike," he said, unknowingly interrupting her runaway admiration.

"I'm sure no one will take us for that," C.G. murmured, settling herself deeper in the leather seat, all too aware of how easily she could reach out and touch his hand, ruffle his hair. . .she clasped her hands firmly together on her lap and squeezed 'til her knuckles turned white.

❀

Drake was tense. It was all he could do to keep from reaching out to touch C.G.'s hand or ruffle her hair. His attraction to her was far stronger than he'd realized, and being only inches apart in the Vette didn't help keep his libido in check one bit.

No desk separated them here, as it did in her office. No other people looked on, as they could at the bank.

He smelled her perfume, heard more perfectly the lilt in her voice, the gentle Southern accent, and he knew his willpower was going to be put to the test before this trip was over.

Now was the perfect time to find out if she was off-limits. No use tying himself into romantic knots if she was committed to another man. "So, C.G. Grady, are you ready to answer the question I've put to you twice now?"

"What question is that?" she asked him innocently.

"Is there a special man in your life?"

There was a long pause before she answered, "No, there's not."

"I find that hard to believe."

"Thank you." She blushed, and he was amazed. When was the last time he'd seen a woman blush?

Then she caught him off guard by boldly asking, "How about you?"

"Not married. Not engaged," he told her, then stopped himself just in time from saying, "But falling in love," an incredulous thought that had just sailed into his mind.

"Divorced?" she asked.

He laughed then. "Not that either. What other personal information would you like to know about me?" He captured her gaze and held it with his, and the most powerful feeling swept over him, that of a great contest beginning, a battle of wills. He wanted her, and she knew it. She was drawn to him, and he knew it.

"Frankly, Mr. Forrest," she said with considerable verve, "I couldn't care less about your personal life."

Drake laughed heartily, and the boisterous sound reverberated through the Corvette, telling them both that he didn't believe her and that they had moved to the second stage in their relationship: They were no longer strangers.

Chapter 11

The countryside they traveled through was like a timeless picture, its verdant hills dotted with tall pines, hardwood forests, and fat, black cattle grazing by ponds and streams. Houses, set far back from the road, nestled among healthy green grass and flower or vegetable gardens tenderly cared for and abundant in the rich red clay of Georgia. Occasionally there were two or three long rectangular chicken houses standing end to end, old and abandoned, their roofs rusted and dilapidated.

Far more present were small brick churches with white shutters, particularly Baptist but sometimes a Methodist or Church of God. They sat on knolls and hills, open land around them, with white steeples pointing to the sky as if to say, "Our Father is in heaven," and they reminded passersby that people worshiped in this county.

Lying quietly beside most of these churches were graveyards, neatly trimmed and colorful with bouquets of fresh and fake flowers at nearly every headstone.

C.G. pointed out to Drake various scenes of interest, but neither of them were forgetting his lengthy laughter over her assertion that she didn't care a whit about his personal life. They knew the mood had changed between them. They chatted amiably about serious things and not-so-serious things. They laughed together. They were silent at times, enjoying the sun-bright summer scenery.

Then, about halfway to Blue Ridge, C.G. realized what was happening: She was enjoying herself with him. It had to stop. She did not want to be his friend. Well, not his good friend. They would be working together for many months to come, and she absolutely was not going to get involved with him, even though every part of her was affected by Drake Forrest's very presence.

They took a corner marked thirty miles per hour at forty-five, and C.G., who found herself nearly in Drake's lap, complained, "Does everyone from California drive fast?" He'd told her he'd grown up there and graduated from a university in southern California.

"Am I going too fast?"

"For me but obviously not for you." She sighed with relief when the road straightened out and she could sit up.

❀

Drake looked over at her, saw the paleness of her face, and realized only her ladylike demeanor had prevented her from demanding he slow down, which even he now knew he should do on this winding, two-lane country road.

They were approaching an old building on the left labeled Smith's General Store, and Drake pulled into the graveled parking lot and stopped the car.

The store looked like it had stood on this spot for a hundred years and hadn't received a lick of paint since the original coat. There was rust around the metal door and windows that one could hardly see through.

"Let's get a soft drink," he suggested, reaching over to touch her hands, which were clenched together. Expressionless, she pulled her hands away from him.

Unfastening his seat belt, he gingerly got out of the car and hurried over to C.G.'s side and opened her door. She just sat there until he extended his hand to help her out. For a moment he thought she wasn't going to accept his offer, but then, without looking at him, she put her hand in his and squeezed it for support as she raised herself from the seat.

Her fingers were cold and trembling, and he wasn't egotistical enough to think it was because he was holding them. She was scared. Or sick.

"Are you okay?" he asked, feeling concerned and guilty.

"No."

"Is your stomach upset?"

"Yes."

"Do you have a headache?"

"Yes."

"You should have told me to slow down a long time ago," he gently chastised her.

"I'm not a backseat driver."

"But you were sitting in the front," he said with a grin. "Do curving roads bother you?"

"Only when I'm the passenger."

"C.G., I'm sorry."

She pushed by him and went into the store and walked straight to an old Coke machine. He followed her. Now there were dapples of perspiration on her upper lip, and he hoped she wasn't going to throw up, although better here than in his Vette.

"What do you want?" he asked, fishing change from his pocket.

"A Seven-Up or Sprite, please, and thank you."

"For what? Making you sick?"

The coins dropped down and the machine grumbled as it spat out its possession. Drake opened the can for her and watched, concerned, as she took a small sip. Then another.

What a jerk I am, he thought.

She closed her eyes and shuddered, then slowly opened them and looked at him. Drake stopped breathing. Her eyes, so large and expressive, like fine blue Wedgwood, with a darker rim around the iris, wrapped him in their beauty and captured his heart. He could not and did not want to look away.

In that moment, he knew she was precious to him and that he wanted to take care of her.

"I really do apologize for speeding," he said, wishing he could take her sickness on himself.

She smiled wanly and laid a gentle hand on his arm, which seared his flesh. "I should have told you how I get. It's my own fault for trying to be brave."

"You are brave."

"Stupid, you mean."

"You're wonderful."

Their gaze took on a new depth, telling each other that something was happening between them, and Drake put his hand over C.G.'s, which was still on his arm, and leaned closer to her.

She did not move away, and when he kissed her—lightly, not hurriedly—a rush of joy plunged from his head to his feet, and Drake felt as though this were the first kiss he had ever given a woman. To him, at this moment, it was the first kiss that had real meaning.

He was in love.

"Can I help you folks?" A rough voice from behind them interrupted their tender moment, and Drake glared at the bearded old man for his inexcusable clumsiness in not noticing they were not interested in store merchandise.

"We're fine," Drake said, hating to leave the soft lips he had just enjoyed, hating to allow space to come between him and C.G. With irritation, he jammed some more coins into the ancient Coke machine and waited 'til it gave him a Classic Coke, his favorite. Then he took a long swig.

"Well, just look around," the man said. "If you don't see what you want, ask for it." He ambled off.

Drake looked at C.G. and was delighted to see she was trying to keep from giggling. She must be feeling better; therefore, he was feeling better, too.

"I think I'll browse a bit," she said. "I'll be ready to go again in a few minutes."

"Take your time," Drake insisted, reaching out to caress her cheek. "We don't have to rush. We won't rush any more today. On this whole trip."

C.G. gave him a you've-got-to-be-kidding look, as though not believing that he was willing to travel at less than warp speed.

"I'm going to check out the fishing gear. I see some over there." He pointed.

"Oh, I'll look, too."

"Don't tell me you're a fisherman."

"Absolutely not. I'm a fisherwoman."

Drake chuckled. "I stand corrected."

"My daddy taught me to fish when I was only seven. I have a knack for it."

Drake's eyebrows raised. "A knack?"

"Yes, although sometimes I think it's because I have red hair."

He laughed out loud. "You're putting me on."

"No," she insisted. "Whenever I go out with other people, I always catch fish, even when no one else does. I think, as a redheaded person, I have some unique scent on my hands that fish die for. Literally."

"Now I've heard everything." He placed his hand lightly on the back of her waist and directed her toward the aisle that had shelf after shelf of baits, lures, poles, and accessories.

They examined the merchandise, exchanging comments, and Drake was amazed to find a woman who loved fishing as much as he did, although one would never know it in counting the number of times he'd been fishing in the last five years. Where had his free time gone? Certainly not for fishing.

He remembered seeing a sign a mile or so back that had pointed to the Toccoa River. Why not buy a bunch of gear and go spend an hour on the bank fishing? Even before the thought was fully formed in his mind, he knew he wouldn't do it. He had forgotten how to be spontaneous.

"I don't believe your theory, you know," he said to C.G., and she gave him a frown.

"Is that a challenge, Mr. Forrest?"

"Sure is, Miss Grady, if you're not afraid to take it."

"Afraid? Sir, I'll fish you under the dock. Or bank. Or wherever we go to prove my point."

"It's a date."

❈

C.G. took in a quick breath and realized what she'd just agreed to, which she couldn't agree to, and wouldn't.

Hoping Drake would understand, she said gently, "I don't think that's a good idea."

"What isn't? Our fishing together?"

"Our having a date to go fishing."

"Why?"

C.G. put down a package of spinner bait. This was an awkward moment. She knew she would enjoy being with Drake, fishing, or doing absolutely anything at all. She was liking him far more than she should. She had even let him kiss her, which had been a big mistake. She had to stop what was happening right now, before things got out of hand.

"I'd enjoy fishing with you, Drake, but we both know we should not socialize since we have to work together for months. That would inevitably lead to. . . complications."

"Complications," he said reflectively, as if tasting the word in his mouth to see if he liked it or not.

She waited for his reaction, not knowing him well enough to even guess what that might be, but when he began nodding his head up and down, she thought he understood and shared her feelings.

"So you think there will be complications, C.G., if we start dating while we're working together?" he said.

"Yes, don't you?"

"Yep. In fact. . ." With one hand he cupped her chin and slowly, very slowly, moved his face toward hers and left a lingering kiss on both her cheeks. ". . .I intend to bring on all the complications I can."

She gaped at him.

"Consider yourself warned, Miss Grady. From this moment on, you're mine."

Chapter 12

Drake walked jauntily out of the store into the bright sunlight, and C.G. stared after him, watching the screen door slam behind him, not believing what she'd just heard. She was his? He was staking a claim on her, as though she were a piece of property with no say in the matter?

The grizzled old man behind the counter kept looking from Drake to C.G., then to Drake, then back to C.G. He knew what was coming, and it didn't take long.

A smoldering surge of adrenaline sent C.G. charging after Drake, where she caught up with him at the front of the car and squarely placed herself in front of him.

With barely controlled anger she said, "I'm warned, am I? I'm yours, am I?" She reached up and tweaked his nose—hard.

"Hey, cut that out."

Her eyes were swirling dark storm clouds. "Do I leap into your arms now or wait 'til I'm bidden?"

"Whichever." His grin was devilish.

She reached for his nose again, but his hand caught her wrist. "One bruised nose a day is enough, thanks. Why are you upset?"

C.G. struggled to be free of him, but he wouldn't let her go. "I don't appreciate the fact that you have decided I am going to be yours. Don't I have a say?"

"You did. You said we weren't going to get involved because of possible complications."

"And then you said you were going to bring on all the complications you could, and from that moment on I was yours."

"That's about it."

"No, it isn't."

"I know you like me, C.G. You know I like you. So why fight our feelings for each other?"

"I need a whole lot more than physical feelings for a man before I enter a relationship."

"What do you need? Whatever it is, I'll give it to you."

He was calm and sure of himself, and C.G. knew he hadn't a clue what a Christian woman wanted in the man she'd love.

He let her wrist go as she shook her head sadly. "You're not the man for me, Drake."

"Explain why not, when I know you're as attracted to me as I am to you."

"I can't deny the attraction, but I won't foster it."

"Why?"

"Because years ago I learned that there are family men and there are businessmen. You are a businessman. In love with the business. Married to the business. First comes the business, then making money; finally wife and children come in last."

"Aren't you being a little judgmental for only knowing me a few days?"

She tilted her chin up in determination. "I don't think so, from the conversations we've had. I've known your type before."

They stood, staring at each other for long moments while each tried to figure out the other, until C.G. finally decided she was foolish to even be having this conversation. Drake Forrest was just a man used to getting his way, in business as well as with women. What he wanted he took. Well, he would not have her.

"There will never be anything between us, Drake. Now, let's get on to Blue Ridge." She turned sharply and strode to the car and got in.

Drake still stood where he'd been, only now his hands were on his waist and he was staring at her thoughtfully.

"Blue Ridge it is," he agreed, and when he got into the car, he didn't slam the door or say anything harsh to her, which she'd thought he would do.

In fact, his whole demeanor was that of a man who had plotted his course, run into an obstacle, cleared it out of the path, and was on his way again.

When he began to whistle, C.G. got worried. She hadn't said or done a thing to deter him.

"I think there's more to your resistance of me than that I'm a dedicated businessman," he said after five minutes of driving.

"No, I just recognize a workaholic when I see one, and that attitude has already changed your life."

"How so?"

"You don't have time for God because you're too bent on accomplishing."

"So I'm not acceptable because I don't do certain things? I told you I was raised in the church."

"But not attending now."

"I still read the Bible. Do I have to read it so many minutes a day to be a 'real Christian'? I still pray. Do I have to be on my knees at certain times in order to be okay in your eyes?"

C.G. looked at him gravely. "Don't mock my beliefs, Drake."

"Those aren't beliefs; they're traditions. C.G., I'm a decent man. A moral man."

"I'm sure you are." The tone of her voice showed she meant it.

"But that's not good enough for you?"

"It's not a question of your being good enough; it's a question of priorities. I want more than just a good man, a well-intentioned man. I want a man who loves the Lord and His principles as much as I do and wants to live by those standards every day."

When he did not respond she added, "I think you know what I mean."

He reached for her hand, took it, and held it up to his lips. "Yes, I do know, but that still isn't going to stop me from wanting you."

C.G. took her hand away from him. "It should."

❈

He grinned, his familiar self-confidence surging to the fore once again. "I'm a confident man," he said. "One of two things is going to happen in our future together: Either I'm going to learn to put other things before business and become the sterling Christian man you want, or you're going to change your mind about how important those are in a relationship."

He smiled the challenge over to her and was not expecting her to jab him lightly in the arm.

"There's a third possibility that you've overlooked, Mr. Forrest."

"Oh? What's that?"

"It's that neither of us will change our minds, and we'll go our separate ways."

He almost stopped the car to take her in his arms and kiss that smug look off her mouth. She was so sure of herself, what she wanted from life and a man. Well, they'd see which one of them gave in.

For the rest of the drive to Blue Ridge, they did not raise the question of their relationship again, but they did talk a little, of unimportant things. Both of them, though, knew a line had been drawn in the sand.

Drake expected C.G. to step over that line and give in to him, regardless of his relentless ambition and lukewarm commitment to God.

❈

C.G. knew she wouldn't but hoped Drake could someday find meaning in a faith that had once been his.

In the meantime, she was wise enough to know she should guard her heart carefully. There was a lot about this man she admired and probably more she would come to admire if they pursued a personal relationship. Better to close off her feelings right now before she was involved, rather than later when real complications could arise.

She tried to relax and enjoy the interesting countryside where people weeded in their front yards or sat in monstrous oak rockers on their front porches and big, scruffy dogs laid out by metal mailboxes at the end of their owners' driveways and watched the traffic, or lack of it, go by in either direction.

They passed antique shops that didn't have a single car parked in front and old stores that were being swallowed up by that wonder weed of the South, kudzu, which crept up telephone posts, along fences, and over anything else in its relentless path to control its territory, sometimes growing as much as a foot a day.

Gazing over a particularly prolific valley of the leafy, green vine, C.G. started to smile as it suddenly took on the personification of Drake Forrest. Would he give up on her now that he knew she was serious about not marrying a man wedded to his work, or would he pursue her relentlessly, like the thorny tendrils of the kudzu vine, attempting to claim her despite her resistance, just as the kudzu dominated anything in its way?

She laughed out loud.

"What's so funny?" he asked.

"Kudzu. Just kudzu."

To his puzzled look, she offered no explanation, but she would never look at the stuff again without thinking of Drake Forrest.

※

Drake wondered if C.G.'s thinking of kudzu had anything to do with him. Failing to see any connection, he was, nonetheless, glad she was in a good mood and not put off by their serious statements of position a few minutes before.

"So," he said, "tell me what C.G. stands for."

C.G. shook her head back and forth.

"State secret, huh?"

"That's right."

"Not even to be revealed to good friends who promise not to tell the news media?"

She turned and mouthed the word *no*.

"I want to be your friend, C.G. Grady."

"As well as my sweetheart?"

"Yes, what could be better?"

"One is fine; the other impossible."

He didn't argue with her, but he wasn't changing his plan one bit. He knew a good thing when he saw it, and C.G. Grady was the finest woman he'd met in a month of Sundays.

Chapter 13

They arrived in Blue Ridge, population 1,400, elevation 1,750 feet, two hours after they'd started from Cheston, but finding Gwen Johnson's house proved a challenge. She'd obviously left out some part of the directions, and it was when they were turning around to go back the way they'd come that the first disaster struck.

Drake pulled into a long driveway and was starting to back out when C.G. warned, "Be careful of the ditch on either side of the drive. There's tall grass covering it."

"Not to worry," Drake responded cheerfully, looking over his right shoulder. "Everything's under control."

That's when he cut the corner too soon, and the right rear of the Corvette slipped into the ditch.

C.G. cried out and clutched Drake's arm, thankful that in this intimate car he was so close. A word slipped out of his mouth that was not one C.G. would have used, but she understood its meaning and Drake's frustration.

He put the car in forward gear and tried to go ahead, but the right rear of the Vette was grounded. They were royally stuck, though not dangerously so, for the ditch was not deep.

Drake got out to assess the damage and assured C.G. she'd be okay if she stayed inside, which she did, dreading to think what might be wrong with his lovely, expensive car. "We'll have to get a tow truck," he yelled from behind the car after a minute's examination. "I'll go up to the house to make the call."

In a minute he was back. "No one's home."

Obviously he was disgusted, but he wasn't mad, and C.G. knew why: He was a problem solver. After initial frustration, his orderly mind kicked into gear, attacking the problem, not wasting energy on temper. She liked that.

"I don't see another house on this road," he said, leaning his arms through the open window of the driver's side, "so we'll have to walk."

"We?"

"I won't leave you here alone since I have no idea how far the nearest house is or how long I'll be gone." He gave her a lopsided grin of contrition. "Sorry about this."

She shrugged. "Accidents happen." She didn't vocalize the fact that in the high heat and humidity, they'd be soaked with sweat in a matter of minutes. Not something to look forward to.

Climbing across the driver's seat, C.G. got out, helped by Drake's strong hands, and the two of them were just starting to walk away when a massive Chevy truck rumbled down the road toward them. Drake waved his arms, the truck stopped, and a big, burly man, carrying more than two hundred pounds on a short frame, got out and walked toward them.

"Y'all need some help?" he asked, his deep, gravelly voice matching the two-days' growth of beard on his face.

"Afraid so," Drake answered. "Do you have a chain?"

"Yes, Sir. We'll have that baby outta there in a jiffy." His eyes traveled from one end of the gleaming Corvette to the other. "Sure is one fine car."

"That she is."

In less than five minutes the Vette was on level ground and Drake was shaking the man's hand. "I can't thank you enough. Your coming along just when you did, here in the middle of nowhere, was a miracle."

"Could be." The big man smiled broadly, revealing one missing tooth right in front.

Drake reached for his billfold, but the man stopped his hand. "No need for that, Sir." He reached into his own pocket and pulled something out and handed it to Drake. "Have a good one," he yelled, getting back in his truck. He drove away.

C.G. went over to Drake and looked at what the man had given him. It was a pewter cross, small enough to fit in the palm of a hand.

"I didn't even get his name," Drake said quietly, staring at the cross, then down the road toward the truck that had just disappeared over a hill.

All C.G. could think was what a marvelous testimony to leave behind after a work of kindness.

Drake was quiet during the rest of the drive to Gwen Johnson's house, which they found in another few minutes, and C.G. respected that silence, only interrupting it to give directions. But when they finally arrived and parked in the small driveway of the one-story cedar home, Drake said, "I need to get under the car to see if there's anything wrong."

"Oh, I hope nothing is," C.G. responded.

"Me, too, but I won't drive home without checking."

"Of course not. Here comes Gwen."

A tall, slim career woman in her early forties, with short, wavy hair, came out on the front porch and greeted them, her effervescent personality immediately apparent.

"Oh, C.G., I'm sorry to have caused you so much trouble, to make you drive all this way. How do you do, Mr. Forrest; I'm honored to meet you. If there's anything I can do to make your work easier, please let me know. Gracious, isn't this a hot day? Just feel that humidity. Let's go inside."

It was a pretty house, not spacious but neat, done in peach and blue, the colors repeating themselves in the furniture and accessories. Mostly, it was a cheerful place with oversized windows that let in lots of Georgia sunshine. And it was air-conditioned, for which both C.G. and Drake were thankful.

"I've put the folder you want to look at on the kitchen table," Gwen told C.G. and Drake, mostly Drake, C.G. noticed. "And I'll busy myself in an office down in the basement. If you need me, just call down the stairs. There's coffee already brewed, and iced tea and soft drinks in the refrigerator. Help yourself. Chocolate chip cookies are in the cookie jar, and I've made tuna sandwiches for lunch—"

"Gwen, Gwen," C.G. stopped her. "You've gone to too much trouble for us."

"It was no trouble at all," Gwen insisted. Turning to Drake she said, "I think it's exciting that we're going to be a part of Georgia National."

"It's a major step," Drake said with a smile that would turn any woman's head. He then explained about their accident.

"How awful," Gwen commiserated. "That beautiful car. Those awful ditches."

"I need to check it out for damage, although I won't know much 'til I get it jacked up. Let's just hope we can get home tonight."

C.G.'s eyes widened. "You think there's that possibility?"

"Could be."

"Can I help you in any way?" Gwen volunteered. "Hold something?"

"Thanks, I'd appreciate that."

He and Gwen started out the door, but he turned back. "Start without me on those bills, C.G. I'll be in as soon as I can."

C.G. was irritated with herself for not offering to help, too. As she made her way to the table to start her work, she could not help but think how easily Drake gathered women to him: Susie Black at the bank, and now Gwen Johnson.

I am not jealous, C.G. told herself, and she pulled the bills from the file and began her research, but she knew exactly when ten minutes had passed and Drake and Gwen were still not back in the house with word on the damage to the car.

When she heard them laughing outside, it galled her that Drake had been in such an all-fired hurry to get here, get the information, and get home, but now he had enough time to chat and laugh with a woman he'd only just met.

"We're in trouble," Drake called out as he burst into the house with Gwen following close behind.

C.G. stood up to get the news.

"The oil pan's been ruptured. There's a leak."

"That's bad, isn't it?"

"We don't go anywhere until it's fixed. Hopefully a local garage has another one that'll fit." He turned to Gwen. "Could you recommend a place? Or a mechanic? I want someone good; no weekend hotshot."

"I know just the man," Gwen declared, grinning from ear to ear as if she had just won a million dollars. "Henry Jenkins. Most folks in town use him. There's nothing he doesn't know about cars."

"Great. Can you give me his number?"

"I'll do better than that, Drake; I'll call him for you myself."

C.G. sat down. *I am not jealous*, she thought, wishing Gwen weren't quite so efficient and already on a first-name basis with Drake.

While he talked to the mechanic about the Corvette, Gwen poured him some iced tea from a large, glass pitcher in the refrigerator, then took a half-dozen plump, chocolate chip cookies from a cookie jar and set them on the table with his drink.

C.G. cleared her throat. She was thirsty and hungry.

Gwen giggled. "C.G., I'm sorry. I've overlooked you. What can I get you to drink?"

"Anything diet will be fine."

"Okay."

Gwen fixed her a Diet Dr. Pepper but didn't give her a plate of cookies. "May I have one of Drake's cookies, Gwen? They look delicious."

"Silly me," Gwen exclaimed. "Of course. Help yourself. I have lots more for the man."

For the man, but not for me, C.G. surmised.

She knew the cookies would be delicious. They were. She knew they would still be warm. They were. She had always liked Gwen Johnson. That might soon change. She stuffed another cookie into her mouth, despite how many calories it contained.

Drake plunked the phone back on its receiver. "Like I said, we're in trouble." He came over to the table and faced the women. "Henry knows he can fix the Vette."

"I knew he could," Gwen exclaimed, clapping her hands enthusiastically. C.G. remained quiet.

"The problem is he doesn't have an oil pan on hand at his garage. So he's going to check Cleveland or Cheston at the dealerships there, and if they have one he'll go pick it up, then come here to put it on."

"Does he think he'll find one?" C.G. asked, seeing what kind of trouble they could be in if Henry couldn't locate just what was needed. It was Saturday. Tomorrow was Sunday and, in most of the surrounding small towns, nearly every business would be closed. They might not get the Corvette fixed 'til Monday.

Tonight Jeffrey Brandon was taking her to dinner.

The worst problem, of course, was the possibility of spending the night under the same roof as Drake.

"You can have faith in Henry," Gwen declared, putting more cookies on the plate to replace the ones C.G. had taken, winning for herself Drake's dynamite smile of appreciation. "If he says he'll find one, he will. And if he finds one, he'll work overtime to put it on."

Drake nodded. "That's what he told me."

Gwen sat down in a chair next to him. "But on the wee chance that the car can't be fixed, you don't have to worry about where to spend the night. You can stay right here."

"Oh?"

"Yes."

C.G. coughed.

"You and C.G., of course."

"How many bedrooms do you have, Gwen?" C.G. asked, sure there was hardly 1,500 square feet in the house.

"I have two."

"Two?"

"Two."

C.G. and Drake looked at each other, and she was sure she saw one corner of his mouth raise. *If he thinks I'll spend the night in the same house with him, getting cozy, he has another thing to learn about what kind of a man will win my heart. Certainly not one who has only one thing on his mind.*

Chapter 14

L et's cross that bridge when we come to it," Drake suggested.

"Good idea," Gwen agreed, rising. "I'll leave you two to your task. I'll be downstairs if you need me."

After she was gone, Drake said, "Gwen is great, isn't she?" He gobbled down the last chocolate chip.

"A regular lamb," C.G. agreed, her eyes down, trying to concentrate on the pages before her, looking for the designation that would identify an analog line.

She didn't want to think of the fact that not only had she missed going with the singles today, but she might also miss seeing Jeffrey tonight if they couldn't get the car fixed early, not to mention her greatest concern—spending even more time than necessary with Drake Forrest.

Back at Smith's General Store he had made it abundantly clear where he wanted and intended for their relationship to go. Well, he might know his own mind, but she knew her mind as well: There was not going to be a relationship.

It took less time than they'd expected to locate the billing code that identified the number of analog data circuits Ashford Bank and Trust utilized. There were fifteen.

That was more than long enough, however, for Gwen to come back up to the kitchen from her basement office and fix them whopping tuna sandwiches on hoagie rolls for lunch, accompanied by fresh, sliced tomatoes and homemade brownies.

At the end of the meal, C.G. was ready for a nap but opted instead to sit outside on the front porch while Drake called the garage to see how Henry's search for an oil pan was progressing.

When he joined her a few minutes later, it was easy to deduce from the stern look on his face that he had not heard what he'd wanted.

"Henry's found the pan," he told her, "but it's in Atlanta, and it will be three or four hours before he can get it, come by here, and replace the ruptured one."

His exasperated sigh led C.G. to say, "You're thinking we'll be lucky to get it on today at all, aren't you?"

"Right."

Drake sat down beside her, both feet solidly on the ground, so the swing did not move.

"This is proving to be a costly trip," C.G. said. "You're losing not only a lot of your valuable time, but money for your car as well."

Drake nodded. "That's the truth. Things better go smoother than this from now on, or we'll never get this acquisition sewed up by the end of the year."

"Sure we will," C.G. insisted. "Things like this just happen, that's all."

"Not with me, they don't."

C.G. frowned. "I take it you're saying that with proper planning and careful supervision, problems don't arise."

"Precisely."

"How would you have planned not to back into that ditch that damaged the car?"

He threw her a thoughtful look, then began to smile. He also started the swing moving back and forth. "That was worse than bad planning," he said. "It was just plain dumb driving."

"It was an accident."

"So says the eternal optimist. That's what you are, isn't it?"

C.G. thought for a moment. "I guess so. I much prefer to find a positive solution than wallow in self-recrimination."

Drake chuckled and put his arm around the back of the swing. "No wonder you're different than any woman I've ever known."

"That's a broad statement."

"But true." He turned to face her, his eyes studying her lips. "You are different, C.G. Grady. I don't know all the reasons why yet, but I will someday soon."

He leaned forward to kiss her, but C.G. put a hand between them.

The swing stopped, and C.G. wasn't breathing. The natural woman in her wanted Drake's kiss. The rational woman knew it shouldn't happen.

She lowered her hand from his strong, firm mouth, down to his chest, where she felt the vibrant beating of his heart. And it matched her own.

"I want to kiss you, C.G.," Drake whispered, his eyes imploring her to forget her resolve and surrender to the delicious moment of his tenderness.

"I. . .I want it, too."

"Then let me—" He leaned toward her, but she backed away from him.

"Please don't tempt me."

He didn't smile, and she was glad. She didn't want his pursuit of her to be a game for him, a pleasant challenge to add zest to the tedious chore of merging two banks.

"Can I tempt you?"

"Of course. I'm not made of stone."

"No, you're not, but you're as exquisite as the finest marble statue of any Greek goddess."

C.G. laughed lightly. "I am not a goddess."

"You could be in my eyes."

She shook her head no. "You need to be seeing God."

"Maybe I see Him in you."

C.G. took a deep breath and let it out very slowly. Was she being a good witness for Jesus? Somehow she doubted it, for Drake didn't seem to understand what she was trying to say about priorities. "I wasn't playing hard to get earlier today, Drake," she said, "when I told you I don't want a relationship with a workaholic."

"You keep using that word, C.G., but it does not apply to me."

"No?"

"I love my work. I'm good at it. I work hard and long hours. What's wrong with that?"

"Nothing, as long as it doesn't make you give up more important things."

Drake stopped the swing and looked at her. "Who gave up important things, C.G., and turned you against ambitious men?"

He'd thought she wouldn't tell him, but she did, and rapidly.

"My uncle is rarely home, hasn't taken a vacation for years, misses many special events that involve his wife and children. But he makes lots of money.

"Dottie's husband wants to be top cop, so he works double shifts, volunteers for extra duty, and isn't even aware that Dottie is on the verge of having an affair with his best friend.

"I had a fiancé who thought so much of marrying me that he said on the night we were planning our honeymoon, 'You don't mind if I schedule a meeting with some associates in Miami, do you? An all-day meeting will really cement a number of tentative business relationships.' His ambition severed our relationship."

Drake looked seriously into her eyes. "I am not those men, C.G. When I marry, I'll give a hundred percent of myself to my wife and family, and I'll never miss my children's baseball games or vocal recitals."

Even as he said the words that sounded so right, Drake searched his heart and wondered if he would keep those promises. He was a man of ambition. A man who didn't really know how to put anything else before his work. C.G. was probably right to steer clear of him.

He started the swing moving again.

If he were smart he'd say, Okay, let's forget the whole thing. If he were smart. But something about C.G. made him think she had some insight into living that was escaping him at the present. Maybe he *needed* her more than he *wanted* her.

"Are you against the accumulation of wealth?" he asked her.

She gaped at him. "Absolutely not. I'm not naive or simple, Mr. Forrest. I fully intend to drive a Porsche myself someday. In order to get that car, though, I'm not going to give up what's really important—a full relationship with Jesus Christ, a knowledge that I'm walking in His will and that I can call on Him at any time to guide me and give me His peace. What could be more wonderful than that?"

The phone rang, and Drake jumped up and was already at the door when Gwen met him on the other side of it.

"That wasn't Henry," she told him. "Sorry."

He grunted. "Well, I can make this day productive while I'm waiting. Gwen, do you know the circuit identification numbers for the Blue Ridge branch?"

She wrinkled her forehead. "No, I don't. Why do you need them?"

"We're changing the analog data lines to digital, so in order to disconnect the proper circuit, I need its exact identification number. All the numbers will be on your network interface, probably in some equipment room where the circuits are terminated."

"We have a small room that's little more than a closet where the phone company has installed all the circuits," Gwen told him. "It's nothing fancy. Just a piece of mounted plywood that has various jacks on it."

"That's what I need."

Gwen's eyes brightened. "Shall we go now?"

"Sure."

Drake turned to C.G. "Would you mind staying here, C.G., in case Henry calls or comes over?"

❦

C.G. did most definitely mind playing baby-sitter to his sports car while he and Gwen spent time in a tiny closet at the bank, but she could hardly admit that.

"Of course I'll stay," she assured him.

"That's my girl," he said exuberantly, and Gwen's head snapped around nearly 180 degrees to stare at C.G.

Chapter 15

D rake went off to the bank with Gwen, and C.G. read a magazine and glanced every five minutes at the clock above the kitchen sink. If Henry didn't come sooner than expected, she was going to miss her six o'clock date with Jeffrey and would have no way to get in touch with him. She would hate him thinking she had stood him up.

Though her mind was filled with imaginings of what Drake and Gwen were doing at the bank, she just kept turning the pages of the magazine, seeing very little of what lay on them.

How can I be so attracted to someone who is the epitome of what I do not want in a man? she questioned herself. Ambition and success were admirable traits. She had them both herself, though to a much lesser degree than Drake Forrest.

He, however, was in the big leagues and had given up his spiritual life to get there. Could he change? Learn to put his work after his relationship with God and his family?

She had known of too many women who had married men with problems, sure they would change once they had their wives and families, only to have that dream shattered with the reality that people don't often change—unless they have a personal encounter with the God of the universe, and His Son, Jesus Christ.

The trouble was, Drake was already a Christian, though he was out of fellowship with God. He knew the Scriptures, knew the kind of life he should be leading, but he had chosen another way instead. He was worshiping success at any cost rather than worshiping the God who loved him and had died for him.

C.G. gripped the magazine to her breast and prayed for wisdom in her relationship with Drake. He was a determined man, and he wanted her. He would not give up his campaign to win her. How could she keep from falling in love with him and still be his friend?

When she heard a car door slam in the driveway an hour later, she raced to the window, hoping it was Henry. It wasn't. Drake and Gwen were back and walking toward the house.

C.G. took a deep breath to calm her racing heart and hoped her face wasn't flushed. She'd missed him. She'd missed Drake as though he were special and important to her, a person she wanted to be around a lot.

"Hi," he called out to her with a grin when she opened the door and greeted them. He looked pleased, which had to mean he'd found what he was looking for or had enjoyed himself with Gwen.

C.G. chastised herself for thinking that. It was all Dottie's fault for putting the idea into her head that Drake Forrest was a womanizer. Here at the house his behavior toward Gwen had been perfectly circumspect. Still, C.G. couldn't help wondering just how small that closet at the bank was.

Gwen's facial expression was a stark contrast to Drake's. While she was not out-and-out scowling, she was not a happy camper either.

Drake bounded up the porch steps and stopped in front of C.G., his eyes drinking her in.

"Miss me?" he asked. She knew he was probably teasing, and she answered in kind, in her best Scarlett O'Hara imitation.

"I couldn't concentrate on a thing while you were gone. My poor head was just a muddle."

Drake laughed uproariously and turned to say something to Gwen, but she swept past them both and into the house before he got a word out, allowing the screen door to bang closed behind her.

C.G. looked up at Drake. "What happened?"

His gaze became serious, along with the slant of his mouth. "Nothing, C.G. Absolutely nothing."

"I see." And she did, and she was glad. For some reason she wanted to know that Drake was smarter than to fall for Gwen's homespun designs on him. It seemed he had been loyal, too, to his declaration that he wanted C.G. to be the woman in his life.

"Has Henry called?" he asked, his eyes flitting back to his car.

"No. Sorry."

But just as the words were spoken, a beat-up, rattling old blue Ford 250 pickup truck groaned into the driveway. On its side was painted, probably in the 1940s, the identification "Henry's Garage," and under it the words, "We do it right."

Drake's relieved look turned to one of grave concern, and C.G. wondered if he would actually turn over his forty-thousand-dollar baby to this grizzled man of indeterminate age who groaned getting out of the truck, whose huge belly protruded from greasy suspendered pants, and who moved with all the speed of an ancient turtle.

"Hi y'all," he called out, and Drake hurried to meet him. "Didn't have to go to Atlanta after all," he explained his early arrival. "Friend of mine in Ellijay had just what you need."

"Great!" Drake exclaimed.

A few minutes later the Vette was up on a hydraulic jack and Drake was squatted beside Henry, sharing an animated conversation that had as its focus their mutual love affair with this particular make of automobile. One would think they'd known each other all their lives instead of just five minutes.

C.G. sat on the swing and admired the litheness of Drake's body as he stooped, or stood, or bent over. He was in great physical condition, moving with a fluidity that came from honed muscles and regular exercise. He certainly was one appealing combination of mind and body that she couldn't help but admire.

Then something happened that showed another side of him. A small boy, aged eight or nine, dirty, poorly clothed, and in bare feet, with bushy, unkempt hair, came shuffling down the sidewalk. He looked unhappy, and his little shoulders heaved now and then, as if he'd been crying and was trying to stop but couldn't.

The sound of Drake and Henry talking caused him to look up, and C.G. almost laughed out loud at how big his eyes grew when he saw the gleaming black car, the likes of which, it was easy to guess, he'd never seen before.

He stopped where he was while his mouth slowly dropped open. He became a statue, not moving, barely breathing, but his eyes darted back and forth from the car to Drake and back again to the Vette.

It was several minutes until Drake noticed him. Then he smiled and called out to him. "Do you want to see the car?"

The boy stood where he was, not moving an inch, just staring.

"It's all right," Drake assured him, taking a step toward him, which made the boy move backward defensively. "You can see it better close up." Drake stood quietly, not moving, but smiling until the youngster slowly, cautiously inched his way forward.

"It's a Corvette," Drake said, his hands locked behind his back.

When the boy was close enough to touch it, he did not do so but put his hands behind his back, just like Drake, who then began a painstakingly slow walk around the magnificent machine. The boy imitated him, and C.G. held her hand over her mouth, wishing she had a camera with which to capture the moment.

"I can't let you get in until the car comes off the jack," Drake said, "but I'll take you for a ride later if you'd like."

The boy gawked up at him, amazed at the invitation, as was C.G. who hadn't thought Drake would want so dirty a tyke in his immaculate automobile.

The boy stayed, squatting down beside Drake and watching the work in progress, just like the big man was doing while he talked with Henry. It was a Norman Rockwell slice of American life, three males united for a moment by a common love for a gorgeous hunk of metal.

Gwen came out of the house and joined C.G. on the swing. She seemed perkier and smiled as she whispered, "Henry's the best. He may not look like much, but there's no one within a hundred miles who knows more about cars than he does."

"That's good. Did everything go okay at the bank?"

"Yes, fine." Gwen turned and look straight at C.G. "Is there something going on between you and Drake Forrest?"

C.G.'s eyes widened in surprise. "No, Gwen, nothing."

"Mmm, you could have fooled me. He must have asked me a dozen questions about you."

"He's probably checking out my qualifications to stay on once the acquisition is completed. I was told by one of our vice presidents that not everyone will keep his or her job."

"Is that so? Oh, I hope I keep mine."

"I do, too, Gwen. You're good here. We can depend on you."

Gwen looked surprised with the compliment. "Thanks. I appreciate knowing that." She looked over at Drake and began to shake her head back and forth. "I don't think that's the reason he was asking questions about you," she said.

"You don't?"

"Nope, because he came right out and asked me why you're not married."

Gwen got up and went back into the house, leaving C.G. stunned and wanting to know what the other questions were. So, C.G. thought, *he isn't giving up on me, after all, and doesn't care if others know of his intentions.*

The object of her thoughts jogged over to the porch and gave her a winsome smile. A lock of hair splayed over his forehead and there was grease on his fingers, but the radiant look in his eye told her he was having a glorious time.

"Henry says we'll be on our way in five minutes." He looked at his watch. "Add to that another ten or so. I'd like to take Danny for a ride, if you don't mind."

C.G. smiled warmly even while she thought of Jeffrey Brandon standing on her front porch in just a few hours, receiving no answer to his knock. "I wouldn't mind at all. He's thrilled with the attention you're giving him."

"He's a good kid. Bright. We'll still get back to Cheston by five-thirty," he promised, then gave her a mischievous grin and added, "even if I don't drive fast. I know that's later than either of us wanted, but at least we won't have to spend the night here." His expression grew serious. "Would you have minded?"

"It would have been awkward, don't you think?"

"No, I don't, because I would have had Gwen drive me to a motel. There's one not far from the bank."

"Oh."

❀

Drake didn't quite know what to make of C.G. Grady. On the one hand she was sophisticated, mature, and well educated, as evidenced by her position with the bank and her appearance, which showed style and good taste. On the other hand, there were moments when he caught an innocence about her, as though she were on unfamiliar territory being with a man.

Surely, at her age, she must have had one or two meaningful experiences with someone. Women didn't save themselves any more for the man they married. Not like his mother and her mother before her had done. Times were different nowadays. Self-gratification was accepted as the norm. Self-restraint was unusual.

He knew any number of women who would have used such a situation as he and C.G. had faced to foster a more intimate relationship with him. C.G., however, struck him as a woman who was not interested in that kind of liaison. She wanted more from a man. She deserved more.

He looked at her with new eyes, knowing more than ever that he wanted her in his life. For how long or how seriously, he wasn't sure, but he knew he had at least four months to win her over, and there was no doubt at all in his mind that he would do just that.

Chapter 16

Henry finished the Vette, and C.G. went out to meet Drake's newest friend, little Danny, and watched with pleasure when the boy's eyes grew huge and unbelieving as Drake made good on his invitation to take a ride in the fancy car.

The "ten-minute ride" that Drake had promised turned into fifteen, and C.G.'s heart sank, knowing she could never get home and changed before Jeffrey came to take her to dinner.

They said good-bye to Gwen and thanked her for the lunch and snacks and other help, and when they went to get into the car, Drake surprised C.G. by suggesting she drive home.

"Are you kidding?" she asked. "You'd trust me with your baby?"

"I'd trust you with anything, C.G." His eyes softened. "Besides, you'll be more comfortable, won't you, behind the wheel? And less likely to throw up if you're not sailing from side to side around those four hundred curves between here and Cheston." He winked at her.

"Ah, I see. So your grand gesture is not altruistic after all?"

"I always take care of what's mine."

❦

At exactly 5:32 P.M., they drove onto the winding, private, graveled road that led to C.G.'s house. It had been a dream driving the Corvette, and C.G. had thoroughly enjoyed doing so, with the top down, the wind whipping her hair.

Now, though, there were other things to do. Because of everything that had happened, she was going to have far too little time to get herself ready for her dinner date with Jeffrey.

She scrambled out of the car before Drake even had a grip on the door handle on his side and went to the front and waited for him and said, "I'm sorry the day was such a mess, but we did get what we went after, and now you can work tomorrow to your heart's content. I guess I'll see you on Monday."

She turned and ran up the three steps to the porch, knowing she'd been babbling, hoping he hadn't picked up on her nervousness.

"Yes, it was a good day, C.G.," Drake agreed, and instead of leaving, he sauntered slowly across the front of her one-story country home, scanning the curtained windows, the three hanging baskets of geraniums along the front of the porch, the dried arrangement of magnolia blossoms fastened to the front door.

"This is really nice. Yours?"

"Mine and the bank's." C.G. got out her keys. Hopefully, he'd get the message. He didn't.

"This porch is wide," he commented, stepping up on it and going to one of two heavy, maple rocking chairs. He eased his long frame into it and gave a long and deep sigh. "I could sit here all night."

C.G.'s palms were moist.

"Do you use it a lot?" he asked, looking out across her finely mowed lawn, groups of marigolds and zinnias scattered here and there.

"Yes. I like to read here." The key was in the door. She unlocked it. "Well, Drake, I must say good-bye." She watched him turn, a surprised expression on his face as he slowly rose to his feet.

"Am I being given the bum's rush?" he asked.

"Not at all," C.G. exclaimed, embarrassed, mentally ticking off exactly how long it would take her to shower, apply fresh makeup, and select an outfit to wear. She must have been unconvincing because Drake came up to her and said, "You have plans for this evening, don't you?"

"Well, yes, I do."

He looked at her long and hard. "You should have told me."

"Probably."

"Why didn't you?"

C.G. didn't know what to say. After all, it wasn't as though she were doing something wrong, that she was going out with someone else behind his back.

"It doesn't matter," she said, trying to sound offhanded, as though the whole situation was minor. "I'm here now, so—"

Drake's hands captured her shoulders and held her firmly. "Oh, but it does matter, C.G. Why didn't you tell me you were going out?"

"It wouldn't have made any difference. We couldn't have gotten the car fixed any sooner. True?"

Besides, what could she say that wouldn't sound ridiculous: I have this date, but it's not with someone I care about—at least I don't think I care about him, although maybe I could someday, but really I wish I were going out with you instead?

She hesitated too long because Drake's eyebrows raised, as though he had just figured something out.

"It's a man, isn't it?" Those same brows dipped in an ominous frown. "You're expecting him at any minute, and you don't want him finding me here." His hands tightened on her arms.

"I need time to get ready."

400

"You're gorgeous like you are."

Did he see her like that? Even after the long day? She couldn't have a shred of makeup on. Her hair had been blown to smithereens in the convertible.

C.G. wanted to look away from him but couldn't. In his eyes, for the briefest of moments, she saw something she had not seen before in him: uncertainty, and it took her breath away. Drake Forrest knew his abilities, his power to make things happen. Here, with her, he was not in control, not able to make things happen the way he wanted them to.

"What's his name?" he asked, his tone knife sharp.

Hearing his question, asked as if he had every right to know what she did every moment of her life, caused C.G. to turn out of his grasp and reach for the door handle. But before she could open it, Drake's hand was on hers.

"Is he someone special, C.G.?"

Now she was irritated. What gave him the right to ask such a question? She stabbed him with a look as sharp as his previous words. "I really don't have time to discuss my love life, Drake."

"Love life?"

Rats. Poor choice of words. "I have to get ready."

"Fine. Go right ahead." Surprisingly, he released her, and his change of mood from interrogation to cooperation left her wary.

"Go ahead? No more personal none-of-your-business questions?"

"Nope." He spun on his heels and walked to one of the rockers and sat down. Puzzled, C.G. followed him. "What are you doing? I thought you were leaving."

"Before meeting your date? Not on your life, Sweetheart."

"I'm not your sweetheart, Drake Forrest, and I have not invited you to meet my date." C.G. glanced at her watch. Quarter to six. She'd never get ready in time.

"I'm inviting myself," Drake replied.

"Why?" She was getting exasperated.

The look of innocence he gave her was worth a thousand words. "To see if he's worthy of you."

"What?"

"Which, of course, I know right now that he isn't."

"Drake Forrest, get off my porch. Get off my property." C.G. plunked her hands on her hips and faced him with grit.

He just smiled and said softly, "Make me."

C.G. wanted to wring his neck. Of course, she'd have about as much chance to do that successfully as she would in physically evicting him from the premises. He was a big man, with at least a seventy-pound advantage over her, not to mention strong, powerful hands and a determination to match the most aggressive bulldog.

She turned abruptly and stormed to her front door, yanked it open, heard his soft chuckle, and slammed the door once she was inside.

The nerve of that scoundrel, she fumed, stomping into her bedroom, flinging open the closet door, seeing absolutely not one thing she could wear that night, then deciding on kelly green slacks and a matching long-sleeved blouse, neither of which fit her very well, but what difference did it make anyway? Drake was going to be there when Jeffrey arrived, and Drake would ruin the evening before it even started.

She hurried through her shower, heard Drake whistling on the front porch, then heard the crunch on gravel as a car came up her driveway.

She peeked through the window and saw Jeffrey getting out of the car. *Oh, no,* she groaned, standing there dripping wet. *I have to throw something on to go out and greet him before Drake sends him packing.*

But it was too late for that. The men were shaking hands. The men were talking. The men were sitting down in the rockers.

Chapter 17

Frantically C.G. dried herself off, dried her hair, got dressed, added gold earrings and some dangly bracelets to her outfit, which didn't look as bad as she'd thought it would as it defined her figure nicely without being suggestive.

Stepping out on the porch fifteen minutes later, the animated conversation Jeffrey and Drake were having about baseball abruptly ended. Both jumped to their feet as she walked toward them.

She had to admit it was a heady sensation to see pure, male admiration from both of them, but it was in Drake's eyes that she saw a devilish grin that made her want to kick his shins.

"I see you've met each other," she tried to say without malice in her voice.

"Yes." Jeffrey came over to her. "Drake tells me you're working together and just had a rough day in Blue Ridge. He explained why you're running late."

"Did he?"

C.G. turned her eyes to Drake, who nodded, innocence personified. She could only imagine what else he'd told Jeffrey, or what impression he'd given about their relationship.

"Well, folks, I have to be going," Drake said cheerfully. "It was nice meeting you, Jeffrey. Enjoy your dinner." He turned to C.G., who was thrown off guard by his intent to leave. She'd half believed he would ask to join them for the evening.

The two men shook hands, and Drake turned to C.G. "Could you walk me to the car, C.G.? I have something to tell you."

"About the acquisition?" she asked sweetly.

"Yes, of course."

"Excuse me, Jeffrey, I'll be right back," she told him.

At Drake's Corvette, he turned and gave her a winning smile. "Have a good time."

His accepting attitude made her suspicious. "Why do I think there's more to that good wish than a good wish?"

"There's nothing at all misleading in it. I hope you enjoy yourself. Jeffrey's a neat guy."

"You think so?" She was amazed. She'd half thought Drake would have driven him off. Hadn't he claimed her as his own back at Smith's General Store? Was he giving up on her already? Of course, why shouldn't he, since she'd told him in no uncertain terms that she wasn't even looking for a man, much less a man like him?

"Did Jeffrey tell you he's a minister?"

"Sure did. Sounds like he has quite a church down in Florida."

"I haven't seen it, but from what he says, it's dynamic and growing."

"Lucky for those kids to have a man like him to guide them."

C.G. knew something was missing here, and she found out what it was in the next words out of Drake's mouth.

"The kids are lucky, like I said, but you realize, of course, that Jeffrey Brandon is not the man for you." The confident look on his face was maddening.

"You've decided that, have you?"

He nodded. "That's right. It's easy to see. Oh, he's a nice guy. Genuine. Committed."

"But?"

"Not the man for you."

"Well, thank you for informing me. I never would have figured it out for myself."

Drake fixed on her a look that could only be construed as that of a male caveman claiming his female. "I told you back at the general store that you were mine. And I meant it. Jeffrey Brandon is no threat to me."

He climbed into the Vette while C.G. seethed.

He started the engine. "Oh, by the way, what time should I pick you up tomorrow?"

"Tomorrow?"

"Yes. I'm taking you to church."

"You're what?"

Drake laughed. "You know, Miss Grady, you ask a lot of questions. What time does the service start?"

"I go for Sunday school. Way too early for you."

"Not at all. What time?"

"I usually leave at nine o'clock, but I am not going with you."

"Why not?"

C.G. stepped closer to the car to be sure Jeffrey couldn't hear her words. "This won't work, Drake, this sudden interest in going to church when I know you gave it up long ago. It's nothing more than a cheap attempt to get on my good side."

"You're wrong, C.G. You've made me see the light. The error of my ways—"

"Oh, please, stop. You can go to church every day for the next year and still not be the kind of Christian man I want and need."

"I understand that, but this is, at least, a start."

"Then find any church you want, and go to it."

"I want to go to yours."

"Fine, but not with me."

"Why not with you?"

"Because I won't be manipulated." She leaned over and glared at him. "Do you think I'm that naive to believe your sudden change of heart is genuine?"

"Okay, but it will be on your conscience if I decide not to go tomorrow because I won't know anyone."

"Poor excuse for staying away."

"If I never find the way back to church. . ."

"All right, all right. Pick me up here at nine o'clock, but I warn you, Drake; if you're not sincere in this, you won't get as much as a smile out of me the rest of the time we work together."

"See you then." And he drove the Corvette slowly down the driveway while C.G. condemned herself for falling into what surely must be a honeycombed trap.

Drake's mother's home-cooked meal of beef stew, slow-cooked for sixteen hours in a Crock-Pot, bakery-style blueberry muffins, and pumpkin pie for dessert was his father's favorite. It was also Drake's.

After apologizing for being late, then eating more than he should have, he sat in his parents' living room and listened to what they'd been doing lately and felt contented in a way he knew he hadn't been for a long time.

His dad, a tall, virile man of sixty with a flat stomach and a full head of brown hair that was once red, a retired firefighter, sat in his favorite recliner and recounted what he was doing in the rose garden and in his basement workshop. "That circular saw you got me for Christmas makes easy work of cutting landscape timbers," he told Drake.

"I'm glad you're using it, Dad."

Despite his father's recitation of activity, Drake noticed a decided lethargy about him. He hoped it was just routine tiredness.

"He always puts the tools you give him to good use," his mother insisted.

She looked particularly pretty to Drake tonight, wearing a wide-legged, one-piece hostess outfit of black and lavender that emphasized her still-slender waist. Her soft blond hair was newly styled in a full, stacked cut that swept toward her cheeks, and her aqua eyes danced with love, which Drake felt strongly every time she looked at him.

He, of course, was urged by his parents to tell them about his life, and he got a little lengthy in explaining the bank acquisition.

"Tell us more about this person you're working with at Ashford Bank and Trust," his mother urged.

She had listened carefully to her son for nearly a half hour and had picked up on a pattern: No matter what subject Drake talked about, he invariably came back to this "person" he was working with to coordinate the acquisition. So far he had said she was nice, intelligent, capable, and had a sense of humor. It was what he had not said that worried her.

"Is she young?" his mom asked.

"Younger than me."

"Pretty?"

"Very."

"Married?"

"Single."

❦

Katherine took a long, slow breath. "Would you both excuse me for a minute?"

As quickly as she could, she went to the farthest room in the house and called Jane Grady.

"We're going to have to step up our efforts," she told her matchmaking partner. "My son is interested in another woman."

"Oh, no."

"What's worse is that they'll be working together for months."

"Does it sound serious?" Jane asked.

"I'm reading between the lines at this point, Jane, but we need to do more than send our children written teasers. Is your Chryssie showing any interest in my son?"

Jane giggled. "So far she thinks he's a dog."

"A dog?" Katherine responded indignantly. "Jane!"

"It's not what you think. Chryssie got the wrong impression from my veiled teasers and thinks her father and I are getting her a cocker spaniel."

Katherine laughed. "She's going to be a bit surprised, don't you think, when she meets Drake?"

"I'll correct that impression the next time I talk with her."

"You'd better make it soon. Tonight, if you can."

"I'll try. Do you think it's time to send a picture?"

Katherine thought a moment, then said, "I suppose, although I wish they could come to appreciate each other's sterling qualities first. Why are young people so hung up on good looks nowadays?"

"To tell the truth, Katherine, I think they were in our day, too."

"Perhaps you're right. Anyway, when we see each other at Bible study this week, let's exchange pictures. Small ones, of course. I think an 8 X 10 color would be too hard a sell, don't you?"

"Yes. See you on Tuesday."

Chapter 18

Back in the living room, Drake's mother went to a tall bookcase and pulled from one of the shelves several picture albums. Sitting down on the sofa next to her son, she said, "Let's look these over, shall we? They bring back so many wonderful memories."

Drake loved looking at family pictures, even ones of him when he was younger and looked funny, at least to his own eyes.

"Look at this one, Mother." Drake pointed to the picture used for his high school yearbook.

"You look so young there, Dear."

"That's because I was. Look how light my hair is. It's getting darker."

"That's what happens to blonds, I guess. Where's your graduation picture from college?"

They found it, and Drake was surprised at how much he had changed in the intervening years. His face was more defined now, cheeks narrower, his eyes more intense. He had a little less hair, too, but not by much.

His mother was now skimming rapidly through the pages. "What are you looking for?" he asked her.

"Don't we have a current picture of you? One that shows how devastatingly handsome you are?"

Drake laughed and his father guffawed. "Did we have one that showed that?"

"Yes, Kevin, we must have." She was getting frustrated as she flipped over one page after another. "All these pictures, and not one I could give to—" She stopped abruptly.

"Give to whom, Mother?"

"Well. . .to anyone. . .who needs one. . ."

Drake threw his hand down on the photo album she was holding on her lap. "Don't tell me you're looking for a picture to show this mystery woman I'm supposed to fall in love with on your recommendation."

"Mystery woman?" his father questioned.

Drake turned to him. "Hasn't Mother told you she's been sending me little teasers of information about the daughter of some friend of hers she thinks is perfect for me?"

"Katherine, you never told me," Kevin Forrest blustered. "Who is this person?"

"She's Jane's daughter, Kevin. I'm sure I've mentioned her to you?"

"I don't remember you doing so."

"Oh, I must have." She was flustered with two men staring at her as though she had just committed murder. She deliberately had not mentioned Chryssie Grady to Kevin because he would have been against the idea. Men never put any faith in matchmaking. But mothers did, and she wasn't giving up on getting Chryssie together with Drake.

Her son stood up abruptly, closed the book on her lap, scooped the other albums up in his arms, and returned them to the proper shelf. "Enough of looking at pictures."

"Drake, you're being uncooperative."

He gave her a patient grin. "Yes, I am."

"But she's a lovely girl."

"I appreciate your wanting to help my love life along, but I'm not interested."

"How can you say that when you've never met her?" his mother questioned. "Weren't you at all intrigued with the information I sent you about her?"

"No."

"I don't believe it."

"Believe it, Mother. I want to do my own looking."

"You can't be everywhere at once. That's why God created mothers—to help."

Drake chuckled and came back to the sofa. Giving his mother a kiss on the cheek, he said nicely, "I know your heart is in the right place, but I want you to give up this matchmaking."

Her lower lip jutted out in a pout that made both Drake and his father laugh. "I can't," she said.

"Why not?" Drake wanted to know.

"Because this girl is right for you. If you would just meet her—"

"No."

"Once?"

"I think I'll have another piece of pie. Dad, would you like one?"

"Sure."

"Mother?"

She shook her head no, still pouting.

Drake sprang to his feet and fled to the kitchen where he cut two big pieces of pie and began to pour himself a glass of ice cold milk.

He hoped he hadn't hurt his mother's feelings. She was a sweetheart, a wonderful woman who loved him unconditionally and thought she had his best interests at heart.

What she could never do, though, in a million years was pick out the right woman for him. Someone he could love and admire forever. Someone like C.G. Grady.

The glass filled up and milk ran over onto the kitchen counter, and Drake didn't even notice as he stared off into space. He was thinking of C.G. and of going to church with her the next day.

He only snapped back to reality when a flashbulb went off and he heard the automatic advance of a 35mm camera. Looking up, startled, he saw his mother, a smug grin on her face, holding the camera that had done the deed.

"Motherrrr!" he yelled after her as she scurried from the room and milk ran off the edge of the counter and onto his shoes.

🌼

Drake picked C.G. up at nine o'clock and took her to church. On the way they stopped at the house of a Mrs. Ingles, a shut-in who only got out rarely, because of severe arthritis. C.G. took her some homemade peanut butter cookies, Mrs. Ingles's favorite, and a small African violet.

"Our Helping Hands ministry cleans her house and brings her groceries," C.G. explained on the way. "On days when she feels well, one of us will take her shopping for whatever she needs."

"How many people are in your group?" he asked.

"A dozen or so. We have no set schedule with anyone but attend to needs as they arise." Her eyes misted. "It's a very satisfying ministry."

"A depressing one."

"Oh, no, not at all. To wipe away tears and ease anxiety, maybe bring a smile to someone who has little to smile about—what could be more rewarding in this life?"

Drake was more in love with C.G. than ever.

The newly built church where C.G. attended was located on a rocky hill. One looked up to see its brick form and white steeple rising toward the sky, then looked around to see the eye-catching landscape of pansies and azalea bushes sitting in islands of dark pine straw. There was no grass yet, but there was a view from the parking lot of Lake Lanier in the distance.

Although the building was only one year old, the congregation had been in Cheston for decades. There were ninety or so families who worshiped together and shared each others' triumphs and burdens, and love was there.

Drake felt it when he was warmly welcomed in the singles' Sunday school class after being introduced by C.G. to those present. The teacher, Helen Douglas, an attractive brunette with shoulder-length hair, a lawyer in her forties, was friendly, funny, spiritually mature, and understanding of what it was like to be an adult single in a world of pairs.

Drake realized, as the group read Scripture and discussed it, that he was happy with much of his life but lonely for someone to share it with.

He made only one comment during the class, about the problem of finding women to date who could hold a man's interest. "I've dated beautiful women. I've dated intelligent and successful women, but after a few months the relationship is still shallow."

"That's why taking our time is important in getting to know someone," the teacher said. "Rushing into too serious a relationship can lead to all kinds of problems. Take it slow. Don't let physical desires overshadow the more important goal of learning what a person is all about. Take it slow," she repeated. "We can't afford to damage our lives by recklessly pursuing a relationship that might not be good for us."

Drake glanced at C.G. and found her looking back at him. The shimmering blue of her eyes held in their depths the very same question he was debating himself: Could they have something meaningful together if they took it slow? He'd never been a man to go slowly. He didn't like the word or its connotation for inaction. He had a quick mind and a rare ability to make accurate decisions in a short time. He had a reputation for it.

Now, though, after listening to this wise Sunday school teacher and reading Scripture that advocated patience and control, he was beginning to rethink his campaign to win C.G. He wasn't giving up. Not one bit. It might be wise, though, to slow down and plan a different strategy.

Fast or slow, C.G. was going to be his.

Chapter 19

Drake took C.G. to lunch after church, then drove her home where they sat in his car for a few minutes and just talked. He did not attempt to kiss her. He wanted to; oh, how he wanted to, but he knew C.G. suspected he had only gone to church to get on her good side. And she was right. His motive had been far from pure. He told her so.

"What I didn't expect," he went on, "was to feel a strange hunger for something I haven't had in my life for a very long time."

"It's the God vacuum in our hearts that can't be filled with anything or anyone other than God Himself," she explained.

"I was so sure it wouldn't mean anything to me—being in church, hearing and singing the familiar hymns, listening to the choir." He shifted in the seat so he could look directly at C.G. "The singles' class was great. Then your pastor threw me a curve, speaking, as he did, with great conviction on the subject 'For what shall it profit a man, if he shall gain the whole world, and lose his own soul?'

"The logic and encouragement of his words were meant for me, C.G. They spoke to my heart. I'm a man who owns a lot of the world. I've struggled to get to the top and have made it. But have I lost something more important along the way?

"I'm not sure yet. I'm still trying to sort out things in my head. All I know is that I've thought for too many years that success is proven by material possessions. To get those rewards, I've done my share of underhanded things, lost friends, and even made enemies. I don't have a best friend because I don't have time for one. I don't have a wife and children because I concentrate on myself and my own needs and desires.

"C.G." He took her hand. "How long ago did the pastor decide to preach on that text which has gripped my conscience, a man who hasn't gone to church for ten years?

"Why was I chosen by Georgia National Bank to oversee the merging of the databases of the two banks?" He paused, drinking in every feature of C.G.'s face. "Why are you the person I have to work with?"

"Those are a lot of questions, Drake. Do you know any of the answers?"

"Not a one, so far, but I'm pretty sure God is leading me to something step by step, and I'd better pay attention."

A month later, C.G. sat in her office, trying to concentrate. On the corner of her desk were a dozen pale yellow roses, sent to her by Drake. She couldn't take her eyes off them. The petals were fragrant and delicate and reminded her of the gentle touch of his hands when he'd presented them to her. She also saw the thorns.

"Daydreaming of Prince Charming again?" Her assistant, Dottie Westfall, breezed into the room and collapsed in the vinyl chair in front of C.G.'s desk. "Last week it was Godiva chocolates. The week before a hardcover book you've been wanting for weeks, tied with silver ribbon. Just as I was beginning to think there wasn't a romantic man left in the universe, along comes Drake Forrest and sweeps you off your feet."

C.G. gave her a look of disdain. "I'm not swept off. . .yet. I'm taking my time in making up my mind."

Dottie laughed out loud. "Really? Have you looked at yourself in the mirror the past few weeks? You're dewey-eyed—"

"I'm not."

"Radiant."

"Well. . ."

"And distracted."

"Distracted?"

"That's what I call it when you break off conversation in the middle of a sentence to stare out into the lobby and ignore the person speaking to you, which has been me, more than once. C.G., my friend, you're dancing on the precipice."

"Of what?"

"Falling in love, if you haven't already." Dottie leaned forward and folded her arms on the desk. "With Drake Forrest. Admit it."

C.G. clucked her tongue against her teeth. "That's ridiculous, Dottie. I haven't known him long enough."

Since that first Sunday, when Drake had gone to church with her just to win her affections, and admitted the same afterward, he'd gone every week, and Sunday evenings, and for midweek Bible study, too. He was not a man to take things slowly, he'd told her, and she knew that from watching him at work. She just prayed he wasn't rushing into a recommitment that would be short-lived.

As far as their relationship was going, he was wooing her slowly and carefully in exquisitely thoughtful ways meant to defuse her natural wariness of him and his intentions. She knew this; he did not deny it. The fact that he was honest with her about his plans to bring her into his life led her, strangely, to trust him, but still she would not give in wholly until she knew he really was a changed man.

"You're doing it again." Dottie's soft chuckle drew C.G. from her contemplation, and she had to smile at herself. Her thoughts were never far from the man who had strode tall and strong into her life and planned to stay. At least for awhile.

"I give up," Dottie exclaimed, hoisting herself out of the chair. "I'm amazed you keep your job when your mind is so often elsewhere."

She left with a cheery good-bye, and C.G. didn't even know why she'd come to see her until she saw a file folder in front of her with information she'd asked Dottie for.

I'd better get a grip on myself, she thought. *What if one of the vice presidents sees me the way Dottie does?*

She rose and took the file to her credenza where she put it in a drawer after taking some papers out. The task completed, her eyes fell on the picture of her parents, the one Drake had been so interested in the first day he'd been there.

Poor Mom, she thought. Looking back over the past month, C.G. realized her mother had been acting strangely. First of all, there was the conversation they'd had the day after Drake had taken her to church, when she'd gone to her parents' home for dinner. While putting away the leftovers, her mother had said, "Chryssie, I must clear up a misunderstanding."

That's when she'd learned that the adorable cocker spaniel she'd been expecting as a gift from her parents was really a grown man whom she was expected to dutifully meet and fall in love with, then marry.

"He's highly intelligent, dependable, protective, successful—" Her mother had recited previously given information.

"Don't forget the mischievous eyes."

"Oh, yes."

"Mom, how could you be trying to set me up with this stranger? You know how I feel about blind dates and matchmaking."

"Yes, I do, but this man is exceptional. One of a kind. When you meet him—"

"I don't want to meet him, Mom."

"You'll like him, I know. I'm going to send you a picture of him."

C.G. groaned and decided not to be too hard on her mom, whose heart, after all, was in the right place because she wanted what she thought was best for C.G.

"How do you happen to know this man?" C.G. asked.

"He's the son of a good friend of mine."

"Have you met him?"

"No, Chryssie, but his mother has told me enough so that I'm sure he's just what you need."

"You make him sound like Pepto Bismol."

"Not at all. He's quite handsome, successful, and—"

"Mom, is he a Christian?"

There was silence and C.G. was surprised. Her mother felt the same way she did about the importance of a man and a woman sharing a strong faith. "He grew up in the church, Chryssie, and just needs the love of a good woman to bring him back. His parents have been praying for just that for years. And you know what it says in Proverbs 22:6 [NKJV]."

"Yes. 'Train up a child in the way he should go, and when he is old he will not depart from it.' Still, he doesn't sound right for me, Mom."

"Well, of course there are no guarantees, but I think once you meet him and go out with him for awhile, you'll know whether he's right for you or not. And you could be a powerful influence on him for good."

"Mom, there's another man in my life right now who may turn out to be important." Then she told her mother about Drake, not by name or physical description, but that they worked together and were attracted to each other and that he, too, was searching for a spiritual life. "Probably nothing will come of our friendship," C.G. told her mom, "but I don't think I can handle two men at the same time."

She hoped she hadn't hurt her mother's feelings. "Do you understand where I'm coming from, Mom?"

"Yes, of course. Now, Chryssie, do you have a good photo of yourself? Just a small one. I've looked everywhere and can't find any that show your true personality that I can send to him."

C.G.'s heart lurched. "Him?"

"Why, yes, dear, the man we've been talking about for ten minutes. I heard what you said about this other man, but until something permanent is decided with him, I think you should keep your options open, and my friend's son is worth consideration. So please look through your pictures, and bring me something as soon as you can; otherwise I'll give his mother whatever I have. His mother is going to give me a picture of him as well. That may make him more interesting to you."

C.G. didn't know whether to laugh or cry.

A week later, when an envelope arrived in the mail with the words "PHOTO— DO NOT BEND" on the cover, she was not even tempted to open it, so turned off was she to the idea of two mothers scrambling to get their children together.

She put the photo envelope on a pile of newspapers in the kitchen, afraid to throw it out but not planning to look at it in the near future either.

Then she lost it. It had been inadvertently tossed out with the papers, she guessed, and she felt appropriately guilty, knowing all the trouble her mother had gone to to get this picture to her. What was she going to say when her mother asked what she thought of him, this mystery man? She knew she could not lie to her mother, and C.G. dreaded the conversation to come.

414

Chapter 20

I t came four days later, when she met her mom after work to do some shopping together.

"Well, what did you think of his picture?" C.G.'s mom asked, as eager as a teenager over her manipulations. "Isn't he handsome? Doesn't his face show what a strong, dependable man he is?"

"Mom. . .I—"

"My friend said it wasn't the best picture of him. He was distracted when she took it."

"Mom. . .please—"

"She's going to try to get another one, but I guess he's stubborn. Doesn't want to meet you."

C.G. gasped with relief. "There you go, Mom. He doesn't want to meet me. I don't want to meet him. That should be the end of it."

Her mom looked at C.G. as though she had just materialized from outer space. "The end of it?" she cried. Then she shook her head. "The end of it will come only after the two of you sit down and get to know one other. Then, if you really find there is no common ground upon which to build a lasting friendship—"

"Motherrrr—"

"Then, and then only, will it be over." She stood to her feet, her facial muscles taut. She was not happy with her daughter's attitude. C.G. knew the look well. "You may pay for lunch," her mother announced and left the restaurant ahead of C.G. and said precious little all the way to her home.

Before leaving the car, her mom asked, "By the way, you haven't told me what you thought of the man's picture." She turned in the seat of C.G.'s Mercury Cougar and waited.

C.G. cleared her throat and admitted softly, "I lost it."

She was not surprised when her mother got out of the car without saying a word. C.G. rolled down the window and called after her, "I didn't mean to."

She received no reply.

❈

Being a forgiving person, her mother called her in a few days, as cheerful as ever. No mention was made of the episode, and neither did she ask for a picture of C.G.

Sitting at her desk now at the bank, C.G. felt guilty because she had not sent

415

her a picture. She knew she was being unusually stubborn about this match-making. Would it be so horrible for her to go along with the plan?

What could be the worst thing to happen? She wouldn't be forced to marry this stranger at gunpoint. All she had to do was meet him once, then tell her mother there was no way in a year of frozen Mondays that she wanted to see him again. There. Simple.

One thing she knew, this man, whoever he was, could not be better-looking than Drake. Or as smart. Or as successful. Or as attentive. Or as much fun to be with.

"C.G.? C.G.?"

She finally heard the voice of her assistant, James Wyatt, and she knew she'd been daydreaming, just like Dottie had said.

"Yes, James, what can I do for you?"

He was looking at her strangely, and beside him was a dowdy-looking woman who just had to be his mother. They had the same scowl, the same small mouth, the same straight nose that looked too short for the long face.

"C.G. I want you to meet my mother, Hilda Wyatt. Mom, this is C.G. Grady. We work together."

"She's your boss, don't you mean?" Mrs. Wyatt leaned forward and squinted as she looked C.G. up and down. "She's young but not as pretty as you said."

Now it was James who was embarrassed.

"Mom's visiting me for awhile," he explained, "from Iowa, and she wanted to see where I work."

"How nice. How long will you be here, Mrs. Wyatt?"

"Until I decide to go home," came the curt reply.

She began walking around C.G.'s office, inspecting everything closely. "Why is her office so big and yours is so small?" she addressed James, not C.G.

"I'm Miss Grady's assistant," James told his mother.

"Does that mean you have to have such a dingy, tiny office?" She glared at C.G.

"James is a valuable worker here at the bank," C.G. said. "I couldn't get along without him."

"Why don't you give him a bigger office, then? And a raise? He earns next to nothing."

Poor James. C.G. felt sorry for him. An indefinite stay from his mother was not going to be easy for him.

"Come on, Mother. I'll show you the rest of the bank." He turned to C.G. "Thanks for meeting her." He already looked exhausted.

"It was my pleasure." She turned to shake hands with Mrs. Wyatt and say something else, but the woman was toddling out the door, and as she did, she ran one finger over the top of the credenza, found just enough dust to have made the gesture worthwhile, and gave a little grunt of satisfaction as she moved into the lobby.

❀

C.G. began to think Dottie was right about her being in love with Drake. He had been out of town for over a week, visiting the other bank branches, getting pertinent information, as he had in Blue Ridge, and C.G. couldn't believe how much she missed him.

At work, knowing he wasn't in his office, she felt a strange emptiness.

At noon, eating alone, she thought of the times Drake had taken her out for lunch, or had ordered in salads or pizza, or had brought in something he'd made himself, like the Italian meat loaf that was scrumptious. She'd been surprised he could cook, having thought he was always too busy to take the time to do it.

She had relented in her determination to remain aloof from him when she'd learned from her Sunday school teacher that Drake was in counseling with the pastor. "I don't know what it's about, of course," Helen had said, "but he must be serious about getting back into fellowship."

C.G. wanted to believe that, wanted to know he was sincere in his spiritual search.

It would be one thing for him to go to church with her; anyone could do that without really caring. But to talk with the pastor—well, there had to be something substantive about their conversations.

Drake came back on a Wednesday. C.G. saw him in the lobby and stood up and moved out from behind her desk but dared not go farther, for she knew she wanted to fly into his arms.

Susie Black called to him from behind her teller's window, but he only gave her a wave of the hand in greeting. His eyes were on C.G. all the time that his long, powerful strides carried him the distance to her office, where he closed the door behind him and wrapped her in a look of pure adulation.

"I've missed you, Miss Grady."

"I've missed you, too."

"Do you know how much I want to take you in my arms? Right now? Kiss you? And I wouldn't care if everyone in the whole bank sees us."

C.G. nodded nervously, knowing she wanted him to do exactly that. They couldn't, of course, because they were at work, where decorum had to be maintained; but his eyes feasting on her and the rigid way he stood, barely controlling his urge to do just what he'd said, let C.G. know how strong his feelings for her were.

"I'm glad you're back."

He took a step toward her. "I'm not sure how good my work was; my mind was distracted."

She reached down and took one of his roses from its vase and held it to her

417

nostrils. "Thank you for these. I love roses."

"I love you."

He crossed the rest of the room and cradled her face in his hands, leaning over her, lowering his head until he kissed her.

The rose C.G. was holding fell to the floor as she released it to clutch his arms. "Oh, Drake, I love you, too," she said when he released her.

Over his shoulder she saw several of the tellers, including Susie Black, staring at them in amazement through her office window.

Her heart tumbled about in its cavity, its rhythm erratic as she tried to cope with Drake's saying he loved her and her pledging the same.

"We've known each other such a short time," she said, stepping back from him before she did something impulsive, like throw her arms around his neck and kiss him ardently.

"Yes, but you're not like any woman I've ever known."

She felt a stab of insecurity, knowing there had been other women in his life. Had he told any of them he loved them? Was his telling her now just a line to get what he wanted?

With legs none too steady, C.G. leaned against her desk and said, "I think we should talk about this somewhere else."

Drake smiled. "Good idea. Then I can convince you of my feelings."

C.G. felt a rush of joy as well as one of caution. She wanted to ask him about his counseling with the pastor, wanted reassurance that he was serious about his coming back to the Lord and wasn't just playing a game to win her for a season.

He saw the concern in her eyes and brushed her cheek with the back of two fingers. "Don't worry, Love." An eagerness exploded over his features. "I have tickets for the gospel concert tonight at the community center. Will you go with me?"

"Yes. I wanted to hear the quartet. They're fantastic. When did you get the tickets?"

"The first night I went to see the pastor."

"The pastor?"

He smiled and daringly kissed the end of her nose. "I'll tell you about it later."

Chapter 21

The concert was inspiring, thrilling, and even fun as the various musical numbers dealt with the joy of being a child of God, as well as the pain of being separated from Him.

It was unlikely that any person in the sold-out auditorium was not moved toward a deeper walk with the Lord. C.G. hoped that Drake was, too.

"There's a place I want you to see," he told her after the concert, and he took her to his apartment, which was on the fifth floor of a sophisticated complex in the prestigious Buckhead area of north Atlanta.

Walking through the various rooms, C.G. saw the rugged individualism of Drake's personality carried out in the furnishings and accessories with which he surrounded himself. She could see him sprawled on the formidable bone-leather sofa and matching love seat in the great room, pacing over the elegant forest green carpet that extended from room to room throughout the entire apartment, turning on the tall brass lamps, polishing the marble, almost-life-sized horse's head on the wood and brass coffee table, explaining the detailed mountain mural over the fireplace that stretched fifteen feet, and nurturing the bonsai forest of pine trees on the mantel.

None of the furnishings crowded the rooms but rather left ample space to move around and through, even in Drake's den, where a cherry wood home theater system took up one entire wall, and some bookcases covered two others.

C.G. examined the hardcover books there, which were mostly nonfiction, biographies, history, and mysteries; and she was surprised to find a whole section of Christian and religious books, too, ranging through the centuries from Josephus to Luther, John Wesley to C. S. Lewis. Swindoll, Schuller, Dobson, Graham, and Peale stood with the others.

She turned to Drake. "You can't have read all these?" she questioned.

He chuckled. "Not hardly. I just got them. But I'm making a dent. I've read three a week so far."

"Three? You must be a fast reader."

"Yes, fast."

As opposed to slow, C.G. thought, *which is what we are supposed to be doing in getting to know each other.*

On a round, cherry wood table beside a high-backed upholstered chair, C.G. saw a burgundy leather volume of Oswald Chambers's classic book, *My Utmost for*

His Highest. On its cover, imprinted in gold, was Drake's name.

She sat down in the chair and picked up the book, admiring its feel, the smell of genuine leather, the fragility of the gilt-edged pages. "I've always wanted this book," she said. "My parents have a copy, and I read it once years ago but have wanted one of my own."

With a smile, Drake went to one of the doors of the entertainment center, opened it, and brought out a small package wrapped in burgundy paper, tied with a gold ribbon. He handed it to her and sat down on a love seat on the other side of the table to watch her.

"What's this?" she asked but knew from how it felt that it was a book. Her eyes widened and she stared at him. "It's not. . . It couldn't be. . ."

Carefully, she slid the ribbon off the package and opened the paper without ripping it. Inside was a matching copy of Chambers's book in burgundy leather, only with her own name imprinted in gold on the cover.

She gasped. "Oh, Drake, it's beautiful. And precious." She gazed deeply into his eyes, which were filled with delight because she was so happy. "I'll treasure it and read it every day."

Where a slender, burgundy ribbon marked a spot, she opened it and read the day's heading, "The Spontaneity of Love," and the Scripture portion from 1 Corinthians 13.

Her eyes filled with tears. How thoughtful he was. This, coupled with his diligent study of faith in the books he'd bought for his library, left C.G. with little doubt that he was a changed man. But would it last?

She leaned toward him, as he did toward her, and they kissed, sweet and lingering. "Thank you, Drake."

"I know the book will bless you, C.G. It already has me."

He told her then about his meetings with Pastor Horton.

"He's great, isn't he?" she said. "Down-to-earth? Understanding?"

"Agreed. Our talks together became a one-on-one discipling course. He figured me out pretty quick, that I was a materialistic guy who wanted to succeed more than anything."

"Which you've done."

"Yes, but at what price? Without going into a sermon, I know there's nothing wrong with being successful, but I gave up important things to be so."

❦

From a Source not his own, Drake found the words to explain. "No more. God is now first in my life, C.G., and will remain so. I want to be in His service. I want to know I'm walking where He wants me to walk."

She clapped her hands like a child. "I'm thrilled for you, Drake. There's nothing in this world more satisfying than being right with God. There's unbelievable happiness, hope, contentment. . .oh, now you're a whole man. You're complete in Him."

He smiled, then became serious. "I want you to know, C.G., that my relationship with God is not tied with you. If you walk away from me right now and I never see you again, I still want to grow and stay in the center of God's will."

C.G. moved over to the love seat and put her arm through his and laid her head on his shoulder. "I pray that will always be your commitment, Drake."

They sat there, quietly enjoying the closeness of the moment, until Drake said, "You think my decision was a hasty one, don't you?"

C.G. sat up, her expression thoughtful. "You must admit, Drake, that it happened quickly. You go to church with me one Sunday, and boom, there you are, a dedicated Christian again."

"It wasn't quite that fast, but, yes, it does sound as though I did it—or pretended to do it—just to win you over."

"I don't want to think that."

"You don't have to." He placed his hands on her upper arms and held her away from him so he could focus on her questioning blue eyes that made him giddy inside.

"C.G., I've always been a decisive man. I make my living by rational and logical thinking. While there can be deep emotion in being a Christian, for me, after listening to the Sunday school lesson and the pastor's sermon, then talking with him, it was a logical and rational decision to turn my life over to God. Completely. There weren't tears or fireworks for me, but I know it's real."

C.G. smiled. " ' "Come now, and let us reason together, says the Lord." ' "

"Isaiah 1:18 [NKJV]. I learned that one as a kid, but it was meant for me. I'm a reasoning kind of guy."

"Yes, you are, and what you're saying makes sense."

He stood up and she did, too. "It's getting late," he said. "Do you want to see the rest of the apartment or go home?"

"I want to see everything the fifty-cent tour allows me to see."

"You got it, Lady." He went to the impressive entertainment center and turned on his CD player. Soft, classical music floated through the whole house as they resumed a leisurely exploration.

A half hour later, they were sitting at the oval table in his cheerful breakfast nook, sipping glasses of sweetened iced tea, and Drake knew she belonged there. Her presence had left an image he would remember and feel long after she was gone—her moving through each room of his apartment, standing near this window, sitting in this chair, touching his books, complimenting his taste.

Before C.G., there had been a few friends—though not close ones—and a few women—though not meaningful ones. There had been places to go, things to do, but nothing that mattered much. He was a man consumed with the joy his work brought him, and when he got home he wanted to relax, more likely than not by reading the latest technical journal in his field.

Thinking back on his rather lone-wolf existence, he supposed that was the price to be paid for becoming the best in his field, and he knew he was the best.

But now what? With a thriving career, plenty of money, and a fine place to live, where was the next challenge? What things did he still need?

He had learned in the past weeks that things didn't speak to him in that golden voice of C.G.'s. Things didn't look at him with admiration and feel soft the way her lips did beneath his.

He and Pastor Horton had spoken of material things and how there's nothing wrong with acquiring them, as long as they don't take priority over a relationship with God.

He reached over and took C.G.'s hand and gently pressed the back of it to his lips. "Sweetheart, look at me." She did, and his heart warmed to the vibrant attention she gave him, her eyes shimmering blue pools under the glow of the polished brass chandelier above the table.

He was scared. More than scared—he was petrified that she'd say no. Turn him down. Never speak to him again.

For the first time in his adult life, Drake Forrest thought he might fail.

"C.G.," he began, then stopped.

"Yes?" The porcelain ivory of her forehead raised in question, and he longed to smooth it with his fingers.

Drake took a deep breath. *Here we go, Lord. Help me, will You?* With a tremor in his voice that reminded him of his high school days, he said, while squeezing her hand, "C.G., I love you. Will you marry me?"

422

Chapter 22

C.G.'s eyes became giant saucers of surprise, then puzzlement, and she said nothing, just stared at him. He felt the moments as an eternity.

"C.G.? What are you thinking?"

She swallowed. "I don't know what to say."

"Yes would be simple."

"I. . .I can't say that, Drake."

"Why? Because you don't trust me?"

"I'm sure you're sincere."

"Now. But only time will prove how deep my commitment is, right?"

"Yes."

"You told me you love me."

"I do, but. . ."

"What?"

"It's too soon to make so major a commitment. We've known each other such a short time, and even though you're counseling with Pastor Horton and have made a recommitment. . ."

She paused, and he knew she didn't want to express her doubts out loud, but he knew what they were.

"You still wonder if my sudden return to church may be just to win you. Isn't that right?"

"No, no, not at all. I believe you when you say you've turned your life back to the Lord and. . .and I'm thrilled that you want to marry me."

Her hands were cold and trembling, and he wanted desperately to make them warm and calm again.

"But we need time to be sure of our love."

Drake caressed her hands, then kissed the palms of both. "I will wait for you forever." His words were barely audible, but he knew she'd heard them when she reached up to a shock of his hair that had fallen across his forehead and gently, with her fingers, blended it back in place. Her touch made him shiver, gave him life and hope, and he knew he would do whatever it took to make her his.

He leaned forward then, and with one hand raised her face to meet his kiss, which was tentative at first, as though he had no right to be doing it, but when she did not pull away and even leaned into the kiss, he groaned and moved closer.

His hands felt the silken skin of her face; he smelled the delicious scent of perfume that she wore. It reminded him of honeysuckle—sweet, intoxicating, filling the air with dreams, and he stood and pulled her into his arms in a fierce embrace and deepened the kiss that was not like any he had ever experienced before.

She was his. She loved him.

They stepped back and opened their eyes at the same time, and C.G. knew with her heart she was where she wanted to be: with Drake, in his arms, in his life.

Her rational mind, though, cautioned her to wait, to be sure.

"I'd like for you to talk with Pastor Horton," Drake said. "Get his impression of me and my intentions."

She gave him a tender smile. "I'd rather make up my own mind, Sir." She broke away from him and went into the great room to retrieve her purse.

"I take it your answer is no to my proposal?" he asked.

"For now."

"So I should let the preacher go home, the one I've hidden in the laundry room all night who was going to marry us?"

"Most definitely." C.G. laughed, and the sweet sound of her voice only reinforced Drake's fascination with her. He really would have married her right then if her answer had been yes. It wasn't easy for him to wait, but he would, because he understood her hesitation and respected her wishes. She was wise and good, a lethal combination that made him love her all the more.

"I'd better get you home," he said. "As it is, we're both probably going to fall asleep at work tomorrow."

As he escorted C.G. toward the front door, he saw on the polished wood table in the foyer a stack of mail, and the envelope on top was in the familiar hand of his mother. He knew the big, red letters "PHOTO, DO NOT BEND" sprawled along one edge meant there was a picture inside of "the perfect woman" she wanted him to meet.

With a chuckle of patience toward his mother who never let go of a good project once she got started on it, he picked up the envelope, excused himself from C.G., and strode into the kitchen, where he tore it into four pieces—without opening it and looking at the picture inside—and dropped it into his trash compactor. Turning the knob to the right, with satisfaction he heard the grinding of the arm as it lowered to crush the envelope and its contents among the garbage and other trash.

"I don't need your matchmaking, Mother," he said softly. "I've found the perfect woman for me. All by myself."

He went to join C.G.

❋

"What have you done to that man?" Dottie asked C.G. a week after the memorable night when Drake had told her he loved her and asked her to marry him.

"What man are you referring to?" C.G. asked innocently, keeping her head down as she calculated a long row of complicated figures involving a comparison of voice and data communications for all twelve branches of Ashford Bank and Trust.

Dottie plunked down in the seat in front of C.G.'s desk and clucked her tongue. "I'm talking about that gorgeous male Drake Forrest, who is trying his best to act as though you're nothing more to him than wallpaper, only he can't keep the glaze out of his eyes when he looks at you or the longing from his voice."

"Oh, that man." C.G. peered up at Dottie. "Is he acting strangely?"

Dottie shook her head back and forth in disbelief. "Do you two really think you're fooling anyone? Well, I take that back. Susie Black is so dense she still thinks she has a chance with Drake. Have you noticed how she falls all over herself trying to do things for him?"

C.G. grimaced. "Yes, I have noticed."

"So, great boss, tell me all the details of your torrid romance."

"I can't tell you anything, Dottie. Not yet. Maybe someday."

Dottie squinted her eyes. "Ooo, that sounds serious."

"Could be, but we have to maintain a proper professional relationship here at the bank."

"I understand. Has he told you he's madly in love with you?"

C.G. looked over Dottie's shoulder and said nothing.

"Does he want to sweep you up in his arms and take you away from all this?" She waved her arm in a grand arc.

When C.G. still said nothing, Dottie grunted. "Okay, okay, I get the idea, but I want to be the first to know. . .when there is something to know."

Dottie walked out of the office just as Drake came in. "Hi there," Dottie said to him, giving him a look C.G. was sure he would recognize as awareness of "the situation."

"Dottie," he responded with a smile, though he was looking at C.G. with large blue eyes filled with the same yearning she was feeling for him.

"Miss Grady, is that comparison of voice and data communications ready for me?" He stopped a respectable distance in front of her desk.

"Almost, Mr. Forrest. I'll have it on your desk in a half hour."

"Good."

Trying not to smile, he said, "I'll pick you up for the theater right after work. *The Sound of Music* is one of my favorite plays."

"Mine, too."

"We'll have dinner first, in Atlanta, at the Plantation House. It's new, and they say the atmosphere takes you back a hundred and fifty years."

"I've never been there. It sounds. . .wonderful." The words came from deep in her throat, and Drake reacted to them and took a step toward her but then stopped when James Wyatt shuffled into the office.

"Oh, Mr. Forrest. Here are the figures you wanted." He handed a large manila folder to Drake, and C.G. wondered what was in it. Drake hadn't told her James was working on a special project for him. She didn't like not being included.

"Thanks, James. You do good work," Drake said.

Has he done other things for Drake? C.G. wondered, staring at a thrilled James who was preening from the compliment, his shoulders thrown back, his chin raised.

Drake gave him his full attention. "How long have you worked here, James?"

"Three years."

"Plan to stay forever?"

James gulped. "I don't know. I guess that depends on what opens up, or if I have a good offer somewhere else."

Drake smiled. "It's good to have a career plan. Know where you want to be in five years. Ten years."

"Yes, Sir. I have some ideas on that."

"I'd like to hear them."

Drake turned to C.G. "I'll expect that report on my desk, then, in a half hour."

"It will be there," she said, *along with a few questions,* she wanted to add. Since when had James and Drake become buddy-buddy? It almost sounded as if Drake had some job in mind for James. What could it be?

When Drake left, she and James talked over some business, and then she asked him what he'd given Drake.

"Just a comparison of voice and data communications for the past year."

C.G. frowned. That's exactly what Drake was waiting for from her. Why would he ask James for the same figures unless he didn't think he could trust hers?

C.G. felt a nagging concern over what was happening and planned to ask Drake about it as soon as she took the report to his office.

A half hour later, armed with the statistics he'd requested, C.G. went to his secluded office to give them to him. He wasn't there, so she sat down and waited ten minutes, then left because she had an appointment with one of the vice presidents. She placed the folder with the information in the center of his desk and was frustrated because she hadn't been able to ask him about James.

Chapter 23

C.G., why haven't I received that report from you?"

It was Drake asking the question as she poured herself some coffee from the hospitality area in the bank's lobby. The stern expression on his face told her he was not happy with her.

"I left the folder on your desk more than an hour ago," she explained with a forced smile. She hadn't cared for his tone of voice and hoped no one else had heard him. Being reprimanded in public was not what professional colleagues did to one another.

"On my desk?" he questioned.

"Yes."

"Well, it's not there now."

C.G. frowned. "Maybe you moved it without realizing what it was."

"I don't think so."

"Why don't we go and look?"

Without waiting for his approval, C.G. moved quickly across the lobby and down the hall to Drake's office. Together they scanned his desk and the other furniture in the room, but the folder was not there.

"I don't understand what happened to it," C.G. exclaimed. "I put it right here." She tapped the center of Drake's desk. "You were gone, so I waited a few minutes, then had to get to a meeting with Mr. Cole—"

"C.G., I need that report." His words were sharp.

She slowly crossed her arms over her chest and said, "Really? Didn't you get the same figures from James Wyatt? Why must you have them from me, too? Actually," she went on before he could answer, "I'm puzzled why you would ask the same report of both of us."

"Now don't get miffed, C.G.," Drake said, coming up to her and taking both her hands in his. "This is the way I do things. With any important information, I get it from at least two sources, sometimes even three. You wouldn't believe how many errors creep into vital statistics. Yes, it's extra work originally, but in the long run it cuts costs and saves valuable time."

The logic of his procedure was not lost on her, but C.G. still felt he should have come to her, as division manager, and told her what he was doing.

"I'm sorry if you feel I overstepped your authority."

"I do feel that, but I understand your method."

He gave her a lopsided grin. "Good. Shall we kiss and make up?" He put his arms around her waist and gave her a quick peck, but it still sent shivers to her toes.

They had just broken their embrace when James Wyatt appeared behind them.

"C.G., I picked up this folder by accident earlier when I came to see Mr. Forrest. I'd put some of my own work down on the desk while I waited for him to come back, and when he didn't, I grabbed up what I thought was mine, but it included yours as well."

He held the folder out to her, and C.G. flipped it open, checked its contents, then handed it to Drake. "I believe this is what you wanted."

He took it with a straight face, although she saw the regret in his eyes. "Thank you, Miss Grady."

James left, and as soon as he was gone, Drake moved toward C.G. "Now where were we?"

C.G. scooted toward the door. "I'm out of here. Some of us have work to do and can't stand around being kissed and held in someone's arms."

She hurried back to her office and quickly sat down, for her legs were weak. Another minute in Drake Forrest's arms, and she would not even have noticed if the president of the bank had walked in and discovered them together.

❀

Something was wrong, very wrong. While her personal relationship with Drake was deepening each time they were together, their business relationship was subtly changing. And C.G. didn't know why.

Looking back over the past three weeks, strange things had happened. Mysterious things she could not explain, but all had pointed to her as being inept in managing the Information Systems Division.

It had started with the comparison of voice and data communications that Drake had asked for from both her and James. Incredibly, James's figures had been correct, while Drake had found several glaring, sloppy errors in hers. The matter was made worse because it proved to be an inaccurate transfer of numbers, so silly a mistake a first-year employee would not have made it. But it looked as though she had.

She was sure she hadn't, of course, but she also couldn't explain it.

Maybe Dottie was right in saying she was distracted thinking of Drake. It was getting harder every day at the bank to pretend he was only someone she worked with and not the man she loved.

Oh, yes, she loved him, completely.

Seeing Drake, hearing his voice, working side by side with him without reaching over and touching his hand or his face, or running her fingers through

428

his hair, was far more difficult than she'd thought it would be when she'd insisted the night he proclaimed his love for her and asked her to marry him that they wait before making a permanent commitment to each other.

They were already committed, more and more every moment they spent together. Drake was a wonderful man. A solid, dependable man who solved complicated problems at work easily and just as easily fixed the leaky faucet in her kitchen sink. He mowed grass and painted fences and didn't mind strolling through a shopping mall.

They read together, current books as well as the Scriptures, and they had long discussions over doctrinal issues and how to live a Christ-centered life. His insight into the human character was amazing, and C.G. knew he was allowing God to bring him wisdom.

So it was no wonder she had trouble concentrating on anything other than him. She remembered Dottie saying, "I'm amazed you keep your job when your mind is so often elsewhere."

Then there was the important meeting Drake called, which was to be attended by her, Dottie, and James, to present them with a Proposed Implementation Plan. She was a half hour late, and Drake was livid. Controlled livid, because he was a professional, but livid nonetheless.

"It's nice of you to join us, Miss Grady," he ground out the words. "The three of us have gotten better acquainted waiting for you."

C.G. was puzzled. "I've been in a meeting with four other division managers until just now. According to my calendar, we were to meet at eleven o'clock—" she looked at her watch— "which it is now—exactly. What's the problem?"

"The problem is that our meeting was scheduled for ten-thirty." Fiery dark eyes met hers and condemned her. In Drake Forrest's time frame, there was no excuse for lateness or misunderstanding.

C.G. distinctly remembered seeing the time on her calendar that morning before she'd gone to her other meeting. She was not about to blame her secretary for putting down the wrong time, which must be the explanation.

"I'm here now," she said with a little smile, which was not returned by Drake, though both Dottie and James looked sorry for her. "Shall we proceed?"

C.G. didn't really understand why Dottie and James were there anyway. Drake could have given her the information, and she could have passed it on to them on a need-to-know basis. For some reason, he wanted all three of them informed of what was going on. Was this another indication that he didn't trust her capabilities?

"As you know," Drake told them, "the acquisition date for Georgia National to take over Ashford Bank and Trust is set for December 15. Implementation of the merging of the databases of both banks will be December 1. We'll switch to digital here at the main branch first but leave the analog service in place so the other branches can still communicate until we convert all the branches to digital, one branch a day."

He handed them a ten-page document entitled "Proposed Implementation Plan" which listed the date the new system would be installed in each branch, the name and number of the equipment vendor doing the work, the name of each branch manager and phone numbers to that bank, contacts for the three telephone companies being used in the particular region each serviced, and the names and numbers of assistants in his office and his secretary should he need to be contacted. The document gave November 15 as the date when a Final Implementation Plan would be on C.G.'s desk.

"That does it." Abruptly, Drake stood and ended the meeting.

Dottie and James made a hasty retreat, but C.G. stayed, knowing she had to apologize even though she still did not understand the mix-up and wasn't happy with the fact that Drake was so upset by it.

※

Drake wanted to forget that C.G. had been late, but he couldn't. He was beginning to worry about her reliability. In the beginning, her work had been excellent and her cooperation and quick facilitating of needed information had made his job easier. But lately inconsistencies were occurring that neither he nor she could explain.

Soon his contact at Georgia National Bank was going to ask if C.G. and her assistants should remain in their positions when the acquisition was completed. A month ago Drake would have given an immediate yes to all three. Today, he was reconsidering C.G., and he was in pain.

He loved this woman with his whole heart. He knew she was intelligent, capable, witty, lovable—his mind quickly turned from her business acumen to her adorable personality.

It had been the hardest thing he'd ever done to work closely with her here at the bank. His mind kept wandering down the hallway to her office where he imagined her sitting, her soft, expressive hands working the computer keyboard or holding the telephone, her eyes scanning information, her voice speaking—that voice he relished when it spoke his name and thanked him for every small thing he did for her.

She was his love. But he just might have to recommend she be fired from her job.

430

Chapter 24

"Chryssie, I have a favor to ask of you."

"Sure, Mom. What is it?"

It was a week before Thanksgiving, and mother and daughter, along with three other women, were in the church basement sorting through shelves of canned goods and boxes of food for what would be used to provide a Thanksgiving dinner for the homeless in the area.

C.G. and her mom were part of the Helping Hands ministry, which collected food, clothing, and medical supplies throughout the year for the needy. C.G. particularly enjoyed helping at Thanksgiving and Christmas.

"I don't want you to say no until you've heard everything I have to say."

Properly warned, C.G. agreed.

"You know I've been trying to get you to meet a certain man whom I think you would like."

"Yes, Mom."

"You have steadfastly resisted my efforts."

"Yes, Mom."

Mom put some cans of pumpkin pie mix down on a nearby table and faced her daughter. "Chryssie, I'm asking you, for my sake, to just meet this man once."

"Mom. . ."

"I'm embarrassed that you've been so stubborn. His mother is a good friend of mine, and I hate to keep telling her that I'm getting no cooperation from you."

C.G. gave her mom a hug, then stepped back and looked at her. "I'm not doing this to be difficult. Honestly. I know you think this man would be good for me, but I've told you I'm seeing someone, and we're pretty serious."

"Then why haven't your father or I met him?"

"We just want to be sure, so we're taking it one day at a time. I think soon I'll be able to bring him to the house to meet you."

Her mother looked so crestfallen that C.G. felt sorry for her. She imagined it hadn't been easy for her to constantly tell her friend that her daughter showed no interest in her son. It also showed disrespect for her mother's wishes.

"Mom, you told me once this man doesn't really want to meet me either."

"Well. . .yes. . .he's very busy with a project at work that leaves him almost no time at all for a social life. That's the reason, probably. But his mother feels just as strongly as I do that once you meet each other, you'll find common ground. She's most impressed by you."

"I've never met her."

"I've described you to her."

"Dare I ask what you said?"

Her mom patted C.G. on the cheek. "I simply told her the truth, that you are marvelous, and bright, and loving, and sophisticated. What man in his right mind wouldn't want you?"

"Don't you think that was a bit of oversell, Mom?"

"Absolutely not. In any case, I just wish you would consent to meeting him. For lunch. That's all. Nothing major. Just lunch." She gave C.G. a pleading look. "Just lunch. How bad could that be?"

C.G. sighed. "Okay, Mom, I'll meet him, but just for lunch."

"Oh, Chryssie," her mother exclaimed, her eyes bright with excitement, "that's wonderful. Thank you. I'll set it up. I wouldn't be surprised if someday you thank me for being so stubborn about this."

"We're talking lunch here, Mom, not marriage for life."

"I'll call my friend, Katherine, and set it up," her mother gushed. "Oh, she'll be so pleased."

They hugged each other, and C.G. decided not to confide that the only reason she'd agreed to see the man was to end her mother's silly maneuvering once and for all. She'd meet him, report no interest at all, and that would be the end of it.

She, of course, wanted no other man but Drake. They were closer than ever away from work, but at the bank the tension between them was worsening, and Drake was being more and more friendly with James Wyatt. C.G. didn't want to think why.

It was only later when she was home that C.G. realized she didn't even know the man's name. It didn't matter, though, because he wasn't going to be a part of her life, not when she was in love with Drake Forrest, and was going to marry him.

Yes, she'd known she wanted to marry him for weeks now, but she still thought it too soon to make such a major commitment. If their love for each other was real and lasting, it could stand the test of a few more months of waiting.

She felt sorry for her mother, though, who really believed her friend's son was the man for her. C.G. hoped she would not be too disappointed when it didn't work out the way she'd wanted.

❀

"Drake, Drake, you'll never guess what's going to happen."

Drake's mom was at her son's apartment, having brought him some sour cream chocolate cake. She'd also invited him home for Thanksgiving dinner. Her brother and sister-in-law and their two children, Drake's teenage cousins, were going to be there, too. They all got along well, and it would be an enjoyable day.

"What's going to happen, Mother?" Drake asked, trying to decide which he enjoyed most, the rich chocolaty taste of the cake itself, or the old-fashioned fudge icing with which it was frosted.

"Jane's daughter has finally agreed to meet you."

Drake choked on a big chunk of cake that slipped down the wrong way. This endless project of his mother's to match him up with a friend's daughter was getting on his nerves.

He was in love with C.G. Grady and was going to marry her. He knew she wanted the same thing, although she had still not agreed to be his wife.

They'd spent nearly every evening together for months now and had discovered their similarities and differences and had survived a few disagreements. Most importantly, they now shared the same faith.

"Did you hear what I said, Drake?" his mother went on. "Jane's daughter, Chryssie, has agreed to have lunch with you."

"Is that her name—Chryssie?" He snorted and gave his mother a discouraging look. "Sounds like a Barbie doll, Mother, not a real, live woman."

"Chryssie's not like that at all," she persisted. "She's very intelligent and has a prestigious job. In computers. Just like you."

Drake groaned. "But, Mother, I've told you I'm seeing someone now and it's serious."

"Oh? Then why haven't your father and I met her?"

"You will. Soon. We're just taking a little time to be sure it's right."

"In the meantime, though, won't you agree to meet with Chryssie? It's only for lunch. Just lunch. Oh, Drake, I've worked for months on this. You can't turn me down now."

Drake gave her a bear hug. After chocolate cake and cold milk, how could a man say no to his mother? "All right, I'll have lunch with this Chryssie person, but only on the condition that you understand it's just for lunch. Don't go making honeymoon reservations for us in Hawaii."

"Drake, don't be ridiculous." She smiled. "Actually, you might prefer the Caribbean."

"I'll decide on the restaurant," Drake said firmly.

"Fine."

He took his mother by the shoulders and gave her a special look of indulgent love. "I'm sorry you're going to be disappointed in this meeting, Mother, because you will be. I'm in love with the most wonderful woman in the world, and her name is not Chryssie."

❧

In her hand C.G. held the Final Implementation Plan that Drake had given her, right on time, as everything he did was right on time.

He was an amazing man, and having worked with him these past four months, she had come to respect him tremendously and understand why he was in such demand by the top companies in the country. When he gave his word, he stood by it. When he made a decision, he made it happen.

He was not easy to work with, or forgiving of mistakes, or understanding of sloppy work; but he was fair, and he worked harder than anyone else to complete a project on schedule.

She looked at the plan again, she being the only one to have received it, not Dottie and James, as they had the proposed plan.

The final plan included order documentation for the three phone companies they had to use and for the twelve branches, each of which would receive separate bills. Carefully itemized were the new billing numbers, circuit I.D. numbers, service order numbers, and the installation dates Drake had ordered.

Additionally, there were the billing numbers for the old analog circuits, their circuit I.D. numbers, disconnect order numbers, and the date service was to be disconnected. Impressive. Perfect.

The word "perfect" made her think of the man her mother had been trying to get her together with. Well, today her wish was coming true: C.G. was meeting him for lunch at the Magnolia Tree, a charming downtown restaurant with a reputation for excellent and innovative cuisine. He had suggested it, through his mother, through her mother to her, and C.G. gave him credit for having good taste.

She'd worn a lightweight ivory wool suit with fabric buttons down the front and at the wrists. The jacket was long and slimming, looked just as nice unbuttoned, and was accented by a gold lapel pin at the shoulder in the shape of a rose. Matching gold earrings shone to advantage, for her hair was swept back in a tiny French twist with a small gold comb at its base.

She hadn't dressed up for him, for the suit was one she often wore to the office, but she did want to look her best, for the sake of her mother.

C.G. went to the rest room, checked her makeup, and added a dab of perfume behind both ears. Why she was nervous she did not know, for this was going to be the first and last lunch she would have with Mr. Perfect.

Back in her office, she took her purse out of the drawer and withdrew her car keys from it.

She did not notice that Drake's Final Implementation Plan was not in the same position it had been in when she'd left.

Chapter 25

Walking out to her car, C.G. realized she was dreading this lunch, wishing she had never agreed to meet this man. What could possibly come from it except her mother being disappointed that the two of them would not become a couple?

Because she'd lost the picture her mom had sent her of him and had not received another, she had no idea what he looked like. Interestingly, though, his name was Drake. She had never known a Drake in her life, and now she was in love with one and about to meet another.

She wondered if this Drake was as embarrassed about the matchmaking as she was and would be just as glad as she when this obligatory lunch was over.

It only took her five minutes to drive to the downtown square, and parking was easy. She entered the restaurant, a small but elegant place with crisp honey gold tablecloths, matching napkins, fresh flowers in delicate vases, and fifties music playing softly in the background.

When she gave her name, she was shown to a table by the hostess, who told her that her companion would arrive soon. "He's just called to say he will be delayed but only shortly."

"Thank you."

C.G. sat down in the corner booth and the hostess asked, "Would you like anything to drink while you wait?"

"Just water, please. With lemon."

The hostess walked away and C.G. took a deep breath, almost glad she had another moment or two to compose herself.

In her single life she had had two blind dates, and while neither had been disastrous, both had been boring to the point she would have enjoyed herself more being at home watching Sesame Street.

Her water arrived, and she sipped it gratefully, her throat suddenly dry. Looking slowly around the room, from one table to another, she speculated on the life story of each person. She even tried putting names to the jolly grandmother, the pouty teenager, the shy, dark-haired beauty whose hand was being held by a man with red hair.

At the front of the restaurant she saw her hostess talking to someone, and when the man stepped around her, C.G. gasped.

It was Drake.

She choked on her water and spilled a little when she set the glass down with a clunk on the table.

How can I explain what I'm doing here? she thought in panic. *Will he believe that I'm meeting a man for lunch in whom I have absolutely no interest?*

She hurriedly picked up the large menu and put it in front of her face, but it was too late. He'd seen her and was coming toward her table.

"C.G., what are you doing here?"

Picking up on the vehemence in his voice, she slowly lowered the menu and prepared to tell her implausible story when she was stopped by the look of raw fury on his face. Every muscle along his cheekbones was taut, as was the hard line of his mouth across his teeth. His eyes blazed; his nostrils flared.

"Drake, what's the matter with you? What's happened?"

His eyes bored into her. "The game is over, Mata Hari." The words cut sharper than any knife could have.

C.G. started to get up, but Drake pushed her back down, a powerful hand digging into her shoulder. The look he pierced her with was one she never wanted to see again. It was hard, almost cruel, and it told her that she was in serious trouble. But why?

"What made you do it?" he growled, leaning over her, his face only inches from her own. "Why did you risk your reputation as well as mine?"

C.G. was speechless, having no idea what he was talking about.

"Well, I'm here to inform you that you didn't get away with it. You've been found out, and believe me when I say that I'll see to it you never work another day in this business again!"

C.G. gulped and her mouth fell open in disbelief at what she was hearing. She had never seen Drake so angry and threatening.

Pushing his hand from her shoulder, she said as steadily as she could, "You'd better explain what you're talking about, because I haven't a clue."

"Really? Try explaining why you want to sabotage the acquisition."

"What?!"

He sat down close beside her, and she could feel the warmth of his breath on her cheeks. "You're good, C.G., very good. That innocent look you wear so effectively perfectly covers your deceit."

"Drake, just tell me what you're talking about." She was getting frustrated and annoyed at being accused of some horrendous crime of which she had absolutely no knowledge. She was also amazed and disappointed that Drake could think her guilty of something so terrible.

"The installation dates of the new circuits—why did you change them?"

"I didn't. Good heavens, why would I? That's your responsibility."

Drake glared at her, and slammed his arm across the back of the booth in a gesture C.G. could only assume was his way of telling her she could not escape him. But why would she want to?

A muscle twitched just below his right eye and the hand that lay on the table flexed and did not relax.

"I have proof that you called the three phone companies we're working with and changed the installation dates of the new circuits."

"Proof? That's impossible, because I did not call anyone."

"When I contacted the companies to verify that the circuits would be installed on the dates I ordered, I was told they'd been changed. 'By whom?' I asked each of the service reps."

"Do you mean someone can change those dates over the phone?"

Drake grunted. "Oh, no, one must have written verification for a new installation date request."

C.G. straightened her back and looked him straight on. "They did not get that from me, Drake."

He leaned even closer. "Oh, yes, they did, Miss Grady. Each of the service reps has on file a fax from you, signed by you, on Ashford Bank and Trust stationery."

C.G. felt like she'd been stabbed. She could hardly breathe. "That's. . .that's impossible."

"I saw them. All three requests, with your signature, which I compared with others I got from your secretary, Greta."

She knew Drake was barely holding his temper. He looked as though he hated her, and she understood why. If the change had not been caught in time, there would have been chaos, not to mention that his reputation would have been seriously damaged, if not ruined altogether.

He thought she'd betrayed him, so she understood his rage, but she also knew he loved her, and shouldn't he be believing her and trying to find out what really happened?

Tears gathered in her eyes and slid down her cheeks.

"Oh, please," he roared, and nearby customers looked up, startled. "Don't play the poor, wrongly accused woman with me."

Suddenly the anger left him, and anguish took its place. "How could you have done this to me, C.G.? To your own bank?" He looked as if he were going to cry any moment, and her spirit rallied a little at the realization that he still cared and was trying to figure out what had happened.

She reached out and put her hands on both sides of his face. "Drake, believe me, I did not do this. I can't explain it. I don't know how the phone companies got my signature on the letters, but it was not from me." She said the last words slowly, with great emphasis.

Drake grabbed her wrists and hung on tightly. "No one, C.G.—and I mean no one—interferes with my work and gets away with it."

Flinging her hands away from him, he sprang to his feet, then leaned back over the table and glared at her. "I don't know why you made me fall in love with you—"

"Made you?" C.G. cried, scooting out of the booth and bravely confronting him. "Made you? If I remember correctly, Mr. Forrest, you were the one who decided you felt that way about me, almost as soon as you met me, while I was trying to keep my distance from you."

"A clever game, obviously."

"It was no game, and you know it. You've just rededicated your life to the Lord. How can you judge me so harshly? So unfairly? I'm a sister in Christ."

"I have facts!" he roared and pounded the table with one fist, rattling the dishes and sending one coffee cup crashing to the floor. "You betrayed me!"

The hostess hurried over to them and said firmly, "Please leave our restaurant and continue your argument somewhere else."

C.G. gasped in extreme embarrassment and covered her mouth with her hand. She felt sick to her stomach. Turning, she ran from the restaurant without looking back, praying Drake would not follow her.

She ran all the way to her car and drove to the bank with tears streaming down her cheeks, not realizing she had abandoned lunch with her mother's friend's son.

In her mind she heard, over and over, Drake's stinging words: "You betrayed me! You betrayed me!"

She wanted to go home. How could she go back into the bank after what had happened? Who else knew what Drake had just told her?

Her heart was pounding fearfully when she entered the doors, and she walked on unsteady legs toward her office. No one gaped at her; the tellers paid no attention; even Greta gave her a cheerful, "Hi, how was lunch?"

At her desk, she collapsed into her chair just at the moment she knew she could not take another step. Her breathing was shallow and her face was bathed in sweat.

She half expected Drake to come barging into the bank, into her office, and continue his diatribe against her. But he didn't come.

Ten minutes went by before C.G. felt in control of herself. She was ashamed of her unprofessional argument with Drake, in public, no less, and wished she could have stood up to him without tears, but she hadn't.

How was she going to convince Drake that the "proof" he had was not reliable?

Then another cold, deadly thought struck her mind: Someone had written three letters in her name requesting changes of dates on the installation of the circuits.

Someone had forged her signature.

Someone wanted to destroy her career.

Chapter 26

The ringing of the phone jarred C.G. from her thoughts on the incredible realization that someone was playing with her career.

"C.G., this is Gerald Ramey. Please come to my office immediately." The phone went dead with an ominous click, and C.G. knew what was coming.

With zombie-like steps she made her way to the large, corner office of the bank's president, a tall, heavily built man with thinning white hair, with whom she had always gotten along well. She listened to him accuse her of the heinous act of sabotage.

He showed her the faxed letters under her signature, and C.G. had to admit they looked genuine.

Though Mr. Ramey did give her a chance to defend herself, he sternly concluded, "In the face of this irrefutable evidence that Drake Forrest has brought me, I have no choice but to relieve you of all responsibility for the Information Systems Division."

She was fired.

"Please gather your personal belongings and leave the bank immediately," the president said.

C.G. stared at him. "But, Sir, I'm willing to stay a few weeks until you find someone else, or until I can prove my innocence."

He did not smile at her but stood to his feet behind his desk, and from the un-compromising expression on his face, C.G. knew the matter was decided. There was no hope of understanding. And she couldn't blame him. If a man with the reputation of Drake Forrest reported such a contemptible act by a bank employee, what else could be done but to get the traitor off the premises immediately?

"Mr. Ramey, I am not guilty of what I'm accused of," she told him one last time. "Please let me stay and try to clear my name."

"No, Miss Grady. But I can promise you there will be a full-scale investigation, and if you are found innocent, you will be contacted." Then his eyes became kinder. "You have been an outstanding employee up to this time. We thank you for all your efforts on behalf of Ashford Bank and Trust. Good-bye." He did not offer her his hand.

It took C.G. thirty minutes to clear her desk and credenza of personal things, for she could not get herself to move quickly. Dottie and James came in, aghast at what had happened, both offering to quit in protest, but she insisted they stay and help Drake.

"How can you want us to help your enemy?" Dottie cried.

"I'm going to punch him in the nose," James said, and when C.G. imagined the skinny, underdeveloped James taking on the formidable, muscled Drake, she almost laughed but didn't. James meant what he said; he wanted to defend her, and she appreciated his support more than she could tell him.

She gave each of her two assistants a hug and said, "I don't know how I'm going to prove my innocence, but I swear to you that I did not do what I'm accused of."

"Of course you didn't," Dottie insisted, "and believe me, C.G., James and I will do everything we can here to find out the truth and get you reinstated."

They left, and C.G. was ready to leave, too, but there was one more thing she had to do: She had to go and see Drake.

❀

Drake heard her open his door and come into his office, and he dreaded looking up. His heart was a twisted mass of agony and he didn't know how to deal with his love for C.G. and his fury at her betrayal of him. *Why, Lord? Why?* he questioned.

"Drake, I. . .I came to say good-bye."

He stood up, but he wasn't prepared for the anguish he saw etched on her usually serene features. Though her face clearly showed where rivulets of tears had slid over her cheeks, she had never looked more beautiful to him—like a martyr going to her death, which was an apt description for, because of him, she had just experienced the death of her career. Mr. Ramey had called him the minute he'd finished with C.G. and told him she'd been fired.

It had taken all of Drake's willpower not to rush to her office and take her in his arms and tell her it was all right, that he knew it was a terrible mistake, that he would find who had done this vile thing, and would make her life right again. He had wanted to do that, but he hadn't. Facts were facts, and he had the evidence on his desk. C.G. was guilty!

Warring against his noble nature that insisted this woman he loved was an angel who would never betray him and her bank was the dark side of his nature that ridiculed him for being a sucker, falling in love with a woman he barely knew and getting involved with the church he'd abandoned years ago.

Satan put him on the rack and made him question his new commitment, C.G.'s spirituality, and where God had been when this "crime" had been perpetrated against him and his employer.

In an instant of time, all these thoughts crashed through his head, vying for supremacy, and Drake was more confused and angry than he could ever remember being.

He was a man who would not be made a fool of, and C.G. Grady had done exactly that. Fortunately, he had discovered her act before havoc had been created among the many branches of the two banks involved.

Now she was here, daring to face him. She was saying good-bye.

"Good-bye, Miss Grady."

Those were the only words he could say. The only safe ones. He wanted to rail at her; he wanted to tell her he adored her.

She gave him a tiny little smile that broke his heart and said quietly, "I have no explanation for what happened, but as God is my Savior, Drake, I did not do it."

"Stop it! Don't bring God into this as your witness."

He wanted to throw something, physically vent his wrath at the impossibility of what had happened.

But it had happened, and he could not look C.G. in the eye, so he turned his back to her and folded his arms across his chest.

There was not a sound in the room. The very air stopped moving, and Drake thought he would never breathe again.

Then he heard the click of his door being closed, and he whirled around and found the space where she'd been standing empty. She was gone. Out of his office. Out of his life.

"Oh, God," he groaned, covering his face with his hands, "what is the truth here?" He waited for a thunderbolt from heaven to tell him, but all that he heard was a deafening silence.

❧

In his apartment that night, Drake forgot to turn on the lights, and he sat in his great room alone in the shadows, in total quiet, and wondered what he could do to make the numbness go away.

He hadn't eaten all day. He was lethargic one minute and restless the next. The loss he felt was excruciating because it attacked him personally as well as professionally.

"Why, C.G.? Why?" he moaned.

Leaning over, his hands on his knees, he gazed down at the carpet, searching for meaning out of the worst day in his life.

None of it made sense. What could possibly be C.G.'s motive for doing such a crazy thing?

First of all, she was a Christian, a genuine, loving follower of the Lord. He wouldn't have thought her capable of such deceit. Could she have fooled him all these months into thinking she was honest and trustworthy? Wouldn't he have seen any deviation in her behavior, sensed a frustration or anger or greed that would drive her to betray her own bank and him?

Secondly, she was an intelligent woman, organized and logical in her thinking. Surely she must have known she'd be caught either before or after the crisis. Her signature was on the letters, for Pete's sake. It had been child's play for him to find it.

He stood up and paced the room in a frenzy then, running his hands repeatedly through his hair. "She's innocent. She has to be. C.G.'s too smart to have done such a dumb thing. Too clever."

He stopped and studied the empty fireplace, which was swept clean of winter's ashes. "So, if she's not guilty, then who is dumb enough to pull a stunt like this?" he questioned. "Who wants to hurt C.G.?"

He determined to find out.

❀

C.G. waited 'til the next day to tell her parents the unbelievable story of what had happened to her at the bank. She also apologized to her mother for not keeping the date with her friend's son.

"Sweetheart, how terrible for you," her mother moaned, taking her child in her arms and comforting her. "Why don't you come home for a few days? Let us take care of you while you're hurting."

C.G. drew back and smiled appreciatively. "I'm a grown woman, Mom. I have to take care of myself."

"Which you do admirably. But not now, when you're wounded, when you need time to recuperate and forgive."

"Forgive?"

"Yes, forgive that horrible man who got you fired; forgive the bank for not standing by you. Forgive, or this can destroy you, eat away your self-confidence, and strip you of your ambition to succeed."

"Oh, Mom, at what am I supposed to succeed? My career is ruined. No bank will ever hire me, nor will any other institution."

C.G.'s mom took her daughter to a gleaming, waist-high walnut table upon which sat a huge, old family Bible from the 1800s. "This was your great-grandfather's," she said to C.G., opening the heavy, ornate leather cover. "Read what he wrote there in 1898."

C.G. leaned over the Bible she'd seen all the days of her life and read words she'd read many times before, in the hand of a man she'd never known: "There is no problem that cannot be solved by reading this Book."

She sighed and closed the cover and turned to her mother. "I know that's true, and I know some passages I need to review that will help me through this."

Her mother smiled. "Then stay with us a few days and study. Find peace here in what used to be your home."

C.G. finally agreed and walked a little quicker up the familiar stairs to the sage-and peach-colored room that once had been hers, in which she'd grown from a little girl to a young lady and had left when she'd gone away to college in another city.

Her parents used it now for a guest room, and even though it didn't have her knickknacks on the dresser and her wild animal posters on the wall, it was still her room, and her mind flooded with poignant memories of happy days spent here.

She sank down on the bed, stared up at the ceiling, and whispered, "Dear God, I don't know what to do. I don't know if I can forgive Drake. Guide me, please." Then a tremendous sob escaped her, and she cried herself to sleep.

Chapter 27

The few days C.G. had originally planned to spend with her parents extended longer, as her mother persuaded her to help with a Christmas party she was having for her church missionary group, and her father told her he'd missed their nightly chess games.

With no job, no income, no man to love, and Christmas only two weeks away, C.G. faced the holiday with little enthusiasm. Even decorating her parents' house, shopping with her mother for gifts, caroling door-to-door with the singles' group from church, and being constantly reminded by jingles on the radio and television that this was the season to be jolly, she was sad and discouraged. Nothing in her life was going right, and she didn't know why.

She steadfastly read her great-grandfather's Bible and prayed for wisdom. She found comfort in many of David's Psalms written when he'd been oppressed and misunderstood and pursued by enemies and treacherous family.

One of the most comforting was from Psalm 27:11–14: "Teach me Your way, O Lord, and lead me in a smooth path, because of my enemies. Do not deliver me to the will of my adversaries; for false witnesses have risen against me, and such as breathe out violence. I would have lost heart, unless I had believed that I would see the goodness of the Lord in the land of the living. Wait on the Lord; be of good courage, and He shall strengthen your heart; wait, I say, on the Lord!"

Just as David had believed that God was his Deliverer, his light, and his salvation, C.G. also clung to that belief, knowing that God was walking with her through this dark valley.

She hadn't heard from Drake since the day she had been fired, and the temptation to call him or go to his apartment was almost overpowering at times, but she had enough pride not to throw herself at him. His love for her had not been strong enough for him to believe in her innocence, no matter what the evidence against her, and accepting this appalling fact was particularly hurtful.

Though she'd been looking for a job with any eligible company from Atlanta to north Georgia, C.G. had been unsuccessful. The question inevitably posed by the interviewer, "Why did you leave your last position?" was a painful one to answer honestly, and though she'd been tempted to simply say she'd quit, she knew she could not out-and-out lie. No one wanted her.

She didn't give up trying to clear her name, and she made some calls or went to the various phone companies in an attempt to talk with someone who could help her discover who had falsely represented her.

Each party would not talk with her, and though they displayed various reactions to her story, from sympathy to disbelief, she learned nothing from them until one day, during her second visit to the friendliest service representative, who said to her, "You know, your voice sounds different in person than it did on the phone when you first called about changing the installation date."

"How do you mean?" C.G.'s heart began to race.

"You sounded much older then and. . .grouchier. Like you were having a bad day." *What older woman could have called the phone company and impersonated me?* C.G. pondered. She went through all the possibilities, and none of them made sense.

What if it were a younger woman, just trying to sound older? That introduced a whole new set of characters, and at the top of the list was Susie Black, except that C.G. just didn't think Susie had the knowledge to pull off something so complicated.

She called Dottie at the bank and Dottie agreed. Discussing various candidates, neither could think of someone who would want to destroy C.G.

"You were one of the most popular people here," Dottie insisted, in frustration. "It's been awful without you."

✸

From Dottie, C.G. learned that the acquisition took place on schedule, the equipment changes were implemented without a problem, and that Drake Forrest was only at the bank one or two days a week. "Troubleshooting mostly. James and I are handling the workload until they hire someone to take your place, but the bank personnel see now that that isn't going to be easy. You were a whiz."

There was an awkward silence and then Dottie added, "Oh, phooey, I'm going to stick my nose into your business and ask. Have you heard from Drake at all?"

"No, Dottie, I haven't."

"The bum. How could he turn on you like he did? Not believe in you?"

"He could have lost his reputation over what almost happened."

"And that's more important than believing in the woman he loves and fighting for her?"

"Dottie, I really don't want to talk about this."

"Sure, sure. But listen, I've been doing some snooping around here, and I have an idea who the troublemaker is."

"You do?"

"I'll get back to you in a few days. I may need your help."

"Oh, Dottie, I'll do anything to clear my name."

"Remember that statement."

445

"Well, almost anything," C.G. amended.

❀

Drake's mouth went dry when he got the phone call from his mother: "Your father has had a stroke, Dear. The doctor says it will be touch and go for a few days. Can you come home?"

"Of course. I'm on my way."

Drake's father made it through the dangerous days and was allowed to go home from the hospital a week later. Drake spent as much time as he could with his parents, but it was not easy. The bank acquisition had taken place as scheduled, and his work there was nearly finished, but it still required him to be there at least a couple days a week to be sure things stayed on track.

In addition, he had just signed a contract worth hundreds of thousands of dollars with an Atlanta brokerage firm that would keep him and his firm involved in the latest technology for at least two years.

He was back to his old, familiar grind of working day and night to keep life on target, except he still made time for church, prayer, and Bible study. And he'd had more than one talk with Pastor Horton about C.G.

He knew he needed strength beyond his own to carry him through and that God would provide.

He missed working with the people at Ashford Bank and Trust, now part of the Georgia National Bank family. After C.G. had been fired, Dottie and James, particularly James, had been a big help to him. In fact, every time he'd turned around, there was James, volunteering to do something, anything to get on Drake's good side.

It hadn't taken many such occasions for Drake to realize what James wanted: C.G.'s job.

Losing C.G. was something Drake still had not gotten over, even though at first, when he'd been faced with evidence that she had betrayed him, he was sure he'd never forgive her or want to speak to her again.

Since those early days, he'd thought endlessly about it, coming eventually to the conclusion that C.G. could not possibly have done what he'd blamed her for.

Painstakingly, he'd tried to find out who the real guilty party was, doing so as carefully as he could without arousing suspicion. It had not been easy; the person had covered his or her tracks well.

Drake wanted desperately to see C.G. and to let her know he was working to exonerate her, but he didn't want to give her false hope and take her through more pain if he wasn't successful.

As difficult as it was to stay away from her, he made himself do so, praying all the time that she'd still be there when he came to rescue her.

Now he was facing another crisis: Not many days after his father got home

446

from the hospital, his mother fell in the driveway and broke her kneecap.

Her mending rendered her immobile, in a plaster cast from ankle to hip, in which she would stay for ten days or so; then she'd be put in a fiberglass cast for at least another two months. The doctor told Drake that total healing could take up to a year.

"When is it all going to stop, Lord?" Drake prayed more than once, feeling intensely the buffeting of the storm around him. He was not enjoying the Christmas season at all.

He moved home to help out: cooking, cleaning, fixing, decorating for Christmas, and buying gifts. He was frazzled, and what time he could give away from his several business requirements was pitifully inadequate. He determined to hire some temporary help.

"Oh, you don't have to do that, Dear," his mother told him when he approached her with the idea. "The church is going to start sending in food three days a week, as well as someone to clean."

"You're kidding."

She smiled. "Being a Christian is more than sitting in a pew one hour a week."

"I know, but that's a lot to do for you and Dad."

"It's a service the people are happy to give, in Christ's name."

With relief, Drake went off to work each day and returned home to find nourishing food in the refrigerator, the house sparkling clean, and his father and mother mending. How blessed his parents were to have their lives surrounded by a "family" of believers who cared about each other.

If only he could mend C.G.'s life.

Chapter 28

"Chryssie, I have a favor to ask of you."

It was nine o'clock in the morning, three days before Christmas, and her mother was dashing about the house scooping up wrapping paper, ribbons, and bows, and stuffing them into a huge shopping bag to take to the church to use for decorating the gifts to be given to the Sunday school children.

"I was supposed to go to a friend's house today to clean. Her husband's had a stroke, and she's broken her kneecap. Can you believe it? But I forgot I'm also to be at the church to help wrap gifts. It's an all-day activity."

"Say no more, Mom; I'll be happy to pinch-hit for you. What's the address?"

While C.G. was indeed happy to help out her mother, she hated the fact that she had the time to do so. She still didn't have a job, and future prospects were grim. It was hard to get into the Christmas spirit, though she tried not to let her frustration show and concern her parents.

Her mother handed her a piece of paper. "Katherine will appreciate anything you can do, Dear. She's a good friend."

C.G. smiled. Her mother had dozens of good friends, for she was a charming woman whose style and grace, as well as caring nature, just made people want to be around her.

C.G. came to realize that this friend, however, was different from the others. The first hint came at the front door when the attractive woman on crutches, in her midfifties with ash blond hair, introduced herself as Katherine Forrest. The last name touched a tender spot in C.G.'s heart, and she battled not to be overwhelmed with remorse that she and Drake Forrest were no longer together.

Every day she half expected to hear from him, but in the weeks since she'd left the bank, he had neither called nor written, and she knew this because she went back to her house often to check her mailbox and answering machine.

The second indication that Katherine Forrest was indeed a good friend of her mother's, a very good friend, came when C.G. was dusting the master bedroom. There on the dresser was a picture of a strikingly handsome man in tennis togs, with the racket held firmly in front of him and a determined look on his face.

C.G. found herself staring at Drake Forrest.

"Oh, no," she groaned out loud. "This can't be his parents' home." She remembered Drake telling her they lived in the city, and he had mentioned the street, but she had forgotten it until now—until she found herself in the parental home of the man who had destroyed her career unjustly.

She wanted to pick up the picture and throw it through the window. She wanted to pick up the picture and hold it to her heart. Instead, she finished the housework and fixed a light lunch for Mr. and Mrs. Forrest, who were kind and appreciative and made it easy to see where Drake got his loving side.

Every time C.G. looked at Katherine Forrest she saw Drake, for their facial features and coloring were similar. It was from his father that he got his gruffness of manner and the straight set of his shoulders.

She stayed longer than she'd expected, doing this and that, her reason honestly being to help these unfortunate people. Added to that, though she wouldn't have admitted it, was the bittersweet experience of feeling Drake's presence. Did she still love him? Or despise him?

"He was an easy child to raise," Katherine Forrest told C.G. about Drake, not knowing the two of them knew each other—and well. The two women were in the small white and blue kitchen with its collection of teapots sitting on a long shelf above the cabinets, and C.G. was fixing the older woman a cup of tea.

"Even as a child Drake understood the adult mind. All we had to do was explain why we were saying no or yes, and he reasoned it out for himself that it was in his best interest to trust us. That doesn't mean he didn't have a temper or want his own way occasionally." Mrs. Forrest laughed lightly. "I can show you the closet door he put his fist through one time."

C.G. looked surprised.

"He's been very good to us, and we're proud of his success. Even though he's extremely busy these days with a new client, he stays here as much as he can and does all kinds of things for us. Bless his heart. He offered to hire some temporary help, but we really don't need it with him being here and the church helping as it does."

She gave C.G. an especially warm smile. "Jane, of course, has been a real blessing, and we appreciate all she's done for us, and for sending you to us, Chryssie. You've been a dear today, giving us far more time than you should have."

"I was happy to do so, Mrs. Forrest."

"You really should meet my son, Drake. The two of you would hit it off, I'm sure." She looked at her watch. "In fact, he should be here any minute."

C.G. caught her breath. The possibility of Drake finding her there sent her blood pressure rising.

"If there's nothing else you need me for today, then I'll go," she anxiously told Mrs. Forrest, suddenly desperate to be gone.

For weeks she'd been wanting to see Drake, talk to him, see if he'd had a change of heart, but since she had not heard one word from him, the prospect of being face-to-face with the man who had not believed her and had caused her firing made her intensely uncomfortable.

She had prayed for the courage to forgive him; seeing him in person would tell her whether or not she had been able to. Only she didn't really want to see him.

"Please call my mother or me if there's anything at all you need," she said to Katherine Forrest, who squeezed her hands and said, "You're an angel. I wish my son would find someone as wonderful as you to love." There was a decided twinkle in her eye, and C.G. wondered if she ever played matchmaker as her own mother was doing.

After a quick good-bye, she was out the door, brushing tears from her eyes as she scurried toward her car.

Deep in thought over her own troubles, and looking down at the sidewalk, she did not hear the footsteps approaching until she ran right into. . .someone. Powerful hands grasped her shoulders to keep her from falling, and when she looked up, she almost fainted.

It was Drake.

"C.G.? What are you doing here?"

The sound of his voice sent a thrill through her. The strength of his hands almost made her forget what he had done.

Straightening herself, she backed away from his support and looked into the intense blue eyes of the man she thought she had known so well. They drew her to him as deeply as his words, but she knew there was no point in dreaming of a love that was no longer possible.

"I did some work for your folks."

"What kind of work?"

"Light housework. Straightening up. Lunch."

Drake looked puzzled. "Why are you doing that? Mother said some folks from the church would be cleaning and cooking."

"It was my mother's request. She was going to help your folks today but then couldn't, so she asked me to instead. Since I have nothing better to do. . ."

The words hung in the air, and Drake commented, "No, that's not what you're trained for, is it?"

Not knowing what to say to that remark, or being up to having an altercation with him, C.G. stepped around him and started again for her car.

Drake followed. "C.G., I want you to know how sorry I am about what happened at the bank."

She whirled around and stared at him. "You're sorry? Now you say you're sorry? I could have used your sympathy and understanding back then. I was innocent, but I couldn't convince you of that, and I haven't been able to find any proof to clear my name. So, Mr. Forrest, I'm unemployable at the moment, thanks to you being so sure I was the one who tried to sabotage the acquisition. For a man who told me you loved me, you sure didn't stick around when the going got tough."

She fumbled with her key, trying to unlock the car door, but her hands wouldn't cooperate. They were shaking.

Drake's hands covered hers, stopping her efforts. "C.G., we need to talk."

"I have nothing to say to you. Let me go."

Surprisingly he did, and all the way home C.G. was torn between anger toward him for giving up on her so easily and her own wish they were together again.

"That's impossible," she said out loud, "and you'd better accept it, Girl. Drake Forrest is out of your life forever."

Chapter 29

Drake longed to tell C.G. what he'd been piecing together about the tragedy of her losing her job, but he couldn't—yet. The guilty party was not quite in the net.

The look on her face when she'd seen him seared his conscience. She had suffered professional humiliation and personal betrayal—both of them at his hands—and her tired, sad eyes betrayed her devastation. He wouldn't blame her if she never forgave him.

Despite her accusatory words, he had not felt venom from her. Only an honest asking of how he could have misjudged her so horribly. He didn't know himself.

Going into his parents' house, he listened to ten minutes of his mother's ravings about how wonderful "the Grady girl" was. He would have liked to have told her that he was in love with that Grady girl, wanted to marry her, and still would, as soon as certain things were worked out. And they would be worked out.

※

Katherine called Jane. "Your daughter is a jewel and will be a perfect wife for my son."

"Thank you for thinking so. Between losing her job and her friendship with this man at work, the poor child has been suffering, and I didn't want to suggest another meeting with your son after their lunch date didn't materialize. But with Christmas right around the corner, this may be the perfect time to get them together. After all, what season is more romantic and filled with hope than Christmas?"

"I agree. What shall we do?"

"Why not have them go with us to the community singing of *The Messiah* on Christmas Eve? Could you manage that with your crutches?"

"Drake will help. Kevin can't go, of course, but my brother will be here visiting and will keep him company."

"All right. Afterward, we could come back here for some refreshments."

"And find some way to leave the young people alone."

Jane Grady laughed. "Aren't we wicked, Katherine Forrest?"

"Not at all, Jane Grady. We're only doing what any self-respecting mother would do: Find the very best daughter- and son-in-law possible."

"Do you think we should tell them they'll be meeting each other?"

There was a long pause before Katherine said, "No."

They giggled and then prayed over the phone.

❀

"C.G., this is Dottie. You need to come down to the bank right away."

It was nine o'clock at night, two nights before Christmas.

"Why are you whispering? What's happening?"

"I'll explain when you get here. Park in the shopping center lot. Come to the side door." She hung up.

❀

It was humid and dark when C.G. stepped out of her car. Feeling strangely like a secret agent rendezvousing with a foreign spy, she walked cautiously toward the back of the bank. There were no cars in its parking lot.

She passed the drive-up window and arrived at the small side door employees used to come and go after hours.

It was armed with a security system, but she wouldn't have dreamed of punching in the numbers. That's all she needed to seal her criminal reputation forever—to be caught breaking into a bank where she no longer worked.

The door suddenly opened, and a hand reached out and pulled her inside. She started to scream until she saw that it was Dottie.

"Dottie! Why this cloak-and-dagger stuff?" C.G. questioned, feeling her skin start to crawl. She wasn't adventurous by nature.

"We don't want anyone to know we're here."

"Why?"

"Because we're going to find evidence on who framed you."

"We are?"

"Yes. Now go to James's office and wait for me. Don't turn the lights on. Keep the door open."

C.G. did as she was told, but her heart was pounding. What if someone else at the bank decided to work late? What if James came?

She got to his office and sat down on the only chair he had and tried to keep from fidgeting. She didn't like being there. With the lights off it was pitch-dark, for there were no windows either facing the lobby or the outside of the building. She strained to listen for Dottie. What was this all about anyway?

The motion of a body passing by alerted her to the fact that someone had come into the office, and she jumped up to flee when she was caught—in the arms of Drake Forrest.

"What are you doing here?" she exclaimed, aghast. "Where's Dottie?"

"Here I am." The small lamp on the corner of James' desk was turned on, and C.G. blinked to adjust her vision.

"Why are we here?" C.G. asked. "Why is Drake here?"

"Because he and I think we know who the culprit is who cost you your job, C.G., and we're looking for evidence."

"You and Drake?"

Drake moved closer to her. "It seems Dottie and I have been working separately toward the same goal."

"Really?" So he did care. He believed in her after all. C.G.'s heart swelled with joy, and she thanked God for answering her prayer and almost burst out singing.

Drake swept her into his arms and gave her a long and hungry kiss, then held her close. "I've missed you, C.G. Forgive me for not believing you right from the start."

"Come on, you two," Dottie said impatiently. "You can make up later. We have work to do."

C.G. couldn't leave the warmth of Drake's arms. Nothing else really mattered as long as he believed in her and knew she hadn't betrayed him. But this wasn't the time to mend fences.

"Yes, let's get on with it," she agreed, turning out of his embrace and hugging Dottie.

Nervously she looked over her shoulder, to the now-closed door, positive they would be caught at any moment. She definitely was not into breaking and entering, although technically they weren't doing that because Dottie was an employee, but it felt like it to C.G.

"What are we doing in James's office?" she asked. "I don't think he would take kindly to us being here."

Dottie grunted. "C.G., after I show you two files, you won't care a whit what James Wyatt thinks."

❀

Every year on Christmas Eve, the United Methodist Church of Cheston hosted a community sing-along of *The Messiah*. It was a treasured evening for the three to four hundred people who attended and sang the magnificent oratorio from well-worn copies.

The sanctuary was tastefully decorated with tall candles and sprigs of evergreen, and the pipe organ played Christmas hymns as people took their seats.

Jane and Jonathan Grady arrived with Chryssie and walked down the right aisle.

Katherine Forrest hobbled carefully down the left aisle, on her crutches, aided by her handsome son Drake.

The Gradys went to the center section, the seventh row from the front.

Drake's mom pointed Drake to the seventh row, center section.

Chryssie's mom told Chryssie to go in first.

Drake's mother insisted Drake go in first.

The families met.

Drake and C.G.'s eyes found each other. Then they smiled.

Jane and Katherine hardly breathed, so intent were they on watching the looks on the faces of their children as they met for the first time. They just prayed that there would be an initial interest, a small spark that might grow in time into a significant love. They sighed as the fruition of their long months of match-making came to an end.

"C.G.," her mother said, "may I present the man I've been telling you about. Drake Forrest."

"Drake, this is Chryssie Grady," Katherine Forrest introduced.

With a roguish smile, Drake leaned forward and lingeringly kissed C.G. on the cheek. "What a beautiful name—Chryssie. I've been looking forward to meeting you."

Katherine Forrest's eyes grew round.

"And I you, Mr. Forrest. My mother tells me you are strong, dependable, adorable, protective. . .oh, yes—" she leaned toward him— "and have mischievous eyes."

Jane Grady's eyebrows slid to the ceiling.

"I wonder if we're supposed to fall in love now or wait 'til after the concert," Drake questioned, gazing at his mother, whose mouth was strangely open.

"I'm afraid we'll have to wait, Drake darling," C.G. answered, "as the choir is entering and the soloists."

Jane Grady sank into her chair, stunned.

C.G. and Drake sat down and reached out to each other, their hands locking while they gazed at each other in rapturous attention.

"I must say, Miss Grady, that my mother was absolutely correct when she described you as sophisticated and beautiful, smart, and possessing a peaches-and-cream complexion. You also sing?"

"Yes, I do."

"I'm anxious to hear you."

Katherine Forrest leaned forward to hear every word. Jane Grady leaned back and closed her eyes.

"How's it going?" Jonathan Grady asked his wife, glancing over at his daughter holding hands with a man he'd never met.

He received no answer. For once in their lives, Katherine Forrest and Jane Grady were speechless.

Chapter 30

During intermission, the audience adjourned to a lovely fellowship hall where Christmas cookies and cakes, cheeses, and punch were being served.

"Excuse us, please," Drake said to the mothers and C.G.'s father, and before they had a chance to say anything, he whisked C.G. across the room and through the first door he saw. It happened to be a clothes closet—a small clothes closet, at that—with folding chairs stacked along one side. There was barely room for the two of them and the chairs.

"What are you—?" C.G.'s words were lost when Drake's mouth captured hers in an ardent and prolonged kiss. They clung together, relishing being together, and didn't hear the pounding on the door.

"Don't you think we should tell our mothers we finally figured out we are the object of their matchmaking?" C.G. suggested.

"Later." Drake caressed her face with his fingertips and gazed at her with intense emotion. "I can hardly believe everything worked out between us last night in the bank when Dottie called us in."

"And I'm grateful that finding those pages in James's office on which he practiced forging my signature and the copies of the new installation date requests he instigated were enough to convince you *and* the bank president that James, and not I, was the one who had tried to sabotage the acquisition."

"So he could get rid of you and take your place."

"I still can't believe that timid James was so vicious."

"And that he was responsible for all the other mysterious things that happened, that I blamed you for."

"Like the wrong information sent to you that very first day and the file I'd left on your desk, which James claimed to accidentally have taken."

"The rat."

"Don't forget the figure changes he made in that report you asked both of us to do for you."

"And the wrong time being inserted onto your calendar that made you late for an important meeting with the four of us." Drake growled in disgust. "James always hated working for a woman."

"How do you know that?"

"I began to suspect there was more to James than we realized because he tried too hard to get on my good side. Once I figured he wanted your job, I became his buddy, continued to proclaim your guilt, and soon found out what a frustrated and angry young man he really is."

"But we always got along."

"You thought."

"For him to use his mother as my voice was really incredible. That one time I met her, I knew she wanted more success for her son, but I never would have guessed she would go to such lengths to obtain it."

"Fortunately, that one service rep you found a few weeks ago who thought your voice didn't match the one she'd heard the first time was willing to co-operate with the police and recognized James's mother's voice as the one pretending to be you."

C.G. slipped her arms around Drake's waist and laid her head against his shoulder. "It's fortunate for me I had two people who loved me enough to work to clear my name."

"I can't accept any plaudits, C.G.," Drake admitted. "I was an insensitive jerk who was more concerned over my own ego and career than with yours. I should have known you could never do anything so dishonest."

He choked on the words, and C.G. saw tears in his eyes that filled her with wonder at the depth of his caring.

"You were a true Christian, C.G., to forgive me as you did. Once I realized you had to be innocent, I prayed many long hours for wisdom to sort out the whole mess."

"I did, too." She touched his cheek tenderly. "Isn't it comforting to know God was working in both our lives to bring us together?"

"With a little help from our mothers."

Drake drew her back into his arms and was kissing her thoroughly when the door was suddenly flung open and there stood their mothers.

"What are you two doing in there?" Drake's mom asked sharply.

"Getting acquainted, Mother, just as you wanted," Drake answered.

"You've barely been introduced," C.G.'s mom pronounced sternly. "C.G., please show some decorum. You're acting. . .common."

"I can't help it, Mom. You were right. He's everything I want in a man. In a husband."

"Husband?" her mother exclaimed, gaping first at her daughter, then at her friend, Katherine, wondering what kind of calamity the two of them had unleashed.

Their plan had been to introduce Drake and Chryssie, have them like each other enough to start dating, and then a year later they could get married. Ending up in each other's arms in a clothes closet at church was not at all according to plan.

"Come out of there, please," Drake's mother ordered, and C.G. and Drake obeyed, still holding hands and trying to keep from laughing.

When they entered the fellowship hall, the two mothers threw anxious glances every direction to see if anyone they knew had seen their children coming out of a very small closet, flushed in the faces and hanging on to each other like newlyweds.

Just as the mothers began to breathe easier, Drake turned to C.G. and said, "Since we're going to get married, don't you think you should tell me your real name?"

"Married?" his mother screeched.

Drake nodded, and C.G. did, too.

"It's Chrysanthemum Geraldine." She shuddered and Drake kept a perfectly straight face.

"Chrysanthemum Geraldine? What an unusual name."

"There's nothing wrong with it, young man," C.G.'s mom insisted.

"You're absolutely right, Mrs. Grady," Drake agreed. "May I ask why you chose it?" Now he understood why C.G. used C.G. at work. Imagine someone signing Chrysanthemum Geraldine Grady ten times a day, and who'd believe the name anyway?

"My husband and I," and she looked around her, but Jonathan Grady was nowhere to be seen, "named her Chrysanthemum because we met each other at a famous botanical garden in south Georgia, while walking through the chrysanthemum display."

"I see," Drake said, grateful they hadn't been in a rhubarb patch.

"Geraldine is my maternal grandmother's name."

"Thank you."

They noticed the people filing back into the sanctuary.

"We'd better go back in," Drake's mother said.

"Yes," C.G.'s mom agreed, and they both started for the door but stopped when Drake and C.G. did not follow them.

"Aren't you two coming?" her mother asked.

C.G. and Drake were gazing at each other with unmistakable love in their eyes.

"We'll be right there," Drake said. "I have a very important question to ask of C.G. But first, she and I have a confession to make," and they told their mothers about working together and falling in love, which was why they had had no interest in meeting this "perfect" man and woman who'd been picked out for them.

The mothers were unbelieving, then amazed, then intrigued, then delighted at how the situation had turned out.

As they walked away from their happy children, they giggled softly and winked at each other, and Jane said to Katherine, "They're a match made in heaven, don't you agree?"

"Absolutely. Isn't it fortunate we got them together?"

With self-satisfied grins, they made their way to their seats in the sanctuary just as the orchestra music began.

Back in the fellowship hall, which was entirely empty now, Drake took C.G. in his arms, kissed her hungrily, and asked, "You will marry me, won't you, Chrysanthemum Geraldine?"

Looking into his powerfully persuasive eyes, C.G. murmured, "Yes, Drake Forrest. And thank you."

"For what?"

"Helping me redeem my honor and my career. I love you."

"And I love you."

Drake took C.G. into his arms, and they stood together in the center of the room and listened to the swelling of the music as it magnificently portrayed the glory of God.

The miracle of Christmas became the miracle of their finding each other and coming to love each other despite unforeseen obstacles.

Silently they pledged themselves to serve forever this Christ, born to set them free and give them life everlasting.

KATHLEEN YAPP
Kathleen lives in Georgia with her husband, Ken; they have four children and six grandchildren. She is an accomplished writer of both contemporary and historical romances.

A Letter to Our Readers

Dear Readers:

In order that we might better contribute to your reading enjoyment, we would appreciate your taking a few minutes to respond to the following questions. When completed, please return to the following: Fiction Editor, Barbour Publishing, Inc., P.O. Box 719, Uhrichsville, OH 44683.

1. Did you enjoy reading *Georgia?*
   ❑ Very much—I would like to see more books like this.
   ❑ Moderately—I would have enjoyed it more if _____
   _____
   _____

2. What influenced your decision to purchase this book?
   (Check those that apply.)
   ❑ Cover   ❑ Back cover copy   ❑ Title   ❑ Price
   ❑ Friends   ❑ Publicity   ❑ Other

3. Which story was your favorite?
   ❑ *Heaven's Child*   ❑ *Restore the Joy*
   ❑ *On Wings of Song*   ❑ *A Match Made in Heaven*

4. Please check your age range:
   ❑ Under 18   ❑ 18–24   ❑ 25–34
   ❑ 35–45   ❑ 46–55   ❑ Over 55

5. How many hours per week do you read? _____

Name _____

Occupation _____

Address _____

City _____ State _____ Zip _____

E-mail _____

HEARTSONG ❤ PRESENTS

Love Stories
Are Rated G!

That's for godly, gratifying, and of course, great! If you love a thrilling love story but don't appreciate the sordidness of some popular paperback romances, **Heartsong Presents** is for you. In fact, **Heartsong Presents** is the premiere inspirational romance book club featuring love stories where Christian faith is the primary ingredient in a marriage relationship.

Sign up today to receive your first set of four, never-before-published Christian romances. Send no money now; you will receive a bill with the first shipment. You may cancel at any time without obligation, and if you aren't completely satisfied with any selection, you may return the books for an immediate refund!

Imagine. . .four new romances every four weeks—two historical, two contemporary—with men and women like you who long to meet the one God has chosen as the love of their lives. . .all for the low price of $10.99 postpaid.

To join, simply complete the coupon below and mail to the address provided. **Heartsong Presents** romances are rated G for another reason: They'll arrive Godspeed!